PRAISE FOR **WITHOUT WARNING**

"Delivers all the action and techno-detail that any Clancy fan could wish for."
—ROBERT BUETTNER, author of *Orphanage*

"Greasy realism, noxious clouds from burning American cities, currency collapse, mass panic, survival of the fittest, and the triumph of the human spirit all help to make *Without Warning* an absolutely cracking read."
—SF Site

"Narrated with crisp, fluid expertise, Birmingham's ultra-bloody and violent yarn exerts a dreadful, morbid fascination. Three volumes of this should satisfy the most avid cravings."
—*Kirkus Reviews*

"John Birmingham's new book is even better than the Axis of Time series, which is saying something. It's a modern, even postmodern alternate history where the people who wish the United States would go away get what they wished for, and the consequences are meticulously, horrifically worked out in compelling detail through the eyes of a medley of interesting, well-developed characters and tightly plotted action."
—S. M. STIRLING, author of *Island in the Sea of Time*

PRAISE FOR THE AXIS OF TIME TRILOGY

"[Birmingham] describes military hardware with an exuberance and virtuosity that's positively Clancyesque . . . [and] shows a suprisingly tender touch with his characters, who react to their unexpected time trip with authentic, believable anguish."
—*Time* on *Weapons of Choice*

BY JOHN BIRMINGHAM
(published by Del Rey Books)

Without Warning
After America

THE AXIS OF TIME TRILOGY
Weapons of Choice
Designated Targets
Final Impact

WITHOUT WARNING

JOHN BIRMINGHAM

BALLANTINE BOOKS • NEW YORK

2010 Del Rey Mass Market Edition

Copyright © 2009 by John Birmingham
Excerpt from *After America* by John Birmingham copyright © 2010 by John Birmingham

Published in the United States by Del Rey, an imprint of The Random House Publishing Group, a division of Random House, Inc., New York.

DEL REY is a registered trademark and the Del Rey colophon is a trademark of Random House, Inc.

Originally published in hardcover in the United States by Del Rey, an imprint of The Random House Publishing Group, a division of Random House, Inc., in 2009.

This book contains an excerpt from the forthcoming book *After America* by John Birmingham. This excerpt has been set for this edition only and may not reflect the final content of the forthcoming edition.

Cartographic art by Laurie Whiddon, Map Illustrations

ISBN 978-0-345-50290-2

Printed in the United States of America

www.delreybooks.com

9 8 7 6 5 4 3 2 1

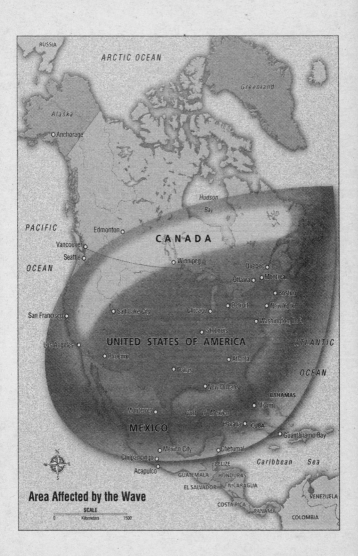

Area Affected by the Wave

SCALE

0   Kilometers   1500

FIRST DAY

March 14, 2003

01

The killer awoke, surrounded by strangers. An IV line dripped clear fluid through a long, thick needle punched into the back of her right hand. Surgical tape held the silver spike in place and tugged at the fine blond hairs growing there. The strangers—all women—leaned in, their faces knotted with anxiety, apparently for her. But she stared instead at her hands, which lay in her lap on a thin brown blanket. They looked strong, even masculine. She turned them over, examining them. The nails were cut short. Calluses disfigured her knuckles, the heels of both palms, and the sides of her hands, from the base of both little fingers down to her wrists. The more she stared, the more unsettled she became. Like the women gathered around her bed, those hands were completely alien to her. She had no idea who she was.

"Cathy? Are you all right?"

"Nurse!" somebody called out.

The strangers, three of them, seemed to launch themselves at her bed, and she felt herself tense up, but they simply wanted to comfort her.

"Doctor. She's awake," one of them said in French.

She felt soft hands patting her down, stroking her the way you might comfort a child who's suffered a bad fright. *Cathy*—that wasn't her name, was it?—Cathy tried not to panic or to show how much she didn't want any of these women touching her. They looked like freaks, not the sort of people she'd want as friends. And then she remembered. They weren't her friends.

They were her mission. And her name wasn't Cathy. It was Caitlin.

4 · JOHN BIRMINGHAM

The women were dressed in cheap clothing, layered for warmth. Falling back into the pillows, recovering from an uncontrolled moment of vertigo into which she had fallen, Caitlin Monroe composed herself. She was in a hospital bed, and in spite of the apparent poverty of her "friends," the private room was expensively fitted out. The youngest of the women wore a brown suede jacket, frayed at the cuffs and elbows and festooned with colorful protest buttons. A stylized white bird. A rainbow. A collection of slogans: *Halliburton Watch. Who Would Jesus Bomb?* And *Resistance Is Fertile.*

Caitlin took a sip of water from a squeeze bottle by the bed.

"I'm sorry," she croaked. "What happened to me?"

She received a pat on the leg from an older, red-haired woman wearing a white T-shirt over some sort of lumpy hand-made sweater. *Celia.* "Auntie" Celia, although she wasn't related to anyone in the room. Auntie Celia had very obviously chosen the strange ensemble to show off the writing on her shirt, which read *If you are not outraged you are not paying attention.*

"Doctor!" cried the other older woman, who had just moved to the doorway.

Maggie. An American, like Caitlin. And there the similarity ended. Maggie the American was short and barrel-chested and pushing fifty, where Caitlin was tall, athletic, and young.

She felt around under her blanket and came up with a plastic control stick for the bed.

"Try this," she offered, passing the controller to the young girl she knew as Monique, a pretty, raven-haired French-woman. "See, the red call button. That'll bring 'em." Then, gently touching the bandages that swaddled her head, she asked, "Where am I?"

"You're in a private room, at the Pitié-Salpêtrière Hospital in Paris," explained Monique. "Paris, France," she added self-consciously.

Caitlin smiled weakly. "Okay. I remember that Paris is in France." She paused. "And now I am, too, I guess. How did I get here? I don't remember much after coming out of the Chun-nel on the bus."

The large American woman standing over by the door to her room—*Maggie, try to remember her fucking name!*—turned away from her post.

"Fascist asswipes, that's how. Attacked us outside of Calais."

"Skinheads," explained Monique. "And you were *magnifique*!"

"I was?"

"Oh yes," the French girl enthused. She looked no more than seventeen years old, but Caitlin knew her to be twenty-two. She knew a lot about Monique. The others chorused their agreement. "These National Front fascists, Le Pen's bullyboys, they stopped the bus and began pulling us out, hitting and kicking us. You stood up to them, Cathy. You fought with them. Slowed them down long enough for the union men to reach us and drive them away."

"Union men?"

"Workers," Maggie informed her. "Comrades from the docks at Calais. We'll meet up with them and the others in Berlin. For the next rally, if you're up for it. We really gotta keep Bush on the back foot. Mobilize the fucking streets against him."

Caitlin tried to reach for any memories of the incident, but it was like grabbing at blocks of smoke. She must have taken a real pounding in the fight.

"I see," she said, but really she didn't. "So I beat on these losers?"

Monique smiled brightly for the first time.

"You are one of our tough guys, no? It was your surfing. You told us you always had to fight for your place on the waves. *Really* fight. You once punched a man off his board for . . . what was it . . . dropping in?"

Caitlin felt as though a great iron flywheel in her mind had suddenly clunked into place. Her cover story. To these women she was Cathy Mercure. Semipro wave rider. Ranked forty-sixth in the world. Part-time organizer for the Sea Shepherd Conservation Society, a deep green militant environmental group famous for direct and occasionally violent confrontations with any number of easily demonized ecovillains. Ocean dumpers, long-line tuna boats, Japanese whale killers. They were all good for a TV-friendly touch-up by the Sea Shepherds. But that was her cover. Her jacket.

She took another sip of cool water and closed her eyes for a moment.

Her real name was Caitlin Monroe. She was a senior field agent with Echelon, a magic box hidden within the budgets of a dozen or more intelligence agencies, only half of them American. She was a killer, and these women were—for a half second, she had no idea. And then the memory came back. Clear and hard. These women were not her targets, but they would lead her to the target.

Al-Banna.

Caitlin cursed softly under her breath. She had no idea what day it was. No idea how long she'd been out, or what had transpired in that time.

"Are you all right?"

It was the French girl, Monique. The reason she was here, with these flakes.

"I'm cool," said Caitlin. "Do you mind?" she asked, pointing at the television that hung from the ceiling. "I feel like I'm lost or something. How'd the peace march go?"

"Brilliant!" said the redheaded woman. Auntie Celia.

She was a Londoner with a whining accent like an ice pick in the eardrums. "There was 'undreds of thousands of people," she said. "Chirac sent a message and all. Berlin's gonna be huge."

"Really?" said Caitlin, feigning enthusiasm. "That's great. Was there anything on the news about it? Or the war?" she continued, pointedly looking at the television.

"Oh sorry," muttered Monique as she dug another controller out of the blankets on Caitlin's bed. Or Cathy's bed, as she would have thought of it.

A flick of the remote and the screen lit up.

"CNN?" asked Caitlin.

Monique flicked through the channels, but couldn't find the news network. White noise and static hissed out of the television from channel 13, where it should have been. She shrugged. There was nothing on MSNBC either, just an empty studio, but all of the French-language channels were available, as was BBC World.

"Can we watch the Beeb then?" asked Celia. "Me French, you know, it's not the best."

Caitlin really just wanted to carve out a couple of minutes to herself, where she could get her head back in the game. Her injuries must be serious, having put her under for three days, and although her cover was still intact, she didn't want to take any chances. She needed to reestablish contact with

Echelon. They'd have maintained overwatch while she was out. They could bring her back up to . . .

"Eh up? What's this then?" blurted Celia.

Everyone's eyes fixed on the screen, where an impeccably groomed Eurasian woman with a perfectly modulated BBC voice was struggling to maintain her composure. ". . . vanished. Communications links are apparently intact and fully functional, but remain unresponsive. Inbound commercial flights are either returning to their points of origin or diverting to Halifax and Quebec in Canada, or to airports throughout the West Indies, which remain unaffected so far."

The women all began to chatter at once, much to Caitlin's annoyance. On-screen the BBC's flustered anchorwoman explained that the "event horizon" seemed to extend down past Mexico City, out into the Gulf, swallowing most of Cuba, encompassing all of the continental U.S. and a big chunk of southeastern Canada, including Montreal. Caitlin had no idea yet what she meant by the term "event horizon," but it didn't sound friendly. A hammer started pounding on the inside of her head as she watched the reporter stumble through the rest of her read.

". . . from a Canadian airbase have not returned. U.S. naval flights out of Guantánamo Bay at the southern tip of Cuba have likewise dropped out of contact at the same point, seventy kilometers north of the base. Reuters is reporting that attempts by U.S. military commanders at Guantánamo to contact the Castro government in Havana have also failed."

Caitlin realized that the background buzz of the hospital had died away in the last few minutes. She heard a metallic clatter as a tray fell to the floor somewhere nearby. Caitlin had a passing acquaintance with the Pitié-Salpêtrière. There had to be nearly three thousand people in this hospital, and at that moment they were all silent. The only human sounds came from the television sets that hung in every room and ward, a discordant clashing of French and English voices, all of them speaking in the same clipped, urgent tone.

"The prime minister, Mr. Blair, has released a statement calling for calm and promising to devote the full resources of the British government to resolving the crisis. A Ministry of Defence spokesman confirmed that British forces have gone onto full alert, but that NATO headquarters in Brussels has not yet issued any such orders. The prime minister rejected calls by the Liberal Democrats to immediately recall British forces deployed in the Middle East for expected operations against the regime of Saddam Hussein."

"That'd be fuckin' right," Auntie Celia said quietly to herself.

The reporter was about to speak again when she stopped, placing a hand to one ear, obviously taking instructions from her producer.

"Right, thank you," she said before continuing.

"We have just received these pictures from a commercial satellite that passed over the eastern seaboard of America a short time ago."

The screen filled with black-and-white still shots of New York. The imagery was not as sharp as some of the mil-grade stuff Caitlin had seen over the years, but it was good enough to pick out individual vehicles and quite small buildings.

"This picture shows the center of New York, as of twenty-three minutes ago," said the reporter. "Our technical department has cleaned up the image, allowing us to pull into a much tighter focus."

Caitlin recognized Times Square from above. She quickly estimated the virtual height as being about two thousand meters, before the view reformatted down to something much closer, probably about five or six hundred feet. The Beeb's IT guys were good. It was a remarkably clear image, but profoundly disturbing. Her brief curse was lost in the gasps and swearing of the other women. Fires, frozen in one frame of satellite imagery, burned throughout the square, where hundreds of cars had smashed into each other. Smoke and flames also poured from a few buildings. Buses and yellow cabs had run up onto the sidewalks and in some cases right into shop fronts and building façades. But nothing else moved. The photograph seemed to have captured an unnatural, ghostly moment. Not because they were looking at a still shot of a great metropolis in the grip of some weird, inexplicable disaster, but because nowhere in that eerie black-and-white image of one of the busiest cities in the world was there a single human being to be seen.

02

Washington State

The lower reaches of the Cascades never failed to impress James Kipper. Dropping his backpack for a five-minute rest and a drink of water, he rewarded himself for the morning's trek with a moment staring down the long, deeply wooded valley up which he had climbed. Snow lay in patches along the well-beaten trail, and dropped in wet clumps from the sagging branches of fir and pine that covered the gentle slopes below him in a dense green carpet. He loved it out here. Nature was so powerful, the hand of man so light, you could have been hundreds of years removed from the twenty-first century. The brisk but unseasonably sunny morning had made hiking up the remote valley a rare pleasure for the senses. The air was fragrant with sap and the rich brown mulch of earth warmed by sun for the first time in months. A breeze, just strong enough to set the treetops swaying, carried the natural white noise of a nearby stream, running heavy with an early melt. As he stood at the edge of a small plateau he could imagine the landscape below dotted with castles and mounted knights. He was the father of a little girl just lately in school; knights and castles and fairy tales were seldom far from his mind these days.

Kipper sucked in a draft of air so clean and cold it hurt all the way down into his chest. But it hurt *good*. The temperature hadn't snuck much past the mid-fifties, but he was well dressed for the hike, and could even feel sweat trickling down the inside of his arms. Another mouthful of icy spring water added pleasantly to the discordant sensations of feeling both hot and cold. His breath plumed out in front of him, and his stomach rumbled, reminding the engineer that it had been four hours since his last substantial meal, a bowl of pork sausages and beans cooked over the coals at his campsite a few miles farther downrange. Kipper unzipped his Gore-Tex jacket and fished around inside for the protein bar he'd stored in one of the many pockets before setting out that morning. It would be satisfyingly warm and chewy by now.

He frowned at the buzzing in one of the pockets. A second later the trilling of his satellite phone punched him back into the real world. The phone was a concession to his wife, Barb. Three days a year he was allowed to run around in the woods by himself, but as a former New Yorker, Barb had "issues" with his "nature-boy shtick" and insisted that if he was going to go commune with the elves he should at least take a sat phone and GPS locator beacon with him. "So we can find your body before the coyotes and buzzards are finished with it," she said.

He took out the heavy lump of hated technology, scowling at the small screen as he realized it wasn't even her on the line. The number looked to be someone at City Hall.

Well, now I'm really pissed, he thought. Only his wife and the park rangers were supposed to have this number, and true to her promise Barb had never actually used it. But apparently she'd gone and given it to some pinhead at work.

Unless of course it's telemarketers. Please God, don't let it be telemarketers.

He was simultaneously dreading and relishing the prospect as he answered. If this was some asshole in New Delhi trying to sell him a time-share apartment . . .

"Kipper. You there?"

The chief engineer of the Seattle City Council closed his eyes and exhaled.

"Hey, Barney. This better be good, man."

Whoever had decided they had something worth interrupting his precious hiking holiday had chosen the messenger well. Barney Tench was his closest friend and probably the only person who could call him right now, safe in the knowledge that he would survive the encounter.

"It ain't good, Jimmy," said Tench, and for the first time Kipper noticed the tremor in his friend's voice. Was he scared?

When he spoke again he sounded like he'd just survived a train wreck. Like he was terrified.

"It's fucked, man. Totally fucked. You gotta get back here

right now. I know it's your break and all, but we need you, right now."

Kipper shivered as a single bead of sweat trickled down his spine before hitting a patch of thermal underwear and being absorbed.

"What's up, Barn? Just tell me what's going on."

Tench groaned.

"That's it, Jimmy. Nobody knows. Could be a war. Could be a fucking comet strike. We don't know."

"A what?"

His surroundings were completely forgotten now. All of James Kipper's attention was focused down the invisible connection to his friend and colleague back in the city. A friend who seemed to have lost his marbles.

"What d'you mean a comet or a war, Barney? What's going on?"

"The whole country is gone, Jimmy. All of it, 'cept us. And Alaska I guess. Even Canada's gone. Most of it, anyway, in the east."

The ice water he'd just swallowed was sitting very heavily in his stomach, as though he'd gulped down a gallon of the stuff instead of just a mouthful. That might have been anger. He was beginning to suspect that this was some sort of prank. Tench was famous for them. When they'd been rooming together in college he'd fabricated an entire gala ball at the Grand Hyatt, convincing a couple of college babes to hand out "free," "strictly limited" tickets on campuses all over town. Tench and Kipper had got as drunk as lords sitting in the lobby bar, dressed in rented tuxedos, watching hundreds of students waving their bogus ball tickets in the face of a bewildered hotel manager. Barney Tench was more than capable of fucking with someone's head for a laugh. Especially Kipper's.

"Gone where, Barney?" he growled. "You're not making any sense."

"Just gone, Jimmy. Just fucking gone." His voice was scaling higher with every word he said. "Turn on your locator beacon. There's a National Guard chopper headed your way soon. They're gonna pick you up and transfer you to a plane somewhere. A C-130 or something, they said. One of them big fat ones. It'll get you straight in here. Council's called an emergency meeting. All heads of department. Governor's office is sending a team, although nobody can find Gary Locke. His schedule had him in transit today. In the air," he added, as though that explained everything.

"Barney, is my family safe?" asked Kipper.

"They're fine, buddy, they're fine. Barb gave me your number. Look, I gotta go. The guard can fill you in. I got a thousand calls to make now that I found you. Just fire up that beacon, sit your ass down, and wait."

"Bar . . ."

But the line cut out.

"What the fuck was that about?" he muttered. Shaking his head, Kipper knelt in front of his pack and popped the snap lock on the pocket containing his personal locator beacon, a lightweight ACR Terrafix unit. He powered up the little yellow device and couldn't help searching the skies, even though he knew his ride was probably still an hour away. Assuming it came at all, and Barney wasn't now roaring with laughter, about to fall backward off his chair. Who knew?

Subzero air torrents high above him stretched a few scraps of cloud into long white ribbons, streaming away toward the coast. He caught sight of a giant hawk as it dived into the valley, wings folded back.

"Someone's about to get eaten," he thought aloud.

Then he noticed the contrail, maybe twenty miles farther north. The sky was crisscrossed with contrails during the colder months, great white arcs of vapor trailing the jetliners as they headed for Seattle, or the Pacific and the long haul to Japan or down to Honolulu. There seemed to be fewer than usual, just this one actually, and he had never seen a plane tracking that low over the Cascades before. His unease at the weird call from Barney tightened into alarm as he watched the slow arc of the aircraft and realized it wasn't going to clear the mountains toward which it was headed.

"No," he whispered, aware that he almost never spoke aloud on his hiking trips, and that he was positively yapping his head off today. "No, don't."

His mouth was dry, and he drank from his canteen without thinking. The cold water hit his clenched stomach like acid, and for a second he thought he might vomit. That faraway plane, a thin tube of metal enfolding—what? a hundred, two hundred souls?—slowly, gracefully, inexorably speared itself into the side of a mountain, impacting just over the snow line, freeing great blossoming petals of dirty yellow flame to roll away into the morning air.

"Ah shit."

Kipper shook his head, and took a few steps toward the small, roiling ball of fire before he stopped himself. He would never make it, and anyway he had to stay here and wait for the chopper. He apparently had his own disaster to deal with.

Still, he had to do something.

He keyed 911 into his sat phone, glancing down momentarily to check that he'd gotten the numbers right. He could at least call this in. Maybe someone had survived. A ridiculous thought, which he recognized as such as soon as he'd had it. But he couldn't just stand by with his thumb in his ass, taking in the view, could he?

"Nine-one-one, which service do you require?"

The dispatcher sounded harried, and just as freaked out as Barney had been. But then, Kipper thought, that was probably her normal state of being.

"This is James Kipper, chief engineer, Seattle City Council. I've just seen a passenger plane crash. A big jet."

The dispatcher's voice seemed nearly mechanical, washed free of human affect by the multiple layers of impossibly complicated technology required to allow Kipper to speak to her from the side of this mountain in the middle of nowhere.

"Sir, what is your location and the location of the incident?"

As Kipper told her that he was in the lower reaches of the Cascades, and read his location off the GPS beacon, the soft rumble of the titanic explosion finally reached him.

"Sir, please repeat. Are you outside the metro area?"

"Yes, damn it. I just watched this plane go down in the mountains. It was flying out of the east and it got too low and . . ."

"Are you outside the Seattle metro area, sir?"

"Yes, I . . ."

"Your call has been logged sir, but we cannot dispatch anyone right now. Please hang up and leave the line free for genuine emergency calls."

And with that he was cut off.

"What the fuck?" he said, loud enough to startle a flight of birds from a nearby tree. A mass of snow, disturbed by their takeoff, fell to the ground with a soft, wet crunch. Twenty miles to the north a pillar of dark smoke climbed away into the hard blue sky. A secondary explosion bloomed silently in the heart of the maelstrom on the face of the granite peak. Kipper was still staring at the phone in disbelief when the sound reached him.

Seattle, Washington

The parking lot of the supermarket on Broadway East could be a challenge at the best of times. Barbara's little Honda had picked up three mystery scratches and dents there over the past six months. But today it felt like genuine hell. With one hand she was trying to steer a heavily laden cart sporting at least two malfunctioning wheels, while carrying a sobbing child on her other arm and attempting to redial Kipper's number on her cell phone. The Safeway parking lot was full of hysterics and loons, some of them normal people who'd gone over the edge, but also some full-time nutbars who'd turned up with sandwich boards urging everyone to "REPENT" as the "HOUR OF DOOM" was "*AT HAND!!!!*" The signs looked quite professional, as though they'd been prepared much earlier for just this occasion. Barb had taken a small measure of childish joy from clipping one of the Jesus freaks with the corner of her fast-moving, barely controlled metal shopping cart.

She was less pleased with the long scrape she gouged out of the paintwork as she stumbled and lost her grip on the cart just as they made it to the car.

"Shit!"

Suzie, who at six years old was way too big to be carried, one-armed or otherwise, for more than a few steps, struggled to clamber deeper into Barbara Kipper's embrace. "I'm scared, Mommy," she cried.

Struggling with her daughter, Barbara lost her grip on the cell phone, a cheap flip-top model, which fell to the asphalt and broke into two.

"Oh shit! Oh . . . I'm sorry, sweetheart. Mommy's sorry. Just hop down, okay, and . . ."

Suzie, who had buried her face in Barbara's neck, shook her head and wailed, "*Noooo.*"

"Suffer the little children unto him, good lady . . ."

Barb spun around to find that one of the nuts had followed her through the heaving crush of the parking lot and was holding aloft a small branch of some sort, waving it as if to bless her.

"Suffer the little . . ."

"I'll fucking suffer you to get the hell away from me, you god-damned freak. You're scaring the bejesus out of my daughter."

She fixed him with such a baleful stare that he actually seemed to recoil, but Barbara, who was normally so conscious of others' feelings, felt not the least bit contrite. This place was a madhouse. It was as though people had gone berserk or something when the first news came through, and these holy fucking lunatics were only making it worse. She managed somehow to lower a clinging Suzie to the ground while digging her keys out and thumbing the car's electronic lock. It opened with a reassuring *bleep-bloop,* lessening her fears that whatever had happened, it might have put the zap on all the electrics. Some bearded panic merchant had jumped up onto a checkout in the store to announce that an electromagnetic "event" had taken out all the circuits, everywhere. Unfortunately for him the automatic conveyor belt on which he was standing was entirely functional and jerked forward, pulling his feet out from under him. The last Barb had seen of him he was lying on the floor of Safeway with a badly broken ankle.

His theatrics, the almost instant viral panic that had seemed to flash through everyone, a couple of fender benders in the parking lot, followed by the inevitable blare of horns, the trilling of alarms, and the increasingly ugly screams of abuse . . . it had all been enough to upset Suzie so badly she was shivering, begging to know where Daddy was, and whether it was "mine eleven" happening again. Barbara Kipper soothed her as best she could while pushing the child into the backseat, where her stuffed panda, Poofy Bear, might at least provide some comfort.

She popped the hatch and transferred the shopping bags as quickly as possible, with no idea how she was going to get them away from here. The lot was a gridlocked nightmare, with people increasingly desperate to get away, backing and crunch-ing into each other, while more turned up every minute, pre-sumably to panic-buy a year's worth of discount Pop-Tarts and boxed mac-'n'-cheese, the specials of the day.

A short distance away two men were squaring up for a fight. An actual fight. One was huge, enormously obese, while the other looked tall and fit. God only knew what they were pissed at each other about. Maybe the big guy got the last of the Pop-Tarts. They circled each other, feinting and throwing out air punches, and then, much to her surprise, the thinner of the two bent over and charged the other guy like a rhino, head-butting him in the gut. They went down in a tangle as police or maybe ambulance sirens seemed to be closing in from somewhere nearby.

Barbara shook her head in disgust and threw the last of her groceries into the hatch.

Having unloaded the cart, she didn't dare push it back to the collection bay for fear of leaving Suzie alone for even a moment. She could have killed Kipper at that point. He would choose this of all weeks to disappear into the mountains.

As soon as she voiced the thought in her mind, her heart lurched forward.

Disappeared.

No, he wasn't gone, too. He was fine. He'd left a hiking plan with her and the park rangers, and as soon as she'd called them they said there was no way he would have been anywhere near the edge of this . . . effect . . . event . . . whatever it was. It was on the far side of the mountains. They said he'd be cool. Barney said the same thing.

She began shaking anyway, an uncontrolled shudder that seized her whole body as dizziness threatened to steal her legs from under her. Biting down on a knuckle until she drew blood helped focus her mind away from the terror that wanted to swamp her. The pain was something sharp and real, something on which to focus. And as soon as she did, Barb was embarrassed that she'd let herself get so frantic. She gathered up the broken pieces of her cell phone and tossed them into the front passenger seat before moving around to the driver's door. She was going to hit the shopping cart if she backed out, but she really didn't care. Getting Suzie away from here was more important.

"Is Daddy all right, Mommy? Is he okay?" her daughter asked as soon as Barb had the door closed. It shut out some of the chaos and madness but meant that Suzie could see without any distractions just how disturbed her mother was.

"He's fine, sweetheart," she said as calmly as she could manage. "His friends from work are phoning him and sending a helicopter just for him. To bring him home. He'll be back later, don't worry."

"But what if he got *eaten,* Mommy? I heard a man in the store say everyone was *eaten.* Everyone."

"Daddy is fine," she repeated as calmly as possible, even as her head reeled with the insanity of it all. "And nobody was eaten, Suzie. I don't know what's happened, but nobody was eaten. That's just silly talk. Now strap yourself in, sweetie. This is going to be very dangerous."

The young girl snapped her seat belt to show that she'd already done so, and Barb apologized for not noticing. She keyed the ignition, which worked perfectly, and slowly but resolutely backed out of her parking space, pushing the cart aside with the rear bumper. A few more scrapes and scratches then. The view out of the back window was bedlam, with people swarming and vehicles everywhere. Barb gritted her teeth and kept moving, even as she butted up against other shoppers who didn't move out of her way. Some hammered on the window, one guy punching it so hard it cracked, causing Suzie to squeal in fear. But Barbara Kipper refused to stop, believing that to do so would see them trapped. She was only making a walking pace, but kept going. Not for the first time was she grateful for driving a small car in this parking lot. While SUVs and sedans soon got themselves jammed together, almost like broken teeth on a zipper, she was able to thread, very slowly and determinedly, through the crowd, until she made it to a small hedge line at the edge of the lot and gunned the little Honda right on through it. The car didn't like it much, and the scratching of branches on the paintwork was hideous. She almost certainly knocked the wheels out of alignment mounting the curb, but she was suddenly able to press the accelerator and break free onto Harvard Avenue. They bounced and hit the road with a terrible, metallic crunch. But at least they were out.

As they drove away in heavy traffic, Barb was certain she heard the pop of gunfire.

She couldn't help but keep looking at the phone, wondering if Barney had got through to Kip.

03

Somebody must have tipped off the ragheads, because they were wailing up a storm. Long ululating cries of "*Allahu akbar*" rolled around the dusty confines of Camp Delta, drifting over the razor wire. General Musso heard them as tinny voices emanating from the speakers of a nearby computer in the situation room of the naval op center—a grand title for such a modest facility, a demountable hut with heavy gray air-conditioning units rumbling away at the windows. It was a relatively mild Caribbean day outside; almost but not quite balmy. The brigadier general knew he could probably run up and down the nearest of the scrubby low-rise hills that surrounded this part of the base without raising much of a sweat. But the room was stuffy. Dozens of laptops had been plugged into the existing cluster of workstations, and they were all running hard, dumping waste heat into a space that was already overcrowded with at least three times as many occupants as normal.

Having given up on the computers in frustration, however, Tusk Musso leaned over the old map table, gripping the back of a swivel chair, biting down hard on the urge to pick it up and throw it through the window. He was so angry, and—just quietly—so weirded out, that there was a fair chance he could have heaved that sucker all the way down to the water's edge. The bay was deep cerulean blue, almost perfectly still, and the chair would have made a satisfying splash. Unfortunately, Musso was the ranking officer on the base that day and everybody was looking to him for answers. Guantánamo's naval commander, Captain Cimines, was missing, apparently along with about three hundred million of his countrymen, and a whole heap of Mexicans and Canucks into the bargain. *And Cubans, too,* Musso reminded himself. *Let's not forget our old buds just over the wire.*

"What are the locals up to, Georgie?" he rumbled. His aide, Lieutenant Colonel George Stavros, delivered one brief shake of the head.

"Still hopping around, sir. Looks like someone really kicked over their anthill. Our guys have counted at least two hundred of them bugging out."

"But nothing coming our way, yet?"

"No, sir. Santiago and Baracoa are still quiet. A few crowds building. But nothing too big."

Musso nodded slowly. He was a huge man, with a head resembling a solid block of white granite resting atop a tree trunk of a neck. Even that simple gesture spoke of enormous reserves of power. He shifted his gaze from the antique, analog reality of the map table with its little wooden and plastic markers across to the banks of flat screens that even now were refusing to tell him anything about what was going on such a short distance to the north. The faces of the men and women around him were a study in barely constrained anxiety. They were a mixed service group about two dozen strong, representing all the arms of the U.S. military which had a stake in Guantánamo, mostly navy and marines, but with a few army and air force types thrown in. There was even one lone coast guard rep, mournfully staring at the map table, wondering what could possibly have happened to his little boat. The cutter had dropped out of contact. It was easily found on radar, but would not respond to his hail.

Musso had no permanent connection to Guantánamo. He'd been sent down to review operations at Delta, the first task of a new job, a *desk* job back in D.C. that he really hadn't wanted. A genuine shooting war was about to begin in the Middle East, and here he was, on a fucking day trip to Gitmo, making sure a bunch of jihadi wack jobs were getting their asses wiped for them with silken handkerchiefs, not copies of the Koran. It was almost enough to test a man's faith, and more than enough to make him regret the international law degree he'd taken as a younger marine. It had seemed like a good idea at the time. A fallback, his old man had called it, in case he didn't take to the Corps with any enthusiasm. Musso stood erect, folded his arms as though examining a really shitty used-car deal, and grunted.

"Okay. Let's take inventory. What do we know for certain?" he asked, and began ticking the answers off on his fingers. "Thirty-three minutes ago we lost contact with CONUS for two minutes. We had nothing but static on the phones, sat links, the Net, broadcast TV, radio. Everything. Then, all of our comm links are functioning again, but we get no response to anything we send home. All our other links are fine. Pearl. NATO. ANZUS. CENTCOM in Qatar, but *not* Tampa. All responding and wanting to know what the hell is going on. But we have no fucking idea. I mean, look at that. What the hell is that about?"

The Marine Corps lawyer waved his hand at a bank of TV monitors. They were all tuned into U.S. news networks, which should have been pumping out their inane babble 24/7. With the war in Iraq only days away, the global audience for reports out of America and the Middle East was huge and nigh on insatiable. But there was the Atlanta studio of CNN, back after a few minutes of static, devoid of life. The anchor desk sat in center frame, and dozens of TV and computer screens flickered away in the background, but nobody from CNN was to be seen. The same over at Fox. Bill O'Reilly's chair was empty. Bloomberg still filled most of one monitor with garishly bright cascades of financial data, but the little picture window in one corner where you'd normally find a couple of dark-suited bizoids droning on about acquisitions and mergers was occupied by a couple of chairs, what looked like some smoldering rags, and nothing else. Meanwhile another bank of screens running satellite feeds from Europe and Asia was fully operational, and peopled by increasingly worried talking heads, none of whom could explain what was happening in North America.

"Anybody?" asked Musso, not really expecting an answer.

The silence might have become unbearable had it not been broken by a young ensign, who coughed nervously at the edge of the huddle.

"Excuse me, General," she said.

Musso bit down on an irrational urge to snap at her, instead keeping his voice as level and nonthreatening as he could.

"Yes, Ms. . . . ?"

"Oschin, sir. I thought you might need to look at these. I've streamed vision from eighteen webcams onto a couple of monitors at my workstation. These cams are all in high-volume, public areas, General. Grand Central in New York. Daley Plaza in Chicago, that sort of thing . . ."

Ensign Oschin, who was obviously uncomfortable addressing such a high-powered group, seemed to run down like a windup toy at that point. Musso noticed a couple of army officers glaring at her for having interrupted the big kids at play.

"Go on, Ensign," he reassured her, giving the army jerkoffs a cold hard glare. "What's your point?"

Oschin stood a full inch taller. "They're live feeds, sir. From all over the country. And there's nobody in them. Anywhere."

That information fell like a lead weight into a dark, bottomless well, tumbling down out of sight. No one spoke as Musso held Oschin's gaze, seeing the fear gnawing away at her carefully arranged professional mask. He could taste a trace of bile at the back of his throat, and he was unable to stop his thoughts straying to his family back home in Galveston. The boys would both be in school, and Marlene would be up to her elbows in blue rinse at the salon. He allowed himself the indulgence of a quick, wordless prayer on their behalf.

"Can you patch it through onto the main displays?" he asked.

"Aye, sir."

"Then do so please, as quickly as you can."

Oschin, a small nervous woman, spun around and retreated to the safety of her workstation, whipping her fingers across the keyboard in a blur. Other sysops who'd been less successful in their own endeavors to raise anyone stateside snuck peeks over their shoulders at the results of her work as two large Sony flat-panels hanging from the ceiling suddenly filled with multiple windows displaying scenes from across the U.S. Oschin appeared at the map table again with a laser pointer. She laid the red dot on the first window in the upper left-hand quadrant of the nearest screen.

"With your permission, General?"

"Of course."

"That's the Mall of America. Local time, 1320 hours. You're looking at the main food court."

It was empty. A small fire burned in one concession stand, and it looked as though sprinklers might have tripped, but the image quality wasn't clear enough to be certain. It reminded Musso of an old zombie flick he'd watched as a kid. *Dawn of the Dead* or something. For some reason his flesh cr...

the memory, even though he'd thought the movie was a dumb-ass piece of crap the first time he'd seen it. Oschin flicked the laser pointer over the next three windows as a group.

"Disneyland, California. Local time 1120 hours. You're look-ing at the concourse just inside the main entrance. Then you have Space Mountain in Tomorrowland. And finally Mickey's Toontown."

Again, the pictures were poor in quality, but no less disturb-ing because of it. Not a soul moved anywhere in them. A breeze pushed litter around the main concourse, where some sort of golf buggy had run up onto a gutter and tipped over. The young officer, her voice quavering, laid the red dot on a couple of piles of smoking rags.

"I think they may have been clothes, sir."

Nobody replied, possibly because they all felt as sick in the gut as Musso. Oschin waited a second, then made her way through the rest of the image windows. Crown Center in Kansas City. Half a dozen cams from UCLA's Berkeley cam-pus. A mortgage brokers' convention in Toledo. The main strip in Vegas—which looked like Satan's wrecking yard, with cars all piled into each other and burning fiercely. Venice Beach. JFK Airport. The Strand in Galveston.

Musso arranged his features into a blank façade for that one. He'd already recognized the scene before Oschin had explained to the others what they were looking at. Down in his meat, right down in the oldest animal parts of his being, he knew his fam-ily was gone.

Oblivious of the personal import of what she'd just shown him, Ensign Oschin carried on, cycling through a list of public gathering places that should have been teeming with people. All of them abandoned, or empty, or . . . what?

"It's the Rapture," whispered an army major standing directly across the table from Musso. One of the two who'd unsettled Oschin a few minutes ago. "The end of days."

Musso spoke up loudly and aggressively, smacking down on the first sign of anyone in this command unraveling.

"Major, if it was the Rapture don't you think *you'd* be gone
? And where are the sinners? Don't they get to stay and
?me I heard, this thing has a defined horizon,

Chastened and not a little put out, the major, whose name tag read CLARENCE, clamped his mouth shut again.

Musso wished, for once in his life, that someone were giving him orders as opposed to the other way around. This was one football he didn't want to run with. He didn't know what to make of the video streaming out of his homeland. After 9/11 he hadn't thought anything could surprise him again. He'd been ready for the day he flicked on the television and saw mushroom clouds blooming over an American city. But this . . . this was bullshit.

"Allahu akbar. Allahu akbar."

The distinct popping sound of gunfire in the middle distance crackled out of a speaker set. Then came the screams.

"George," growled Musso.

"I'm on it, sir."

His aide hurried out of the room to track down the source of this new disturbance. Musso waited for more shots, but none came.

"Okay," he said. "I'm not sending any more assets into this thing, whatever it is. I think we've established that it's a no-go zone."

Both of the helicopters he'd ordered to fly north over international waters had apparently crashed soon after crossing the line that now defined the edge of the phenomenon.

"Okay. Let's call up PACOM . . ." he started to say.

"General, pardon me, sir? Permission to report?"

A fresh-faced marine butterbar in full battle rattle appeared in the doorway, his dark features unaffected by the recent turn of events.

"Go ahead," said Musso.

"It's the Cubans, sir. They've sent a delegation in through the minefield. They want to talk. Matter of fact, they're dying to. One of their vehicles hit a mine coming in and the others just kept on rolling."

Musso stretched and rolled his neck, which had begun to ache with a deep muscle cramp. He was probably hunching his shoulders again. Marlene said she could tell a mile off when he was really pissed, because he seized up like the hunchback of Notre Dame.

(Marlene . . . Ohmigod . . .)

"Okay," he said. "Disarm t

few miles closer to it, whatever it is. They might have seen something we haven't."

The lieutenant acknowledged the order and hurried away, weaving around Stavros, who returned at the same moment.

"I'm afraid a bunch of our guests decided to charge a guard detail," he said, explaining the gunshots of just a few minutes ago. Things were moving so quickly that Musso had stopped caring about the incident as soon as it didn't escalate. "Two dead, five wounded. They've heard that something is up. They think Osama's set off a nuke or something. The camps are locked down now."

Musso took in the report and decided it didn't need any more of his attention.

"Folks, right now, I gotta say this. I don't think bin Laden or any of those raghead motherfuckers had anything to do with this. I think it's much bigger, but what the hell it is, I have no idea."

The live feed from Oschin's webcam trawl stuttered along above his head. Mocking them all.

I wish it was just a nuke, thought Musso, but he kept it to himself.

04

Pacific Ocean, 600 nm west of Acapulco

The old sailboat was a twin-masted forty-footer carved out of thousand-year-old Huon pine from the Tasmanian highlands, a

museum piece. She'd placed third on cor-
way back in 1953, and in
to make it to the
plaything of a

builder, a manufacturing tycoon, two dot-com millionaires, and Pete Holder.

Pete knew he was never going to be anywhere near as wealthy as any of the *Diamantina*'s former skippers—although the dot-com guys had tanked badly a couple of years ago and were probably down to their last two or three million now, hence the bargain-basement price he'd paid for the old girl. Not that he gave a shit. The Australian government issued his passport, but he considered himself a citizen of the waves, and for the past eight years, after taking a redundancy payment from his old job as a rig boss for Shell, he'd been devoted entirely to the pursuit of the world's most fantastic lifestyle. Mostly that involved meandering from one secret surf break to the next, putting in a few weeks at the Maldives, cutting down the Indonesian archipelago to Nias, booming across the Pacific to chase triple-overhead sets off northern California. And sometimes, of course, to pay for this life of pure indulgence, it meant loading the boat up with half a ton of compressed ganja and running the gauntlet of international supernarcs like the DEA and AFP.

Even worse were the state-sponsored but highly autonomous shakedown artists, like the crooked Indonesian navy commodore he'd tangled with in Bali last year, or the Peruvian *federales* he thought he'd paid off in Callao only to have them come back a day later saying they'd "lost" their very generous bribe and would be in need of another of the same value within twenty-four hours—unless Señor Pedro felt like seeing out his days as a slave in a manganese mine deep in the jungles of *la Montaña*. Pete had transferred the money within two hours and never sailed into the territorial waters of Peru again.

As he watched Fifi and Jules, moving around to clear away the remains of lunch, the veteran smuggler catalogued all of the near misses he'd survived over the years. It was a sobering exercise, one he forced himself to endure before every new payday. Bad luck he couldn't control, but with good planning and preparation he could at least minimize opportunities for the ever-fickle finger of fate to insert itself firmly into ḥᵘvoid-Hubris and stupidity, on the other hand, werᵉ̄ be dammed if able. They were the principal mᵉˢ ̣ᵗˢⁱᵒlder was a survivor. selection thinned out hiˢ he was going t᷂ᵒ

"Mr. Peter, sir?"

Lee had snuck up on him again. A Malaccan Chinese from a three-hundred-year-long line of pirates, Mr. Lee was always doing that. Pete tried to rearrange his features into a sunny smile, but Lee knew him too well and responded with a pitying shake of the head. Pete was notorious for his ill temper in the hours leading up to a job, and try as he might to control it, his face was always clouded and dark until they were safely away. Frankly, he resented the necessity for the whole smuggling business and would have done almost anything short of getting a normal job to avoid it.

"Hey, Lee. What's up, mate?"

Pete tried for a light tone, the sort of thing his fellow Tasmanian Errol Flynn might have pulled off if he'd gone into smuggling and full-time surf bummery. Instead he came off as clipped and nervous. He noticed Fifi and Jules throw a curious glance back his way. They'd only been with him for about eighteen months, but like Mr. Lee they'd learned to read his moods with an almost preternatural accuracy. It was the legacy of living so close together and taking things right up to the edge.

"Something is up, Mr. Peter."

"Okay. I'm waiting."

Jeez, he wished he could *loosen* up.

"The *Pong Su,* she is changing course, sir. She will not meet up with us if she continues on her new heading."

Pete was dressed in ripped board shorts and a sun-faded sky-blue cotton shirt. The Tropic of Cancer was well north of them, and the day would have been uncomfortably warm were it not for a gentle sou'wester that only just bellied out the sails but did little to dry the sweat pooling between the breasts of his female crew.

"Come see. I show," said Lee.

Jules finished scraping a plate of grilled fish scraps over the side and used the dish to shade her eyes as she straightened up.

"Is there something the matter, Pete?" she called out in her ~~posh~~ English accent, what his mother would have called

"Dunno, ~~~~"

just in case. You ~~~~."

"Righty-o," she said.

chores with added vigor. Bou~~~~ the Let's be ready to split

~~~~you're ready."

twenties and resembled each other closely enough that Pete had long ago taken to calling them "the twins," even though Jules was a Brit, a trust-fund exile from Surrey, while Fifi had run away from a trailer park in Oregon at the age of fifteen. They brought a rare and valuable mix of skills to the *Diamantina*. Jules had a master's in accountancy from the London School of Economics, and her father, the late Lord Balwyn, had been a two-time winner of the Fastnet race and a board member of the Royal Thames Yacht Club. Or had been, until Scotland Yard had come calling at the manor one day with a warrant for his arrest on 129 charges of fraud and tax evasion.

Fifi, the ship's cook, had not even finished high school, and her only inheritance was genetic. Her mom, one of Larry Flynt's very first *Hustler* models, had bequeathed her some good looks and a mighty fine ass, but apart from an explosive temper and a morally flexible attitude to life's manifold challenges, that was about it. And compared with her mom, she was still kind of uptight. She'd left home after her fourth "stepdad," the aptly named Randy, a shiftless, unemployed crab-pot repairman, had suggested they have a threesome and go on *Springer* to tell their story. He'd heard they could score a trip to Chicago, a free stay in a motel, and two hundred dollars cash for expenses.

Fifi was on the road with her thumb in the air about half an hour later.

She was a great cook, however. And hell on mag wheels with a loaded weapon.

He could hear the twins rummaging through the gun locker just beyond the forward bulkhead as he sat at the nav station and tried to make sense of the screens in front of him. Even with air-conditioning it was hot belowdecks, and the prospect of a transfer going bad gave the confines of the boat a claustrophobic feeling. The *Diamantina* was fitted out for high luxury, thanks to her former owners, and Pete was able to sink into a soft leather swivel chair adapted for maritime use from a Herman Miller original, but nothing about sitting in front of the flat-panel displays in the small nook outside his personal cabin made him happy. He could see immediately what Lee was talking about as he watched a computer-generated track of the *Pong Su,* the North Korean freighter scheduled to swap four million dollars' worth of perfectly counterfeited U.S. currency for a "full stick," one million dollars' worth of the real deal bundled away in the *Diamantina*'s stronghold. That money represented the profits of three high-risk dope runs from Mexico up to California. Currency fraud wasn't the sort of business they normally got into, but the blowout in Bali had left him few options. The four large he could trade in Mexico for two million U.S. real, a profit of one hundred percent.

Or that was the plan, anyway.

But forty minutes ago the *Pong Su* had deviated sharply off course, and was apparently running rudderless. It looked for all the world as though she'd lost steering.

"No good, Mr. Peter," avowed Lee. "Look here, and here, too."

It was only then that Pete realized the *Pong Su* wasn't the only ship in trouble. Five other vessels within the *Diamantina*'s radar bubble had all likewise veered off course and appeared to be heading out of the designated shipping lanes.

"Pete, you'd better come up on deck. There's something very strange happening off to the north."

It was Jules, with Fifi at her elbow right behind her.

After cleaning up, they had changed into their rigs for the handover. Both were now dressed in ballistic vests and wearing combat harnesses weighed down with reloads for the Vietnam-era M16s and grenade launchers that they would take from the armory fifteen minutes before the rendezvous. But Pete Holder was beginning to doubt there'd be any rendezvous today, or ever.

"What do you mean strange?"

"I mean odd, weird, right out of the bloody ordinary, Pete. It looks like a storm front came out of that heat haze to the north, but . . . well . . . you'll need to see for yourself."

Grunting in frustration, he pushed himself up out of the chair and hurried up on deck. Moving forward to the bow, shielding his eyes, he saw immediately what she meant. Far to the north of them half the sky seemed to be taken up with the queerest, most exotic-looking storm front he'd ever seen. It appeared to sparkle and hang still in the air. It must have been a long way distant, because it appeared from beneath the horizon and climbed away into the stratosphere. Just standing, watching it, he felt insignificant and deeply vulnerable.

"Radio's not working!" Fifi called out from below.

"Radio's fine . . ." he started to say, then stopped. They'd been monitoring the airwaves for any U.S. or Mexican government traffic, using the yacht's high-gain antennae to eavesdrop on coast guard and navy signals, a constant background chatter. It was only when Fifi pointed out the silence from the radio that he realized he'd heard nothing from it in more than half an hour. Frowning at the bizarre weather up ahead, he hastened back belowdecks.

Mr. Lee was flicking switches and twirling dials on the M802 marine radio. It was only then that they picked up the babble of some commercial station down in Acapulco, where a DJ was reading in heavily accented English a local police order imposing an immediate curfew, which would remain in effect until contact with the central government was "reestablished."

"Oh, bugger this . . ." muttered Pete at the unpleasant feeling of déjà vu. It transported him back to the day he'd woken up late in the morning, dockside in Santa Monica, after a hard night's partying with his then relatively new crewmates. He'd spent nearly the entire day mooching around, drinking Irish coffee and napping off his hangover. It had been September 11, 2001, and he'd missed almost all of the day that had changed the world. Only Lee's return from the city in the afternoon had alerted him to the news from the East Coast. As he sat belowdecks again, sweat leaking out of his armpits and trickling down his sides, listening to an increasingly hysterical radio jock talking about "*la catástrofe*" and watching the strange, ghostly track of those five ships to the north, Pete Holder felt as though time had folded back in on itself.

"I dunno what's happened," he said, "but I got a sick feeling about this. And about that weird fucking storm front. I'm gonna go with my gut. Mr. Lee, let's make ready for a fast run, sou'-sou'west. Keep a watch on the *Pong Su.* If nothing changes we're gonna blow this off in fifteen minutes. I want to put some serious miles between us and . . . whatever."

The *Diamantina* slipped through a light swell, pushed on by a freshening breeze. Mr. Lee had the wheel, as phlegmatic in the face of the world's end as he had been staring down the barrel of an M16 in Bali. Pete wondered what, if anything, would upset him.

Not that it mattered, because between himself and the twins there was plenty of freaking out to go round.

"Zombie Jew on a fucking Zimmer frame," said Fifi.

"What?" said Pete.

"It's redneck for 'Christ on a crutch,' Pete. Let's stay on the ball, shall we?" said Jules.

The three smugglers were crouched in front of the Samsung monitor, a brand-new twenty-three-inch flat screen Pete had picked up back in La Paz during a night of tequila shots and hard bartering with an Italian yachtsman of long acquaintance. CNN's Asia bureau, reporting out of the network's regional HQ in Hong Kong, ran in a small window taking up about a quarter of the screen. Jules had plugged into the live web feed via an Iridium phone, and if they watched it much longer they'd need all of the money in the hold to pay this month's bill.

If it ever arrived.

Pete's eyes flicked over to the GPS window, which showed them retreating from the abandoned rendezvous with the *Pong Su* at eleven knots. The North Korean ship was still describing a long, lazy arc that would eventually see it run aground somewhere near Mazatlán, in the next day or so. Pete, the only one of them to have a seat in front of the display, had to rub his eyes. Like an addicted gamer, he'd been staring so hard at the screen he hadn't blinked in a long while. He shook his head as he rubbed the irritation away, his vision blurring slightly when he refocused on the window in which footage of a major highway crash was now running.

He couldn't get his head around the pictures that had come in from a small Canadian local news team, some guys out of Edmonton according to the dateline. The image seemed to be out of focus or something. He could tell they were looking at a big pileup on a six-lane highway, but everything was indistinct, as though viewed through poorly blown glass.

"The effect is stationary," the heavily accented Quebecois voice-over assured everyone. "Mounted police at the scene are not allowing anyone to approach the phenomenon after the loss of the two fire engines."

Blurred, wavering vision of two fire trucks came up, both of them overturned in a deep ditch by the side of the road. A few hundred meters beyond them a large pileup of vehicles burned freely.

"Oh, man, this is really putting the zap on my head," Fifi muttered.

"We really need to think this through," said Jules, in her oddly cool, high-tone manner. "This could be quite awful."

Pete rubbed at his three-day beard, completely lost for an answer. For a few minutes, a little earlier, he'd actually thought of heading north to raid an empty city. He could have sailed into Santa Monica and picked up a super-yacht, provisioned her for a year, filled the leftover space with jewels and ammo. But CNN had convinced him otherwise. It was abundantly clear that you could go into the "storm front" that had appeared to their north, but you'd never come back. What was the old Argentine phrase? It "disappeared" people.

"I think we might shoot through to my old stomping ground," he said. "Hobart looks far enough away to me. And I know people there. We can move this money in a flash."

"But what if it starts growing?" asked Fifi, with a sharp edge to her voice. "What if it just eats up the whole world? Like the Blob or something?"

Pete gave her his most open, honest face.

"Then we're fucked, darlin'. Aren't we?"

"Pete . . . ?"

It was Jules, if anything looking even more concerned than before. The worry lines between her eyes were virtual canyons now.

"How fast can we get to Hobart?"

"Why?" he asked. Jules had a postgraduate degree in keeping a stiff upper lip, probably thanks to her old man. If she thought something even worse was coming their way, it really didn't bear thinking about.

"Because nobody will want greenbacks if Uncle Sam's beamed up to the *Enterprise* and flown away for good."

The bow of the yacht sliced into the face of a larger than normal wave, throwing them all slightly off balance. The *Diamantina* climbed up and over the crest, slamming down hard on the far side with a great, hollow boom. Fifi and Jules braced themselves against the nearest bulkhead. Pete hung on to the arms of his chair. On the computer screen, Stan Grant interviewed a physicist from the Hong Kong University of Science and Technology, but Pete Holder had already tuned out. Jules was right. If this was a permanent deal they had very little time before their hard-earned stick was worth less than a handful of Polish zlotys.

"You're right," he said tonelessly. "We have to get back onshore and change our money over. Do we know if the Caymans are affected? Or the Canal?"

"We can find out." Jules nodded at the screen. "But, Pete, I don't think we can get there in time. We have to get onshore as soon as we can. Somewhere big enough to convert the money, but far enough removed from . . . whatever it is . . . that blind panic hasn't taken over yet."

"Acapulco's still there," said Fifi. "But it's locked down, accordin' to the radio."

"That might be a good thing." Jules shrugged. "They keep a lid on things long enough, we might just get in and out. Otherwise we'd have to run down to Guatemala or El Salvador."

Pete chewed his lower lip, sucking the salt from it as he pondered the unfolding disaster. A window displaying the Google news page refreshed, informing him that nearly three thousand stories had already been filed on the phenomenon; none of them from North America. The bright blue hyperlinks all led to European and Asian sites. One, from Agence France-Presse, reported that trading had been suspended on the London, Tokyo, and Sydney stock exchanges. Just beneath it, a Novosti report out of Moscow claimed that the Russian armed forces had all been called into barracks and placed on high alert. Pete adjusted his balance as the *Diamantina* slipped sideways down the face of another large wave.

"You're right," he concluded. "We've got to get in somewhere fast. This feels like a big bucket of shit about to tip over and bury the whole world. Let's head for Acapulco."

"You sure?" said Fifi, her usually sunny features darkened by real fear. "That's close to the . . . thing."

"I know," said Pete. "But I got friends there. Well, contacts anyway. And the effect's not moving."

For now, he thought.

05

The shock and awe was not long in coming. Coalition head-quarters in Qatar was a focal point of communications links, neutron-star-dense, not all of them controlled by the military. Hundreds of journalists had gathered there to report on the invasion of Iraq, and many if not all of them enjoyed direct voice and data access to their own headquarters and, of course, to the wider global media. The "incident," as it was now being referred to, occurred shortly before a scheduled press briefing in the main media room, giving the assembled journalists just long enough to work up a fine head of blind panic and to warn their colleagues who might have been disinclined to attend the tightly scripted and mostly useless briefing that for once "the follies" might be worth a look. Bret Melton couldn't believe the turnout. Normally this room was only half full, but today every seat was taken, and in the back half even the aisles were full. He doubted it had anything to do with the scheduled appearance of the British and Australian task force comman-ders to do their first joint conference with General Franks.

Indeed, neither Franks nor the junior Coalition partners were anywhere to be seen as a USAF colonel took the podium. Melton, a former ranger, was a nine-year veteran of the *Army Times* foreign desk and knew most of the U.S. military's Qatar-based flack handlers by first names. He had never seen the air force bird before. He keyed on his Dictaphone as soon as the officer appeared, ensuring that the first twenty seconds of his recording was taken up with the jabbering crescendo of two hundred plus colleagues all shouting individual questions at the front of the room. He had no trouble resisting the urge to join in the raucous assault on the dignity of the briefer. What would be the point? Melton waited for the chaos to die down. The colonel did nothing to calm the room. He merely placed a sheaf of papers on the podium and stood at ease examining the unruly mob with cool aloofness. Nearly a minute and a half after he had first entered the room, the reporters slowly, gradually quieted down and resumed their seats like shamefaced school-children. As if to make the point about who precisely was in charge, the colonel's eyes traversed his audience with a cold, mechanical detachment.

Melton readied his pen to take notes. His Sony recorder was working perfectly, but that was exactly when you couldn't trust the damn things.

"Ladies and gentlemen, my name is Colonel Yost, and I will be taking your briefing tonight in place of Generals Franks and Wall and Brigadier McNairn. They have been indisposed by developments but will make themselves available for questioning as soon as possible."

An Italian TV producer sitting directly in front of Melton leapt to his feet and called out, "When?"

Yost fixed him with a killing stare and waited a full three seconds before answering.

"As. Soon. As. Possible."

A further glare delivered as a broadside to most of the room cut off any more interruptions.

"As you know, communications links to North America have been severed, not just from CENTCOM, but more generally, across both the civilian and military spectrums," said Yost. "Answering speculation as to why, how, and by whom is not my responsibility today. It may be yours, but you won't get your answers here. CENTCOM is endeavoring to reestablish contact as quickly as possible. We have already confirmed links with the Pacific, European, and, *I emphasize, some* elements of the Northern Command. For those of you who do not know, NORTHCOM is the unified military command responsible for operations in the U.S., Mexico, Canada, and the northern Caribbean."

Melton didn't bother to jot down the explanation. He was familiar with all of the U.S. commands, having worked in each of them at some time, but he did note that Yost didn't claim to be in contact with NORTHCOM proper, just "elements" of it. That could mean a big ass-kicking setup like Fort Lewis, outside of Seattle, or it might mean he'd phoned a guard post somewhere on the outskirts of Juneau or Guantánamo.

"Have you seen the photos, Colonel? The French satellite photos? Of your cities. Can you tell us what has happened to them?"

Melton recognized the voice of Sayad al-Mirsaad, the al-Jazeera correspondent who was forever in danger of being thrown off the base. Yost leveled the same robotic stare at him that he'd used to silence the Italian provocateur, but Melton knew his Jordanian colleague wouldn't be so easily cowed. Al-Mirsaad remained on his feet, hands on hips, almost inviting him to reach over and take a swing.

"They are gone, Colonel. They are all gone. An act of God, no less. How could it be otherwise?"

Yost jumped in before a flood tide of voices could drown him out.

"It could very easily be anything but, *Mr.* al-Mirsaad. You are not there. You haven't seen anything for yourself. All you know is that you can't get a phone call through, and somebody is selling very expensive pictures of what looks to me like computer-generated video game imagery. If I were you I'd go read your H. G. Wells before I pushed the panic button, sir."

Melton smirked quietly as he filled his notepad with short-hand. He had to score that one to Yost, although the classical sci-fi reference seemed lost on the Jordanian as well as most of the other foreign journalists in the room. For himself, he didn't mind a bit of trashy reading when he was stretched out in business class, thirty thousand feet up. But he lived and worked in the real world, just like the men and women he wrote about, and while the *Army Times* correspondent couldn't possibly imagine what sort of technical clusterfuck or psy-war hoax they were dealing with, he had no doubt the explanation was more prosaic than alien space bats or the hand of God.

He hadn't had time to view the still shots on BBC World. He'd been too busy trying and failing to get through to the head office back in Virginia. If he had to make a bet, however, he'd lay his money on some kind of killer software virus, probably written up by guerrilla hackers in Russia or Malaysia as a protest against the imminent war, not to mention as a personal shot at glory in the bizarro underground. A hit like this, just days before the start of the war, would instantly transform some zitty college dropout into a hypercelebrity superhacker. A pity for them they'd never be able to cash in with Nike endorsements or a Coke ad. Best they could hope for was a virtual hand job on some malware chat site. Fuckwits. Just a few months ago he'd freelanced a three-thousand-word feature on digital security for Stratfor.com that the *Times* didn't want. He'd come away with mixed feelings: utter contempt for the social misfits and losers who were the creators of so many of the most destructive programs, and an unshakable certainty that one day one of them was going to pull some stunt that did real-world damage to real-world lives. Perhaps this was it.

Somebody from Agence France-Presse jumped to his feet demanding to know—the French reporters always sounded like they were *demanding* this or that—how the Coalition expected to maintain the integrity of its communications in any conflict with Iraq, given the "total collapse" of its network this morning. It was a good question, one Melton had wondered about, and he was surprised to see that Yost looked almost relieved to get it.

"Our theater-level networks remain fully functional, intact, and secure," he said. "General Franks is in complete control of all Coalition forces in situ. That is simply not an issue. The U.S. and its allies are ready and willing to carry out any order from their national command authorities. Whatever the mission, we will accomplish it. Thank you. This briefing is at an end. You will be kept informed of any developments via the media center."

Yost nodded curtly, gathered up his papers, and walked away from the rostrum as hundreds of seated reporters suddenly leapt to their feet to hurl questions at him. Melton stood with them. In the sudden outburst all he'd heard was a single question shouted by Sayad al-Mirsaad before anyone else.

"What national command authority? They're gone . . ."

It's an intensely frustrating experience for a newsman to find himself cut off from the biggest story of the day, and Bret Melton felt as though he was cut off from the biggest story of all time. That's not to say that there was nothing to report from Qatar. The press conference had broken up in chaos, and the headquarters of the Coalition forces was seething with all of the mad energy of a giant ants' nest that had been rudely kicked open. But in spite of all the activity as the military spooled up its response to whatever had happened on the other side of the globe, Melton knew that a more immediate story was available a short plane ride away: the inevitable eruption of the Arab world when it realized that America was gone.

It was unbelievable, insane, and completely fucking outrageous.

It was gone.

He'd eaten nearly half a roll of antacid pills in the last hour as he tried to accept the situation. Sitting by himself in a crowded canteen roaring with the voices of dozens of reporters who'd crowded in for the free Wi-Fi and chilled air, Melton had surfed the web frantically looking for something, anything that might expose the morning's news as a gigantic fraud. All he managed to do was convince himself that nobody, no state or group and certainly no individual, could pull off such an enormous scam. The disappearance was real.

He thumbed another couple of Rolaids into his mouth, sucking at them despondently as he clicked through a series of windows. News reports. Canadian TV shots. webcam feeds. He'd searched dozens of chat sites, which had "lost" most of their participants hours ago, their last messages often ending in midsentence. It was a visit to an online gaming site that convinced him, however. He had a little-used subscription to Blizzard.net that he'd set up when researching a piece about the possibility of using multiplayer combat sims as a recruiting tool. Everywhere he went in the virtual worlds, he found CGI avatars standing mutely, awaiting instructions from their creators. Beneath them, in the small windows given over to character dialogue, there were reams of increasingly bemused, uneasy, and then fearful comments from players who'd logged on from areas outside North America. Most tellingly, almost nobody was now online, the survivors having abandoned the game servers for news sites or perhaps even the real world.

"A dark day, my friend. A very dark day."

Melton looked up from the eerie stillness of a window running a multiplayer version of Diablo. Sayad al-Mirsaad, the al-Jazeera correspondent, stood over him.

"Do you mind?" he asked, indicating the seat in front of Melton.

"Of course not," he said distractedly. "Sit down, Sadie."

His Jordanian colleague had given up protesting the American's use of the slightly offensive nickname, finally accepting some time ago that it was meant affectionately. He was regularly called much worse by some of Melton's countrymen.

"I can see from your face you are a believer now, yes?" said al-Mirsaad without a hint of irony. He and Melton were both educated men, both men of strong faith, and they had passed many late hours in Qatar discussing theology and politics.

The former ranger shrugged and let his hand fly up in a gesture that was part resignation, part expression of utter futility. He didn't reply. Around him the reporters roared on, all holding forth on their own ideas and bullshit conspiracy theories. An unpleasant energy pervaded the room, setting his teeth on edge. In contrast, al-Mirsaad appeared to be almost as depressed as he was.

"Not everyone will think it's a bad day, Sadie," Melton said at last. "Some asshole's gonna be sending a lot of extra prayers upstairs tonight, thanking their God for getting rid of the great Satan."

He watched al-Mirsaad closely, but he seemed almost as upset as any American.

"Then they would be fools," replied the Jordanian. "Ultimately everything is God's will, but this is not His work. In the affairs of men, the will of Allah is known through the actions of men. This . . . this is something else."

"I think so, too." Melton nodded. "But it doesn't mean . . ."

"Hey, shut the fuck up!" somebody yelled from across the room. "It's Saddam."

The name acted like a spell, laying a hush over the room as Melton twisted around in his plastic chair to get a view of a television screen high on the wall behind him. The Iraqi leader appeared there, beaming like a pirate king who'd fallen ass-backward into a huge pile of both kinds of booty. The electronic watermark in the top right-hand corner of the screen belonged to the al-Jazeera network, and the report was in Arabic.

"What's it saying?" somebody asked. Melton glanced back at al-Mirsaad for a translation, but before he could answer, an educated English voice rang out over the heads of the crowd. A handsome, well-groomed young man with South Asian features and an impeccable Etonian accent stood on a chair to get a clear view of the TV. Melton thought he recognized him. A BBC producer.

"It's saying Hussein appeared briefly before a crowd at one of his palaces about forty minutes ago," the man called out.

The footage showed a beaming dictator. Melton thought he was smiling so much that if he'd been a cartoon character the top of his head would have fallen off. Dressed in army greens and sporting a black beret, he fired six rounds from a pistol into the air as a small coterie of unctuously smiling generals watched and a no-doubt-handpicked crowd exploded into spasms of joy and tyrannophilia. Hussein began talking and an Arab voice-over cut in, after a few seconds, paraphrasing him. The English producer translated as the room full of journalists remained unnaturally still and quiet.

"He's saying that Allah the merciful, the Almighty, has swept the crusaders from the very heart of their castle . . . from the very face of the earth which they defiled with their presence. He's calling on General Franks to come out of his spider hole, to fight right now. He's demanding that all of the Arab world rise up and throw out the invaders . . . and their dogs and puppets in Riyadh and Kuwait and Qatar . . . and he's promising to lead a coalition of the fedayeen, the honorable, to drive the infidel and the apostate out of the holy lands."

The Iraqi leader punched out a few more gunshots before spreading his arms wide and retreating inside the palace. Probably to haul ass to an underground bunker before a Tomahawk caught him out in the open, thought Melton. He raised an eye at al-Mirsaad, and the Jordanian nodded, confirming the accuracy of the BBC man's translation. Within a second the room was in an uproar again, even louder and somehow denser this time. Melton shifted in his seat and rolled his shoulders in a vain attempt to shrug off a growing sense of frustration.

He had no family back in the States. He was an only child, and his parents, who'd had him late in life, were both dead. For the first time in what felt a long and lonesome existence, he was glad to be on his own in the world. His work didn't lend itself to stable relationships, and although he'd never had trouble finding women to date, none had ever lasted beyond a few weeks. Now, perversely, he was thankful for that. What must it be like for those poor fuckers around him who had family back home? A cursory glance around the canteen told him they were the ones whose voices were loudest, and whose faces were the most strained.

"What will you do, Bret?" asked al-Mirsaad.

He was about to throw out the standard reply of "my job" when it occurred to him what a ridiculous answer that would be. Did he even have a job anymore? His month's salary and travel allowance were due to be automatically deposited overnight. Would they go through? He had no idea.

"I don't know," he answered honestly, raising his voice to be heard over the tumult. "What about you?"

Al-Mirsaad seemed almost ashamed.

"I have an assignment in Palestine," he said. "They are celebrating there. Dancing in the streets. A big party. But soon I think there will be fighting, no?"

"Fighting?" muttered Bret Melton, as he contemplated the loss of his whole world, and the prospect of what remained falling to pieces beneath his feet. "I reckon so."

06

Pitié-Salpêtrière Hospital, Paris

A harried-looking man wearing a white coat over a dark suit appeared at the door and pushed past Maggie. Poleaxed by the TV news, she barely noticed him. The physician seemed to do his level best to ignore all of them, including Caitlin, even as he questioned her. A name tag on his white jacket read COLBERT.

"Any pain? Discomfort? Anything?" he asked in French, addressing the query to his watch, which he was examining as though it was the most fascinating trinket in the world.

"Yes, Doctor," she replied, in the same language. "When I tried to turn my head. My neck is very sore and I feel . . ."

She stopped short. To judge by the wide-eyed surprise on Monique's face, the young woman had not known she could speak French.

Shit.

"Yes?" he asked, still in French. "You feel what?"

"My neck . . . is very stiff and sore," she said, slowly, in English. "It hurts so much to turn it, I get sick. And I have a terrible ache in my head all the time."

Monique's hand fell away from hers. The young woman stared at her as if she had grown a new limb. The others were still fixated on the BBC. More commercial satellite imagery, from all over the North American continent, was becoming available every minute. Forty-five minutes after the short burst of white noise that shut down all communication with the richest, most powerful nation in the world—and big chunks of the countries bordering her to the north and south—the truth was unavoidable. They were gone.

Caitlin had woken into some sort of Kafkaesque nightmare, and for a moment she clutched at the hope that it might just be an actual nightmare, or even a psychotic break, perhaps the result of an acquired brain injury.

"But you told us you could not speak French," Monique said.

"Fookin' 'ell, lookit that."

"Ms. Mercure, I'm afraid I have some bad news for you . . ."

Dr. Colbert was still mechanically checking his watch.

No shit, Sherlock, thought Caitlin.

Monique, like the doctor, was also phase-locked in her own little world.

"But you *told* us. You told us you could not speak French."

Caitlin stared at her, as the world broke up into jagged mirror shards of meaning and insanity. She improvised as best she could.

"I don't speak it very well. It's embarrassing to even try. You guys are like so hard-core about it, with all the eye rolling and the shrugging. I mean, you know, *lighten up.*"

The doctor saved her by cutting her off at that point, speaking in English.

"Excuse me. But my patient is very ill. Now is not twenty-questions time. Now is . . ."

"*Fook me!*"

Auntie Celia's extra-loud cry finally brought everyone's attention back to the TV, where a top-down image of Manhattan was displayed. Caitlin momentarily thought it might have been archival footage of the 9/11 attacks. Great plumes of black smoke curled away from collapsed high-rise buildings that burned at their cores like active volcanoes. But she quickly saw that there were too many of them, too widely spread over the island, at least eight or nine that she could count immediately.

". . . if repeated across the country, the death toll might run into the millions," read the anchorwoman.

"Everyone's gone," said Maggie in a flat voice. "This is fucked. *Where have they gone?*"

". . . At any one time many thousands of aircraft are aloft over the U.S., many of them above densely populated cities."

The coverage switched to grainy video taken from a weather-cam, somewhere high above Manhattan. As Caitlin watched, numb and disbelieving, a Singapore Airlines jumbo jet plowed into the side of the Chrysler Building, one wing spinning offscreen.

Something snagged in Caitlin's conscious mind. Something that she had almost missed.

"I'm ill?" she asked, suddenly picking up on the qualification the doctor had made. "I'm sick? Not just injured?"

Irrationally, she reached for the thought, hoping it might explain the psychotic bullshit on the television.

Dr. Colbert nodded distractedly. Now that he was watching the TV he seemed unable to wrench his attention away from it. The screen switched to a series of shots detailing the moments just before and after a giant tanker slammed into a wharf in a city she didn't recognize. Two frames showed it heading straight in to the dockside. The next two captured the impact, with the front quarter of the supertanker crumpling back in on itself while the water around the vessel churned white and dockside cranes began to topple. A single frame caught the moment of detonation amidships, a blossom of white light spilling from the ruptured hull. And then the entire length of the supertanker was consumed by the birth of a dwarf star.

Maggie started swearing at the TV again, a stream of disconnected curses. Auntie Celia softly repeated the same thing over and over again.

"Fookin' 'ell . . . fookin' 'ell . . ."

Every time she said it, she unfolded and refolded her arms, like a malfunctioning animatronic figure. Monique, however, was refusing to even look at the screen anymore.

"You said you could not speak French at all," she said.

Dr. Colbert shook his head like a dog emerging from water and waved her away with his clipboard, addressing himself only half to Caitlin. His eyes remained fixed on the catastrophe as it unfolded a few feet above the end of the bed.

"We have done scans while you were unconscious. You have a lesion on your hippocampus, a part of the brain intimately involved in the organization of memory. It may be a tumor," he said in English. "But we need to take a biopsy to ascertain its nature. It may be serious. Much more serious than the injuries that brought you here. They are uncomfortable, but they can be dealt with."

Caitlin Monroe had been an Echelon field agent for nearly five years. She had been intensively trained for three years before that. Her entire adult life she had lived in a crazy maze where every step she took, every corner she turned, she faced the possibility of betrayal and death. She had adapted to a contingent existence where nothing was taken for granted. She had faced her own potential annihilation so many times that a doctor telling her she might be dying was completely passé. At least on a normal day.

But this was a thousand miles from being a normal day, and for once Caitlin found the idea of her life ending a completely novel and unsettling concept. It stuck in her mind, a barbed, immovable object that tugged painfully whenever she tried to pull at it.

"I'm dying?"

"No," said Colbert. "But . . ."

The television went blank, the screen a dead black void.

"What the . . ."

Two words of plain white type appeared.

TRANSMISSION INTERRUPTED.

"Holy shit, it's happing here now!" said Maggie.

"No!" said Caitlin, cutting off an outbreak of panic. They could all hear cries of alarm and distress from other rooms on the hospital floor. "Just wait."

STAND BY FOR AN ANNOUNCEMENT BY HM GOVERNMENT.

"Check the French news channels," she said. "See if they're still on. And the English sports channels."

Monique abandoned the task of glaring at her to flip channels with the remote. As Caitlin had expected, the continental stations were still broadcasting, as were Sky Racing and the English football channels. Even the end of the world wouldn't be allowed to interfere with interminable replays of last year's Champions League.

"It's nothing," Caitlin assured them, rubbing at her throbbing temples with one hand, the one trailing slightly fewer sensor leads. "The government has taken control of the news broadcasters. It's standard procedure in a national emergency. Just watch . . . And Doc . . . what's your name again?"

"Colbert."

"Dr. Colbert. I'm not dying?"

He gave the impression of a man greatly relieved to find himself back on familiar ground.

"Not yet. But you could, without proper treatment. You are not yet incapacitated but the lesion might well require intense therapy and very soon. But we can treat you as an outpatient for the moment . . . We need your bed." He shrugged, smiling for the first time, almost apologetically.

A single, high-pitched tone filled the room for one second before the TV screen came back to life. Tony Blair was sitting at a desk in a book-lined room with a British flag prominently draped from a pole behind him. His eyes were haunted, and even beneath a very professional makeup job his skin looked blotchy and sallow.

"G . . . good evening," he stammered.

Colbert wasn't kidding about needing the bed. An hour later, still swaddled in bandages, trailing one rogue sensor lead that had become entangled with her unwashed hair, Caitlin Monroe was still in-character as Cathy Mercure, attempting to sign herself out of the Pitié-Salpêtrière while shaking off what she'd come to think of as her "secret squirrel detail." The motley trio of professional antiwarmongers had closed around her like a fist as she'd dragged herself out of bed, dressed, and pushed her way through corridors now crowded with panicky idiots.

Caitlin was surprised at the hysterical undertow that was already running so strongly in the Pitié-Salpêtrière. But then, the place was full of people who were already stressed out and had nothing much to do beyond watching television while they waited for some sort of traumatic medical procedure. On the way down to checkout she witnessed any number of pedal-to-the-metal, full-bore freak-outs. One woman even barreled right into her; a large, bug-eyed Parisian Mack truck, she knocked Maggie right off her feet, screaming about the end of days before disappearing down the hallway with her enormous, deeply dimpled butt swinging free in the rear of a badly strung hospital gown.

"I'll be a lot better off out of here," Caitlin assured her companions.

Apart from Monique, who remained suspicious after discovering Caitlin's hidden gift for her native tongue, the secret squirrels weren't doing much better than any of the ranting, unbalanced Frenchies around them. Maggie, after picking herself up off the floor, was blabbering on about needing to phone her sister in Connecticut. And Auntie Celia had settled on a never-ending string of curses and oaths as her favored response. They'd all made perfunctory efforts to get her to stay in the hospital, to argue with Colbert that she was too ill to move, but Caitlin could tell that each was spinning off into her own little world of free-floating and violently unstable anxiety. The whole city was probably going to be like this. The whole fucking world.

For her part, she didn't know what to think about the news out of the States. It was bordering on schizoid. But she did know that even if this all turned out to be some postmillennial *War of the Worlds* shakedown, if she'd been cut off from Echelon, she was traveling blind and unarmed in a world of predators. She had to run to ground as soon as possible, reestablish contact with Wales Larrison, her controller, and get some updated instructions. Christ only knew what had gone down while she'd been out of it. Plus, of course, Monique was eyeing her with increasing suspicion.

A single television suspended from the ceiling in the main waiting room had drawn a huge pool of onlookers, all muttering and gasping at every new revelation from the French-language news service. Caitlin ignored it. She was having trouble negotiating her release with the large, distracted black woman on the front desk. Like everyone else she seemed incapable of dragging her attention away from the TV for more than a few seconds. Monique tugged at her elbow, saying in French, "*I want to speak to you,*" while Maggie, who had spied a bank of pay phones, exclaimed, "All righty then!"

She took off past Caitlin and Monique and her head suddenly burst open.

Ropy strands of blood, bone chips, and gobbets of brain tissue splattered everybody within two meters. As Maggie's oversize, badly dressed, and utterly lifeless frame began to drop to the floor, Caitlin was already in midair, having launched herself without thought toward the nearest cover. She sailed over the counter, crashing bodily into the nurse with whom she'd been making so little headway. A cheap pink radio exploded on top of a filing cabinet. The screams began as the hundred or more people crammed into the foyer finally realized that somebody was shooting into their midst, but Caitlin was already on the move, belly-crawling toward an open door that she hoped would give onto another exit point.

"Wait!"

She felt a hand on her ankle and lashed back with a heel strike, only checking the move as she recognized the voice. Monique. The blow still caught the French girl heavily on one cheek, and she cried out in pain. Caitlin swore and reached back behind her, grabbing Monique by her collar and roughly dragging her up into a crouching run. She slipped once, losing her footing and painfully twisting one knee. "*Move,*" she yelled. "*If you want to live, move your ass!*"

Behind them a riot had seemingly erupted. She heard two muffled shots and the crash of breaking glass, barely masked by the uproar of the terrorized crowd. A frightened nurse stood in their way, her eyes wide and staring. Caitlin elbowed her aside and made for a doorway behind her.

"What is happening?" cried Monique before Caitlin cut her off.

"Shut up and run!"

Crashing out into the corridor, they ran headlong into a couple of security guards, one fat and wheezing and another who looked like he might have started his career as a public security professional back in the days of the Maginot Line. "That way," yelled

Caitlin, throwing a glance back over her shoulder, where she caught the briefest glimpse of pandemonium in the hospital foyer. Snaking around the guards, she sped up again, turning left and right, slamming through a series of swinging rubber doors without regard for who or what she might find on the other side. She'd let go of Monique and didn't much care whether she was keeping up or not, as she blew through yet another set of swinging doors, crashing into an orderly and the trolley he'd been pushing. It tipped over and fell to the tiles with a great metallic clattering of medical instruments and stainless-steel bowls. Never stopping, Caitlin swooped down on a foil package, slipping it into her sleeve as she hurried on.

"Wait, Cathy, wait."

Monique was still with her.

They'd found the treatment area of the hospital's emergency ward, and even by the usually chaotic standards of an ER their entrance drew attention. With no televisions in this ward and almost everyone distracted by whatever injuries or raging illnesses had gained them access to the overstretched facility, the sudden noisy appearance of two women, covered in gore and moving at great speed with no apparent regard for their own safety or anybody else's, caused heads to turn and all conversation to halt. Monique was obviously about to start demanding answers, and looked like she might just put down roots on the spot where she'd slid to a halt. A formidable gray-haired woman in a matron's uniform started moving toward them with her head down and eyes glaring murderously. She put Caitlin in mind of a big blue bulldozer.

"What the hell are you doing?" asked Monique. "What is going on?"

Before Caitlin could answer, or even just spin around and keep running, the same heavy rubber doors swung inward and two men, both of them armed, muscled through. They were dressed in suits, one of them badly bloodstained, and their eyes swept the room, quickly settling on their quarry. Caitlin knew there was no chance of running.

Two bullets took the formidable-looking matron in the chest, throwing her through the air and rendering her a whole lot less imposing as her body crashed into a bed and dropped to the floor, twitching and pulsing extravagant amounts of blood onto the yellowing tiles. Monique screamed and ducked, covering her ears with both hands. Her cries were lost in the bedlam as patients and medical staff exploded into panic. Having no cover and no safe exit, Caitlin took the only option left. She attacked.

One of her assailants had been caught with an empty magazine, leaving his partner as the primary threat. She grabbed the only ranged weapons on hand, a couple of stainless-steel bowls, and launched them with great force like bright metal Frisbees directly at his head. He had no choice but to duck and weave, firing anyway, the bullets heading downrange unaimed, uncontrolled. One splattered an IV bag. Another struck a patient in one arm. Taking the foil pack from inside the sleeve at her wrist as she charged, Caitlin stripped the silver wrapping away from a disposable scalpel, and focusing her *kiai,* her war shout, into the very center of her target, she closed the short distance between them as quickly as she could.

To those normal, mortal beings around her, she moved as a fluid blur of violent action, suddenly airborne, one long leg pistoning out and into the sternum of the armed attacker. The gun fired again, bringing down a shower of plaster dust from the ceiling as he slammed backward into a wall. His head struck a metal oxygen tap with a wet crunch, and he began a slow drop to the ground, trailing a greasy organic smear down the wall. Without pause Caitlin's whole body swept around in a small, self-contained tornado, one foot lashing out to strike squarely at the gun hand of her second foe, who had just jacked in a fresh mag as she struck. The pistol, a Glock 23, discharged a single round, shattering an overhead fluorescent light. Turning tightly with the direction of the kick, getting right inside the circle of her man, Caitlin shot out her free hand, grabbing his wrist, extending it up, and slamming her other arm in under the elbow to snap the vulnerable joint with a terrible crack. In a flash, her weapon hand whipped backward and she opened his throat with the razor-sharp scalpel. A geyser of hot blood spilled out in a rush as she continued to spin, dragging the bulk of her victim around between her and the first man. Only then did she strip the Glock from the weak, rubbery grip of the man, who was already slumping out of her grasp. She felt fingers breaking as she wrenched it away.

In the space of less than three seconds she stood over

her would-be killers. The pistol was already cocked. Two loud, flat cracks rang out and she finished off the prone figure by the wall. A slight shift in stance as she swung around and double-tapped the man at her feet, even though his life was already bleeding out of him. Almost no thought went into the actions. She hadn't indulged herself in the luxury of conscious thought since the two of them had burst into the ER. She had simply reacted, her mind and body running along tracks that had been laid down for her by thousands of hours of training.

"*No!*" screamed a voice. Monique's. "*What are you? You fucking monster!*"

I'm Echelon, thought Caitlin, as she took the weapon from the lifeless hand of the first man she had killed. The ER was unnaturally still all around her. No one had yet recovered from the shock of such extreme and unexpected violence. Her gun hand seemed to float toward the weeping French girl. A slow, inhuman movement, machinelike in its lack of compassion. Monique was no longer an asset, a resource to be exploited for the mission. She was a loose end.

07

Guantánamo Bay naval base, Cuba

The Cuban officer's salute was crisp, and his posture ramrod-straight, but his eyes betrayed confusion and anxiety. Musso returned the salute before dropping into a more relaxed posture. The two men stood in a bare office, borrowed for the meeting. Until two days ago it had been the domain of a navy lieutenant, but he had transferred back home, and nobody had yet arrived to fill his berth. *And five'll get you fifty that nobody ever will,* Musso thought bleakly.

"Major," he said, to open the discussion, "welcome to Guantánamo Naval Station."

Major Eladio Núñez bobbed his head up and down in an agitated fashion.

"Would you care to sit?" asked Musso.

"*Sí*. Thank you."

Núñez dropped into a chair with some relief. His aide, a captain, remained at attention by the door. Lieutenant Colonel Stavros stood at ease by the cheap government-issue desk on which Musso had leaned back. Outside, the base was locked down on its highest alert. Two marines in full battle rattle double-timed past. They were ready. The question was simple enough. Ready for what?

"This . . . ah . . . this is very difficult . . . you understand?" said Núñez. He leaned forward, his hands rubbing together nervously. "We do not . . . I don't . . ."

"You've lost contact with Havana," Musso offered.

"*Sí*. But more than that. Something strange. A few miles to the north of my position. A sort of heat curtain. We can see the land behind it, through a haze, and it looks normal. But nothing, or no people, move there. There is a town, not far beyond the line, on the road north. Nothing. Not a soul."

Musso nodded. Núñez was deeply agitated, but Musso was not so stupid as to make any judgments about the man's character on that basis. The major had been chosen by the Cuban military to face off a mortal enemy squatting on the very soil of his motherland. He would be neither a fool nor a coward.

"Have you sent anybody in?" he asked. "To investigate."

The captain standing by the door moved fractionally. A tic flickered under one eye. Núñez nodded.

"*Sí*. Yes. I send in some scouts. They appear to, uh, to disappear in the heat haze. It was very thick, very powerful, no? Near the effect? It seemed much hotter. And so my men they walk in, slowly. They . . ."

He groped for the right word.

"They shimmer? Yes? In the haze? And they are gone."

"Just gone?" asked Stavros.

Núñez nodded vigorously. "Yes. Sometimes the haze seems to shift, like a curtain, just for a second, and we can see farther down the road, say two hundred meters. It is like looking into a fish tank, yes, in a restaurant? It is a very strange sight. Like a curtain of air? I do not see how that can be but it . . . ah . . ." He rolled his hands in a helpless gesture, seeking the right words again. "You can see this curtain. But the scouts, they never emerge on the far side. Their uniforms. They fall in a heap. Charred and smoking."

Musso frowned. He thought he understood what Núñez was describing. The heat wall sounded a little like a blast wave, the front of supercompressed air that moves outward from the point of an explosion. But in this case it wasn't moving, or compressed. It merely hung in the air "like a curtain," as Núñez had called it.

Musso cleared his throat.

"Major, my own observers reported some of your men . . . heading north . . ."

"Yes," he said bitterly. "They abandoned their posts."

"And they ran into the haze?"

Núñez nodded, almost looking satisfied.

"Yes. There was no need to shoot them. They have gone, too."

"I see," said Musso. "And what would you like us to do?"

Núñez shifted uncomfortably in his seat, looking around, surprised at last to find himself in the devil's lair. He sighed.

"We would like help. We are not a tin pot dictator's ship," he said, forcing Musso to suppress a grin for the first time that morning. "We have been intercepting your satellite news services. We know this is beyond the normal. Something terrible and large is happening. We need to know what. To prepare."

Musso folded his arms and let his chin rest on his chest.

"This 'curtain' of air," he said after a brief moment of quiet. "Is it stable? Is it moving, expanding at all?"

Núñez appeared deeply troubled by the question. "Like I said. It is a giant curtain and like a curtain, it moves as if blown by the wind, sweeping over the countryside like a curtain blows in a window."

Musso had to suppress a shiver that started at the base of his spine and ran up into his shoulders. The idea of this thing moving an inch was disturbing at a cellular level.

"Major, how much is it moving? Have you been able to determine any limits?"

Núñez bobbed his head up and down.

"It seems to . . . billow . . . is that your word? It seems to billow like a sail, up to fifteen or twenty meters. It seems random.

Just like a curtain or the branches of a tree moving in the breeze. But if it sweeps over you . . . poof! You are gone."

"Well, we need to know more about it, about the parameters under which it operates. But neither of us can send any more of our people in," said Musso.

"I know," Núñez agreed. "We have watched your planes and ships, no? The pilots and sailors, they have been taken, too."

"What about a Predator?" suggested Stavros. "I understand there's a unit on base. The effect doesn't seem to interfere with electronics. Perhaps we could send one up and into the affected area."

Musso gave Núñez an inquiring look.

"How d'you feel about that, Major? We could send an unmanned drone up, but we'd be violating your airspace. I would need a written authorization from your senior officer."

Part of him marveled at how deeply ingrained the ass-covering reflex was, but what the hell was he supposed to do?

"I am the senior officer, now," said Núñez as he began patting his pockets. "My colonel was in Havana, and Lieutenant Colonel Lorenz drove into the haze before we realized what it was. His car went off the road and burned."

Stavros handed him a pen and notepad. The Cuban began scribbling immediately. Nobody spoke while he wrote. Musso walked over to the window. It was coming on for midday and the sun beat down fiercely on the base. A flagpole across the compound outside cast only a short dagger of shadow, the Stars and Stripes hanging limp in the humidity. Guantánamo was not a major fleet base. It had been established as a coaling station, not the most glamorous of postings, long before it became a famous prison camp. Down in the bay, a couple of tugs and a single minesweeper lay at anchor close to shore. It was a scene entirely normal, even banal.

"Here," said Núñez, handing the slip of paper to Stavros. "You may countersign as a witness. I have authorized Brigadier General Musso to deploy surveillance assets into Cuban territory on a temporary basis, with myself to administratively supervise such deployments in each and every instance."

"Fine," said Musso.

In fact there were any number of red flags sticking out of such an arrangement, and under normal circumstances Núñez would have guaranteed himself a trip to prison, or even a blindfold and last cigarette, by writing out such an order. If he was willing to put his nuts in the grinder, Musso could hardly quibble.

"Goddamn."

Lieutenant Colonel Stavros was the first to speak, and he said it all.

"Goddamn is right," agreed Musso.

"*Madre de Dios,*" muttered Núñez.

His very presence in the situation room would have been unthinkable only hours earlier, and two heavily built MPs were shadowing his every move, but Musso wasn't expecting any trouble. Nor was he expecting any repercussions from having allowed an enemy officer into one of the nerve centers of the U.S. military to watch some of its newest technology in action. There had been some quiet and very forceful dissent from the army's senior representatives on base, a military police colonel and a signal corps major, no less. But they had been overruled with extreme prejudice.

"Empty," said Núñez. "Completely empty."

"Goddamn," whispered Stavros again. A single bead of sweat trickled down his temple even though the blue-lit room, buried thirty meters below ground, was nearly as cold as a beer fridge. Fear sweat, sour and musky, filled the space. Holguín, a city of more than three hundred souls, scrolled down the plasma screen in front of them. It lay nearly a hundred klicks away to the north, well within the Predator's range. But Musso intended to push the aircraft on, deeper into Cuban airspace. It was going to go down in hostile territory. Or what had been hostile territory this morning. Musso was already thinking of it as no-man's-land now. Quite literally.

The sysop controlling the surveillance bird had dropped its altitude to three hundred meters, a height at which the Predator's cameras could easily pick out very fine detail on the streets below. In fact, so low was she flying and so close had the operator pulled in the view that the real-time feed was a blur, and Musso, like the other observers, was instead examining slo-mo replays on the other monitors. In one, the Calixto García Park, right in the middle of the city's downtown area, rolled into view. Another showed the giant Cervecería Bucanero brewery—a joint venture with the Canadian brewer

Labatt. It was aflame, but nobody was fighting the blaze. On some monitors beautifully decaying Spanish colonial architecture sat cheek by jowl with aesthetically worthless cement office blocks and warehouses. Winding streets gave onto cobblestone plazas and the town's surprisingly rich cultural district, wherein half a dozen museums, galleries, and libraries all stood.

Not a solitary human figure moved anywhere.

"You know what else I don't see," said Musso. "Dogs. Or birds. Or animals of any kind."

"Damn," said Stavros. "You're right."

Unlike the satellite images they'd been watching on the European and Asian news services, the Predator fed live video, and although the streets of Holquín were not nearly as crowded with vehicular traffic as an American city of comparable size, they were still choked with the wreckage of hundreds of cars, many of them burning, which had apparently all lost their drivers at the same time. A thickening layer of smoke hung over the city, stirred only slightly by a gathering breeze.

"General Musso, sir?"

"Yes, son," Musso answered without looking away from the eerie scenes.

"I have PACOM on line for you, sir."

Musso accepted a pair of headphones with a mike attached, fitting them on and walking over to a far corner.

"This is Musso," he said, quietly.

"General," came a brusque reply in a rather refined New England accent. "Admiral James Ritchie here. Glad to hear you're still with us. You seem to be on the front line of this . . . phenomenon."

"Close enough, sir. It's touched down about seventy klicks north of here. Admiral, if you don't mind me asking, do you have information about the situation in CONUS? All we're getting is the news feeds out of Europe and Asia."

"No," complained Ritchie. "We're not doing much better. Some of my people have managed to take control of the Keyhole over Havana. That's what I'm pushing through to you now, but we've got nothing from home yet. I take it there's no chance we'll get a real pair of eyeballs on this today?"

Musso shook his head, holding the earphones in place as he did so. The set was way too small for him and kept slipping off.

"No, sir. Whatever this thing is, it's specifically targeted for an antipersonnel effect. We lost a few people to it before we realized. The Cubans lost a lot more, for what it's worth. But there seems to be no interference with electronic signals or equipment. I guess it's something akin to a neutron bomb. Takes out the people and leaves the infrastructure in place."

Even as he said it, the rational part of his mind rebelled. He was talking about his wife and children. They were part of the "antipersonnel effect." They had to have "shimmered away," just like all of Núñez's men. Just like everyone north of here.

They'll be fine, he repeated over and over. *They'll be fine and they'll be home soon.*

Ritchie's voice crackled in the headset, and Musso wondered if he'd spoken too soon about signal interference, but the audio came good again.

"Okay, well, have a look at the video my people are sending you. There's about twelve minutes' worth. Then we'll talk again. I'm going to call a videoconference of the . . . the available theater commands in twenty minutes."

The admiral sounded like an old man.

He'd have family at home, too. But this was worse than losing a family. Much, much worse.

The videoconference, hosted out of Pearl, drew in high-level participants from all the theater commands, including himself as the senior officer "available" from NORTHCOM. That's how they were putting it. Not "surviving," just "available." For Musso, the fact that he was sitting in was a bad, bad sign.

He was enthroned behind the desk of the "unavailable" commander of Guantánamo Naval Station, in a small, bare office just off the base war room. Beads of moisture sweated from gray concrete walls, and no personal touches softened the utilitarian space. Even the Sony plasma screens on the desk had been set up by a couple of navy techs ten minutes earlier, to give him some privacy during the linkup. One panel was layered with multiple windows running civilian news feeds and restricted military data channels. In one of them he saw live top-down footage of Washington, with English-language subtitles laid in over the original Cyrillic script. There was no explanation for the Russian source material. It might have been hacked, or purchased, or simply offered for free. Another small riddle to add to the all-enveloping mystery of why the city in the satellite footage was entirely devoid of human life. At least half of Washington was visible in the pop-up window. Musso could see dozens of fires burning out of control, unattended by a single soul. It was amazing how the human mind could adapt to the most irrational, outrageous insults. He'd already accepted, down in his bones, that what had happened was real, and that there would be no reversing it. But his balls still tried to crawl up into his belly as he considered the vision of a depopulated American capital. Perhaps it was the Russian captioning.

"Links secure."

The disembodied female voice could have originated anywhere, but Musso supposed it belonged to a comms specialist somewhere in Pearl. The screen devoted to the conference divided in two, with the face of Admiral James Ritchie taking up half the real estate, while four smaller windows carried the heads or acting heads of the other unified theater commands. Apart from General Jones, the Marine Corps officer in charge of U.S. forces in Europe, Musso didn't know any of them personally. But of course he knew *of* Tommy Franks, the CENTCOM boss. The long, weathered face was famous the world over as commander of the Coalition arrayed against Saddam Hussein. Musso could only imagine what sort of pressure he must be under right now. Franks had a naturally melancholy appearance to begin with, and Musso thought it even more deeply lined and puffy-eyed than normal. By way of contrast, a fresh-faced woman, Lieutenant Colonel Susie Pileggi, occupied the frame set aside for the senior "available" officer of the Southern Command. With SOUTHCOM's main HQ in Miami lying well behind the event horizon, seniority fell to her as acting commander of Joint Task Force Bravo in Honduras. She was based at Soto Cano Air Base, about ten miles south of Comayagua. Like Musso himself, and Admiral Ritchie, whose superior, Admiral Fargo, had been in Washington this morning, Pileggi had found herself thrust into the rumble seat by the absence of her own boss back in the U.S. It reminded him of war games in which he'd played a very minor role back at the start of his career, role-playing a massive Soviet nuclear strike that all but destroyed the United States and her government.

Franks was the ranking officer among them, but he deferred to Ritchie, who wasn't burdened with managing a looming war in the Middle East, and who had the full resources of PACOM at his disposal. The admiral, like all of them, appeared tense, and when he spoke it was with a clipped tone that Musso recognized. He'd heard the same serrated edge on his own words whenever he'd opened his mouth today.

"I'll recap what we *do* know," said Ritchie, "before moving on to the much greater issue of what we don't."

Musso watched four heads, including his own, nod in acknowledgment.

"As of three hours, fourteen minutes ago, an event of unknown origin appears to have wiped human habitation from an area estimated at just over four million square miles . . ."

Musso found his throat closing involuntarily. His wife and children were deep inside that four million square miles. His whole country was, close enough. His life.

"We have not yet mapped the exact perimeter of the effect," Ritchie continued. "But we have good estimates that it lies in a *very* rough ovoid shape that covers ninety percent of the contiguous U.S. mainland states, half of Canada, and all of Mexico above a line extending from a point a few miles north of Chilpancingo on the west coast to Chetumal on the east and extending through the Gulf to transect Cuba seventy klicks north of Guantánamo. Of the big mainland U.S. cities, only Seattle appears to lie outside the area. The governor's office in Olympia has declared a state of emergency, imposed a curfew, and called out the guard."

Musso couldn't keep the surprise off his face. Nor could Susie Pileggi, he noted. He hadn't seen any mention of Seattle in the news bulletins. As if reading his thoughts, Ritchie explained.

"General Blackstone at Fort Lewis sent troops into the local media outlets to forestall a panic. The . . . uh . . . governor and deputy are . . . unaccounted for. So are some of the city council people for Seattle. Apparently they were at some conference in Spokane. Behind the event horizon. An estimated four hundred million people were caught within the affected zone," Ritchie continued. "At this stage we have no information or even speculation about what may have happened to them, whether the effect is permanent, a natural phenomenon, or technologically based. We've been monitoring the reaction from any potentially hostile governments and none are behaving in any way that would give rise to a suspicion that they played any role in this."

"What's happening in Beijing?" asked Tommy Franks.

Ritchie appeared to direct his answer to a spot just over Musso's shoulder as he addressed the image of Franks on a screen thousands of miles away.

"The army is pouring onto the streets in every major provincial capital, General. Martial law has been declared but none of the PLA's force-projection assets have been mobilized. Nonetheless our own counterstrike forces are at Defcon Two, just in case."

Ice water pooled in Musso's guts. Ritchie had ordered his nuclear submarines to stand ready should the need arise to reduce the communist giant to a vast crematorium. It raised an immediate question. Who would authorize any such strike? Again, Ritchie seemed to be one step ahead of him.

"I'm afraid before we proceed any further," he said, "we need to discuss where the executive authority now lies."

"There's no designated survivor?" asked Tommy Franks.

Ritchie shook his head.

The further into this they got, the bleaker it grew, thought Musso. The designated survivor was a cabinet member nominated to remain apart from the other—was it sixteen or seventeen?—people in the presidential line of succession, a civilian analogue of the chain of command. The system only really operated when the executive branch was gathered in one place, such as during a State of the Union address, but it wasn't the time to play semantics. If they couldn't legitimately find somebody to step into the office of president, then any military actions they took would have no legal basis.

"Elaine Chao, the secretary of labor, is in Geneva," said Ritchie, "at a UN conference. But she is specifically barred from the line of succession because she's not a natural-born citizen. As best we can tell, there is nobody from the line . . . available."

"You mean alive," said Musso, unable to accept the euphemism any longer. "There is nobody else *alive*. In the line of succession. Back home. Anywhere within the area affected. You'll excuse me for speaking out of turn, but I think we need to start responding to this on the basis of a worst-case scenario. It's permanent. We cannot change it. They are not coming back, and if we screw up, a lot more people are going to die."

Silence greeted him, and Musso immediately regretted his lack of tact. There was a reason he was never to going to ascend to the rarefied heights of a theater command, the same reason he'd been slated for forced retirement in the next twelve months. Finally, General Jones broke the moment, speaking from Brussels.

"Well said, Tusk. The world's been knocked flat on its ass, wondering what hit it. But that's going to change within a day or two. And all hell is going to break loose. You can bet on it."

"Gentlemen, if I might?"

The testosterone had been ramping up very quickly. The intrusion of a softer, female voice seemed to calm things a little. Lieutenant Colonel Pileggi smiled out of the monitor at Musso, at all of them.

"We all took an oath to defend the Constitution of the United States. No matter what catastrophe has overtaken us, that oath and the Constitution still stand. Millions of American citizens are still with us. Some of them back home, in the unaffected Northwest. Most of them scattered around the world. I don't know the exact figures but there must be—what?—four or five million Americans overseas on any given day. There are embassies, consulates, military bases and personnel, the sinews of government, if you will. But it is a government *of the people*. Not of us. If we are to act, it must be as servants of the American people, no matter how few or far-flung they may be."

Pileggi spoke with controlled passion. Nobody spoke at all until Tommy Franks's thick Oklahoma drawl poured out of the speakers.

"Granted, Colonel, we can't just pick a president out of a hat. But we need to act and damn quick. I've got close to a quarter million men and women out here in the desert waiting on orders to go. Saddam has even more waiting to receive us, and a lockerful of dirty weapons ready to fire off. I got millions of potential enemy combatants all around me. Israel sitting on top of her nukes. And that asshole bin Laden spooking around in back of it all. Pretty soon I'm gonna have to shit or get off the pot, and either way now it's gonna make a helluva goddamn mess. You are right. It ain't my decision to make. But somebody *has* to make it, and I don't see anybody we can turn to."

Pileggi nodded.

"In the end, we have to turn to our citizens," she said. "But given the extreme nature of the immediate crisis I suggest we return to first principles. We are a representative democracy. I suggest we find the senior surviving *elected* representative. If we can't lay hands on anyone from the federal level, then we go to state, to the governor of Alaska, or Hawaii or Washington State. We frog-march them into office if necessary, for a strictly limited period, pending an election of a new Congress and executive."

"Sounds like a plan," said Franks.

"Consider it done," said Ritchie.

Musso watched him drop his hand to make a few handwritten notes.

"If and when we do find someone to assume executive responsibility," the admiral continued, "we will need to be ready to do whatever is needed of us. General Musso, you're the closest of us to the phenomenon. It might be time to tell us what you know."

What I know? he thought. *What I know is that we've been fucked three ways from Sunday.*

When he spoke, however, it was in the same brusque style as his peers.

"The edge of the effect, the event horizon, manifested itself as an observable atmospheric phenomenon, seventy kilometers north of my position at Guantánamo," he began.

08

"He's . . . Barb. The Air . . . Guard picked him . . . ago . . . and later . . . for now . . ."

"Barney? You're breaking up. I can't hear more than two words in five. Did you say Kip was fine? Is he okay?"

The phone beeped in her ear, the connection lost.

Barbara Kipper slammed the handset down in its cradle. It'd taken her nearly an hour, trawling around in hellacious traffic, to find a pay phone that actually worked. Twice she had been stopped by soldiers who had informed her, politely enough, that a curfew was in place and she'd need to get home. But Barb knew that given the traffic, home wasn't going to be that easy to reach, and she *needed* to talk to Kip. Only for a moment. Just to make sure he was safe.

She was convinced that the phone companies let their booths fall into disrepair to force everyone into buying cells. Not that they were worth anything today. The network was melting down. She got through to Barney Tench on her eighth attempt, and even then the interference had been so bad it was hardly worth it.

But Kip was okay, wasn't he? Barney had said that. The guard had picked him up somehow and was flying him back? Or driving. Or whatever. But he *would* be back "later." She realized she was shaking and close to tears.

"Are you all right, lady? Are you done with the phone? I really need to call my mom is all. She's in San Francisco this week. Visiting her pop. And you know. I *really* need to call her now."

Barb came out of her trance with a start. The young man, a

boy really, in front of her had almost pushed his way into the booth. He was dressed in some sort of uniform. A Wendy's employee, she realized, and his eyes were large and fearful, darting over her shoulder to lock on the phone as if it were a life preserver in high seas.

"Can I just get in, ma'am? And use the phone? You made your call and . . ."

"It's okay. I'm sorry," said Barb. "Let me get out of your way."

He waited until she was half out of the cramped space before pushing in past her. On any other day it would have set off all of her old New York alarms, made her think she was being mugged. But the kid had eyes only for the phone.

"Good luck," she said. "With your mom."

He muttered thanks and began feeding coins into the slot.

She hurried back to the car, where Suzie was sitting up in the front seat, keeping an eye on her. She'd parked outside a bar and grill near the corner of Northeast 106th and Fourth Street, far enough away from the Bellevue Square mall to have avoided the traffic snarl that had frozen the streets for a few blocks around there, but even so, the road network here was peaked out, too. Nobody, it seemed, wanted to be at a desk, and thousands of people had poured onto the streets in their cars, all hoping to get home or to their kids or partners. Maybe it was the dumbass curfew, too, she thought acidly. Nobody wanted to get stuck away from home today. The sun flared off windshields in hundreds of small supernovas, horns blared, and thousands more people on foot picked their way through the slow-moving traffic, all of them looking frantic to be somewhere else. It was like 9/11 except in the burbs.

Barbara climbed back into the Honda and strapped in, keying the ignition and searching the radio band for a reasonable voice. The national stations were off-line, and many of the locals had thrown open their switchboards to a rising cacophony of nutbars and crazies.

"Mommy, did you get my treat?" asked Suzie.

Barb squeezed shut her eyes. She'd promised Suzie a small chocolate or another piece of candy if she sat quietly through her mother's increasingly anxious search for a working public phone. And of course, in the rush and the worry, she'd completely forgotten. The sharp, rising inflection in Suzie's voice, which was quavering toward a tantrum, meant she couldn't put it off.

"I'm sorry, sweetie. Mommy forgot. But, I've . . . uh . . . I've got some gum here. Would you like some gum?"

She fished a packet of Dubble Bubble out of the coins and scrunched-up gas receipts in the cup holder.

"But, Mommy, I'm not allowed to have gum. You know that I . . ."

"Today, you can have gum," she said, more brusquely than she'd wanted to. "Here, knock yourself out."

She tossed back the packet and immediately regretted it. Suzie was always a little more sensitive to Barb than to Kipper—admittedly because Barb tended to have a sharper tongue. Her lower lip was trembling, and the glassy sheen in her eyes warned of imminent tears. A tension headache began drilling in behind Barbara's temples.

". . . estimates of the dead or missing run into the hundreds of millions," declared a somber voice on the radio. "A joint statement from the governor's office and the commander of Fort Lewis advises people in the metro area to stay off the roads, keeping them clear for emergency service vehicles and military transport. The curfew will be enforced . . ."

Barb flicked off the radio with some irritation. It couldn't have been helping Suzie's mood.

"I want Daddy," she sobbed, as the tears finally arrived. "I want Daddy home. I don't want him eaten."

"It's all right, darling. It's all right."

But the collapse had begun, and within seconds her daughter was a heaving, squalling ball of misery in the back of the car.

Where the fuck are you, Kip? thought Barbara.

"Goddamn. That mother's gotta be twenty miles high."

"Higher, sir," the airman informed him. "Seems to fold over somewhere up in the mesosphere."

Kipper nodded but said nothing. Better to keep your mouth shut and be thought a fool than to open it and confirm the fact, as his granddad used to say. Pops Kipper was full of such quips for all occasions. He used to keep a dictionary of quotations on the kitchen table at his place, ready to deploy somebody else's wit at a moment's notice.

Christ knows what he'd have said about this, thought Kip, as they banked down and away to the west to begin their long approach to Seattle. The C-130 wasn't designed for scenic flights, but even through her small, grimy windows he was afforded a scarifying view of the energy wave that ran in both directions right out to the very edge of the world—and over it. He was the only passenger in the plane, a service laid on especially for him by the military at the city's request. He'd linked up with it on some no-name airstrip out in the boonies, delivered there after a helicopter ride that had left him white-knuckled and nauseated.

The loadmaster—that's what they were called, he was sure—stayed glued to the window nearest his perch at the rear ramp, jamming his head up hard against the Plexiglas to keep an eye on the phenomenon as their course change took it out of direct view. It was far enough away from Seattle that people couldn't see it from the ground, the airman told him, which Kip thought a small mercy. The city would be a nuthouse if you could. Probably was anyway, he reflected. The flight crew, after exhausting the possibilities of speculation and conspiracy theory when the vast, shimmering wall had first hove into view, was restricting itself to terse monosyllables as they prepped the craft for descent and approach.

"I reckon it came from space," said the airman, a native of New Orleans to judge by his accent. "Something like a black hole that brushed up against us."

He was young, with a smattering of pimples on his fleshy pink jowls.

"Black holes don't really brush up against anything," said Kipper. "They suck in whole planets and crush them to a singularity."

He'd seen that on the Discovery Channel once. It made him feel better to have something to say.

"A singu-what now, sir?" asked the airman.

"A singularity," said Kipper. "It's, uh, where energy and matter get crushed down into a single state that is so small it's almost not even there."

"Shit," said the young man. "Well, I guess that ain't no singularity out there."

"Nope," agreed Kipper. "Guess not."

"Do you know what we're gonna do about it, sir, to turn it off?"

Kipper could see from the strain around the boy's eyes that he was really asking another question. *How are we gonna make this better? How are we going to get our world back?*

"Son," said Kipper, who felt old enough to call the airman that, "you and I are going to do our jobs. And somebody, somewhere else, is gonna see to punching the lights out on this motherfucker."

"So you think it can be turned off, sir?"

The need in the boy's voice was almost painful.

Kipper tried for a nonchalant shrug.

"I'm an engineer. I was always taught that if something can be turned on, it can be turned off," he said.

But he didn't believe that for a second. Not after seeing the thing with his own eyes.

By the time his flight touched down at Sea-Tac, Kipper had almost forgotten the crash back in the Cascades. As the young guardsman who'd strapped him into his seat in the Blackhawk back in the mountains had explained, there were almost certainly no people on that flight anyway. They'd been "disappeared." The phrase gave him a twitchy feeling. It was redolent of the bad old days in Chile, where he'd done some contract work for Arthur Andersen on a power-station project back in the eighties. People by the thousands got "disappeared" there. As frightening as that had been, however, it was also comprehensible. Bunch of assholes who looked like they'd been tricked out as opera villains in military drag had simply decided to murder anyone who looked sideways at them.

What he'd seen as soon as the chopper lifted clear of the deep valley in which he'd been trekking was entirely *in*comprehensible. The brooding mass of the Cascades still blocked from view a good deal of what the guardsmen were calling "the wave," but the goddamned thing was reared up so high he could still see it anyway, soaring off toward space somewhere beyond the skyline of the ranges. That was bad enough, but what they'd told him about the effect of this "wave" had drilled a cold, dead finger bone into his heart. Hundreds of millions of people, gone. Whole cities, close enough to the whole country, empty. Ships plowing into ports and exploding. Cars just veering off the road, uncontrolled, crashing into each other because nobody was behind the wheel. Planes falling out of the sky, as he'd seen with his very own eyes earlier that day. It'd been happening all over. Still was, in fact. The Air National Guard had jets up right now, waiting for half a dozen flights whose tracks were due to take them over Seattle. They'd been authorized to shoot them down well short of the city.

Kipper caught himself obsessively twisting and wrenching one of the straps on his backpack as he tried to imagine what had happened, what bizarre correlation of physical forces might have done such a thing. He couldn't think of a single explanation. He was a civil engineer, a good one, but he maintained a professional interest in related fields, and indeed in most of the hard sciences. As a young boy he'd wanted to be an astronaut—who hadn't?—but he wasn't one for uniforms and taking orders and sucking up a lot of chickenshit nonsense. So he'd refused to go down the path his old man had been pushing him toward, a career in the air force. He loved building things, not blowing them up. He'd never quite gotten the bug out of his system, though, and a lot of his downtime consisted of reading the sort of scientific journals to which he might have contributed had he pulled on a space suit for real, instead of just in his dreams.

But nothing he'd ever read or learned or seen in his private or professional experience went one inch toward explaining what the hell had happened while he'd been off on his precious fucking nature walk.

As the C-130 dropped toward the tarmac with a dense, industrial roar, Kipper shook himself out of his thoughts like a dog throwing off pond water. The plane touched down on a patch of concrete apron north of the control tower, affording him a good view of both runways and the terminal complex. He could see right away that things weren't normal. There was an unusually large number of planes on the ground, and none taking off. In one glance he could make out the logos of half a dozen stranded carriers. Midwest. JetBlue. Frontier. China Airlines. They all had flights parked by terminals they wouldn't normally use. A bunch of 737s and MD-80s from Alaska Airlines had huddled together, a bit like an old wagon train, down near the fire station, while a collection of jumbos and long haulers from overseas had gathered at the southern end of the airport. As his plane rumbled along the tarmac, a United Airlines Airbus aborted a landing with a scream of turbines and a building roar as she heaved herself back into the sky again. Kipper craned out of the cabin to see if he could spot whatever had gone wrong, but the guardsmen were already popping harnesses and hurrying him out of the aircraft.

"This way, sir," a woman in a Nomex flight suit yelled at him, pressing a firm hand on his shoulder. "Follow me."

Kipper did as he was told, crouching slightly for no good reason. It just seemed appropriate. The airport was a thunderbowl of screaming engines, jet exhaust, and speeding vehicles, all of it controlled in some vague, chaotic way by hundreds of scurrying, shouting men and women in coveralls and earphones. There were a lot more military uniforms than he was used to seeing, as well. The engineer allowed himself to be led across to a waiting pickup with city markings, where Barney Tench, a huge unkempt figure in khaki drill pants and a faded blue shirt, was waiting for him, looking worried.

Tench came forward, holding out his hand, shaking his head.

"Man, am I glad to you see you, buddy," he called out over the background roar. "Thought we might have lost you up there, Kip. We lost a lot of people upstate. I think Locke's gone, Owen, too. Nobody can find the mayor either, but Nickells wasn't scheduled to be out of town, so maybe he'll turn up. It's chaos, man. Fucking chaos."

His friend sounded unbalanced, which was one of the more disturbing developments of the morning. Barney Tench was usually as phlegmatic as a statue. Nothing upset him. It was why Kipper had insisted on hauling him in all the way from Pittsburgh when he'd taken the city engineer's job. There'd been some grumbling about him hiring an old college beer buddy, but that had fallen away as Barn had settled into the job. You couldn't ask for a better right-hand man.

Except that at this moment, his strong right hand was trembling and pale.

Kipper threw his gear in the back of the truck, yelled his thanks to the aircrew who'd picked him up, and climbed up into the driver's-side seat, motioning for Barney to follow.

"Okay, Barn, gimme the keys. I'll drive, you chill the fuck out, and we'll deal with this like we would any problem. Step by step. First. Has anyone spoken to Barbara since you got my number off her? She'll be freaking out wanting to know I'm okay."

Barney had the good grace to look guilty.

"I'm sorry, Kip. It's just been a hell of a morning. And I . . . well . . ."

"Okay. Give me your cell. I'll call her now."

Barney shook his head.

"No point, man. The nets are jammed. Your sat phone might work, though."

Kipper took a small, calming breath. "Okay. Two minutes."

Kipper hopped out again, and hurried around to retrieve his phone from the backpack in which he'd stored it. The signal strength was good, and he was relieved to get a clear dial tone. The call to Barb's phone, however, stalled before it began. A recorded voice told him that due to higher than normal demand, his call could not be connected. Kip grunted and tried their home phone number, an old-fashioned landline. It went through to voice mail on the fifth ring.

"Hi, honey. It's me. They got me. I'm back safe. I have to go into the city. When you get home and get this message, stay there. Don't go out again, okay? Things are gonna be crazy for a while. Love you. Love to Suzie, too."

He hung up, hoping that would forestall a scene later on. If Barb wasn't at home it probably meant they were caught up in some traffic jam somewhere, hopefully not for too long. Some of the roads had looked like parking lots on the flight in. It was going to take them a while to drive into town.

"Okay, let's get going," he said, climbing back into the cabin.

They pulled away, with Kipper driving south, toward the main terminal building. As they approached, he could tell it was crowded, with thousands of people lining the big glass windows that looked out over the tarmac.

"You got any idea what's going on, Barn, beyond the headlines?" he asked.

"Wish I did, Kip. This is like a horror movie. First I heard this morning was Ross Reynolds on KUOW saying he thought we'd been nuked or something. Communications went down. Civil-defense alarms went off. Chaos and fucking madness."

"But it wasn't an attack?"

Kipper threaded past a knot of distressed-looking travelers who were making their way toward a transit bus from a Horizon Air Dash 8. Then he accelerated toward a vehicle exit up ahead.

"You've seen that thing, haven't you? Not unless we got attacked by the Death Star or something. Right now the whole fucking world is just as weirded out as us."

Kipper waved off a security guard who seemed intent on holding them up, and accelerated past, paying no respect at all to his frantically waving clipboard.

The F-150 bounced up and down at they hit the outer road surface, and Kip wrenched them around before accelerating toward the next exit. There appeared to be a couple of dozen soldiers on duty around the airport, although what role they were playing he couldn't tell. Mostly they seemed to be doing traffic control, barring any civilians from leaving the facility. *That's gonna end in tears,* he thought. Seattle wasn't the sort of town where folks took well to being dicked around by crew cuts and camouflage. It was a righteous certainty that if he stuck his head outside right now he'd hear some would-be grunge god caterwauling about "fascists" and "Nazis."

"I'm sorry," said Kipper. "I didn't think, Barney. You got family, back East."

Barney breathed deeply and nodded.

"Everyone has somebody. So do you."

Kipper said nothing.

His immediate family was here, thank Christ. But his dad was in Kansas City. And he had a sister in New York. Their mother had died three years back. New York and KC, of course, were both behind the Wave.

He knew now why Barney had sounded so bad on the phone. There were some good folks on the city council, as well as a fair leavening of pinheads. But if Seattle was on the front line of a fight against something with the power to zap a whole continent, they were all in deep, deep shit.

09

Pacific Ocean, 570 nm west of Acapulco

"Man, I vote we stay the hell away from that," said Fifi.

It looked like Hollywood's idea of a mid-ocean tsunami, a mind-fucking wall of water that stretched across the horizon and reached miles into the sky—which was utter bullshit, of course. The *Diamantina* had struck two tsunamis in the time that Pete had been her skipper, both of them over a thousand nautical miles away from any coast, neither of them even noticeable as they passed under the hull. The thing to the north was nothing like a tsunami. And they were sailing closer to it with every minute.

"No arguments from me, sweetheart," he agreed. "We'll keep a safe distance."

"That's *not* what I said," she insisted.

"And how close is that?" asked Jules with a much cooler demeanor. "That bloody thing starts *below* the horizon, Pete. God knows how high it is. If it wanted to reach out and grab us it probably could."

Pete Holder swung under the boom of the mainmast to get a better view. He frowned.

"I don't think it's going to grab anyone, Jules. It's not alive. It's not even moving."

"Whatever," she said with real exasperation. Whenever she was pissed off with him her voice became even more clipped and correct than normal. "If we have to do this, let's get it done, and then get the hell out of here, shall we?"

By "this" she meant boarding the luxury cruiser they'd intercepted on their run toward the Mexican coast. The vessel, an enormous aluminum and composite superyacht, was obviously unmanned. It wasn't drifting, but the engines were pushing it along on a southerly heading at just a nudge over six knots. It had emerged from behind the screen of the energy wave two hours earlier, easily visible on the *Diamantina*'s radar. Pete had thought nothing of it until Mr. Lee had come to drag him away from the news feed on the computer. Lee's incomparable pirate's eye had spotted something very special on the horizon.

The empty yacht—the crew had to be dead or "gone"—presented as a brilliant white blade on the deep blue of the Pacific. It almost hurt to look at the thing, so brightly did it gleam in the tropical sun. From the bridge it dropped through four decks before kissing the waterline, where he would have guessed it was maybe 230 or even 240 feet in length. A big twin-engine game fisher hanging from two cranes in a dedicated docking bay at the stern would have easily outsized the *Diamantina* all on its own. Instead it looked like a toy, which in a way it was. A rich man's plaything. Pete could see other, slightly smaller vessels stowed away in the rear dock.

"It's like a fucking amphibious assault ship for the go-go party crowd." He whistled.

Not a soul moved anywhere on the open decks, and behind her the impossible, iridescent wall of coherent energy raised itself high into the heavens.

"You're going to steal it, aren't you?" said Jules in a resigned voice.

"No. I'm going to salvage her." Pete grinned, his first real, sunny smile in hours. "Keep her safe from the sort of villainous rogues one meets around these parts. I'm sure if the owners ever make it back from the Twilight Zone there'll be a more than generous reward for her return."

Jules rolled her eyes. Fifi nodded uncertainly. Her eyes never left the horizon.

"I dunno, Pete. We're coming up on that thing. We're much closer than you thought was safe coupla hours back. It's like it's curving toward us or something."

"Mr. Lee, could you bring us alongside her?" said Pete, ignoring Fifi's quite reasonable point. Selective deafness was a useful skill he'd picked up from his mother.

The old Chinese pirate grinned and began to swing their helm over on a converging course with the slow, aimless track of the yacht. As they drew closer Pete noted the name on the stern. *The Aussie Rules.*

He whistled, both at the unexpected connection with home, and the very strong feeling that he knew this boat from somewhere. It was maddening though, he couldn't remember where. There was little time to ponder the mystery, as he busied himself with preparations for the boarding. Truth was, he was no happier than Fifi about their proximity to the vast standing wave that filled the northern sky, but if his instincts played out, this baby might be the answer to their prayers. It could be that the superyacht was too hot to hold on to even with the world collapsing around his ears, but she'd be packed to the gunnels with all sorts of goodies they could trade for jewels or gold. He had a feeling that the world's definition of wealth was going to get back to basics very quickly.

"Steady as she goes, Mr. Lee. Steady now."

Over the next five minutes Lee brought the *Diamantina* alongside the immense bulk of the yacht. Even with the sun high overhead, they sailed in the shade of the much larger vessel. Lee matched their speed to that of their quarry, and then slowly dialed down the engines, slipping back toward the docking bay at the vessel's stern. Pete could tell that the yacht had been well cared for. Anyone who could afford to buy such a magnificent craft could obviously afford to lavish attention on her. Her hull was free of any buildup below the waterline. The portholes were all crystal clear, the glass freshly cleaned, possibly even this morning. As they drew level with the docking bay, Lee edged their speed back up again, holding position perfectly, just a foot away. Pete gave him a nod and a wink before stepping off. The little Chinaman stood at the wheel, as though organically connected to the *Diamantina* through it. He didn't move much, but when he did it was in perfect sync with the swell, the light chop, and the grosser, sluggish movement of the other vessel.

"We cool?" asked Pete.

Fifi and Jules, both of them back in their combat rigs, agreed in turn.

"Okay," he said, "let's fuck this cat."

Lady Julianne Balwyn was not, at first blush, the sort of fabulous creature one might expect to find gracing one of England's older landed families. She had the bearing, the soft beauty, and the polished vowels of a woman whose family had enjoyed hundreds of years of privilege and favor. But in her case, as with her father, something had gone wrong. Lord Balwyn, a spectacular wastrel and confidence man, had told her more than once that Sir Francis Drake had added his seed to the Balwyn family line, accounting for the freebooters and blackguards who regularly popped up in their history, and whether it was true or not—Jules was smart enough to take *everything* her father said with a mountain of salt—it was undeniable that in the last Lord Balwyn's eldest daughter, the family's propensity for throwing up the occasional black sheep had reached a very particular zenith.

As she cross-decked from the *Diamantina* to the superyacht, however, she found herself once again grateful to her father for instilling in her such a bleak, pragmatic, Nietzschean view of humanity. While Pete, their putative leader, was lost in an uncontrolled moment of fanboy worship, Jules kept her head down and her poo in one sock.

A favorite saying of Daddy's.

"Holy shit," cried Pete. "You know what, I really think this *is* Greg Norman's yacht."

"Who?" asked Fifi.

"You know," said Pete, who was now *very* excited. "The golfer? The Great White Shark? A terrible fuckin' choker, actually, but a great businessman. I think he designed a lot of golf courses when he wasn't losing PGA playoffs. Talk about money for nothing and your chicks for free. Although, you know, your lady golfers, there's a reason those chicks are free. Anyway, I'm pretty sure this is his yacht. Or was."

"You think so?" Jules deadpanned, as they stood by a large swimming pool, inlaid with a stylized shark motif. She held a solid gold putter in one hand and in the other a white straw hat, both sporting the same cartoon outline of a great white.

"Greg who?" asked Fifi.

Pete shook his head despairingly.

"If it ain't NASCAR it just ain't real for you, is it, sweetheart?"

"What's up with NASCAR?"

Before Pete could answer, Jules cut him off, snapping her fingers.

"Excuse me, people? End of the world over here? Greg Norman's yacht getting all *Marie Celeste* on us? Let's maintain our focus, shall we?"

"Sorry," said Pete. "It's just, you know, it's *the Shark,* baby!"

"Stupid fucking game anyway," muttered Fifi. "Buncha fat-ass white guys in ugly pants, driving around in those faggy little carts . . ."

"Fifi." Jules's voice took on a warning edge. She was fond of her white-trash friend, but managing the bimbo eruptions was a full-time job.

"*Got it,* got it," said Fifi. "Maintaining focus."

"Come on, let's have a little look-see," said Jules. She slipped her carbine over one shoulder and took out a handgun, a Beretta Px4, even though she wasn't expecting to find anyone on board. They'd been calling out since boarding, but it had the same feeling as knocking on the door of an empty house. She knew they were alone. The ever-suspicious Fifi, however, kept a sawed-off shotgun to hand with a shell racked in the tube. Her thumb stroked the safety, ready to flick it off at the slightest provocation.

They stood by the pool, located on the second of four upper decks, the sun glinting fiercely off the water as it slowly sloshed around with the gentle motion of the boat. The tip of the *Diamantina*'s mainmast rolled through a small arc a few meters away. By leaning over the polished rail, Jules could see the top of Mr. Lee's bald head a long way below. The pool looked to be about ten meters long, with four round black stools peeping above the waterline at the far end, where they abutted a full bar with its own beer taps and all the fixings for a high-end cocktail party. A large plate of fruit salad, wilted in the heat, lay untouched in the center of the polished hardwood bar top. White padded cushions lay along both sides of the pool, with pillows scattered here and there. She could read Pete like a cheap novel and knew that it was all he could do to resist diving in and asking the girls to set him up a margarita. To move things along she strode forward, taking the port-side companionway.

"*Hello,*" she called out. "Is anyone on board? Do you need help?"

"Oh, fuck!" Fifi cried out. "Oh, gross me out!"

Jules spun around, but no obvious threat had emerged from anywhere. Rather, Fifi was dancing about as if she'd trodden in something nasty.

Which she had.

"Oh, goddamn! This is worse than rendered hog fat."

"What is it?" asked Jules, as she hurried over, just one step behind Pete.

"Gawd, that is nasty," he said, suddenly pulling up.

Before them on the deck was a pile of burned clothes out of which had leaked a couple of gallons of the vilest-looking green-black substance Jules had ever seen.

"What is it?" shrieked Fifi, who was losing it, badly.

"I think it might have been the shark," muttered Pete, rubbing at his face. He gingerly toed a straw hat away from the mess. "Ugh. Darlin', I really think you ought to throw those shoes of yours over the side."

Fifi shook her head, disgust acid-etched into her features.

"Man, I don't wanna touch that gunk. What is it?"

Jules leaned over and peered at the toxic ooze.

"I think Pete's right," she said. "I think it used to be someone."

"What happened to them?" asked Fifi with a quavering voice.

The only answer was the hiss of the Pacific sliding past the hull a long way below them.

"How many of those things are there?" she asked, tiptoeing over to the gunwale and using a pistol to ease off her deck shoes.

"Careful you don't shoot yourself in the foot," warned Pete.

She shuddered.

"Couldn't be no worse than getting this crap on me. What if it's like the Blob? What if I turn into that . . . stuff?"

Jules could clearly hear the approaching edge of hysteria in her friend's voice.

She strode over, put a steadying hand on Fifi's shoulder, reached down, and pulled off the shoe she'd been trying to dislodge, before tossing it into the sea. Some of the oozing substance ended up on her hand, but she wiped that off on her shirt.

"It's gross. But it's not the Blob," she said. "We'll have to clean up if they're all like this. It'll be a devilish health hazard otherwise. What do you think, Pete? How many would have been on board?"

The Australian shrugged. "Dunno, sweetheart. At a guess, a boat this size, well over a dozen, maybe even twenty, but some of them would have been cooks, bartenders, cleaners, and so on. Perhaps even a caddy. There'll be a crew manifest somewhere."

"Do you think he was on it, you know, when they got zapped?" she asked, indicating the straw hat with a nod.

Pete stared at the obscene mess on the polished deck. He looked very grim.

"The Shark? I dunno. Could have been. Unless he lent it out to someone. Or ran charters. I don't think he did, though. I read somewhere that he kept this baby very much to himself."

It did raise other, more pressing questions in Jules's mind. If it was the golfer's yacht—and the mess in front of them wasn't him—then he was definitely going to want it back. And if they had to make a run Down Under, to put some serious distance between themselves and whatever had happened to the U.S., there'd be no hiding this yacht anywhere. It *would* be noticed.

"I suppose we'd best have a look around then," she said. "Fifi, maybe you could find a pair of shoes somewhere."

Fifi nodded, looking sickly.

They moved farther up toward the bow.

Another pile of clothes, a uniform belonging to a crew member, lay at the bottom of the steps up to the next deck, oozing the same putrescent substance.

"Man, I am so not looking forward to swabbing that up," muttered Pete.

"Maybe we should blow this off," suggested Fifi. "I really don't dig this at all, Pete. It's freaking me out. You know this is the bit in the movie where you're sitting there yelling at the screen, '*Get off the boat, you fucking dumbasses!*' "

Jules and Pete both ignored her, stepping through a doorway.

A cool curtain of chilled air washed over them. The yacht's climate-control system was obviously unaffected by the loss of the crew. It kept the interior of the boat at a perfect twenty-one degrees Celsius. A small readout just inside the hatch confirmed the fact.

Jules whistled in appreciation.

The shock of cold air hadn't pulled her up short. It was the full-blown opulence of the interior fit-out. Unlike the *Diamantina*, where you could never forget that you were on a small boat, Norman's yacht seemed designed to provide the experience of stepping into a grand European hotel at sea. Polished wood paneling glowed with a soft red warmth. Brass gleamed. Thick woolen carpets covered the floor. As she got over the surprise and moved on, Jules briefly caught sight of huge staterooms, lavishly furnished with antique tables and cabinets and massive, overstuffed armchairs. Oil paintings hung from the walls wherever they turned. Here a bush scene—from Australia, she presumed. There, an enormous portrait of four white dogs. A grand staircase connected the decks above and below them, again looking as though it would not be out of place in a French palace or grand Italian villa.

Jules counted another seven piles of clothes and organic matter as they explored.

The surroundings seemed to overwhelm Fifi, who momentarily forgot her fear and disgust.

"Man, this is like a hotel or something," she said. "A real hotel, too. Not just a Motel 6. This is more like a Holiday Inn."

"In here," said Jules, leading them into a private cinema where two rows of plush royal-blue lounges faced a giant widescreen TV. She thanked God there were no putrescent rag piles in here.

"Pete, do you think you could work some video magic?"

"Mate, there's gotta be more than five hundred channels on this thing," he said, waving a black plastic remote control at the screen. Immediately, the sound came booming up, making them all jump.

"News would be good."

"Okay, don't rush me," he said. After some brief fiddling he brought up a news service. BBC World, according to the electronic watermark in the corner of the screen.

". . . broke out between riot police and residents of the largely Muslim suburb after a man was arrested for allegedly stopping cars and demanding that the occupants join in the celebrations."

"What the hell's that about?" said Fifi.

Jules took the control from Pete and thumbed off the sound as she searched for a program guide.

"It happened last time, too."

"Last time?"

"Nine eleven."

"That's great," said Pete as the big flat Sony filled with images of burning cars and shops. "But we need to move our arses before someone else tries to grab this boat out from under them."

Fifi, who by now had recovered from her earlier fright, shrugged and hefted her sawed-off shottie. "Let 'em try."

"Someone with more guns," he added.

Mr. Lee looked over the main controls one last time, shaking his head, sadly.

"Yes, we can do this," he said, somewhat paradoxically. "But not for long. We will need engineering johnnies, for begin."

Pete nodded. They'd just come from inspecting the lower decks, specifically the engine room, which had gleamed whiter and cleaner than any human space he'd ever seen before, save for the remains of three more crew members. If you could ignore them, puddled on the floor, it was like the photos you sometimes saw of microchip plants in Taiwan. Not a speck of dust or grease anywhere. The boat was running perfectly for the moment, following a computer-controlled track to the south, but it was such a huge, complicated piece of machinery that there was no guarantee they'd be able to cope if anything went wrong. He allowed himself a little Captain Kirk moment, swiveling in the main command chair as Fifi and Jules reclined on a padded bench at the rear of the cabin. Late-afternoon light flooded in through the huge windows, bathing them all in a deepening golden glow. All in all it felt more like they were kicking back at the Bellagio in Vegas than scoping out a hijack at sea.

"We could get crew," said Pete. "I know some guys in Acapulco, and down Panama way. German Willy still runs out of the canal zone. And Stan Lusevic, and Shoeless Dan."

"Jesus Christ, Pete!" protested Jules. "Are we putting together a crew or a sheltered workshop for retired drunks and dick pullers?"

"Yes," Mr. Lee agreed. "German Willy, too much drinking, too much willy. Other two morons. Without shoes. No good, Mr. Pete. No good."

"Okay," he conceded. "I take your point. But Lee's also right about needing crew if we're going to be doing anything other than selling this boat off at the first safe port we can find."

Jules smiled wryly at him from deep inside the luxurious royal-blue padding of the bench that occupied the entire rear bulkhead. "Pete, I thought we were just minding this old tub for the Shark."

Pete smiled sadly and shook his head.

"The Shark's gone, baby." He spared a glance at two viscous stains on the nonslip floor where Mr. Lee had cleaned up another two pools of human ooze and empty clothing. True to form, it hadn't seemed to bother him.

"Most everyone north of here is gone for good," Pete continued. "You've seen the news. If we're *lucky* this'll be some kind of space-monkey invasion, because at least then we'll have someone to maintain order."

"Like *Planet of the Apes*," said Fifi in all seriousness.

"Sure, sweetheart, if you like. But me, I reckon the universe, or merciful Allah or the Great Pumpkin or whatever, sneezed and blew the good ol' US of A right out of its arse, which as we've seen, a lot of people think of as A Good Deal. But me, I reckon it means we're about three days away from a Hobbesian fucking meltdown."

Fifi's blank look spoke volumes for a formal education that had ended when she was only thirteen years old.

"Thomas Hobbes, darling," explained Jules. "A Brit. He invented the idea of the violent clusterfuck, with everyone fighting each other. Like a Jackie Chan movie. Or a cage-wrestling free-for-all on the telly. You know, *Smackdown* or *Spankdown* or whatever it's called."

"Right," agreed Pete, waving his hand in the general direction of the energy wave. "That thing out there, most people won't realize it yet, but that thing has thrown us into a state of fucking nature, a war of all against all, darlin'. And I've been wondering whether the safest option might be to ride it out in the South Pacific for a couple of years. Island-hop. Trade a bit. Stay one step ahead of the chaos, because it's coming, believe me."

"Already here," said Lee.

"What's that?" asked Pete, spinning in his captain's chair.

Lee was standing a few feet away, splitting his attention between a radar screen and an enormous pair of Zeiss binoculars, mounted on a pivot stand, through which he'd been watching the southern horizon. He'd peer through the glasses, check the screen, and peer through the glasses again, finally grunting once, emphatically.

"Twelve miles sou'-sou'east, Mr. Peter. Three go-fast boats I see. They making over sixty knots."

"Heading?" asked Jules before Pete could open his mouth.

"Straight for us, I'll bet," said Pete in a flat, fatalistic voice.

Mr. Lee nodded. "Straight for us."

"They packin'?" asked Fifi, suddenly on her feet, shotgun in hand. "You think I should go get the worm?"

"Too far away, cannot see," said Lee.

"They're packin'," sighed Pete. "Come on," he said, pushing himself up out of the chair. "It's started. And yeah, Fifi. Go break out the worm, and get your cannon, too."

"Awesome."

10

Pitié-Salpêtrière Hospital, Paris

"NO!"

The French girl's shriek was a raw, animal sound. Within it roiled pain, violation, horror, and outrage. Her face, a mask of dark, primal emotions, raged at Caitlin over the unwavering muzzle of the Glock 23. The assassin had long ago stopped counting the number of men and women whose last seconds she'd seen through crosshairs or iron gun sights, and she knew from that face that Monique's cry was not a plea for life. It was a scream of protest at what had already been taken from her. Trust and intimacy and a whole world in which Caitlin—or Cathy, as Monique knew her—was a friend, and not a liar and murderer.

A hot flush washed over her, dizzying, unexpected.

She let her gun hand fall to her side, tired of it all. And they might still use Monique to get to al-Banna.

"If you stay here you will die," she said. "Come with me right now, and you might live."

The emergency room remained a still life by Goya. The first cries of staff and patients had been silenced by the shots she'd fired into the heads of her would-be killers—or captors. As Caitlin turned for the exit a spasm of movement passed through the onlookers, as each flinched away from the line of her gaze. One man in a white coat, a doctor most likely, took a few hesitant steps in her direction, but a shake of her head and a casual wave of the pistol in his direction arrested any further advance. Caitlin did not check to see whether Monique was following her. She knew the girl would. Walking quickly but calmly toward a set of sliding doors, she stripped off her bloodied chambray shirt. The white T-shirt underneath was stained pink, but she hid the worst of it with a black leather motorcycle jacket, lifted from the corner of a bed on which a man with a heavily bandaged head lay unconscious. It was too big for her but would have to do for now. The guns, identical models, went into a couple of zippered pockets, and she plucked the last of the sensor leads from her filthy hair. A roll of thick surgical tape from a bedside tray went into another pocket. In the last few steps she turned and walked backward, scanning the room quickly for any more pursuers. Monique was glaring at her with unalloyed loathing, but she was following just a few feet behind, victim of a type of Stockholm syndrome that Caitlin had seen and exploited many times before.

The doors closed on the Pitié-Salpêtrière with a chime and the protesting grumble of old rubber wheels in dirty guide rails. Early evening had come with a hard frost, and she shivered inside the jacket, thankful for its warmth. Transport was her first and most urgent need, then shelter. When they were safely hidden she would contact Wales, her overwatch coordinator. Her cover was blown. Her image and the fight in the emergency room had certainly been captured on hospital security video.

"Where the fuck are we going, Cathy? What are you going to do? You killed those men. Murdered them."

Monique's tone was shrill, accusatory.

Caitlin shrugged her off, scanning the cars parked in front of the building as she hastened down the steps. A blue Renault Fuego had caught her eye, a good car, easily stolen, and as close to invisible in Paris as she could get on short notice. The front passenger-side window was open a crack.

"It's not the same," she said.

"What do you mean?" Monique demanded to know, hurrying to catch up beside her. Sirens were audible, but there seemed to be hundreds of them, the distinctive warble and wail coming from all points of the compass. The city was alive with their discordant, jangling sound. Traffic along the roads around the hospital grounds was heavy, but grinding forward in fits and starts. She could see the strobing lights of both police and ambulance vehicles in three separate places. It was impossible to tell whether they were headed in her direction.

"Killing and murdering are not the same thing. I killed them, sure. But I had good reason. That isn't murder. It's self-defense."

"Self-defense!" Monique made a grab for her arm but Caitlin slipped out of her grip with practiced ease. "You expect me to believe that! You attacked them and killed them like . . . a . . . machine. A thing. You are no activist. You are no surfer!"

Monique spat the last word at her.

"Well, I used to surf, but I'm also a soldier," said Caitlin. "Now get in the fucking car, if you want to get out of this alive. Those men back there, they were soldiers, too, like me. And there'll be more of them looking for us."

Caitlin retrieved one of the pistols and swung the butt of the handle into the window, smashing it open and causing Monique to jump with surprise. There were more than a dozen witnesses watching her but none made any attempt to intervene as she popped the lock. More people came spilling out of the ER doors, some of them pointing in her direction, but none made any move toward her. It wouldn't be long, however, before hospital security, or the gendarmes, or something worse turned up.

"Clock's a-tickin', Monique. Hop in."

The front seat of the Fuego was cluttered with papers, a bag of onions, and a clutch from which spilled a checkbook, iPod, cell phone, makeup, and more keys.

"Jesus Christ," said Caitlin. "Why not just get a big fucking bumper sticker that says 'Steal My Stuff?' "

She snatched a sturdy-looking steel pen from the jumble of items and used it to lever her way into the car's accessory circuits, cracking open the plastic cover beneath the wheel with a couple of violent jerks. She sensed Monique hovering outside and swept the detritus from the seat. "Just get in. We're running out of time."

The French girl climbed in carefully, as if unwilling to touch the belongings of the unknown owner. Caitlin swore softly as she sparked the engine to life, giving herself a small electrical shock in the process. A brief glance over her shoulder revealed a growing knot of people on the steps of the hospital, all of them gesturing in her direction, some of them shouting. She threw the car into reverse, stamped on the gas, and peeled out backward from the parking slot with a squeal and the harsh smell of burned rubber, reefing on the hand brake to tighten her turning circle. Both she and Monique jerked forward in their seats and she slammed the disk brakes, changed gear, and accelerated away, barely missing the taillights of an adjacent Fiat.

"You are not Cathy Mercure, are you?" asked Monique as they negotiated a twisting course through the parking lot toward the exit and out into the traffic stream.

Caitlin's first, unthinking reaction was to lie. Deceit and betrayal were so deeply ingrained by her training and the demands of her work that they had become elements of her true nature. But unless she was psychotic, her mission concerns were no longer relevant. Something bigger had happened, something infinitely worse than anything she had been prepared to fight. A painful throbbing on the injured side of her head grew more insistent as she allowed herself to contemplate anything beyond fight or flight for the first time since the shooting had begun back at the hospital.

"No," she conceded to Monique. "I'm not Cathy Mercure. My name's Caitlin. That's all you need to know. That, and also that you're in a lot of trouble."

Blaring horns and some muffled Gallic abuse greeted their high-speed entry into the crowded Parisian road net. Caitlin opted to cut across the main flow of traffic, where they would be jammed in place, and forced her way through an intersection onto a lesser boulevard. She wasn't familiar with the road, but it had everything she wanted right at that moment. It was navigable at a good speed and it was taking them away from the place where somebody had just tried to put the zap on her.

"*I'm* in trouble?" protested Monique. "I have not killed anybody or stolen a car. *I* am not some sort of criminal. I did not get my friends shot back at . . ."

Her voice hitched and cracked as the emotional blowback of

the battle at the Pitié-Salpêtrière finally struck her. She had seen at least one of her friends shot down in front of her eyes, before watching another morph into a homicidal destroyer. Monique's mouth gaped and her shoulders trembled as a squall of wild animus blew through her. Caitlin rammed the little blue car through a series of gear changes as she threaded a course through a thicker pulse of traffic. When they cleared the moving obstruction, she plucked a couple of paper tissues from a box jammed into the cup holder that lay between them.

"I didn't get your friends killed, Monique," she said firmly, but quietly. "I didn't pull that trigger. But I took down the assholes who did. They're avenged, for what it's worth."

"*Nothing! It's worth nothing,*" shouted Monique, as the tears came at last.

"Fair enough." Caitlin shrugged, checking the mirrors for any sign of pursuit as she dialed back on their speed to blend into the surrounding traffic flow, and began to look for a landmark with which she could place them. She didn't fancy asking the French girl for anything just yet. The street had narrowed to just one lane running in each direction. Stunted, leafless trees lined the footpath, which was thick with people hurrying home from work, or out to dinner in one of the many bistros and wine bars that huddled up close together on the ground floors of the old four- and five-story buildings. Warm golden light spilled out through their windows, which gave onto brief glimpses of packed tables and bars at which drinkers stood beneath thick clouds of cigarette smoke. For all the cosmopolitan charm it was all so conventional. Had she been able to drive along here twenty-four hours earlier, Caitlin was certain she would have passed by almost exactly the same scene. Surely the only topic of conversation at those crowded tables would be the day's news from the U.S., but from the driver's seat of the stolen Renault, she could not tell.

Beside her, Monique was trying valiantly to control her crying, but she had already gone through at least a third of the tissues. She searched inside a pocket for a small flip-top cell phone, sniffling as she tried to key in a number. Caitlin slapped it out of her hands.

"What the fuck are you doing? Don't you read your own conspiracy theories? You can be tracked with that thing. In fact . . ."

She reached over roughly and jammed her hand between Monique's legs to retrieve the little Samsung.

"I'm just calling Billy!" she protested. "He can come for me. I don't want to be alone with you, or anywhere near you, whoever you are."

Monique gasped in shock as Caitlin threw the phone out the window.

"It won't be Billy who comes for you if you make that call, darlin'. It'll be more guys in ties, toting big fucking guns."

"You bitch! That was my phone!" cried Monique, genuinely affronted.

"No. That was a chip tracking your every movement," said Caitlin. "And forget about your boyfriend. His phone is being monitored, too."

Caitlin checked her watch. They had been driving for nearly fifteen minutes, more than enough time for their descriptions and the car's plate to have been pushed out over the police nets.

"We have to change cars, Monique," she said. "I'm going to pull off the street up ahead at that corner and ditch this ride. I'm gonna ask you to come with me, but I'm not going to make you."

She allowed herself a brief, measuring glance at her passenger. Monique's eyes were puffy, and tear tracks had washed runnels of makeup from her face. It must have been expertly applied. Caitlin hadn't even noticed before. She was upset, naturally, but she was angry, too. Very angry.

"Why should I come with you? I should go right to the police and report you."

"You could do that," she said as she turned the wheel to take them off the narrow street and into an even narrower alleyway. "But those men I killed? The men who shot Maggie in the head? They were from your state security service. Secret police, if you like. If you walk in to the gendarmes and tell them what happened, your details will go onto their network and within half an hour more guys like that will turn up at the police station and take you away. The cops won't stop them. But they will stop you from leaving if you try."

"But why? That is ridiculous."

Caitlin pulled over, running their wheels up onto the very narrow footpath. It couldn't have been more than two feet wide. She was glad she hadn't had to reverse park. Her head and neck were aching painfully.

"They were after me, and I was with you, so now they're after you, too. You have family? They're being watched. Your boyfriend? Him too. It's not you. It's me. Your security service is conducting a hard target search for *me,* and as of half an hour ago, you are the key. Every phone call you have made for the last five years, every address you've lived at, or just stayed at, that can be tracked is being tracked. Every movement across every border, every purchase with your credit card, every trans-action in your bank account, every mailing list your name appears on, every e-mail you've ever sent, every chat room or website you've ever visited, every Net search you've ever done, they are all being sifted and analyzed right now, by people *way* smarter than you, because you are alive, and free, and running from them. With me."

Monique shook her head, refusing to believe what she was hearing. As she spoke, her words became clipped and fiercer.

"This is bullshit. *You* are bullshit. You come to us as a friend. You say you are against the war. But you are part of the war. You are a killer just like Bush and Blair. Those men, if they were from the police or the secret service, it was their duty to arrest you. And you killed them and got Maggie killed as well."

Monique's anger overwhelmed her and she emphasized her last point by slapping at Caitlin's face. The American woman brushed off the ineffectual blows with one swift hand, not even flinching as Monique cried out with frustration and attempted to rake out her eyes. Caitlin grabbed one of the girl's hands and turned it sharply back in on the wrist, making her gasp with pain and shock.

"Knock it off, princess. I didn't come here to hurt you or your dumbass friends. I came to protect you."

"What?"

Three young men, obviously drunk and in high spirits, came around the corner and past the car, banging on the windows and calling out to the two women to come out and play, to have a drink and celebrate with them. Caitlin glared at them, but they just laughed. One held up two fingers in a V and stuck his tongue between them, waggling it obscenely. This was obvi-ously the funniest thing his friends had seen all night, and they fell into the cobbled roadway, laughing hysterically.

"Assholes," muttered Caitlin.

"What did you . . ."

"I said, *assholes*."

"*Non*. What did you say about *protecting* us?"

The drunks helped each other off the cold, damp road surface and continued on their way to the next bar, one of them turning awkwardly to grab his crotch and give it a bit of a squeeze for the benefit of the two dykes.

"See what you are missing, ladies?"

"How could you have been protecting us?" Monique repeated, ignoring her oafish countrymen. "From those skinheads at the tunnel? You couldn't have known about that."

Caitlin opened the door and stepped out, taking a handful of banknotes from the handbag with her. She left the door ajar. The Renault would not be here for long. Monique squeezed out on the other side, the car's proximity to a brick wall making for a tight fit. The wall was covered with an inch of peeling posters, most of them for awful French rock bands, but the uppermost layer calling for a "National Day of Action" to stop the "Anglo War." That was the gig her merry little band had been headed for when set upon by the National Front thugs who got lucky and put her in the hospital.

Where I got lucky and caught a fucking brain tumor!

Caitlin had to stop for a moment and lean against the wall as her head reeled. Whether it was from the illness, her injuries, or an adrenaline backwash she couldn't tell. She stood still, closed her eyes, and sucked in a long draft of air. It was unpleasantly cold now, but the alleyway still reeked of garbage and dog shit, the signature smell of Paris behind the coffee and *pain au chocolat*.

"Are you all right?" Monique asked grudgingly.

"I'll be fine. Just give me a second."

And the dizzy spell did pass quickly. She felt a little lightheaded as they stepped off toward the high street again, but nothing too crippling. Monique supported Caitlin at the elbow anyway, a gesture she was happy to accept.

"You didn't answer my question," she said, a little petulantly. "What did you mean before, about protecting us?"

"You wouldn't believe me, not yet."

"Try me."

"No. If we're still alive in a few days, I'll tell you, and you will believe me, every word I say. But for now, no. Come with me, or make your own way home, where they'll be waiting for you. It's all the same to me."

They stopped at the intersection, where bright lights and heavy foot traffic created an effect a little like stepping back into the real world from some underground realm. A bus rumbled by, coughing thick gouts of acrid smoke into the air. Shoes scuffed and clicked on wet, gray flagstones, and around them roared hundreds of voices, all discussing the same thing: "the Disappearance."

Caitlin's heart sank. She had been hoping irrationally that the apparent normality of the street scene spoke of some disorder within her, some malady of the brain caused by her illness, that had manifested itself as a perverse hallucination of cataclysm. But no. The Parisians were agog with the news, and confirming for her that it was real was the sound of so many voices raised in good cheer and even merriment. That is what the three jerks who'd abused them before were drinking to. A world without America.

"*Fucking assholes.*"

"*Pardonnez-moi?*"

"Sorry. Didn't think I was speaking aloud," said Caitlin. "It's nothing. We've got to get moving. Let's go."

They set off again, heading uphill. Caitlin's eyes swept the road and the sidewalk ahead of them on both sides of the street for any sign of hostile action, but all she could see was late-rush-hour traffic and throngs of boulevardiers, many of them seemingly toasting the day. Not all, admittedly. Here and there arguments raged in that Gallic way, all sound and fury without any real danger of violent contention.

". . . It is a disaster, I tell you, a world-ending disaster . . ."

"No. A second chance is what we have been gifted by the gods . . ."

"So. You are a believer now, eh?"

". . . this will mean horror, horror on an unimaginable scale . . ."

". . . I shall be leaving for my farm this very night. Mark my words. Leave the city now or you will have . . ."

"All I will have is another glass of Billecart . . ."

Caitlin set her mouth in a grim, thin line and pushed on with her head down. Monique fell silent beside her. After a few minutes it became obvious that for each individual who saw the Disappearance as a malign catastrophe, another two or three thought it a fine thing. From the snatches of conversation she picked up as they hurried along it seemed that in this part of the world at least, a rough consensus had settled on a conspiracy theory about the Americans having destroyed themselves when testing some superweapon for use in Iraq. Nobody seemed to imagine that any such fate might befall them here in Paris. But then, if they did, they'd hardly be out scarfing down aperitif and dinner, would they? Perhaps the freeways out of the city were jammed with more people like the man she'd heard planning to leave for his farm later that night. Although why he thought he'd be safe there from something that gobbled whole continents was a mystery.

"I am sorry."

Caitlin almost didn't hear her. Monique's voice was small and timid and nearly lost in the roar of the busy street.

"What?"

"I am sorry, Cathy—Caitlin. I can hear what they are saying as well as you. It is disgraceful. Drinking to a tragedy. Saying your people deserved it."

"Oh, fuck that," replied Caitlin in pitch-perfect French. She really didn't want to get tagged as an American at the moment. "This is one street, Monique. One little neighborhood where people of like minds will gather all the time. It's just human nature. If some Algerian madman set off a nuke in Paris I could take you straight to a food court in any city in the U.S. and it'd take me all of three seconds to find some fat, doughnut-sucking slob who said you deserved it. People everywhere are fucked, that's all."

"No. Not everyone . . . Caitlin. Some people are led by the better angels."

At that moment they passed a café outside which stood a small, elderly gentleman in a black jacket and red beret, both hands holding the crook of a walking stick, which he was banging into the ground for emphasis while arguing with a couple of men who looked to be a fraction of his age.

"I was with the Americans at Carentan. I saw them shed their blood for France. You dishonor them and you dishonor France with this rubbish talk . . ."

Caitlin gifted the old man with a sad smile and a wink as she passed by. A siren brought her head up slowly, lest she draw attention to herself, but it was a fire engine a block over. She caught a glimpse of it muscling through traffic as they crossed an intersection.

"Down here," she said, veering off toward a line of parked cars in a street of private houses and apartments. Only one shop, a liquor store, was open.

"Are you going to steal another car?" Monique asked warily.

No, thought Caitlin. *I'm going to buy a couple of magnums of champagne and pass them around the surrender monkey set back there to help celebrate the cosmic cornholing of the great Satan.*

Aloud she simply said, "You got it."

Three minutes later they were cutting back across town in a gray Volvo station wagon, a late model V40. A suction cup held a black plastic cradle to the windshield just below the rearview mirror. Caitlin leaned across Monique as they came to a red light, popping the glove compartment open.

"Sweet," she said as she pulled out a small Magellan Meridian GPS receiver. "Is there a power cord in there? Look for a sort of flexi cord and an adapter to plug into the cigarette lighter."

Monique couldn't find one, but the little yellow and black unit had three-quarters of a charge anyway. Caitlin powered it up as the light changed and waited for the chime that would tell them it had linked to enough satellites to fix their position. A frustrating few minutes passed during which time she had to force herself to concentrate on the road. As full darkness covered the city, she could see the telltale glow of fires burning on the outskirts of the old center, explaining the large number of emergency vehicles. Apparently not everyone was content to celebrate with a smirk and a snifter of Courvoisier.

The Magellan chimed once, eliciting a small "Oh!" from Monique.

"Is this us? Here, near the rue Ricaut?"

"Yeah. That's us. Does it have a route function? Can you work out how to get us to . . ."

The windshield suddenly cracked and starred with a huge, hollow boom.

Event horizon, Cuba

As a boy, Tusk Musso had loved visiting the city with his grandfather. For the Musso clan, that meant New York, the greatest city in the world. In the whole goddamned history of the world, except maybe for Rome, according to his grandpa Vinnie Musso. There was a game they played, which Grandpa insisted little Tusk never tell his mother about, where they lay on the sidewalk at the base of the highest building they could find, and then just stared up at this monster looming over them, looking like it went all the way to heaven. They had to be quick before the cops or security guards chased them off. The very first time they'd done it, when Tusk was only six, it had been a cool, overcast day, with a slight breeze dragging clouds across a lowering sky, and it looked for all the world like the Chrysler Building was gonna fall right down on top of them. Tusk had squealed with laughter, and not a little fear. He wasn't allowed to say anything to Momma about it, of course, because she would've had a blue fit if she'd known that Grandpa Vinnie, whom she considered a *very* poor influence at best, had been letting her precious bundle roll around on the filthy pavement with the dog turds and cigarette butts.

Thank God they're long gone, he thought, as he stood about two hundred yards back from the base of the event horizon and craned his head back to watch it climb away to heaven, feeling as small and insignificant as he had all those years ago at the feet of the tallest buildings in the world. Clouds drifted overhead, and Musso narrowed his eyes against the still-intense glare of the day and watched as a patch of white that reminded him of a Spanish galleon floated serenely into the silvery haze at the edge of the affected area. At that distance it created an effect similar to a stationary waterfall, all glistening silver hanging down like a curtain.

And like a curtain, it moved. Not much, just a lazy drift back and forth, across the ground, no more than a couple of yards in either direction—just enough to wake up the primitive creature dwelling in the darkest parts of Musso's mind, to fill him with an atavistic fear of whatever danger lay in the darkness just outside the mouth of the cave.

Musso the modern, rational man, dressed in a short-sleeved khaki shirt and olive-drab pants, ground down on that ancient terror and watched, fascinated, as the cloud drifted into the energy wave. It seemed completely unaffected as it passed through. Its form became less distinct on the far side, but it was discernibly the same shape and size.

"Seen any birds fly into it, or out of it?" he asked, still peering upward.

Major Núñez shook his head. "None. Some of my men say they saw large flights of birds moving away from here earlier today, but I do not know where they came from. And there are none here now. Not one."

Musso dropped his gaze. They stood by the crumbling edge of a two-lane road, the asphalt surface shimmering in the heat a few hundred yards behind them, a natural phenomenon. The much more powerful haze directly in front was decidedly unnatural. The small convoy of Hummers and Cuban vehicles had pulled up ten minutes ago, and his heart was still beating hard from the sight. Any last, lingering doubts placed in the way of belief by his rational mind had been banished as soon as he'd seen the haze. Visible from well over the horizon, it not only reached up to the stratosphere, it curved away toward the horizon in both directions like a giant standing wave, raised by an unknowable deity.

It was alien.

It sat there, in front of him, utterly removed from any human context to give it meaning. He had no idea what it was, and having seen it for himself he doubted that anybody ever would.

"You still got nothing, Lieutenant Kwan?" he said.

Lieutenant Jenny Kwan shook her head. She seemed too young to Musso, almost baby-faced, but she was one of the smartest, scariest individuals he'd ever met. An MIT grad,

Kwan was a marine first lieutenant, the boss of an incident response unit, a bland name for a bunch of very smart people trained to look for and respond to some of the worst things in the world—chemical, biological, and nuclear weapons. Her crew and equipment took up three of the seven Humvees that had driven deep into Cuban territory, escorted by Major Núñez and a platoon of his men in a couple of old Soviet-era BMP-2s. Musso had to hand it to the Cubans. This monstrosity wasn't an abstract proposition for them, something to be intuited from indirect evidence provided by weblinks or satellite data. It was sitting literally a stone's throw away, bisecting their country. Given all that, he was impressed by their professionalism and no-bullshit attitude, although Núñez had probably picked his Praetorian guard for this gig.

They helped Lieutenant Kwan whenever she asked for it, and kept to themselves when she didn't. Not that Kwan was having any luck with her equipment. No matter what sensors or sniffers or magic wands she waved at the haze, it made not a damn bit of difference.

"According to my readings, General, that thing isn't even there," she said.

"Uh-huh," he muttered. They'd had the same result plugging into FAA and weather satellites back at Gitmo. As far as their technology was concerned, the haze didn't exist.

He could feel the warmth leaking out of the late afternoon as the sun dropped toward a line of low, scrubby hills in the west. There was a faint but noticeable dry heat radiating from the haze, but that was all.

"Care to take a closer look, Major?" he said.

Núñez shook his head. "No. But what else is to be done?"

The Cuban officer took the first steps away from the convoy, toward the new edge of the known world. Musso fell in beside him as they cautiously approached the barrier. The country hereabouts was little different from the area around Guantánamo. Both were nestled at the edge of the Sierra Maestra range, the remnants of huge fractured slabs of continental plate raised from the ocean floor over millions of years by tectonic impact, volcanic eruptions, and the hundred-thousand-gigaton blast of the Chicxulub comet punching into the surface of the planet just a short distance away some sixty-five million years ago. The Maestra was a perfect guerrilla territory, a vast contrary maze of steep valleys, volcanic dikes, abrupt fault lines, and nearly impenetrable karst areas, all riven with limestone caves and covered in dense forest. The ranges gave out on the far side of the haze, smoothing out into the low, rolling plains that made up nearly two-thirds of Cuba's land surface. For all of the earth-shattering violence that had gone into creating this environment over the aeons, it was nothing compared with the immediate spectacle of the static energy wave.

Musso was able to make out the lowland steppes on the far side without much trouble. Nothing moved there. Núñez had compared it to looking through a waterfall, but to his mind it was more like a few layers of plastic wrap. He stooped down to pick up a rock as they walked, wondering what would happen if he threw it in. Núñez slowed as they approached the face. It appeared to billow, like a sail. They stopped about fifty yards away.

"I would not think it safe to get much closer," Núñez said.

"I wouldn't argue with that, Major," agreed Musso. "Let's just accept that we're both possessed of stainless-steel *cojones* and take it nice and careful from here."

He could see a burned-out car wreck on the far side, near a bend in the road, and wondered if that's where Núñez's superior officer had disappeared. This close to it, he avoided looking up. The scale of the thing was enough to give him a teetering sense of vertigo without making it any worse by craning his head back. He turned around to check on his people. They were all watching anxiously, their bodies rigid with anticipation. Suddenly there was a whooshing noise and he saw them all jump, like an audience in a horror movie frightened by a cheap stunt.

"What the fuck?" he said, turning to Núñez.

But the Cuban was gone.

The cries of his comrades and of Núñez's men reached him a moment later.

"Run, General! Get the hell outta there!"

Admiral Ritchie found his eyes straying from the television news broadcast to the silver-framed picture of his daughter on the desk in front of him. The photograph was old. Nancy was nineteen now, but on his desk she remained forever three, holding a small bear, sucking her thumb, and staring off a thousand miles into the distance.

He had to tear his eyes away. It was almost too painful to bear. She should be all right. She was supposed to fly out for Europe this morning. But they had heard nothing from her.

Had she made the flight? Had it escaped the Wave? He didn't know. His wife was frantically trying to find out, but without much luck.

With a grinding effort of will, Ritchie turned his attention back to work.

Thank God for cable news, at least, he thought. He had wondered if he might have to press the governor's office for a declaration of martial law, fearing that panic and violence would be inevitable as the population of the islands digested what was happening. But far from sending mobs onto the street, the wall-to-wall media coverage, all of it sourced from Asia and Europe, seemed to be keeping Hawaii's civilian population glued to their TV and computer screens. Every available police officer had been called in, and a battalion apiece of marines and soldiers were hurriedly tooling up with crowd-control gear, just in case, although all of the reports he'd received so far had the streets half deserted. Hopefully they wouldn't be needed. The surf breaks off the north shore were a little less crowded than usual, but not much. Apparently even the end of the world wasn't going to interfere with some people's search for the perfect wave.

"Governor's office called, sir."

Ritchie looked up from the drifts of paperwork that covered every square inch of his desk. A couple of pages had even dropped to the floor. His PA, Captain McKinney, bent forward and retrieved them.

"Yes, Andrew? Good news, I hope?"

"Mixed, Admiral. Curfew starts at 1800 sharp tonight. They couldn't agree on the rationing, though. But they have organized emergency flights from Tokyo and Sydney for any perishables or medical supplies that run low. The national security committees of both the Japanese and Australian cabinets are still meeting, but their local liaison staff has passed on messages from both prime ministers that they'll give us whatever help we need."

They're the ones who'll be needing help soon enough, thought Ritchie. But aloud he only said, "Well, that's something at least. For now."

The armed forces had considerable stockpiles of rations and medical supplies on the islands, but they didn't store items like insulin for diabetics, or drugs for treating cancer or a dozen other common maladies. Ritchie couldn't help wondering just how much of a supply of antidepressants there was in Hawaii, and how many people were likely to kill themselves or suffer heart attacks or stress-related strokes in the next few days. Given the number of tourists from the mainland here, probably lots.

Nearly two and a half decades earlier he'd written his master's dissertation at Annapolis on the navy's crisis management at Pearl Harbor. He'd been scathingly critical of their efforts on December 7, 1941. Now, faced with his very own calamity, he had to wonder if he would have done any better. There was just so much to do and so little to do it with. Events had accelerated to a point where he would possibly never catch up.

"Thank you, Captain," he grunted, dismissing young McKinney, just as an officer in army greens appeared at his door.

"Colonel Maccomb, Admiral. I have your updates if you have a moment."

Ritchie didn't, but waved the man in anyway. Maccomb looked like he had run all the way over from the 500th Military Intelligence Brigade, a decent hike in the midday heat of the equatorial sun. PACOM was just months away from taking possession of a new headquarters, the Nimitz-MacArthur Pacific Command Center, which would have centralized everybody in one modern facility. It looked like they'd be sticking with the old campus now, however, necessitating a lot of time wasting as his subordinates ran all over the island.

"Sit down, Colonel. Give it to me as quickly as you can without losing track of the story."

The intelligence officer nodded brusquely, snapped a sheaf of paper in his hand, and worked down a series of bullet points.

"Both of our alliance partners in the AOR have either activated their treaties, or will have within twenty-four hours. Land elements of the Japanese Self-Defense Forces have been recalled to barracks, the naval forces are making preparations to put out to sea, and the air force is already flying CAP over the home islands. The Aussies have called up their reserves and moved all of their remaining high-readiness forces onto alert . . ."

"Remaining?"

"Yes, sir. They have a special forces group, a squadron of Hornets, and a naval task force in the Gulf with us, for Iraq."

Ritchie nodded.

"All of the other regional powers have gone to varying states of high alert. Taiwan has been placed under martial law, and the armed forces have put Plan Orange into effect. South Korea has declared that a curfew will come into effect as of 2200 tonight. Their forces and ours are ready, watching the DMZ, but Pyongyang is sitting very, very still. There's been nothing on their media at all."

"And China?"

Maccomb gnawed at the inside of his mouth like a man with a lifelong chaw habit.

"They've put a lot of troops onto the streets, and our satellite cover shows a lot of activity around the Taiwan Strait batteries, but the force-projection capabilities they do have remain dormant for the moment. They're as spooked as anyone, and they know we still have the forces in theater to check them if necessary."

Ritchie nodded, feeling a headache building behind his eyeballs.

"That's a dreadfully dangerous amount of hardware and armed men moving around."

"Yes, sir," agreed Maccomb. "It is."

"It just reached out and took him," said Kwan, a little breathlessly. "Like, I dunno, like a sort of liquid metal blob or something. Faster than anything I've ever seen."

Musso nodded. He didn't trust himself to speak just yet. His heart was still going like a rat in a trap, and he recognized the hollow, shaky feeling of having dodged a bullet, or something just as nasty. Musso had been a marine for longer than he had been anything else in his life. He knew war from the inside, the way an addict knows his poison. He knew what it was like to make a ball of himself, tight and small, like a clenched fist, as death zipped like a swarm of bees through the air all around him. He knew too well the fragility of the human body, the way that war respects not age, not courage, gender, righteousness, intelligence, or any of the limitless personal touchstones that everyone thinks will get them through, just before everyone starts dying. He had held in his arms grown men reduced to bloodied rags and cooling meat by a few dumb grams of flying metal. He had carried a little Somali girl in his hands, no more than two she would have been, her poor tiny body burned and disintegrating as he ran for a medic. He knew the filth and horror of war as a contagion buried just beneath the surface of his own skin.

He knew fear.

But he had never known it as he had in the few seconds after Núñez was consumed. Fear like a rancid, suppurating pustule that suddenly burst all sweet and bilious in his guts, flooding his mouth and throat and stomach with a distillation of terror in its primal state.

He was going to be a few moments getting over it.

The Cubans, he saw, had freaked the hell out, but were holding it together under the lash of Núñez's deputy, Captain someone-or-other. Musso couldn't recall his name. His people were no less upset, although they were hiding it a little better. Everyone had withdrawn back up the road toward Guantánamo, pulling over to the side about five hundred meters from their original position. The energy wave hadn't altered in the slightest.

Musso released a ragged breath.

"Okay. As of now, nobody gets within five hundred meters of that thing, okay? I can't tell the Cubans what to do, of course, but I'm guessing they won't argue."

Kwan nodded and looked around for the nameless captain.

"I don't even know if he speaks English, sir."

"Me neither," he said. "Get someone to translate. Your sergeant, Gutteres, he's sharp. Put him on liaison if you can spare him."

"Julio's specialty is binary nerve agents. I don't think I'll be needing him," she said flatly.

Kwan saluted and turned away to find their new translator. Musso took a sip of chilled sports drink from an insulated bottle. They had withdrawn to a spot on a slight rise where a small clearing allowed all of the vehicles to pull off the shoulder. The Americans were still attempting to take readings from something that their equipment told them wasn't there. The Cubans had gathered into a loose line under the watchful if anxious gaze of their latest commanding officer. They were sure going through them at a fair clip.

Musso calmed his breathing. His heart rate had dropped back to something a little more reasonable, and the unpleasant low-grade voltage that had been buzzing away just under his skin had finally died down. He couldn't help but wonder where Núñez had gone. If anywhere. That led naturally to thoughts of his wife and kids and what had happened to them. His stomach turned over again. Another slug from the drink bottle and he put it away, pushing off the side of the Humvee and walking over to his radioman, determinedly trying to ignore his personal anxieties.

"Corporal, can you hook me up with Pearl, via Gitmo?"

"No problem, General. Just give me a moment."

Musso left him to it, taking a minute to talk to the Cubans' new CO. Jenny Kwan and Sergeant Gutteres were deep into a three-way conference with the scared-looking officer, who snapped rigidly to attention when he saw Musso approaching. The marine gave him a tired smile and a nod in reply.

"How're we doing, Lieutenant?" he asked Kwan.

"Pretty good, sir. Captain Álvarez here speaks pretty good English. A hell of lot better than my Spanish at any rate. Sergeant Gutteres is filling in the blanks."

Musso addressed the Cuban directly. "I'm sorry about Major Núñez. He seemed a good man and an excellent officer."

"He was," Álvarez replied. "We liked him. All the men liked him very much."

"Well, Captain, I'm about to seek guidance from my superiors, but for myself, I'd like us to keep talking, to help each other out if and when we can. I'd suggest you try and find someone further up your chain of command to report to, but son, you need to prepare yourself for the possibility that you *are* it."

Sergeant Gutteres had begun translating quietly as soon as he'd seen Álvarez struggling to keep up with Musso. He finished a few seconds after the general. Captain Álvarez grimaced a little at the thought that he might well be the sole surviving authority figure in his country, but to his credit he sucked it up and gave the Americanos his sternest warrior's face.

"Cooperation, yes, General," he answered. "Perhaps, in this emergency, we might discuss a joint command, no? A combination command?"

At the look of incomprehension on Musso's face, he launched into a burst of Spanish. Gutteres waited, taking it all in, before passing on the gist of what he'd said.

"Long story short, General, Álvarez is offering to *temporarily* place his men under your command. He emphasizes the temporary nature of the arrangement."

Musso nodded. He understood that the Cuban was covering himself against the unlikely eventuality that they might click their heels three times and find that everything had returned to normal, in which case he'd probably need to seek immediate asylum.

"You do me an honor, Captain," said Musso, nodding to Gutteres to make sure he translated the phrase literally. "Your men have comported themselves with great bravery and forbearance today. They are a credit to your country, and it would be a privilege to serve with them, however *temporary* the arrangement might be."

Álvarez, who seemed more than happy with that, asked if he might borrow the sergeant to speak to his men. Musso agreed, laying a light hand on Gutteres's shoulder before he left them. "Take it easy, son. A light touch is called for. Let Álvarez do any yelling and butt kicking that's required."

"Got it, General."

His radio operator indicated from the command Humvee that he'd established the link to Pearl, and Musso exchanged a salute and, less formally, a handshake with his newest subordinate before hurrying back.

"It's Admiral Ritchie, sir."

"Thank you," said Musso, as he took the handset. "Admiral, it's General Musso, sir. I'm afraid I have some more bad news."

Ritchie hung up when he was done with Musso. He didn't know which was more disturbing, the way the energy barrier had reached out and snatched Major Núñez when he strayed too close, or the fact that the surviving Cubans had been so neutered by the events of the day that they had effectively surrendered control of their territory, or what was left of it, to the United States . . . or what was left of *it*.

A terrible melancholy had settled upon his spirit in the last hour or so. He hadn't noticed it stealing up on him, but having received Musso's report he found himself in a bleaker frame of mind than he could recall having known before. He could hear an increasing hubbub outside his office as more and more people poured into PACOM headquarters. Hundreds of phones appeared to be ringing, and so many voices competed with one another to get *their* message through, to have *their* tiny part of this unfolding nightmare recognized as important, that the normally hushed environs of the command center reminded him of the stock exchange in New York. He'd visited there with his wife and daughter a few months before 9/11.

"Admiral."

"I'm sorry," he said, a little roughly, pretending he'd been lost in thought about something more than his own personal tragedy. His PA was at the door.

"It's General Franks, sir. On a secure line from Qatar. He says elements of the Iraqi army are leaving their entrenched positions and appear to be heading toward the border with Kuwait."

Just for a second Ritchie thought his heart might have stopped. Then he realized it had simply jumped. It felt as though it had gathered itself up and tried to leap right out of his chest. He felt momentarily dizzy and covered it by nodding as he leaned back in his chair.

"Patch him through if you would. Any other good news?"

"The Israelis have moved extra units into the Gaza Strip. A street party there got out of hand and turned into a riot. One of their guys got shot trying to close it down."

"A street party?" Ritchie couldn't keep the dismay out of his voice.

"They're breaking out all over, sir. *All* over. Plenty in the Mideast, of course. But plenty more in Europe, even Britain, in some of the northern areas, with big . . . ah . . . migrant populations."

"You mean big Muslim populations."

"Yes, sir."

"Very well. Patch General Franks through to me here."

Ritchie had a few seconds alone to himself before Franks came on the line. *My God,* he thought, silently. *This is going to turn bad even quicker than I thought.*

12

"Shoeless fuckin' Dan," spat Pete, with no joy in his voice at the arrival of such an old, esteemed colleague.

"And all of his little toes," said Mr. Lee, shooting a wide, gap-toothed grin at Pete. To add to the effect he raised one eyebrow and winked, a most disconcerting sight. "Flippant humor, Mr. Pete? To ease tensions before confrontation."

Pete forced a wan smile in spite of himself. Shoeless Dan was no laughing matter. The dude dealt in some high-octane villainy. Word was, he'd once filled the hold of a Liberian freighter with a couple of hundred orphans for the Chechen maf'. Unspoiled children paid off at the same dollar-per-key rate as good heroin if you could get them into the right wholesale chain. Dan denied it, of course, but not all that strenuously. It added to his mystique, which he needed, given the incurable fungal infection that had turned his feet into putrescent, oozing slabs of meat. The things were grotesque, as big as footballs when they really swelled up, and never smelling any sweeter than a rancid wheel of Spanish cheese.

He knew his boats, though. And he knew the smuggling biz.

"Flippant humor, Mr. Lee." Pete nodded while watching the go-fast boats split up and peel off to come at the yacht from opposite sides. "Does Chinese culture even do flippancy?"

"Mr. John Woo, yes," said Lee. "Central Committee of Communist Party, not so much."

"Who is the more Confucian, then?" asked Pete, following Dan's boat through a pair of binoculars.

"Not Confucian," said Lee, raising both eyebrows and positively beaming at his skipper with all of his remaining teeth on show. "Just confusing."

The old Chinaman held up one hand in triumph. Pete allowed himself a genuine smile that crinkled the net of lines at the corners of his eyes as he smacked out a high five. It might well be the last smile of his life.

"Mr. Lee, John Woo doesn't know shit about Chinese action heroes if he doesn't know you . . . Now, let's deal with this shoeless fuckwit, shall we? I won't have his stinky fucking plates of meat oozing and peeling all over my new boat. Take her up to thirteen knots, if you will. We'll leave a little bit of tiger in the tank for later, if needed."

Lee fitted a set of headphones over his ears, plugged them into a digital radio clipped onto his sun-faded canvas pants, and opened the throttles on the big boat's massive Caterpillar engines, unleashing a stampede from the fifteen hundred horsepower contained in each. Acceleration was smooth and instantaneous. Pete felt himself rocking back on his heels as they leapt forward, and Mr. Lee began a series of sharp tacking maneuvers to make any boarding operations as difficult as possible. The radio in Pete's hand crackled to life. It was Jules.

"We're in position, Pete."

"Good work, Julesy. Keep your finger on the trigger. Big-boy rules today."

He signed off and moved over to the port side of the bridge, where he could see one cigarette boat slowing down and looping in and out, attempting to match its course and speed to the yacht. There were six men crammed into the small cockpit, all of them toting weapons. Shoeless Dan was standing by the wheel, one hand on the windshield, the other waving madly at the bridge of the *Aussie Rules*. He'd know Pete was on board. The *Diamantina* was roped to the stern, bumping along in their wake.

Dan stood about six-two in his perennially bare feet, but he added another nine or ten inches to his height with the largest 'fro Pete had ever seen on a white man. The fact that Dan was afflicted with red hair made him stand out even more dramatically from his brown-skinned crew. He was yelling, to no effect, grinning like a hyena on crystal meth.

Pete glanced at Lee, an unspoken question passing between them. Lee nodded brusquely that he had the helm under control. The Chinaman suddenly spun the wheel hard aport in response to a radio call from one of the girls. Pete plucked a handset from the console a few feet down from Lee and powered up the yacht's loudspeakers. He was going to tell Dan to back off or get blown away. Unfortunately he hit the wrong switch, punching through an audio feed from the media room, where BBC World was running an ad for an upcoming repeat of *Pride and Prejudice* on UKTV.

". . . it is happy for you that you possess the talent of flattering with delicacy," boomed the giant luxury yacht. "May I ask whether these pleasing attentions proceed from the impulse of the moment, or are the result of previous study?"

The effect upon the Mexicans was salutary. They began shooting.

"Oh, for fuck's sake," cursed Jules.

She didn't know whether Pete had done that on purpose or not—he had a pretty inappropriate sense of humor—but the result was the same. Whatever small chance they had of talking Dan down suddenly disappeared, and they were now committed to a shoot-out in which they were outnumbered plenty to one. Hunkered down on the pool deck, where she'd been quietly watching the boat in which Shoeless Dan was traveling, she popped up from cover, and squeezed off a couple of bursts from the M16 as the go-fast made a sudden turn and ran in toward the docking bay. Both vessels were moving erratically at speed and most of her clip missed, but at least one of the men flew back in his seat as his head suddenly appeared to lose its structural integrity. A red mist painted the other passengers in the boat as it came around violently and laid on speed for the bow to get out of Jules's line of fire.

She performed a quick and dirty bit of math, swung the 16 around, and angled the barrel upward at about sixty degrees. The grenade launcher triggered with a hollow thump, sending a single 40-mm high-explosive round downrange. Jules was running forward, crouched low and swapping out her spent mag, well before it hit. She tensed up, waiting for the detonation, but it never came. The round dropped into the sea without exploding.

"Oh, for fuck's sake."

Yes, she tended to repeat herself under pressure.

"Lee!" she yelled into the radio. "Target One is heading forward."

"I see him, Miss Julianne," Mr. Lee replied, his voice calm in her earphones, like that of a parent soothing a distressed child.

The yacht veered across the path of the smaller boat without warning, nearly throwing Jules over the safety rail. She'd just regained her footing when Pete crashed into her. He'd emerged unexpectedly from a doorway, carrying a sawed-off shotgun he'd taken from Fifi. The cut-down stock slammed painfully into her unprotected arm, numbing it.

"Jesus, Pete. Watch out!"

"Sorry, darlin', didn't see you. Heads down!"

He quickly raised the weapon and fired, the blast making her ears ring. Pete worked the slide and fired again and again, until he'd emptied the entire load, then he dropped and rolled onto his back as Jules jumped up and loosed off a series of clattering bursts. The first went nowhere near the go-fast. She had had to squint into a lowering sun and had simply hosed out some fire in the general direction of the boat. The second went a little closer as she adjusted her aim, but the shots flew over the heads of the men as Lee tacked again and she lost balance. The third blast, which emptied her clip, raked the foredeck of the boat, sending bright chips of metal and polished fiberglass flying and twinkling into the salt air and late-afternoon sun. A muffled *whoomp* and a satisfying flash told her something vital had gone up, but before she could nail them with a round from the grenade launcher, Pete dragged her down, just as a line of automatic fire ripped along the bulkhead behind her with a heavy, industrial hammering sound. A hot steel chip grazed one cheek, burning her.

"Shit," she gasped. "Thanks, Pete. Owe you a blowie for that one."

"Consider me blown," shouted Pete over the uproar. "Gimme the sixteen and a couple of mags, take my shottie and get back to Fifi at the loading dock. She's got at least one of the pricks on her case. Crazy fucker jumped onto the diving platform on a flyby."

"Okay. Got it," she shouted, fishing two full magazines out of her combat harness.

From the rear of the yacht she heard the unmistakable hammering of Fifi's favorite gun, a Russian PKM.

They quickly exchanged weapons, and he stuffed the reloads in his cargo pockets as she spun around.

Pete headed forward.

Jules found her shipmate crouched low at the bow of a SeaVee dive boat that hung next to the big custom-built sport fisher on the lower deck at the rear of the yacht.

"Sorry, Julesy," said Fifi. "Asshole got on when his buds had me pinned down. I put a lot of fire down there but don't know whether I even winged him. A frag woulda been nice to roll down on him."

It was hard to hear her over the tumult of gunfire and snarling engine noise.

Jules patted her on the back, where she'd slung "the worm," a rocket launcher Pete had acquired on their last trip to the Maldives. It was stamped with Australian army markings and serial numbers, and had probably been stolen from the garrison on Timor. They had only one warshot for it, and Pete forever had to remind Fifi that she couldn't fire off a practice round. She'd been desperate to light that sucker up since he'd bought the thing.

"You leave this guy to me, babe," said Jules. "We really need you to nail one of those fuckers out there. Pete's working on Shoeless Dan's ride. That leaves the other one for you. Think you can take him with that thing?"

She indicated the launcher on Fifi's back.

Fifi suddenly hauled up her PKM and punched out a short, angry burst that chewed big, expensive chunks of paneling out of the yacht down by the steps to the diving platform. A heavy, Soviet-era design, the gun was powerful enough to be used as an antiaircraft weapon. The uproar when she fired it was enormous. Jules's ears were already ringing from the shotgun blasts a few minutes earlier, and now they began to hum a single deep tone to let her know they'd suffered some real damage.

"Sorry!" shouted Fifi. "Saw him again. Asshole has only two ways up onto the deck. Those stairs down there. You have to move across from one side to the other all the fucking time to check that he hasn't snuck up. Can't keep an eye on both at once, you see. But then he can't be in both places at once either. He's packing some kinda light fully-auto. Maybe an Uzi or an MP5. And yeah, I can put a hurtin' on that other fucker, no problemo."

"Okay," said Jules. "You go."

Her own voice sounded dull and very distant to her, as though her head had been packed in cotton.

She flicked the safety off her shotgun as Fifi moved away. The yacht was still weaving an erratic course, changing tack without warning as Mr. Lee strived to prevent their attackers from boarding any more men. Bent low, Jules couldn't see the go-fast boats, but the deep growling of their engines as they maneuvered around the larger vessel was loud and constant. Distance and the sheer mass of the superyacht often muted the pop and crackle of gunfire from Shoeless Dan's men, but the impact of their rounds hitting home was often deafening, as they crashed into metal or glass just overhead.

Jules shifted position, scowling furiously. The boat deck was crowded with three big vessels, and at least half a dozen Jet Skis, all of which provided excellent cover, but also denied her a clear line of sight to her target. It was also a terrible fucking mess, totally ripped up by hundreds of rounds of ammunition. Her guy was trapped a level down, where he'd come aboard on the diving platform. Conceivably, if she could find a position that covered both sets of stairs up onto the boat deck, she could keep him pinned down until the others were free to help her. But then, she wasn't familiar with the design of the yacht, and it was more than possible that he might be able to work his way up and behind her via an internal route directly from the docking bay. She didn't see any way of avoiding a direct confrontation with the little prick.

Despite the late hour, the sun was still putting out a fierce heat that made all her clothes sticky with sweat. Her tongue felt dry and swollen, and she had trouble swallowing. The yacht swung hard astarboard, nearly throwing her to the deck, but she used the momentum to push forward a few more feet to where a couple of black Jet Skis lay under the keel of the biggest of the auxiliary vessels, the forty-two-footer. That gave her a better view. She could now see at least part of the other staircase, but it also left her a good deal more exposed.

She caught a flash of long matted hair, and blasted away at it, to be rewarded with a strangled cry. Jules didn't think the wound was mortal. A Remington made a horrible mess of a human head when it struck with full force, and she saw no evidence of that. Most likely a couple of pellets hit home and raked out some skin and bone. But nothing fatal.

"Time to double down, Lady Balwyn," she muttered to herself, summoning up her courage with a phrase her father had often used.

A *whoosh* and a sudden explosive *roar* told her that Fifi had launched her rocket. Without thinking, without waiting, Jules leapt up and ran forward, racking another shell into the breech and squeezing it off. The shotgun boomed in her hands. She racked the slide again.

Boom.

She'd made the head of the stairs and fired down into the well.

Boom.

But the boarder was nowhere to be seen.

Damn!

He must have moved over. Bloody tracks led away to the other side of the boat. There was one particularly large splatter, but it wasn't flecked with bone chips or brain flecks, and so mostly likely wasn't evidence of a killing stroke. Still moving as quickly as she could in the pitching, treacherous conditions, she attempted to rack another shell, but the Remington clicked empty.

Oh for fuck's . . .

And then she was on top of him.

A small wiry man, deeply tanned, his bare torso covered in dense, brightly colored swirls of tattoo ink. He was waving a gun around, but was apparently blinded. His face was bathed in blood, and the flesh from his nose up had been badly torn by a few pellets of buckshot.

He fired wildly at the sound of her approach, unloading the better part of an MP5 mag at her, but Jules was already diving before he pulled the trigger. Head tucked in, heart pounding, she crashed into his thighs and knocked him backward into a set of air tanks on the diving platform. Awkwardly, but with all of her strength, she slammed the butt of the shotgun into the soft fleshy part of his upper arm, paralyzing it, and trying to lock the injured limb under her knee as they wrestled.

The rank, sour stink of his sweat mingled badly with the coppery smell of blood and something richer, nastier. He writhed about beneath her weight, much stronger and quicker than she, but badly wounded and handicapped by his lack of clear vision.

For her part, Jules was restricted by having to keep so much weight on his gun arm. Knowing she couldn't win a battle of strength or endurance, she dragged the empty shotgun around and smashed the stock into his face. He screamed with rage and pain, and redoubled his efforts to get out from under her, but three more blows, the last one caving in his forehead, ended any resistance.

The body twitched and shuddered and then went limp as his bowels voided themselves all over her legs.

She gagged, but just managed to hold it together. Snatching the MP5 from his twitching fingers, she crawled to her feet with the muzzle trained on him the whole time. Her leg muscles were rubbery and weak, and her knees folded up beneath her as she backed away.

Sitting with her legs splayed out in front of her, covered in gore and worse, she took a minute or so to realize that she couldn't hear any more gunfire. And then, after a few moments where all she could manage was to breathe and tremble uncontrollably, she realized that for the first time all day, she'd forgotten about the energy wave that had swept away most of America.

"Clubfoot dickhead," Pete murmured through clenched teeth as he dived back inside the yacht to avoid getting his head shot off on his journey toward the bow. "We didn't have to do it like this." They were taking on a terrifying amount of fire now, in spite of the damage Jules had done to Dan's boat. It spoke volumes for the benefit of simply having more fingers on triggers than the other guy. Dan was handing them some serious fucking grief, and it pissed him off mightily. He hadn't been allowed to enjoy a single day as the master of Greg Norman's superyacht before some skanky barefoot shiteater in a Carrot Top fright wig came along and ruined everything by poking holes in his beautiful new boat with a ridiculous amount of automatic gunfire. He had no idea how Dan had come to be out here; probably he'd just loaded up and headed out looking for targets of opportunity as soon as his tiny peabrain had realized that the *federales* and the USN were *permanente desaparecidos*. Frankly, Pete couldn't give a shit. He'd have happily had Dan along as a sidekick, had they been able to berth unmolested at Acapulco, and had Dan agreed to a rigid schedule of foot powder treatments. But this—he emerged onto a forward deck and immediately ducked beneath a couple of rounds from something heavy and unpleasant, a forty-five most likely—*this* was bullshit, and a total liberty and tantamount to taking the fucking piss.

He kept low and swapped out the mag that Jules had been using. The sun was in the last stage of a long dive in the west, which gave him a momentary advantage as the go-fast sped out of the yacht's long shadow. He saw half of Dan's crew suddenly throw their hands up to shade their eyes from the burnt orange brilliance of the sun's rays. This was it. Slowly, and with infinitely more calm than he actually felt, Pete Holder stood up, knees bent slightly to allow him to adjust for movement of the deck. He took careful aim and squeezed off an entire clip in four discrete bursts, forcing himself to drop the iron sight back on the cockpit after each salvo.

"Excuse me, Daniel," he said to himself. "But cheeky little fuckers sometimes need a good smack on the arse."

The effect of taking the time to aim properly rather than just banging away was devastating. The first round stitched up Shoeless Dan, raking a line of fire up his fat belly, punching him backward out of the boat. The last Pete saw of him was a pair of blackened, swollen feet as they spun up and over the side. The next two bursts cut down all of the remaining men, bar one, who had the presence of mind to duck out of sight. The yacht climbed up a small wave while he was hiding, but Pete bent loose at the knees, keeping the gun sight on the cockpit of the cigarette boat the whole time. His stomach clenched tightly, and he could feel his anus puckering in fear, but he maintained the stance, even as a couple of rounds strayed up from the battle at the stern of the ship.

"Come on," he whispered to himself. "Just pop your ugly mug up and . . ."

He'd fired before making any conscious decision to do so. The last surviving Mexican in Shoeless Dan's boat suddenly leapt up and tried to snap off a couple of shots while grabbing the steering wheel and spooling up the engines. It was a hopeless, desperate thing to do, and it killed him. Pete sent at least half a dozen rounds downrange, and while only three intersected the target, they hit him in the back of the neck, tearing through bone and meat with enough force to sever the head. The body was jerked upright and tossed over the side. The head appeared to drop to the floor of the boat.

Nausea and revulsion boiled up inside him, but he sucked in a mouthful of air. It reeked of smoke and gunpowder, which didn't really help, but there was nothing for it. He had to push on. He turned to run for the stern just in time to see a line of white smoke snake out from the deck above him.

"Eat the worm, motherfuckers!"

It was Fifi, yelling from somewhere up on the pool deck.

His eyes instinctively followed the path of the rocket down through the air and into the side of the second go-fast boat, which blew apart as the warhead speared into her, just above the waterline behind the crew cabin. Pete ducked as debris and shrapnel flew out from the point of impact with enough speed to kill anyone who happened to be in the way. Unfortunately, that described his situation precisely. His old knees weren't as quick or as flexible as they'd once been, and a fist-sized chunk of red-hot steel neatly took off the top third of his head.

He staggered back a few steps before his knees buckled underneath him and he fell to the deck, vaguely aware in his last moments of life that he had, after all, been fucked by the fickle finger of fate.

"Bugger . . ." he croaked with his last breath.

The disinfectant stung, but it was the least of Jules's myriad hurts. She seemed to exist within a tornado of pain, of dull aches and sharp, shooting agonies of bruised muscle and tortured bone. Apart from Mr. Lee, who was smiling as he dabbed at the deep cut on her cheek, they had all taken damage during the fight with Shoeless Dan. Fifi had one arm in a sling, and was limping from a flesh wound to her thigh. Lee finished up by gently pressing a thick bandage into place high on her wounded cheek and handing her a couple of blue capsules. The small pharmacy on the yacht had given up a treasure trove of sedatives and balms.

"For the pain, Miss Julianne."

"Thanks," she replied in a dry, cracked voice.

Jules popped her pills and washed them down with a mouthful of gin and tonic, prepared for her by Fifi.

"Would it be churlish, at this point, to remind everyone that a couple of hours ago, Pete had Shoeless Dan tagged as a reliable chap and potential crewmate?"

Fifi sniffed and shook her head.

"He was always a fucking softie, Pete. I loved him so much." Her face crumpled and she let herself go, releasing a high-pitched keening sound that turned into a series of wails and sobs.

"It would be ungracious and beneath a lady of your breeding, Miss Julianne," said Lee, whose own face was a mask, carved from ancient teak.

Darkness had fallen outside, or a sort of darkness. It glowed with a noticeable red hue thrown off by the energy wave, which was now eighty nautical miles to their north, but still visible. The three survivors had bathed and changed after cleaning up the worst of the damage and bloodshed. While they were at it, they got rid of the last remains of the former crew members, too. It hadn't been such a bad job, compared with washing away the carnage of battle.

They'd wrapped Pete's body in a blanket and stored him in one of the galley's huge freezer units. He'd once told Jules that if he ever bought it, he'd want his ashes scattered at an awesome surf break somewhere. Wouldn't matter which one. Maverick's. Pipe. Margaret River. They were all good. Just as long as it was pumping when he took his last ride.

They had gathered in the upper salon, one of the cozier, less formal spaces. A couple of olive-green two-seater lounges, hugely overstuffed and obscenely comfortable, sat around two sides of a giant brown ottoman. A pair of white single-seaters took up one other side, where floor to ceiling bifold windows gave onto an expansive view of the sea far below. Jules had bathed for two hours to rid herself of the stink of the man she'd killed, and the irrational guilt she felt at living when Pete hadn't. A couple of hundred dollars' worth of French toiletries had helped a little with the former, although she still felt as if some corruption had worked its way under her skin. And she knew she was going to be down about Pete for weeks. It was harsh, but she was more affected by his death than by the weird shit happening to the north.

She sipped at her drink, feeling lonely and abandoned, stretched out on the lounge, burrowing deeper into the waffle-weave bathrobe she'd found in one of the cabins. "You know what," she sighed. "Dan was always a bit of a maddie, but even he wouldn't start a fight like that without good reason."

"He had good reason," said Fifi, who'd recovered some of her composure. "Fuckin' Jane Austen on full volume. Drives me nuts when you play those vids, Julesy."

Jules smiled sadly. Fifi still held a grudge for getting her arse dragged into *Sense and Sensibility* by Julianne once. She'd thought she was seeing the sequel to *Dumb and Dumber.*

"It'd make me go for the gun locker, too," mumbled her friend. "Stupid m . . . mo . . . motherfucker," she said before lapsing back into tears.

Jules downed her drink in one long pull and stood up unsteadily, looking for the gin bottle.

"I'm sorry about Pete," she said. "I'll cry myself to sleep later, but we don't have time to wallow. This Twilight Zone rubbish is going to upset the apple cart in the worst way possible, and it will likely happen very quickly. I suspect Dan was simply ahead of the curve. Well, him or someone who paid him. His operation didn't normally run to go-fast boats, or hired banditos."

"Shoeless Dan always most unimpressive," said Mr. Lee as he cleared away the first-aid kit. "First I ever hear of him was of redheaded giant trying to sell stolen dog food to Vietnam criminals. Tried to say real dog in can. Vietnam tie bag of cans to Shoeless Dan and throw him in water. Only escapes because they cannot tie knot well."

"No," said Jules as she handed Fifi a Tasmanian beer. "They probably tied those knots fine. But there were some things Dan did know well. Knots, sails, boats, tides, who'd take a bribe and who wouldn't, the range and speed of every coast guard cutter in the Keys, anything to do with smuggling by sea and he was good for it. But piracy was not his gig."

"Yeah, well, he surely wasn't worth a pinch of shit as one," sniffed Fifi.

"So, what was the story today?" asked Jules as she picked a sandwich from a silver platter on the ottoman in front of her. She wasn't really hungry. It was just something to do. Fifi had found half a turkey and a leg of Iberian ham in one of the giant double-door refrigerators down in the main galley, and she'd thrown together a small feast of cold cuts and salad. She wasn't eating either, and Jules suspected that preparing the meal was more about therapy than hunger. Long before Fifi had taken up smuggling she had qualified as a commercial chef.

Fresh rolls, slathered with melting butter, lay in a pile next to a big bowl of baby spinach leaves, walnuts, pear, and Parmesan slivers. The drugs Jules had taken had begun a slow waltz with her gin and tonic, and she let the warm waves of sleepiness wash over her.

"Yeats, my friends. The story today was Yeats," she said, answering her own question, if somewhat impenetrably. "The center cannot hold. Mere anarchy is loosed upon the world. That's where we are right now. On the edge of anarchy."

13

Honolulu, Hawaii

The early-evening drive down to the governor's residence was enough to convince James Ritchie that the islands were going to go down a tube at high speed unless someone got their act together. The curfew seemed to have had no effect, and the state government had no interest in enforcing it. Thousands of people were milling about the streets, many of them agitated and besieging any place they could buy emergency supplies of food and water. Large, increasingly unstable crowds had gathered outside travel agencies and airline shop fronts, which remained open well after normal business hours. Every gas station had a trail of vehicles snaking away from its pumps, leading Ritchie to wonder where the hell they thought they were going to escape to in their SUVs and family sedans.

His latest reports from Gitmo and Canada spoke of a strange glow, as if from a distant furnace, emanating from the energy wave, and as their route down to the Capitol District allowed Ritchie glimpses of the Pacific reaching away back east, he couldn't shake the impression of a sunset that seemed denser and richer than normal. Long slow lines of surf banked up in sets of three off the beach at Waikiki, a strong offshore breeze blowing thick foam back off the lip as they crested. The weird, almost ethereal light lent the spray a bright, burnished cherry color, and seemed to paint the mass of surfers and body boarders bright pink as they carved up the barrels.

The Capitol District was less crowded, probably because it offered little in the way of supplies that could be bought up and hoarded. Police and state troopers were out in force, however, and the pulsing lights of more than a dozen Honolulu PD squad cars bathed the district in a rich, electric red that overwhelmed the ethereal light Ritchie had noticed before. His BlackBerry buzzed as the staff car swung off Beretania Street and in through the gates of the capitol building. It was his wife.

NANCY IS OK! FLEW OUT OF O'HARE THS MNG. IN LONDON. WILL CALL L8R.

A hollow opened in the admiral's chest and filled with heat, but it subsided quickly and he was left with a loose feeling in his bowels and a giddy, almost guilty sense of relief. His only child had been scheduled to fly out of the U.S. this week for a year's travel through Europe and Asia. But Nancy was a bit of a free spirit—an "airhead," he might have said, were she anyone other than his own—and organization was not her strong point. She was just as likely to miss a flight as catch one, and her trip had already been rescheduled twice for that very reason. Ritchie had spent the entire day trying to cope with the end of the world while stomping down on a feeling of utter hopelessness verging on panic for his baby girl. He had spoken to nobody about it. Everyone had people somewhere back home and his first responsibility was to the nation, not to himself or even his family. But he shivered uncontrollably as tears filled his eyes, hot and stinging, and he had to hold his breath to forestall a sob.

Damn, he cursed silently. *What a time to crack up.*

"You all right, sir?"

He kept his eyes shielded from the driver by pretending to

stare out the window at plastic barricades that were going up around the House. What the hell were they in aid of? They wouldn't stop the Wave if it came rushing at them from over the horizon, and the populace was more likely to storm a well-stocked 7-Eleven than the state legislature.

"I'm okay," he grunted, when he had his voice back under control. "It's just a message from my wife, that's all. Our daughter is fine. She flew out of Chicago this morning, before this business hit."

Ritchie wasn't sure why he felt the need to say anything. Perhaps to make it seem real to himself. It wasn't the sort of thing he'd normally discuss with anyone outside of his family, let alone a driver from the car pool.

"That's great news, sir," said the young sailor behind the wheel, a new guy Ritchie had met only forty minutes ago. He sounded genuinely happy, and Ritchie couldn't help but wonder where the lad hailed from and whether he had family back stateside himself.

"Thank you, son," he said as they pulled up at the edge of a crowded parking lot. "But a lot of people weren't as lucky as me today."

The lot was packed solid. Men and women in expensive-looking business wear hurried about with no apparent reason to their movements. He supposed that the civilian arm of government had gone over to emergency procedures as quickly and completely as the military. Until now, he'd been concerned only with the latter, but the governor's office had requested his presence at this meeting as a matter of the highest urgency, and Ritchie had seen no alternative to attending. Apart from Seattle, which was perilously close to the event horizon, and Alaska, which was sparsely populated and still largely undeveloped, Hawaii was pretty much all that was left of the United States. But while she could defend herself, given the concentration of military forces in the islands, Ritchie wasn't sure she could feed herself for much more than a few days. And with a quarter of a million men and women to pull out of a war in the Middle East, he really didn't need to be distracted by food riots in his own backyard.

"Shall I park, here, sir?" his driver asked. "You don't want to get jammed in is all, Admiral."

"No," said Ritchie. "Good point. Take the car back out of

here. Get yourself something to eat, and then park somewhere in the district, but not here. This place is a mess. I've got your number. I'll call you when I need you."

"Yes, sir. Thank you, sir."

Ritchie was pleased to see that the sailor checked the charge on his cell phone before answering. Just because he was young didn't mean he was dumb.

"I'm sorry, sailor. What's your name? I didn't catch it in the rush before."

"Seaman Horvath, sir."

"Okay. Good work, Horvath. Take a break. I suspect I'll be a little while."

Stale sweat, fading perfume, and air rebreathed so many times it tasted sick and wrong. The contrast with his own headquarters couldn't have been starker. Ritchie hit the corridors of the state capitol and ran headlong into mayhem. Spiraling turmoil seemed to be the general operating principle, the sort of witless hysteria you might expect on amateurs' night at a Chechen bordello. Ritchie was buffeted by staffers and aides as they double-timed from office to office. A woman swerved to miss him, all elbows and high heels, and crashed into a copy machine that had apparently been pushed into the hallway. She spilled a couple of hundred loose-leaf pages over the carpet, cursing like a chief petty officer as she dropped to the floor to gather them up. Hundreds of voices competed in the cramped space as people spoke over and past each other, all of them convinced that their own particular order, or request, or fragmented rumor was the most important piece of that moment's puzzle. The media were everywhere, wolf packs of TV and print reporters threading through the upheaval, firing up shoulder-mounted cameras and thrusting microphones into the face of anybody who seemed remotely responsible for anything. Ritchie gripped his briefcase a little harder and pushed forward lest . . .

"Admiral. Yo! Admiral. Is the military taking over? Is there going to be martial law?"

And before he could dive into a side passage or broom closet one of the packs had suddenly fallen on him. Bright white light seared the backs of his eyes, temporarily blinding him and forcing him to squint against the harsh glare.

"Admiral. Are you here to take over? Are you going to run the emergency response?"

Ritchie couldn't see who was asking the damn-fool questions, but he could sense a sudden press in the crowd around him as maybe a dozen or more reporters turned their attention toward the only symbol of authority in the immediate area: a man in a short-sleeved khaki navy uniform sporting four stars on his collar. A jabbering crush of journalists surged toward him, and without thinking he barked out an order.

"Stand back, please. Have some dignity, would you!"

Ah, damn it!

He'd reacted instinctively, allowing his dismay and surprise at the chaotic scene to get the better of him. But to his relief it actually seemed to work. There was a noticeable lessening of the disarray immediately around him, and Ritchie made an impulse decision to go with it.

"First off, drop the lights, please. I'm not answering any questions standing here like a piece of roadkill in the spotlight. Second, hell no. I'm not here to take over. What's up with you people? You're not children. Stop acting like them. Governor Lingle asked me here this evening to discuss what aid the armed forces of the United States of America might render to the civil power. And that is it. I don't declare martial law. I don't give orders. I follow them. And if you don't mind, I'm going to do just that."

Before he could step off and continue his journey, however, a small birdlike woman with enormous black hair pushed a microphone into his path.

"What can you tell us about what's happened on the mainland, Admiral? Have the military been monitoring the phenomenon? What are you going to do about it?"

Ritchie was tempted to push past her, but he couldn't help noticing how the ambient roar that had filled the entire building just a few minutes earlier had died away completely. A flicker of color behind the phalanx of reporters answered any questions he might have had about why. He could see himself on a television monitor in a room across the hall. This was probably going out live across the island. Possibly around the world. The urge to sit down, sigh, and rub his eyes was nearly overwhelming, but these people needed leadership and certainty just as much as any bunch of kids taking fire from the enemy. In the absence of anyone to provide that leadership, the buck seemed to have stopped at his feet for the moment. The admiral didn't see any point in fudging the issue. He slowly bent and carefully placed his briefcase on a desk, the black, dead eyes of the TV cameras following every move. It gave him time to compose his thoughts. When he stood up again he spoke into near silence.

"Something terrible has happened back home," he said. "If you'll excuse me. My family is originally from New Hampshire. I can't tell you a lot of what you need to know right now. I can't say exactly what has happened, how or why. But you are right. We have been looking hard at this thing, throwing every asset we have at it. We've lost some more people in doing that, but I want to emphasize one very important point. Much of our armed forces were outside of the continental U.S. as of this morning. They remain intact and ready to make any sacrifice, to take any action necessary to protect you, the American people who are listening to this. Our friends and allies are helping us, too, and with that help we *will* get through this, I promise you."

A beat of half a second's silence followed his speech before the media pack erupted again, firing questions and demands for information at him. He was just about to wave them away when a booming Southern accent cut through the pandemonium.

"That'll be all for now, thank you, ladies and gentlemen. You heard the admiral. He does have a very important meeting to get to. Governor Lingle will address you all live right after it—and no, I can't say for sure when that will be, but you've definitely got a couple of hours to go get your horses fed and watered."

The man's voice was so powerful, his delivery so sure, it quelled the incipient press riot almost immediately. Ritchie was grateful, but bemused. As a resident of the islands he was familiar with some of the public faces of the state administration, even though Governor Lingle had not been in office long. But this massive, roaring bear of a man was new to him, and Ritchie didn't see how he could have missed such a figure—or a voice.

He was impeccably if heavily dressed in a three-piece blue pin-striped suit, and he took Ritchie gently but firmly by the elbow and propelled him through the ruck of journalists.

"Keep smiling," he muttered. "Don't let your fingers get

anywhere near their mouths. And check to see if you still have your wallet and watch on the other side."

His self-appointed guardian operated as a gentle but unstoppable battering ram, carving a path not just through the crush of reporters and cameramen, but also through the throngs of civil servants beyond them, many of whom stood and gawped at Ritchie when he passed by, almost as if he were some kind of celebrity.

"Guess I've had my fifteen minutes of fame," he said.

"Not if you got any more performances like that up your sleeve," his companion replied somewhat grimly. "Wish I could get a few others to turn it on like that. Jed Culver, by the way. Of the Louisiana bar. Originally. I run a consultancy out of D.C. of late."

Ritchie awkwardly swapped his briefcase from one hand to the other and they shook.

"Admiral James Ritchie, Mr. Culver. You didn't sound like a local boy."

Culver steered him around a corner and past a couple of security guards who were doing a good job of pissing off a dozen or more staffers who insisted that they had good reason to be admitted to the inner sanctum. That's what this part of the building felt like. It was less crowded and much quieter, and events didn't seem to be spinning out of control quite so badly here.

"I was lucky enough to be on vacation with my family," said Culver. "My immediate family at least, thank God. Anyway, I saw the news this morning and figured I would lend a hand if they wanted. Lingle's main press handler was stateside."

"You've done a lot of press management then?"

"Oh, yes. Real press, too. Hard men like Jimmy Breslin and Chip Brown. Not like these pussies. That was a great speech before, you know. Really nailed a few heads to the wall. That's what we need right now. A big goddamned hammer and a whole bucket o' nails to get things secured 'fore they start flying off all over."

They pulled up outside a closed office door. There was an indefatigable energy to Culver that you couldn't help liking. A lot of spare mass was expensively hidden away under that designer suit, but he looked like a man who could plow on for days at a time without a break. The island was probably lucky to have him. The heavyset lawyer rapped on the door and waited half a beat before pushing on into an anteroom furnished with two desks, behind which sat a couple of very stressed-out young women. One had three phones clamped to her ears and was writing notes on multiple pads. The other was stabbing at her telephone's keypad, listening for a second, slamming down the receiver, and repeating the process all over again.

"Governor ready?" asked Culver. "I got the admiral. Pulled him from the mouths of the lions by my own hand."

The second receptionist, the one having so much trouble making her call, nodded at them. "Go on through, Mr. Culver," she said tersely. "They're waiting."

As Culver led him through, a thought occurred to Ritchie.

"Why pack the suit, if you're on vacation, Mr. Culver?"

The lawyer smiled back over his shoulder.

"Ah, you're a man who thinks like my good wife, sir. Come on, meet the governor."

Culver seemed unnaturally assured of his place, given that he was little more than an interloper, but he'd obviously been of some help to the administration through the madness of the last twelve hours. There were any number of legitimate government officers trapped behind the velvet rope down the corridor who had more claim to be here than him. But here he was, and there they were, frozen out by a couple of state-sponsored bouncers. In a way, it gave Ritchie some hope. Perhaps things weren't as disorganized as they'd seemed.

Governor Lingle was waiting for them just inside the office, flanked by a couple of suits. Her eyes were framed by the same haunted appearance he was beginning to recognize on everyone. If he looked in the mirror he'd doubtless see the same expression staring back.

"Admiral, thank you for coming down," said Lingle, sounding very tired. "I understand you must be very busy. Please, sit down. We'll get on with this as quickly as we can."

"Thank you, ma'am," said Ritchie, shaking her hand and then those of the other people in the room, whom the governor introduced as heads of various departments.

"How did the city look to you, Admiral, on your drive down here?" she asked.

Ritchie didn't see any point in weasel words.

"Your curfew isn't holding, ma'am. It's being widely ignored. The state troopers and police are using a very light hand. I wouldn't say there was panic on the streets, but the stores will run empty very soon, and then you'll see some real fear and probably some violence. There's a lot of people trying to get out, tourists I suppose, although who knows. If you want my advice, do everything you can to get them on a plane with all dispatch."

Lingle nodded and pursed her lips. Her staffers' reactions were mixed. One bristled, two others nodded vigorously. Jed Culver remained impassive.

"I don't want to see any more troops on my streets. In fact, I'd prefer not to see any out there at all, Admiral, and I'm sure you'd rather not have to employ your people here either, but it might not be a bad idea to prepare for the worst anyway. I'm sure you must have a plan in some bottom drawer somewhere for this sort of thing."

"Not really," he said, shaking his head. "But there'll be something somewhere about aid to the civil power in situations of extreme crisis—a mega tsunami or supervolcano or something. It shouldn't be beyond our abilities to adapt. But Madam Governor, if I may, there is a related issue I'd like to raise very briefly, that of executive authority."

Culver and Lingle did an odd, unrehearsed double act. The lawyer leaned forward keenly on his chair, while the governor rubbed her eyes and sat back in her own.

"Go on, Admiral."

Ritchie snapped open his briefcase and handed over a sheaf of documents.

"I had the JAG office here run up this briefer for you, ma'am. It's about the line of succession. Realistically, the president isn't coming back. Nor any of the cabinet or other nominated successors. In terms of elected officials who can assume the office of the presidency, it's you, the deputy governor in Juneau, or maybe the Speaker of the state house in Washington."

"Oh," said Lingle, as an uncomfortable stillness wrapped itself around the room. "So, which one of us?"

Ritchie glanced over at Culver, who was now watching him like a rattler.

"Frankly, ma'am, it could be any of you. There is no statute or precedent covering a disaster of this magnitude. Between you and me, we may have to make it up as we go."

Culver eased himself back a little. His shoulders, which had been noticeably hunched up, relaxed.

"He's right, Madam Governor," the lawyer offered, unbidden. "There is no procedure for dealing with this. Even a nuclear war would not have decapitated the government as cleanly and completely. The admiral is correct in that we need to make it up as we go. And we *do* need to act. I'm sure Admiral Ritchie is thinking of his comrades in the Gulf, and that's only reasonable, but there are still millions of U.S. citizens who haven't been taken up, or whatever, by this thing, and they need to be protected."

"But can we protect them from the Wave?" she asked. "My understanding is that you have no idea what it is, Admiral."

Before Ritchie could answer, Culver butted in again.

"That may be so, ma'am, but that's not what I mean. Maybe that thing will gobble us all up before breakfast. In which case, too bad. But the world is a cruel and unusual enough place even without bad *Star Trek* episodes suddenly leaping off the screen at us."

One of the younger aides couldn't help himself.

"There was a *Star Trek* episode . . . ?"

Culver shrugged. "I'm extemporizing."

"Oh. Okay."

"Gentlemen," said Lingle, "I'll read these tonight, I promise. But you've seen what's happening out there. My immediate responsibility is to the people of Hawaii. That's who I was elected to serve and protect, and for now, that is the extent of my office. Admiral, I can understand, given the situation in Iraq, why you need to resolve this, but for now can I suggest that you simply use whatever chain of command has survived the day? You know what you have to do and how to do it. I presume you won't be going ahead with any attack?"

Everyone in the room was suddenly staring at him, hard. Ritchie had spent decades in the military, and every cell in his body rebelled at the idea of having to discuss operational issues in a forum such as this, but what choice did he have?

"Madam Governor," he began, "given the circumstances, no, at this stage we are not intending to commence hostilities. For one thing, as I've made clear, we have no executive authority to begin a war."

"Bush signing a bit of paper wouldn't have given you . . ."

"Quiet, Jim," Lingle snapped at the staffer who'd spoken out of turn. "It's not the time or the place. Go on, Admiral."

Ritchie ignored the distraction.

"But in any event, that decision may be taken out of our hands if the Iraqis themselves attack."

"Is that likely?" asked Lingle. "It would be suicide for them."

"Yes," said Ritchie. "But rationality went down the toilet today if you didn't notice."

A few moments of silence followed, with everyone locked inside their own thoughts.

"Well," said Lingle at last. "As I said, you have an intact chain of command. Use it as necessary. For now, we have our own problem right here. These islands cannot feed themselves. There isn't going to be any food coming from the mainland, and people are going to starve if we don't get it from somewhere else, and soon."

14

Third Infantry Division staging area, Kuwait

The nighttime desert was a crumpled drift of blue-white silk below the chopper, which was all hot metal and grease and the suffocating body odor of soldiers. In the gloom it enfolded him like an unpleasant memory as they rushed out to the divisional staging area. Bret Melton had jumped out of helicopters and into another war not far from here, not long ago, and at times riding out toward the line he had wondered if he'd be doing the same thing in another ten years. And ten more after that, forever and ever amen. Now he knew that he wouldn't.

The thundering engine and rotors made normal conversation impossible, but the four troopers in the cabin with him all needed to talk, to know what was happening back in the real world. In the faint glow leaking through from the cockpit their faces were hollowed-out and haunted. They all knew him, or knew of him. As a former ranger, Melton was a popular embed. His shit was stowed according to regs and he could be trusted. He was as close to a believer as an outsider could be. The questions started as soon as they recognized him hitching the flight back to Third Infantry Division.

"What the fuck's happening, man?"

"What about our families?"

"Is it a fucking attack or what, dude?"

He'd done his best to explain what he knew, but really, what *did* he know? As Melton had laid it out for them, bellowing over the thump of the rotor blades, the looks on their faces had made him feel like a mental case. They gaped in horror and disbelief as he described what he'd seen and heard—and how could he blame them? He couldn't really believe it himself. He sounded authentically mad. After twenty minutes they'd all lapsed into silence, and the rest of the flight passed in a sort of stunned, half-catatonic state. Melton knew that by the time these guys relayed the news to their friends it'd be totally bent out of shape, but he didn't see much point to holding anything back. Everything they were defending was gone. Their homes and loved ones. Everything. They had a right to know. In fact, that was the only reason he was still here. He had open tickets back to Paris and could check out any time he wanted, but he could no more fly out to Paris than he could to New York now. Ever since he'd left the army, after Somalia, he'd had one faith, one love from which he could not be diverted: the telling of soldiers' stories.

The pilot's voice came through, a clipped monotone announcing that they were five minutes out. Melton craned around on his perch and briefly popped his head out into the slipstream. The First Brigade Combat Team's desert base wasn't totally blacked out, but it was much darker than the last time he'd come in, three days ago. Even so, under the moon it still glowed as a bed of pearls in the wide vessel of shadows that was the desert at night. On a satellite image the tent city and masses of equipment would show up as a vast glowing metropolis of blood and iron, but what the hell. There was no sense in making it easy for Saddam.

They flew in low, flaring and pivoting for the touchdown on a steel mesh landing pad. A storm of gritty, stinging sand blasted into the cabin, scouring any exposed skin and working its way in through the layers of clothing Melton had drawn tightly around himself. One of the soldiers slapped him on the shoulder and grimly mouthed, "Thanks anyway, buddy," before leaping out and hurrying off, bent double. The *Army Times* correspondent—or was he a *former* correspondent now?—followed the others out into the chill darkness, intending to head for the tent where some of the journalists maintained a rudimentary press club with a small stash of carefully hoarded bourbon and beer.

"*Mr. Melton? Sir?*"

"Lieutenant Euler?"

Melton recognized him immediately. The platoon commander, who at six and a half feet was forced into a very exaggerated stoop by the Blackhawk's spinning rotors, hurried forward and took Melton by the elbow, steering him away from his intended heading.

"Captain wants to see you, sir. We're getting set to roll on fifteen minutes' notice."

"Roll where?"

"Don't know, sir. But Captain Lohberger needs you over at headquarters. The squadron commander will want to hear what you have to say as well."

"About what's happened back home?"

"Yes, sir."

Both men carefully stood up as they cleared the track of the rotor blades. Melton hoisted his backpack into a slightly more comfortable position and tried to take in as much as he could of his surroundings. Something was going to happen soon and it left a weird coppery taste in the back of his mouth. They hurried down from the rise of the makeshift helipad, diving into a small tent city that was laid out on a strict grid pattern, much of it obscured by the tan camouflage nets. Away from the overwhelming din of the chopper he began to hear shouts and curses as noncoms wrangled their squads toward assembly points while junior officers like Euler gathered up platoons and began clicking them into larger units for deployment into the field. He could hear the whine of Abrams gas turbines and the snarl of Bradley fighting vehicles somewhere nearby, and overlaying it all was the ceaseless thumping of rotor blades as dozens of helicopters pirouetted through the inky black sky above them. The metallic, oily taste of diesel mixed with the grit and dust kicked up by the Blackhawk and filled his sinuses. He pulled out a rag and blew his nose, knowing full well that the snot would be blood-flecked from the dirt.

"Do you mind if I ask you a question, sir?" said Euler, as they double-timed past a tent where a group of men in uniforms and berets he recognized as British SAS was hunkered around a table. One of the commandos leveled a hard stare at him and flicked the tent flap closed.

"Is it true, sir? What we've been hearing?"

Melton squinted against the sand, which was already coating the inside of his mouth and nostrils.

"I don't know what you've heard, exactly, Lieutenant. But it's gone. Home. Everyone there has gone."

Euler's face twisted in a mask of despair.

"I'd heard it was a jihad attack. Bioweapons or nukes or something. Took out a bunch of cities."

They turned a corner, nearly running into a couple of MPs.

"Watch where you're going, asshole," one of them barked, surprising Melton with a female voice. She was built thicker and closer to the ground than he. He muttered a hasty apology and drove on.

"No. This is nothing to do with them. Unless it was merciful fucking Allah, of course, like Saddam is telling everyone. But nobody knows. Some kinda weird energy bubble or something. Seems to have zapped all the primates inside its boundary. Some of them gone. Some of them just sort of turned into mush."

"Primates?" Euler looked aghast. "And mush?"

"Just before I took off, that was the latest on CNN. Some Japanese blogger checking webcams of the San Diego Zoo noticed that all the monkeys were gone. Didn't take long to work out from there."

"Holy shit," said the lieutenant in a small, choked voice that was completely at odds with his towering frame and full battle rattle. The reporter knew exactly what was going through his mind. He'd seen that same reaction many times today. Lieutenant Euler was counting his losses. Children and partner if he had them. Mom and dad, ditto. Brothers. Sisters. Old friends and new. Neighbors. Faces on the streets where he once lived, even if he didn't know their names. Ex-girlfriends. Classmates from school. A widening circle of personal history, all of it sucked away in some freakish moment when the laws of physics got turned inside out. Any moment now he'd look around, like a child who'd woken up in a strange room, trying to figure out where he was and how to put everything back in its place.

There.

"I'm sorry," said Melton, but Euler just shook his head.

"This sucks," he breathed. "Everyone?"

"Most everyone," he confirmed. "Seattle's still there. Alaska. Coupla places in Canada. That's it, though."

"Man . . . oh, shit, here we are."

They stepped into a large frame tent, one of the newer types, which came with power outlets and lighting. It was nicer than the Korean War–era GP Mediums he used to spend time in. Melton recognized the tense, guarded body language of men who were used to facing the worst possible situations, but had never really expected anything *this* bad. He was almost rocked back on his heels by the concentrated force of their attention when they recognized him.

"Come in, gentlemen. We're pressed for time here, Bret."

Melton nodded a quick greeting at Captain Christian Lohberger, Bravo Troop CO, 5/7 Cav, and the only man in the tent who routinely used Melton's first name. Everyone else referred to him as sir, or Mr. Melton. Being called "sir" beat "hooah" or "rangers lead the way," which Melton had found increasingly annoying over the years, especially hearing the ranger war cry from pukes who most definitely were not rangers and were never going to be rangers. And as a former grunt, the "sir" thing had greatly amused him at first. Nothing much amused him at the moment, however.

"I'm guessing that's not why you wanted to see me," he said.

Lohberger shook his head and cut straight to the bone. "No. We're getting nothing but smoke blown up our asses from Division on down. What the hell is going on?"

Melton dropped his bag by the trestle table, on which a map of the Kuwaiti-Iraqi borderlands rested. It was covered in a swirl of red and blue lines and unit markings. The faces around the tent were grim and focused entirely on him.

"Well," he began, "what I knew when I caught the chopper back this afternoon . . ."

By the time Bret finished, Lohberger's first sergeant had fetched the squadron's commander and command sergeant major.

"Sweet mother of God," grunted Sergeant Major Bo Jaanson, a gnarled stump of old wood who looked like he might well have seen the Nazis off at the Singfried line. Melton had given them the superconcentrated version of the hours he'd spent plugged into the European and Asian news feeds, finishing up with the news of the "monkey" discovery—fresh when he'd stepped off the tarmac in Qatar, but probably superseded by some new madness in the hours since.

The leadership cadre was otherwise speechless. Outside the slowly billowing walls of the tent in which they stood, the squadron continued to gather its strength. Yesterday it had seemed utterly formidable. Now Melton felt like a bug sitting on a mound kicked over by laughing, moronic gods.

"Thanks anyway," said Lohberger at last. "It's been hard not knowing anything."

Bret shrugged helplessly.

"I'm only telling you what I got off the satellite feed and web. I wouldn't call it gospel, but . . . you know . . ."

The men were all younger than he, the platoon commanders by a considerable margin. Some of them would have young families of their own. Lohberger, at thirty, was something of a grand old man. He sucked in a deep breath and looked at the map as though he'd found some kind of nasty porn stash in his daughter's bedroom.

"Okay. There's nothing we can do about it from here, not right now anyway," he declared. "We know a lot more than we did ten minutes ago, but nothing that changes what we have to do in the next couple of hours."

His voice and manner were hard. Melton observed a stiffening of postures and facial expressions among the other men in the room, a turning away from anxiety and doubts, as men jammed them down somewhere deep, at least for the next little while.

"Do you mind if I ask what's gonna go down here?" said Melton.

"Nope," Lohberger replied. "You're gonna be in on it soon enough."

He jabbed a finger at the map table. Melton read the map plan, named OPLAN Katie. It looked like someone's joke of a Cold War–era Forward Defense at Fulda Gap write-up. He started to feel ill. Katie bar the door indeed, Melton thought, not seeing the humor in the battle plan's name.

"Saddam's moving toward us. He's pulled a lot of his guys out of those useless fucking trenches they dug and put them on the road heading this way."

"Holy shit."

"Yeah. Like we don't have enough to think about."

Melton leaned forward to examine OPLAN Katie on the transparent acetate. The basic plan had all coalition forces moving forward out of Kuwait as originally planned. On the map was one phase line, a graphic control measure called Phase Line Katie, that ran through the Sulaybat Depression. All of the units in the coalition were to hold that phase line and attrit any Iraqi force approaching it. The Brits with the First UK Division were still assigned the chore of dealing with Basra. Melton choked back any criticism of the plan. Getting into an urban firefight, especially now, didn't seem to make any sense at all. It negated almost all of the coalition forces' technological and military advantages.

5/7 Cav's objective was Jalibah Airfield, marked as Objective Marne.

The Mog all over again, he thought. It explained why everyone in the tent looked pale and sweaty.

What idiot came up with this plan? He kept that question to himself and asked a different one. "Any idea which units?"

Command Sergeant Major Jaanson volunteered the answer. "The crap ones. Militia. Fedayeen. Reserve forces. A couple of Republican Guard units, but from the way they're moving they look like their job is to keep a gun at the back of those other guys heading into the meat grinder."

The *Army Times* reporter glanced at Lohberger for confirmation and received a brusque nod. "We've seen a couple of firefights break out within the Iraqi ranks. Guard units chewing over militia who tried to break off the advance."

Melton couldn't help it. He pointed at Phase Line Katie. "Surely you are not going to attack them, are you?"

Captain Lohberger shrugged as his squadron commander, a lieutenant colonel, left the tent for a meeting with the brigade commander.

"Well, the Kuwaitis don't want us fighting on their soil. So that is why we are moving forward. They are taking positions on the coalition's western flank inside Iraqi territory just on the other side of Wadi al-Batin. These base camps are not the best defensive positions anyway, so we may as well follow the first tenet of warfare," Lohberger said.

"Engage the enemy as far forward as possible," Melton said, nodding.

"Hooah, rangers lead the way," said Lohberger, who did have a ranger tab on his uniform and thus, in Melton's mind, the right to talk like one. Still, Bret winced anyway while Lohberger continued. "The plan is that coalition air power will conduct the air war as before, going for command and control. They'll take out the bridges as well, which should make our life a bit easier. Close air will stomp anyone who gets over those obstacles, then our arty engages them. Whatever is left is our meat, Bret."

Melton didn't ask the obvious question.

Why?

Why the hell did any of them have to be here now? Saddam was no longer a threat to America, was he? And if the wing nuts were right, and it was all just about the oil, and fattening up Halliburton's balance sheet so that Dick Cheney could retire in comfort . . . well, again, so what? Cheney was gone. And Bush. And the hundreds of millions of Americans they said they were defending. Melton had to shake his head to clear the buzz of conflicting thoughts crowding each other out. Why the hell didn't they just pack up and leave the whole sorry mess behind?

Of course that begged the question of where they might go.

Hawaii? Alaska? The Pacific Northwest? Frankly, he couldn't see anyone staying in Seattle if they could find a way out. Not with that hungry fucking bubble buzzing away just down the road.

Lohberger finished and let the air force liaison, also known as the ALO, start his portion of the briefing. Bret found his thoughts drifting once the ALO, a major who liked to dip Oreos in his Scotch, had taken over. His private thoughts, a tangle of confused memories and fresh trauma, were interrupted by Jaanson and Euler.

"You all right, sir?" Sergeant Major Jaanson asked.

The briefing was over. Melton blushed at having been caught so badly. He'd seen plenty of others zoning out through the day. Men and women just standing, staring into the middle distance, eyes unfocused and faces slack. The worst ones looked like they'd come out of a session of electroconvulsive therapy. It was a mild form of shock, he supposed, as the rational mind shut down its higher functions to let the hindbrain deal with the violation it felt. In millions of years of evolution humans had never been confronted by a threat like the energy wave. It was going to take some adapting, getting used to. Assuming the goddamned thing didn't end up swallowing the whole world, of course.

"Sorry," he said. "It's been a helluva day. I'm a bit out of it."

"That's fine," said Lieutenant Euler, who looked to have recovered a good deal of his composure. "You'll have time to shower, change, and get some food into you, sir. Then you'll need to get your gear together and find my Bradley. We're on thirty minutes' readiness, but I want my guys ready to rock in ten."

"Outstanding," said Melton, his voice flat with weariness and just a touch of sarcasm. The meeting was breaking up around them as Lohberger's men set to their duties with almost discernible relief that they had something to keep them busy.

"I'll send someone to get you from the reporters' billet, Mr. Melton," said Jaanson. "Don't stray from there, okay?"

"Okay. I won't take long. I was already packed to move anyway."

As they left the tent he could see that a change had come over the camp. The activity he'd noted on arriving had greatly intensified. Hundreds of men, all of them in full combat harness, hurried about in regimented groups, raising thick clouds of dust. The rattle of their equipment and the dull thudding of boots was loud enough to nearly drown out the shouts and curses of their NCOs. Nearly, but not quite. Humvees snarled and rumbled, and a flight of jet fighters turned long, lazy circles high overhead.

Melton hurried back to his tent. He'd spent more than enough time in camp to move with confidence through the organized bedlam and located the six-man canvas shelter without trouble. Inside he found that his colleagues had already departed. There was a note from Patricia Escalon on his cot, but otherwise nothing to show for the small civilian community they'd built up over the weeks. He slumped down on the bed and allowed himself a few moments of rest. He would need to eat, and a quick shower wouldn't be a bad idea. It might be weeks before he could wash again. Instead of moving, however, Melton found himself immobilized by a bone-deep lassitude.

What the fuck is the point of any of it now?

His throat tightened and he felt tears beginning to well. Sitting up quickly, he rubbed the moisture from his eyes and sucked in a deep breath. Now was not the time to be falling to pieces. Chances were, things were gonna get a shitload worse in the next few weeks. Even if the bubble didn't move an inch ever again, you couldn't punch a hole in the world like that and expect life to continue as normal. How long could the military hold together, for instance? They couldn't be resupplied for very long. And who was going to pay for them?

Who was going to pay for him?

His paper was gone. He could ride out with the Cav and dutifully file his copy. For now the Net was still working and his e-mails would zip through the myriad channels of fiber and copper wire all the way back to the *Army Times* server. But there they would sit, unread, forever. He had no idea whether his pay would go into his account as scheduled. Possibly it might, if the process was automated. But how long would that last? And how long would anyone go on accepting U.S. dollars anyway? For that matter, could the world economy even expect to survive the sudden disappearance of its beating heart? He didn't think so. Not when he gave it any real thought.

Sayad al-Mirsaad had been right. This was the end of things.

15

Thirteenth arrondissement, Paris

Monique screamed as the windshield crashed and bulged inward, threatening to shatter. Rather than hitting the brakes, Caitlin sped up, awkwardly pawing inside her stolen leather jacket for one of the pistols she'd taken back at the hospital. The wheel jerked in her free hand and a dramatic shudder ran through the body of the Volvo as they struck something with a loud thud. She heard a cry and sensed rather than saw a dark shape fly through the air. The dense spiderweb of cracks in the windshield made it impossible to know exactly what was going on outside. Caitlin hammered at the safety glass with the butt of the gun, using her peripheral vision and one-handed driving to keep to the road.

"Would you shut the fuck up and help me out here?" she yelled at the screaming Monique, eliciting a couple of ineffectual taps at the glass from the girl in the passenger seat. It popped out just as they struck the tail end of a Mercedes with a massive metallic crash and a sudden jerk back into the middle of the road. Both women could now see dozens of people scattering from the roadway in front of their moving vehicle. They seemed to be fighting among themselves, although several were focused solely on their car. Monique hunched down as more rocks came flying at them, one bouncing off the hood to slam into her shoulder. She cried out in pain and Caitlin reached across, grabbed a handful of her jacket, and violently jerked her down so that she was no longer exposed to the improvised missiles flying directly at them. The American enjoyed no such luxury and had to drive while dodging and weaving.

They had come around a sharp bend into a street fight, or riot. A normal person would have slowed down, fearful of injuring or even killing a pedestrian, even as they were targeted with a fusillade of torn-up cobblestones, bottles, and broken bricks. Caitlin set her mouth in a grim line and, hunching behind the wheel for the minimal protection it offered, deliberately pointed the Volvo into the center of a mass of youths blocking the road ahead of them. She didn't sound the horn or wave them away. She simply drove at them, implacably increasing her speed as they drew closer. A few of the braver or dumber among them hurled a couple more rocks, but they were poorly directed and none managed to hit the body of the car. The group lost its coherence rapidly as the men—they were all young, dark-skinned men—dived for the relative safety of the sidewalk. One, his head swathed in a black and white kaffiyeh, was a fraction too late, and one of the car's headlights caught his foot in midair, spinning him off the arc of his dive and into the side of a grocery van. His scream was snatched away by the speed of their passage.

"What is happening? Who are they?" cried Monique in distress.

"*Arabs,*" shouted Caitlin, over the roar of the wind pouring into the car. Youths from the city's outer suburbs, who were normally never found in the old quarters in such numbers. In a few mad moments the car was through the confrontation and back into clear space, as Caitlin swung through a roundabout and took the exit farthest from the direction in which they'd just come. She tried to organize her impressions in a coherent fashion, organizing a random series of images into something she could understand and maybe even use. It wasn't just a riot. It was a brawl. The crowd, which she would have put at somewhere between seventy and one hundred strong, seemed almost evenly split between young white men and women, and perhaps a slightly larger number of African- and Arabian-looking youths. All of the latter had been males, as far as she could tell. The clash appeared undirected, and was probably a fight between the sort of moronic drunks she and Monique had encountered a little earlier, and a pack of Muslim yahoos, stoned on kef or possibly drunk as well. In her experience, for all of their sanctimonious posturing, many of the thugs from Paris's Muslim districts liked a drink as much as the next hoodie.

Still doesn't explain what they're doing all the way in here, though.

A quick check of the GPS navigator placed them within a few blocks of the Parc de Choisy, a locale Caitlin knew well from a previous mission, a much quicker, cleaner job to shut down an official from the French trade ministry who had been selling perfectly mocked-up end-user certificates to a Lashkar-e-Taiba cell.

"Jeez, those were the days," she sighed to herself.

She swerved onto the avenue Edison and almost immediately threw the car into a hairpin turn around a small, arrow-shaped traffic island to run southeast alongside the park down the rue Charles Moreau. She was going to have to ditch the Volvo very soon. It had taken a horrible beating in the short time she'd been driving it and was certain to attract the attention of the gendarmes before long. In the seat next to her, covered in small diamonds of shattered windshield glass, Monique had curled up in a tight little ball and was shaking violently. The yellow wash of sodium lamps gave her features a gaunt, malarial cast. Caitlin dropped through the gears and pulled over under the budding canopy of an ancient oak tree.

"Come on," she said. "We're ditching the ride."

"*Non,*" replied the French girl in a flat, affectless voice.

"Fine. Die here then. Or in a cell at Noisy-le-Sec."

Monique turned an empty, uncomprehending face to her.

"There's an old fort there. Run by the action division of your DGSE. Spent some time there a few years ago. It sucked. Believe me, you don't want to find out firsthand. So sit there if you want, but I'm outta here."

She grabbed the handbag left behind by the car's owner, tossing in the phone, GPS unit, iPod, and wallet before heading off toward the park. She smiled at finding an unused McDonald's towelette in one of the pockets of the bag—*you should be ashamed of yourself, mademoiselle*—and ripped it open, cleaning the worst of the blood from her face and hands. The park was beautiful at night, just as she remembered it. Soft white spotlights underlit trees budding with the first intimation of the coming spring. She briefly consulted the GPS and took her bearings. The screen seemed overly bright, and she dimmed it a fraction, so as not to degrade her night vision too badly. With time to think, she could finally place herself within a mental map of the city as she understood it: a matrix of bolt-holes, safe houses, escape routes, dead drops, rat runs, friendly and hostile camps, and, naturally, history; a personal and professional history of assignments, targets, milk runs, black-bag jobs, and wetwork. An ocean of wetwork these past few years.

There was an apartment she could access on the rue de la Sablière over in the next arrondissement, but it was a good hour's walk away, possibly more, and Caitlin did not fancy being exposed on foot for so long, especially given her condition. She had already taken to thinking of the tumor as My Condition. She would have to steal another vehicle, if possible. A car door slammed behind her and she heard boot heels hammering on the road surface as Monique chased after her.

"Please, wait for me. I am scared."

"Everyone's scared," said Caitlin as she drew up. "Trick is to push through anyway. Come on."

They crossed an open area of the park, where the city put on moonlight cinema in the summer, always showing French films, and usually only those that had been filmed in the surrounding district. *And they call us insular,* she thought, before experiencing a weird episode of doublethink. *Of course, there is no us anymore.* This part of town was relatively quiet, but sirens still reached them from across the metro area, and from the banlieue, she imagined, the outer suburbs where generations of North African and Middle Eastern migrants had created their own pinched and grim little fiefs in the tenements and public housing projects of Paris. Caitlin was as familiar with them, with the slums and dangerous, gunned-up shariatowns like Clichy-sous-Bois, as she was with the global Paris of Montmartre, the Louvre, and the avenue Montaigne.

"Do you think everything will be all right?" Monique asked in a small, mousy voice.

Caitlin stopped dead in her tracks. They were halfway across the darkened park, two figures who stood out from the handful of wandering, self-obsessed lovers by the tension evident in their every interchange. Stiff limbs, jerky movements, voices pitched too high and sharp-edged like broken glass in the night.

"No, Monique. Everything is not going to be all right."

She faced her captive companion square-on, hands to hips, jaw jutting out as her teeth ground together painfully. Pain like a cold knife behind one eyeball welled up from nowhere.

"Start. Paying. Attention, sweetheart. Someone is trying to roll me up, and you with me. Hundreds of millions of people disappeared today. Important people, too. The guarantors of life as you know it. Even if they all get beamed back down tomorrow morning with nothing to show for it but a sore ass from the alien butt probing they got, the world would still never be the same. Your city is falling apart. The whole fucking world is falling apart. What do you think will happen? You'll all suck down a few celebratory bottles of Lafitte now that the Left Bank is the center of the world again? Everyone will wake up tomorrow and go, hey, isn't this cool, we don't have to worry about big ol' fat-assed America ruining everything with her shitty fucking movies, and fast food, and violence? Is that what you think? Huh?"

Her delivery grew more intense and unbalanced with each question, until by the end of her little speech, Caitlin knew she was ranting but couldn't stop. Monique withered away under the lashing, shrinking into herself and dropping her eyes until she looked like a small child being shouted at by the scariest grown-up she'd ever met. Caitlin regretted her loss of control immediately. It was stupid and unprofessional, not at all the sort of thing she'd normally do, especially out in the field with hostiles on her case. She saw a couple of teenaged boys on push-bikes pointing at them, but there was no aggressive intent to the gesture. They merely seemed to be amused by the crazy woman, and had probably picked up on her American accent.

"Look, I'm sorry," she said in French, running a hand through lank, greasy hair. "It's been a helluva day, and it ain't getting any better."

"I am sorry, too," Monique replied in a small but surprisingly strong voice. "You have lost everything, *non*? You had family?"

Caitlin nodded, a dark-blue wave of sadness breaking over her at the thought of her parents and siblings, now gone.

"What will you do . . . *Caitlin*?"

She was still unsure of that name and pronounced it with extra care.

"You cannot go home and cannot stay here. You are a spy, yes? A killer? I suppose you know how to disappear?"

They resumed walking through the park, heading northwest, back toward the old center of Paris, but still away from the hospital and the fighting they had happened across before.

Caitlin smiled sadly. "I'm better at making people disappear than doing it myself. I have . . . well, let's not go there. You shouldn't even know any of this. It's only that things have changed so much, and . . . well . . . I'm sorta swinging out here on my own now."

They passed a homeless man, making himself a bed on a wooden bench, balling up a copy of *Le Figaro* for a pillow. He smiled at them, a wide toothless grin, and doffed his filthy cloth cap as they passed. Monique stopped and handed him a couple of crumpled banknotes.

"Merci, mademoiselle, merci."

"You know," said Caitlin a minute later as they neared the edge of the Parc de Choisy, "that guy back there doesn't know it, but he has a bunch of skill sets that are about to put him back at the top of the food chain."

"Why?" asked Monique.

"He's a survivor."

"I need to rest and eat," said Caitlin half an hour later, as they left behind the unattractive, modernist high-rise district of the Centre Commercial Italie on the rue Vandrezanne. Seven roads met in a great starburst of an intersection a short distance away. Some of them were major arterials, like Bobillot, which ran back into the huge roundabout at the place d'Italie. Others were smaller, tree-lined streets, on which cafés dealing in simple fare survived on local custom rather than the tourist trade. Monique steered her into one such venue, grabbing a table near the door, which Caitlin immediately rejected in favor of another where she could sit with her back to the wall and watch the entrance and the street.

"Does this place have a toilet out the back?" she asked. "Do we have access through the kitchen?"

"I don't know." Monique shrugged. "I come here sometimes, but I've never had to ask. Why? Do you need to go?"

"No," she said. "But we need another exit. Indulge me and ask them."

Monique rolled her eyes, which Caitlin took as a good sign. She was throwing off her shock, reasserting herself. Still, she did as the American asked. While she chatted with the owner, Caitlin sat and leaned up against the redbrick wall. Faded posters of beach scenes in New Caledonia had been tacked up around the café, and they looked mightily inviting. She felt her head swimming with exhaustion and forced her eyes open, gesturing to the one waiter and asking for a double shot of espresso.

"I'll teach this tumor to mess with me," she muttered to herself.

After the violence at the hospital, and an hour or more on the run, she could have wept with relief at being able to just sit somewhere comfortable and warm, where people weren't hunting her. Nine other patrons were scattered about in ones and twos, and such conversation as she could hear was all about "*la Disparition.*" The Disappearance. She ignored it as best she could. The café smelled of baking bread, fried garlic, and roast lamb. A man at the table next to her supped at a bowl of soup in which floated big white chunks of fish meat and black mussel shells. He tore small pieces of bread from a baguette and dipped them into the stock, washing it down with a glass of wine poured from a bottle with no label. Caitlin's stomach rumbled in protest and saliva leaked into her mouth. Her coffee arrived just as Monique returned.

"There is a convenience out the back. You have to go through the kitchen and they do not normally allow it, but I have told them you have just been diagnosed with a cancer and they relented."

Caitlin favored her with a crooked half smile.

"Nobody wants to disappoint the cancer girl. Good work, Monique. You're learning."

"I am," she nodded, even seeming a little pleased. "The toilet is in a separate block, in a small yard that opens onto an alleyway. The alleyway runs in both directions, linking up with rue Bobillot and Moulin des Prés."

"Damn." The American whistled. "You could do this for a living, sweetheart."

She spooned a single sugar into the coffee and threw it down in one go.

"I ordered some toasted sandwiches, *croque monsieur,*" said Monique. "I thought you would want something simple."

"And fast," she added, dropping her voice. "We have to get to the apartment as soon as we can. See if I can contact anyone from my shop."

Two straw baskets arrived, brimming with thick, toasted white bread wrapped around ham, Gruyère cheese, and French mustard. Two glasses and a bottle of house wine landed next to them, a nameless *vin blanc*. Monique poured herself a glass and drained it in two swallows before filling Caitlin's and refilling her own. Dark half moons stood out under her eyes, which were puffy and red from crying. Her hand shook as she poured, but not so much that she spilled any. Caitlin took a careful sip of her own but was more interested in the food. The bread had been dipped in egg and pan-fried in butter, with more melted cheese drizzled on the outside. Her eyes watered with the intensity of flavors as she bit into the moist, heavy slab. Right then it seemed like the finest meal she had ever tasted. She wanted to close her eyes and savor each bite, but her training demanded that she continually scan their surroundings and the entrance to the café for any threats. Apart from the heart attack she was holding in her greasy hands, however, there was nothing.

They ate in silence for five minutes, chewing through their meals and sipping at the wine. Unspoken, but lying between them like a dead curse, was the fate of Monique's friends. She had not mentioned them again, but Caitlin could tell they were on her mind. She didn't raise the issue herself, not wanting to unsettle the precarious emotional balance that Monique seemed to have achieved. There would be time for that later. Perhaps.

She ordered another coffee and paid for the entire bill when it came, but didn't finish her wine. Even a few mouthfuls had left her feeling light-headed and dizzy. It would have been luxurious to stay in the café for a few hours, drinking and smoking Gitanes as though all was right with the world, but Caitlin hauled herself to her feet as soon as she'd downed the second espresso.

"Come on," she said. "Let's go."

The American headed out through the kitchen toward the rear of the café. The owner nodded and tutted and tried to look as sympathetic as he could for the pretty cancer girl, although his eyes kept slipping back to the bank note. The kitchen was cramped and narrow, with crammed shelves running all the way up to a high ceiling. A woman in a stained apron gave them a querying look but the owner, her husband most likely, shushed her with one word, "*Cancer.*"

Caitlin shut her eyes for a few seconds before pushing open the screen door and stepping out into the small darkened parking lot. A single pallid globe struggled to illuminate the courtyard in which two scooters and a battered old van were parked. She had shifted the guns into easy reach, but there was nothing in the scene to alarm her.

"Well, my Spidey senses ain't tingling," she told Monique, who gave her a weird look in return. "We're fine," she explained.

Two blocks later, she found a couple of bicycles chained to a cast-iron railing in front of a white, Moorish-looking tenement, and was pondering how to break the chains when Monique admonished her.

"Please, Cathy . . . sorry, *Caitlin*. Bicycles? Look at them. They are not expensive models, no? The people who ride these do so because they cannot afford a car. Do not steal them, please. They will not be insured. You will only be spreading more misery."

Caitlin's irritation at the scolding was transitory. She was feeling quite ill now, and was coming to think she would need Monique to get through the next couple of days if she was unable to make contact with Echelon. It was better that the girl was feeling more confident, even if it meant she'd be less malleable and, frankly, more of a pain in the ass.

"Fine," she conceded. "No bikes. But we are gonna need some wheels soon. If we get caught out in the open on foot we're dead."

The resumed their journey toward the fourteenth arrondissement, walking against the flow of one-way traffic along the Butte aux Cailles, which was alive with throngs of younger Parisians, all of them wealthy and well dressed, hopping from bars to clubs and restaurants as if this were a normal evening with a warm spring in the offing. The buildings here were smaller, with steeply pitched alpine roofs, and tended to be given over to commercial concerns, chichi diners and exclusive clubs, and the two fugitives stood out in their cheap, unwashed clothes. A few bookstores remained open for late-night browsers, and apple trees lined the street, perfuming the air with sticky pink blossoms. The sidewalk in front of the cafés and bistros had been colonized by clusters of small round tables, all covered in immaculate white linen, and playing host to lovers, friends, gourmands, and modern boulevardiers. Monique's cluster of angry political badges and sewn-on patches drew a score of withering glances and even open sneers. Caitlin tried to arrange her face in as neutral a fashion as possible, but something about her must have tripped warning beacons for most of those they passed by. In contrast with Monique, nobody looked her in the eye or dared make any snide, slanting comment about her bloodstained pants and leather jacket.

Two police cars and an ambulance went rushing by at one point, forcing Caitlin to softly squeeze Monique's arm and remind her to "be cool." She felt terribly exposed on the expensive strip, and wondered whether it might be wiser to dive into a side street, but the GPS indicated that the route they were walking would get them quickly to the apartment opposite the Montparnasse cemetery. The longer she was out on the street, the more imperative her need for shelter. She hadn't said anything yet, but her headache was getting worse, and now she was beginning to suffer from such severe nausea that it was possible she might lose her dinner all over the sidewalk. She had to get to that apartment. There she'd find shelter, weapons, money, clothes, and, just possibly, somebody from Echelon waiting to bring her in. Possibly even Wales. Although, what the fuck "bring her in" meant at the end of a day like this was a mystery. Perhaps a flight to London on one of the agency's black renditions—if the French were still allowing them. Nothing that had gone down in the last few hours gave her any confidence on that score. She was certain the muscle at the hospital had been French secret service. But she had no idea why they'd come in hot.

If they wanted to parlez, why not just ask nicely?

Even though she was an undeclared operative, an assassin no less, working on their turf, there had been no call for that bullshit back at the Salpêtrière. This wasn't the movies. You didn't draw down on somebody and start banging away without serious fucking reason.

"Caitlin?"

Monique's voice was quiet but thick with emotion. They had passed out of the busy, well-lit entertainment district and were back on the quieter streets. Caitlin checked the navigator, estimating that they had about twenty minutes to go before reaching the apartment. She'd have to decide very soon about stealing another car, or sneaking up on the building through the cemetery, investing a couple of hours in surveillance before heading in. Beside her, Monique's eyes had welled up again, and her shoulders were hitching beneath the thick jacket she wore.

"You thinking about your friends?"

"They were your friends, too, Caitlin. Or at least I thought . . ."

They were my mission, she thought. But aloud she said, "I liked them all right. Celia could be a self-righteous bore. And Maggie was kind of embarrassing, but . . ."

She shrugged off the rest of whatever she had been planning to say, not wanting to upset Monique further, but also not wanting to construct a series of defensive lies around her previous actions. Thunder, distant and muffled, rolled over the city, although there didn't appear to be a cloud anywhere in the sky. The city lights blotted out most of the stars, but only a few wispy strands of gray drifted across the face of the moon. Monique didn't appear to notice, and Caitlin said nothing. The French girl was upset enough without being told that something big had just exploded a few miles away.

"I feel so guilty . . . about the hospital. About Maggie and Celia and . . ."

"It's natural," said Caitlin. "It happens. You can't understand why they got zapped and you didn't. You keep telling yourself you should have done something, anything, to change it. You obsessively pick away at the memory like a wound, wondering if one small thing here or there might have changed it all, and kept them alive."

"Yes," she admitted in a small voice.

They stopped at the steps of a narrow-fronted building. Flickering blue-green light behind a set of drawn curtains in the ground-floor apartment indicated the presence of a television. Probably tuned into a news service. Sirens, police and fire service, swooped by a few streets away.

"Well, don't," said Caitlin. "You're gonna have to let it go at some point, Monique. May as well be now. Your friends got taken out by a couple of guys you would have called fascists just yesterday. I took them down in return. For what it's worth, that's about as much balance as the world ever achieves."

Monique's eyes looked hurt and almost resentful, but Caitlin continued anyway.

"This isn't over. I don't know why I've been targeted like this, whether it has anything to do with what happened back home today. But it isn't over. They'll keep coming until they get what they want, or we get away. You need to toughen up, Monique. And you need to understand that I will not let them take me or you without paying a heavy fucking price. Some people have been killed. Some more will go that way before I'm done. And that's just in our little world, which nobody knows about, 'cept us and the guys who are hunting us. The rest of the world? It'll be a shitload worse."

They'd started walking again, slowly, passing under the branches of an ancient oak tree that covered a street corner in front of a small, darkened art gallery.

"What do you mean, worse?" asked Monique. "How can that be so?"

Caitlin laughed, although it was more of a bitter little cough, really.

"Well, those guys at the hospital, and me, for that matter. We have our ways. You'd think them wrong, barbaric even. But if you understand the game and its rules, you can at least act with some sense of things playing themselves out right, one way or another."

Which is why that splatterfest at the hospital was so fucking out there. *It simply shouldn't have gone down like that.*

Caitlin stopped again, this time fixing Monique with a hard stare.

"But the Disappearance, you cannot underestimate how much that is going to fuck things up. I have to get out of Paris, out of France altogether. But so do you, if you want to survive. You ever read the English philosopher Hobbes? You're French, right? You read philosophy with your croissant in the morning, *non*? Man exists in a state of nature? A war of all against all? That's what modern society cured, at least so it didn't interfere with the lives of people like you. People like me, on the other hand, we were still out there, getting bloody with it. But Monique, listen to me. We're all outside now and a hard fuckin' rain is gonna fall. You need to find shelter."

"How bad do you think it will be?" she asked.

"I'm a pessimist," said Caitlin as they crossed a road where the traffic lights seemed to have failed. "I think it'll be totally fucking medieval. Pogroms. Food riots. Blood in the fucking streets. Maybe that's just me. Whatever. But your friends? They're not gonna miss much in the next little while."

"The living will envy the dead, you mean?"

"That's a bit too Metallica for me, but yeah, if you like. Economies are going to collapse all over the world. Not just slow down, or go a little wobbly. They will collapse like the Twin Towers into smoking fuckin' rubble and anyone standing around underneath is gonna get smashed flat. Modern society is too complex to survive a shock like this. A simpler world, yeah, no worries. People would grow food in their back gardens. Cart water from the well. Live harder and closer to the bone for a few years. But you got what, fifteen million people in the greater metro area of Paris? How are they going to move around, how are they going to feed themselves and their families in two weeks when the stores are empty because there's no more gas at the pumps?"

Monique tilted her head and gave Caitlin a quizzical look. "But why would . . ."

"Why will the gas run out? Think of where it comes from, Monique. Think about what's going to happen there now that the evil global overlord is no longer around to oppress everyone into behaving themselves. Think about what's going to happen to the evil world financial system now that the planet's greatest debtor nation has winked out of existence and won't be meeting its loan repayments to anyone. Think about what happens when you take the lid off Pandora's box and everything that we forgot about history comes spilling out to bite you in the ass. Do you know how unusual it is, in human history, for children to be able to grow up in a place like this?" She waved her hands around to take in the city. "Never knowing the fear of someone riding over the horizon to steal their family's crops and burn their fucking hut to the ground? All as a prelude to snatching them up as slaves for the rest of their miserable fucking lives? *That's* normality, baby. *That's* life as it has been lived by most human beings through most of our history. *That's* what I've been fighting my entire adult life, variations on *that* theme. *That's* what America protected you from. And now she's gone. And you are all alone in the world. Except for me."

They had reached the edge of the Montparnasse cemetery, a vast pool of darkness in the city of light. Monique's lip was pushed out, giving her the appearance of a petulant child. She obviously didn't want to hear any more, but neither did she argue with Caitlin.

The assassin checked their position, relying on memory now rather than the GPS device. They were on the far side of the graveyard from the safe house. It was time to get to work.

"Listen," she said. "We're going in here, and I'm going to go ahead some and check out the situation at the apartment. See if it's been tumbled. If they got my number they might be rolling up the whole network. Are you going to be okay if I can stash you somewhere for a few hours?"

Monique looked alarmed. "A few hours?"

"It's okay," Caitlin assured her. "I have a layup point in here. Something I set up myself. You'll be safe there. But alone. I need to recon the place, or else we could be walking into something like the hospital all over again. Will you be okay with that? Are you strong enough?"

Monique shivered as she contemplated the fields of the dead stretching away from them into the dark.

"I will try," she promised.

"Cool," said Caitlin, slapping her on the shoulder. "That's all anyone can ever ask. Let's go."

Two vans had mounted the curb outside the apartment, a no-parking zone, and lights burned inside the third-floor apartment. Four or five men moved about inside without any pretense at stealth, turning the place over. Three hundred yards away, stretched out on a cracked, weed-covered grave site overhung by an ancient elm, Caitlin was able to observe them unmolested. She had no scope or binoculars, but that hardly mattered. Their very presence was enough to alert her.

The apartment was an Echelon safe harbor, a first sanctum known only to her and her controller, Wales Larrison. He should have been waiting for her there. Indeed, he might well have been. He could be tied to a chair somewhere inside right now, taking the first of many beatings that lay in his immediate future. Caitlin had no way of telling unless she was willing to stake out the scene for much longer than was prudent. She closed her eyes and slowed her breathing as a new wave of dizziness and nausea rolled over her. She couldn't leave Monique on her own at the layup point farther back in the cemetery for too much longer, and she couldn't interdict the search of the safe house in her current condition with no backup, minimal equipment, and no idea what sort of opposing force she'd encounter.

"I'm sorry, Wales," she mouthed silently, before slowly crawling backward into the darkness of the cemetery.

She didn't know whether her illness was affecting her judgment as badly as she knew it had affected her physical abilities, but Caitlin was annoyed and not a little perturbed to find herself feeling scared and lost. The shooters at the hospital were state-sponsored muscle—of that she was sure. And the team at the apartment looked like pros, too. From what little she could glimpse, they were taking the place apart in a precise, methodical fashion. Thinking it through again, if she had to bet on it, she'd lay down good money that they were French secret service, probably the action division of the DGSE, the designated point men for securing the Republic against the intrigues and depredations of Echelon.

What the hell they were up to, what greater scheme they served, she had no idea. It was obviously related to the day's events—such frontal assaults on a "sister" service were almost unprecedented—but she could not be sure how.

What she did know was that her control cell was compromised and she would need to get herself to safety. To a U.S. or British military facility somewhere on the continent. Across the Channel, to friendly ground. Or, as a very last resort, to one of the diplomatic missions of Echelon's member nations, the old, English-speaking democracies.

As soon as the last idea occurred to her, she dismissed it. If the French were aggressively rolling up Echelon cells, they'd be staking out the embassies and consulates.

No. She was on her own.

ONE WEEK

March 21, 2003

16

"I don't want you going out there again, Kip. You look *sick*."

Barb looked worse than him, he thought, but it wouldn't be worth his life to point that out, of course. Her eyes stared at him from within dark hollows. She'd had little more than an hour or two of sleep a night for the last week. The old bathrobe clutched nervously just below her throat was dirty, and her dark hair was lank and greasy. Nobody had been allowed to run water for three days now, because of the contamination. They were living on what they had stored in pots and bottles and the old claw-foot tub upstairs in the half-renovated bathroom. Kipper needed to get in to work to see if he could change that today.

"Barb, I'm not sick. I'm fine. They've been checking us every day. Army doctors. Guys who specialize in chemical war and stuff. We're fine. We got those biosuits, but we don't even need them anymore."

Unfortunately, she would not be dissuaded.

"Kip, you have a family to look after . . ."

"And I am looking after them," he countered, with some irritation. "I am the guy who can turn on your taps again. I am the guy who makes sure the power is there when you flick the switch. Me. Nobody else. It's my job, Barb. I have to go."

He wondered why she was so much worse this morning. The pollutant storms were clearing out. The toxic soup he'd had to brave last Tuesday to get into the city had been truly scary. The army had sent some sort of pressure-sealed armored vehicle for him, something they were going to fight Saddam or the old Russians with, and all of the troops were suited up in NBC gear.

"This is insane, James."

Uh-oh. He knew he was in trouble when she called him that.

"We should be thinking about getting out of here," Barb continued. "Not hanging around. Deb and Steve flew out for New Zealand, yesterday. They're not coming back. They're too smart. But your martyr complex is going to see us die here. Isn't it?"

He controlled the anger that threatened to flare up between them, reminding himself that Barb had nothing to do but sit in the house, like the rest of the city, staring out the windows at toxic rain. She must be going batshit by now.

And, he remembered at that very moment, she was also premenstrual.

"Okay," he said as calmly as he could without shading over into anything that might be mistaken for a patronizing tone. "Deb was born in New Zealand, so they could do that. They got out on a government charter. There aren't any other flights leaving because no airlines will fly in here anymore. So leaving isn't an option. Yet."

"But it's got to be, Kip. We can't feed ourselves. We'll starve soon."

"We won't," he said. "I've got all those freeze-dried camping rations down in the basement. Remember? The ones you gave me all that grief over when I bought them cheap. We've got at least two months' worth."

She shook her head and her eyes hardened.

"That's not what I'm talking about and you know it. The city is starving. They're going to have to evacuate people before long. You know that, James. You must have been talking about it at council."

He tried to speak but she rode in over him.

"And when it happens, *we're* going, mister. All of us. To New Zealand or Tasmania or fucking Bora-Bora. Anywhere but here."

Suzie, who appeared at the kitchen door to complain that *Bear in the Big Blue House* wasn't on, saved him any further escalation. None of her shows were on. *Jo-Jo's Circus, Little Einsteins, The Wiggles,* they had all disappeared offscreen days ago. And every day she grew more upset with their absence. The only TV and radio now available carried Emergency Broadcast System updates. Warnings about dangerous acid levels in the rain.

Information about food and gas rationing. Handy hints for postapocalypse homeowners about fortifying their neighborhoods and establishing Citizens Watch Committees. And pleas for information on "saboteurs and subversives" from the so-called Resistance. None of which impressed the hell out of a little girl who was bored and terrified in about equal measure.

"I want my shows back, Daddy," she said. "Can't you make the army men put them on?"

"Can't you watch a video, sweetheart? One of the movies I brought back?"

"I've watched them all a million times," she complained, in a rising whine. "It's not fair."

He looked to Barb for help but she wasn't giving him an inch. She simply folded her arms and raised one eyebrow. Very much aware that she'd be dealing with this all day, he didn't dare find fault with that response.

"Tell you what, princess," he said as he dropped to her level on one knee. "I've got to get to work but I promise I will bring home some new videos, ones you haven't seen yet. Okay?"

"Can you get *Piglet's Big Movie*?" she asked, suddenly brightening.

"Sure," he said, without thinking. "*Piglet's Big Movie*. No problemo."

He felt rather than saw Barb tense up beside him.

"You run along and get dressed for Mommy now. And no playing outside yet. Maybe tomorrow."

"But D-a-a-a-a-d-d-y . . ."

"*Maybe* tomorrow. No promises."

As she scampered away he rose to his feet again with a feeling of trepidation.

"You already made a promise you can't keep."

"Sorry?"

"The Piglet movie. It's not on DVD. It was supposed to be on at the Cineplex this week. She's been looking forward to it all year. But you wouldn't know that, would you?"

His wife turned around and stalked off down the hall.

Oh, for Chrissakes.

Kip stood in the kitchen, clenching and unclenching his fists, trying to breathe slowly. Blood was rushing through his head, and he desperately wanted to say something stupid, but long, hard-won experience kept him quiet. He knew he should follow

Barb and work things out, but he also knew that doing so would involve him in at least an hour's worth of apologies he didn't feel like making and maddening, circular discussions of his manifest failings on the home front. He was already late, and couldn't afford to miss the convoy out to the dam on Chester Morse Lake. Plus, he had to check on the food-aid distribution centers that were kicking off their operations this morning. One of them had been raided by some anarchist fools late last night. Kip hadn't gotten back to sleep after the cops had called him about it. There'd doubtless be interminable meetings about that today.

So he simply did not have time to get caught up in domestic trench warfare. It wasn't just a job anymore. People's lives rested on his decisions.

He knew he'd regret it before the day was done, but Kipper grabbed his car keys and travel pass and walked out through the kitchen door. The headache that had been building eased off a little as soon as he stepped outside and sucked in some fresh air. Well, not fresh, exactly. He could still taste the sharp, chemical tang in his mouth, in spite of the prevailing winds carrying most of the pollutants from the south away over the last twenty-four hours. A gigantic low over the Bering Strait had drawn up enormous volumes of ash and smoke from the conflagration in the Los Angeles basin while a weird, contrary ridge of high pressure to the east had held the lowering toxic clouds over the Pacific Northwest for two days.

Seattle's chief engineer squinted into the morning sun for the first time in days, and tried not to think about what his family had been breathing into their lungs. He'd sealed the house as best he could—better than most would have managed—by rigging up an air lock and filter chamber in the spare room at the back. Barb had initially been none too impressed at the sacrifice of their best cotton sheets and the new Panasonic air-conditioning unit they'd bought last summer, but the appearance of the towering, septic fog bank on the southern horizon quickly brought her around. When power supply allowed, he maintained a rough overpressure by running the reverse cycle heating and keeping the fireplace in the living room stoked at all times. Hopefully it would be enough.

Kipper stepped off the porch and started down the wet concrete pathway to his vehicle, the same F-150 pickup he'd driven in from the airport on the first day. He felt both guilt and relief at leaving Barb and Suzie behind. The house was large and comfortable, like most on Mercer Island, but it had felt like a cell while they'd been confined inside during the worst of the fallout period, as thousands of tons of toxic waste from the burning of LA had hung over the entire city and its surrounds. Barb's immaculately maintained garden had turned brown and died as though soaked in defoliant. Stopping at his front gate to survey the rest of the street, he could see that they weren't alone. Mercer Island was a high-tone enclave, and Deerford Drive, perched on the edge of the lake and snuggled up against Groveland Park, was one of its better addresses. Truth be known, it was all a bit precious for Kipper, but Barb's family was Manhattan royalty—or had been, he reminded himself, grimly—and she was used to moving among "a better class of persons."

"People like us," she would tease, smirking, knowing that the rude inhabitants of the cheap seats at a Wrestlemania show were more Kipper's sort of people than any of their opera-loving, sherry-sipping neighbors.

Thinking about her family made him feel even worse. She had cried all through the night of the Disappearance, after wasting hours calling every number she knew back on the East Coast. Her parents, her brothers and sisters, uncles, aunts, old friends. All gone. Kip almost turned on his heels and went back inside, but momentum carried him forward. He *had* to get to work.

The street was sorry-looking and deserted. Nothing moved in a gray landscape of dying trees, brown lawn, and wilted flower beds. Rain had washed away the worst of the fallout, but blackened, soggy clumps of mud and ash had collected at natural choke points in the gutter, behind the wheels of parked cars, and in small ponds of sludge where the ground dipped and runoff normally collected. Normally lush green and manicured to within an inch of its life, Deerford Drive was now sadly unkempt. Kipper shivered in the bleak chill of the morning. It had been unnaturally dark for most of the past week, with the sun completely blotted out, but prevailing weather patterns had finally pushed away the worst of the airborne waste, and although the day was by no means sunny, it was at least a good deal brighter. That wouldn't necessarily last, however.

Hundreds of cities and towns were ablaze across North

America. The entire continent was pouring out vast noxious plumes as the infernos spread with nobody and nothing to stop them, save for the occasional, and completely futile, automated firefighting system. He'd seen satellite photos of it on the web, and once on a local news show, before FEMA took over the airwaves. If he hadn't known better he'd have bet good money that an angry rash of supersized volcanoes had suddenly erupted all over the U.S. and up into Canada. Vast, slow-moving geysers of smoke, thousands of miles long, trailed away east from city after city. The Atlantic and most of Europe was now blanketed, with the wave front due to pass over the Urals in a day or two. It wouldn't be long before it had circled the Northern Hemisphere and reappeared back over Deerford.

"Mr. Kipper! Mr. Kipper. Hello!"

Jolted by the unexpected cry, Kipper got his mask in place. He knew the voice only too well. Mrs. Heinemann from number forty-three.

"Is it safe now? Is it safe to go out, Mr. Kipper?"

"Well, you'd better hope so, Mrs. Heinemann. Because you'll be in trouble otherwise, won't you?"

The woman was a wire-framed ninety-eight pounds of faded Jewish American Princess. Never married. Never got over it. At fifty-something, perhaps even sixty-odd, give or take some plastic surgery and a high degree of elasticity in her actual birth date, she'd poured all of her considerable energies into her self-appointed role as block capo of the neighborhood. Without a husband or children to harass and make miserable, she busied herself with other people's "problems"—situations that, generally speaking, nobody had recognized as a problem until Mrs. Heinemann became involved.

And yes, she was *Mrs.* Heinemann. Unless you wanted an ear bashing out of your thoughtlessness and lack of consideration for the cruel vicissitudes that had left her single when so many other, undeserving women had chanced upon partners and offspring. Dressed in a bright green and salmon-pink sweat suit, gathered at the ankles and wrists with elastic bands, and sporting a plastic shower cap and handkerchief face mask, she hurried up the slight incline in the street toward him, firing from the lip as she advanced.

"I'm so glad I caught you, Mr. Kipper. I haven't seen anyone out and about all week. This terrible situation, you know. And the curfew. So is it safe now? Can we move about? It's just that I have very little food in the house. And neither does anyone else. Mrs. Deever at thirty-six, with her two little ones. She needs formula, Mr. Kipper. And sweet Jane at twenty-nine, the retarded girl, she needs her medication. The Songnamichans, that very large Hindu family, he's a Microsoft manager, well, they must nearly be eating the wallpaper by now with all those children. What *is* to be done, Mr. Kipper? *What is to be done?*"

She'd arrived right in front of him by then, yapping the whole time, a classic demonstration of fire and movement. He hadn't had a chance to speak or retreat. But her questions gave him the opportunity he needed.

"Mrs. Heinemann," he said forcefully. "You need to get back inside right now. It is not safe out here yet. We haven't had a chance to take any measurements of air or water quality. I'm only out here because it's my job. You need to get back inside where it's safe this very minute. Go on. Right now. Don't delay. And don't drag any mud into the house with you. You'll need to strip off, bag up that outfit, and scrub yourself thoroughly. You still got water stored in the house? Good. Then get going. Right now!"

He made sure his delivery was every bit as rapid and incontestable as her own. He waved her back toward her own house, shaking his head and brooking no backchat. In his peripheral vision he could see curtains twitching aside in a couple of houses, and he made sure that everyone watching could see that he didn't want anybody wandering around until it was safe.

"But Mr. Kipper . . ."

"No! Move along now. Go on, Mrs. Heinemann. You've no business endangering yourself out here. Now git. Go and decontaminate yourself."

He took her upper arm in a deliberate grip and gave her a hurry-on toward home.

"Oh, my. Oh, dear," she murmured as she toddled off at high speed.

Shaking his head, he returned to the pickup and climbed in, carefully knocking any mud from his boots before doing so, mostly for the benefit of his audience. The cabin was cold and still smelled of the McDonald's family meal he'd brought home late on the first day of the Disappearance. He'd also picked up a whole heap of canned fruit and eighty gallons of spring water in big ten-gallon plastic bottles, but that was the extent of any hoarding he felt necessary, because of all those freeze-dried, vacuum-sealed meals he'd bought in bulk near the end of last year from some camping store that had closed down. Man, hadn't Barb changed her tune on that little purchase? He'd got himself a new one torn at the time.

The engine needed turning over a couple of times before the truck grumbled into life, sounding louder than usual in the unnatural stillness of the morning. He checked the fuel gauge as soon as he had power, making sure he hadn't been siphoned. The city council's Emergency Management Committee had banned the sale of gasoline for "nonessential" purposes on the second day, but hadn't had the manpower—or the will, in his opinion—to enforce the measure when thousands of people ignored it and started queuing at gas stations. They bid up the price to near fifty dollars a gallon at one point. That was when the army had rolled out of Fort Lewis to lock down the city and get everyone off the streets as the sky had blackened and the rain turned to acid.

Kipper's truck had three-quarters of a tank, and he could still get more from a council depot without any trouble. But that'd change. No commercial shipping or air traffic had come into Seattle for five days, and he didn't expect any in the foreseeable future. The only supplies they could draw on were aid shipments: food from Australia and New Zealand, one supertanker of petroleum so far from Taiwan, and more food and medical supplies from Japan. It was enough to keep things ticking over, if it kept coming, and if people didn't panic. Two big fucking "if"s.

The island was quiet, and people were sticking to the curfew. Mostly. Kipper searched the radio dial for anything besides the recorded EBS messages, which told him nothing new, and said nothing about the raid on the food bank. He picked up a scratchy, inconsistent transmission from somewhere in Canada, but it was all electronic dance music, which in his book was worse than nothing. Sighing, he punched the button to cut off the radio and pulled away from the curb, wondering what the hell he was going to do about *Piglet's Big Movie.*

His route took him along West Mercer Way. Normally a quiet, tree-lined drive through some of the more exclusive real estate the island had to offer, it felt eerily deserted, with sodden rubbish and leaf litter strewn along its length. He took the Homer Hadley floating bridge across Lake Washington into the city, and again found it hard to get his head around the empty lanes. At this time of the morning traffic should have been crawling over the span, bumper to bumper. There was some vehicular movement, however. Mobile army patrols stopped him three times. Then there were the roadblocks and checkpoints he hit on another four occasions. His pass, countersigned by three city councillors and the ubiquitous General Blackstone, carried him through each obstacle, but he understood why there were so few people about. After the food riot down at Ivar's Salmon House under the I-5 bridge on day three, and a shootout at the 7-Eleven on Denny Way that left four people dead following an argument over who was going to get the last of the frozen pizza subs, the army had put away its smiley face. Three young men, who'd have been thought of as burglars a week earlier, got shot down as "looters" while trying to make off with a carton of frozen hamburgers from the Wendy's on Rainier Avenue that evening. A vagrant, emerging from a Dumpster behind a KFC the following day, was cut in half by automatic-weapon fire from an armored fighting vehicle. Far from attempting to cover up the incidents, the same General Blackstone who'd scrawled the signature on Kipper's "transit documents" appeared on television and the radio to detail exactly what had happened and to assure the citizens of Seattle that it would happen again to anyone who broke curfew and attempted to steal from their fellow citizens by "subverting" the rationing system.

Things went quiet around the city after that.

Talk radio and a couple of current-affairs shows on the local TV networks had raged against the "injustice," but that defiance was short-lived, lasting only as long as it took four Humvees full of troops to roll into their parking lots. Some lawyers who arrived at City Hall to serve papers on the administration for First Amendment violations were still in custody somewhere. There'd been no more open dissent and, incidentally, no more food riots or "looting" either. But the self-proclaimed Resistance appeared shortly afterward in the form of an e-mail spammed throughout the city warning of a fascist takeover and promising to "take back the streets."

Kipper wasn't happy about any of it—how the hell could you be?—but on the other hand he knew how desperate the situation was, and just how easily it could spin totally out of control. He really hoped this Blackstone asshole would see sense and ease off the thumbscrews a little. People were hurting and scared. You couldn't keep the whole city under house arrest indefinitely. And he could only pray that this dumbass Resistance thing turned out to be a bunch of dope-addled bullshit artists. God knows Seattle was full of *them*. A few more stunts like last night's stupidity at the food bank and they could totally fuck things up.

Speaking of which . . .

He hauled the wheel around, crossing over the median strip and pointing the truck toward Fourth Avenue South, where the main food-distribution center for the CBD was located, at a Costco wholesale warehouse near the train yards.

He wanted to see for himself how the food-aid system was working.

The signal strength meter on his cell phone was near full and he called Barney on hands-free as the pickup swung around Rizal Park.

It seemed a small wonder that the call went through, until he remembered that "unauthorized civilians" were barred from using the cell network for anything other than emergencies.

Kipper shook his head and scowled at a measure he thought of as totally unnecessary and counterproductive. It wasn't like the Wave had just appeared and people were going to be melting the phone company servers with millions of calls. It was just more repression for no good reason. Exactly the sort of nonsense that fueled the paranoid dementia of idiots and conspiracy loons.

His temper was building again as he chewed over the many poor decisions that had been made in the previous week, and it was only Barney's answering the call that short-circuited a bout of foulmouthed, solitary cussing. His friend's voice filled the cabin, sounding flat and tinny, as everyone's did on speakerphone.

" 'Sup, buddy."

"Hey, Barn. I'm heading over to Costco right now to check things out. You on your way?"

"About four or five minutes away. I'm just coming over the First Avenue Bridge. Heather should already be there. She overnighted in town to be there early."

"Oh, okay. I didn't know that. Good for her."

Kipper was taken aback for a second. Heather Cosgrove was a young civil-engineering graduate on a six-month internship with his road-maintenance guys, all of whom except for her had been at a conference in Spokane when the Wave hit. If he was giving out a prize for Most Freaked Out, Heather was an unbackable favorite. She was from Minneapolis, and apart from her job, she had nothing left.

"It's spooky, isn't it?" said Barney, completely oblivious. "Without any traffic. Like a doomsday movie or something."

"Yeah," said Kip, getting his head back in the game. "Listen, did you hear about the raid last night?"

Barney snorted down the line.

"Dunno that I'd call it a raid, man. What I heard was, two dreadlocked jerks got stoned and tried to steal a pallet full of Cheetos from the food bank on South Graham."

"Well, d'you hear they got shot?"

The speakerphone hissed quietly for a second, as Kipper swung down the off ramp at South Forest Street.

"No. Sorry. I didn't hear that," said Barney. "Who told you?"

"Cops rang at about two this morning."

"Why'd they call you? Why not one of the councillors?"

"Said they couldn't raise them."

Barney laughed. "That'd be right."

17

An Nasiriyah, Iraq

"Fedayeen!"

The warning cry came from the man at point, a fraction of a second before the hammering of automatic-weapon fire started up. The Cav troopers, veterans now of urban warfare as meat grinder, moved for cover as though every man had been jabbed with a stun gun. The dismounted cavalry scouts were fast and flowed like quicksilver, pouring themselves into doorways, around stone walls, and down behind piles of rubble that made vehicle movement all but impossible through the narrow streets of An Nasiriyah. The M3A2 Bradley cavalry fighting vehicles followed them when and where they could. A couple of squads of infantry, with their M2A2 Bradley infantry fighting vehicles, joined them when they moved into the town.

Melton moved with them, the instincts and experience of his own time in the rangers, and a decade of combat reportage since, rubbing up hard against fatigue and aging muscles. He landed next to Specialist Alcibiades, burrowing in under the protection of a massive, broken beam of concrete and rebar as small-arms fire chewed up the mud-brick walls of the street, zipping less than a foot overhead.

Melton had picked up an M4 for his own protection moments before they entered Iraq. Nobody said word one to him. After the carbine, he picked up some MOLLE web gear and some ammo pouches. He already had a matching dark blue set of Level III body armor and a Kevlar helmet. The army issued him a protective mask and MOPP gear in case someone dropped some germs or chemicals on them, but he had always been one of the skeptics on the WMD front.

In any case, the fighting was simply too chaotic and disordered for him to rely on anyone else to look after him. In the labyrinthine warren of souks, alleys, cut-throughs, and ragged streets of the towns and villages in which they'd been fighting, you never knew when you were going to have some asshole suddenly appear right in front of you with murder in his eyes. He hadn't needed the carbine yet, for which he was grateful. Still, he flicked the selector from safe to semi and waited. Alcibiades let rip with two short bursts, holding his own M4 up over the cover and firing blind. The Bradleys added the hum and mechanical metal-punching beat to the chaotic audio mix, sending twenty-five mike-mike into buildings without a care for possible civilian casualties.

When the specialist came back down, he spit a green stream in the sand, his cheeks bulging from a wad of chew. "Fuckin' ragheads."

The volume of fire going downrange was impressive and deafening, nearly drowning out the shouts of Lieutenant Euler and his noncoms as they organized the counterambush with the infantry troops who had linked up with them.

Melton did his best to collect himself and commit to memory as many details as possible. He would write notes out later, when the immediate danger had passed, and his hands, hopefully, weren't shaking too much. As always the head rush of contact was giddy and horrifying, a glassy funnel of light and color down which you fell as soon as you realized somebody was trying to take your life. Melton found it harder to deal with as a reporter than he had as a soldier, perhaps because he was older and wiser, perhaps because now he had nothing to distract him from the experience. Indeed, having the experience and recording it for others were his sole reasons for being there. He couldn't shut down and get on with whatever task the sergeant or corporals assigned him. He played his part by opening his senses to the madness of battle, letting it burn its terrors directly onto his cortex.

He savored the taste of the dust in his mouth, the gritty, choking, dog-shit-and-tangy-metallic-diesel flavor of it. He noted the struggle of a green, bejeweled bug caught in a wad of gum stuck to the side of Alcibiades's boot. Tried to freeze in his memory the smell of the man next to him, a cloying miasma of body odor, stale farts, and wintergreen Skoal brand chewing tobacco. He studied the contours of the street, the way the ancient biscuit-colored buildings snaked away, slightly uphill. The yellow-green, foul-smelling stream of raw sewage and trash that flowed downslope toward him. The soldiers themselves, some cool and frosty, others sweating but focused, most of them scared out of their minds.

Lieutenant Euler took shelter behind a pockmarked stone pillar that might well have stood on the same spot since the time of Muhammad. He was on the radio with a map in his hand, looking at something Melton couldn't see. The radio operator kept security, his carbine traversing along the rooftops, looking for snipers, RPG gunners, or any other Iraqi in desperate need of a new weeping asshole in the middle of their forehead.

Top Jaanson was doing the standard shoot, move, and communicate drill, moving the soldiers, infantry and cavalry both, around the restricted battle space of the narrow street like a brutal chess master. Some soldiers would balk while others would execute on command. With some, Jaanson calmed them with a pat on the shoulder and a few fatherly words the way one would handle a terrified horse. With others, it was a boot imprint on the ass.

Melton couldn't help but smile, having been there himself.

He saw a bird, swooping up and away to escape the sudden eruption of slaughter, suddenly fly apart in a spray of feather and blood as some stray round punched right through its frail body. The remains dropped into the dust, raising a small puff of dirt, and the body twitched for a few seconds as dumb electrical storms raged through its shattered nervous system.

Alcibiades saw it, too. "Fuck me, man. Not safe for man or beast in this motherfucker. I say call in Air and let them fucking hammer this place back to the Stone Age."

"Hooah," Melton said before he could stop himself. He tapped Al on the shoulder. "Got any dip, Specialist?"

Specialist Alcibiades pulled a can from his hip pocket. "Got a whole log before we left. I'm about half through it so you'd better make me look good. Hooah?"

Melton took the can of Skoal and nodded. "Hooah, Specialist. Fucking hooah."

The dip in his mouth and the can returned to Alcibiades, he tried to lock himself down on reality. But no matter how hard he tried to anchor himself in the real world, time always seemed to warp and stretch, before snapping back on these moments, almost as though it, too, had become an actor in the conflict, constantly turning and folding in on itself to better examine the deeds of the frail, ridiculous little creatures who raged through its currents. It might have been four minutes or many hours before the Apaches arrived overhead and announced themselves with a whoosh of rockets and the industrial thumpety-thump-thump-thump of their thirty-mike-mike chain guns. Half the street ahead of them disintegrated, quite literally, flying apart under the kinetic hammer of high-velocity explosive ordnance. Blocks of sandstone and dried mud shattered and crumbled, releasing their mass in the form of thick powdery clouds to drift away on the warm sirocco passing over the village.

"Apaches will do," croaked Alcibiades. "I feel like dancing every time they play my tune. Sing it, fuckers!"

Melton stayed down, rub-fucking the ground, as the fire from the soldiers of the Rock of the Marne tapered off. For a brief interlude, silence as heavy as an old coat lay over them. He heard the crunch of boots moving across broken masonry through the ringing in his ears. The rattle of equipment as men darted forward. The metallic click and slide of a mag being swapped out. Slowly, carefully, he raised his head over the cover. Their concrete beam had been badly chewed over by gunfire. Pockmarks and dark scores pitted and scarred the surface. One rusted spike of rebar glistened in the sun, a silver fang sliced out of its dull, reddish length by the impact of a single bullet. Melton let his peripheral vision take over for a second, scanning for any movement that would indicate the presence of a lingering threat. A window pushed open to accommodate the barrel of a sniper's rifle. A door creaking backward into a darkened hut, from whence some maniac in a dynamite vest might emerge shouting "Saddam is great!" before detonating himself. But there was nothing. The Apaches had cleaned up the ambush, and probably a fair number of unlucky innocents as well.

Alcibiades arose beside him like an apparition, the muzzle of his rifle sweeping through a narrow arc in front of them, covering the men who were scoping out the rubble under which their attackers had died. Melton waited for the call of "Medic!"

It never came. Whatever injuries the troopers had taken did not require immediate intervention. He kept his personal weapon to hand but consciously dialed back on the tension compressing his whole body into an impacted mass of nerve endings. They'd survived another one. The brigade and most of the Third Infantry Division had been remarkably lucky so far. Less than twenty KIA after days of fighting, and all of them lost in close-quarters battles like this one. Out on the desert plains, where they'd first engaged the Iraqis, it had been a pure slaughter. Nobody had any idea of the enemy's casualties, but in this sector alone it ran into the thousands. Perhaps more than ten thousand by now.

Lieutenant Euler appeared beside him, handing back a receiver to his radio operator.

"D'you get all that, sir?" he asked. "Gotta keep the folks at home informed."

It was an attempt at light banter, but the young officer's eyes were too tired and far away to carry it off. *Sleep when you are dead* became the unofficial motto of the soldiers. Bret Melton nodded absently and spit into the ground, the nicotine slowly infiltrating his wired nervous system.

"Any casualties, Lieutenant?" he asked.

Euler shook his head.

"Nothing serious. No sucking chest wounds or lost limbs so I'll count myself a happy man. Worthless fedayeen fucktards. Sometimes I think they shoot high and wide, praying to get fucking captured."

Saddam's volunteer militia had borne the brunt of the fighting in the crossroads towns, and although they'd handed out some grief here and there, as a fighting force they seemed to be tasked with holding up the coalition and making them "waste" ammunition and lives. The coalition didn't have the troops to provide EPW facilities, so without an order per se, the higher-ups let it be known that there would be no quarter. Some units in Third ID had taken up the old practice of flying a black flag from an antenna. It didn't take long for the Iraqis to figure out what that meant.

As a tactic, Melton had to admit that sending your worthless troops forward as bullet catchers made some sense. Everyone knew they weren't pushing on to Baghdad now, that'd be insane. The British and U.S. forces executing Operation Katie in southern Iraq were planning to leave the whole leprous mess to fester on its own when they were gone. That was assuming they could kick the Kuwaitis and the Saudis off so they could actually get the hell out of Dodge. The tiny Polish and Australian special-forces contingents were already gone, what missions they'd originally been assigned now irrelevant. And Saddam was openly mocking them from Baghdad, whipping up a perfect storm of pan-Arab hysteria at his "defeat" of the infidel crusaders.

Well, not openly. Not since we dropped that JDAM on Uday.

Saddam still made appearances in the open, but they were never televised live, and they never lasted very long. They did hit the mark, though. The allied air campaign went forward pretty much as originally planned, from what Melton heard the air force liaison say, attempting to decapitate his command-and-control systems. The only difference was that coalition air power destroyed bridges they originally needed. But as long as the fat little fucker survived to taunt them, his stature only grew. He was openly comparing himself to Saladin now, declaring himself the reborn leader of the faithful.

The crackle of gunfire drifted in over the rooftops of the surviving buildings from somewhere to the west, another element of Third ID conducting sweep-and-clear ops to make sure that everyone, ladie dadie everyone, could withdraw through this shithole without getting nickel-and-dimed to death by snipers and suicide bombers and the half-assed incompetents tricked out like Arab ninjas who called themselves the Fedayeen Saddam.

Euler's men were moving toward one of the remaining intact bridges, in tandem with another platoon taking a parallel route two streets over. Apaches from the squadron's air cav component buzzed about high overhead, waiting to pounce on any resistance. When Operation Katie went into effect, the rule book was thrown out along with it. Melton remembered Captain Lohberger saying, *Fuck the rules of engagement,* before he buttoned up his Bradley so many days ago. Somebody seemed to have handed Third ID's commander, Major General Blount, an open checkbook.

No one took any chances. If a building needed to be swept, soldiers tossed frags through the door, then the M249 SAW gunner sprayed the room before they went in. If the Iraqis decided a mosque prayer tower made a pretty good forward observation post, an MPAT round from one of 5/7's M1 Abrams tanks chopped it down. If they used a school or a hospital for a fort, the division's artillery hammered it with one-five-five or MLRS rounds.

No one took any chances anymore.

"Who you writin' for now, anyway, Bret?" Alcibiades was beside him, his eyes hidden behind the silver of a pair of Ray-Bans. They gave him an insectile appearance as he scanned the blasted remains of the thoroughfare ahead, the muzzle of his rifle tracking the movements of his head with mechanical precision. "*Army Times* is gone, right? Like everything else."

Unlike the officers, most of the grunts just called him by his first name. He didn't have to work hard to fit in with them.

"Headquarters is, but we've got field offices in Europe and Korea," said Melton, not that he had had any luck getting in touch with any of them. "And worse comes to worst, there is always *Stars and Stripes,* I suppose. I had some contacts from my freelance days, foreign websites and magazines, you know, British mostly. I'm filing for them now. The war's not nearly as big a story as it would have been. But it's up there."

They formed up again with Alcibiades's scout team, picking their way through the rubble, stepping over tumbledown walls and mounds of pulverized mud brick. Melton stood on something soft and yielding, and before he could stop himself he glanced down and saw the tiny arm beneath his soiled boots. It ended in ragged flesh and a stump of white bone, just after the elbow joint.

He spit on the ground next to the remains and whispered, "Yeah. Fuck the rules of engagement. Hooah."

Lieutenant Euler's Bradley, Fiddler's Green, was burning a few hundred yards short of the bridge over the Euphrates. One of the crew had made it out, only to be shot down from a window in one of the low-rise, ferroconcrete bunkers that passed for apartments in this part of Nasiriyah. His crewmates had not escaped.

"They've got a fucking howitzer in one of those buildings with the muzzle aimed into the street. Or maybe a T72. I can't tell, damn it," said Euler, who was blessed not to be in the Bradley at the time. The binoculars came down from his eyes as he turned away from the corner to address his squad leaders.

"Fuck me runnin'. Either it is Republican Guard or someone who has got their shit wired tight," Euler said.

Melton chanced a quick peek around the corner, darting his head out and back like a nervous chipmunk. He took a sight picture of the disabled Brad. The rear troop hatch was gone and the turret was missing. Rounds cooked off in the main body, one at a time, with the sound of an M80 firecracker under a steel bucket. It made a hollow thump with each cook-off. Thick, oily smoke poured from the commander's hatch, and flames burned at the rear of the chassis.

Euler spoke quickly and privately with his platoon sergeant, while Melton fell back to give the two some space. After a few words, Euler held his hand out to his radio operator for the handset of their SINCGARS radio.

"Airstrike," said Alcibiades as he spat into the ground. "Betcha this week's pay the LT will call in some A10s. Probably gonna flatten a coupla blocks."

"We ain't getting paid this month," said Bakic, one of his buddies.

"Still gonna be an . . ."

"What the fuck!"

Euler hadn't shouted, but the force of his exclamation had drawn all the attention back on him. He was talking on the radio, and everyone listened to his side of the exchange, which didn't tell them much.

"What d'you fucking mean . . ." Euler paused while the voice on the other end shouted loud enough for Melton to hear a time-honored army phrase.

Remember your military bearing, soldier.

"Okay, if the ALO can't get me air, then what about . . . ?" Euler pulled off his K-pot and threw it at the wall across from him.

"You gotta be fucking kidding me . . ." Euler continued, obviously not impressed by the previous admonishment about military bearing. "How about some goddamned fucking fire support then?"

The handset shouted back, leaving Euler to shake his head some more. He signed off and threw the handset back at his radio operator. His noncoms pulled in closer, concern acid-etched into all of their faces. A few shook their heads as he relayed to them the details of whatever shit sandwich they'd just been handed.

"Goddamn," muttered one of the sergeants, loud enough for Melton to hear. The enlisted men around him strained to pick up a few clues without being too obvious about it. They were spread out along a side street running between two shops, both of which had been cleared not fifteen minutes earlier. Euler had men inside both, and crawling around on the rooftops, denying the high ground to any hostiles. Anxiety crept stealthily down the line of soldiers, as men who'd been sitting in the dirt, catching a few minutes' respite, picked up on the changed atmospherics in the leadership group and slowly began to attend to them. Eyes that had been closed cracked open, heads turned almost imperceptibly, bodies shifted just a little bit, leaning in toward the lieutenant, hoping to catch some scrap of information that might provide a clue as to what mess they'd stepped in now.

At last the NCOs dispersed down the line, carrying the news with them. Corporal Shetty, a short, dense African-American version of the Thing from *The Fantastic Four*, rumbled over, his face a study in disgust.

"Choppers had to bug out," he informed them, and suddenly Melton realized for the first time that the constant droning thud of the Apaches and Blackhawks that had shepherded them through the dusty maze of An Nasiriyah was missing. He saw men craning their heads upward all along the shadowed alleyway as they heard the news.

Alcibiades asked the obvious question. "Why?"

Shetty glared at him, as if the absence were his fault.

"Fucking Iranians," he said, as if those two words were enough. When they were found to be patently not enough, however, he continued.

"Iran declared war on America an hour ago. Their air force is up and trying to punch through, to get to us. It is a full-on furball out in the Gulf. Hundreds of speedboats and Jet Skis. All of 'em suicide runners. They been swarmin' the navy. Air force and some British units are mixing it up with the Iranian planes right now, trying to keep 'em off us, here."

"Holy shit," said Alcibiades, his swarthy features paling noticeably.

"Yeah, anyway. Choppers are outta here for the moment. If we want air cover, we gotta call in A10s, and they're only coming when they can get their own cover. It's fucked up."

"Shit, what about arty then?" Some private; he was a replacement pulled out of the division's 123rd Signal Battalion and it showed every time he nearly shot himself in the foot with his M16. Melton stayed far away from him, because it was going to end in tears for that commo puke. He knew it in his bones.

"They're busy hammering a column of Republican Guard who are trying to get to us here," Shetty said. "So no artillery, no air, nothing but buffalo soldiers and the grunts."

Melton yawned so hard he nearly swallowed his stale wad of chew. He was exhausted but it was a nervous gesture, too, one of his personal "tells" that he was under pressure. He fingered the crap out of his mouth, took a sip from his CamelBak, and tapped Corporal Shetty on the shoulder.

"Corporal, is it just Iran? Do we know if anyone else is moving? Syria? Israel maybe?"

The noncom's head swiveled like a gun turret. Back and forth, once.

"Dunno, Mr. Melton. You'd be better placed to find out than any of us, if your satellite phone is working."

"Battery's dead. Went down yesterday and I haven't been able to recharge," Melton said. "Sat coverage has gotten awfully spotty of late anyway."

Shetty took that piece of news like a dustbowl farmer absorbing yet another month without rain. Such was life.

"Lieutenant's talking with Lohberger, getting instructions," he said. "If we can't hammer down the bad guys with air support, it makes this whole deal a lot fucking harder."

"But the brass still wants this bridge," Melton said without any real enthusiasm.

"Yup," said Shetty. "They still want it. Why they want it, I've no fucking clue but they still want it."

"Man, this is totally fucked," said Bakic. "What the fuck are we even doing here? It sure as shit ain't paying the rent anymore."

"What we're doing here, bitch," growled Shetty, "is trying to get the fuck outta the Hood without losing too many worthless motherfuckers like you along the way. That good enough reason for you? Or would you like to just lay down your fucking arms and walk out there and tell the towelheads, 'Yo, dogs. My bad. I'm gonna ease on up outta here and head back to my new crib up in Alaska, yo.' Is that what you want to do, Private?"

The chastened soldier mumbled something like "Sorry Corporal, no Corporal," and devoted himself to the intense study of the dirt at his feet. Up and down the line, similar scenes played themselves out as the men dealt with the shock of losing their air cover and gaining a new enemy. Melton checked his watch. It was late afternoon, shading toward sunset in maybe an hour or so. He wondered if Third ID would wait until dark, when the Americans' night-vision equipment would return to them a significant advantage. On the other hand, the power of a unit like 5/7 Cav lay in its mobility. It was a "terrible swift sword" in movement, cutting through anything that got in its way. Sitting here like this merely invited the Iraqis to gather their forces around them, especially when they couldn't be targeted for destruction from the air.

Euler was back on the radio within a few minutes, his head bent and shoulders hunched tightly forward as though he was attempting to contain some new piece of shit news from getting free. Figuring on being stationary for a while, Melton opened a chili mac MRE and stuck the shit-brown spoon down into the contents. He chewed on the meaty mac combo joylessly and washed it down with a drink of warm water. The other men all used the break as best suited them. Some ate, some dozed, one pissed his name up against an ancient wall. Everyone sipped some water or mixed some flavored drink mix from their MREs in a water bottle. Most of their PX-bought pougie bait had run out days ago, along with most of Alcibiades's chew.

At least the shade of the alleyway was a blessed relief from the oppressive heat of day. Even with the sun dropping toward the edge of the world, fighting in this temperature was a crippling business. Keeping the troops' fluids up was proving as difficult as clearing a block of fedayeen. Melton craned his neck back, stretching it far enough to work out a few kinks with a distinct, cracking sound. The sky was lightly clouded, and the glare had faded somewhat from its painful intensity in the middle of the day. He searched in vain for any sign of the so-called Disappearance Effect, the "nuclear winter" that had fallen on western Europe with the arrival of billions of tons of particulate matter, released into the atmosphere by the burning cities of North America. There was nothing to see. Maybe it was all bullshit. He couldn't tell. He was as cut off from the wider world as everyone else in the unit.

It was in that position, leaned back against the wall of the gutted building, squinting slightly into the hot gray sky, that he saw the dark blur of the mortar round as it dropped toward them. The cry of "*Incoming!*" arose in his head but never reached his mouth as another round smacked into the rooftop corner at the far end of the alleyway, detonating with a bone-cracking roar and a deadly spray of shrapnel. Men screamed out warnings and dived for what little cover existed in the narrow passageway. A few made it through a single door halfway down. A couple of others scrambled through a hole in the wall blown out by a grenade hours earlier.

Oh, fuck, Melton thought. He got down and tried to fuck the ground, to become one with it while he looked for a better patch of cover than nothing at all. An open shop front across the street looked promising.

He was on his feet, then, unaware of how he'd made it up off his ass so quickly. More rounds were dropping on their position with enough accuracy to suggest that they'd been presighted by the Iraqis, who were waiting for just such an opportunity. Many of them impacted the roofline but one speared right down into the constricted space, exploding with a terrible force that lifted Melton off the ground, turning him over and over.

He twisted slowly, impossibly through the air. His mind, detached from the dead, stringless puppet of his body, pulled free with a discernible tug. He watched himself falling back to earth with bricks and clods of dirt, with the disembodied arms and legs of his friends, with clattering pieces of steel and burning splinters of wood. Bret Melton, formerly of the U.S. Army Rangers, twirled oh so slowly through clear air, up so high he imagined he could see the entire town of An Nasiriyah below him. The savage close-quarters battles that still raged around choke points and contested streets. The ruined block where they had been ambushed in another life. Hundreds of Iraqi soldiers and militia fighters running toward his position. And beyond that. He could see the deserts stretching away toward the mountains in the far north. He could see the ships of the U.S. fleet as they raked at skies full of Iranian fighters. And perhaps, at the dimmest edge of vision and consciousness, he could see an empty realm, the burning land that he had once known as home. The lost continent of America.

Melton saw all of these things. Or thought he did, before he fell back to earth and into darkness.

18

Safe house, seventeenth arrondissement, Paris

She was sick. Increasingly nauseated, and occasionally close to vomiting. Caitlin had no idea whether it was a side effect of the headache, which had been constant for three days now, or an entirely new symptom of whatever was eating her brain from the inside out. Of course, it could also be a result of breathing in the soupy miasma of toxins and burned chemicals that had rolled over the city three days ago and stayed. The charred, atomized memory of America. Some *Guardian* writer with a very dark sense of humor and a taste for Delillo had named it the "airborne toxic event," and the name had stuck.

French government warnings played on a loop across every radio station, advising listeners to stay indoors whenever possible. Caitlin couldn't believe anyone would need telling twice. Millions of dead seabirds had washed up on the coast of western France just before the tsunami of pollutants had arrived, and thousands of pigeons—flying rats, as she thought of them—had been dropping from the sick, leaden skies over Paris ever since. She could see dozens of little gray carcasses from the apartment window. City council workers had already cleaned the streets below of twitching, broken birds, but that was on Tuesday, and they hadn't been back.

The few times Caitlin had ventured outside to stock up on fresh food she'd returned with her eyes stinging and her airways burned. It reminded her of the time she'd done a job in Lin-fen, a city in China's Shanxi Province where you could feel the acids and poisons leaching through your skin every minute you were exposed.

She splashed a handful of cold water on her waxy face. She looked bad. Bruised, puffy eyes. Hollow cheeks. All the lines on her face etched too long and deep. Then again, almost everyone in Paris looked like that now. There weren't too many parties celebrating the new world order these days. People were either keeping to themselves, holed up with their families, or they were out in mobs, heedless of the poisoned atmosphere. The ring of fire surrounding the old core of the city was due to them. What had begun as small-scale opportunistic looting had escalated into a rolling series of street battles between the police and ever-greater numbers of rioters from the outer suburbs. In the last twenty-four hours the radio had carried reports of wider clashes, between "migrant gangs" and "white youths."

Between Muslim wack jobs and fascist skinheads, Caitlin thought to herself. The first sparks.

She scrubbed her face with a damp cloth before toweling off. The old bathroom at the rear of the apartment, a dark, depressing closet tiled in deep green and featuring a small faded yellow tub, wasn't the most flattering place in which to examine herself in a mirror. But there was nowhere else in the tiny apartment. The setup was very basic, funded entirely from a black discretionary account that she'd kept off the books at Echelon. One bed. A couch and a table. A bar fridge in the kitchenette, a two-ring gas burner, a microwave oven. And a small armory under the floorboards in the bathroom where she had also stashed some money—increasingly useless—and three passports, ditto. Nobody knew about this place. Not even Wales.

And for now, at least, it remained off the grid, undiscovered by her hunters, and relatively safe, unlike the first sanctum near the cemetery. It made sense, she supposed. If they'd known to try grabbing her up at the hospital, they had probably taken down her control cell, and possibly even the whole Echelon network.

Normally, she'd be gone by now. Disappeared from the map. But her illness seemed to grow worse by the day, and she had realized with horror some time ago that she actually needed Monique's help just to get through the day. A lone run through hostile territory was out of the question.

And anyway, where could she go?

Wales was uncontactable, probably because they'd grabbed him. The cell structure of Echelon's wetwork sections meant she was floating, alone. There were no convenient fronts or trapdoors through which she could slip. Beyond a few dead drops and compromised layup points, the network had no permanent presence on the continent. No outposts or operational centers. Just a transient pool of operators, like her, who came and went with each mission. And she was being hunted.

But why now? What was the fucking point?

A small tic tugged at her cheek in the fly-spotted bathroom mirror. "Relatively safe" didn't really mean much in Paris at the moment. Caitlin pulled down on a string, killing the power to the bare bulb that hung from the ceiling. She couldn't be sure it would come back on when next she needed it. The city's electricity supply was getting patchy. They'd been blacked out for three hours yesterday, and this morning the water had run brown and cold from all of the taps.

She padded down the short hallway, so as not to disturb

Monique, who was sleeping in the single bedroom. It was well after midnight, and the only light spilled in through the large windows overlooking an intersection. She moved up to the nearest one, careful not to silhouette herself. Dead birds still littered the cobblestones. She watched as a thin, scabrous dog carried off one of the bodies. The lights of the old city center provided a pale illumination under the thick blanket of smog, while the fires burning out in the otherwise darkened suburbs threw a harder, eldritch glare over the world below.

Caitlin had never had to use the hideout before. She only ever leased these places as a fail-safe, a fallback position, taking them for a maximum of six months before switching to a new address. After setting one up she would almost never return, unless her cover was blown, and that had happened only once, six years earlier in Berlin. It had convinced her of the need for a bolt-hole, no matter how much expense and hassle were involved in maintaining one without the direct logistical support of Echelon.

After staring out the window for a few minutes she realized that her nausea had eased, replaced by a hollow feeling in her stomach. Hunger. With one last glance at the deserted streets outside, Caitlin padded through to the kitchen to prepare a meal. It was late, but if she didn't feed herself now, she might not have the chance for another day. She'd been eating when she could, to fuel up for the long periods when her body simply rejected anything but water and breath mints. For some reason the mints seemed to help with the queasiness. She suppressed a sigh as she entered the tiny kitchen, not bothering with the light, which had blown earlier.

Besides the small box of prohibitively expensive fruit and vegetables Monique had bought on her last expedition, two weeks' worth of dried and tinned food remained, although given her reduced appetite it would probably last longer, maybe even a month. Caitlin ran the tap for a minute, which helped to thin out the brown tea-stained tint of the water. Satisfied that the quality wouldn't improve any more, she filled a pot and added a pinch of salt, setting it down on a gas burner. The pretty blue flame that flared up at the touch of a match was a pleasant surprise. The building's gas supply had been interrupted the previous day. As she worked, her hunger came roaring back and she decided to chance a slightly heavier meal.

She diced a brown onion and set it aside before opening a can of Italian tuna and breaking the chunks into a bowl. Another tin gave up four deep red Roma tomatoes swimming in their own thick sauce. Saliva began to squirt into her mouth, and she felt almost dizzy with new hunger and the prospect of a decent meal. She had no idea why her nausea had cleared, but she wasn't going to waste the opportunity. There was a hunk of nearly dried-out bacon in the small fridge and Caitlin diced that up, frying it with the onion in the oil from the tuna. One last shriveled mushroom went into the pan, which was spitting and popping as the meat cooked.

When the water boiled, Caitlin added a thick sheaf of dried spaghetti, pushing the long yellow stalks under as they softened. The tuna went into the frying pan, followed by the tomatoes and their sauce. She dialed the heat right back to a simmer while the pasta cooked. It was an old and much-loved dish, one of only three meals her dad had been able to cook. One-eyed Egyptians. Shit on a shingle. And this bad boy right here. She knew nowadays that the recipe was a variation on an old Italian standard, usually made with porcini mushrooms and their soak, but for Caitlin it had always been "Dad's big pasta sauce" and as a teenager she had begged him to cook up buckets of the stuff to freeze and take away on surfing holidays. After seven or eight hours of carving up the big sets off northern California she could inhale three bowls worth.

The small domestic scene in front of her blurred and disappeared behind diamonds and blue sapphires of light as tears filled her eyes. She rubbed away the moisture with the back of her hand. Her parents, of course, hadn't known the exact nature of her work, but her dad, an old air force man, had filled in some of the blanks for himself. He never asked Caitlin why a bureaucrat from the U.S. Information Service had to travel so frequently, or spend so much time out of contact. He never asked how a junior civil servant came to acquire such an impressive array of scars, broken bones, and deep-tissue injuries over the years, and when other family members did, she explained them away as surf injuries. But he had taken her aside at a family wedding a while ago, just after she'd returned from four months "out of contact" in the aftermath of 9/11, and he'd told her that he knew his little girl was doing "good work," and that she needed to know that her family loved her and was very, very proud of her. Dave Monroe, a veteran of Tricky Dick Nixon's undeclared war in Cambodia, had held his daughter's gaze for what felt like an eternity, and while no more words had passed between them, understanding did. He knew his daughter was a soldier.

"Caitlin?"

She had heard Monique shuffling up the hallway and rubbed the last of her tears away before the French girl had caught her in a moment of weakness. Still, her eyes were red-rimmed and glassy as she turned around, holding the onion skin by way of explanation. The French girl seemed to think nothing of it. She herself was very sensitive to the smell. It had probably awoken her.

"You are hungry then?" she asked. "You don't feel sick anymore?"

There was a keen edge of hope to Monique's questions. For a muddleheaded idealist, she had proven herself to be a lot tougher and more reliable than Caitlin had thought possible. Long accustomed to isolation and loneliness, Caitlin had allowed herself to relax just a little around her companion. She drained the pasta and poured it into a large serving bowl, tipping the rich, steaming sauce over it straight away. "For now I'm fine," she said. "So I'm going to eat, if you want to join me. A bit late for dinner, I know, but I have to take what I can get at the moment."

"I'm hungry, too," Monique conceded. "I have not eaten since this morning. It is so difficult to get good food, *non*?"

Caitlin ladled two large servings of the meal into a couple of old china bowls that had seen better days. "It doesn't help that we can't move about freely because of me," she said. "I'm sorry about that, Monique. I'm sorry you got caught up in all this."

"All this?" The French girl gestured expansively, taking in the disintegrating city, and a whole world of hurt beyond it. "*This* is not your doing. This would have happened whether we had ever met or not. Look out there. It is so sad. People behaving so badly toward each other. That is not your doing."

She gestured toward the window where Caitlin had been standing earlier. With the apartment in darkness, the fires burning through the outer burbs stood out prominently against large swaths of blacked-out city. Here and there blue and red strobes marked the passage of emergency vehicles, but they looked . . . inadequate. Paris was heading toward a tipping point. Caitlin doubted most of the city's residents realized that yet. Not down in their marrow, anyway. As soon as they truly understood what was coming, the unrest of the present moment would probably give way to savage anarchy. It would be a little while yet, however. The civilized mind was slow and deeply reluctant to throw off the habits of a lifetime. It meant that Caitlin and Monique still had a chance to escape.

They moved through to stand by the window as they forked up the pasta. It had become something of a ritual between them, a way to push back the walls. It wasn't so much a problem for Caitlin, but Monique very much felt the press of claustrophobia as their time in the hideout dragged on, and the city itself seemed to contract around them, the sky lowering, the streets becoming mean and pinched and increasingly filthy. And of course, there were hunters, somewhere out there, still looking for them. The lack of a police response to the events at the hospital, the appearance of more anonymous gunned-up suits and the vans outside Caitlin's other, "official" safe house, did more to convince Monique that she'd been caught up in something weird and dangerous than anything Caitlin had said. She was not a believer. She hadn't gone across to the dark side, as the American wryly put it. But she was more trusting of Caitlin than she had been, more willing to go along with her call.

They ate in silence, enjoying the luxury of being warm, dry, and well fed in a world that had turned inexplicably hostile, just a few inches away, on the other side of a windowpane.

The recipe wasn't perfect, but it was close enough to her dad's to be both comforting and upsetting to Caitlin. She had accepted the fact of her family's death. They were gone, and the shock of it was doubly unsettling because she had never expected to outlive them. The familiar scent and taste of the dish brought home a flood of memories and threatened an even greater flood of tears. She would allow herself to grieve later. She knew that such feelings couldn't be bottled up without doing damage. But likewise, she was not ready to let her guard down in front of Monique, no matter how much closer they had become under the stresses of the last week. In the end, she told herself, the French girl was just a contact on a job that had gone wrong.

"We can't stay here, you know," she said. "We will have to get going, and soon."

"But where? And how?" asked Monique. "Travel is so

difficult for everyone right now. And for you it is worse. Where would you even go?"

Caitlin nodded. Three men ran through the intersection below, all of them young and white. Two had shaved heads but the third wore his lank, dark hair in a ponytail. They seemed to be laughing, but running as fast as they could. Whether toward or away from something she could not tell. She waited for some further development but the cobbled street, wet with acidic rain and glowing a sick, jaundiced yellow under the streetlamps, remained deserted.

"Things are better in England," said Caitlin. "The government seems to have a stronger grip."

"Social fascists." Monique shrugged. "And racist, too. Putting the army on the streets like that. And only in the Muslim districts, of course."

Caitlin didn't rise to the bait. There was no passion in the delivery. It was almost as though her companion was reciting a lesson by rote. A few days ago Caitlin would have argued with her, pointed out that the army had gone where the violence was worst. But she stayed silent, and Monique abandoned her polemic, switching to a practical protest.

"How would you get there?" she asked. "The borders are closed."

"I'm not a tourist, baby."

"No. I suppose not. But you are still hunted, *non*?"

"*We* are still being hunted," Caitlin reminded her.

"Do you think? Really? Don't you think they have bigger problems? After all, you are no longer working on your mission, are you?"

For the first time in many days an accusing tone crept back into Monique's voice, but unlike the first twenty-four hours after their escape from the hospital, it was unaccompanied by any whining or hectoring. If Caitlin wasn't mistaken, Monique was almost gently mocking her.

"No," she admitted. "The mission's been scrubbed. By me. By circumstance. Or whatever. My priority now is getting the hell outta Dodge, and I will take you with me, if you still want to come. But if you believe you're safe here, I'll go alone."

Monique held her gaze for a long moment, lifting her chin in an almost defiant gesture.

"What was your mission, Caitlin? Why did you lie to us? Why did those men kill Maggie and the others?"

Caitlin shook her head as she put down the empty bowl.

"I don't know why they were killed, Monique. I've told you that. It was probably just a fuckup. I don't think it had anything to do with my *mission,* although it obviously had something to do with me, since I'm the one they were trying to grab up."

"But we were your mission. Your *target.*"

She said the word with more venom than Caitlin was expecting.

"No, you weren't," the American replied, trying to sound soothing without being patronizing. She paused then, on the verge of a significant departure. To go on would be to acknowledge that not just the mission but her whole world had been scrubbed. She stared out the window, looking at but not really seeing the bleak scene below. She missed Wales, missed the security of knowing that he was out there somewhere, watching her back, keeping her safe.

She felt guilty at being unable to help him, but of course there was no way of knowing whether he was even in the country when the Disappearance went down. He might well have been out of Paris or out of France altogether, especially with her laid up at the hospital for so long.

Her training reasserted itself. Putting aside pointless speculation, she had to go with what she knew, addressing the situation right in front of her.

"You were going to lead me to my target," she explained. "To a man, a blind recruiter, called al-Banna."

Monique looked confused.

"But I don't know any blind men."

Caitlin shook her head. "Sorry, jargon. Al-Banna's not blind. You are. He had targeted your group as mules, carriers. You were going to take something back to the UK for him."

"What bullshit." And in an instant the old Monique was back, her face an angry mask of disbelief. "I've never heard of this al-Banna. None of the others mentioned such a name. Do you take us for fools?"

Caitlin kept her face professionally blank at that question, but Monique seemed not to notice. A switch had flipped over somewhere, and a torrent of impacted rage released.

"We are not idiots, you know, Caitlin. We are not *blind* or even one-eyed, like *some.* We saw oppression and violence on all sides. Not just you and your masters. I have worked as a volunteer in a women's shelter, I have seen what happens under the burqa, *non*? The broken arms, the smashed ribs and bruises everywhere. Do not imagine that just because we opposed your stupid oil war we did not understand the nature of your enemies. You were as bad as each other. They may even have been worse, possibly, but they lacked your *means*. So please, this stupid conspiracy of yours, don't imagine that . . ."

"Monique," Caitlin sighed, tired from a bone-deep weariness. The inertia and fatigue in her voice seemed to trip the other girl up.

"What?"

Caitlin shook her head.

"Sweetheart, you'd already been recruited."

"What do you mean?" she demanded to know. "By who?"

Caitlin squared off and gave it to her cold.

"Your boyfriend."

19

Acapulco Yacht Club, Acapulco

The Gurkhas were a real find, the first stroke of good luck they'd had in a week. The Nepalese warriors were long famed as members of one of the finest regiments in the British army. Fearsomeness alone did not make them special, however. The world wasn't short of violent men. The Gurkhas were special because they combined a well-deserved reputation for savagery in battle with an equally well-founded renown for disciplined professionalism. The British army had recruited Gurkha infantry since the 1850s, and thousands still served in the regiment named for them. Such fame had they earned that former members were in high demand by private security concerns all over the world. Of course, this, too, made them little different from the old boys of any of the world's A-list military outfits, but for Jules the five Gurkha warriors standing before her were of singular appeal because they had, until a week ago, been employed as shipboard security by the Carnival cruise line, headquartered in Florida.

Unfortunately the Disappearance had robbed them of an employer and any way of getting home. Julianne chewed at the stub of a pencil while she pondered exactly how much *legitimate* work she might have for them, but she pushed that thought to one side. For now, she needed some tough, reliable men who wouldn't fall apart if you pointed a gun at them and who, just as important, she could trust not to sell her out.

"So, Mr. Shah, how long did you serve in the regiment?"

"Twelve years, ma'am," replied the short but powerful-looking man who acted as the group leader. His accent was quite polished, for a sergeant from Nepal. "Four years as a private soldier. Eight as a noncommissioned officer."

"A sergeant?"

"For the last six, yes, ma'am."

Jules nodded as she scanned the employment history of the five men. The minimum any had served was six years. Shah had the longest stretch at twelve. He was the only one who'd risen above corporal, making him the natural leader, even though they no longer took Her Majesty's coin. Jules was thankful for that. It made negotiating with them a simpler affair.

She leaned back in the old wooden chair behind a scarred table on which sat a small pile of papers, the men's résumés, and a loaded handgun within easy reach: a big shiny Mac-10, unsafed and set to full auto, for which she had traded away her former skipper's beloved yacht. The beautiful wooden cruiser had been worth the gun, a thousand rounds of ammunition, two Mexican army M16s, one crate of 5.56 mm reloads, and a half-pallet of rice, milk biscuits, and flour, all packed tightly into bags stamped A GIFT FROM THE PEOPLE OF AMERICA—USAID. The guns and stores were secured in a cage behind the Gurkhas. She would have preferred to transfer them to the yacht, but had decided with Fifi and Mr. Lee that hiring reliable security was their first priority.

"Do you mind if I ask why you left the Cunard line?" she

asked. The men had all been employed by the premier British cruise line, and some had even worked on the *QE2*. In her admittedly biased opinion, signing on with the Florida-based party-boat operators was not the first step on the happy staircase to success.

"Downsizing," said Shah. Coming from him, the Western technobabble sounded weird and alien. "The labor hire firm that subcontracted our services to Cunard was bought out by P&O, who were taken over by Carnival a year later. We were transferred to their Caribbean operations a fortnight ago. We were to pick up our next berth here at Acapulco."

The former sergeant shrugged as a way of finishing his explanation.

Jules sighed. "Say no more."

The small shed she'd hired at the yacht club just down from the Avenue de las Américas was a long way from the resort town's tourist center, but she could make out the beachfront apartments and hotels through a greasy, unwashed window to her right. One of the bigger towers was ablaze, with flames leaping high over the top floor. It was a moot point whether anybody was trying to put it out. Most likely not. The lower floors were probably being looted as she sat there.

"Well, Mr. Shah. My father would have been impressed with your regimental connections. He was a navy man, but he didn't hold with all that interservice rubbish. And he thought very highly of Cunard. It's a pity you got shafted like that."

She didn't mention that the old rogue had been banned by Cunard for cheating at cards on a cruise through the Med ten years earlier. Mr. Shah looked like the sort of chap who'd throw card cheats over the side. Only a swift return of the swindled funds and an abject apology to his victims had kept the police from becoming involved. Instead she continued, "I'd be very keen to take on you and your men, Shah, but there are two issues we need to settle. One I don't see causing much difficulty; the other, however, we'll have to see."

Julianne spoke directly and forcefully, never taking her eyes off the man she was addressing. Behind him, his companions remained as immobile as stone dogs.

"First, this won't be a pleasure cruise. My ship, which you

should know straight off we boarded and took over after the original crew disappeared behind the event horizon last week, has already been attacked once. My captain was killed, and in turn we killed every one of the pirates attempting to seize the vessel. I do not expect that that will be the last trouble we see. I cannot guarantee anyone's safety, quite the contrary, but we will endeavor to avoid whatever hazards we can."

She gestured back over his shoulder to the view of downtown Acapulco.

"I probably don't need to tell you that things are going to get worse, do I?"

"No," agreed Shah. "The risks are acceptable. And your second point?"

"Payment," she said. "And length of contract. Without a stable currency in which to negotiate we are stuck with bartering for your services. As a minimum I promise free passage to the port of your choosing in Asia, at which point our business together will be deemed complete. Right now, I cannot give you a schedule. We might get there in a few weeks. It could be six months. Over and above passage, you'll require payment. I'm happy to hear any suggestions you might have about how we calculate a reasonable figure."

Shah nodded slowly, his eyes peering into an unknowable future. She noted that he didn't consult his men.

"Gold," he said at last. "We shall settle on an amount of gold, the value to be calculated at the end of the cruise, based on an equivalent pay scale to that which we would have earned with Carnival, plus hazard pay at current regimental rates, for each day spent in combat. The pay of any man killed or totally and permanently disabled to be delivered to his family by those surviving along with a compensation payment to the value of his entire contracted fee. As to length of service, we would insist on an end to the contract within twelve months of its commencement."

It was Jules's turn to nod sagely and give the impression of hard thought. She quickly toted up what she was getting into and figured it to be worth about half of their current liquid assets. A lot, in other words. On the other hand, there would doubtless be ample opportunity for "salvage" in the near future. And, if she could just get to the Caymans before everything turned completely pear-shaped, she might be able to access her own accounts, and maybe even Pete's. Beyond that broad-brush plan to cash up and lay in stores, she wasn't sure what they would do. Lee was no more interested in returning to his home village than she was in heading for England, where there were still warrants out for her arrest on charges relating to the money her father had sent her. As for Fifi, whatever sorry excuse for home and hearth she'd once had was now lost behind the energy wave. It was possible they might well end up going with Pete's original plan and heading for Tasmania. It was far enough from everywhere to be safe, surely, and he'd insisted it was one of the few places in the world that would still be able to feed itself following a core meltdown of the old world order.

After a moment's consideration she glanced at the men behind Shah.

"Do you mind if I talk to your men?" she asked him.

"No. Ask them what you will."

"Are you men okay with that offer? Do you need to discuss it?"

The briefest of nonverbal conferences took place, with each quickly exchanging glances, shrugs, and nods with the others.

"That will be acceptable," said the man standing nearest to Mr. Shah. Jules was pretty certain it was a former corporal, Birendra. His first name was as long as a Himalayan mountain path, and just as difficult to negotiate.

"Good-o, then," said Jules. "Mr. Shah, if you would like to work out the precise figures we shall draw up a contract today. I'd like to get some of your men out to the yacht as soon as possible, but I will need two of you here with me over the next couple of days as we take on crew."

Shah grunted in affirmation and, she was sure, nearly saluted her.

"Corporal Birendra will take Subba and Sharma out to the vessel. I will remain with Thapa and you."

"Okay," said Jules, still unsure who was who, other than Shah and possibly Birendra. She did note the use of the military rank, too. "I imagine you fellows will have personal effects you want to pick up. And I suppose there's a bill for your accommodation to be worked out?"

"Yes and no," said Shah. "We have personal items to gather. For the last week, however, we have provided security to our hotel in return for lodging. No bill."

And soon after you're gone, no hotel, Jules thought to herself.

"Just one other thing, Mr. Shah. Or would you prefer 'Sergeant'?"

"That is your choice, miss."

"Okay then. Your men here. I'm sorry to have to ask, and I mean no disrespect, but do they all speak good English? It's just that it could be an issue in a tight spot, couldn't it?"

Shah's face split open into a wide grin.

"The Queen's English, ma'am. With a touch of 'sarf' London, from the instructor in their barracks."

"All right." Jules smiled. "That will do fine. If you would like to detail a small party to pick up your gear from the hotel, I'll draft up some paper for you to check and sign if acceptable. Then I'll need your help transferring those stores behind you to my boat. We'll run out to the yacht, you can meet the others, secure the ship, and then you and I and Mr. . . . Thapa, was it? We'll get back on shore and round up some reliable crew."

Shah indicated his agreement but he had one more question.

"Do we have a destination, miss?"

"Please, Jules will be fine. And no, I have no idea where we are headed initially. Just the hell away from here and that bloody wave."

It was late before they returned to port. Shah's men loaded the cruiser in less than an hour, but motoring to and from the *Aussie Rules* was a six-hour round-trip. For now the marina's own security staff, boosted by some freelance heavies, were more than up to the task of securing her boat and the small dockside lockup against any looters, but that wouldn't always be the case. She was quietly relieved when Thapa took up watch on the forty-two-footer, while she and Mr. Shah plotted their next move.

It was coming up on ten at night, and the yacht club was well lit, courtesy of a diesel-fired generator she could hear droning away in the distance. Incredibly, she could also hear music, laughter, and the tinkle of glasses drifting across from the more expensive berths, where a large number of luxury yachts were docked, one of them as big as her own. Apparently the owners and their guests had enough money and muscle to convince themselves that they could remain unaffected by events outside the marina. Not all of the berths were occupied, however. Jules calculated that a third were empty, the boats that normally filled them having lit out already. But of those who had stayed, it seemed most were intent on pretending they could hold back grim reality with good cheer, and hired guns.

Acapulco proper, however, was a patchwork of light and dark. From the flying deck of the cruiser, parts of the city looked entirely normal. Lights twinkled in houses and apartments, traffic streamed along the waterfront, and throngs of people were visible through the big pair of Zeiss binoculars she'd brought back from the *Rules*. Elsewhere, chaos reigned. Buildings burned, and the pop and crackle of gunfire was constant. Sirens had wailed through the first few nights, but they were becoming less frequent. In fact, Jules couldn't recall the last time she'd noticed one. She poured three cups of coffee and silently thanked God that the thick blanket of toxic waste released by the burning of hundreds of empty American cities had drifted east, and not south. She was convinced this place would be falling apart a lot more quickly if a nuclear winter had descended as it had in Europe.

"Thapa. Come get your brew," barked Shah, as he handed a steaming mug down to the heavily armed rifleman on the deck below. Thapa took his drink with a grateful bow of the head and a smile for Jules, making her feel much better about having to hire and trust so many strangers with guns.

She couldn't help wondering how Pete would have played all this. Badly, she guessed, given that his first thought had been to team up with Shoeless Dan, just a couple of hours before Dan had attacked and killed him. She still missed the old fool, though. They'd been good friends, even if Pete had just a little too much of the surf bum about him in a situation like this. He took his business seriously, and he was a smart bloke who'd played the odds as well as any she knew of. But in the end he was like so many Australians she'd met, ultimately prone to falling back on a naive, almost childish belief that everything would work out for the best.

Nothing in Julianne Balwyn's life led her to believe that. To an outsider, to someone like Shah for instance, she must surely appear as just one more rich oik, the lucky child of old landed gentry, wasting the advantages of the best schools, an ancient title, and a thousand years of hereditary privilege. For Jules, however, her old life was an anxious, contingent affair, where the pressure to maintain appearances was grossly aggravated by the manifest inadequacies of two parents whose laziness and selfishness were exceeded only by their sense of entitlement. She was well rid of all that bullshit.

"Okay," she said. "We're not going to need bartenders or butlers, but looking over the old crew manifest, we will easily need more than a dozen warm bods to run the engine room, the bridge, the IT systems, and general deck duties. Probably be an idea to have a ship's doctor, if we can find one, too. A proper helmsman who could handle the tub in a bad blow. A navigator for when the GPS goes down. I mean, where does it end? How do I pay them all?"

Shah swallowed his coffee in one long draw.

"You don't," he said with a single, emphatic shake of the head. "They pay you."

"Beg pardon?"

Jules was perplexed, but intrigued. In reply her new security chief held up the empty mug.

"This coffee, Miss Julianne. It came from your own stores. But if you had bought it here, on shore, today, it would have cost you twenty-five euros."

That caused a raised eyebrow but on reflection it shouldn't have. She already knew that raging inflation and currency collapse had reduced the worth of the greenbacks they'd had stowed away in the *Diamantina* to a fraction of their face value. That's why she'd got rid of them so quickly. The small office and waterfront store she'd rented here for five days had cost fifty thousand U.S. dollars up front. Now it would probably be a six-figure sum, but she was a lot more sanguine about that than she had been a week earlier. As soon as they'd hit port she'd moved to unload most of the cash as quickly as possible, and had managed to get forty cents on the dollar, taken in the form of fuel, stores, gold, medicine, and arms, most of it now safely aboard the *Aussie Rules*.

Shah moved to the railing of the boat's flying bridge and gestured at the party scenes around the marina.

"For now, these people are comfortable," he said. "They have food, shelter, safety, power."

He turned away and pointed to the brighter, more chaotic

nighttime scene of Acapulco central, where uncontrolled fires dueled with neon and fluorescent light to hold back the darkness.

"Over there," he continued, "some people are still fine, but many are beginning to suffer and to fear for themselves. Soon, everyone will be afraid. Especially Americans. A cup of coffee, a loaf of bread, it could be worth more than your life. People will pay you to get them away from that."

"American refugees?" She pondered the thought aloud. The richest, whitest refugees in the world. It was a bizarre thought, but entirely logical when you thought about where events were headed, or indeed where they were right now. "Where would we take them? Alaska? Hawaii? The last I heard, people were leaving Hawaii, not going there. I don't think they're even letting new people in. Same with Seattle, I think. Aid shipments in, flights out and that's it."

Shah moved his shoulder almost imperceptibly. His version of a shrug.

"If you have English-speaking passengers take them to an English-speaking port. England. New Zealand. Australia. They are not closed, and they will accept refugees, especially with money."

"By the time we got there, any money they had would be worthless," countered Jules.

"U.S. dollars, certainly," he agreed. "But yen, or pounds or euros. Some surviving currency. They will be acceptable. At least to us, in the short term, for the purposes of provisioning. It would help you, too, Miss Julianne," he added, with a knowing smile.

"How so?"

"The yacht is not yours, no? The owner, a famous man, the original passengers and crew, they are gone. But even so, you will have to have some legitimate reason for having taken her over. Ferrying refugees away from danger, especially Americans to friendly countries, to friendly *frightened* countries, it could make your passage into any harbor much less difficult. You could be a hero, a rescuer, not a villain and a smuggler."

His eyes glinted with real humor in the dark.

"You're not quite the ramrod-straight do-it-by-the-book type you first appear, are you, Sergeant?"

"No good sergeant is, Miss Julianne."

Jules let her eyes wander over the distant vista of the city as it disintegrated. Long strings of beaded light, the headlights of cars leaving town, wound up into the hills behind the bay. Campfires burned here and there, pushing back the blackness, while occasional flashes of light betrayed either cameras or gunfire. A huge blaze had engulfed a high-rise tower, the flames shooting upward like a giant roman candle, and yet not far away she could see candy-colored neon and a pair of searchlights, picking out a nightclub where local rumor had it you could still dine and drink as though nothing had happened, as long as you could meet the very steep cover charge.

"Okay," said Jules, making up her mind. "Crew first. They work for their passage or they get left behind. We'll start here, at the marina, put out word that we're offering a berth to qualified hands. But you and I might head out tonight, hit the right bars, gather the first of our flock. We can trawl the international hotels tomorrow, looking for passengers."

"And to where will we offer passage, Miss Julianne?"

"Somewhere big and safe and far away. Somewhere the toxic cloud won't reach. Somewhere that can feed itself. Defend itself, if need be."

Shah gave her a quizzical look, inviting her to go on. Jules nodded at a framed photograph fixed to the starboard bulkhead. It showed the boat's previous owner, Greg Norman, teeing off at Royal Sydney.

"In for a penny, in for a pound. Let's take his boat back home for him, shall we?"

20

The scientist droned on, baffling everyone with his impenetrable waffle and jargonbluster, and in the end it all came to "We don't know shit."

"The phenomenon remains nonresponsive to magnetic resonance scans," said Professor Griffiths, a small, round, redheaded toad of a man who'd added yet one more element of misery to Tusk Musso's existence since his arrival at Gitmo with the National Laboratory team to study the Wave.

"The precise mechanism by which the phenomenon effects the transubstantiation of certain organic matter to energistic potential and organic tailings remains nonobvious," he burbled on, as Musso surreptitiously checked his watch. Griffiths and his eggheads had flown in from Seattle, via Pearl, and Musso remained convinced that Mad Jack Blackstone had facilitated the move as some sort of malicious practical joke. Given the paucity of findings the Nat Lab guys had so far turned up, Griffiths chewed up an enormous amount of Musso's time and energy with resource requests he simply could not fulfill.

"Our investigations continue," the scientist concluded.

Man, I hope that's a conclusion, thought Tusk.

"Any questions?" asked the marine, standing and addressing the room. Everyone remained unnaturally still. They had learned never to give Griffiths an opening. Ask him how high the Wave went and you were liable to get a half-hour dissertation on electron orbits.

"Very good," said Tusk, hurriedly. "Bang-up presentation there, Doc, as always. You keep at it. Get back to us with anything new, of course. But don't feel the need to interrupt your research otherwise . . ."

"Well, about my research, General. This exclusion zone you've established along the line of the phenomenon . . ."

"Is not open for discussion . . . Sergeant!"

A Marine Corps gunny rolled up to the podium like an Abrams tank with the throttles thrown wide open. He double-timed Professor Griffiths out of the conference room, closing the door firmly behind them.

Tusk relaxed slightly.

He wasn't being unfair. Everyone had been intrigued and even a little excited when Griffiths had arrived with two pallets full of scientific equipment, but exposure to the man, coupled with a rapid realization that neither he nor anyone else had yet figured out jack shit about the Wave, tended to dampen that enthusiasm.

And he was a five-star pain in the ass.

"Okay," said Musso with more relief than was seemly. "I can see we lost two or three KIA from boredom there. Not a bad result. Ensign Oschin, you got my PowerPoint files ready?"

"The file's coming online now, sir."

"Thank you, Oschin. Put it straight up."

Tusk Musso rubbed at a freshly scabbed-over blood spot on his shaved head. He'd knocked a small divot out of himself fucking around under a desk earlier, fixing up a data cable that'd come loose. His fingers came away with a few tacky spots of blood and he had to pat down the wound with a piece of tissue paper while he waited for the vision from the Global Hawks.

Two of the giant, experimental UAVs were over the continental U.S. at that moment, covering Miami and Kansas City. In contrast to the first moments after the Disappearance, when everyone had been wired and speeding on fear of the unknown, the feeling in the expanded op center was now resigned and somber. Everyone knew what to expect from the footage. Empty cities. Deserted streets. Massive pileups on the road networks. Some burning buildings, many more charred ruins. Stillness. Ditches and craters of burning ruins in the fields where aircraft had gone down over what many called "flyover country" in the Midwest. Where there should be cattle or horses, there were charred spots and grassfires, especially in West Texas.

Megafires still blazed across the length of America, spewing unknowable tonnages of pollution into the atmosphere. Thankfully, there had been only two meltdowns in a couple of older nuclear plants when the auto shutdowns failed, at Browns Ferry in Alabama and Hartsville, South Carolina. On the other hand, many coal-fired plants went up for want of human attention or computer intervention. But in these two metro centers, at least, the worst of the conflagration was over. Indeed, it had never really started. Cold, soaking rain had hosed down most of the initial outbreaks in KC. And an airliner had speared into a power station in Miami, killing the grid before an untended waffle iron or hair curler was able to burn down half the city. Satellite imagery confirmed that similar strokes of luck had spared dozens of other cities, but hundreds more had been incinerated. Thousands, if you counted all the minor towns and burgs that had gone up for one reason or another.

"Miami on the right-hand screen. KC to the left, General."

Musso thanked Ensign Oschin again, even though the two cities didn't look much alike, and there was no trouble telling one from the other. The footage of Kansas City was trisected by a meeting of the Kansas and Missouri rivers in the center of the metropolis. No beaches, that was for certain. Musso had been to nearby Fort Leavenworth during the course of his career for some joint forces training with the U.S. Army. It had been the coldest winter he had ever experienced, and he certainly wasn't eager to go back there anytime soon.

"Okay," said Musso, as he turned to address the tightly packed group of officers seated on plastic chairs behind him. "This is a highlight package, cut together an hour ago from twelve hours of coverage by our two Hawks."

Fifteen men and women had squeezed into the small room for the briefing, including Lieutenant Colonel Pileggi, who'd flown up from Joint Task Force Bravo in Honduras the previous day. The senior SOUTHCOM representative sat in the front row with a notepad and pen at the ready. She and Musso were supposed to present a plan to Ritchie that evening to evacuate any and all U.S. citizens who wanted to go, from south and central America to an as-yet-undetermined location. It meant moving hundreds of thousands of people God only knew where. But certainly not to Gitmo. It already had a diabolical refugee problem.

Musso thumbed a control stick and brought up the first set of images. Still shots from the downtown areas of both cities.

"I'm afraid there's nothing new to report here," he said. "Just better imaging than we've had so far. The power grid in both cities has failed, meaning there's less chance of a catastrophic urban firestorm starting, although spot fires continue to break out here and there for whatever reason."

Musso examined the Kansas City screen, which displayed the footage of a burned-out QuikTrip on Armor Boulevard, across from a U.S. post office and a couple of larger buildings in Northtown. He never could keep all of Kansas City's various townships and municipalities straight when he was there. The Heart of America bridge, along with the Paseo and Hannibal bridges, showed evidence of multivehicle pileups, some of which had combusted and later burned out in the schizophrenic weather of the Midwest. A train had derailed on the ASB bridge next to the Heart of America and dumped itself into the Muddy Mo. One of the towers, he couldn't tell which one, looked like it had been slashed with something, probably a Cessna or a Learjet from the downtown airport.

On the other screen a Wal-Mart supercenter on Eighty-eighth Street in Miami had been reduced to a smoldering shell. Several watercraft in a variety of flavors and sizes had washed up on the beaches and canals. Musso couldn't help but be struck by the similarity to images stolen from blasted landscapes throughout the Balkans and in Kuwait after the Iraqi invasion. There was one major difference, of course. No bodies.

"We chose these two cities for the Hawks, partly because they remain comparatively undamaged and also because local weather patterns have temporarily cleared away some of the pollutants choking the air pretty much everywhere else. That won't last."

He thumbed the control again, and the twinned displays appeared to blink, as they switched to a different video stream.

"You're now looking at imaging taken from Montgomery, Memphis, and St. Louis as the first bird made its way up to KC."

The screens reformatted into a series of windows, all showing bleak, gray landscapes that reminded Musso of photographs of old industrial towns, where soggy ash and acid rain permanently blanketed the landscape, leaching the color from everything. A couple of low grunts and a curse or two were evidence that some capacity to be surprised remained in his audience.

"This nuclear-winter effect has been replicated across the continental U.S., although not uniformly. As you might expect, the concentrations of airborne pollutants are most dense at the source, and data from our weather satellites indicates that a significantly thick tail measuring about a hundred and fifty to two hundred miles extends east from each of the largest cities to have burned. In some areas of the country, in certain parts of the Rockies and on the West Coast well to the north and south of the LA basin, the concentration of particulates is not yet at critical levels. Because of a low-pressure system sitting off the coast last week, Seattle did suffer some contamination from the megafires that burned out Portland and Spokane, but that system moved east and dragged a good deal of the plume with it."

The scratch on his head was bleeding again, forcing Musso to dab at it with another tissue. He patted down his pockets, unable to find one, until Colonel Pileggi passed him a Kleenex from a handbag down by her feet.

"Thanks, Susan. Feels like I'm bleeding out here."

"Don't worry, General. Chicks dig scars."

A strained chuckle ran through the tightly packed group and eased just a little of the utter hopelessness that had begun to take hold. Musso turned back to the briefing with at least some sense of purpose.

"Okay. Average temperatures under the particulate cloud are up to twenty degrees cooler than average, although again that varies from one locale to another. The variations are much more pronounced inland than by the sea, and proximity to a major source has an effect, too."

"That solves Gore's global-warming problem." Major Clarence snorted.

"Quiet on deck," Colonel Stavros shouted.

Musso ignored the distraction and brought up satellite coverage of the Eurasian landmass.

"The plume has moved across Europe and is within two days of reaching the eastern seaboard of China. It is largely contained within the Northern Hemisphere between thirty and sixty degrees latitude. The climatic effects are less severe than on the North American continent, but they remain significant, and I'm told they'll probably deteriorate for another two to three weeks, before stabilizing for six to twelve months."

"There's a lot of wiggle room in those figures, General," said Pileggi, as she looked up from scribbling in her notebook.

"Enough of a margin to mean the difference between a lot of people living and dying," he agreed. "I've been on to PACOM to tighten them up, but that's as good as they'll commit to for now. You know what scientists are like," he added, shaking his head. The specter of Professor Griffiths still haunted the briefing room.

The display returned to top-down street scenes in Miami and KC. Not a living thing moved anywhere in either city.

"The weather data are important to us because they directly affect our mission, the evacuation of all U.S. citizens who want it, to a secure location, *as yet to be determined.*" Musso turned to Pileggi while he dabbed at his cut again. "Your airfield is going to be vital in that effort, especially if we evacuate to Australia, New Zealand, or our allies in Asia."

"I understand, sir. If I may, what about defense assets?" Pileggi asked. "Castro is gone, but Chávez isn't. I do not have any air cover to speak of outside of our allies in the region, and their air power isn't quite up to dealing with Hugo if he gets froggy. Plus, we're going to need to secure the Canal."

"I know," agreed Musso. "I've been on to PACOM about it. Pearl's promising whatever they can spare, but at the moment, that's nothing."

The colonel persisted anyway.

"If they're serious about the refugee problem they need to find that support," she said. "My staff have planned our side of any evacuation based on being able to ship people through Panama. If the government collapses—a pretty good bet—that canal is going to stop working. These locks are a century old and require ground crews to run them. At some very narrow points, the ships are actually pulled by tugs. All of these locations are extremely vulnerable to attack."

Musso threw up his hands.

"I know all about it, Colonel. But at the moment, it's a tenth-order issue for them. I'll see what I can do to change that. We need to plan for the worst, though."

"There are some contingency plans, but they are almost uniformly awful," said Pileggi. "Some ships could try to head to

Nicaragua and cross there. Most of Nicaragua can be crossed by traveling upriver to a point where the trip overland to the Pacific side is maybe eight to ten miles. The navy could pick up folks on the other side, but it would require heavy combat power on the ground to secure any transit, especially if Nicaragua goes under. Alternately, a convoy could sail around the tip of South America. But that route is vulnerable to Chávez and his navy. I also imagine there will be a significant rise in piracy throughout those waters should there be a breakdown in state control. Another option is to disembark any civilians on the Atlantic side of the Canal Zone, where our own forces could establish a defensive position of sorts. Those civilians would then be escorted overland to the Pacific side or to a usable airfield. Another nightmare."

"I'll talk to Ritchie," said Musso.

There was no avoiding it. More than a hundred civilian craft lay at anchor down in the bay, most of them carrying U.S. nationals who'd gravitated to the nearest and most obvious symbol of American power still in existence in this part of the world. Just feeding them and supplying enough fresh water each day was a herculean challenge. They couldn't stay. But moving them was a nontrivial problem, too. From Musso's perspective, maintaining control of the Canal was still a number-one priority for the United States. At least in the short term. He was responsible for the transport and protection of any American refugees who requested it, and that meant putting most of them through Panama. Where they went after that was a matter for diplomatic negotiations under way at Pearl.

"It's the low season for tourism, so we have plenty of spare beds, but nobody's figured out how it would work. Who'd pay? What arrangements might we need over the longer course? Whether you'd be looking at permanent resettlement and residency or eventual citizenship? But Canberra has authorized me to assure you that we'll take as many as you can send."

Admiral Ritchie thanked the Australian ambassador—the new ambassador, of course. The previous one had disappeared in Washington. His colleague from New Zealand added that her government would likewise accommodate as many "displaced U.S. citizens" as possible. New Zealand's diplomat preferred not to use the term "refugee" and had twisted herself into linguistic knots once or twice trying to avoid it.

Ritchie placed a checkmark in a small hand-drawn box next to the letters "A/NZ." He looked over to the Japanese consul general, seated near the window giving onto a pleasant view of the small garden outside his office. A riot of color framed the small, dark-suited man, a pink and orange spray of flowering bougainvillea.

"Mr. Ude?"

"My government is more than happy for you to initially house as many of your countrymen and women as you can within your military facilities on our soil, and with the suspension of the academic year, there are a number of temporary rooms available on some college campuses . . ."

Ritchie couldn't help but notice the heavy qualifications in that statement, and he could feel the "but" coming somewhere in the next few seconds.

"However," Mr. Ude continued, "you will appreciate that accommodation is severely limited on the Home Islands, and cultural factors mean that resettling many of your citizens within our borders is likely to be so difficult as to be . . . unfeasible."

Ritchie stamped down on his annoyance and cut to the point.

"But you'll take them in, for now, if we bring them?"

Ude nodded, seemingly thankful for having something to offer. "Yes. Within such limits as are to be confirmed by my government."

Ritchie checked the box next to "Japan" but then placed a small question mark after it and wrote "Limits." A similar notation sat next to "France," which maintained a number of colonial outposts in the Pacific, all of them well served by tourist infrastructure. In fact, a small forest of question marks surrounded the check he'd placed next to France. His direct negotiations with the authorities in Nouméa and the decolonized French territory of Vanuatu had initially gone well, but they had since referred all of his inquiries to Paris, and getting any kind of timely or useful response from Chirac or de Villepin was becoming nigh on impossible. Still, with firm commitments to help from Australia, New Zealand, Brazil, and Chile, in addition to all of the larger independent island states such as Fiji, Ritchie could begin to stitch together a patchwork of temporary refuge for most of the five million souls in the American Diaspora. He had about a quarter of a million berths he could call on throughout the rest of the region, but Ude was right. Countries like Japan and Korea weren't swimming in spare room, and many Westerners simply would not cope with the culture shock of being dropped in there at the best of times.

Ritchie twice tapped the ballpoint of his pen on the notepaper, as if sealing the deal, and leaned back from the conference table around which sat a dozen civilians, most of them foreigners. The only American not wearing a uniform was the lawyer Jed Culver, sitting in for Governor Lingle's office. His blue pinstriped suit was every bit as crisp as the day they'd met at the state capitol, and Ritchie could only wonder where the man was getting it cleaned. He surely couldn't have brought more than one suit on vacation, could he?

Culver's presence, although much appreciated for the way he could smoothly negotiate a passage through the most impenetrable thicket of bullshit, only served to remind Ritchie that very little had been done to settle the issue of executive authority. Indeed, given the mess in Seattle, it was only getting worse. General Blackstone was cracking heads there, but Ritchie was beginning to wonder whether he was stomping down a little too hard. He'd virtually cut the state off from the outside world, save for aid shipments and chartered flights for foreign nationals. And under any other circumstances you'd have to describe some of his tactics as a touch excessive. But Ritchie had no time to go meddling in Blackstone's command with a ten-thousand-mile screwdriver. Stopping that nut-hatch city from imploding was probably beyond the abilities of any normal man. Mad Jack was welcome to the job.

Ritchie turned to the lawyer now, formally introducing him to the meeting.

"Mr. Culver, who's here as a representative of the governor, the highest civilian authority we have at the moment, has a number of issues he needs to work through with you ladies and gentlemen regarding humanitarian aid and any possible resettlement scheduling."

"Thank you, Admiral," said Culver, smiling at the group.

"But if you'll excuse me," Ritchie added, "I'm not needed for the next part of this meeting, and I do have an important teleconference. Please, stay seated . . ."

He waved the Japanese ambassador back down into his chair and withdrew as Culver thanked the diplomats for their countries' help so far.

An aide was waiting for him at the door and ushered Ritchie down the hallway to a temporary communications room he'd ordered set up a few days earlier. Running hither and yon across the scattered PACOM campus was a frustrating time sink, and he had moved quickly to consolidate his most important functions right here in the old white stone colonial building where he'd been quartered before the Disappearance.

"Generals Musso and Franks are online, Admiral. But I'm afraid the secure link to Brussels is out, so we can't get General Jones in conference," explained his aide, a navy commander named Oakshott. "Also, I'm still having trouble getting Fort Lewis online."

"Well, keep on it," grumbled Ritchie. "I know we've got links dropping out everywhere but this system was supposed to survive a first strike so I don't see why it should be so goddamn flaky now."

"No, sir. We're on it, but it's not just the links, Admiral."

Oakshott handed him a sealed envelope with a red stamp. TOP SECRET—ECHELON. YOUR EYES ONLY.

"What the hell now?" grumbled Ritchie as they turned into the comms facility, which had quickly been christened "the Radio Shack" by the lower ranks. "Just excuse me, for one moment, Commander. If you'll apologize to the generals for the delay."

"Yes, sir."

Ritchie took himself off into a small alcove attached to the main communications office, shutting a soundproof door behind him. The space was cramped, not much bigger than a closet, which indeed it had once been. He tore open the brown envelope and read the few lines of text, cursing under his breath as the import of the message became clear.

"That's all we fucking need."

He crumpled the communiqué before regaining control of his temper, smoothing it out, and replacing it in the envelope as he hurried over to the bank of monitors where he could see video images of Musso and Franks.

"Commander, safe-hand this back to my office, would you, and wait for me there. I'll reply when I'm done with the conference."

"Aye, sir."

Ritchie settled himself into a chair in front of the big flat screen, nodding at Musso and Franks. There were only four sysops in the small room, all of them cleared to the level of Top Secret Absolute. One of them handed him a headset, which he fitted on himself before speaking.

"Please excuse the delay, gentlemen. Unavoidable, I'm afraid."

On-screen, both men nodded. They were all dealing with the unavoidable on a daily basis.

Ritchie continued.

"First point. This secure channel may not be secure. I'll explain by encrypted path later, but assume it's been compromised for now."

He noted the immediate reaction of the two officers. They didn't go into a flap, but there was a noticeable stiffening of the sinews.

"Okay. We still have business to do. I've just come from a meeting with some of our regional allies and partners, and we now have firmed up commitments from them to absorb any refugee flows. Some firmer than others, of course, but we can proceed with Operation Uplift."

Musso's relief was palpable. He appeared to exhale a long, pent-up breath.

"General Musso, I'll send you a schedule of receiving ports in an hour. If you could get back to me soonest with a concept for getting any U.S. nationals who want to get out of the SOUTHCOM area I'll start organizing transport assets for you."

Musso thanked him and appeared to scratch out a note to himself.

"General Franks, Uplift doesn't concern you as much in the immediate future, but it will when you've disengaged from the current operation. With a mind to my precaution about communications security, you want to update me with your latest?"

The commander of the coalition forces in the Gulf looked as though he was chewing on nettleweed. He took a moment to gather his thoughts, obviously choosing what he could say over a possibly compromised channel.

"I have multiple situations evolving and deteriorating, sir. OPLAN Katie is reaching the limits of its effectiveness. I have the Kuwaiti government screaming at my liaison not to pull out of the theater and citing line and verse of our treaty obligations; the Saudis and our other allies are doing the same," Franks said.

Marvelous, Ritchie thought. *Just marvelous.*

"The Kuwaiti armed forces are presently engaged along their front in the Wadi al-Batin region to the west of our lines. The British and the marines are heavily engaged against an Iranian armored sweep through al-Basra toward their lines." Frank ticked those items off of a sheaf of paper. "We are heavily attritting any force sent against us regardless of their origin or nationality."

Franks hadn't said anything that wasn't being reported by various surviving news networks. He was sticking to the public and the knowable. Ritchie wasn't surprised.

General Franks continued. "The Iranians have contested our air supremacy over the theater. At present, I've limited myself to asset defense."

Ritchie pursed his lips and grunted an acknowledgment of Franks's vague allusions to the fact that the Iranian air force and navy were probably doing their best to try and sink every coalition ship in the Persian Gulf.

Those Kilo subs of theirs will be a nightmare to find in the Gulf, Ritchie thought. He had half a mind to hammer their so-called regional allies into sending their air and naval assets out to help hunt the Iranians down, citing the same treaties they were currently being hammered with.

"General, execute OPLAN Damocles," Ritchie said. No one listening should know what that was. If they watched their news feeds, they'd know soon enough. *But did I step over the line? Hell, where is the line?*

Frank paused for a mere second before saying, "Copy that, Admiral."

See how the Iranians like that, Ritchie thought before he continued.

"We're in dangerous, uncharted waters here, gentlemen, if you'll forgive me the maritime analogy. This isn't just a military problem. It's political, but we have no political authority to lead us, and frankly I don't see that changing any time soon. The civilian leadership here is barely coping with local respon-sibilities. Just feeding the islands and maintaining order is keeping Governor Lingle busy twenty-five hours a day. She makes the point, quite reasonably, that she can do infinitely more in her current office. After all, her state government instrumentalities remain completely intact and functional, whereas nearly everything at the federal level has disappeared. I get the same line from Alaska and Washington State. They might be bucketing out a sinking boat, but we're asking them to give up the bucket and the boat just to help us out. I don't think we should plan for a new executive to emerge any time soon. Certainly not soon enough to deal with your immediate concerns, General Franks."

A brusque nod from Franks signaled his agreement.

"So, what do I do, Jim?"

The words seemed to come from outside Ritchie.

"If there is no political solution, we will have to find a military one. And fast."

21

Safe house, seventeenth arrondissement, Paris

Sleep finally claimed her, but only after hours of pain, dulled in the end by a dangerously large dose of Advil. The argument with Monique had been titanic and galvanizing and she feared that it had cost her more than a few hours' rest. Caitlin felt as though something vital had torn inside her head. She had lost her temper, and lashed out physically at one point, pushing Monique away from her, which only served to reinforce the French girl's certainty that she held the moral high ground. After the initial shock of being pushed into the wall, Caitlin was sure she'd seen a smile and a small measure of triumph on Monique's face.

"So, in the end it is always the same, Caitlin, yes? If you cannot win by reason you will do so with violence."

Caitlin had been unable to reply. She'd staggered backward, suddenly losing her balance to a strong surge of nausea and a blinding stab of pain behind one eye. She'd collapsed and vomited up all of her dinner.

Monique was beside her immediately.

She had to hand it to the chick, she didn't hold grudges. From a crazed harpy, screeching at Caitlin that she knew *nothing* about her boyfriend, she had switched without hesitation, propping her up, wiping the sick from Caitlin's face with the sleeve of her shirt, helping her over to the tatty, uncomfortable couch, where she lay shivering for the next hour, sipping a glass of cloudy, brackish tap water. She had even apologized repeatedly for upsetting Caitlin when she was so ill.

She was genuinely remorseful. Caitlin didn't know whether to be aggravated or touched, and in the end it hadn't mattered. She was too sick to care. Sleep had been possible only after taking the painkillers, and she'd managed that only after three attempts. Her stomach was rebellious and disinclined to keep anything down. Eventually, however, she had drifted into a feverish, unsatisfying, and fitful doze, waking frequently, or thinking she had, but never gaining full consciousness. The couch was just a few inches too short for her to stretch out comfortably, and the cushions were old and hard. She was so tired and drained, however, that it didn't matter. Her body needed to rest.

She found some peace by emptying her mind of all the troubles piling up around them, and imagining herself young again. Really young. Perhaps fifteen or sixteen, a family beach holiday in Baja. Her dad was newly retired. Her older brother Dom was just about to leave home to take up a basketball scholarship all the way over in Vermont. Mom was still healthy. She lay shivering in the darkness of the small, unheated apartment in a city tearing itself apart, and recalled an endless couple of weeks surfing, swimming, and hiking with her family. She managed a sad, lonesome smile at the memory of the surfing lessons she'd tried to give her parents. Her mother had wisely begged off after ten minutes, but Dad, he'd always been up for anything, and without the air force telling him what he could do with his life 24/7, Dave Monroe vowed that he would spend whatever was left of it living as a surf bum. He was *probably* joking. He already had a civilian job lined up with an air freight company run by a couple of buds who'd handed in their uniforms a few years before he did. But it was nice, Caitlin thought, to have him there to herself, with no prospect that he would ever again be called away to some Third World suckhole to get shot at by wack jobs and savages. It was nice to think of him living a life of ease if only for a little while. And it was a pure delight when she finally taught him to stand up and dial into a little baby wave that carried him all of ten or twelve feet, whooping and hollering before he went A-over-T into the drink. She fell asleep with that happy memory as her last thought.

It didn't last. Nightmares tormented her, some vivid, some half remembered. Her family was gone, and she was left to wander a world denuded of love and kindness. She dreamed herself in a city she did not quite recognize, where decomposing bodies hung from lampposts. Swinging on rotted ropes, they twisted in the breeze and revealed themselves as her family. Wales. Even Monique. She ran and ran through the dream, deeper into a city where children labored under the whip and scourge to build pyramids of severed heads, where monsters capered and ghouls in human form held dominion over all. Every barbarous malignancy of human nature was free to bloom and run free. She passed through this landscape of horrors as a shade, unable to act, invisible to victim and tormentor alike. Every now and then she would come awake with her heart hammering and her mouth dry and she would attempt to find the happy place where she swam and played with her father in the surf off Baja, but to close her eyes meant falling back into dreams where the whole world had become a charnel house.

In the early hours of morning, sometime before the inky blackness of night gave way to the slightest hint of gray dawn, she dreamed herself imprisoned in a cell, somewhere in the old fortress of Noisy-le-Sec. Her captors had beaten her, told her that as a "floater," a deniable asset, she was already dead. She lay on an old cobblestone floor, in a pool of her own vomit and blood, her eyes closed almost shut by swelling. Two teeth were loose, probably knocked free of their roots. The pain from them alone was a hard, white supernova burning one side of her face.

She could hear voices discussing her. Guttural French, a smattering of German, and a few snatches of Arabic.

"She is already a ghost. Let us be finished with it now."

"But the Americans, they know . . ."

"But they can do nothing! She is Echelon. She does not exist."

"They dare to send her against us. They should learn that such impudence is always punished."

"There will be reprisals."

"But of course!"

"Oh, it is fine for you, al-Banna, you are not . . ."

She tried to wrench herself back toward consciousness.

Al-Banna. Her target. Monique's "boyfriend."

"It is all right for you. You are safe."

"Nobody is safe."

"She is not just a spy. She is a killer of the most dangerous kind."

"Then ensure that she does not kill again."

"Bilal, it is not easy . . ."

Caitlin's head felt as though it were wrapped in heavy blankets. Exhaustion and illness weighed her down, pressing her back into sleep, but a small part of her, an echo of her waking consciousness, forced her up out of troubled sleep. The dream came apart like mist before a hard wind. Her head reeled with dizziness, but she was immediately aware that the horrendous pain and nausea had gone. Not just eased, but gone, at least for the moment. She became aware of everything. Her position, jackknifed on the short, uncomfortable couch. The threadbare blanket with which Monique had covered her. The smell of the meal she had cooked the previous evening and the rank stench of her having thrown it up. The predawn darkness, tinted just the faintest orange by the glow of a far-off blaze. The ticking of a windup clock. Footsteps padding about in the apartment above her. And Monique's voice, talking to someone. Just her voice and occasional blank spots in the rhythm of a muttered conversation.

She was on the phone.

A jolt ran though Caitlin's body, propelling her up off the couch and across the room. The sudden change left her balance reeling, and she barked her shin painfully on a table leg, cursing but hurrying on. A phone call!

"Mother of Christ," she hissed.

She heard Monique's voice falter, just before the beep of a terminated cell-phone call reached her.

"What the fuck are you doing? I said no calls! Who was that, Monique? Who was it?"

Caitlin found her in the kitchen, pressed into a corner, looking scared.

"I am sorry. I'm so sorry, it's just I was frightened."

The room was dark, the only light the residual glow of the tiny screen on a new Nokia. It painted her features a garish yellow, before winking out and leaving them in darkness.

"Another fucking phone! Did you call your boyfriend, Monique?"

Caitlin's voice was flat and hard, a sheet of stamped iron slamming down between them.

"Did you call Bilal?"

Her reply was an almost inaudible squeak.

"I'm sorry, Caitlin. I had to talk to him. I had . . ."

"Jesus Christ, Monique. How many times did I tell you, no calls to anyone. Let alone your boyfriend the terrorist."

"He is *not* a terrorist . . ."

"Oh, I'm sorry. Did he pinky-promise you that? Cross his heart and hope to die? Well then, I guess that's all right. I'll just go back to bed."

Caitlin spun on her heels and stalked away, heading for the bathroom, where she tugged on the string to power up the one exposed bulb, before bending down to rip back a sheet of moldy linoleum, exposing the wooden boards beneath. She reached one finger through a knothole, gave a tug, and the board came away. Another pull removed the piece of wood beside it. A thick, buff-colored folder came out first. She sensed Monique coming up behind her but said nothing, busying herself with emptying the small arsenal she had stashed away beneath the floor.

No conversation passed between them. The only sound was Caitlin's breathing and the metallic rattle of weaponry and ammunition coming up out of the hiding place. She could feel Monique wanting to say something; the air was almost alive with the tension growing between them. Caitlin didn't trust herself to respond rationally, however, so she decided to short-circuit any confrontation.

"There's a sports bag in the bedroom, would you please get it for me?" she asked, in as reasonable a tone as she could manage.

"Okay," replied Monique in a small, frightened voice.

She returned a few moments later with an old Adidas bag, empty save for a few shopping items from their last trip out. Batteries, a flashlight. Some energy bars. Caitlin began stuffing the guns and ammo into the bag.

"I am sorry, Caitlin . . . it's just . . . I was . . ."

"Forget it," she snapped. "It's my fault. I should have checked. I should have taken the phone off you. You were always going to call someone. I should be apologizing. I've lost my edge. This fucking tumor or whatever. The Disappearance. It's fucked me up, and we are going to get killed because of it. Not because you made a mistake. That's just . . . you. You're not trained. You have no experience. You don't think things through the way you need to now."

She finished topping off the bag with the three passports and a stack of currency. After a pause she tossed the greenbacks. They were just deadweight now. The euros, about fifteen grand's worth, still had some residual value. Probably about half the purchasing power they'd had a week back. Caitlin hurried though to the small living area.

"I'm outta here. You can stay or come with me. If you stay, there's a good chance men will be here with guns very soon."

"Because of my call."

"Because of your call. To *Bilal.*" Caitlin turned and looked at her for the first time that morning. "If you come, there'll still be men with guns. At first it'll be like at the hospital. Professionals, playing by the rules. Even if the rules have changed and I don't know what the fuck they are anymore, there *will* be rules. But soon, very soon . . . no more rules. Just violence like you cannot imagine. You will have to change, Monique. You will have to grow up."

"To be more like you?" Her tone was reproachful, almost sarcastic.

"To be like me. And Bilal."

At that Monique rolled her eyes again, and Caitlin pushed past her, not wanting to be delayed by another tantrum. She retrieved a small backpack from the bedroom and began cramming food into it. Trail food that she'd picked up from a camping store. Freeze-dried meals and energy bars and couple of

British surplus MRE packages. It was getting lighter outside; the light of the fires beyond the edge of the old city were throwing less of a dramatic light on the low, scudding toxic clouds that hung over Paris.

That hang over everything, she reminded herself.

"I am sorry . . ."

"Would you for Chrissakes stop saying that and pack. We have to get out of here," Caitlin insisted. "Come on."

She led Monique through to the bedroom and pointed at another small backpack.

"Pack clothes and food. More of the latter," she ordered.

"Okay. Okay. But you are wrong about Bilal. I told him what you said . . ."

"A week ago that would have gotten you killed, but right now, slow packing is what's threatening to end your life. Come on, move."

Caitlin's ears pricked up at the distant howl of a siren. Her heart jumped forward a beat but the sound tapered off. As Monique began to fill her pack with more supplies, Caitlin retrieved a pistol from the weapon bag. A Glock 19 for herself and a .38 revolver for Monique, if needed.

"So what did he say, exactly, your boyfriend, that is?"

Monique cinched shut the top flap, and flapped her arms theatrically. "He said you were crazy. He was very understanding. He thought the Disappearance had driven you mad. There have been many instances among the Americans in Germany. Suicides. Breakdowns and such."

"So he's in Germany? At Neukölln, perhaps?"

Monique froze, a suspicious glare fixed on her face.

Caitlin smiled.

"That's right. I know where he lives. With his mom. Be cool. He is so off my to-do list now. Remember, I'm unemployed as of last week."

The other woman eyed her doubtfully but finally swung the pack over her shoulder, ready to go. Caitlin rushed to put on a fresh pair of socks. She slipped into her old boots, donned the leather jacket she'd stolen from the hospital, and loaded up. She wouldn't normally hit the streets loaded down with so much artillery, but any encounter they had with the cops was going to turn nasty anyway. She had no doubt both she and Monique were on watch lists with every agency of the state by now. The only question for her was whether the state would fall apart before it laid hands on them.

She checked her watch.

5:45 a.m.

Fifteen minutes until the curfew was over. Fifteen minutes they probably didn't have.

At least the drizzle had stopped for now. She could see that the pavement and road were still slicked with acidic rain, but for now they could move about without the irritation of burning skin and stinging eyes. Caitlin checked the room for the last time, making sure they weren't leaving some vital piece of gear behind in the rush. The GPS batteries were dead, but the satellite system itself, or at least the link to it, was increasingly patchy, so the unit stayed on the table where she'd dropped it. Between them they knew enough of the city to get away.

There was nothing to identify her. Unless the French security service had her DNA on file somewhere, and anyway, that sort of obsessiveness was no longer necessary. She'd already been blown. Echelon was gone. She was simply looking to save her own skin now, not to maintain operational security. It was liberating in a way. She could play a lot faster and looser because there were no rules. They might just make it.

If her illness didn't finish her off first.

As soon as they hit the street both women were struck by the strength of the contamination still befouling the air. Caitlin had a flashback to her first time in India, when she'd stepped into a small curry house and had to step out again immediately, her eyes streaming and her throat burning from the dense mist of powdered chili dust she'd inhaled. This wasn't quite that bad. It was at least bearable. But the deterioration in the atmosphere was still severe. At ground level the number of dead birds was spectacular. Perhaps the night had claimed more of them. They did not quite carpet the ground, but it was impossible to walk in a straight line for more than a few meters without stepping on one.

"Man," said Caitlin. "This sucks. We should have masks. Let's get going. I want to find us a car with good filters."

A week ago Monique would have protested and held them up. Now she nodded somberly and hurried to keep up with her companion. Avoiding the birds, many of which still twitched and flapped feebly with the last sparks of life, slowed them somewhat, and the noxious ether quickly burned their lungs and air passages. Caitlin had chosen an apartment in the seventeenth arrondissement, where the working-class tenements of Place de Clichy edged into the red-light district of Pigalle. There was still an abundance of smaller, cheaper rooms to be had in the area, one of the most densely populated in the capital. The brothels and strip clubs, the unlicensed bars and underground gaming halls all helped create an outré environment where the police and other, more dangerous state actors were unwelcome.

"Why are you doing this, Caitlin? Why are you helping? Surely you could move more quickly on your own. You must still have friends left in the city. On the continent. You could disappear."

"My friends have been disappeared already, Monique. My network's been rolled up. Those guys at the first apartment I tried to take us to? They were turning it over. My controller should have been there, to get me out. Maybe he was and they grabbed him, maybe he wasn't. But I haven't been able to contact him or anyone. The numbers I had, the Internet addresses, they're all dead. And the Net's useless anyway. It's falling apart. The people are gone, if they were back home. And missing, if they were here. But mostly they're gone. And I have to assume all of my contacts have been compromised. I'm on my own, and in case you hadn't noticed, I'm a hospital case, an invalid."

They stopped outside a patisserie. It should have been open by now but the shop front remained closed and the blinds were shut.

"I could sell you some line of bullshit, darlin'. That was a specialty of mine. You might not believe it, but I'm a bit of an empath. I have no trouble putting myself in somebody else's shoes. Just before I kill them, or arrange to have someone else kill them."

Monique blanched and moved on, picking her way through dead birds. Caitlin stepped up beside her, scanning the streets ahead for a vehicle. In this part of town, however, few people drove, and cars were few and far between. The streets were narrow, and there was no garaging available for cars. Everyone rode the Métro or walked. Caitlin went on.

"But there's no point shitting you, is there? You know the deal already. What I am. What I was doing."

"Oui." Monique shrugged.

"Bottom line is, I need you. I'm fucked up with this . . . tumor, whatever. The effects come and go. I'm cool right now. But I still feel like shit, and I can never tell when I'm gonna lose it. Fall on my ass. Pass out. Who knows what? So I could give you a line about how I'm responsible for you, how I got you into this mess and honor demands that I get us both out. But the fact is, I'm fucked and I need your help. I have nobody else in what's left of the world."

They came around a bend in the street and spied a minibus, but a man was loading his family into it, with about a month's worth of supplies by the look of all the boxes and bags of food he was manhandling into the cabin. Monique caught Caitlin scoping them out and was about to object but the assassin smiled crookedly.

"Don't worry. I'm not about to wax a bunch of kids and steal their ride. You have to have more faith in me. I know it's hard for you to believe, but people like that, normal, decent folks, in the end *they* were my mission. Protecting them."

Monique examined her with wry detachment, almost tripping on a dead pigeon from not watching her footing.

"Not them so much, Caitlin. They are French. And you are not. I know enough now about your world to understand what that means. You told me about Noisy-le-Sec, remember. And this Echelon is no secret. There have been books and news stories written. And a French government investigation. I read about it in *Le Monde*. Not so secret, no? It is a well-documented conspiracy of the English-speaking world."

Caitlin smiled.

"There are knowns, and there are unknowns, Monique. But you're right in one sense. Sometimes governments, agencies, whatever, they might set themselves against each other, but I'm talking about the wider picture. People like that . . ." She nodded at the family now loading the last of their number into the bus. "People like that, who want nothing more than to go about their own business, raising their kids, keeping them safe, giving them whatever chances they can to do better . . . the world they want to make is worth fighting for. They are worth defending."

"Against my boyfriend?" asked Monique, giving full vent to her sarcasm.

Caitlin stopped and held Monique's gaze.

"Yes."

"Oh for Chrissakes . . ."

They started moving again. Monique's shoulders had hunched forward and she was holding her arms stiffly by her sides. Caitlin recognized the signal. She was furious again.

She sighed.

"Bilal Hans Baumer," she said, and immediately caught Monique's attention.

"You know his name!"

She looked both surprised and wary.

"Of course I know his name, darlin'. He was my target."

She dropped into her best Schwarzenegger: "I haff extensiff files."

The French girl didn't get the reference. Caitlin pushed on regardless.

"Bilal Hans Baumer. Date of birth May 5, 1974. Hamburg, Germany. Parents, separated. A German auto mechanic, Hans Baumer, and Turkish mother, Fabia Shah. His father named him Wilhelm, but he was a drinker and abandoned the family after losing his job in 1978. His mother was a reformist Muslim. Her bother Abu came to act as a surrogate father for the boy after Hans took off. Abu had always called him Bilal instead of Wilhelm. The name stuck. Don't stop walking. Come on, we've got a lot of ground to cover."

Monique had come to a halt just meters from the back of the minibus. The father, who'd been about to climb into the driver's seat, caught her eye. He looked guilty, as though she had caught him doing something shameful. Monique favored him with a shaky smile, and he nodded, taking in their backpacks and the appearance of flight that hung about them.

"*Bonjour,*" said Caitlin as they passed. "*Bonne chance.*"

"*Bonne chance.*" He nodded back before climbing in and closing the door with a slam. Caitlin scanned the back of the van, thinking of asking for a lift, but it was crammed full with children, adults, boxes, suitcases, and food.

"Why are you telling me this?" asked Monique as the bus pulled away.

Caitlin kept walking.

"Through Abu, Bilal came to meet other lost boys, most of them the products of failed unions between German men and migrant women. His mother still lives in the council flat where he grew up. She works for the City Council records department. She is inordinately proud of his achievements. He is one of the few young men in the neighborhood to finish school, let alone university. He has a real job, and would have represented Germany in volleyball at the Athens Olympics."

A few people were beginning to show up on the streets now, some of them also dressed for hiking. Another family emerged from an apartment block just across the street. The children were crying, complaining about the way their eyes stung and how it hurt to breathe. A young man rode past on a bicycle, wearing goggles and a painter's disposable mask. He rang his bell as he passed them, fluttering his eyebrows. It drew a brief smile from Caitlin, made her feel a little better. But still she continued.

"Bilal is tall and rangy with light olive skin. Thick, wiry hair, colored a dark, almost caramel blond. He has wide shoulders, long well-muscled arms and legs. No fat. Deep brown eyes, so brown they almost appear black from more than a few feet away. A ready smile that seems to spark off a high level of nervous energy. He rarely sits still for more than a moment and is given to little jumps and skips when he is excited. He talks with his hands."

Monique was staring at her now, almost walking into a pole at one point. Her eyes were wide and anxious. Caitlin had never met Bilal, but she had just described him perfectly.

"His uncle Abu encouraged him to remain in school and proceed to university while many of the young men around him had simply gone onto welfare. Abu funded his education and supported his mother. As Bilal Baumer he had studied the German equivalent of sports science and became a qualified personal fitness instructor, first working for a health-insurance company, providing physiotherapy and rehab training for older clients, and later moving to a gym, where he proved very popular with the female clientele. I believe that is how you met, in fact, when he took you for a complimentary training session at a women-only gym in Berlin, when you were in the city eight months ago."

Monique now looked physically ill, but Caitlin gave her no respite.

"Bilal took up beach volleyball after a trip to Sardinia in

1995 and became a German regional champion with his partner Jurgen Müller. Their run to the Olympics was cut short by
Müller's acceptance into the Deutsche Marine."

They had stopped walking and now stood on the edge of the
gutter while Caitlin quickly checked up and down the street for
any signs that they were being followed. It seemed clear. She
spoke without emotion, simply recalling the facts from the
dossier she had committed to memory as soon as her case controller had handed her the file on the al-Qaeda recruiter known
as al-Banna.

"He grew up in the Berlin suburb of Neukölln, where
migrants form just under half the total population. Three generations of Turks are mixed in with Eastern Europeans and some
North Africans. Most of the Turks don't speak German or even
go to school. Unemployment is eighty percent, and the city
spends three-quarters of its budget on welfare."

"Stop it, please. Just stop," begged Monique. "What is the
point of all this?"

"The point, Monique, is that Bilal Baumer is not your
boyfriend. Do you know why he has never agreed to move to be
closer to you?"

"His work, he . . ."

Caitlin smiled gently.

"His work, or at least the job he uses as a cover, his personal
training, could follow him anywhere. He's good at his job. His
cover job. He has EU citizenship. The health funds that employ
him would do so anywhere. You know all this. You've always
known."

Caitlin stepped closer, moving into Monique's personal
space. Her voice, which she had kept flat and free of emotion
while reciting from her memory of the target file, now grew
softer, more understanding.

"Like a lot of women, you don't have perfect self-esteem.
You could not believe that such a good-looking, intelligent,
caring man, a good man, would be attracted to you. Part of you
always believed you didn't really deserve somebody like *Billy*
and you assumed, possibly without ever thinking it aloud, that
he was keeping his distance until someone better came along."

Monique's eyes had filled with tears and she was shaking her
head in jerky little spasms.

"No."

"So you wore all of his bullshit excuses about work and his mother and needing to stay in contact with his community. You were pathetically grateful when he traveled to see you, but you covered most of the miles in that relationship, didn't you, honey? And you had to wonder sometimes, when he was away with a client, or traveling for work, whether there might be some other girl he was stringing along, because he was a catch and a half, wasn't he?"

A nod this time, just the smallest movement but a crucial acknowledgment that Caitlin wasn't entirely wrong. She could have said something about how Monique was also drawn to Bilal because he was simultaneously dangerous and safe. A young man from a Muslim background, politically aware if not active, but fiercely secular in his outlook. Not at all like the bearded wing nuts whose medieval views on women would make it impossible for an enlightened feminist like Monique to have anything to do with them. But of course, to lay it out as brutally as that would break the tenuous connection she had established.

"Monique, you were right. You were not his only one."

A small groan escaped the throat of the distressed young woman. Judging the time to be right, Caitlin reached into her jacket and produced the envelope she'd removed from the folder hidden under the floorboards back at the apartment. She shook out a handful of surveillance shots, good-quality high-def color photos of Baumer entwined with two separate women. The date stamps marked them as having been taken in the last six months.

"He also successfully targeted a Belgian student," said Caitlin as Monique took the photographs with a shaking hand. "Anya Delvaux, a part-time canvasser for Greenpeace in Brussels, and Sofia Calderon, an activist documentary maker from Barcelona."

Monique had started to sway on her feet, and her face grew blotchy, with irregular patches of high color fading quickly into bloodlessness.

"An auteur?"

"Well, a *would-be* auteur. Sofia's posted a few vids on the Net, entered a competition or two, but she still pays the bills as a waitress."

The uppermost photograph showed Baumer and the Spaniard, a tall, rather extravagant beauty, dry-humping each other in a park. The tears were flowing freely now, but silently, as Monique attempted to control her free-falling emotions.

"You . . . you seem to know them well. These women."

She leafed through the other photographs with an unsteady hand, blinking large tears onto them and gasping at some of the more intimate encounters.

"Oh, my God," she said in a tiny voice. "You must have similar photographs of . . ."

"Of you," Caitlin finished for her. "I'm sorry, but yes. I do. Or I did. When I selected you as my objective, my target, I filed them."

The effort to dam up her feelings failed at last, and with a series of hitching sobs, Monique suddenly came apart, wailing and crying like a child who suddenly realizes she is lost and alone. Caitlin placed a hand on her elbow and steered her through the carpet of twitching birds toward a side street, which was still deserted. The avenue on which they stood was beginning to come to life. It was nowhere near as busy as it would have been on a normal day, but here and there individuals were venturing out.

The photos spilled from Monique's fingers, falling into the contaminated mud and refuse of the street. Caitlin was forced to bend over and pick them up.

It saved her life.

22

U.S. Army Combat Support Hospital, Camp New Jersey, Kuwait

Everything came back slowly, from a great distance. Awareness, senses, memory, and pain. Oh yeah, there was plenty of that. Everything was so dim and far away that the actual transition to consciousness was not immediately real, and for an age he hovered on the far side of a morphine dream, unable and unwilling to pull himself back to reality. In the end, the pain made it impossible to hide. Whatever drugs he'd been given were beginning to wear off and Melton had a dizzying, sick-making instant of realization that he was in pain. Real pain, seated in more places throughout his broken body than he cared to catalogue.

"Goddamn," he muttered.

"Hurts like a bitch, don't it, sir?"

The voice was loud and obnoxiously cheerful. Familiar, too, in its smooth rap cadences. But he felt as though everything in his head, every thought and memory, had been violently jostled out of place by the explosion that must have put him here.

Where?

His eyelids were gummy and difficult to force open, but force them he did, blinking and raising a hand to rub away the crust that had formed while he slept. Or at least he tried to. His shoulder throbbed abysmally, as though he'd reinjured the old wound picked up so many moons ago at ranger parachute school.

"Damn!"

"Yeah. You'll want to lie still, until the nurse comes to get you. Don't go getting no ideas though. It's a male nurse. Skinny, ugly little fucker, too. He'll jam a bedpan sideways up your ass if you give him any stick."

"Corporal Shetty?"

"Uh-huh. Bits of me."

Their surroundings slowly came into focus. Melton was lying on a cot in a tent. On either side of him lay more men in uniform, some heavily bandaged, some apparently undamaged, at least on the outside. A fine layer of sand covered the plywood floors, and through a flap a short distance away he could see the fierce, white light of the desert. He noticed the thrum of a heavy-duty air-con unit, keeping them cool. It looked as hot as a furnace outside. He slowly turned his head toward Shetty's voice, noticing immediately that the corporal was short one limb. His left arm had disappeared just above the elbow.

"Yeah, gonna have to work extra hard scratching my ass now," he said. "And that was my natural ass-scratching hand, too. Least I still got an ass, though. And my nuts."

He gave his groin a reassuring squeeze with his remaining hand.

"Where are we?" asked Melton. His voice was cracked and he reached for a squeeze bottle of water on the small stand next to his bed. It was warm and tasted slightly metallic, but still felt like sweet dew in his parched mouth.

"We scored an evac slot," said Shetty. "Don't know where from exactly. They're not saying. But I'd bet Kuwait or Qatar if I had to . . . if I had any money. Germany is our next stop."

Now fully awake, if still groggy at the edges, Melton found himself unpleasantly aware of just how much he hurt. His entire body seemed to ache, but here and there, more intense pain warned him of some very special hurts that he'd picked up. Shetty seemed to read his mind.

"You're not doing too badly, Mr. Melton," he explained. "Doc told me you lost a finger off your right hand. A big chunk of shoulder meat. You lost about half of your ranger tattoo. And you got peppered with shrapnel and one big hunk of wooden window casement. Had a splinter as big as Florida stuck in your ass, apparently. Doc said that hunk of wood coulda been a thousand years old. Said they shoulda had an archaeologist dig it outta your butt."

Melton forced a weak smile, more in recognition of Shetty's attempt to cheer him up than any genuine amusement. He carefully levered himself up on his elbows to have a look about. The tent was about as big as a tennis court and housed something like sixty or seventy cots. All of them were occupied. He was surrounded by a forest of IV lines and blood bags, but very little specialized equipment.

Shetty was on the other side of his cot, propped up on a couple of dirty-looking pillows, one stump of an arm heavily bandaged. He was smoking Kools with his free, intact hand.

"Glad to have you back, Mr. Melton. You're the only familiar face in here. They got guys from all over, but nobody from my platoon."

"How bad?" asked Melton.

Shetty's eyes clouded over slightly.

"They fucked us up three ways from Sunday, sir. The lieutenant's dead. Sar'nt Jaanson. Everyone in my squad. About fifteen guys all up, most of 'em in that alley. There just weren't nowhere to go. You and me, we got blown clear into a little shop. That's what saved us."

"Holy shit," he muttered. "I'm sorry, Corporal. I really am."

"I know, sir. You're a good guy. The boys, they liked having you along with them."

A jet flew low overhead, the screaming whine cycling up quickly and shaking Melton's rib cage from the inside out. The dull thud of chopper blades emerged from the tail end of the cacophony. He tried to move around to face Shetty but only succeeded in setting off a small supernova of pain in his left shoulder. Waves of gray washed out his vision, and a thin layer of sweat broke out all over his body. He started shaking.

"Take it easy, sir," said the wounded noncom. "You're going to be a while getting better."

Somewhere down the row of cots to his left a man began screaming. There was no warning, no cycling up. His shrieks suddenly filled the entire tent and brought two orderlies running. Melton turned his head as far as he dared but could only see what was happening at the very limit of his peripheral vision. The medics appeared to inject the soldier, and a few seconds later he dropped back into unconsciousness. The reporter gave up and eased himself back into his pillows.

"So, you know what's been happening, Corporal? Here? Back home? Anywhere?"

Shetty drew on his cigarette and shrugged. Melton wondered idly how he'd managed to get one in and light up. There were no oxygen tents nearby, or flammable chemicals that he could see. But he was sure there had to be a rule against smoking in a hospital tent. Yeah. There would definitely be A Rule.

"You were out of it a coupla days, sir. You missed a lot of stuff. We're fighting Iran and Iraq now. Expecting to have to fight pretty much everyone between here and wherever we're bugging out to, probably Europe. Maybe the Pacific somewhere, but the Kuwaitis and the Saudis aren't too happy about that so it's all up in the air. And it ain't just us. Israel has called up all of its reserves. Everything they got is ready to go, on a fucking hair trigger is what I heard. Had my first walk outta here just this morning. Over to the mess tent. Guy there, a reporter like you, he told me the only reason the Arabs ain't invaded Israel, or tried to, so far is the bomb. That Ariel Sharon, he went on al-Jazeera and just straight up said yep, we got it, in fact we got over two hundred of 'em, and then he read out a list of cities they'd nuke if anyone so much as looked at 'em wrong."

"Holy shit," muttered Melton.

"Yeah. Rules are changing. Even so, the Israeli army is fighting right now. They've gone into those Palestinian areas—what is it again?—that Left Bank Gaza joint, I can never keep that shit straight. Anyway, the Israelis have put a world of hurt on 'em. They're fighting Hamas, the PLO, a whole bunch of fruit-and-nut-bar Islamic wack jobs. They pretty much hammered Arafat's guy's flat. But Hamas is shooting lotsa rockets at 'em from Lebanon or something. Everyone thinks they're gonna get nuked."

Melton felt dizzy and had to sip at his water bottle and lie back with his eyes closed.

"What about Iraq? What's happening with them? You said we're fighting Iran, too, now. I sort of remember something about that before getting clobbered but it's all hazy. My head feels like mush, you know."

"Well, they ain't allies or anything. It's more like a street fight where everyone's piling in. Do you remember the Iranians had sent all them little speedboats into the Gulf waters? Half of them suicide bombers? They got some good fucking licks in early, too, before we started sinking anything that didn't belong to the coalition. They got a couple of our cruisers, sank a British destroyer, tagged some Australian boat full of clearance divers. It was fucking chaos for an hour or so, and then the skies were full of fucking MiGs. Iranian. Iraqi. Our guys were raking 'em out of the air, but these things were unloading hundreds of bombs and missiles, and some of 'em got through. Fucking Scuds started landing on us—well, not us here, but right on some port where the Brits were fighting a bunch of Republican Guards and those fedayeen motherfuckers. These fucking Scuds, man, they don't discriminate, they're dropping like rain, killing everybody. Iraqis, Brits, a buncha marines happened to be in the wrong place. It's fucking madness. A brawl, not a war."

Melton was about to say "What about Washington?" when he remembered that Washington was gone, or empty at least. Instead he asked, "So, what happened. Is it settled now?"

Shetty smiled without humor.

"You know how I said rules have changed. Well, of course there ain't nobody in Washington to prod us in the ass. General Franks, he just gets on the blower to some admiral back in

Pearl. He's like the new chairman of the Joint Chiefs or something, and he says, I'm gonna kill these motherfuckers if it's cool with you. And the admiral didn't have to run it past no Senate committee or congressional circle jerk. He just goes, yeah, sure, kill 'em all."

Shetty drew in the last of his smoke, and with one quick little move, almost like a magic trick, he twisted and squeezed out the butt between his fingers, before pocketing the remains to throw away later.

"So?" asked Melton. "What happened?"

"It's happening right now," said the nuggety corporal. "Navy and air force turned around, dismantled the Iranians' air defense net. Then they demolished their fields. Last I heard, Baghdad and Tehran were getting taken apart by cruise missiles, and . . ." He leaned over as if to impart some grave national secret. ". . . I heard there's a hundred or more B-52s flying in from the Pacific right now and they're gonna carpet bomb what's left of both cities. None of this pinprick surgical-strike bullshit. We're just gonna smash 'em flat. Give those raghead motherfuckers something to think about next time they feel like pissing us off. Lets the Chinese know the big dog's still in the yard, too. I heard they tossed a coupla missiles over Taiwan's way this morning."

Melton tried to take it all in. He doubted there were a hundred B-52s available now, but he suspected that Shetty probably had the broad outlines of what was happening more or less right. Everything was beginning to unravel. The politics of it were pretty much irrelevant. All that mattered now was getting the hell out and hunkering down somewhere safe.

But where?

He drifted off into a long fitful doze, and when he awoke Shetty was sleeping, the ward seemed quieter, and the bright, hard edge had come off the day outside. Melton felt a little better, a little less muddleheaded and fragile. He still hurt all over, but being able to identify the injuries behind his pain allowed him to put each of his many hurts into a box and file it away. It didn't decrease the pain, but it sure helped dealing with it. Pain could be endured a lot more easily when you knew where it came from and when it was likely to recede.

"Mr. Melton, you're awake, that's good."

Bret turned his head carefully toward the male voice. A thin, exhausted-looking corpsman with deep purple smudges under his eyes appeared to have just noticed him and was advancing with a clipboard. He appeared to be of Italian or maybe Greek extraction, and was obviously running close to the ragged edge of a complete physical breakdown. It was a look you got used to around soldiers. When you saw it on rear-echelon personnel it was never a good sign.

"What's your name, son?" he asked. He had about fifteen years on the kid, and probably had more time in service than him, too, so he felt comfortable taking the liberty.

"Deftereos, sir. Tony Deftereos."

Then he seemed to remember himself.

"Hospital corpsman, Fifteenth MEU, sir . . . I've been told to watch out for you."

"You're navy? What are you doing here?"

"Oh, you know. Chaos. Madness. The usual. My ship got hit by a Jet Ski."

"A what?"

"A fucking Jet Ski, sir. Pardon my language. Full of explosives. So here I am, looking after you, as per my orders."

"From who?" asked Melton, somewhat nonplussed.

"Corporal Shetty, sir. He said he'd stomp me if he woke up and found out anything had happened to you."

Melton looked across at the maimed black soldier lying in the bed next to his, and realized that he was the closest thing he had to family or friend. At least in this part of the world. Possibly anywhere. He felt that familiar, irrational swelling of affection for someone he didn't really know, beyond having faced mortal danger with them.

"I'm sure he didn't mean it, Corpsman," smiled Melton. "Corporal Shetty is a gentle soul, a friend of lost animals and small children. He wouldn't hurt anyone."

Deftereos looked most uncertain.

"Well, I promised him I'd keep an eye on you, sir. If you feel up to it, the doc would like you to answer some questions for him."

"I'd shrug, but I've got a big hole in my shoulder and it really hurts. What d'you need to know?"

Deftereos took him through a standard posttrauma questionnaire, which wasn't all that different from the experience a civilian might have answering an ER survey at a hospital, except for questions about exposure to chemical or biological weapons and so on. By the time they were done Melton felt a little hungry and asked if he might have something to eat. The corpsman checked a note at the end of his bed and nodded.

"Nothing heavy, sir. A cup of soup, maybe, to begin with."

"Thanks. Listen . . . Tony, wasn't it? Your hear anything from back home? About what happened. Have there been any developments the last few days while I've been out of it?"

A sad shake of the head was the initial reaction.

"No, sir. Nobody's had any word out of home. And the news coverage we were getting, you know, satellite photos and webcams and stuff? It's drying up, because of the firestorms. Some whole cities have gone up. Not just a couple of blocks here and there. The whole thing, sir. They reckon the clouds are like a nuclear winter or something over Europe. Like when Saddam torched those oil wells in the last war. Only much worse."

Melton remembered that from before he checked out. He recalled resting in the alleyway, looking straight up at a hard blue sky and wishing some of those clouds would drift south and cool things down a bit. He tried to recall some more details but it was like pushing those same dirty, polluted clouds around the inside of his head. Nothing really cleared up.

"I'm not feeling too bad," he told the corpsman. "D'you think I could get up and walk over to the mess tent for my soup?"

Deftereos grimaced slightly. "In fact, I was gonna ask if you could, sir. We're real shorthanded here. Doc's written that you should be mobile by now. You got no leg or spinal injuries, nothing internal. Just have to watch your sutures on the shoulder and some stitching on your rear end, where they took out some real big splinter. You'll have to move slowly, is all. I'm sorry, sir," he said again.

"That's fine," grunted Melton as he pulled himself up. "If you could just give me a hand up that'd be great."

He bit down hard on the pain that welled up as he arose from the bed. No stranger to injuries and discomfort, he knew he'd have to get used to moving around with both. He was very much a nonessential part of this operation and considered himself lucky to have made it this far. It seemed that a lot of the boys he'd been covering hadn't. A mild headspin unbalanced him and he leaned against Deftereos, but it passed with a few deep breaths.

"You gonna be okay, sir?" asked the corpsman.

Melton nodded. "I'll be fine. You get back to looking after your patients. Just give me some directions."

Deftereos pointed at the main tent flap as a puff of wind caught it. Melton could see a throng of uniformed personnel hurrying in both directions outside.

"You head out, turn left, and move through three intersections, then it's on your left again. About a hundred and fifty yards. You won't miss it."

Melton thanked him and began the slow shuffle out of the tent. It remained quiet in there, with most of the wounded men sleeping in their cots. A few orderlies and corpsmen moved about checking on them. Some were in scrubs, some were in their desert fatigues, a mix of various services, something that wouldn't normally happen in an Army Combat Support Hospital. But regardless of their branch not one spared him as much as a glance. He was walking and mostly in one piece. He just wasn't a priority.

He felt adrift, disconnected from the world. He understood Shetty's feelings about not wanting to let go of the familiar. He'd never been part of a unit that'd been shattered before, but it sounded like that's what had happened to Euler's platoon. He'd embedded with them, nearly died with them, been right there in among them as they fought their way through southern Iraq. It had been such a bullshit mission in one way, rushing forward to engage the Iraqis who'd attacked them, just to give themselves enough elbow room to get the hell out of Iraq when the war was all but called off by events, or just the Event, back home.

The tent opened up onto a thoroughfare, a wide street of sand in yet another huge, military camp, laid out as always on a grid pattern. Soldiers and marines moved about in groups of two and larger, all in full battle rattle, many with a bad case of the thousand-yard stare. Melton blinked at the raw power of the sun after the relative gloom of the tent's interior. The field hospital enjoyed the benefit of a slight rise in an otherwise flat landscape, affording a view of the frame tents, generators, and vehicles. The Combat Support Hospital was attached to a number of other units in the area, near as he could tell. A five-ton truck rolled past him, filled with body bags, the bumper number clearly defined. HHC 703rd MSB.

"Jesus," he said, watching the REMF vehicle roll down toward a container. "I've died and gone to the rear."

The truck stopped in front of the container, where a detail of soldiers waited. With great care, two soldiers at a time removed a single body bag from the truck and carried it into the container. Melton could see a refrigeration unit attached to the side. A couple of soldiers from the Third ID glanced at the body, then looked away. Melton overheard them as they passed.

"Those poor dumb bastards really got zapped," one specialist said.

"Glad I wasn't there," the other, a private first class, replied. "Stupid fucking mission anyway."

"Amen to that," Melton said under his breath.

He gazed over a vista of thousands of tents and makeshift arrangements of prefab huts, motorized trailers, converted shipping containers, vehicle parks, supply depots, and chopper pads. A cluster of antennas sprouted next to a tight knot of command vehicles and shelters. The camp had to cover a couple of klicks of real estate, thought Melton. He cautiously craned his head skyward, and could pick out the twinkling points and occasional contrails of at least a dozen jets flying CAP.

"Division Main will want that on the double," someone said to an underling. The underling nodded to the soldier, who was standing in the back of a communications shelter. Melton read the bumper number without thinking.

123 Sig BN.

"Guess that commo puke didn't have to worry about shooting himself in the foot after all," he thought aloud. "Must be at Third ID's main camp."

Now, where that was, he had no idea.

The ground was rockier, harder than he remembered from that last big post. It made walking a little more treacherous for someone with his injuries, but it also meant that there was marginally less grit and sand in the air. From the lowering position of the sun he estimated the time as being quite late in the day, maybe 1600 or more. His watch was missing. There was only room enough for foot traffic in this part of the base, and it was heavily congested. Everyone was fully armed, as though expecting the enemy to appear around the corner at any moment, but people made way for him as he shuffled off in the direction of the mess tent.

It was slow going. His whole body was stiff, and every movement seemed to threaten new rips and tears in those parts of him that had already been sundered apart and put back together. Melton desperately wanted to know what had happened while he'd been out of it. What had become of "his" platoon? Who'd lived and died? And what had gone down in the wider world? The little he'd picked up from Shetty and Deftereos wasn't reassuring. He had the impression of a world that had already tipped over the brink and was now falling toward destruction.

It took him a while and a good deal of discomfort to cover the short distance to the mess, and he felt worn out when he'd done it, but satisfied, too, as though he'd proved to himself that he wasn't a total cot case. Pushing in through the fly-screen doors he found about half of the tables occupied by service men and women whose working routines obviously had them out of sync with the bulk of the camp. He recognized marines and army personnel, some foreign uniforms, possibly Australian special forces. There was even one table of USN sailors looking very much out of place. The hum of the room was subdued, with many of the diners watching a television that hung from a pole near one end of the space. Nobody appeared to be enjoying the show, some sort of news broadcast. Melton was desperate for information, but also weak with hunger. His appetite had come roaring up as he shuffled toward the mess with its familiar smell of fried meat, grease, and instant coffee. He was salivating heavily, and his stomach actually seemed to twist itself into a knot in the effort to move him toward a folding table where a female on KP duty smiled at him.

"Can I help you, sir?" the specialist asked. Melton couldn't read her name tape. It was covered by her body armor. "We got some burgers and fries that are sorta fresh. And you look like you need feeding up."

He shook his head but smiled.

"Got any soup?"

She turned toward the giant metal pots sitting on a big field oven behind her.

"Got some beef stew in one of them, sir. I could add a bit of water if you like. That'd almost be like soup, wouldn't it? Just chunkier."

"Chunky is good," said Melton.

The army specialist even helped him over to a table where he could watch the TV, which surprised him. No one was ever cheerful to be put on KP duty. A minute or two later he was sitting on a poncho liner she loaned him, trying to ignore the sharp pain from his butt sutures, dunking a bread roll into the thick dark stew of chuck steak and vegetables. His ranger buddies would have given him a ration of shit for accepting the snivel gear, but his ass hurt, and as far as he was concerned, he wasn't a ranger anymore.

"You ain't a ranger with that haircut."

Melton turned to an air force sergeant and noticed that the remains of his ranger tattoo was visible on his left shoulder. For some, it'd be fighting words, but Melton just wasn't wired that way. The sergeant inhaled a chili mac and green beans with a good-natured grin. Bret reached his hand over to shake.

"Reporter these days. Bret Melton, *Army Times*. Or I was until last week," Melton replied. "But no, I'm not in the army anymore."

"Sergeant Anderson. Michael Anderson," he said. "But you can call me Micky if you want. You look pretty badly shot up there, Bret. You mind if I call you Bret? You get caught up with the marines?"

He shook his head.

"5/7 Cav. At An Nasiriyah."

The sergeant nodded sagely but said, "Didn't hear about that. But then, there's been a helluva lotta fighting here and there. They're still patching my C-130 back together after all the fire we took from the Iranians getting in here. Copilot didn't make it. Hell of a ride, I'll tell you. Two burning and two turning and I don't mean jets. Your guys, the ones you embedded with, they okay?"

"Afraid not. We got caught in a bad spot. They mortared the shit out of us . . . I don't even know how we got out."

The realization had just struck him. He really did have no idea why he was alive. Shetty hadn't explained how they had escaped, only that they'd been blown into a building of some sort. A shop or something. One of the other platoons must have fought their way over to drag them out. Hadn't they lost air support just before the mortars started to fall?

He found himself slipping away into reverie and consciously pulled himself back into the present.

"Sorry, Sergeant . . . I mean . . . Micky. I've only just woken up. Been out of it since we got hit. But no, I don't think many guys made it."

"I'm sorry," he said quietly. "But at least you weren't with the marines at Abadan. Man, what a fucking mess."

He didn't explain further. Another forkful of chili mac effectively silenced him. Melton gingerly dunked his bread into the rich broth of beef stew and tried to focus on the TV screen. He recognized BBC World's business news presenter, Dharshini David, on the screen. Her normally dark, full lips seemed pale and pressed tightly together, and her eyes were haunted and nervous. It was hard to hear what she was saying but a tagline rolling across the bottom of the screen, and a small picture window hovering beside her head, implied that there had been a massive banking collapse in Europe. The little video window carried footage of black-clad riot police; he recognized them as French CRS, baton-charging a huge crowd laying siege to an old, colonnaded building. He assumed it was a financial institution that had run out of money. The scene switched to London, where even bigger crowds waited a lot more patiently outside a large Barclay's bank in the city. A man in a dark blue suit made some sort of announcement to them and they reacted with catcalls and jeering, but there was no violence. The presenter then threw to an interview with a frightened-looking woman who was holding on to two children.

"Any idea what that's about, Micky?"

Sergeant Anderson glanced quickly over his shoulder at the television and shrugged. "Something about the banks falling over." He grunted in disgust. "Welcome to my world. I haven't been paid yet. Not that it matters, since my ex gets half of it. Or . . . she used to, I suppose."

He stabbed at the chili mac. "But at least I'm not going hungry."

Yet, thought Melton.

23

Seattle, Washington

He could tell there was a problem from two blocks away. Two women, one of them covered in blood, ran past his car, hair streaming behind, eyes bugging out. Kipper nearly gift-wrapped a telephone pole trying to follow them in his mirror. When he looked up, saw the danger, and jerked the pickup back onto a safe course with one wrenching pull on the steering wheel, he could see more people running toward him, many of them pounding up the middle of the road, which was free of any vehicles save his own. With his heart beating quickly, Kip pulled up and wound down his window, immediately becoming aware of a distant siren.

He hopped out and tried to flag down somebody to ask what had happened—it had to be a problem with the food bank—but nobody would stop. A couple of young men abused him when he tried to hop into their path.

"Get out of the way, you crazy old fuck. D'you wanna get killed, too?"

And then he realized that the crackling, popping sound he could hear was gunfire.

Shit.

Kipper jumped back into his truck, but before stomping on the gas, he redialed Barney, who answered on the second ring.

"What's happening, boss man?"

"Something's gone wrong, Barn. Very fucking wrong. I'm about two blocks from Costco and I can hear shots and there's all sorts of people running past me. Some of them bleeding."

A string of oaths burst out of the earpiece.

"It sounds like cops are coming. But get on the phone

anyway. Make sure they get here before the army. Those ass-holes should have been here already. They turn up now, they're just as likely to kill anyone they see moving . . . Oh, and ambu-lances, too. I think we're gonna need lots of ambulances."

At that moment a weeping woman ran past, holding up one hand, from which a couple of fingers had clearly been removed by a gunshot. Kipper had no idea how she kept going, given the amount of blood she was losing.

Barney didn't answer. He'd already hung up.

Kipper's head was reeling and he felt distinctly ill. This was his fault. The food banks had been his idea, a way to ensure that the aid shipments coming in from across the Pacific were distributed in a rational, effective manner. It wasn't the sort of thing he should have been involved with; as the city engineer he already had a full dance card with the utilities. But the elected councillors had frozen like rabbits on the road, and they had let him run with the program. He'd personally negotiated the use of the Costco facilities with company management, who'd assigned dozens of their own stock-control specialists to the job and cleared their warehouse space of all nonessential items. He and Barney had been expecting all sorts of teething problems on the first day, but nothing like this.

Heather.

An image of his nervy intern sprang up unbidden: a big pair of Bambi eyes staring out at him from under a short blond bob as her hands twisted in her lap like small, white otters, con-stantly moving over and around each other.

"Oh, fuck," he muttered, stamping on the accelerator and punching the horn.

The truck leapt forward, scattering the fleeing mob in front of it.

Many of the people running toward him still paid no heed in their desire to flee whatever had happened at Costco, forcing him to slow down some. By the time he made South Bradford Street the crowds were thinning out, with most people having already fled and dispersed. He rolled down his window and lis-tened for gunfire but heard only screams and cries and the growing wail of sirens.

Kipper threw the pickup onto the sidewalk and into the park-ing lot at the northern end of the giant wholesale warehouse. Immediately he saw bodies, a lot of them lying still, and people who were so badly wounded they could not flee. But no shooting. Costco warehouse staff were everywhere, easily identifiable by their brightly colored vests, many of them tending to the injured. Of the army, who were supposed to have provided a security detail, there was no sign. Nor of the cops or other emergency services, although he could hear them approaching.

Kip turned off the engine and stepped down warily. His senses seemed to be unnaturally alive, and even though this part of the city was a gray, industrial area, he could never recall seeing colors so vibrant as the red and blue of the giant Costco sign high up on the building. His hearing, too, was amped up, with every cry and moan disturbingly clear. Small stones crunched on the tarmac beneath his feet, and the engine block of the F-150 ticked loudly as it cooled down. And he gagged as the smell of violent death flooded his nostrils.

Barney's car, an old mud-splattered Chevy C10, came flying up the road and screeched to a halt under a tree at the entrance to the lot. The squeal of his tires caused some people to jump and shy away a few steps. Barney climbed out, and raised one massive hand, pointing toward the warehouse. Kipper saw Heather standing there, a small, forlorn figure in blue jeans and a Minneapolis Twins sweater. Even from a distance Kip could see that she was shaking violently. The two men hurried over to her, picking their way through the carnage.

"Heather! Yo, Heather," Barney called out.

She didn't seem to hear him at first, but her slack features became animated when she finally recognized her colleagues. She immediately burst into tears as Kipper folded the quivering young woman up in his arms.

"It's all right, kid. Everything's gonna be fine. It's all right."

He didn't attempt to question her for at least two minutes. Barney stood by and occasionally patted her shoulder, but obviously felt the need to be doing more.

"Kip, I'm gonna see if I can scare up somebody from the company. See if they can tell me what happened."

"Good idea," nodded Kipper. "I'll be here. You got the cops and the ambulance, right?"

"Done deal. They'll be here, even if the fucking army won't."

In fact the first squad cars were already screaming to a halt at the edge of the lot, disgorging officers, who emerged guns ready but unsure of where to aim them.

Barney kept his hands held up in clear view and walked carefully over toward them.

"Can you tell me what happened, Heather? Can you do that yet, darlin'?" asked Kip.

A small, tentative nod was all he got in reply. Her whole body was still shaking uncontrollably as she pushed away from him. She rubbed at her arms, folded them, and started rubbing again.

"There were m-maybe a thousand people here, when I got in at six," she said, unsteadily. "They all had transit passes and ration vouchers, just like we planned."

Heather stared around the parking lot as if seeing it for the first time. Her face contorted, and Kip was sure she was about to start crying again, but she got it under control. Her voice was small, and seemed forever on the edge of breaking into a thousand little shards.

"Th . . . they were just fine. Everyone waiting their turn, until these three pickups arrived." She pointed with a shaky hand at a couple of abandoned trucks a hundred yards away. Kipper could only see two of them, but didn't interrupt her.

"A-about a dozen guys," she stammered. "All armed, and they like, just *pushed in.*"

Kipper shook his head.

"What about the army, the cops? Where were they? There was supposed to be a platoon of soldiers here to help out."

Heather volleyed back his headshake with one of her own, throwing in a nervous, exaggerated shrug for good measure.

"I don't know. But these guys, like I said, they just started pushing their way to the front, and some people are yelling at them, some are just getting out of the way. And this one guy, some big guy in a lumber jacket, a big red lumber jacket, he just steps in front of them and puts his hand up like a traffic cop or something."

"Okay," said Kipper. "Go on," he said in a quiet voice.

"Well, one of these jerks, from the pickups, he had like an ax handle or something, and he just buttswipes this dude with it. Totally wiped him out. He goes down and then the shooting starts."

"The pickup truck guys, the looters, they started shooting people?" asked Kipper, his voice rising.

"Nope. They *got* shot. Or at least the one with the ax handle did. He dropped the lumberjack dude, looked like he was about to start wailing on him with that club, next thing you know, somebody blew him away. Two or three shots, I don't know. But there's blood everywhere, people screaming, and *then* the real shooting started."

Kipper felt as though he was going to vomit.

There had to be more than a dozen lifeless bodies lying around in the parking lot. There'd probably be more in the streets beyond.

Where the fuck were the army guys? They were supposed to be here. They'd insisted on it, in fact.

"How about you, Heather? Are you okay? You got a little blood on you, darlin'. You're not hurt, are you?"

"I don't know where all the guns came from," she said. "But once they were out, it was like everyone was armed. Everyone was shooting. I've never seen anything like it. There was a little girl . . . standing just near me . . . she was screaming and crying for . . . for her mom . . . and . . ."

The young woman broke down completely as the morning's blood and horror overwhelmed her.

Barney reappeared with a police officer, an older-looking man with sergeant's stripes.

"You in charge here, sir?" he asked, almost accusingly.

"What? Yes, no . . . well I . . ."

Kipper pulled himself together.

"My name's Kipper," he said. "James Kipper, city engineer. We were starting our food-aid program here this morning. The city's running the program, with help from Costco, here at least, but the army was supposed to be doing the site management and security. So, no, I'm not in charge. Nobody was, by the look of things."

The cop took in the scene with unalloyed disgust on his face.

"You know, the fucking city could have just used us. This wouldn't have happened on my watch, I tell you."

More cops were arriving and the first of the paramedics were charging around, doing triage.

"I don't make these choices, Sergeant. I'm like you. A civil servant. We do as we're told."

It sounded weak and worthless as it came out of his mouth, and Kipper immediately regretted speaking.

The cop fixed him with a baleful glare.

"Well, don't you be wandering off, Mr. Kipper. I'll be needing to speak to you again."

He turned his back on them with that and trotted over to a couple of uniformed officers, barking orders as he went.

"Jesus, what a fucking mess," said Barney. "This is just so fucking typical of trusting those assholes at Fort Lewis to do anything but blow shit up."

"Uh-huh," grunted Kip. "We'd better find out what broke down, do what we can to help, then get back to council. We'll call them, tell them what's happened."

Barney looked troubled.

"I tried, Kip. But none of them are available."

"What d'you mean?" he snapped, instantly regretting it. "Sorry. It's just that I keep hearing this. It's bullshit. Where are they?"

Barney shrugged. "I even tried a few home phones. Their cells. Nothing. Offices back at Municipal Tower. Same result every time. You just get routed into the phone menu hell out at Fort Lewis."

"Why? How come our calls are going out there?"

"Not ours," said Barney. "Just any calls to the councillors."

Kip started walking Heather over toward an ambulance. She was looking shocky and pale, and he wanted to get her cared for as quickly as possible. The paramedics, however, would have their hands full with more serious casualties.

"Heather, I'm going to get someone to run you out to the hospital . . . no, scratch that. They'll be overloaded. Do you have a doctor in town? Someone we can call?"

She shook her head.

"No, but I've been to a clinic near my apartment a couple of times. I got food poisoning my first week here."

"Jeez, Seattle's been good to you, hasn't it? Okay. Barn, you think you could drive Heather over to this clinic? Get her checked out. Don't take any shit from them. It's city business."

"No problem."

"Okay, you guys go now. Fuck the cops, they know where to find you. I'll deal with them. Off you go."

He shooed them away, keeping an eye on the sergeant who had his back turned to them.

A long line of ambulances was speeding down Fourth Avenue South toward them, and he could hear a chopper, more than one, approaching from the city. Hopefully it would be a medical flight. The media couldn't take their helicopters anywhere without written authority from Fort Lewis. The entire state had been declared a no-fly zone. To "secure" the city's airspace and approaches. It was bullshit, of course. There were no more unpiloted, empty aircraft headed for Seattle. They'd all crashed within hours of the Disappearance. But General Blackstone hadn't gotten around to removing the restrictions.

Well, for once, Kipper was glad of it.

He could really do without having to deal with a lot of jackass reporters this morning.

Nearly six hours later he finally made it through the last checkpoint on Fifth Avenue, where a couple of Humvees with ring-mounted machine guns blocked access to the Municipal Tower, the city's administrative center. A kid with the name tag MEYER read his papers, stamping his feet in the cold while his breath plumed in the frigid air. He didn't look at all pleased to be out in the open. The sun had disappeared again, and a light drizzle was drifting down from the leaden sky. It stung Kipper's eyes, as he waited for his papers, taking him back to childhood memories of swimming in pools with way too much chlorine.

"Looks fine, sir," said Private Meyer. Or was it Specialist Meyer? He never really knew where he was with these military types. "Just park as normal and head on through. Major McCutcheon is waiting to see you."

Kipper was about to walk away when he pulled himself up.

"Sorry, who's waiting to see me?"

Young Meyer consulted his clipboard again.

"Major McCutcheon, sir."

"I don't know any McCutcheon, son. Major or otherwise. What's it about? Unless he's come to explain where your guys got to this morning instead of guarding my food bank, I'm not interested."

Meyer looked severely discomfited.

"Sorry, sir. I don't know why he came to see you. He's General Blackstone's aide, if that helps."

Kipper blinked away the burning rain that ran into his eyes.

"Well, no it doesn't . . . but . . . damn it. McCutcheon, you said?"

"Yes, sir, Major Ty McCutcheon. Waiting for you inside, sir. In the . . . ah . . . deputy mayor's office."

"Okay. Thanks."

He stalked off. If nothing else, this McCutcheon might make a convenient punching bag. God knows he needed one after this morning.

Forced to take a spot a good long walk from the tower, he didn't recognize many of the vehicles, and noted that a fair amount of military transport had arrived, too. The thin mist of rain started to thicken, falling more heavily and forcing him to hurry. He no more wanted to be out in it than poor Private Meyer. Two more guards, both of them toting rifles, greeted him at the door, eyeballed his papers, and reminded him that he had an appointment with Major McCutcheon. Kipper tried to shake off his anger with the rain and pushed past them into the heated and slightly humid interior of the building.

He could tell immediately that many more folks were in residence than was normal, many of them, perhaps most, out-of-towners. Every fourth man or woman was dressed in a military uniform. A couple of very expensive suits were wrapped around some very polished Eastern accents, too, but not many. And Canadians seemed to pop up at every corner, announcing their presence with a rising inflection and an "*eh!*" for every occasion. None of the newcomers recognized him, but here and there he caught a despairing look from a city employee. He had no idea how many people knew about the fuckup at Costco. It certainly hadn't been on the radio as he'd driven in. Those stations still operating were given over to official announcements spliced in between wall-to-wall music, and none of the official announcements had made any mention of the trouble this morning.

By the time he'd reached the deputy mayor's office, he'd calmed down a little, and decided to ditch the meeting with this McCutcheon guy. He was going to be far too busy with all of the blowback from the food-bank disaster and opted instead to attempt an end run to his own office.

"Yo! Kipper! You made it, man, good to see you. Come in, dude. We need to talk."

The engineer nearly jumped out of his boots.

The army officer—or was he army? They had majors in the air force, too, didn't they?—was a lean, forty-something man with a bristling gray crew cut. He looked the part, but sounded like a surf bum. A Californian, maybe?

There was no avoiding him, though, so Kipper set his features and made the best of it.

"You're McCutcheon, right? Did you come in here to explain what the hell happened at Costco? You guys were supposed to be there guarding the handout. You insisted on it, as I recall." As soon as Kipper started to speak, all of his bottled-up rage and frustration spilled out. He was nearly shouting by the time he'd finished. "All that bullshit about major security operations being an army gig now. But I got eighteen people dead, and the entire fucking city locked down again. It's not good enough, Major."

"No, it's not," countered a gruff voice from somewhere behind McCutcheon. "Now get your ass in here, son, and help us sort it out."

Kipper pushed in through the door, surprised to find another uniformed man in the chair behind the deputy mayor's desk. This one was older, bald, and much thicker-set than McCutcheon.

"Who the hell are you?" he asked, as the major closed the door behind them.

The man, who was dressed in fatigues like McCutcheon, gestured at a chair. "General Jackson Blackstone," he said. "Sit down."

Kipper blinked and froze.

"You. You're the fucking idiot who insisted that the army would handle security this morning. Great fucking work out there, guys. Top-shelf effort."

"Sit. Down."

Blackstone's voice came out in a low growl.

McCutcheon pressed Kipper toward the chair, placing a hand gently on his elbow.

"Yeah, sorry, not our finest hour," he said. "We sent two platoons over to that marketplace that got hit last night. It's a snafu, Kipper. I'm sorry. It happens. Come on. We need to talk."

"You're damn right we need to talk," said Kip. "And what's

with the invasion?" he asked, gesturing to take in the hordes of military personnel swarming the building. "Is the army taking over or something?"

McCutcheon remained unaffected by his hostility.

"Naw," he said. "We just stand out because of our superior grooming and fashion sense. Really, if it weren't for that, you wouldn't even know we were here. Come on, come in. I'm not army, by the way. I'm air force. Special liaison to the civil power, for now. General Blackstone is army, and cochair of the Special Means Committee."

The air force officer fetched a coffeepot from the sideboard. The office was crowded with paper files, maps, and electronic equipment, all of it military issue.

"You want java?" asked McCutcheon. "It's fresh. But the milk's not. I got some very nasty military-issue creamer, if you want?"

He held up an olive-drab container with a white plastic slide top on it by way of explanation. Kipper grunted, asking for a mug of black, no sugar.

"Damn, that's hard core," said McCutcheon. "You sure you've never been in the service?"

Kipper nodded grumpily. "I'm certain. People shouting at me just pisses me off."

"Well, fair enough then. You gotta love the shouting, or it's just not the life for you. How's your family, by the way? They pulling through okay, got enough supplies?"

Kipper shook his head in exasperation.

"Look, what the fuck is this? I have a major disaster on my hands. Eighteen people dead. And you call me in here to make fucking small talk."

The major walked over to the door and carefully closed it, cutting off the growing hubbub from the corridor outside.

General Blackstone spoke up as he did so.

"The last time I checked," he said, "we had a lot more than eighteen dead. When last I checked, our casualty count was well over three hundred million, Mr. Kipper. So I have some sour news for you, sir. Get over this morning. It was a minor fuckup. There will be more of them."

"A minor . . ."

"That's right. And there will be more of them. More death. More chaos. Get used to it. And get used to dealing with it.

Because if we don't deal, it's game over here. In this city. Everywhere."

Kipper waved away the cup of coffee McCutcheon held out.

"What are you talking about? If this morning was your idea of dealing with things, then yeah, we're fucked."

"Look, this is kinda delicate," said the air force man, taking a perch on the edge of the desk, where he could look down on Kipper. "We've got a bit of a problem with the council, I'm afraid."

Kipper shrugged. He'd wondered how on earth the military was going to go on working so closely with a group of people who were almost their antithesis. "Well, apart from this morning, things do seem to be getting done," he offered. "All my department's requests are going straight through the Special Means Committee and getting approved without any questions. What's the problem?"

McCutcheon sort of whistled inward, which Kipper recognized as the universal sign of bad news coming.

"Well, the thing is, we don't really have a Special Means Committee," he confessed.

"What?" asked Kipper, completely dumbfounded.

Blackstone leaned forward.

"I had them arrested three days ago."

McCutcheon actually looked embarrassed for a second.

"Yeah. And we've been kinda winging it ever since."

24

Playa Revolcadero, Acapulco

The roadblock was almost professional: four old cars arranged in a herringbone pattern that forced any oncoming traffic to slow to a crawl as it negotiated a winding course through the obstruction. A dozen armed men, locals by the look of them, lounged on the hoods and inside the vehicles, passing around bottles of no-name tequila and Dos Equis lager, and smoking an assortment of cigarettes and reefer.

"We could take that left," suggested Fifi, pointing to a narrow side street, which remained open to traffic, just before the roadblock.

"No," said Shah without hesitation. "Too narrow. Nowhere to go. And they have weapons on the roofline and windows above. We must reverse immediately or go through."

"Drive on," said Jules. "But slowly. Don't spook them. They're probably just shaking down the *turistas*. I'm sure we can talk them around to leaving us be."

She lifted the dark gray Franchi SPAS-12 autoshotgun from the improvised gun rack Shah had installed on the dashboard of the Jeep Cherokee, and jacked a round into the chamber. Behind the wheel Sergeant Shah—they'd all taken to calling him that now—slowed the vehicle and made sure his own weapons cache, a pair of MP5s, was close to hand. In the backseat Thapa and Fifi readied themselves.

They had almost managed to drive right up to the edge of Acapulco Diamante, the most exclusive tourist enclave in the city, but the roadblock brought them to a halt a couple of hundred meters from the start of the private resorts and clubs. Jules had been expecting trouble even earlier, which was why the jeep was equipped with so much firepower. Until now, however, the sight of a few gun barrels lazily produced out of the windows had been enough to negotiate passage through the town, where most of the violence they encountered was still small-scale and anarchic.

"Sergeant Shah, if you wouldn't mind, I think Fifi and I will handle the negotiations. A prominent display of your willingness to kill anybody who interferes with us would help, of course."

"Of course, Miss Julianne."

The former noncom brought them to a halt at least twenty-five meters from the blockade. A lot of the men up ahead were carrying rusty revolvers and forty-fives, which were unlikely to hit anything they aimed at more than ten meters away. And most of them appeared to be drunk or stoned, which further called into doubt their chances of deliberately targeting anybody. There was a lot to be said for volume of fire, though, and they had plenty of that to go around.

Jules slipped a pair of sunglasses down over her eyes and stepped out of the jeep, fitting a radio headset. Fifi emerged behind her, already wearing her commo gear, the same sets they'd used back on the *Rules*. Immediately the wolf whistles and catcalls began. It was almost comical, really. It was a hot, bright day and both women were dressed in shorts and hiking boots. Jules wore a Level III-A armored vest over a white T-shirt, but Fifi had only a sleeveless checked L. L. Bean to protect her. She'd knotted it, exposing a long expanse of tanned, finely muscled midriff, and most of the would-be desperadoes were torn between which of the *chiquitas* they wanted to objectify and harass the most.

One guy stood out from the rest, simply because he didn't ogle them or grab his crotch. He just stared cold and hard at the four gunned-up intruders.

"That'd be our guy," Jules whispered into the mike. "He's mine."

"Gotcha," said Fifi, who took her much-loved Russian PKM from Thapa at that moment. Jules was almost certain she felt the ambient temperature drop as her blood began to run cold.

"What's happening back at the car?"

"Both Shah and Thapa are good to go, if they have to."

"Are they being obvious about it?"

"Yup."

"Excellent *and* . . . Good morning, *señor.* This is your turf now, I suppose?"

Jules favored the gang leader with the full wattage of her smile, holding the shotgun so as to squeeze just a little more cleavage up into his face.

"You presume I speak English, no?"

"You look like an intelligent, educated man. Well-traveled and worldly-wise. It's a reasonable assumption." She beamed at him. "Especially when you use big words like 'presume.' "

In fact he looked like the worst sort of bad news. Sober and mean and not likely to be sweet-talked or bullshitted into anything he didn't fully intend to do.

"I am the block *capitán* here now," he informed her. "I coordinate security for the Mayan and Fairmont resorts."

You mean you're shaking them down for protection, she thought.

"Well, that's excellent," said Jules. "Because that is where we are headed this morning. So if you'd like to provide an escort for me and my friend here . . ."

Fifi winked and grinned, while never taking her finger off the trigger of the PK.

"Howdy, *Capitán*."

". . . we'll be on our way," Jules continued. "We have business up there, Mr. . . . ?"

"What business?"

He was instantly on guard, alive to the possibility that somebody might trespass on his turf. She wondered about his backstory. He seemed too smart for a street thug, and yet he'd gathered a vintage crop of them around him. There seemed no obvious structure to his crew, no settled hierarchy of lieutenants or enforcers. He might be telling the truth about them providing a form of security to the resorts. After all, Shah and his men had hired out to do just that to pay for their former lodgings, and of course they were now doing the same for her.

"There are some American citizens in the resorts," she improvised. "Their government has arranged evacuation and we're providing . . ."

"They have no government," he cut in. "It is gone."

"Not all of it." She smiled disarmingly. "Not the part with all of the guns and tanks and stuff. You know. The military. There's a good many of them still hanging around, and if you can still get a news service you'll see that they're organizing safe passage for any U.S. citizen who wants it. We're just part of that service. We're . . . contractors."

She shifted the Franchi, a big, heavy-hitting piece of artillery, just to remind him of his proximity to it.

She dropped her voice, however, so that only she and the *capitán* could hear.

"Let me guess what's happening here, *puta* . . ."

Jules noted the instant flush of anger to his face. She could tell he wanted to bitch-slap her for that, but the shotgun stayed his hand.

"You probably had a couple of your crew back there take a few potshots at some of the guests. Maybe they roughed up a gringo or two. And then you magically appeared to offer your services to preserve them from the attentions of such dreadful ruffians. Of course, a premium service like you're providing doesn't come cheap. There's all the men to pay, the equipment to maintain, and the smokes and the beers and the three-dollar whores don't come cheap, do they? Well, except for the whores. And you plan on, what, holding them here until you've bled them dry? Is that right?"

A quiet smile was all the reply she received. Jules stepped in a little closer. Spoke a little more softly.

"You're obviously the brains of this operation. You look about a hundred times smarter than anybody here. What were you last week? A cop, a soldier, or something?"

He didn't answer, but then he didn't smack her down either. He was listening.

"So think about this, Professor. Think about how much more it costs you to buy a cup of coffee, or a beer, or a taco, than it did two days ago. Think about how the money you've been taking off these fat, white fools is worth less every day than the one before. You've noticed that, haven't you? Because you're the smart one here."

He nodded, almost imperceptibly.

"Think about how *quickly* that's happening. Ask yourself how long it's going to be before the money they have in there—" Jules motioned behind him, toward the protected enclave "—isn't good for anything but wiping your arse. How long will that be? Another week? Maybe two? Their money is going to be worthless a long time before you relieve them of it."

She could see that she'd struck a nerve; now she had to move quickly, before he'd made the logical connection and turned his guns around on the resorts. She moved right into his personal space now, but not in a threatening way. He had a good two or three inches of height on her, and she used it by turning her face up toward his and widening her eyes just a little more.

"This city is falling to pieces. You're part of that, aren't you? You know how it's going to be here very soon and you're setting yourself up as a new power. But you know what, it's not just you. We drove in here this morning. Some places are burning. Some looted. Saw a couple of bodies on the streets here and there. Saw plenty of guys like you, too. The marina where my boat's tied up, they've hired some muscle who would take these faggots of yours down in less than a minute. That's not meant to be insulting. They're just better equipped, better trained, better paid, too, I'd guess. Looks like a lot of ex-military types down at the marina. Like my Mr. Shah and his friend back there."

The *capitán* flicked a glance back at the jeep where the two Gurkhas stood, squat and utterly impassive. Between them they were more heavily armed than his entire crew. They fairly bristled with automatic weaponry, and Thapa even sported a kukri at one hip.

Jules was almost whispering now, softly and gently, like an old lover.

"Not many ex-mil types here though, are there, *Capitán*? Just you, really. You're the only true pro here, which means you know what'll happen if my guys back there open up on you. I'll get shot, almost certainly. Just because I'm standing so close to you. My friend Fifi, with that enormous Russian machine gun, she'll probably make it to cover because she'll put out enough fire to make sure nobody draws a bead on her. And Shah and Thapa, well, look at them. They're cold motherfuckers. They'll do the job. But your guys . . . well . . . I think we both know what'll happen when thousands of rounds of ammunition start heading toward them, don't we? So let's not even go there. Let's see if we can work something out between us, you and me, so that everyone's a winner. Perhaps you could start by telling me your name."

"Miguel Pieraro," he said quietly. "I am not police, no. I was vaquero. A cowboy . . . a boss of cowboys." His shoulders straightened with real pride. "But that was before. I worked in the north, by the border. I worked for an American cattleman, with large herds below the Rio Grande. I ran his business there. He supplied McDonald's."

Pieraro invoked the name of the Golden Arches with reverence and awe. Jules eased back a little, giving him some room. He was a proud man and very obviously cut from finer cloth than his comrades. The chorus of sexual taunts and whistles from the makeshift barricade had died away completely. All of Pieraro's men watched him closely, straining to hear what had passed between *el jefe* and the white slut.

"I will take you in myself," he declared. "We will discuss your proposal. You will have a proposal, yes?"

"I will," she agreed.

He nodded and called out to another man who was sitting on the hood of an old '79 Camaro, reclining against the dirty windshield. The car was a dinosaur, with faded red racing stripes to match a thick coating of rust and dust.

"Roberto, you are in charge here! I will take our new friends through to the Fairmont. Call me on the radio if you need to. The phones are useless."

Jules noted that like Miguel, Roberto was notable for being clean-shaven and sober. Where his boss was a tightly wrapped bundle of steel cord and knotted muscle, Roberto slid from the hood of the car in one fluid movement. He reminded her of a snake, uncoiling in the sun. In Miguel's position, she wouldn't have trusted him to sit the right way around on a toilet seat. Oh well, not her problem.

A few hand gestures from the two men saw their followers hurrying to turn over engines and reverse the cars out of their herringbone arrangement. Pieraro indicated that Jules should follow him, and she signaled Fifi to hurry back to the jeep. With the tension evaporating she allowed herself a few moments to check out the locale as she followed the former cowboy through the gauntlet of leering street toughs. They'd set up their *barricada* across an avenue most of them would formerly never have seen. Fab little fashion shops, jewelry stores, and cafés lined both sides of a street that had only recently been a well-manicured boulevard. She noted a Givenchy, a Prada, and an Armani boutique, all looted and burned out. Rubbish choked the gutters and sidewalks, and a couple of spent brass shell casings twinkled in the late-morning sun. Pieraro stopped at his car, forcing Jules to suppress a snigger. It was a micro, some sort of courtesy vehicle from the Fairmont resort according to the livery, not much more than two doors and four dinky little wheels. Pieraro caught her skeptical expression.

"It is new," he said. "And environ . . . *environmentally* sustainable."

"Does it run on tanning butter or something?" She smirked. She would have taken him for a muscle-car tragic. But then she'd taken him for a crooked cop, too, hadn't she?

"It is just for running about . . . with work," he emphasized.

She made sure the safety was engaged on the shotgun before climbing in. A misfire would probably peel off the entire roof.

"My name is Julianne, by the way. Jules, if you like," she told him as he climbed in and fastened his seat belt. "Do you mind if I ask you something?"

"Will you mind if I don't answer . . . should the question be none of your business?" he said. "I was an honest person . . . Not like you, *señorita, sí*?" he added pointedly.

"Really," said Jules. "Your little shakedown racket back there, you're earning an honest peso with that, are you?"

He started the car but didn't drive off.

"I have a family. Three children. I am providing for them. Those men back there, *my* men now, they have their own to look out for, too. Unlike these people—" He waved a hand to take in all of the Diamante district. —"they have nothing to fall back with. *La Desaparición,* it will hurt the poorest most."

Pieraro pressed on the accelerator and they pulled away.

"Your question, *señorita*?"

Jules shrugged. "I was just wondering how you ended up on that roadblock. But I guess you answered it. Three children. You were what? Holidaying? Visiting relatives?"

Pieraro snorted at the first suggestion.

"My wages, they would not have allowed me to clean the streets of *el Diamante.* I could not holiday here. We were visiting my wife's cousins farther south for a wedding when everyone disappeared. I came as far north as I dared to find work to support them. We have lost everything but our lives."

Jules glanced in the side mirror to check that the others were still with her. The jeep was only a few meters behind. She couldn't get a read on Pieraro at all. He looked like a hard case, and she could detect none of the primitive fear in his eyes that was such a part of the makeup of almost all street thugs, the knowledge that there was always someone harder and meaner than you just around the corner. She could sense anxiety leaking out of him, at the edges, where he couldn't keep his emotions completely nailed down, but it didn't seem personalized. If he was telling the truth about his family that might well explain it. She would have to play him very carefully. In many ways it would be a lot easier if he were a simple gang boss.

"I suppose I should ask how you ended up running that operation. Not a lot of call for herringbone roadblocks, snipers, and intersecting fields of fire in the cattle business, is there? Not even working for Mickey D?"

An arid smile cracked open the dark, sunburned rock of the cowboy's face.

"The catering manager of the resort, an American, once

worked for McDonald's in Houston. I met him on business many years ago. We drank a lot of tequila and he embarrassed himself. Eating the worm like a college boy. Well, he *was* a college boy, I suppose. I looked after him. I knew he had taken the job here so I came looking for work. Any work."

"I see." Jules nodded. "But security work. That's not your business."

"Men are my business. Running cattle and running men. You have never bossed twenty vaquero, no? I have bossed many more. Hard men. Not to be crossed. Much harder than those pissants."

Pieraro threw a contemptuous look back over his shoulder.

"Yeah, I get that. But let me take a shot in the dark. That Roberto guy? He really is ex-military or something, right? He handles the tactical side. Where to place your good shooters. How to set up the roadblock."

The cowboy remained quiet for a moment before finally muttering.

"He is Colombian. AUC. Autodefensas Unidas de Colombia."

"What's that, some sort of fascist coke-smuggling outfit?"

"Paramilitaries," said Pieraro before hurrying on. "So, you have a proposal, Julianne?" He pronounced her name "Chooley."

As the little car wound its way down toward Playa Revolcadero, the signs of breakdown and chaos in the social order became much less evident. The streets remained free of rubbish or indications of conflict. Huge villas and gated resorts sat quietly underneath palms and soaring canopies of transplanted tropicals. Few people moved about, apparently preferring to hunker down behind their high walls, but those who did didn't seem especially fearful or concerned. Jules scanned for any obvious signs of things beginning to fray, but found none. Perhaps Miguel was holding it back for now. She decided to take a punt on his honesty.

"You have three children, Miguel, right?"

"Yes," he answered. "Two girls, and a little boy."

"Would you like to get them away from here? From Mexico, I mean."

There was a slight delay before he answered.

"Very much so. What you said before, it was not all true. But some was. About how things will soon turn for worse. I have seen the worst of people. I know what to expect."

They began to travel downhill through a neighborhood of large modern houses, some of them set back within vast grounds. Jules caught the first sparkles of sunlight on water as glimpses of the bay showed through verdant greenery.

"Okay. Here's your deal. Passage out of Mexico for you and your family if you can help me put together a passenger list. A short one. High-value customers. People who can pay up front, right away, in euros, British pounds, or trade goods. Stones and jewelry, high-end stuff only. Gold, platinum, diamonds, and so on. I have a yacht that can accommodate two dozen passengers and the same number of crew . . . Well, I can accommodate a hell of a lot more, but I'm not interested in more. I'm not running a budget operation."

It was Pieraro's turn to fix her with a measured, vaguely contemptuous look.

"You have misread me today, Julianne. Taken me for something I am not. You, however, I can read very well. I have met your type before. You are not an honest person. You are not good. Good, honest people do not carry themselves with weapons into danger, real danger, like you did before, with such . . . composure, no? You are familiar with men such as that." He jerked his head back in the direction from which they had come. "You have used weapons such as this." A nod toward the SPAS-12. "You have killed people before. Yes?"

"When I had to," she said tightly. "When it was them or me."

"This I understand," he conceded. "But you must understand me now. If I help you, if I entrust to you the lives of my wife and children, your own life, it is entrusted to me then. It is held within my hands. Do you understand? If you give me reason. I will close my hands and take that life from you."

"I understand," said Jules.

Pieraro slowed down and stared into her eyes.

"Good. Then we have a deal."

25

Monique grunted and dropped to the ground like a puppet cut loose from its strings. A single round had felled her. Caitlin went down on the dirt under the angry buzz of bullets zipping overhead.

"Son of a bitch!" She rolled Monique over and grabbed her by the backpack. Strap in hand, Caitlin hauled the young woman toward the door of the nearest apartment block. She didn't pause to think, to examine her surroundings, to question the choices she was already making. Her largest handgun, the Glock 19, had quickly appeared, and it roared, biting huge chunks of wood and masonry from the solid timber apartment door.

Rather than screaming, Monique was gasping and grinding out an arrhythmic series of grunts, like somebody punched in the stomach trying and failing to draw air into their lungs.

Glass shattered, rounds zipped and cracked past her head to chew up the brick façade of the old, run-down tenement. The gunfire echoed against the brick-and-mortar apartment buildings. Caitlin logged the direction and volume of fire, and part of her mind calculated that they faced maybe three or four attackers.

Three? She looked out of the corner of her eye. *No, four attackers.* They emerged from a white van that had turned down her street just a minute ago. Four she could be certain of. But were there more? A second vehicle? A lookout who'd been scoping the street for hours?

Her boot slammed into the door, which flew open and crashed into the wall, and they were suddenly through, into a darkened passage that smelled of boiled cabbage and dog hair.

She dropped Monique on the threadbare carpet running down a long, poorly lit hall and spun back toward the street.

Caitlin holstered her Glock and hauled out both of her Steyr TMPs from the shoulder rigs under her jacket. Safeties flicked off, she held the weapons out around the corner of the door and unloaded both of them into the free fire zone of the rue d'Asnières in the direction of the van. The outgoing fire sounded like canvas sheets ripping in the high wind.

After three bursts, she took a quick peek to her left around the doorway to see what she'd caught.

A civilian, on a bicycle, lying in the center of the road, probably dead. Head shot.

(Shit.)

A small Fiat, faded blue paint, up on the sidewalk down near the rail tracks, smoke or steam pouring from under the hood. One flat tire.

Birds. Dead and dying birds everywhere.

A woman in a bright floral head scarf, cowering in the doorway of an empty boarded-up shop, shielding what looked like a child with her body.

Across the street from her, a dirty white van, parked at a slight angle in the gutter about fifty meters away, sliding cabin door open. One leg hanging out of the interior, twitching. Windshield smashed, horn blaring.

Three identified shooters there. All white males, dressed casually. Armed with FAMAS G2 assault rifles. One behind the van, possible leg wound. One crouched behind another vehicle, a gray, aged Volvo. The last one, aiming from a deeply recessed doorway fifty yards away across the street.

She snapped off two quick bursts at the man in the doorway.

The G2 rounds crashed around her, pulverizing the ancient red brickwork and forcing her to fire blind again. Caitlin emptied the rest of the Steyr magazines with much greater accuracy, however, having sighted her targets; then she turned back into the building and shoulder-charged the first door on the right. It gave way with a crack of splintered wood, and she tumbled into the small sitting room, taking cover below the window ledge, crunching broken glass underfoot.

In one quicksilver motion she slipped off her backpack and poured half a magazine of 9-mm hollow point from the Glock through the smashed windowpane into the street outside, mostly aimed at the shooter behind the Volvo, the closest, easiest target. Chances of nailing him were low, but she could at least keep the fucker bottled up. Monique moaned loudly just outside the room, and glancing back over her shoulder Caitlin saw her legs begin to scythe and kick in reaction to the burning pain that would now be making itself felt. Gut-shot by a military assault rifle. There was gore and leakage everywhere.

Caitlin knew exactly the location of a couple of morphine syrettes in one of the bags, but to attend to Monique would mean ceding the initiative to their would-be killers.

She opened her oversized pack and pulled out the artillery. The pistol-grip Benelli shotgun came first, customized twelve-gauge, extended mag with a sidesaddle shell carrier. Next came the deal closer, a specially cut-down Heckler & Koch UMP 45, with an extended box mag housing thirty rounds of .45-caliber Smith & Wesson goodness. She slung the H&K over her shoulder.

It was a large, excessive arsenal for just one young lady to haul around, but Caitlin very much adhered to her daddy's rule that when it came to guns it was always better to have 'em and not need 'em than the other way around.

She picked up the shotty, jacked a cartridge into the chamber, and poked the muzzle out through the shattered window. The Benelli was loaded with a buck'n'ball combo that gave her a nice spread for quick and dirty area clearance, but still packed a nasty surprise in the form of one larger, molybdenum-disulfide-coated brass slug at the center of the load. Unlike softer malleable rounds, it was armor-piercing and would slice through a car door or ballistic vest without bothering to slow down much.

She methodically pumped half a dozen rounds of buck'n'ball downrange, angling to do some damage to the men behind the vehicles, but occasionally raking a shot along the front of the building to shut down their partner in the recessed doorway. She briefly heard a few distressed cries and more shouting upstairs and the hammering of feet on bare wooden boards, but then the uproar of her sustained gunfire drowned out everything else.

I need to get a handle on this fucking mess, she thought. She was still firing blind, however, attempting to disrupt the flow of her opponent's advance and hoping for a lucky hit.

The briefest of lulls drew her attention upward again, to the sounds of renewed panic. She let loose with another four shells from the shotgun and then ran, reloading, clearing the ruined sitting room and bouncing off the slimy, plastered wall of the apartment's main corridor. She leapt over Monique, who was writhing and crying pitiably—"*Hold on, baby! These fuckers are gonna regret getting out of bed today*"—then sped for the internal staircase, slipping the shotgun over her shoulder and bringing the Heckler & Koch into play.

After bounding up the steps, she swung around at the first level and raced for the front of the building. An open door led onto a small bedroom just ahead, and she rushed in, grateful to find that there was no baby in the cot pushed up against one wall. She thumbed the selector on the machine gun to full auto. One of the reasons she liked the H&K was its relatively low rate of fire, a modest six hundred rounds per minute, which in the hands of an expert operator made the burst mode all but superfluous.

Caitlin looked out the window with a black widow's smile.

Two of the three were crossing the street, giving her a clear line of fire.

"Thank you, gentlemen," she said. "Much obliged."

The operatives both squeezed off covering fire as they crossed the road. The dense rapid crack of their FAMAS rifles was painfully loud. They edged forward, right into her sights.

Her movements were quick and machinelike.

One sharp pull on the trigger shattered the window, and as the men instinctively looked up, she nailed the pair of them with short auto bursts, aiming for the center mass and letting the muzzle drift upward to punch a couple of rounds into their skulls. The first man simply looked surprised, his eyebrows raised comically and mouth a perfect O before five rounds stitched him up from the sternum to the forehead. His head all but disintegrated. The second attacker was fast, well trained, but doomed. He managed to get his muzzle up a few inches and even squeezed off one misdirected round before Caitlin nailed him in the same way. A fan of blood and brain matter painted the side of the car next to which he died.

More. There have to be more of them, she screamed silently at herself.

She didn't pause, leaning back from the exposed position and holding the gun forward, angled down, to let rip at the guy who had been sheltering in the doorway. There was no direct line of sight, but Caitlin fired from memory, confident she could at least keep him pinned down. A woman was screaming nearby, and downstairs she could hear Monique's own guttural cries of pain becoming more ragged and intense, more animalistic in their abandonment.

"Shitfire!" spat Caitlin.

She took half a second to scan her immediate surroundings and plug them into a larger mental map of the world outside. A triangular block, typical of the streets of Paris, was her battlefield.

Time to slip backasswards.

Setting off at a sprint, she charged down the first-floor internal corridor, a dank, evil-smelling space. She headed away from Monique, from the cries of the tenement's occupants, moving as fast as possible for the rear of the building. A closed wooden door loomed ahead of her, and she went straight through it, shoulder-charging the old wooden frame, which disintegrated in a storm of splinters and dust. A faraway part of her mind thought "termites."

She'd been expecting either a small storeroom or water closet. It was the latter, as filthy and unkempt as the rest of the place, but she didn't care. A sash window, gray and completely opaque from grime, opened onto a rear courtyard. The pulley ropes were broken and hung uselessly, one of them trailing its frayed end through a petrified blob of toothpaste. Caitlin ignored it, safed and shouldered her weapons, and hauled herself awkwardly through the window.

It was a straight drop into the muddy courtyard. No shed or ledge to step on. She levered herself out, hung down as far as possible. Then she pushed out and dropped. Her knees folded up under her just as she had been trained by the good folks at the U.S. Army Airborne School at Fort Benning.

There was nothing elegant about the move, which ended with her rolling in the wet earth. The submachine gun squelched underneath her, digging painfully into her ribs, but she mostly kept the Benelli out of the muck, and with no time to check and clean the guns, she chose that as her primary. Pulling more shells from the sidesaddle, she finished reloading on the run toward the small wooden fence separating the courtyard from the next property.

The muted rattling cough of the FAMAS reached her, adding urgency to her flight. As she stood, however, a wave of disorientation swept over her and threatened to steal her balance. Caitlin took one precious second to stand perfectly still, draw in a fresh breath, and attempt to center herself, to gain some measure of control over her traitorous body. Then there was nothing for it but to forge on, leaning forward into the vertigo that seized her and biting down a rising tide of bile trying to erupt upward out of her stomach.

She leapt over the wooden fence, catching her jeans and almost crashing down in a heap on the other side as she lost her footing on a dead pigeon. Her momentum was enough to carry her forward, however, and she brought the shotgun around, flicked off the safety, and jacked a round into the chamber.

In front of her stood the rear door of a building facing onto the rue du Bac d'Asnières, one side of the elongated triangular block. From her point of view the quiet, uncontested side. The van was at the apex of the triangle, flat tires and all.

An empty bakery stood in front of her, if she recalled correctly. *This just might work.*

The small frosted window embedded in the door was covered with a wire grille, but there were no other obvious security measures. No wires, no cams, no back-to-base relays that she could spot. Her head was still spinning and her balance was off, but the door was a stationary target. She drove a powerful side kick into it just inches below the rusted lock. It gave way with a report like a gunshot, and she hurried in as the sound of more automatic fire drifted over the roofline from the street she had just fled. She entered a storeroom, mostly empty, with just two large paper bags of flour lying on the concrete floor. Rats had chewed both of them open. A doorway led through to the baking room, where big commercial ovens stood cold and unattended, presumably for want of supplies. Or perhaps the baker, more closely attuned to the city's increasingly serious hunger, had already taken his family and left.

Caitlin didn't give a shit. She found the door she was looking for, punched through it, and emerged into a flat dismal light that leached through the thick blanket of toxic clouds lowering overhead. Rain started to spatter down again, burning her eyes and exposed skin. A black crow, seemingly unaffected by the pollution, picked at the carcass of a squirrel in the gutter just in front of her. She swore at her lack of goggles, a pair of which lay in the bag she'd left with Monique.

The assassin was caught unawares by the strength of her feeling for the girl. They were not comrades, more allies of convenience, thrown together only because of the extreme circumstances of the last week. And she had never allowed herself to grow attached to a target or an asset, but neither had she ever been diagnosed with a brain tumor or woken up to discover that her whole world had vanished like a dream. As she ignored the increasingly difficult symptoms of her illness and pushed herself to the limits of endurance, Caitlin tried to convince herself that she was simply worried, quite reasonably, at losing the vital support of a key asset.

A rising, ungovernable anger threatened to overwhelm her as she remembered her last sighting of Monique, jackknifed in pain, bleeding out onto the filthy floor of the old tenement. She was a ditz, but she had stuck by Caitlin when, really, she would have been better lighting out on her own. If nothing else, the American owed her a settlement with whoever had shot her.

There were a dozen or more people milling about nervously on this street, flinching at the gunfire. A young man called out a warning in French—"*She's got a gun!*"—and they scattered like birds startled from a tree. Caitlin ran five doors down the street back toward the hairpin corner around which she'd walked with Monique a lifetime ago. When she judged herself far enough along she diverted in through an open garage door of an auto-repair business, yelling that she was the police and warning everyone to get down. She heard more cries of alarm and noted two figures in coveralls cowering out of her way, but ignored them.

This building sat on the point formed by the meeting of the rue and the rue d'Asnières and so it had no back courtyard. The only open ground it boasted was a triangular concrete apron at the apex of the two streets, which appeared to be used as a parking bay for the business. It was possible to cut right through the workshop and emerge, hopefully, behind the white van and the last shooter. She quickly weaved her way through, dodging around a couple of pits over which a new Honda Accord and an ancient Trabant were being gutted by mechanics. A pair of double doors, identical to the ones through which she'd entered, stood ajar, opening onto the wider thoroughfare of the rue d'Asnières. She could just make out the rear of the white van, splattered with blood, and an outstretched hand, lifeless on the sidewalk.

The FAMAS roared again, a long guttural snarl of fully automatic fire, none of it directed at her. Nonetheless her heart lurched forward. She saw smoke and a muzzle flash light up the darkened cave of the apartment entryway where the last shooter had holed up. The doorway of the building in which Monique lay disintegrated as the bullets struck.

Clearing burst, she thought. *Right where she's lying.*

Caitlin took a second to check the shotgun and finish racking shells into the magazine. It was good to go, as near as she could tell. After she reloaded her Glock with a full mag, she stopped to think for a moment.

What if there are more of them? There have to be more of them. Her eyes scanned the windows and rooftops, into stopped cars, taking in the few people still crazy enough to be on the street.

Nothing for it, she told herself. *Surprise is everything.*

The shooters lying on the sidewalk and roadway in front of her were dead. She hurried past the van, covering the man whose legs protruded from the rear cabin, but he, too, was gone. Bled out. The last-known gunman was inside the building, just out of her sight.

She sped up, crouching to drop below the line of the windowsill as she reached the front door. Shotgun up, trigger on a half pull, she took in the sight of Monique lying as still as a fallen log in the dark pool of her own fluids. Her head was a shattered mess of blood, gristle, and gray matter. She was identifiable only because of the stupid little protest badges she still wore on her old jacket. Fury boiled over inside Caitlin's head.

Oh, you filthy cocksucker, Caitlin swore to herself. *You and I will most certainly have a reckoning here directly.*

Bloody footprints led away up the stairs, and she heard the creak of a footfall overhead.

Oh yes, Caitlin thought, pointing her shotgun at the ceiling. *We'll have that reckoning right now.*

She pulled the trigger two, three, four times without giving a second thought to any collateral damage. Not a thought about the families who lived in the building or the cot she had fired over. Each blast gouged giant plumes of plaster dust and atomized floorboard, which erupted and dropped, coating the two women like a snowfall. She was rewarded with a strangled cry and a brief, uncontrolled snarl of gunfire, before a dead weight dropped to the floor above.

She looked over her shoulder, out the door behind her, still wary that someone else might show up. But there was no one in sight.

Taking off at speed again she rushed the steps for the second time that morning. A round in the chamber, the Benelli's muzzle described tight little arcs as she aimed where she expected to find the body.

He was still moving, but barely so. The last shooter, she hoped. Struck three times, once in the femoral artery to judge by the rivers of rich, almost purple lifeblood flowing out of him on the tacky brown carpet. He'd dropped the assault rifle in his dying spasm and Caitlin used her boot to kick it away, never once taking her aim off the back of his head. She heard a door open somewhere and yelled out in French again, "*Police. Get back!*"

The door slammed shut quickly. A child screamed endlessly somewhere in the building.

Cautiously approaching the downed man, she kept her eyes on his hands and feet, aware that even now he might lash out at her. In his position, if at all possible, she would have. But a thick, glutinous, gargling sound told her he was on the way out. She shouldered the Benelli again, where it clanked against the barrel of the Heckler & Koch. Her pistol replaced the long guns, and she dropped a knee right into the small of the man's back, jamming the Glock up against the base of his ear. A pellet had torn off a bite-sized chunk, and she ground the iron gun sight into the bleeding wound for emphasis. He groaned pitiably, but there was very little fight left in him.

"You don't have long, Pepé Le Pew. We both know that," she snarled in French. "But I could make the last few minutes of your miserable fucking life feel like an eternity."

To drive the point home she shifted her balance to focus her weight onto a rib that was protruding from an ugly chest wound. A weak, liquid groan escaped from the man beneath her as she felt a nub of bone dig into her knee.

"Okay. Two questions. First one. Did you shoot my friend downstairs?"

"I don't . . ."

The Glock gouged out a chunk of meat from his ruined ear, and he found the strength for a full-bodied scream.

"Yes. Yes. I did," he babbled. In heavily accented English.

"Question two. Who sent you?"

Lighter pressure was all she required this time.

The answer told her half of what she needed to know.

"Noisy-le-Sec."

An iceberg in her stomach.

Just as she'd thought. They were from the action division of the DGSE.

She didn't bother asking why.

This loser wouldn't have a clue, only a target. Her and Monique.

"Okay I lied. More questions. How many in your team? How many shooters? How many on overwatch?"

"Fuck you," he groaned.

Caitlin drove a short, sharp punch into his injured rib cage and he screamed.

"How many?"

But his howling did not abate. If anything it grew worse.

Her skin crawled, and every nerve ending under it seemed to tingle.

Time to go.

She stood up carefully, making sure to give him no chance of entangling her legs or feet, and then she fired once into the back of his head, silencing the caterwauling cries, before turning and hurrying back downstairs to Monique.

Not that she needed to hurry.

She already knew that her friend—and yes, "friend" *was* appropriate—was dead.

The body lay still and heavy in that telltale way, as though slowly melting into the floor under the pressure of its own dead weight. Black petals of light bloomed in her vision, and her head began to spin again, this time around the axis of a bright, sharp pain. Caitlin staggered against the wall, which seemed to fall away from her. She had to get out. She had to abandon her friend. More killers would be on their way. As the floor rushed up to slam into her face she thought she heard the dull metallic thudding of a helicopter. But it could have been her own heartbeat.

26

He was getting used to the chaotic, tumbling, white-water rush of events, to waking up in different cots, or beds, or a plastic picnic chair at some random transit point. Of course, Melton had experienced plenty of hurry-up-and-wait during his time as a ranger, and although he enjoyed a much greater degree of autonomy in his later career as a civilian correspondent, he was, in the end, still hanging around the army, which had raised "hanging around" to an Olympic standard event, interspersed with short bouts of furious ass haulage and seemingly pointless tail chasing. The thirty-six hours after he awoke in the field hospital featured plenty of each.

He'd been upset on returning from the mess tent to discover that Corporal Shetty was gone, evacuated on a medical flight to Ramstein. He was alone again, without friends or colleagues or even a passing acquaintance, before Corpsman Deftereos returned, this time with a set of three-pattern desert BDUs and a standard-issue brown undershirt and underwear. He was accompanied by an exhausted-looking female doctor, who gave the reporter a perfunctory once-over, checked his stitches, wrote him a prescription for some antibiotics, and signed off a travel order, ripped from a clipboard, and pushed into Melton's pocket.

"Congratulations," she said in a voice devoid of any spark. "You win a no-expenses-paid trip out of my ward and on into the next exciting phase of your own personal mystery tour."

He hadn't even drawn breath to ask what the fuck she was talking about before she was gone, administering more scrips and travel documents like some sort of malfunctioning vending machine. Deftereos, at least, had been a little more helpful, gesturing for him to stay exactly where he was for the next couple of minutes at least. Melton felt abandoned and more alone than he had in a long time as the two of them swept out of the ward, and he was on the verge of simply climbing back into his cot when the corpsman rushed back in, grabbing him by the arm and pulling him upright.

"No, really, you gotta get the hell outta here right now, sir," said Deftereos.

"Why? What's up?"

"What? You think they tell me anything? I don't fucking know, excuse my language, sir."

Deftereos was babbling, and noticeably distracted.

"Look, we just got word that we're shifting at least a third of our cases. Corporal Shetty scored a golden ticket with the Eighty-sixth Airlift while you were out. And you just lucked out with a civilian charter, to London. If I was you, I wouldn't even be here anymore. I'd be a dust ball, on my way to the fucking helipad. Now go!"

He pushed a small bottle of pills into Melton's hand. Vicodin.

"It'll help. With the shoulder and your finger," he said. "Don't worry about your kit. All your stuff has gone ahead. Now you gotta get going, too."

And with that he'd changed out of his scrubs and been given the bum's rush out of the tent and into the dust and harsh sunlight, to join a small throng of the walking wounded, all recently displaced and as thoroughly nonplussed as himself. They had just enough time to work up some really wild theories about battles gone wrong, bioweapon exchanges, hundreds of thousands of American dead and wounded, when a white bus with dark blue Hilton Hotel livery pulled around the corner formed by a pod of air-conditioned shipping containers a hundred yards away, and a navy chief stuck his head out of the rear door, roaring at them to get their worthless carcasses into the vehicle or they'd get left behind for good.

Melton remembered a short ride out to a vast helipad where civilian choppers of all manner and description vied with U.S. military helicopters for landing and takeoff slots. He remembered shuffling onto a Vietnam-era Chinook with an Australian aircrew, but missed a lot of that flight, after downing two of the Vicodin with a swig of warm bottled water. He vaguely recalled half an hour spent in some lavish civilian airport where he was at last able to fill the prescription for his antibiotics, at a markup of about a thousand percent.

Melton slept through a C-130 flight to Qatar, and ended up for a long spell in a giant hangar where hundreds of wounded marines and soldiers were laid out on stretchers if they were lucky, or if they weren't, on a makeshift line of bright orange molded plastic chairs. Groggy from the Vicodin and creeping exhaustion, he made his way toward a small mound of duffel bags that had been colonized by half a dozen Polish commandos. They all seemed in fine fettle, with their equipment stowed neatly in a pile to one side, guarded by one of their own, a huge blond stone monolith of a man.

"*Witam*!" He smiled in greeting, before holding up his hands to forestall a Polish-language landslide. "Sorry. That's all the Polish I know. Besides *piwo* and *piekna dzie . . . dzi . . .*"

"*Dziewczyna*?" grinned a small, wiry, heavily mustachioed man, the men's sergeant to judge by his chevrons. "Not much beer or beautiful ladies around here, my friend. Just stinky American boxheads, yes. Apologies if you are boxhead, too. I say it with love in my heart. And sorrow, too, great sorrow. Please sit, you are wounded, yes?"

Two of the Poles crabbed around and Melton eased himself down onto a couple of kit bags. They seemed wonderfully soft.

"Boxhead? No," he said grunting with relief at getting off his feet. "Not for a long time, anyway. Wounded, yes. Not too bad though. Just missing a few bits and pieces."

"Nothing to stop you enjoying *piwo* or *dziewczyna* though?"

"No." He smiled. "Nothing that bad. My name is Melton, by the way. Bret Melton. I'm a reporter, or was . . ."

He shrugged awkwardly and trailed off. It was simply too much effort to go into his CV, to explain his shift from *Army Times* staffer to itinerant freelancer for a slew of British arms trade mags.

"You guys been waiting for transport long?"

"Eight hours. Not long. Some here have been waiting many days. Some have died here. Not joking now. I am Sergeant Fryderyk Milosz. I do not joke. Pleased to meet you, Melton by-the-way. Okay. That was joke. Polish joke, yes? The best kind. By Pole."

Milosz flashed him a blindingly white grin and raised his

eyebrows with such comic élan that Melton couldn't help but laugh out loud. It hurt his shoulder dreadfully but he gave in to it anyway. It had been a long time since he'd enjoyed the abandon of real laughter. It seemed to loosen up Milosz's men as well, with some of them smiling and nodding, as their own tension and stresses eased off a little.

"We are going home soon," said Milosz. "But you, my friend, where do you go now?"

The man's eyes were dark pools of sympathy.

"London, I think," said Melton. "That's what my travel chit says anyway. After that, well, I don't know that there is an after that."

"No," agreed Milosz, nodding as though Melton had revealed some deeper truth. "Maybe nothing after that, no."

Melton waved his hands as if to say, *What the hell?*

Leaning back and taking in his surroundings, he couldn't help but dwell on how things were unraveling. There had to be nearly a thousand guys crammed into the baking heat of this hangar at the edge of a temporary base in the middle of nowhere. A lot of desert MARPAT, which meant marines. Mixed in with the MARPAT were some army and air force in the three-pattern desert BDUs like the fresh set Melton wore.

Marine, army, the few navy and air force he saw, all had the same look. The long stare, the slumped shoulders, postures crumpled in upon themselves. A few were crying openly, quietly, regardless of the severity of their wounds. Here and there Melton would spot a soldier looking at a snapshot or a Marine watching a saved video file on his laptop. Some were by the door, chain-smoking for lack of anything better to do.

One soldier, from the 101st Airborne, had a collection of dog tags in his fist. He rocked himself back and forth until someone passed him. Melton watched the soldier ask a number of times, "Who should I give these to? Do you know?"

Even when he got an answer, he didn't seem to hear it. He'd go back to rocking, back and forth, until someone else walked past.

A female marine over by a Coke machine covered in Arabic script was smiling, flirting with a half-comatose man on a cot. "When I get home to see my baby girl, it'll be all right. She lives in North Dakota with my grandma. I heard they made it."

Oh boy, Melton thought, taking in the glazed green eyes of the marine, a lance corporal. She looked right past him, not seeing anything but her dead girl smiling back from the past.

To Melton they looked beaten. Like men and women with nothing to live for. Milosz and his small band of brothers, however, they were still tight and looking forward to something. Home, family, a simple fucking ride out of the furnace. It was enough to keep their spirits up. Melton shook his head. Any place where soldiers gathered in great numbers always ended up reeking of sweat and stale breath, cigarettes, ration farts, and something more elemental, an animal smell of violence waiting to turn loose upon the world. But that musky scent had turned rancid and cloying in here. Even Somalia wasn't this bad, Melton thought. The rangers on the whole weren't beaten, nor were those pogues from Tenth Mountain, who'd done better than anyone thought they would.

Desertions, Melton thought. *These folks will desert or simply collapse if someone doesn't give them their spines back real soon.*

The giant metal fans droning away at the edge of the hangar merely pushed the vile atmosphere around, a gaseous slough of ill feeling and desolation. He was familiar with this. It was what happened when men faced the hopelessness of their circumstances and shrugged away any chance of redemption. It was what happened when men who were used to fighting for their lives gave up and said, "What's the point?"

Milosz let him alone for a few moments, but perhaps uncomfortable with the brooding presence that had just insinuated itself into his little group, he toed Melton's boot to regain his attention.

"So, Melton by-the-way. You have a theory, yes?"

It was such a weird, unexpected question that Melton shook his head as though a bug had crawled into his ear.

"Sorry. What do you mean?"

"A theory, about the Disappearance, no? I am interested in theories. Real theories with science and learning, not bugaboo magic for explanation. Like these Muslim pigs and their stupidity about Allah's will. So, your theory. Tell me."

Melton opened his mouth to say something but simply shut it again, shaking his head. Fact was, he'd heard any number of bullshit explanations and crazy-talk gibberish about what might have been behind the catastrophe. He'd heard as many backwoods Christians lay it all at the foot of God as there were bug-eyed imams rejoicing in Allah's vengeance on the infidel.

He'd heard whispers of secret government experiments gone wrong, black-hole laboratories, portals to hell dimensions, and alien space-bat biology missions that had scooped up hundreds of millions of lives with something akin to a giant butterfly net. He hadn't given any of them a second thought.

"I don't know, Sergeant. I don't even begin to know what happened, or why, or whether it can ever be reversed. I figure best analogy is we're like ants whose nest got hit by a lightning strike, or a kid with a magnifying glass on a sunny day. We're ants. What would we know about anything? Either of those things, they'd be the end of the world to us, but you stand outside the situation, you get the context in a way that we don't have, and it's probably something really simple . . . that we're a thousand years from understanding. Possibly we'll never understand it. My bet is, a thousand years from now we'll be back living in caves banging rocks together for a living."

The Polish noncom narrowed his eyes and dipped his head in acknowledgment.

"*This* is a wise man," he said to his troops. "You see. He knows what he cannot know and does not pretend otherwise. This is wisdom, Jerzy."

Milosz pointed to a younger, black-haired youth and spoke in a rapid garble of Polish. Melton had the impression that he was repeating what he'd just said. The young commando shrugged, conceding a point.

"So what about you, Sergeant. No theories for you?"

Milosz smiled sadly.

"It is like you say. People groping through the dark, grasping at this and that, trying to explain what cannot be understood. My question, I ask it of people because it tells me how they are now. Whether they will get through or not."

"You think people will 'get through' based on whether they believe in conspiracy theories, or magic, or the will of God?"

"No. People will survive this; some because of luck. If you have no food to eat, no warmth in the deep of winter, it doesn't matter whether you think little green men or Muhammad broke your world. You will still die frozen and hungry. But if you have enough to eat, just enough, and if you have some shelter and safety, again just enough, then maybe your living or dying might have something to do with whether you fall to madness and superstition, or whether you hold on to your rationality."

A small, indulgent grin sketched itself onto Melton's weathered features.

"You're a materialist then? Of the dialectic school? I thought Poland was done with all that."

"Yes, I am a material thinker, like my father, a mathematician, and you are no boxhead, Melton."

"It's foolish to assume that just because somebody puts on a uniform and takes orders they turn off their brains. You didn't."

"Excellent," beamed Milosz. "It is good to talk like this, Melton. So much of soldiering is crudity and ugliness, yes. But there is more to the profession of arms, and to life itself. We soldier so our children won't. For us, guns. For them, books and easier lives."

Melton gestured helplessly. "I never had any kids. Gotta say I'm real happy about that now." He didn't look back over at the marine lance corporal. She was still talking about her girl in North Dakota. Someone came over, checked the man on the cot, took his pulse. The orderly pulled a blanket over the man's head and made a note on the clipboard, but the lance corporal didn't notice. "But if I had," he continued, "and they hadn't disappeared, I don't know that they'd be looking at an easier life than I had."

"Not now, no," conceded the Pole.

Three trucks pulled up at the vast hangar doors and able-bodied troopers began unloading more litters from their rear cabins. Corpsmen and a few nurses appeared and hurried over to help them, but otherwise there was no appreciable reaction to their arrival. Men still sat and talked in low voices in their own small, closed groups. Country-and-western crooners still clashed with speed-metal shrieks and hardcore rap from dozens of portable stereos. Listless card games of hearts and spades continued without pause. The *bleep-blee-bloop* of Game Boy systems never faltered.

"And what now for you, Sergeant? Home to your families?"

Milosz nodded, but there was a grimness to his expression that belied any sense of release or deliverance. A couple of the other Poles appeared just as somber.

"Home yes. We hope."

He waved his hands in the air, a concession to helplessness.

"If we have not been forgotten. Or abandoned. Or lost."

He shrugged.

"But we may not see our families even if we do get home. There will be much work to be done. Our sort of work."

"Fighting."

"Of course. You have seen what happens when things go bad, Melton. In Polish history, there is much fighting. Russians. Germans. Who knows who will come now? Maybe Tartars and Ottomans again. Once even the Swedes invaded. I doubt they would again. They are a soft people now. But not everyone is soft, no? The jihadi pigs I am fighting in Afghanistan. They are crazy men, but hard. The Iraqis, not so hard, but bad, and led badly. Weak men are often the cruelest. And Russia, a sick place, but still peopled with ruthless boyars and commissars and would-be tyrants. This Putin, watch him. He is an iron fist hanging over all of us. So yes, Melton, fighting. Always fighting. Fighting big, between states. And small, between people for little things. Food, water. Basic things. My brother, I spoke to him for three minutes on American phone yesterday. Nothing he has to eat for two days. Just some dried crackers and little tinned foods for his children. Nothing in market. It is like communism again. And now, with the poison clouds, no harvests I will wager."

His men were nodding, and Melton wondered about their grasp of English. If he recalled correctly, GROM operators needed a working knowledge of at least two languages other than Polish. He supposed there was a fair chance that all of these men did speak English with some fluency, given the Anglophone nature of the coalition. And doubtless this was a topic that had been chewed down to the gristle among them. He wished he had taken notes, or recorded the sergeant's lament. He was sure he could sell a story based solely on snatches of interviews taken with the men in this hangar, or with those men and women with whom he'd traveled to get here. An old, nearly burned-out spark flickered somewhere inside him, and he reached inside his jacket pocket, searching for the digital recorder he kept there. It was gone, but he had a pen and a notebook that he had lifted off someone's desk over the course of his journey from Kuwait to this hangar. His writing hand was uninjured, but holding the pad in his heavily bandaged left hand was awkward.

He looked at the lance corporal by the Arabic Coke machine one last time.

Don't end up like her, he swore to himself.

Melton raised an eyebrow at Milosz and asked, "Would you mind? I don't have any of my gear. My newspaper is gone. But I'm still a reporter. I shouldn't be sitting here on my ass feeling sorry for myself. I should be telling stories. Your stories. Would you mind?"

"Of course not," the sergeant said, holding his arms wide. "I am always interested in hearing myself talk. And these, my poor little bastards, they have no choice. They have to listen. Why should they suffer alone? Yes, Melton, of course you can tell my stories. Where should I start? With our attack on the Mukarayin Dam? Yes, that was us. We flooded Baghdad. Everyone thinks it was Green Berets. Pah. Hollywood pussies! It was GROM."

Melton couldn't help but take a quick glance around to see if any Army Special Forces were around to hear that remark. If they were and they heard, they didn't make themselves known.

Still struggling with his pen and paper, Melton came up short. The Polish special forces were not an old and venerable outfit. They had only been established in 1991. But they already had a rep as a very closed-up shop. You rarely heard of them, and they never did press. Yet here was one of the senior non-coms suddenly happy to give up details of a mission that he would have denied even happened just last week.

Milosz had no trouble translating the American's puzzled look.

"Do not be surprised, Melton. Everything has changed now. I will tell you about Mukarayin because it suits our purposes."

"How so?" he asked.

"It is like I said, there will be much more evil in the world soon. There is already, yes? My country, she has suffered more than most through her history. But not this time. Or not without making others suffer for what they might do to us. I will tell you about Mukarayin because you will tell the world, and then she will know, we Poles will not be plowed under again. You know what most people see when they imagine Polish army? They see horsemen galloping off to charge Hitler's tanks. Brave but stupid. And doomed. But now, if you tell them about Mukarayin, in future when people think about Polish fighting man, they maybe think about that dam blowing high into sky and that mountain of water flooding out and drowning city of Baghdad. They will think twice about wishing evil upon us, yes?"

"Yes," agreed Melton. "I think they will."

It was more than he had imagined writing about. He'd been more interested in Milosz's story of calling home and talking to his brother, of being trapped in the broken machinery of a vast war machine, suddenly cut off and alone in a hostile world. And he did take that interview, but he also filled half of his notebook with stories from every man in Milosz's extended squad— GROM usually operated in teams of four—about blowing the dam that flooded Baghdad.

As he did so, the strangest thing happened. A small audience began to gather around them, just two passing Cav troopers at first, but increasingly building up into a circle of attentive listeners that drew in even more men and women by virtue of its novelty. After ten minutes Melton was sure that more than two hundred people surrounded them, perhaps the majority of the walking wounded in the hangar space. The Polish operators spoke into a rapt silence, but occasionally someone would call out, confirming a detail of their story, or some would clap or cheer like believers at a revival meeting.

The specialist from the 101st Airborne stood over him, with a fistful of the dog tags, his eyes clear now. "Sir?"

"Yes, Specialist?"

"Can I . . . would it be okay if I told you . . ." The specialist held up the dog tags.

There must have been twenty or more of the tags, some of them with blood and skin on them.

"Sure, Specialist," Melton said. "Tell me what happened."

"Hey." A marine stepped forward. "Need a recorder, Mr. Melton?"

Melton took it and smiled. "Just call me Bret."

When the dog tags had been reattached to formerly breathing, living, loving people, the army specialist moved away. The batteries were low, but a Brit stepped forward with a set of AAA batteries. Melton talked to the marine who loaned him the tape recorder until the tape ran out. He took the tape out and offered the recorder to the marine, who had a boy, a girl, and a horse named Eagle back home, but the man shook his head.

"No, Bret. You keep it. You need it more than I do." He fished around in his pocket and pulled out some fresh tapes. "I don't have anyone to record messages for anymore."

The marine stood up, squared his shoulders, and moved out of the hangar. At the door he collected a rifle and a helmet from another marine and they walked out into the searing Qatar daylight.

Melton had no idea where he would place the interviews, or what form they might take. But he kept scribbling and taping, encouraging people to talk about . . . well, whatever they wanted.

"So the bastard was up in the ceiling," Private Adrian Bennet said. "He popped four in my squad before we finally figured out where he was hiding."

"Our convoy got cut off." A Native American army private, Piewesta, shook her head. "We took a hell of a lot of fire and my friend Jessie, she was in the back of the Hummer when we got hit. She didn't make it."

"That was a hell of a mess," someone added. "Five-oh-seventh Support Battalion, right?"

Piewesta nodded.

"The bullets came flying from everywhere," said an Apache pilot, half of his left foot missing. "Hell of a thing, Bret. I thought I was home safe after knocking down those three Iranian helicopters, but then all of this ground fire comes up. Like being trapped in a Mason jar full of lightning bugs. Just wasn't my day to be flying."

Bret noticed that the pilot didn't mention his gunner. Probably didn't make it, he decided.

"She just wouldn't sink," a sailor from the USS *Belleau Wood* said. "That Iranian sub put three torpedoes into her but she wouldn't go down. We were trying to get the fires under control when we got word to abandon ship. We could have saved her but they said resources were tight. Better to scuttle her."

A Tarawa-class LHA lost, Melton thought. Scuttled. The navy hadn't lost a ship that large in combat since World War II.

The sailor smiled. "We got that fucking Kilo sub, though. ASW guys from the *Nimitz* got us some payback on that bitch."

"Hell, yeah," someone else said. Others took up the chorus. "Hell, yeah. Payback."

He heard a seemingly unending stream of combat horror stories. Units cut off or abandoned. Enemies suddenly materializing out of nowhere. Supplies running out. Air cover disappearing. Waves of Iraqi troops flowing toward them, suddenly disappearing inside great roiling walls of flame, or enormous volcanic eruptions of high explosive dropped from miles overhead. He heard small, intimate stories about men killing each other with whatever weapon came to hand. About a female truck driver, trapped in a hostile village, crawling out via the two-thousand-year-old sewage system, and souveniring a couple of old Roman coins she discovered on the way.

Night had fallen, and half of the hangar's floating population had been spirited away before he finally stopped. Both hands ached, but his missing finger tormented him with a particular ferocity, and his wounded shoulder throbbed with a deep, agonizing bass line from having sat hunched over his notes for so long. But Melton thought he had enough material for a whole book, including a wrenching series of personal stories about what people had already lost. Families, home, friends, everything.

He made an effort to gather testimonials from the handful of Europeans present, such as Milosz and his men, and some British tankers whose Challenger had been crippled by a buried mine. Fact was, they would sell the piece in whatever form it took. The hometown market for American stories had literally disappeared. When the Poles finally got their ride out, he was reading over the tale of a Scottish infantryman who'd been separated from his platoon in al-Basra for two days, but whose main concern remained the fate of his family's trout farm after a week of acid rain had killed all the stock. They all shook hands and wished each other well.

"Make them understand that there is a new Poland," said Milosz, taking his hand gently as they parted.

Melton looked around at those who remained. Not quite so many tears now. A few of them were snoring, sound asleep, jerking in the fit of a nightmare somewhere in their past. He heard a couple of guys laughing about a canoe trip they had been on, how drunk they'd been and the silly idiot with the yellow swimming trunks who wouldn't fall into the raft full of college coeds.

It was mid-evening, a cool, almost chilly night, alive with the rumble of distant air operations. He was tired and very hungry, and growing almost claustrophobic having been trapped inside for so long, even in such a large building. The last thing he'd eaten had been a protein bar, four hours earlier, and he just knew the table service in this place was going to suck. Until his transport batch number was called there was nothing for it but to wait. Having lost the pile of Polish duffel bags on which he'd been resting contentedly, he'd moved to one of the uncomfortable plastic chairs dotted about the facility. He remembered the poncho liner, which he still had from the specialist on KP back in Kuwait. Melton wrapped himself in the woodland-green camo snivel gear as the desert daylight heat turned to nighttime frigid. It was there, half asleep, haunted by visions of the mortar attack that had put him in the hospital, that Sayad al-Mirsaad found him.

27

Seattle, Washington

"You've gotta be fucking kidding me!"

Kipper was incredulous, outraged even. In fact, half a dozen emotions blasted through him like a hot desert zephyr on finding out that the military had arrested the elected city councillors, but mostly his feelings arranged themselves around incredulous and outraged.

"You can't do that. It's . . . it's . . ."

"Wrong?" offered General Blackstone.

"Yeah. That's right. It's wrong. It's fucking wrong in so many ways I can't even begin to count them. What? You guys couldn't get your own way so you just threw the switch on a military coup? For Christ's sake, you're dealing with a bunch of frightened, fucked-up nimrods who take three hours to decide which sorta cookies they're gonna serve up at council meetings."

"We knew you'd understand," said McCutcheon without a hint of irony. "That's exactly why we put 'em in the bag. They really do argue about the cookies, don't they? It's a big deal. I watched them do it last week. Amazing, man. Truly fucking amazing. Anyway, while they're banging heads over the catering arrangements *PEOPLE ARE DYING.*"

The last part of his routine he delivered in a parade-ground roar emphasized by pounding a fist on a stack of folders, which burst out from under the blow in an explosion of paper. Kipper jumped and looked over to Blackstone, but the general remained impassive. It was a bad-cop bad-cop routine.

"Look," McCutcheon said, instantly switching back to his usual calm and spookily cheery self. "They haven't been arrested as such. Just detained preventively."

"What the hell do you mean, 'preventively'?"

Blackstone answered for him.

"To prevent them being arrested before they fucked up so badly they really did get a lot of people killed."

"What? Like this morning?"

"Oh, grow up, Kipper," snarled Blackstone. "This is serious. We don't want to take over here. We don't want to take over anywhere. Hell, we're desperate for someone to tell us what to do, but nobody's putting a hand up. Everyone's arguing about fucking cookies."

"Bullshit, General, that's an exaggeration."

"No," said McCutcheon, tag-teaming him again. "It's a metaphor. For pointless, infuriating contention about complete fucking inanities. Like cookies, which I can assure you they did argue about, because somebody said they needed to start conserving food and so they spent three-quarters of an hour debating whether they were entitled to a packet of fucking Oreos at their meetings. This was just last Thursday, by phone hookup, during the worst of the pollutant storm. By phone hookup, Kipper. They were all *at home*. They could have eaten *their own fucking cookies*."

Kipper rubbed his tired, burning eyes, but it only made them sting all the worse.

"So what are you gonna do? Keep arresting people until you get someone you can work with? You gonna go all the way down to the dogcatcher?"

"If we have to," said McCutcheon. "But really, I've met that guy. He's a freak. Got that gimpy eye. Half of one ear chewed off. Wouldn't be a good look for the next president."

"President?"

"Yeah. That's what I'm talking about. We need a president. Pronto. If we don't get a handle on this situation, we're all going to hell in a handbasket."

Kipper bumped up against a filing cabinet, jarring his elbow on the corner.

"Shit! Who the fuck talks like that? Hell in a handbasket?"

McCutcheon's eyes twinkled.

"Granny Mae McCutcheon. Eighty-six this year and still skinning her own beaver . . . Oh, man, that didn't come out right. She's a trapper's wife. Or she was. Granddaddy McCutcheon passed back in '92. It was Clinton that eventually killed him.

Seeing that glad-handing cocksucker take the oath, it was too much . . ."

"Back on message, Major," said Blackstone. "Mr. Kipper. We have some command-and-control issues here, and elsewhere. Here it's bad enough, elsewhere it gets worse by an order of magnitude. That mess at your food bank this morning. That was a C-three issue. That's what happens when command, control, and communication breaks down. Blood. Gets. Spilled."

Kipper's head was reeling. He wondered if the heating had been turned up too high or if any contamination had made it into the building through the filters.

"Do you know anything about the line of succession, Kipper?" asked Blackstone.

"The line of what?"

"Succession," explained McCutcheon. "You know, the president gets whacked in a motorcade, the veep steps up to the plate and *bam!*—any hopes the enemies of freedom had of exploiting our temporary constitutional befuddlement are right down the crapper."

"Are you sure you're an air force guy?"

"Sure. Born and bred. Anyway, the line of succession. Focus, dude. Right? You with me? It's toast. We got nada. Nobody. Everyone we could have tapped for the top job is gone. Everyone we've approached since is like '*Oh, no, don't ask me, I'm too fucking busy. I got this fucking cookie crisis exploding in my face here.*' "

Kipper exhaled a deep breath he hadn't even realized he'd been holding in. That probably explained his dizziness.

"So, what do you want me to do about it?"

"About that? Nothing," said Blackstone. "That's our problem for now. But this city is yours. Kipper, you're now on the executive committee. You and your department heads. I need you to do a better job running this place than we've seen so far."

"Whoa! Wait a second. That's a political position. Only elected officials can sit on the committee."

McCutcheon shrugged.

"Only elected officials on the civilian side. And they're all unavailable now. So General Blackstone is the senior member, and he's appointing you and the other department heads."

"What are we? Your good Germans?"

"No, you're the only people we can rely on to keep this place from falling apart," said McCutcheon.

"You don't get a choice, Kipper," growled Blackstone. "The days of easy choices are over. You've been drafted. You can either get with the program or you can fuck off and we'll find someone who will."

"Jesus Christ, you people . . ."

"Yeah, wrestle with your conscience in bed, if you have to. But you need to decide whether you're going to help pull your city through, or walk away."

It was too much.

Kipper turned and stormed out the door.

Was it his imagination or did the Municipal Tower seem to be even more overrun with military uniforms than he'd thought when he first came in? Kipper shook off the thought. No sense getting paranoid. A lot of the support staff were scurrying about on fast-forward. A few saw him and looked relieved, others seemed even more frightened and just put their heads down, hurrying past.

The soldiers didn't seem to be intimidating anyone. Indeed, some of them looked pretty well spooked, too. But their very presence, in full combat gear, including their weapons, was enough to put the zap on anyone's head. And what the fuck were they carrying arms for anyway, what did . . .

Kipper pulled up in confusion. He'd been so angry, so unbalanced by the meeting with Blackstone and McCutcheon, that he'd stomped right around the corner into the planning department. Cursing quietly, he retraced his steps to the office of the city engineer, his office, a small suite of rooms behind a plain dark wooden door inset with marbled glass. It felt like a holy sanctuary right now. He pushed through, praying that he'd find no military people inside, with their feet up on his desk, guns lying on top of the filing cabinets.

He didn't.

Instead he found Rhonda, his secretary, a large and formidable African-American presence in a room full of frightened white folk.

"Kipper! Thank the Lord at last!" she cried out when she saw him. "We were beginning to worry that they'd arrested you as well."

"Not yet, Ronnie. Not just yet. So you've heard then?"

He smiled wearily at his team, or what was left of it. Barney Tench, his deputy and old college bud, who looked about as glum as Kipper had ever seen him; Marv Basco, the sanitation chief, a dead ringer for Larry from the Three Stooges; Dave Chugg, water, who looked a lot like Curly to Marv's Larry, at least when you stood them next to each other. And Heather. Sweet, fragile, freaked-out little Heather.

"Whoa. What are you doing here, darlin'? You should be at home."

"I wanted to come in," she said, sounding preternaturally calm. He wondered if she'd been medicated. Barney shrugged and shook his head.

"I dropped her at her apartment, Kip. But she talked some dumb grunt into giving her a lift back in."

Kipper sighed.

"Okay. Heather, I'm not sending you home again. But you shouldn't be here. You're in shock. Go and sit yourself down on that couch over there and do not get up again. Ronnie?"

His secretary nodded and bustled the girl as gently as she could over to the old brown couch in the corner. Heather didn't really protest or resist. When he thought about it, Kip understood. She had no friends or family in Seattle. Her work colleagues had been caught behind the Wave in Spokane. The only people she had left in the world were here, in this office. It would have been cruel to send her out again.

"So. You've heard about the council?" he asked.

They all nodded and mumbled that yes, they knew about the arrests now.

"Did you know you've been drafted?" he asked Basco and Chugg. "You're on the emergency committee now."

"No. Nobody's told us anything," said Chugg.

Kipper rubbed his neck, which felt stiff and very sore. He noticed that he still had a smear of dried blood on the back of his hand.

"Well, I met the guy behind the coup d'état a few minutes ago. General Blackstone."

"He's here?" asked Barney.

"Yeah. Hiding down in the deputy mayor's office."

"Did he have any explanation for this morning?"

"Said it was a fuckup, said we should get over it."

"Good Lord!" said Ronnie, who considered *heck* and *gosh darn it* to be pushing the boundaries of decent language. "He said that?"

"Close enough," said Kipper, as he leaned back on his desk. "He pretty much threw everything back on us. Said if we didn't want the city to die, we'd have to step up to the plate."

"And what about the councillors?" asked Barney.

"I have no idea. He's got them detained for protection or some crap somewhere. I dunno what that means, short or long term."

"Well, it sounds like this asshole feels perfectly free to lock up people he doesn't get along with," said Barney. "What'd you tell him, Kip?"

"I didn't give him an answer either way," he said, chewing his lip. "And I'm not happy. I'm a thousand fucking miles from happy. But he's right about one thing. No matter what we think of him, we have a responsibility to the city. We still need to get a handle on food distribution. As of right now there is no market solution to the problem of empty shelves because most of the market disappeared behind the energy wave last week. Priority number one is food. We have enough in aid shipments coming through if it's distributed rationally. If not, this city will die. It'll tear itself apart before we can work out how to feed ourselves."

He paused to look around. Heather had closed her eyes on the couch, but he had everyone else's undivided attention.

"I can't do anything about the politics. I'll talk to the army about letting the councillors go, but we have to proceed on the assumption that they won't. So, despite the fact that everything has changed, I don't see that anything has changed. We have a good plan to pull the city and the state through this. We just need to make it work. Which means we *are* going to need the military's help, no matter how difficult that might be to swallow for now."

Barney Tench shook his head firmly.

"I don't know about that, Kip," he said. "What these guys look like to me is fascists. My mom's family, way back when, they came from Croatia. You only got two types in Croatia. Fascists and commies. That's why Grandpa moved here. To get away from that bullshit. And arresting elected officials, no matter how useless, just because it's convenient. That's fascism. And I can't have any part of it."

"So what are you saying, Barn? You're going on strike? I need you, buddy. The city needs you."

Barney shook his head.

"You think I don't know that, Kip? My family lives here. Anything I won't do for you, I can't do for them either. But this dictatorial bullshit, I can't do. I'm sorry, man. Some things are just too important. I'll leave you a formal letter of resignation before I go. But I will go, and there's nothing you can do to stop me."

Marv Basco dipped his head. "Damn," he said. "Do you think Barney's right, Kip? Do you think we should all just walk off until the army agrees to get back in its box?"

Again, Kipper felt the weight of everybody's anxiety and expectations settle upon him.

"I don't know, Marv. I got no fuckin' idea. But I do know that if there had been a truckload of soldiers at South Street this morning like there was supposed to be, a lot of people would have lived, instead of getting shot down. I admire Barney's strength of conviction, but I can't afford it. I've got half a million people to look after, to feed and shelter. Half a million terrified people at that, all of them looking over their shoulder at that wave wondering if it's gonna decide to gobble them up any time soon. The only reason most of them haven't bugged out overseas is that nobody's willing to come in here and get them. If we still had transport out of here they'd be gone. I'd be gone. Nobody wants to be here, but here we are anyway, trapped. You ever seen what a trapped, hungry, frightened animal can do to itself? To anyone who gets too close? It's not pretty. So, if I can't get them out of here right away, I can at least do something about keeping them fed, and safe from the things I can guard against, like mass fucking psychosis."

He paused then, to calm himself down a bit. He was beginning to lose it, raising his voice and barking his words out. He sighed, and shook his head in apology.

"I'm sorry. But does anybody else feel like Barney? I need to know right now."

Nobody answered.

The burning rain had closed in again, early in the evening. The army's weather guys told him it was due to an isolated pocket of toxins caused by a series of fires that had ripped through Portland two days earlier.

Kipper was glad of the weather in one way. It meant he couldn't see the glow from the Wave. It was visible at night, high up in the tower, as if the devil had thrown open a furnace door on the far side of the mountains to the south. It was a good thing most people couldn't see it—that Barb in particular couldn't see it. He was supposed to go out with some of Blackstone's people tomorrow to inspect the thing "from a safe distance." Whatever the hell that meant. He didn't think he'd be telling Barb about that little day trip. Her idea of a safe distance probably meant Guam.

"I'll be going now, Kip, if that's okay with you?" said Ronnie. "I'll take Heather back to my place. She can sleep on our couch for a while. Poor child. She don't need to be alone."

Kipper turned fractionally and smiled at Ronnie.

"Thanks for staying and helping out, Ron. It was kind of a madhouse here today, wasn't it?"

"It surely was," she agreed. "And are you okay now, boss? Should I be pushing you out this door to your beautiful wife and child?"

"I'll be leaving soon, don't worry. I got no appetite for hanging around here at the moment. It's just that I have no choice."

Ronnie frowned at him.

"Don't talk like that, Kip. There's always choices."

"Yeah, but sometimes they all suck."

"Ha!" she laughed. "You sure you ain't a black man?"

Kipper pressed his face against the cool pane of window glass, beaded with millions of starry droplets of poison.

"Barney won't be the last one, you know."

"How's that?" asked Ronnie.

"A town like Seattle, people aren't going to stand for this takeover. And that's what it is, Ronnie. A military takeover, pure and simple. And I'm helping them do it. I should be stopping them."

"Oh, horse hockey! All you're doing is keeping people warm and safe and fed and watered."

"Keeping the trains running on time?"

"What trains?"

"Sorry. I was being obtuse. What I mean, Ronnie, is that I don't know if I can hold this place together. The council, let alone the city. I wonder if we shouldn't be planning to get the hell out of Dodge. I mean, look at that thing . . ."

She kept her eyes on him, rather than looking at the eldritch glow coming from just over the horizon.

". . . it took everyone, Ronnie. Everyone. Who's to say it's not going to jump out here and take the rest of us in two minutes?"

"Nothing," she replied quietly. "Nothing but my faith in the Lord. I know you're not a praying man, Kip. But I say some extra prayers on your behalf every Sunday to make up. And what the good Lord tells me is that nothing he does is without meaning. It all serves a purpose in the end. His purpose. And I do not believe his purpose would be served by laying another tribulation upon us. What is, *is*. This is for us to endure. For you to bear, Kipper. Whether you're a believer or not."

"I wish I was, Ronnie," he said. "I wish I was."

"So does Jesus, Kipper."

From anyone else, he'd have taken offense. But Ronnie and he went way back and he knew she meant only the best.

"You coming in tomorrow?" he asked.

"As if you need to ask."

"I'm sorry. I'm on the edge of a decision here. I think I'm going to confront Blackstone. Demand that he release the councillors and ease off on the restrictions on people."

"Set my people free?" smiled Ronnie.

"Something like that."

"And what if he throws you in the clink, too?"

"Well, we all have our choices to make, don't we?"

"We do. And I'm sure you'll make the right ones."

Kipper didn't reply at first, instead looking out the window at the largely empty city center. "You look after Heather," he said at last. "She's a good girl, but she's lost."

"She wouldn't be the first stray we took under our care. Or the last, I'll wager. And you look after yourself, Kip. Don't sit here all night. Get yourself home. Your family needs you, too."

"I will, Ronnie. Good night."

He turned back to the window as she left, staring out into the rain. The city was dark, with only a few lights burning here and there in offices where he could see other people moving around working. As he watched, a few of them flickered out, too. He tried to pick out the smoldering red light of the Wave but failed. The weather was really closing in.

Ronnie was right. Time to go home.

The walk back to his car was uncomfortable, the rain constant and stinging. They said a big chemical plant had gone up in the Portland blaze, and he thought he could feel it in the pores of his skin where the water soaked through.

The drive home was thankfully uneventful. No riots. No ambushes. Only the usual military checkpoints, through which he sailed without delay, thanks to a new upgraded pass from Blackstone. He tortured himself the whole way, wondering if he should have followed Barney out the door. If they all should have.

He could see candles burning in the kitchen at home as he pulled up, and a curtain twitched aside. He turned off the motor and hurried up the driveway as the door opened.

"Come in, Kip. Hurry up. That rain's gone bad again they say."

"Hang on, Barb," he said, shaking off as much moisture as he could on the porch, and removing his muddy boots.

"Come on. I've kept some dinner warm by the fire. And I poured you a whiskey."

"Thanks, darlin'. That's just what I need."

"Barney called," she said.

"Oh. He told you."

"Everything . . . I'm so sorry, Kip. All those people. You must feel awful."

He dried off with an old towel she handed him and closed the door. It felt good to shut out the weather.

"Yeah. It wasn't a great day," he said wearily. "And this thing with Barney and the council. I'm just . . ."

Barb shushed him and took him by the arm through the lounge room, where a small fire crackled and glowed in the hearth. A plate, covered in foil, sat near the flames, and a tumbler of whiskey waited for him on the coffee table.

"I'm sorry about this morning," said Barb. "I was a bitch. I shouldn't have put all that pressure on you. I'm sorry."

"Damn."

He squeezed his eyes shut.

"What?"

He looked at his wife helplessly.

"I forgot the fucking Piglet video."

She stared at him for a full second before they both burst out laughing.

28

Admiral Ritchie was right. Jed Culver, of the Louisiana bar, did not take three or four business suits along with him on vacation. He only ever took one, just in case. As soon as he'd learned of the Disappearance, however, he'd gone straight downtown and bought four new outfits, off the rack, but quickly tailored to fit his ample frame. As always they were either blue pin-striped and single-breasted, or charcoal gray, ditto. Two Brooks Brothers. One Zegna. And a rather subdued Armani. He put the charge on one of his European cards, a Visa issued by Barclays Banks in London, where he had worked for three years as an equity partner with Baker & McKenzie before moving home to set up his own firm. The Barclays Visa he normally saved for annual trips to Europe with Marilyn, but as of three days ago none of his U.S.-issued plastic was working. Diners, Amex, and MasterCard, none of them were any good. The local merchants had stopped taking them in payment or their billing systems simply locked up when presented with the account details.

For now, at least, there was no such problem with his English credit card. Even so, aware that some might think his use of credit an imposition on the goodwill and touching naïveté of Mr. Rajiv Singh, the owner of the high-tone gentleman's outfitter on Beretania Street where he bought all four suits, Culver explained exactly how quickly Singh needed to lodge his accounts this month, which was to say, immediately.

"And don't take no guff from those sons a bitches neither," he'd advised. "Get your money fast, and if you're in the market for some further and better advice, get the hell out of the suit business, too. Ain't gonna be much call for all these fancy duds soon."

Mr. Singh had not needed telling twice. Eighty percent of his business came from mainland tourists dropping disgraceful amounts of money on exclusive leisurewear. Business attire was a sideline. The next time Jed Culver drove past the shop it was closed. He never saw Singh again.

"Best damned investment I ever made," he said to himself while climbing into the jacket of his new favorite, the Armani.

"What's that, Jedi Master?" his wife called out, distracted, from the lounge room where she was glued to the television.

Culver tugged at his shirt cuffs as he walked through into the main living area of the Embassy Suites–serviced apartment. Marilyn, his third wife, and definitely his favorite, sat curled up at the end of the lounge nearest the TV, ignoring the glorious vista of Waikiki Beach and Mamala Bay in the floor-to-ceiling picture windows. The pollution storm had not yet reached this far around the world, and the best advice they had was that the worst of it probably wouldn't drift so far south anyway. Intensifying low-pressure systems were likely to draw the poisoned banks of cloud back up to the northern latitudes. Even so, Marilyn, a forty-year-old who looked thirty and sometimes acted twenty, remained at the end of the sofa, a black three-seater covered in a strikingly dense pineapple motif.

She was, he thought fondly, a bear of little brain, but such a beautiful bear, and so cuddly and loving that he couldn't help but love her all the more. She was just so much easier to live with than the harsh, angular, carnivorous bitches he'd married by mistake the first two times. (And if there was one upside to the otherwise unmitigated horror of the last week, it was realizing that those two life-sucking trolls had winked out of existence.) In comparison with Vanda and Louise, Marilyn's needs were simple, if expensive, and she gave him so much in return that he could only worry at the change that had come over her since the Disappearance. What she lacked in book smarts, his wife more than made up for in a vast store of emotional, physical, and spiritual resources. She was a woman who rushed at the edge of life, gleefully, like a child, chasing soap bubbles on the breeze.

Jed had never known her to veg out in front of the tube for such a long stretch of time, unless it was in front of Fashion TV in the weeks before they decamped to London and Paris each year. This last week, however, she'd camped in front of the box, channel-surfing between BBC World, CNN Hong Kong, Sky News, and whatever crisis-of-the-moment bulletins the local network affiliates were putting on air. Right now, she was seemingly mesmerized by an interview with some retired British admiral who wanted to blow up the Channel Tunnel and deploy the Royal Navy "to secure the approaches." Distracted by his murmuring in the bedroom for only a moment, she had now sunk back into video torpor. Jed shook his head and let her be.

Of his children, there was no sign, for which he was happy. Melanie, the only positive reminder of his first marriage, had taken the loss of her world like a physical blow. She hadn't wanted to come to Hawaii, and as soon as she realized that her mother and all of her friends back home were gone she'd spiraled into a black whirlpool of survivor guilt, crying in her bedroom for two days. Roger, three years younger, from one marriage down the line, dealt with the shock by putting on a brittle and entirely counterfeit stoicism as his game face. Jed had worried about it cracking open at some point.

"Have you seen Rog around?" he asked Marilyn, interrupting the Chunnel bomber.

"He's with Debbie," she said, only half paying attention.

"Debbie?"

"A pretty little thing. Down on one of the lower floors. You know. With the Girls Choir from Iowa."

As Marilyn spoke she seemed to emerge from a daze, sitting up and actually dragging her eyes off the screen.

"You met her mom, the air force lady," said his wife. "Remember? At breakfast the other day? When they ran out of muffins and toast."

He did remember now. All of the choir girls had at least one parent with them as a chaperone, and a few had come with all of their immediate family, dampening the shock a little. But Debbie's mother, an air force reservist, had been called back to active duty two days ago, and had been forced to leave her daughter in the care of the tour leaders.

"Oh, yes, I remember her. And Debbie. She is a pretty thing, isn't she?"

He was glad the kids had met, because like kids everywhere

they were totally self-obsessed, and given the current circumstances that was a form of strength.

Marilyn stood up, brightening.

"Yes. And Jedi, the girls are doing a concert tonight, down in the restaurant. Do you think you could get back for that? It would be lovely, don't you think, to do something nice? Everyone will be there, and the hotel manager will be hosting drinks afterward. To keep up our morale. I could wear a new dress. If I went out to buy one."

Another man might have brain-snapped at such vacuous babble, but Culver smiled indulgently. The curfew had been lifted somewhat in the islands, allowing people to get out for strictly rationed supplies, but he had no idea whether Marilyn would be able to find a clothing boutique that was still open, or that would accept her credit cards. Doubtless, knowing her, she would have a wonderful adventure trying, however.

"You knock yourself out, honey. And I will move heaven and earth to be at that concert."

He kissed Marilyn on the top of her head and loitered briefly by the picture window, squinting into the morning glare in the hope of picking his kids out of the small, scattered crowds down on the beach. A large but orderly swell pushed regular sets of clean barreling waves up onto the sand, and he knew that they would be somewhere down there, his children, Debbie, a handful of choir girls, and at least one or two parental chaperones, all playing in the surf, trying to keep their minds away from dark places. They were doing well at it, too, all things considered, and he sent a quick, silent prayer of thanks up to the Lord for that small mercy, especially for his daughter, who had found in her new friends a salve for the loss of so many old ones.

On the television the blustering admiral was gone, replaced by a handsome but harried-looking middle-aged man in a white shirt and bright yellow tie. He stood on what looked like the trading floor of some bank or brokerage house, and his thick East London accent was difficult to follow, but certain words tolled like funeral bells. "Meltdown . . . crisis . . . credit shocks . . . market collapse . . ." A ticker line of breaking news items scrolled across the bottom of the screen. Massed rocket attacks on Israel from southern Lebanon. "Preemptive" Israeli air strikes on dozens of targets in Syria, Iran, and even Egypt.

Another American destroyer, the USS *Hopper*, swarmed by hundreds of Hamas suicide bombers on Jet Skis. Food riots in Berlin. Street fighting between thousands of youths in Paris. More refugees pouring into Guantánamo Bay. A declaration of martial law in six Chinese provinces. A toxic supercell storm forming in the Bay of Biscay.

There was no question in Jed's mind what everyone was doing down on the beach below him. They were trying to ignore the end of the world.

"Bye-bye, honey," he said to Marilyn as he picked up his briefcase and kissed her again, on the forehead this time.

"Okay. I'll see you later, darlin'," she replied, surprising him with a fierce hug that almost pulled the two-hundred-pound lawyer off his feet. When they separated her eyes were puffy and haunted. "Everything's gonna be cool, isn't it, Jedi Master?"

It was one of those questions he wasn't meant to answer truthfully.

"Sure, honey. Everything's gonna be cool."

And he wasn't lying *exactly*. Things would probably be better for his family than most survivors, because Jed Culver had come flying out of the starter's gate, throwing himself at an overwhelmed administration, impressing the hell out of them with his extensive background in disaster management and civil-military relations, two bits of fluff on his résumé that might best be described as completely fictitious. Didn't matter. Nobody was going to be checking his bona fides for a long time, if ever, and the fact was, if you had to put a realistic description on his colorful employment history, you could do no better than saying that Jed Culver got things done and made sure they stayed done.

Indeed, he couldn't think of anyone better qualified to stick his hands into the fire and haul everybody's asses out with a minimum of singeing and whining. And if the price of that was his family getting looked after because he'd snuggled up tight to the surviving power structure, well then that was just a win-win situation, wasn't it? As he squared his shoulders, still powerful from years of college wrestling, and headed out of the apartment, he was already thinking about that power structure, which was becoming one of his more difficult projects. In his briefcase he had letters from four ambassadors, each putting himself forward as interim president until a new Congress or election could be organized. It wasn't a bad idea, stiff-arming a senior diplomat into the job for a strictly limited amount of time. There were decisions that needed to be made at a national executive level that simply weren't getting made. But the four bozos in his briefcase were all political appointments—one of whom he'd actually played a very sly hand in getting set up—and Culver didn't rate a single one of them much higher than a stale sack of shit. Frankly, anyone seeking power at the moment definitely couldn't be trusted with it.

No, they were going to need someone who actually didn't want the job. Someone who was available but who was nothing like him or any of his peers in the shark tank. They were going to need someone honest. As honest as George Washington, or at least a good enough actor that he, or she, could pull it off.

But who?

He was going to have to start doing some digging, finding out what was happening beyond the islands. With winter looming, the Alaskan state government was consumed with the job of making sure its people didn't starve and freeze to death. Seattle and those parts of Washington outside of the Wave's effect seemed to be muddling through after some unpleasantness with riots and looting, although it was hard to tell with news coming out of there in a drip feed. Perhaps that might be the place to start looking.

He stalked through the hotel corridors toward the elevator at the end of the hall, brooding on a tangle of competing thoughts, among them how much emptier the Embassy Suites seemed than just a few days ago. Almost all of the foreign guests had checked out, but there seemed to be fewer Americans in residence, too. Operation Uplift hadn't started yet, and he wondered where they might have gone, since most would have hailed from the mainland. That was less an issue, however, than the lack of maids. Every morning when he'd emerged from his rooms at least three housekeeping trolleys were parked somewhere on his family's floor, but this morning nada. Of course, it might mean nothing, but he made a mental note to check with some of the staff about whether there were problems with their pay, whether some people had just stopped turning up to work, whether there might be any signs of order and organization starting to fall apart. Of the three surviving U.S. states, Hawaii was the least able to sustain itself. Without massive amounts of external assistance the islands would probably be ungovernable, even with a huge armed-forces presence. Both the civilian and military authorities were alive to the very real possibility of starvation and a rapid fraying of the social fabric. Given the shit going down in Europe nobody was sanguine about just muddling through anymore.

He walked into the elevator, which was empty, and punched in the button for the lobby. The elevator stopped only once during the descent, to pick up a German couple and their luggage.

"Howdy." He smiled as they wrestled their bags in. "Heading home?"

"No," the man replied in perfect, clipped English. "We have relatives in Australia we are to visit. Winemakers in the Barossa Valley. Do you know it?"

"No," he admitted. "Not much of a wine drinker, though."

The Germans both nodded as though he'd said something profound.

"So, you think you'll be going home any time soon?" Jed asked when the silence began to stretch out.

"No," the man replied just as quickly as they reached the ground floor. He bowed his head brusquely and said, "My sympathies for your loss," as they squeezed out past Jed with their suitcases.

The foyer would normally have been crowded at this time with guests checking out and conferencegoers arriving for seminars and meetings, but apart from the Germans and half a dozen cabin crew members from some Asian airline, the lobby was mostly deserted. A couple of wet tourists wandered in from the beach with towels thrown over their shoulders, and the glassy, frozen grins of people desperately trying to avoid looking at the yawning abyss that had lately opened in front of them. It was a look Jed was becoming used to. His eyes scanned the floor and he found his driver standing just outside, sneaking in a last-minute cigarette. He'd given the cancer sticks up himself twenty years ago, after successfully representing British American Tobacco in a suit against one of their many former customers. Or victims, as one executive called them in private.

Bobby Kua, his driver, was a native Hawaiian, a surfer, and Jed shook his head ruefully as he saw the boy suck extra hard on the Marlboro to drag in a few more precious carcinogenic lungfuls as soon as he saw the lawyer approaching.

"I'm telling you, Bobby, you'd be a much better surfer if you gave those things away."

"No way, boss," smiled Kua. "I'm already a weapon. Couldn't get any better."

He drew one last, long puff before stubbing out the butt and flicking it into a nearby can. Privately, Jed wondered how long it would be before the young man was pinching off his half-smoked butts to finish them later.

He made a mental note to lay in a few cartons. Within a week or two, some people would sell their souls for nicotine, he was sure.

"So where to, boss?"

"Pearl today," said Culver. "We'll be there all day, too. Then out to the capitol about three-thirty for a meeting. You could probably get away for an hour or so if you needed to. But I'm on a promise to get back here for drinks. Say, seven."

"Got it," said Bobby, leading him over to the nondescript white Chevy Aveo from the government fleet. Gas rationing meant that only the smallest, most fuel-efficient cars could be signed out of the pool for official business, while civilian motorists were restricted to just a few gallons a week, which could only be purchased on alternate days. Rationing had quickly become an unpleasant reality that *everyone* had to deal with. Armed troopers posted at supermarkets and gas stations made sure of that. Appeals to fairness and civic-mindedness shortly after the Disappearance had achieved nothing but the rapid emptying of grocery-store shelves and at least a dozen incidents of serious violence, including one macadamia-caramel-popcorn–related multiple homicide at a supermarket on Kalakaua Avenue.

Culver was grateful that he had no responsibility for the rationing system. It had quickly come to challenge the Disappearance as *the* open wound on talk radio. The first time an American was told by a heavily armed man in combat gear that they couldn't buy *all* the Twinkies they wanted tended to come as a deep existential shock every bit as unnerving as the still unexplained cataclysm back on the mainland. Culver himself had quickly emptied the small bar fridge back at the hotel of liquor and filled it with emergency food supplies, as soon as he noticed that the breakfast buffet in the restaurant was looking a bit spare. Frankly, he'd have been much happier if he could have relocated Marilyn and the kids to Pearl Harbor, just in case things got totally out of hand. But they all insisted on staying at the Embassy Suites, and he was reasonably confident of making himself important enough to grab a safe berth in the event of any European-style uprising.

To that end he strapped himself into the backseat of the car, with room to spread out his documents, and got to work while Bobby drove him through Honolulu. More shops were closed every day now. In fact, apart from bars and heavily guarded food outlets there was very little open, and there were very few people on the streets. Marilyn was probably going to be disappointed in her search for a new cocktail dress. Soldiers and cops comprised most of the foot traffic, in contrast to the first few days, when huge unruly crowds had gathered and surged back and forth, almost like people running without real purpose on the deck of a sinking ship. Together the rationing and curfew systems tended to keep people at home most of the time.

They slowed down to negotiate a large but docile crowd that had gathered at the Fort DeRussy parklands for a food-distribution point run by the army. A dozen trucks were parked in a line before an avenue of olive-drab tents. Soldiers were unloading hundreds of boxes, stacking them in neat piles guarded by colleagues toting rifles. It was still a bizarre, unnatural sight, Americans lined up like victims of a Honduran earthquake to score a bowl of rice or a jar of baby food. Jed pushed the images out of his mind and returned to his papers, making some untidy margin notes on a briefing he had to deliver later that day to a phone hookup between the attorneys general of the surviving states.

Admiral Ritchie was adamant that the armed forces could not continue drifting through the constitutional limbo into which they had been cast. It was not simply a matter of requiring political direction for the course of the hot war they were now fighting in the Middle East. There were security nightmares springing up like poison weeds all over the world as well as some very basic and uncomfortable questions of sustainability for those forces that remained in existence.

"How do we keep going?" Ritchie had asked Jed late last night.

Culver thought the admiral might as well have asked, "Why should we keep going?" He couldn't imagine what was holding together a fighting force that had nothing to fight for anymore, and increasingly lacked the money to do so.

Immediate survival, he supposed. But if and when the immediate peril was no longer, what then? A nation of ten million people—that was the rough estimate of living, breathing American citizens left in the world—a nation that small could not sustain a military even a fraction the size of the one it had at the moment. Especially not with most of the country sealed off behind an impenetrable and utterly mysterious barrier. Frankly, Jed doubted whether the area that remained unaffected on the continent was viable in the medium term anyway. He grunted almost imperceptibly as he briefly thought of all those people stuck in Seattle and just across the border in Vancouver. None of them could be certain some natural fluctuation in the event horizon wouldn't consume them in the blink of an eye, although by that measure, of course, nobody on the planet could really feel safe.

You had to wonder how much of the chaos wrapping itself like giant bat wings around the world was due to the effect of that uncertainty rather than the unsettling effect of simply removing at one stroke the massive political ballast represented by America. Oh, screw it. It was undergrad bullshitting, all of it. The only thing that mattered was fixing the problems he could fix, and for now that meant stabilizing the remnant power of the United States and securing the immediate future of his family.

He flipped open his laptop and began to compose an e-mail to Ritchie. He wanted to bounce a few ideas off the admiral before the conference call in the afternoon.

He typed very deliberately, using the informal style of address he'd cultivated in his dealings with the navy man.

> Hey Ritch, You asked for my thoughts on the line of succession before I wrote them up for the reference group. Well, I'm thinking the only way to punch through all this is to go back to first principles. We've got us a constitutional boondoggle. We need us a constitutional convention to stamp it flat. A short, sharp, butt-kicking convention.
>
> Normally you'd require a vote of two-thirds of the

state legislatures just to get everyone together. It's the only amendatory process available in the absence of a functioning Congress and Senate. The intent of the relevant section of the Constitution, Article 5, is that the "two thirds" would be "two thirds" of all of the states, but that is impossible under present circumstances.

The only available option would be for the three surviving states to declare themselves the only three states and to then call a convention or, more likely, to declare themselves Trustees for the "missing" forty-seven states, and vote those states' interests at a convention called to address the current emergency. The result is the same and is the only mechanism available in my estimation to reconstitute a federal government within the letter of the Constitution.

Jed stopped tapping keys and stared out the window at the passing scenery for a moment. They had turned onto the freeway, which was largely deserted, save for a few Hummers heading downtown from Pearl, and the National Memorial Cemetery was slipping by on the right. He had a great-uncle buried up there. Uncle Lou, on his mom's side. He'd meant to visit the grave site sometime during his vacation but had never made it. He was sure his forebear would understand. Lou Stafford had been killed on Wake Island, the same day the Japanese bombed Pearl Harbor. He'd fought when all seemed hopeless. Given his life so that Jed and his kids could live free. You had to wonder what the old guy would have made of all this, thought Culver, before reminding himself that Lou Stafford was only nineteen when he died. Not much of an old guy, really. The lawyer nodded a quick greeting, which would have to do for now.

He went back to his screen, wondering about the difficulties of assembling a convention along the lines he was proposing. The very nature of the three surviving states might pose problems. Hawaii and Washington, particularly the western half of the state, were very liberal, Democratic-leaning, and, in the case of the latter, not particularly pro-military. Seattle he found notoriously smug and self-righteous, although that might have changed by now. The eastern, agricultural portion of Washington, right up to the event horizon, was heavily Republican, although many of those people had already relocated into temporary shelters in Seattle. Hāwaii had no oil, no real agriculture, and no industry, but it did have a strong military presence. The maritime power alone concentrated here was still greater than that of any other country in the world. Washington had agriculture, industry, and refining capacity but no oil. Alaska had no agriculture, plenty of oil, and decent refining capacity but very little else, particularly people, and what people it did have tended to be very conservative, libertarian Republicans.

He just didn't know whether they could all get together.

With Massachusetts and Mississippi gone, you could award a blue ribbon to Alaska and Washington for taking the "polar opposites" prize. Jed figured that Washington, with its much larger population and resource base, would resist Alaska having a virtual veto over any measures necessary to act within a constitutional framework. And Alaska, for its part, might well see itself as the last bastion of rugged individualism, and would have limited interest in submitting to a drastically revised federal system highly tilted toward nanny statism.

It was going to be worse than the First and Second Continental Congresses, that was for certain. It was going to make the argument over issues like the Articles of Confederation and how much of a person a slave represented look like a middle-school debate class. There wasn't any George Washington around to hold the delegates together or come up with the various compromises they'd need. Any constitutional convention with the three remaining players was going to be a first-class WWE smackdown cage match.

He sighed, already exhausted at the prospect of tying all this together in a neat package with a bright bow that everyone would want to own.

The trick to making this work, he wrote to Ritchie, will be to cram all the wildcats into the bag before they know what's happening.

The key, he thought to himself, is George Washington. If a modern George Dubya didn't exist, Jed Culver was going to have to invent him.

29

He was an operator, possibly a crook, and definitely not to be left alone with the small-change jar. But Admiral James Ritchie couldn't help but warm to Culver the more time he spent with him. There was no reason they should get along, a patrician New Englander from old money with a long family history of noblesse oblige, and a scheming carpetbagger from the bad end of the bayou. Certainly naïveté didn't come into it. Thanks to Colonel Maccomb of the 500th Military Intelligence Brigade, Ritchie was well aware of what kind of a creature Jed Culver was.

A fixer.

He was the operator your troubled multibillion-dollar company called in to quickly and quietly clean up the mess left behind by your recently departed and grotesquely incompetent CEO. He was the man who procured the difficult export license in the hopelessly corrupt but fabulously oil-rich Third World shithole. Or the development approval for your six-star resort on the ecologically fragile tropical island. Or the seemingly impossible negotiated truce between the warring stone-age tribes that was interfering with the profit margins of your hardwood logging operations in the New Guinea highlands. If that didn't work, he hired the heavy hitters who protected your oil-drilling operations in Africa without cutting too deeply into your budget.

Jed Culver was a rolled-gold son of a bitch.

That said, Ritchie had a gut feeling that when the big questions were asked, this glad-handing sack of shit would actually give you a straight answer, especially if that answer was something you didn't want to hear. Perhaps he was a bit like old Joe Kennedy in that way. Ritchie, an avid reader of historical biographies, thought he recognized something in Culver that FDR might have seen in the old bootlegger when appointing him to head the SEC way back in the Depression—a thief you could trust.

The admiral kept all these thoughts to himself, of course, as Culver walked around his office, speaking from notes with his expensive jacket off, shirtsleeves rolled up, and tie raffishly askew. Was the ruffled, big-doofus thing just part of his routine? Probably. With a guy like Culver you had to figure that *everything* was part of the routine. But still, he seemed blessed, if that was the right word, with a frightening appreciation for the worst aspects of human nature, and how they might still be turned to everyone's advantage.

"The only intact chain of command we have left," said Culver, in his soft Southern drawl, "is, of course, your own. But by constitutional tradition, your entire chain remains subordinate to civilian rule and, let me just check back with you, ladies and gentlemen . . ."

Culver looked up from his notes and smiled at the small group of military officers in the room. "Y'all ain't planning a coup d'état, are you?"

From anyone else it would have been a dangerous gamble, an insult to people who had pledged their lives to defending the Constitution, but Culver had a way of smiling and somehow twinkling his eyes that added an unspoken, "Naw, of course you ain't, you're *good* old boys and gals. The Best."

Ritchie even noticed a smile attempting to creep around the corners of the deeply fissured face of General Murphy, the senior army officer on the island. But, for professional reasons, Murphy had long ago banned any semblance of a sunny disposition from his person, and he managed to crush the small grin stone dead. It had no discernible effect on Culver, who carried on.

"Fact is, though, folks, given the scale of disaster we face, precise legality *will* have to give way almost immediately to practicality. As the esteemed Justice Jackson pointed out in *Terminiello v. Chicago,* the Constitution is not a goddamned suicide pact. If we are going to survive we need good government and quick. And given that nobody is much interested in fashioning a military dictatorship out of the ashes of the old Republic, I would suggest that for practical purposes it will initially resemble a patchwork of small- and big-town mayors, the surviving political and administrative leadership, law enforcement, and perhaps . . . no, *definitely,* some religious and community leaders with a large following. Whatever government comes into being out of this nightmare has to *arise* from the ground up, rather than be *imposed* from above."

"Fine words, Mr. Culver," rumbled Murphy. "Brings a tear to the eye. But we're in deep shit, and we need to dig ourselves out of it, *muy pronto.* Adapt, overcome, and drive on."

There were nine military officers in the room. The senior marine nodded in agreement with Murphy's brusque comment. Again, however, Ritchie watched with sneaking admiration as the lawyer let the rebuke wash over him, even turning it around.

"Damn straight," said Culver. "We need this done yesterday. Hell, we needed it as soon as that energy thing crashed down on top of us. But we have to accept that, as scared and fucked up as people are right now, especially those poor bastards who are close enough to the Wave to be able to see it, they *will* adapt. There *will* come a day when it's not the first thing they think of when they wake up in the morning. And they will go back to the old ways of doing things, of each against the other and damn anyone in between. It's just our nature. So whatever we set up now has to have the elegance of our first constitutional principles. It has to allow for the better angels of our nature to sing, because Lord knows the demons are going to be a massed fucking choir over the next little while."

"What exactly are you suggesting, Mr. Culver? Could you take us through your proposal? Step by step."

"Of course, Admiral," said Culver. "Basically, some laws are going to get bruised, if not broken, but even Jefferson would have been cool with that. You know his purchase of my home state, Louisiana, was, to put it bluntly, completely illegal and he *knew* it. But he also knew that the strict observance of the written law, while one of the high duties of a good citizen, is not *the* highest."

Culver stood up straight and appeared to stare off into the middle distance, obviously quoting from the third president of the United States.

" 'The laws of necessity, of self-preservation, of saving our country when in danger, are of higher obligation. To lose our country by a scrupulous adherence to written law would be to lose the law itself, with life, liberty, property and all those who are enjoying them with us; thus absurdly sacrificing the end to the means.' "

Having finished, he leaned forward and placed his hands on the edge of the conference table where they all sat.

"What that means, ladies and gentlemen, is that we are gonna crack some heads together. And fast. And by 'we' I mean the American people, what's left of us."

"I think it might be better if nobody showed up in uniform, flashing their medals and . . . what d'you call that stuff . . . fruit salad?"

Culver gestured toward the campaign ribbons on Ritchie's uniform. He didn't wait for the admiral to reply.

"Fact is, we already got blood spilled in Seattle. People are skittish. Yeah, you guys are the only outfit with the chops to put boot to ass and get it all done, but I promise you that anything that looks even halfway like a military takeover will mean the end of *everything*."

Ritchie clamped down on his surging frustration. Only he and Culver remained in the office, all of the other attendees having returned to their duties. He was hungry and tired, and didn't see himself being able to do anything about either any time soon. The austerity measures he'd ordered for every military establishment in Hawaii were not merely window dressing. Food shortages would become dangerous if strict rationing was not enforced. The islands' airfields were running around the clock, shuttling aid in and people out, but a cascading series of economic crises ripping through global money markets was beginning to bite hard in the real world. Both the Chinese and Japanese governments had quietly ordered container ships loaded with food and medical aid bound for Hawaii to turn around and head home in the last twenty-four hours. Ritchie had savored his cup of coffee at breakfast this morning with sad relish because he wasn't sure when he might get another one.

"Yes, I understand, Mr. Culver," he said, still refusing to give in to the lawyer's insistence that he was just "plain ol' Jed."

"But I am fighting an illegal war. Men and women are going to their deaths on my say-so and not much else. Why are they doing that? No reason. No good reason anyway. We're there because we're there and we can't get our sorry asses out in good order. Hell, we can't even turn to the United Nations for guidance."

"I know you got pressures, Admiral. I know . . ."

"Do you? Really?" Ritchie stood up and walked over to the window. He stared out at the afternoon sunlight, took a deep breath, and turned on Culver.

"I have bagmen from every tin-pot, oil-drenched Dark Ages dictatorship in the Middle East, including the ones we're fighting at this very minute, all banging on my door demanding to know what the U.S. government policy toward them and their vile little country is now. Doesn't matter how many times I tell them I'm not the president, not the government. They don't care. They won't listen. To them, I am the man with my finger on the trigger of what is *still* a very big gun. Big enough to blow them to hell and back. And the worst of it is, I can't just tell them to fuck off because some of them at least I need. I cannot get our people out of there without the help of the Saudis and Kuwaitis and Turks and half a dozen others. But of course, none of them want us to go because they know the whole place will melt down three minutes later. I need clarity, Jed."

Damn it. You're losing it, he thought. *Get your bearing back.*

". . . I need orders from a properly constituted executive. I need to get my people out of that septic mess in the Gulf. I need to know what role we're going to play here, in CONUS, wherever we end up. I need to know what resources we'll have. I need to get on the phone to Tommy Franks and give him and his people some *hope*."

Culver absorbed the mini-tirade with equanimity, waiting him out. When Ritchie was finished he nodded, slowly.

"Okay then. That's what you need. Now this is what I need to get it for you."

Dealing with Culver's Machiavellian schemes was enough to bring his headache roaring back from the dull, middle distance where he'd banished it with a couple of Advils. Ritchie was not at all comfortable being so closely involved in political maneuvers, but the lawyer was right. The United States had been gutted, and one of the very few working and half-intact institutions it had left was the military. He was also right that it would be an intolerable violation of the country's founding principles if the republic became a militarized autarchy in the mad rush of a catastrophe. And then, in mocking contrast to these high ideals, there was brute reality.

"The Israeli envoy is here, Admiral."

Ritchie popped another painkiller and washed it down with a mouthful of tap water from his beloved old VF-84 coffee mug.

"Send him in."

The man who entered the room carrying a briefcase was relatively short, and his gray, wiry hair had retreated at least halfway back over his head. Tel Aviv had dispatched him as their new ambassador, but Ritchie was adamant that he could not be addressed as such because he had not yet formally presented himself to the president. He had flat refused to stand in for the role himself. Nonetheless, Asher Warat was the chosen representative of his government, and as such was deserving of good manners and what few diplomatic niceties Ritchie could extend him.

"Admiral." He smiled, lighting up his wide brown eyes. "Thank you for seeing me. I understand that the demands on your time must be horrendous."

Ritchie gestured for him to take one of the two armchairs directly in front of his desk. The Israeli did so, placing the briefcase by his feet. Through the windows behind Warat the old sailor enjoyed a sweeping view from Halawa Heights down to the harbor, which looked magnificent under a high sun. A few wisps of clouds drifted across a hard blue sky, and the waters of the base sparkled bright silver on dark blue. Stare at it long enough and you could almost believe nothing was wrong with the world. The long, drawn features of his visitor, sitting smack in the middle of that view, indicated otherwise.

"Everyone has their own troubles, Mr. Warat. I'm sure yours are as difficult as mine in their own way."

Warat bobbed his head up and down, and his eyes seemed even more watery and forlorn, which was saying something.

"Life is trouble, Admiral. Especially these days. And I am afraid I am about to make more for you. Much more. Or less, maybe."

Ritchie was instantly alert, the fatigue of the last week

sluicing off of him. The small adrenaline surge didn't help with his headache, however. That just grew worse.

"How so, sir?" he asked guardedly.

Warat checked his watch and seemed to hesitate. He rubbed his fingers together and shifted nervously before checking the time again.

"You will be aware, Admiral, that the strategic circumstances faced by my country have declined precipitously due to the cataclysm, the absolute cataclysm that befell your own."

"Yes," said Ritchie as his heart seemed to slow down and grow to about twice its normal size, pressing painfully against the confines of his chest. Warat hitched his shoulders and chewed at his lower lip. The man was a veritable Wal-Mart for nervous tics and tells.

"Your own forces in the region have come under attack from Saddam, from the mullahs, and from a whore's parlor full of opportunists and crazy men. Hamas. Islamic Jihad. Al-Qaeda."

Ritchie nodded but said nothing. Just that morning they'd lost the USS *Hopper* and two hundred men to a swarm of jihadi suicide attackers on Jet Skis. You don't lose an Aegis destroyer every day, and he wasn't certain when he'd get a replacement. Probably never. It was the sort of thing that would have made headlines all over the world before the Wave. Now it was a minor irrelevancy to most news agencies, obsessed as they were by the accelerating collapse of their own societies. The Israeli envoy glanced quickly at his watch again.

"Your plans to withdraw coalition forces from Iraq and Kuwait, and U.S. forces from the region in general, are understandable," he said, "if shortsighted, in the opinion of my government."

"Well, sir," said Ritchie. "I am afraid the withdrawal is an operational necessity, at the moment. It is not U.S. government policy, as you would be aware. I would characterize it as a tactical withdrawal, not a strategic retreat."

"Or abandonment," said Warat.

"No," agreed Ritchie. "I would not call it abandonment. But right now, our presence there is making things infinitely worse, and I shouldn't have to explain to you, sir, that we cannot sustain our forces even in the short term. Our base is gone. Every missile we fire, every ship we lose, every soldier or sailor or airman who *dies* is a true loss. They *cannot* be replaced."

Warat shrugged and sighed. "We understand, Admiral. We have lost, too. America was our arsenal, and we find ourselves in the same position. Unlike you, however, we can stage no tactical withdrawal. We are trapped within our borders, with nowhere to go. The barbarians are at the gate. You will be aware of that. We are already fighting them. It will be a war of annihilation for one or the other."

Ritchie ceded the point with a wave of the hand, an almost preternatural dread creeping up on him. It was a physical sensation, something he could feel crawling through his body like ice water rising from his nuts. The diplomat checked his watch one last time. He squared his shoulders and looked Ritchie in the eyes without flinching. His voice firmed up, losing the quaver and uncertainty that had haunted it until now.

"Twelve hours ago, we received a secure data package from our highest-placed source within the Republican Guard. His information was so critical that it was cross-checked independently, even though doing so revealed the identity of other sources we had cultivated within the Hussein regime and the Iranian Revolutionary Guards. I am afraid those sources have now been exposed and eliminated. Before losing them, however, we were able to confirm that a convoy of civilian vehicles crossed the border with Iran and traveled without a military escort, but still heavily guarded, to a warehouse on the outskirts of Mosul at 0300 hours local time yesterday. If you will excuse me, Admiral . . ."

Warat leaned over and picked up his briefcase, popping the lid and pulling out a sheaf of papers, which he handed across to Ritchie. Photographs mostly, with a few pages of printed material that appeared to be chemical analyses. The pictures were obviously close surveillance shots, taken covertly by somebody at the warehouse.

"The vehicles you can see in these pictures are standard commercial vans. Two Scania transports, a Volvo truck, a Mack truck, and a Hino heavy diesel truck. The utility vehicles, SUVs I believe you call them, provided the escort. The Hino truck carried a shipping container in which was stored an unknown quantity of uranium hexafluoride. I am afraid we have lost track of it. The other trucks, which we were able to track from the border, to Mosul and onto an Iraqi missile battery, contained weaponized anthrax and botulinum."

Ritchie glanced briefly at the typewritten pages, but he was not a chemist and they meant nothing to him. He assumed that they somehow attested to the contents of the trucks.

"We have no sources within the Iraqi battery, and the exposure of our other assets will have caused Hussein to alter his plans anyway. But we must presume that we now face the mortal danger of a missile strike on Israel with biological agents. Our policy in the face of such threats has always been stated clearly. We will not just retaliate. We will strike preemptively."

Ritchie placed the documents very carefully on his desk. His hand was shaking, and there was nothing he could do to stop it.

"So, my government hereby informs you, as the commander of friendly forces in the region, that as of one hour ago, the Israeli Defense Forces have commenced Operation Megiddo. I am informed by my government that Israeli air force units are currently en route to twelve centers. I have here a list of the targets."

The ambassador passed across a single sheet of paper that Ritchie took with a trembling hand. The Israeli, he noticed, seemed abnormally calm by comparison. He'd apparently done all of his sweating and shaking when he first came in. The list was divided into two parts, labeled "Counter Force" and "Counter Value." The former was a catalogue of military bases and suspected WMD sites such as the Iranian Revolutionary Guard training facility at Hamadan, long suspected also to be the Guards' principal WMD depository. The latter was a short list of cities.

The American officer found it hard to breathe. Baghdad, Tehran, and Damascus were slated for destruction within hours.

"You can't do this," croaked Ritchie. "You'll kill millions, tens of millions of innocent people."

Warat's face was ashen and drawn, but firm.

"Yes, Admiral. We will. It is either that or millions of our people will die."

"But . . ."

Ritchie found it hard to speak. Blood rushed through his ears, and dark spots bloomed in front of his eyes. Warat sensed his difficulty and pressed on.

"We have drawn up the target list in such a way that it should not expose your forces to significant radiological effects, and it will not be necessary to fly through airspace controlled by the coalition. This will not be like 1991, Admiral. We will not require IFF transponder codes; however, the range of some of the longer strikes means that without midair refueling, our planes cannot return home. My government therefore requests the cooperation of the U.S. Air Force in assigning such in-flight refueling assets as we would require to successfully complete all of these missions without needlessly sacrificing our personnel. For many of them it will be a one-way trip."

"Are you mad?"

Ritchie stared at the man, who had the good grace to look embarrassed.

"My government did not expect to receive a positive response to this request, but instructed me to make it anyway."

"Mr. Ambassador . . ." Ritchie faltered, forgetting that Warat had not been formally received and confirmed as ambassador. "Mr. Warat, I am afraid I cannot allow this plan to go ahead. Your government must call its planes back."

"I am afraid they will not do that, Admiral. Under any circumstances. My government is convinced that we face annihilation as a people if we do not act immediately."

"You will be annihilated if you *do*," protested Ritchie.

Warat nodded glumly.

"Anything is possible these days, Admiral."

Ritchie's heart was still thundering in his chest, but his head was at last clearing of the shock and disorientation. He took a deep breath and leaned back in his chair.

"Sir, I am afraid I must inform you that I will direct U.S. forces in theater to interdict this strike and stop it by any means possible. I will further contact our coalition partners and request any and all cooperation they might provide. And, I will immediately inform the governments of the targeted nations that your strike is inbound, and I will assist them in whatever way possible to repel it."

Warat received the rebuke with stoic reserve. Behind him, through the wide glass windows, life went on. Not normally. But it did go on. Some traffic moved through the streets. Children would be playing in suburban backyards as parents did their best to insulate them from the horror of a world collapsing in on itself. High above the idyllic panorama Ritchie saw the sun glint on the wings of a commercial airliner, outbound. For where, he had no idea, but it was undoubtedly full. The Israeli envoy sighed and quickly recovered his composure.

"My government expected that you might react in this fashion, Admiral. It would be the honorable thing for you. However, I must point out that your own forces have degraded the air defense nets of Iran and Iraq to the point where they cannot deny our air forces. And the IAF has done the same to the Syrian air force over the last week of fighting. By warning them, you will do no more than condemn millions to spend their last hours in abject fear."

Ritchie slammed an open hand down on the desk, with a thunderous crash.

"Goddamn you, will you *listen*? You cannot do this and you *must* not. I am ordering my theater commanders to interdict your sorties with deadly force. We *will* shoot you down!"

Warat's chin moved up and down like a bobble-headed doll on a dashboard. His shoulders twitched, and when he spoke he did not look Ritchie in the eye.

"My government has prepared for such an eventuality, Admiral. The weapon packages will be delivered with an escort of IAF fighters. They will engage *any* hostile force that tries to prevent them from accomplishing their mission. Any. Hostile. Force."

"My God," breathed Ritchie. "You'll kill us all. If you do this how long do you imagine it will be before some maniac in New Delhi or Islamabad decides that they need to get the drop on their nemesis? How long will it be before Russia and China decide that things will be a lot simpler with us, here in Hawaii, out of the picture?"

"I cannot answer these questions, Admiral, as you well know. But I *can* tell you that if we do not act, the Jewish people and their state will be wiped out in a second Holocaust. And *you* know that I speak the truth."

Ritchie dropped his head into his hands and rubbed at eyes that burned with a lack of sleep.

"Get out," he said quietly.

30

The envoy had lied. Or rather, he had not told the whole truth, because he did not know it. The targeting list Warat provided to Ritchie was incomplete, as were other details of the attack, including the fact that many of the warheads would be delivered by Jericho II missiles, not piloted aircraft. In addition to the cities and military facilities on the list, the Israeli cabinet had added a further thirty-eight sites. Suspected Iranian nuclear centers in Natanz, Ardakan, Saghand, Gashin, Bushehr, Aral, and Lashkar Abad were all slated for destruction, along with the cities of Tabriz, Qazvin, Shiraz, Yazd, Kerman, Qom, Ahwaz, and Kermanshah. Five of the nuclear-tipped missiles were inbound on Libya as the ambassador sat down with Admiral Ritchie, while another three were headed for military bases near heavily populated Egyptian cities. But one mission, the last to depart, had a very different target. The Aswan High Dam.

Colonel Rudi Molenz sat quietly in the cockpit of his F-15I Ra'am at the end of the main runway of Hatzerim Air Base in the Negev Desert. Tel Aviv and his family lay fifty miles to the north, but the bejeweled cluster of lights would be dimmed tonight, as the city hid itself in the dark. He would not be able to glance back over his shoulder after takeoff and smile at the thought of his two little children safely abed, somewhere in that mass of glowing pearls, surrounded by soft toys and dreaming of Daddy's return. Because there was no guarantee that Daddy would ever be coming home. And worse than that, no certainty that home itself would survive the night or the next day. Behind him, his weapons system officer, Lieutenant Ephron, hummed tunelessly, irritating Molenz, who said nothing. Ephron was nervous, and the flat, atonal droning was his release valve. It was the same before all of their missions. When they finally had a release from the tower, the little putz would shut the fuck up and do his job flawlessly. He always had before.

A brief crackle in the earphones of his bulbous DASH helmet.

"Attention Reach One Ninety, please stand by . . ."

Molenz felt his balls shrivel, and became acutely aware of silence in the back of the cockpit.

The voice crackled in his display and sight helmet again.

"You have clearance to execute Plan Magenta. Preliminary release codes Echo Kilo Four Niner Three Niner Foxtrot."

Molenz had burned the one-use code into his memory but checked the mission pad Velcroed to his leg anyway.

"Release confirmed. Reach One Ninety away."

The enormous power of the aircraft's two F-150 Pratt & Whitney engines came roaring up like an angry leviathan as the pilot's head-up display blinked into life. The caged fury of the jet fighter completely enfolded him, and as always he felt the deep-body thrill of having so much potential power in his hands. Beneath the old familiar sensation, however, lay a dread that ran deeper than anything he had experienced in all the years he had been flying combat missions. It was not the fear of his own death, but of becoming Death itself, because attached to the underside of his Strike Eagle was a thirty-kiloton nuclear warhead in a specially hardened penetrator casing. It was designed to slam into the base of the Aswan High Dam and drill down through ten meters of concrete before birthing a small supernova to atomize much of the dam's solid mass, releasing the superheated waters behind to roar down the Nile Valley like a megatsunami toward Cairo.

Part of him could not believe that he was doing this, that it was even happening. But the two aircraft ripping down the tarmac right after his were real. As were the dozen flights he'd watched leaving earlier for much farther-flung locations. He'd known many of those pilots. Commanded some of them. Trained others. Their good-byes were restrained but heartfelt. Unlike Molenz they were flying single-engine F-16s with modified drop tanks to get them all the way to Iran while flying low and fast through the wastes of northern Iraq. They would traverse the edge of the Kurdish regions, where years of British and American enforcement of the no-fly zone had denuded Iraq of air-defense assets. Even with drop tanks, however, there would not be enough fuel for them to return. Extraction teams were standing by to evac anyone who made it to the preset rendezvous points. But Molenz knew from looking into the men's eyes as they shook hands, and in some cases hugged, that they were going to their deaths.

The Israeli air force flights left in groups of three. One F-15 carried the warhead, while the two escorts carried air-to-air loadouts. Those headed for targets in Iran and Iraq did not expect to encounter any significant resistance en route. The top-secret electronic-warfare suites installed for this mission were designed to maximize the escorts' effectiveness against any allied aircraft they might encounter. It was possible that coalition aircraft might try to stop them, but Molenz and his peers figured they had enough on their plate as it was. They were no threat.

Molenz pulled back on the stick, and the Strike Eagle clawed its way up into the stars. At twenty thousand feet he performed his usual contortionist feat anyway, straining to catch a glimpse of the capital off on the northern horizon. It was definitely dimmer, but not completely blacked out. What would be the point? Modern sensors meant that pilots no longer had to feel their way through darkened enemy airspace, seeking out targets to bomb. Iraqi Scuds had been landing in Israel for days, despite the best efforts of the Patriot batteries and the promises of General Franks that coalition special forces would own the western deserts from where the missile threat originated. The promises meant nothing. The threats issuing from the Iraqi dictator in hiding, however, had to be taken seriously, and since the flooding of Baghdad those threats had become increasingly shrill and apocalyptic. It almost seemed as though Hussein and the Iranian president were racing each other toward a rhetorical abyss.

And now, thought Molenz, *the abyss races toward them.*

Behind him, Ephron ran through another check of the Elisra SPS-2110/A Modified Electronic Warfare System and the LANTIRN pods while Molenz checked the APG-70 terrain-mapping radar. Even in the foulest weather, in the darkest hours of night, the radar provided him with a picture-perfect return from the ground, making it possible to pick out even small targets like mobile batteries tucked away in a dry wadi. The dam was just under four thousand meters in length, and a hundred and eleven meters tall, containing forty-three million cubic meters of concrete and fill; there wasn't much chance of him missing the dam.

Molenz edged their nose around to the south, to skirt Beersheba and trace the length of the border with Jordan, on a course for the headwaters of the Gulf of Aqaba. The three jets flew low and fast, operating up near the edge of full military power, shrieking over the ghostly blue-black desert at Mach 2.5. They maintained radio silence, each man alone with his own thoughts as the demands of the mission allowed. A few minutes before they would overfly the resort city of Eilat, he pushed the stick over and sent them rocketing toward the Egyptian border. Beyond lay the Sinai Peninsula and the rocky wastes of the biblical Wilderness where Moses and the Israelites wandered for so many years. Mountains lay ahead, a jagged-edged void of darkness blotting out the stars corresponding to the image scrolling down the APG-70 screen, bathing him in the softest of glows. During a brief interlude, they traversed a particularly desolate and empty stretch of mountainous wasteland, and the pilot became aware of the beating of his heart. For one perverse second he couldn't help thinking of the millions of hearts he was about to still forever. Pushing the thought away like a fearful specter, he concentrated on the return from the radar and the threat boards. Nothing untoward. The Egyptian air force was steadfastly refusing to offer even the slightest provocation to its neighbor, for fear of unleashing exactly the sort of hellfire that Molenz now carried with him.

They didn't seem to know that he was even in their airspace.

Whatever moral qualms Molenz had suffered before accepting this mission—and they had been many—he had nonetheless volunteered for it. They all had. He would destroy the dam, and doom millions tonight, none of whom had raised a hand against him or his country. But there were millions more who would, who wanted to, and who, even now, were battling with the Egyptian government's security forces on the streets of a dozen cities, attempting to overthrow the Mubarak regime because of its supine response to what they called Zionist aggression. And they were winning. That was the hell of it.

They were winning, and very soon they would sit in the presidential palace and turn their blood-dimmed eyes on his home and his family, and it was wrong and it was tragic, and he might well burn for the sin he was about to commit. But Rudi Molenz was convinced that if Israel did not reach out now, at this very moment, and hammer its mortal enemies into the dust, then the Jewish state and people would surely perish.

He shook his head, a quick constrained movement inside the helmet. They were coming up on the Gulf of Suez, one of the trip points in the flight, where they would be exposed to the radar and weapons of the Western naval forces operating in the area. They had no IFF codes for this flight, and as lead planner for the squadron he knew that an envoy had been dispatched to Hawaii to inform the Americans at the last possible minute what was about to happen. But they would not know just yet. He checked the mission clock.

Fifteen minutes.

In fifteen minutes they would find out.

But in half that time he would be over the target.

The Gulf flashed beneath them and Ephron sat quietly waiting for the warning tones and pings that would tell them they had been painted by the sophisticated arrays of the naval vessels below.

The warning was not long in coming. Three harsh discordant tones sounded, and Lieutenant Ephron went to work, firing up jamming sets and countermeasures. Molenz focused his attention down to a stiletto point, determined to see them through this passing hazard.

It was over as quickly as it had begun. The waters dropped away and suddenly the giant wind farm at Zafarana appeared in the crisp aquamarine glow of his terrain-rendering APG screen. Huge alien-looking structures blurred beneath them, recalling for Molenz an unbidden childhood memory of running alongside a picket fence through which a setting sun had cast its dying rays.

Behind him, Ephron requested permission to arm the warhead.

"Granted," said Molenz. "Primary release code Alpha Two Four Delta Zero Two November Three Two Five One Echo. Confirm."

"Confirmed."

"You are released to arm."

Ephron, whose voice was shaking, busied himself on a small keyboard, tapping out a long series of commands before announcing, "The weapon is armed."

Molenz dry-swallowed.

The port wing dipped thirty degrees and the plane began to track to the south as he leveled off, dropping the flight into the folds of a long valley that ran roughly parallel to the Nile. The faintest silver crescent of light bleeding over the ridgeline to the west would be Luxor, often acclaimed as the world's greatest open-air museum. The temple at Karnak, the Valley of the Kings, the ruins of Thebes, they were all just a few minutes' flying time away.

Molenz pressed on, allowing the Strike Eagle to begin its climb to a safe release height.

As all three birds emerged, screaming from the folds of the ancient valley, he finally saw what he was about to do. Towns and villages clung to the edge of the Nile, their weak, twinkling lights marking its sinuous path through the night like illuminated buoys.

He pressed back into the flight seat, he poured on power for altitude.

Ephron announced from behind him that the automatic targeting system had a lock and requested that Molenz release control of the aircraft to him.

The pilot agreed and felt that brief, awful moment of loss as microprocessors took over. The Eagle rolled and turned to bear down on its target, just like the bird of prey for which it was named.

There was an audible clunk and the plane jumped, suddenly free of the dreadful burden that had fallen away from beneath them.

All three aircraft pitched over and raced due east, away from the terrible thing they had just done.

The warhead slipped quietly down through the warm moist air. It did not whistle or shriek to announce its death dive. A passing sibilant hiss and the whirring of guidance fins at the tail were the only sounds it made. In the nose of the bomb a small electronic device slavishly tracked the laser-designated aim point at the base of the dam, for as long as the warplanes were able to maintain the link. By the time they broke contact to escape the blast, the weapon had already settled into a stable descent. It struck the angled concrete wall of the Aswan High Dam at near supersonic speed with a thunderous boom that shook the entire structure.

Designed·to spear deep into extremely hard, multilayered underground facilities, the penetrator, the elongated narrow-diameter spike of superhardened nickel-cobalt steel alloy, was enhanced with a void-sensing Hard Target Smart Fuze that measured the progress of the warhead into the body of the dam, delaying detonation until an optimal depth had been reached. Israel had long ago learned the art of reducing the size of its nuclear devices without sacrificing their destructive power. Some of the bombs falling on cities through the Middle East at that very moment topped out in the megaton range. The blast and heat and radiation effects they yielded were vastly greater than those of the primitive bombs that the U.S. had dropped on Japan in 1945.

The device that lay, for all of a millisecond, sleeping beneath thousands of millions of tons of cement was modest in comparison, although twice as powerful as the Nagasaki and Hiroshima bombs. It did not need to be a city killer, however. It merely needed to bring down a wall, and did so by instantly turning a significant portion of it into white-hot plasma. The Smart Fuze, having determined that an optimum penetration had been reached, signaled the bomb to compress a sphere of subcritical explosive material around a plutonium core, setting off a fission reaction.

Surrounded as it was by the crushing mass of the Aswan dam, the initial burst of radiation could not escape and so began to rapidly heat the encasing medium to tens of millions of degrees, vaporizing everything within the expanding sphere of gas. Growing toward its maximum size, the fireball cooled rapidly, until it no longer possessed the heat to transform solid mass into gaseous residue. Having disintegrated the wall, however, it did have more than enough thermal power to flash-boil the waters of the dam. The blast front, with nowhere to easily dissipate, transferred much of its energy into a shock wave that sped outward from ground zero, imitating the effect of an earth-shattering quake. It struck the older, smaller original dam wall a little farther downstream like a hammer of the gods.

A few thousand people who lived in the small settlement around the dam died instantly in the explosion, leaving nobody on the ground to witness what happened as the Nile was set free.

High above, however, Molenz had a perfect view and whispered a prayer, asking forgiveness for what he had done. As the immediate effects of the explosion cleared, a mountainous wall of hot, irradiated water was unleashed on the valley below. A giant, boiling wave, over a hundred meters high, began its journey to the sea. It roared out of the huge lake, punched through the mushroom cloud that rose inexorably over the void where one of the great engineering marvels of the world had stood just a few seconds earlier. He could hear nothing in the cockpit, over the roar of the Eagle's twin engines, but the pilot imagined that hearing that monstrous wall of angry, superhot white water rushing toward you would have to sound something like sticking your head inside the F-15's afterburner.

He watched the progress of the wave for as long as he could, saw it sweep over Luxor like a giant ocean dumper rolling over a child's toy at the beach, before something even more terrible caught his eye.

The rising of a new sun, hours before dawn, far off to the north.

Where Cairo once stood.

PACOM HQ, Hawaii

The tremor in Admiral James Ritchie's hand was obvious as he read from the briefing note. He managed to keep his voice steady, though. Wouldn't do to be caught pissing his pants in a room full of civilians.

"Casualties from the immediate effects of the first strike are estimated at eighty-five million," he said. "Further casualties from the breaching of the Aswan dam may double that."

The dozen men and women arrayed around the grand oak table in the governor's dining room were ashen-faced. And some of them were visibly shaking. Governor Lingle had tears in her eyes. The room was crowded and hot, partly because of the amount of audiovisual equipment that had been brought in to effect the teleconference with Anchorage and Olympia, the Washington state capital.

The surviving civilian authorities of the United States of America were in shock. Perhaps even more traumatized than they had been by the Disappearance. Ritchie wasn't sure why. Perhaps it had something to do with the completely inexplicable nature of that event. Perhaps they were all still in a sort of denial. Everyone in this room, however, everyone involved in the conference, had grown up with the specter of nuclear war lurking at the edge of consciousness. It was not merely explicable. It was familiar.

"Indirect deaths, in the short term, from radiation poisoning and injuries, are estimated by our modeling to climb as high as another thirty million over the next month."

He heard somebody curse softly but continued on.

"Medium-term fatalities, from the collapse of governing and societal systems, may double or triple that again," said Ritchie. "There may be unquantifiable effects, farther afield. Millions of bodies and radioactive debris have been flushed out of the Nile delta into the Mediterranean, for instance, where they will contaminate the environment and enter the marine food chain."

A woman sitting by Governor Lingle covered her mouth and ran from the room.

Jed Culver, who had been standing near the door, waiting to speak, yanked it open to let her through. He was sweating profusely, and appeared blotchy and unwell.

"General Franks reports that coordinated attacks on U.S. forces in the area have ceased," said Ritchie. "Iraqi forces are requesting cease-fires or surrendering en masse. Iranian forces are withdrawing. Further, there seems to be no evidence of any national command authority in either country that survived the Israeli strike. In the areas of Iraq still under our nominal control as part of Operation Katie, local Iraqi government leaders have requested humanitarian aid. We have had similar requests from the surviving civilian leadership in Syria and Egypt. Iran has also requested our assistance."

He paused as a Republican state senator from Alaska swore loudly and colorfully.

"Uncoordinated attacks by nonstate actors continue off the coast of Lebanon and in Afghanistan. General Musharraf survived yet another assassination attempt this morning in the aftermath of the attacks. He informed me personally that Pakistan has now gone to full readiness to retaliate against anyone, Israel, India, anyone who even remotely threatens his country."

Ritchie let his hand drop and looked around the room, taking in the cameras beaming his image across the Pacific to Olympia and Anchorage as well.

"I have no national command authority to whom I can turn for orders," he said. "Our own nuclear deterrent is effectively useless without said authority. I can give orders to fire all day and night long, but the commanders of our ballistic missile subs will not follow them without presidential authority. That is why we originally scheduled this meeting. I believe that if we had had such an authority, if we had had a president and even the semblance of an emergency government, this . . . *holocaust* could have been avoided."

He had spoken the word without forethought, but having done so, did not regret it.

"This is not your fault," he said with a mounting and voluble anger that seemed to say just the opposite. "You have all had a hell of a time dealing with the impossible demands of our own emergency. But I promise you, if you cannot come to some sort of working arrangement, if you do not leave this room tonight with a plan to immediately rebuild some basic form of national government, then what happened today will happen again and again and again until the only evidence that civilization ever arose on this planet will be its radioactive ruins."

And with that, he turned and stormed out of the room.

31

Suzie was in the lounge room, watching *Toy Story* with her friend Emma, when Kip heard the news. Emma's mom had a transit pass and voucher for the food bank in Bellevue, and Kip had spent the morning on the phone to Fort Lewis—another "privilege" of his newly elevated status—making sure that this time all of the security that should have been in place *was*. He was running through a checklist of all the aid centers with a Lieutenant Somebody-or-Other when he heard Barbara cry out from across the kitchen.

"Just hang on . . . I'll call you back," he said.

She had the radio on, listening to a news bulletin, which Kipper didn't put much stock in because of the army's control of the airwaves. Yesterday's shootings at Costco, for instance, had been reported as a "serious disturbance," possibly "Resistance-related," which had halted food distribution for the day. Nothing more.

Whatever Barb had just heard, though, had to be something more than the anodyne pap and propaganda that Blackstone's people let out. She was pale-skinned by nature, but at that very moment she looked almost translucent, as though every drop of blood had rushed away from her face. Her hands shook visibly as she raised them to her mouth.

"What is it, Mommy?"

Suzie and Emma had appeared at the door, drawn by the cry of an adult. Both of them wore very grown-up frowns. Kip hustled them back into the lounge room with a promise of "emergency chocolate" from the camping rations before hurrying back to his wife.

"What's up?" he asked. Her eyes were wide with fear.

"A war," she said. "A nuclear war has started."

Kipper's stomach flipped over.

"What d'you mean?"

"It's on the radio," she said in a quavering voice.

He cast a quick look back over his shoulder, but the kids were back watching the movie. He stood next to Barb, who grabbed on and held him tightly. She seemed even more scared than she'd been after the Disappearance.

". . . of sixty million dead in the Nile delta. Israel remains on the highest state of alert, and the Israeli cabinet is meeting in secret. Full-scale fighting continues in the Gaza Strip, West Bank, and southern Lebanon, but hostilities elsewhere in the region have ceased . . ."

The report was short, sourced from somewhere in England to judge by the accent, and frustrating in the brief details it gave of American forces, which were reported to be unaffected, for the moment.

"What if they bomb here, Kip? What will happen?"

"Shh. That's not gonna happen. This is a local thing, over there. It's been coming for a week. It won't affect us."

"But the Chinese or the Russians . . ."

"Barb, we didn't do it. They weren't our bombs. It's not our issue, and even if it was, all of the navy's missile boats are still at sea. I think. Most of them anyway. Nobody is going to bomb us."

Barb was shivering violently, and kept looking over his shoulder to the lounge room, where he could hear Buzz Lightyear hamming it up.

"To infinity. And beyond!"

"You're seeing Blackstone today, right?" said Barbara, almost accusingly.

"Right," he said, with some care.

"Well, if you get one thing out of that useless cocksucker today, make sure it's a good idea about whether we're on a target list. Because I mean it, Kip. We're so gone. We are out of here if he even hints that we might get hit."

"Okay," he said, still holding her. "I can do that. It's the sort of thing I would ask anyway. But you need to stay calm, all right? Don't go losing it in front of the kids. Do you still have everyone coming around for the home-school thing today?"

Barb shook her head, but didn't look up.

"I don't know now."

Kip pushed her away gently. "You should. Suzie needs it. That rain's cleared out and people will be looking for you. They'll be looking *to* you. You need to hang tough, Bub," he said, invoking a pet name he used only in the rarest of circumstances. "I'm not going to sit here for the sake of it. If we had to leave we would. Right away. But if people panic this place will unravel so quickly that nobody will get out. Do you understand?"

Barb looked up and wiped away a few tears. Her eyes were swollen and red, and she had to sniff to clear her nose. But she nodded.

"I'm sorry. It's just . . . on top of everything, you know?"

"I know. Be strong, okay? I do have to go. I have to get to Fort Lewis this morning and pick up a bunch of guys coming up from Olympia."

"You're not driving down there, are you?" she asked, suddenly fearful again. "That's much closer to the Wave."

"No," he assured her. "They stayed in town overnight. They're just coming out to coordinate the relief effort through the rest of the state. What there is of it anyway."

Kipper kept his misgivings to himself, but he really didn't know how much use they'd be. The state government had lost about a third of its people and was still reeling in shock. He couldn't blame them. Seattle would be exactly the same in their position. He just didn't want to get sucked into their death spiral.

"I'll be late. But I will be back. Don't worry. And don't spend the day hovering over the radio while we have power. That stuff means nothing to us now. It's somebody else's problem."

He saw Barbara gather her forces and quell her fears. She was so much smaller than him, but stronger in many ways. He wished he could have taken her to sort out General Blackstone. One of Barb's patented maulings and the old prick would run up the white flag for certain.

He kissed her on the head and went through to say good-bye to Suzie and Emma, knowing it would probably be the last pleasant moment of the day.

"Release them now!"

"Now is not the right time."

"Now is completely the right fucking time or I walk. My people walk. Every fucking city council employee walks, and you can deal with the consequences," said Kipper, pounding at the tabletop for emphasis.

General Blackstone, half hidden in shadow under the shaded light, folded his arms and leaned back, disappearing farther into the darkness.

"The consequences will be that you go down in history as the man who destroyed America," he said, just as implacably.

Kipper snorted. There were at least twice as many military personnel as there were civilians in the underground conference room at Fort Lewis. Blackstone had obviously insisted on scheduling the meeting here to keep them off balance, but Kip was determined that it wasn't going to work. He wished he had Barney with him, though. Two ax handles across the shoulders and dangerously impatient with bullshitters and idiots, he'd have made a great shotgun rider for this mission.

"America is more than just a name on a map," said Kipper. "Or a bunch of business interests. It's not the military. It's not the president. In fact, it's none of those things anymore. It hasn't been since they disappeared. I'm not destroying America. You are, General. America is an idea. Of the people. By the people. You do the math on the rest of it. Because locking up the people's representatives, no matter how useless and fucked up they might be, *that* is destroying the idea of America. And I'm here to tell you that we won't stand for it. Release the councillors now."

Blackstone, who had been sitting back absorbing Kipper's attack, suddenly exploded forward into the light and slammed both open palms down on the table.

"How dare you! You march in here under the pretense of amity and lay down a subversive agenda . . ."

"Oh, please. What are you, channeling McCarthy? The only subversives here, my friend, are toting guns and pretending the fucking Constitution doesn't exist. I'm here to tell you that it does. And if you won't defend it, we will."

Blackstone gaped as though struck, and Kip wondered if he might have gone too far. But no, damn it. He would be heard. Even if it meant that he ended up in the cells, too. He didn't dare take his eyes off Blackstone, lest it be interpreted as weakness, but he could sense the presence of Dave Chugg and Marv

Basco on either side of him, and of the state government people beyond them. They weren't exactly supporting him yet, but they weren't backing Blackstone either.

"Haven't you seen the news, son?" asked the general. "Are you a complete imbecile?"

Kipper smiled, but without warmth.

"The news? Is that what you call it? I've seen the censored bulletins your media people let out."

"Uh-huh," said Blackstone. "And did you happen to notice anything about a nuclear war starting overnight? You think that might affect how you see things? You really want to turn the city over to a bunch of headless fucking chickens who couldn't even decide what cookies they were gonna vote themselves the last time the world was ending? What'll it be this time, Kipper, as the fallout cloud closes in? Deadlock over flavored milk or Kool-Aid?"

"I don't know, General. That'll be up to them. And they'll be judged on their performance or lack of it the next time they go to the polls . . ."

"Oh, my God, man! There won't be a next time!"

"Why, you getting rid of the vote while you're at it?"

"Don't be obtuse."

Kipper closed the manila folder in front of him and scanned the ranks of military personnel arrayed around and behind the general. The only one he recognized was Major McCutcheon, on Blackstone's right. What could they all be thinking, he wondered? They had to take off those uniforms sometime. Surely they didn't want to live in a prison camp at the end of the day.

At least Blackstone hadn't ordered him thrown in irons yet. He let his eyes wander around the room, playing for time. It was an unremarkable concrete block structure, somewhere deep underground. Maps of Seattle and the local area covered most of the walls. Some others had been obscured by hastily hung drop cloths. He had no idea why. Perhaps it was time to roll a hard six.

"How about we ask Admiral Ritchie?" said Kip, turning back to let Blackstone get the full wattage of his stare.

The general wouldn't have made much of a poker player. His lips curved downward, his shoulder rolled. He did everything but run a finger around the inside of his collar and make an exaggerated cartoon gulp. A few of his uniformed officers shifted noticeably in their seats, too. McCutcheon, he noticed, was as still and quiet as a stone.

"Holy crap." The engineer smiled, chancing his hand again. "You haven't told him, have you?"

"I have full authority for line management of the tactical situation here and I . . ."

The blustering tone nailed it.

"Oh, General," said Kipper. "Oh, dear me. We are in trouble, aren't we? My apologies. I mean it. I came in here, all ready to beat you down. But now I see that what I needed to give you was an exit plan, right?"

A long uncomfortable silence greeted that, broken in the end by Major McCutcheon.

"Keep talking."

"An offer?" said Kip. "Truth be known, I don't have one. This has sort of caught me by surprise, but if my colleagues agree to let me take this on the fly . . ." He glanced sideways at Dave and Marv, who nodded, and the state government people, who were now more obviously behind him. "Look, I guess, if you let them go, and apologized for the inconvenience, I could do my very best to make sure that the councillors don't make a meal of it. Unless you've tortured them or anything. You haven't done that, have you?"

He was joking but Blackstone took genuine umbrage.

"They've been quartered more comfortably than any of my people, I'll tell you that."

"They had Xbox and satellite TV," offered Major McCutcheon.

"Well, then, I'm sure they'll see the upside of their imprisonment," said Kipper. "Look, being serious. I can understand why you felt the need to take them out of the decision loop. But you just can't do that, okay? Let them go. Put them back on the Special Means Committee . . ."

He held a hand up to stave off any objections.

". . . but in the meantime we'll set up an *operational* committee, with my heads of department, some guys from state capital, and whoever you feel the need to have on it, and the OC can do the actual grunt work of ensuring that the power stays on and people get fed. Okay? Special Means can discuss . . . I dunno . . . the meaning of life . . . but at Operations we'll actu-

ally get stuff done. Like assigning security to food distribution," he finished, pointedly.

Blackstone let out a long breath and leaned across to consult
in a lowered voice with McCutcheon. After a few moments of
muttered discussion, he leaned forward and nodded.

"All right. You square it with the councillors, or it doesn't
happen. Believe me, Admiral Ritchie is going to be a lot less
interested in what's happening here than in the Middle East for
the next little while."

"Well, let's hope for your sake we don't have to find out,"
said Kipper.

"Is that all?" asked Blackstone. "Can we get on with the
meeting now?"

"No," said Kipper. "All of this 1984 bullshit has to stop, too.
Travel permits and monitoring people's phone calls and shutting down the media. It's convenient in the short term, God
knows I understand that, but it is a road to hell, General. And it
has to stop here and now."

"Are you crazy?" said Blackstone. "Even in normal times,
during natural disasters, the government reserved the right to
temporarily restrict travel, to federalize services, ration supplies, and limit communications. You surely can't be serious
about letting people run around as they please. Think of the
scene at your food bank the other morning. Some controls are
necessary. Especially given that we have a fallout cloud from
the Middle East making its way around the world."

Kipper leaned back and tapped his pen on the table. Some of
what Blackstone said made sense, but he couldn't help but feel
that they were paving a path to hell with good intentions.

"The fallout, we'll deal with. We have some experience
with it now, thanks to the pollutant storms. They were a bit of a
left-handed gift that way, I suppose. But I am serious, General.
This police-state bullshit won't stand. It weakens us in the
long run. I'm going to suggest that one of the first things the
Special Means Committee could do, when it's formed up with
its *elected* members, is look at exactly what restrictions are
necessary."

Blackstone looked like he was going to choke.

"Or we can take it up the line to Admiral Ritchie," Kip suggested helpfully.

"Goddamn, this is why we need a proper chain of command,"

grumbled Blackstone. "These decisions should be no-brainers. Instead I've got a bunch of no-brain pen pushers telling me how to do my job."

Kip sensed Marv Basco stirring beside him. His sanitation chief was slow to anger, but he did hold grudges and he wasn't one for ignoring a personal slight. There was no sense in letting this get out of hand, seeing as how he'd done so much better than he had expected.

"Listen, if an elected official tried this KGB stuff, fine. There's checks and balances to constrain them. And they can always get ass-whupped at the polls. But you're not elected, General. You have force. But you have no power. Nobody *consented* to being ruled by you, and that's what's been happening. Rule by decree. It has to end. We have to get back to first principles. Now more than ever."

Blackstone's hands were clasped, thick fingers knitted together, but they barely moved. He had stilled himself again.

"We will agree to disagree on the necessity of certain emergency measures, Mr. Kipper," he said slowly. "For now, martial law will remain in place, as it remains in place throughout Alaska and Hawaii, without all of the amateur dramatics we've endured here. But I will release your councillors—on the proviso that they understand the extremity of our situation, and the absolute necessity of matching ends to means."

"I will do my best, General," said Kipper, in as conciliatory a manner as he could. "I guess we can get on with business. And I guess that business has to be the Middle East and any fallout that might reach us."

He felt Marv Basco nudge him with an elbow.

"Oh, and on a sort of related topic, we really need to talk about the nuclear plants back behind the Wave. Marv thinks some of them are going to melt down."

32

Everything had been going so well. Pieraro had spoken very quietly to a deputy manager at the Fairmont—the manager being a complete wanker—and between them they had quietly drawn up a short list of potential passengers for Julianne. The deputy manager did not seek transport, merely a cut of the shakedown. A sum was agreed upon. Discreet contacts were made. A meeting was arranged in one of the resort's more expensive bars. It had all taken about four hours, but everything was going swimmingly. And then some fucker turned on the telly.

Even Julianne, who had an unnatural ability to maintain her focus under the worst of circumstances, was blindsided by the reports coming out of the Middle East. If there'd been any upside to recent events, it was the sudden collapse of the media's obsession with that benighted shithole. Even the Iraqi war news still ran a poor second to the Disappearance. But sixty, maybe seventy million dead in a nuclear strike, that did get your attention.

She had gathered a small group of potential customers around a table, sipping cocktails at hyperinflated prices, eating macadamias that weren't *quite* worth their weight in gold. The bar filled up as the day waned, mostly with displaced Americans and wealthy vacationers from Mexico City. Her grandfather Lord Rupert had been in Singapore just before the Japanese took it, and Jules wondered idly if Raffles had felt like this: a genteel outpost surrounded by a gathering darkness. It was hard to tell which group was more desperate: the Americans who filled the room with booming voices and sheer physical presence, or the Mexican elite, whose anxiety was quieter and, if possible, much more extreme. For her purposes, however, only the gringos held any interest. She'd been following enough of the news to know that she could get them into port legitimately at a number of places around the Pacific as part of some deal called Operation Uplift. She could even hit up the remains of the American government for her fuel and supply costs if she felt really cheeky and could be bothered to fill out the appropriate forms for lodgement at the nearest consulate or embassy. The wealthy Mexicans, however, had nothing even resembling the wreckage of a government to lobby foreign capitals on their behalf, and Jules wasn't willing to take the risk of running them all the way to Sydney, only to have some little migration nazi with a clipboard tell her they couldn't land. Pieraro and his family she'd get in somewhere by other means. But that marked the outer limits of her largesse.

So they were sitting at the large table in the coolest, darkest corner of the bar, a small band of superrich refugees, negotiating payment for passage, when the background buzz in the place suddenly spiked upward and drowned out all conversation. Somebody screamed "*No!*" and Jules tensed up, instinctively reached for the pistol hidden in her small carryall, then stayed her hand as she realized that nothing was going down. A small crowd had gathered under a television fixed high in another corner of the bar, and something had set them off. Briefly she fought down a surge of panic, like a rat twisting in her mind, terrified that the Wave had expanded again.

A barman turned up the volume as people argued and shushed each other, and Jules recognized the voice of BBC World presenter Mishal Husain. Poor old Pete'd had the hots for her, and Jules smiled sadly at a memory of him drunk on Jamaican rum, stoned on hash, and growling at the TV exactly what he'd like to be doing to Husain while she burbled on about some EU trade meeting.

She missed him terribly.

"In Tehran alone," read Husain, "it is estimated that three million died in the initial blast and firestorm, which extended more than a dozen miles from ground zero. Many more died quickly from radiation exposure, and experts say that the final toll in that city may reach six million. Other Iranian cities destroyed in the attack include Qom, Isfahan . . ."

Pieraro crossed himself as the news silenced the entire bar for a second. Her Gurkhas, Shah and Thapa, standing a few feet away, providing a formidable barrier to anybody wanting to approach them, did not visibly react. Their eyes continued to sweep the room like cameras.

"That's it. I'm not going to Hawaii," said the construction magnate.

"What?" asked Jules, still straining to hear the telly.

"Pearl Harbor. That's in Hawaii. If there's gonna be a nuclear war it'll get hit for sure. I'm not paying you everything I have left just to get my family turned into fucking shadows on a wall by some Chinese A-bomb."

Cesky was his name. Henry Cesky. A squat, powerful-looking man with coarse black hair and a nose that had obviously been broken more than once. He owned more than a hundred building cranes towering over twelve North American cities. Within half an hour of hearing about the Disappearance he'd transferred as much available cash as he could from his U.S. accounts to a series of shelf companies registered in Vanuatu, using that money to buy gold and diamonds in Acapulco. He was traveling with his second wife and four children, all girls, and as soon as they'd met he'd demanded passage to Hawaii for them and then Seattle for himself.

"I still got an office in Seattle," he'd initially said in a deep, rasping voice that was just barely inflected with the merest trace of eastern Europe under his harsh Brookyn accent. "My girls, they can't go to Seattle. Too close to that fucking wave it is. But I don't mind that. I can handle it. I don't think that fucking thing is going nowhere. So you take me there. Lotta fucking work to be done in the Northwest now. Lotta money to be made. To make up what I lost and what you fucking pirates are stealing from me. But my girls. They go somewhere I know they're safe. Hawaii."

That had been half an hour ago.

Now Cesky's tune was entirely different. "No fucking way do they set foot on those islands. No fucking way do they get within a hundred thousand miles. You take them as far away from this bullshit"—he pointed to the TV screen—"as you can. New Zealand. They filmed that *Lord of the Rings* there. Got some great fucking six-star lodges built for the movie stars. Ends of the fucking earth it is. Went fishing there once. That'd be good. Or Tasmania. Where they got that devil in the cartoon. That's even farther away. But no fucking Pearl Harbor. Not now."

Jules felt like her head was going to spin off. Cesky wasn't the worst of them, not by a long shot. That'd be the porn king, Larry Zood. He didn't look like a porn king. Possibly because he was an Internet porn king, and so looked more like a crooked real-estate broker. But he oozed a sort of preemptive creepiness that assured Jules that he would one day weigh three hundred pounds, wear a bad hairpiece, and still insist on bouncing hotties on his knee. He'd been trying to get Fifi to climb on board since finding out that her mother had been one of the original *Hustler* babes.

"Larry Flynt was a great American hero," he said in all earnestness, before grabbing one of Fifi's boobs and squeezing experimentally. When she peeled his hand away with a painful jujitsu technique, he simply laughed.

"Ow! What a fucking rack. That was totally worth it."

"Jules," said Fifi, between thinly pressed lips. "If this fucking nimrod gets on the boat, he pays twice the going rate."

"Fine by me," she agreed.

"Hey!" protested the porn king.

Jules leaned forward and fixed him with a glare like a pin pushed into a butterfly's back.

"Understand this, Mr. Zood. We are not your bitches. We are people smugglers. Criminals. If you touch any of my crew or any other passenger like that again, I will have Mr. Shah take out his pistol and shoot you in the head. And, yes, you will now pay double the asking rate if you wish to leave this city with us."

Zood held her glare for a few seconds before breaking into an oily grin.

"Money schmoney," he mugged. "I still got plenty to blow. I didn't even have my dough stashed in the U.S. Legally I don't exist there. For tax purposes, you know. Legally I got *disappeared* years ago."

He was drinking heavily and very much amused by his own wit, but Jules could detect a slightly anxious edge to his demeanor.

Having arrived at the table an hour ago with a small imitation Fabergé egg, he'd tossed it to Julianne like a golf ball, demanding to know up front how many of "my bitches" he could take with him.

"Give you one egg per bitch. They're fakes, from Thailand, but the jewels are real. I can leave a few bitches behind. They know that," he said. "Makes 'em extra keen to please, if you know what I mean. But I *will* need some with me. I don't like the water. I don't even like the hot tub they got by the pool over there. So a fucking sea voyage, shit, if you don't mind I'm just gonna bomb myself with crystal meth and stay in my suite getting blown. That's why I need some bitches with me."

She was tempted to shoot him right then and there.

"If you don't mind, Jules, I've got crew to interview back at the marina. I'll see you back there. Better company if you ask me."

"Sure baby, you go. One of Shah's men can escort you back."

Fifi left the table without a backward glance. She was never comfortable around muckety-mucks as she referred to anyone wealthier than a gas station attendant. Except for Jules, of course. Her fall from societal grace and favor meant that she very much met with Fifi's approval.

"You're like Paris or Britney," she often told the English exile. "Rich but cool."

An uncomfortable silence ensued for a moment as Julianne regarded Zood with cold contempt.

Not that her other candidates were much less odious. A property developer and his wife. No kids. Some guy whose family owned a health fund. He had his third wife and one kid with him. A merchant banker, with his very own bank, based in Basel, Switzerland. His mistress. An oil broker. And a couple of trust-fund delinquents, a brother and sister, who seemed not at all put out that their entire family back in Boston was gone. They, like everyone else at the table, had distinguished themselves by striking like rattlers as soon as they knew the score. Cashing out and converting to exactly the sort of high-end trade goods that Jules had known would hold or even increase their value, at least in the short term.

She had trouble keeping their names straight, and was seriously thinking of a cull. Dumping the porn king and his posse of bitches. And possibly Cesky, who struck her as trouble. They were all very demanding people. The trust-fund duo, Phoebe and Jason, had an especially odious sense of entitlement that she recalled from the useless rich kids of her own childhood.

"Will there be staff?" asked Phoebe. "Other than them." She nodded at the Gurkhas.

"We could bring our own, I suppose," her brother mused, not even bothering to refer to Jules. "Hire them here, perhaps? From the resort?"

But Cesky, he was the real quandary. She knew nothing of the construction industry but thought it had to be a tough game. Wasn't it rotten with Mafia money and crooked unions? To make a fortune in it, you would have to be as hard as tungsten, which wouldn't necessarily count him out as a prospect. But she just had a feeling with this bastard that if he got off the leash, you'd suddenly have something like a three-hundred-pound bull mastiff with amphetamine psychosis tearing at your throat.

Then again, she supposed, she could always just have Shah throw him over the side. Her attention wandered back to the television.

"Israeli prime minister Ariel Sharon has warned other regional powers that they will have to disarm immediately, if they do not wish to be attacked in a second round of strikes. The Saudi government has already agreed to immediate talks with Tel Aviv and has stood down its military, which had been on high alert since the outbreak of hostilities with Iraq and Iran."

"Man's a fucking genius," said Cesky. "A fucking devil, but a genius."

"You think he's a genius?" said Zood, arcing up without warning. "A fucking Hitler is more like it. He's a fucking war criminal, Cesky. A mass murderer. He should be fucking stoned to death for the rest of his life."

Cesky laughed in the pornographer's face.

"A name like Zood, you would think that, wouldn't you? Where'd your family come from again? No, lemme guess. They were ass-fucking goats in the Bekaa Valley for the last three thousand years?"

"You fucking Jewish pig!"

Jules caught Pieraro's eye for a half a second, just long enough for an unspoken question.

Where the hell did you find these idiots?

And then the two men were on each other, punching and clawing. Their chairs tipped over and drinks crashed to the floor.

The banker's mistress screamed, knocked down in the sudden eruption. The trust-fund brats simply pushed themselves back to a safe distance and smiled, enjoying the entertainment. Shah and Thapa moved like pouncing tigers, but Pieraro beat them into the fray. A flurry of blows from the Mexican cowboy, a blur of short, vicious punches, laid both men out flat in less than two seconds.

Without consulting anyone, he stood over the prone figures and announced, "You will not be traveling on Ms. Julianne's boat. You will need to make your own arrangements. Do not attempt to answer me back or get to your feet."

Zood opened his mouth to speak and Pieraro suddenly pistoned out one booted foot and kicked him in the face. The man's head flew back with a nasty click and he flipped over, landing on his back. The vaquero turned a stone face on Cesky, who was glaring at him murderously, reminding Jules of an enraged bull. Pieraro absorbed the full force of the man's enmity, never breaking eye contact. Eventually Cesky folded, crabbing away from the table on all fours until he felt that he was at a safe enough distance to stand up.

Two security guards appeared, pushing their way through the throng, which had momentarily turned away from the television, but they stopped in their tracks at a single glance from the Mexican.

"Man," said Phoebe, a little breathlessly. "That was so fucking hot."

"Do you wish to come on the boat, young lady? To escape?" Pieraro asked her.

She flushed noticeably at his attention. Jules recognized it as a purely sexual response.

"Yes," she said.

"Then you will shut the fuck up!" he barked. "And do what you are told when you are told. All of you! Understand?"

The girl flinched but nodded. The others all muttered and mumbled their assent.

Back at the bar, with the prospect of personal violence abated, the crowd reluctantly turned back to the television.

Jules saw Shah acknowledge the vaquero's handling of the situation with the slightest dip of his head.

She had to admit, it *was* pretty fucking cool. None of these rich bastards would give them another moment's trouble. She was sure of it.

And she was wrong.

Acapulco Yacht Club, Acapulco

Fifi liked Mr. Lee. He reminded her of old Lenny Wah, who rescued her when she'd fled her stepfather's dream of a family threesome and cable TV fame via the agency of Jerry Springer. Lenny ran a supercheap Chinese takeout in East Bay, where she'd wound up looking for a cheap meal after running out of money. The meal she got was a comforting fried rice/chow mein combo with a rock-hard spring roll for three-fifty. She also got a job offer, washing dishes in a huge claw-foot tub standing out of view of the customers, in a weed-choked yard out the back of the café. The last dish-monkey had quit two days earlier and Lenny had let the washing build up under a layer of cold, gray, fat-caked water.

"But Lenny was kinda nice," she told Lee. "He had real soft skin, and he smelled of jasmine rice."

"Lenny sounds like a bum, Miss Fifi. He try to make jiggy-jig for dishwashing?"

She snickered.

"Only every fucking day. But he was real nice about it. He didn't get upset when I said no."

"You always said no?"

"Not always."

The old Chinese sea dog rolled his eyes as Thapa showed the next man through to see them. They sat behind a folding card table on the dock of the marina where Jules had berthed the sports fisher while the *Rules* lay offshore, guarded by the remainder of Shah's men. The hasty patch-up work occasioned by the gunfight with Shoeless Dan stood out on the fiberglass hull, and more than a few of their potential recruits spent their interviews nervously eyeing the damage.

The next guy through, an older, potbellied American with a dense map of broken blood vessels coloring his swollen nose, and a fat cigar perched in one corner of his mouth, snorted when he saw it.

"Hot damn! I guess I wouldn't want to see the other guy, eh?"

Fifi glanced over her shoulder to where he'd nodded at the scorch marks and bullet holes. She tried to find the man's name on the list Thapa had provided, but it seemed to have blown away, leaving her with nothing but a cup of flat ginger beer and a bowl of pretzels in front of her.

"The other guy is dead. And who're you, Salty Sam?"

The man grinned, showing off uneven yellow teeth, but his smile seemed warm enough and contained none of the leering suggestion in Zood's eyes back at the hotel.

"Rhino Ross, young lady. Chief petty officer, United States Coast Guard, once upon a time. Nowadays, I run a fishing charter round these parts, or I used to anyway. And whom might I have the pleasure of addressing?"

"Fifi'll do. And this is Mr. Lee. Who's *our* chief . . . petty . . . guy. So we already got one a them. What else can you do for us, *Rhino*?" She paused and regarded him through narrowed eyes. "And did your parents really name you that, or something really gay that you just changed to Rhino?"

Ross smiled again and blew a perfect smoke ring.

"Rhino A. Ross. It's on my passport and birth certificate. Makes me kinda unique, don't you think?" He leaned forward. "And lest you have any doubt whatsoever, it is *good* to be the Rhino. Now, let's get down to brass tacks. A little birdie told me you were looking to crew an oceangoing vessel. Bridge crew in particular, am I right?"

"A little birdie?" said Fifi.

"Yup. Ran his mouth right up to the point I ran a stick through his ass, and toasted him up medium well over some hickory coals. A little scrawny but good eatin'; beak was a little crunchy, though." Another smoke ring punctuated the comment.

Mr. Lee said nothing, contenting himself with a kretek cigarette and a contemplative air. He gazed past Ross, away down the marina, where Fifi could see Thapa standing watch over a dozen men who'd turned up to apply for berths on the *Rules*.

Something about the Rhino's demeanor changed in an instant; his eyes hardened and his voice took on a commanding, almost military tone. "Now, given the size of that sports fisher you got all shot up over there, I figure you've got yourself a real ocean liner stowed away somewhere. And it's gonna have all manner of sensors, radar, communications gear, and other assorted and sundry technological doodads, none of which you know a damn thing about, am I right? Looks more like the starship *Enterprise* than a sailboat to you, right? No. Don't answer. The Rhino is always right. And of course, given all the holes some douche bag has already shot in your runabout, you know what sort of trouble is waiting for you up ahead. So here's the Rhino's iron-clad guaran-goddamned-tee. You take me out to your boat, I'll prove to you that I can run your systems, and then you can get me the hell out of here before this joint blows up. I need to get out of Acapulco, and you need a pro out there, Miss Fifi. Someone who knows these waters and the sort of low-life scum that swims in 'em sometimes. Seems to me that the last thing you need to be worrying about is which button to press when a bunch of bad guys come charging over the horizon with knives between their teeth." With that the Rhino sat back and puffed contentedly on his cigar, releasing a swirling cloud of thick white smoke with a self-satisfied whoosh.

Fifi leaned forward, bunching her boobs up between her arms, to see if the Rhino would drop his gaze. He didn't.

"Would I be right in assuming you'd know one end of a gun from the other, Rhino?"

"Twenty years in service, ma'am. You can assume away, but you know what they say about people who 'assume.' "

She nodded.

"So you said you ran charters. What happened to your boat? Why don't you just get the hell out under your own power?"

The Rhino folded his massive forearms and nodded at her vessel.

"See all the holes in your hull? The ones in mine were a lot bigger. I ran a legitimate business, miss. I don't know what you did before all this, but the fact that you're sitting here tells me it probably wasn't legit, and you had the guns and the balls to fight off whoever came after you. I wasn't so lucky."

Lee exhaled a thin stream of fragrant smoke.

"Mr. Rhino. Your lost boat. Do you know who attacked you?"

The former coast guard chief nodded.

"I do. A local peckerhead, working for a toothfish poacher down south. Said he was recruiting for his bossman. Wouldn't take no for an answer, so he shot up my boat when that's the only answer I had for him."

"Why didn't he shoot you?" asked Fifi.

"Shooting my boat hurt more," he said, quite honestly, she believed.

A lot of folks made the error of mistaking Fifi for some kind of life-sized Sluttymuch Barbie. But she'd been looking out for herself long enough to have developed a wild dog's instinct for sniffing out troublesome men. The job at Lenny's takeout, which quickly morphed into cooking as well as cleaning, had scored her a spot on a catering-industry training course run by a Bay Area businessmen's charity—"guilty fags," she called them—sponsoring college degrees for homeless kids. Her army-surplus cot in the storeroom at Lenny's counted as homeless. Fifi had graduated in the top five of her class, and landed a gig with an LA-based catering firm that specialized in providing "nutritional services" for the military in shitholes-of-the-week like Bosnia and Mogadishu.

She moved a lot more easily through that sort of crowd than the chichi ghetto of West Coast fine dining, and after shacking up with an army ranger for twelve months in the Balkans she could field strip an M4 carbine blindfolded. She also had a lot of experience with men like the Rhino—hard, uncompromising, and occasionally stupid men who were nonetheless decent at heart.

She leaned over to Mr. Lee.

"What d'you think?" she whispered.

"He'll eat too much, but he's okay," replied the Chinaman. "Mr. Pete would have liked him."

"Okay," she said, turning back to the old chief, who had heard everything. "If you brought any gear with you, stow it over there by the ramp. You can start out by helping load stores while we finish talking to those guys."

Fifi waved at the small crowd of hopefuls gathered by the marina gate and watched over by Thapa. The Rhino nodded brusquely and said, "Thanks," before looking around. "You said you wanted some stores loaded?"

"Inside," she said, gesturing to the wooden shed in front of which they sat. "Bags of rice, beans, lots of canned foods. Heavy work. But that won't bother you. You're the Rhino."

"No," he agreed, flashing a stagy grin, and tucked his cigar firmly into the corner of his mouth. He pointed at one of his massive biceps and said around the cigar, "Yeah, it'll be no bother at all since I didn't get these from pettin' kitty cats."

The Rhino paused before ducking his head into the shed. "Oh, one other thing, you got a humidor on that boat?"

Fifi gave a quizzical look.

"Like a hot tub?"

"No darlin', it's a little storage compartment for my Cuban friends here."

The Rhino blew a thin stream of blue smoke into the sky.

Fifi shrugged. "I reckon so. It has everything else."

The last thing she heard as the Rhino nodded his approval and disappeared into the shed was "Oh yeah, it's good to be the Rhino."

MV *Aussie Rules*, 20 nm west of Acapulco

The lambent glow of Acapulco at night, a soft dome of light defining a horizon at the edge of the world in the absolute blackness of night at sea, had changed character, to Jules's eye. It looked less artificial now, less fixed. Suffused by a burnt orange tincture, it flickered and even flared at times.

"Another high-rise, going up," said Fifi.

"I imagine so," Jules agreed.

They worked by starlight and the pale illumination of a red moon. It had been that bloodstained color since the Wave had appeared. The *Aussie Rules* remained blacked out, a precaution against more attacks as the new crew members Fifi and Mr. Lee had chosen helped move supplies from the sports fisher to its mother ship.

Jules was generally pleased with the haul of men and cargo. She'd been a bit taken aback by the Rhino when she'd first met him, especially by the perpetual wreath of cigar smoke that preceded and followed him like London fog, but had quickly come to accept his bluster and bullshit as a well-polished routine. He'd probably been practicing it on tourists for years and had forgotten how not to be in character. She couldn't fault his work ethic or his skill sets, however. He'd fired up whole suites of sensors and arrays in the bridge that had proven completely impenetrable to everyone else. And having done so, he'd gone right back to hauling sacks of rice and fresh-killed meat—very expensive fresh-killed meat—onto the boat deck of the *Rules* and from there off to the freezers. Another odd thing: Every so often he would stop one of the other workers, point to one of his enormous biceps, and say, "You don't get these from pettin' kitty cats," whatever that meant. Odd, very odd.

He stayed out of the ice room with Pete's body in it, though. For now, that was sealed off.

"I'm glad Pieraro kicked the shit out of those assholes," said Fifi as she picked up an LNG canister and hoisted it over her shoulder. Jules grunted as she caught a sack of potatoes thrown up to her by Thapa as though it were no heavier than a bag of cotton candy.

"Bloody hell," she said, struggling not to fall over.

A German man, short but powerful-looking, caught her gently by the elbow.

"Not so good to be falling overboard, no?" He grinned, his teeth standing out in the wine-red light.

"No, thank you . . ." said Jules, reaching for his name. The yacht was beginning to fill up with strangers, and although she tried to commit all of their names and potted histories to memory, there was just so much for her to do each day that she never really felt as if she was getting on top of any one job.

Fifi rescued her. "This is Dietmar. He's German, you know, like hot dogs originally used to be. Anyway, he's our navigator now. He used to work on a container ship."

The German, who looked to be about thirtysomething, nodded enthusiastically as he wrestled the heavy bag of potatoes off Jules before flinging it over his shoulder with as little apparent trouble as Thapa had experienced tossing it at Jules like a feather pillow.

"Okay," she said. "You'll do."

"Yo, Boss Jules!" called out a hoarse, rasping voice. The Rhino. "Where do you want me to stow your boom sticks?"

Jules smiled and nodded at Dietmar again, to thank him for his help. She peered down onto the boat deck, swarming with Gurkhas and new crewmates, and found the Rhino shouldering a wooden box of Mexican army rifles that Shah had secured from somewhere.

The number of things she didn't know about on this yacht was getting bigger and bigger every day.

"Take them through to the gym," she called down. "We're using that as an armory for now. One of the Gurkhas will show you."

"Don't worry. I'll follow my horn. It always knows the way," he replied. "Oh, and where the hell is the humidor that Cap'n Fifi told me about? I've got four boxes of Davidoff Anniversario Number Ones in my ruck and if they dry out you'll find out up close and personal why rhinos are surly beasts."

"Library I think," she called out at his retreating form as another newcomer, an Indian by the look of him, smiled and nodded shyly.

"Engine room?" he asked.

"Follow the Rhino," she said, "but take the second stairwell down two decks. You won't miss it."

She turned around to ask Fifi if she could spare a few minutes to take her through the crew manifest again, but she was gone. Probably chatting up Dietmar on the way to the galley. Julianne took a few moments to just lean on the starboard rail and stare back toward the coastline. They were a good twenty miles out from shore, giving them enough time to see anyone coming at them. The radar, which was now working much more effectively thanks to the Rhino, was showing dozens of vessels within a few nautical miles, but Mr. Lee constantly adjusted their position to maintain a safe distance from any possible contacts. And, she had to admit, she felt much more secure with Shah's men and all of the new arrivals on board.

Not that she'd be staying tonight.

They had to take the smaller boat back to the marina to pick up their passengers and Pieraro and his family in the morning.

Although, looking at the baleful light of the burning city, she had to wonder what sort of fresh hell she'd be sailing into, and whether Pieraro would even make it back in time to rendezvous. He had a four-hundred-mile round trip to retrieve his family tonight, and the roads, if not choked with refugees, would almost certainly be stalked by brigands and highwaymen.

She wondered whether he'd make it, and how long she could afford to wait.

Fairmont resort, Acapulco

College students. More than a thousand of them.

They formed a moat around the entrance of the Fairmont the next morning when she returned with Shah to pick up her passengers and Pieraro. Security had deteriorated all over Acapulco during the night, as though news of the Israeli attack had somehow finally uncapped all of the base animal fears stirred up by the Disappearance. While Mr. Lee and some of Shah's men supervised her newly hired crew in final preparations on board the *Aussie Rules,* now ten miles offshore, at the marina Fifi and Thapa prepped the launch for a quick dash across the bay. Jules had chosen a rendezvous point much closer to the Fairmont to avoid a confrontation with the mob that had gathered at the gates of the marina demanding to be let in. Driving through the city, she could understand their motivation.

Anarchy was loose.

Whatever remnant of order had prevailed until yesterday was gone, and the madness she had been expecting was finally upon them. It was like moving through a city at war with itself. No. It was worse than that, because there were no sides, just a general eruption, a battle of all against all. Packs of young men fell on individuals caught out alone. Larger gangs fell on them in turn. There had been no uniformed police or city authorities visible for days, but even the sort of organized private muscle that had protected places like the marina and the Fairmont resort were much less in evidence, either hunkered down behind high walls and barricades, or simply dissipated as men flaked away to protect their own immediate interests and families. Gunfire, thick oily smoke, occasional explosions, and the mob sounds of fear and rage lay over the entire city.

Driving was a nightmare, with streets frequently choked and impassable.

Only Shah's handling of the all-terrain SUV allowed them any headway through the worst of the snarls. At times he simply mounted the curb and rolled through private yards to dodge some of the blockages. When the roads opened, the former soldier drove quickly and aggressively, twice knocking down small groups of men armed with improvised weapons who attempted to bar their passage along the Escénica roadway as it ran through scrubland in the hills to the west of Revolcadero Beach. The thud of impact as they struck human flesh made her shudder and close her eyes. It was somehow much worse sitting passively in the seat beside Shah. The situation eased somewhat as they came down out of the hills and drove onto the long strip of the dual laneway of the Costera de las Palmas. Sprinklers still sprayed long arcs of recycled water over the empty, bright green golf courses to their left, and the beach-front resorts of Revolcadero on the right had not yet been touched by the violence that gripped the center of Acapulco, but the evidence of accelerating collapse was everywhere. In the long lines of slow-moving cars piled high with personal goods. In the swarms of people sitting on the tarmac at the Aeropuerto Internacional, desperate for flights out, even though no aircraft remained there and none were flying in. And in the mob of seething, chanting American college students laying siege to the gates of the Fairmont, where resort security led a grim effort to hold them at bay.

"What the fuck?" said Jules as Shah slowed and pulled over to the side of the road well away from the mob scene.

"Spring break," said Shah by way of explanation. "Many students on cruise ships from America. Cheap cruises. Very ugly."

"That's great," she said. "But what are they doing here?"

She could see some of Pieraro's street toughs wielding canes and clubs to beat back the Americans, but many of the students seemed prepared to respond in kind. One group in particular had armed themselves with a mix of sporting equipment, some protective gear, and some improvised weapons like baseball bats and even one cricket bat that she could see. They appeared to work as a flying squad, charging from one spot to the next whenever the security men threatened more beatings and mayhem.

"Bit of a fucking cock-up then, Mr. Shah."

"A bit, Miss Julianne."

He started the engine again and pulled back into the slow-moving stream of traffic that rolled straight through the center of the crowd.

"Don't stop," she ordered him. "I'll see if I can get Miguel's attention as we roll past."

Shah nodded and crunched the stick into low gear. There was no moving any faster than a trot anyway, with the road and the dusty shoulder completely choked with foot traffic and hundreds of vehicles. Dozens more had stopped from want of gas and been pushed off the road onto the shoulder, creating obstacles around which flowed the slow-moving river of refugees. The exodus from the city poured through and past the huge knot of young Americans, who all seemed to be carrying expensive backpacks and luggage. More than a few were drunk. As Jules rolled down the window she was struck by the stench of so many people packed in closely together.

"It's bloody hopeless," she said after a few minutes. "I'll have to go in on foot. Turn off up ahead and take the car down to the sand. It can run on sand, can't it?"

Shah nodded. "I shall wait by the cabanas directly out the back. I will not move until you come for me."

Jules thought about taking the shotgun, but settled instead on a concealed pistol, which she carried in a holster on her hip under a long shirt. She was dressed in desert boots, khaki shorts, and a white sea-cotton top, and didn't look all that out of place in the young crowd. She waved off Shah and began to push her way forward. He'd been right. They were mostly young Americans, very obviously vacationing students. She supposed there had to be a few thousand of them in Acapulco at any time of year, but their numbers would probably swell during semester breaks. What the hell they were doing camped out in front of the Fairmont she had no idea, but the deeper she moved into the crowd the uglier and more charged with menace the atmosphere grew, mostly thanks to the same street thugs she'd run into with Shah yesterday. She recognized Pieraro's second-in-command, Roberto, the Colombian guy, standing atop a stone wall, looking splendid in black combat pants and a matching wifebeater. His eyes were hidden behind silver sunglasses and he was sporting some fabulous new bling, but there was no mistaking the brute arrogance and cruelty of the man. He seemed to be enjoying himself, siccing small packs of his men on the gringos whenever they threatened to push too far into the complex, although his goons seemed less enthusiastic about tangling with the mob of drunken, fired-up college jocks who had armed themselves with the sporting gear. They were pretty evenly matched.

It was a wonder gunplay hadn't broken out, but then in contrast with yesterday his men were all armed with clubs and ax handles. The pistols with which they'd manned the roadblock were nowhere in evidence. As Julianne elbowed and squeezed through the crush, she began to attend to the snatches of conversation she heard.

". . . totally. They are picking us up here. Coast guard or something . . ."

"It's the marines, man, I heard marines."

"We're going to Seattle."

"No way. It's Sydney."

Oh, no, thought Jules. *I have a very bad feeling about this.*

She decided to skirt the heart of the mob, pushing out toward the edges and finally getting free of them about a hundred meters farther down the road near the resort's tennis courts. Cutting through a dense forest of artfully arranged palm trees, she looped around the rear of a large apartment complex, emerging near one of the half-dozen swimming pools. They were all deserted today, even the bars at the edge of the water, but over by the artificial lagoon, on the terrace of the Chula Vista restaurant, she found her passengers, their minder Pieraro, and his family. All fifteen of them.

The vaquero looked furious, but he was not nearly as angry as Jules.

She stormed over, fists clenching and unclenching. Everyone but Pieraro flinched and shuffled aside.

"What the *fuck* is going on out there? And who the hell are these people?" she demanded to know. "You told me you had a wife and a couple of kids. You brought half the fucking village with you."

The Mexican's extended family looked to him, with more than a little fear. Jules assumed the woman clinging to his arm was the wife, and the girls crowded around her were their daughters, but the rest had to be a grab bag of aunts, uncles, grandparents, and possibly the village drunk, the village idiot, and the village's drunken idiotic mayor all thrown in for good measure. None of them looked to have a fucking peso between them.

Pieraro disentangled himself from them and moved forward to intercept Julianne as she bulldozed her way through the tables and chairs overlooking the lagoon, knocking one over with a resounding crash. Normally the terrace would have been crowded with guests taking a late breakfast at this time, but the restaurant was closed and seemingly abandoned. She guessed that very few staff had bothered to show up.

"You've got a fucking nerve," she hissed at Pieraro. "I don't know what that balls up out the front is about, but there are about a thousand dumb jock college students out there who seem to think they'll be hitching a ride out of here with us. But they won't, will they, because you've brought half the fucking village of *el Shithole del Diablo* with you!"

Pieraro didn't flare up or push back, insisting in a steady voice, "There is no need to be offensive, Miss Julianne. I am not responsible for the crowd out the front. That was Cesky's doing."

"That putty-nosed toad. What the hell did . . ."

"It's true," called out Phoebe the trust-fund bimbo, looking appreciably less sure of herself than yesterday. "He was so pissed off with you for cutting him out that he marched off yesterday and started telling everyone about the escape plan. It spread. I got three text messages about it."

She held up a cell phone as if to explain. Jules was surprised it still worked. Hers had cut out days ago. She sighed internally. *The rich.* They always had a way.

Her other would-be five-star refugees all nodded glumly.

"Right," said Jules, barely able to contain her exasperation. "Well, we've still got to get you away from here. There is already another lynch party back at the marina, waiting to do you all in for a ticket out of this madhouse. So listen up. You do exactly as I say or you *will* be left behind . . . Miguel. Transport. That was your job . . ."

"I have two buses," he said. "They will take everyone."

"Yeah, and how are they going to get out through that mob in front? I've got Shah parked down on the beach waiting for us. No way will your buses run on soft sand."

"No. But I have not parked them here," he said. "When Miss Saint John"—he indicated Phoebe—"warned me what had happened with Cesky, I hid them down the beach, at the Alberca Heritage. I know the security chief there. A good man."

"How much did that cost?" asked Jules, rubbing her eyes.

"A hundred gallons of gasoline," he answered. "He is leaving with his family this evening."

"Fine," she said through gritted teeth. "And the mob out the front?"

"Roberto will hold them there. He has arranged a number of minibuses from the Fairmont at reception. Everyone thinks they are the escape vehicles."

"And he wants passage, too?"

"No. He sees opportunities here. Mostly he wants me gone. But some payment was involved."

Jules closed her eyes.

"How much?"

The merchant banker, the one with the silicone-enhanced mistress, suddenly spoke up. "It was nothing. Now can we get the hell out of here?"

Jules struggled for his name. Roger . . . Roger . . . Moorhouse.

"So? You paid off Roberto the coke-dealing paramilitary fascist?" she asked incredulously. "Oh, well. That'll turn out fine, I'm sure. He won't be back for another bite of the apple, will he! I mean, do any of you actually need me? Everything seems to be running tickety fucking boo without my input. Perhaps I should just piss off and leave you to get on with it."

"Listen," said Moorhouse, stepping forward. He was a short man with all of the attendant psychological problems. Jules estimated that standing face-to-face with his girlfriend, he'd be smothered by her breast implants. His features were flushed, and he was sweating profusely. "We have had a very stressful morning here. Those people began arriving before dawn. The hotel has been locked down for hours by security men. We were stuck in our rooms, no air-conditioning, no cable, no idea what was happening. If it took a couple of trinkets and baubles to get that Colombian thug to run interference for us, that was well worth it. Now I suggest you start earning your money and get us the hell out of Acapulco."

Tempted to pistol-whip him, Jules merely nodded, silently.

"Right then. Miguel? Can I talk to you? Privately. For two minutes. Do we have two minutes?"

The background roar was building, but not in a way that made her think a boilover was imminent. The vaquero patted his wife on the shoulder and gently rubbed the head of his youngest child, a little boy who was crying silently. He bent down to whisper a few words in his ear before kissing his forehead. With the child settled, for the moment, the two of them walked off to the other side of the terrace.

"This conga line of relatives and . . . whatever. Have you planned on provisions and stores for them? Because I haven't. We had an agreement. Your wife and children. I don't recall agreeing to take all of the supporting cast from *The Three Amigos*."

Pieraro looked physically pained. His next words came out like teeth extracted one after the other.

"If you cannot take them, you cannot. I will explain."

The man's discomfort was so palpable, so deeply etched into the fissures of his sunburned face, that Jules had to look away.

She covered the moment of weakness by pretending to scan the hotel grounds for trouble. Unfortunately, standing right in her line of view were his family, the sorriest, most bedraggled-looking losers she'd seen in a long time. The crowd in front of the hotel was young, middle-class white people with a leavening of upper-echelon Mexicans. They were frightened, but still well fed and used to having their own way. Pieraro's family looked like they would turn around at one word from her and slouch off to their fate.

Jules risked a quick glance at her paying customers. They seemed entirely nonplussed, and she supposed they had no reason to question the arrival of the Pieraro clan. Miguel had clearly established himself as a powerful figure in their eyes only yesterday. If that power meant he could drag along his extended family they would probably accept that. After all, they were all too used to the privileges of power themselves.

The crowd noise intensified, noticeably, spilling over and around the Fairmont's centerpiece architectural statement, the main hotel built in the form of a giant Aztec pyramid. She could see dozens of guests on their balconies hiding from the disturbance outside, and too many of them were pointing at her little group. Time to go.

"Listen," she said. "This isn't over. Not by a fucking long shot. I cannot take all of those people you've brought. I do not have stores for them, and they will not be allowed off the boat at the other end. Not to mention the trouble it's going to cause with everyone who actually paid for their passage. *But.* We don't have time to get into this now. We need to get away from this city. It is going under. Right now. I'll take your extras on today. Take them a safe distance down the coast, away from the city. That's where it's going to be worst. But they will have to get off. Do you understand? You need to talk to them about where that might be. I'm sure they will have relatives somewhere, in some stagnant backwater, who'll take them in. Probably be glad of the extra hands come bean-harvest time. But I can't take them."

She held Pieraro's eyes this time, not flinching away from the falling man she saw in there.

"Because they cannot pay," he said at last, with an air of injured dignity.

"If you want to make me the bitch, okay. Because they

cannot pay. Nobody is going to fuel and provision me if *I* cannot pay. That is the only reason I'm taking those rich arseholes anywhere. They are buying my fuel, my food, my arms and ammunition, and surely even you can see that right now nothing trumps that."

"They have brought their own food," said Pieraro in a dry, flat voice. "Beans. Dried meat. Flour. They will not be a burden."

"Oh, my God, I cannot believe we're even having this discussion. You are not an idiot, Miguel. You know how things are. You know what's coming . . . *fuck,* you know it's already here."

"They are my family, Julianne. My *family.* Do you not have a family of your own?"

His attempt at guilting her out produced only a short, bitter laugh.

"Oh, Miguel, that is *so* not a road to go down with me. Look. We have to move. Now. Get everyone down to the . . . Heritage, was it? Get them onto the buses. We have to get around to the bay, to the big jetty up the beach from the Hyatt. Do you know it? Good. Fifi and Thapa will be waiting there. It is going to be a very crowded trip out to the *Rules.*"

Pieraro closed his eyes.

"Thank you," he said, as if in prayer.

"We are dropping them off, Miguel. Somewhere. Okay?"

"Okay. Somewhere safe."

The crackle of gunfire started, muted by distance and smothered by the sudden roar of an enraged, terrified mob.

"I think Roberto has taken off his smiley face," said Jules. "Let's get the fuck out of here."

33

"Jeez, Julesy. We taking a mariachi band with us? Cool."

Fifi had switched over to a Larry the Cable Guy camouflage baseball cap with the trademark fishhook in the bill. Jules ignored the hat, especially the Confederate flag.

"Don't start, Fifi. Just get them on board."

The trip around the southern headland of Acapulco Bay had not been entirely uneventful. Both Shah and Julianne had been forced to open fire on a couple of makeshift roadblocks that had not been there an hour earlier. The roadblocks were being manned by would-be carjackers. At least she assumed they were carjackers.

Her passengers, paying and nonpaying, poured out of the two beaten-up-looking school buses Pieraro had obtained from God only knew where, and stood blinking in the harsh light, on a massive baking slab of cracked concrete, an empty parking lot overlooking the water. They were all upset, and some of the Americans looked positively ill. The *Aussie Rules*'s giant sports fisher bobbed slowly up and down at the end of the pier, which jutted out more than a hundred meters into the bay. No other craft were moored there, and one look out over the water told her why. Thousands of vessels, from small aluminum dinghies to oceangoing megayachts, were on the move, heading away from shore toward the mouth of the bay. Only the slightest puff of breeze ruffled the ubiquitous palms onshore, but out on the bay the enormous flotilla had churned up a mass of white water.

"Any trouble getting away?" asked Jules.

"Some," admitted Fifi, who was dressed in a denim microskirt and distressed red tee emblazoned with the legend *Zombie Squad—We can handle it from here. We've talked about this on the Internet.* A Marlboro dangled from her lips. Jules wondered what her friend would do when she finally ran out.

She hefted up her PKM. "But we got her done."

Jules winced.

"You didn't kill anyone, did you?"

Fifi rolled her eyes, "Just a few rounds downrange. Jeez, who died and made you Captain Sensible?"

Jules stared past Fifi into a place she wasn't even sure existed. Fifi caught the hint. "Oh. Yeah. Pete. Uh, sorry."

"Fine," said Julianne, throwing up her hands. "Let's just get them on board before we draw another crowd." She could see cars beginning to pull over to the side of the freeway on the hill up above them. Small groups of people were already picking their way down through the scrub, doubtless hoping to clamber on board the boat with them. Across the confusion of the bay, the center of Acapulco was a disaster movie. Fires blazed at so many locations she couldn't count them, but it was eerily quiet, like watching TV with the sound down. After a second she realized why. No sirens, anywhere. The absence was chilling.

"Come on, move your arses," she called out to the dawdling travelers. Phoebe had actually stopped to take pictures with a small digital camera.

"Where the fuck are you going to get them printed?" cried Jules in frustration. "Move!"

Shah and Thapa began herding everyone toward the dock, occasionally glancing back up toward the roadway. A few more cars had pulled over. Pieraro spoke to an old man among his people, who nodded before firing off a scorching fusillade of native oaths and curses and clouting a teenaged boy, who'd stopped dead, transfixed by Fifi's T-shirt. The Mexicans, all hauling heavy sacks of food by the looks of them, began to run down the pier. The Americans, dropping some of their luggage as they went, followed suit as Thapa chivvied them along.

"If you would be so kind as to hurry your arses up now."

"Mr. Shah?" said Jules. "My gun if you please."

The Gurkha sergeant produced her shotgun from the cabin of the SUV, racking a round into the chamber before handing it over to her.

"Thank you," said Jules. She fired three shots into the air

over the heads of the people swarming down the hillside toward them. It had a salutary effect on her own charges as well, speeding their passage down the jetty to a sprint.

"Hell, yeah," enthused Fifi. "Time for a little redneck persuasion."

She let rip with a short, snarling burst from her heavy Russian machine gun, firing into the windows of an abandoned building overlooking the parking lot, shattering a dozen panes of glass. The sound was scarifying, and the small horde descending the slopes stopped and dropped immediately.

"Go, go," said Shah, waving them off toward the boat, where Thapa and Pieraro were hurriedly helping everyone aboard, in some cases by throwing them bodily over the side.

The girls didn't wait to be told twice. They set off at a sprint. A few moments later Jules heard the car start up again, and, looking back over her shoulder, she saw the former soldier drive it onto the jetty. He followed them, stopping halfway down, before turning the wheel to effectively block any further access.

"They'll just crawl over it," said Fifi, leveling the PKM on the makeshift blockade.

"They won't," promised Jules.

Shah climbed out, tossed something into the cabin, and ran as quickly as she'd ever seen a short, refrigerator-shaped man run. A few seconds later, as the first of their desperate pursuers made the start of the pier, the grenade exploded, lifting the vehicle a few inches off the deck, but not moving it far enough to topple it into the water. Everyone ducked. When Jules straightened up, access from the shore was blocked by the burning wreckage.

"Nice work, buddy," said Fifi as Shah trotted up to them. "You like NASCAR at all?"

Smiling like an imp, Shah lifted his shoulders.

"NASCAR. Never heard of it. But I never liked Toyotas much," he said.

Fifi wondered if anyone even drove a Toyota in NASCAR.

Out on the water, it was worse. The sports fisher was big and powerful enough to speed around or muscle through the occasional logjams of smaller craft that blocked its way, and the sight of Pieraro, Thapa, and Shah heavily tooled up and guarding against all attempts at boarding precluded any such misadventures. But Jules still had a hell of a time clearing the bay, on which an unknowable number of vessels jostled for primacy. Where the hell most of them thought they were going, she had no idea. The little runabouts and motor boats and inflatables that numbered in the thousands would founder in even moderate seas, and word from Mr. Lee back on the *Rules* was that storms in the high latitudes had whipped up a bitching four-meter swell on a nasty chaotic cross chop of at least another meter and a half. They were going to have a lot of seasick passengers in less than half an hour. But at least they would survive.

Jules shook her head as she spun the wheel to dodge what looked like a garbage barge barely able to stay afloat under the weight of seven or eight hundred people, all tightly packed onto mounds of rubbish. They were throwing the rotting, malodorous ballast overboard as quickly as they could, but the wake from her sudden turn set the flat-bottomed scow wallowing dangerously, and at least a dozen men and women went over the side. She nudged the throttles forward and tried to ignore their flailing figures. They wouldn't be the last people to drown today.

A cacophony of horns, whistles, sirens, and Klaxons overlay constant screaming and calls for help. The farther out into the bay she took them, the worse it grew. Bodies began to appear in the churning water, some floating near capsized boats, others obviously killed by gunfire. At one point she cut their speed back to allow a small pod of surf skiers to paddle by. They saluted her with their oars before resuming their rhythmic progress.

"How did they get this far?" she said to nobody in particular.

Fifi appeared at her elbow with a couple of chilled Coronas. She watched the surfers for a moment before shrugging.

"Surf breaks get pretty crowded. They're probably used to it. Wanna beer?"

"You have to be fucking kidding . . . oh . . . what the hell. Could you open it for me?"

Fifi popped the tops and passed one to Jules. She kept one hand to the wheel while draining half the cerveza in a couple of long pulls. The crisp, icy cold bite was like an angel's kiss. Indeed, she couldn't recall ever enjoying a beer nearly as much. It was almost obscene.

"You coulda waited, you know," said Fifi. "I cut up some limes."

"Only poofs fruit the beer, sweetheart. What's happening below?"

Fifi finished her own drink and tossed the empty bottle overboard before answering. It crashed into the prow of a ferry, eliciting a raised fist and long string of unintelligible curses from the skipper. She flipped him the finger.

"Miguel's got the mariachi band all stowed away down below. They're cool. No problemo. That fucking prom queen though, and her brother . . ."

"Phoebe and Jason?"

"Yeah, them. They're already arguing with the banker and his boob job about who gets the big cabin."

Jules squeezed her eyes shut for just a second. It was dangerous to have them closed for any longer.

"As long as they keep it down there, I don't give a rat's arse."

A deep, high-powered horn sounded off to starboard. A large container ship had dropped dozens of lines over the side to pick up people struggling in the water. Another big ship, an oil tanker, was heading straight for it. Jules wondered why until she saw the telltale sparkle of gunfire around the bridge.

"Damn, Julesy," said Fifi. "Nobody's in charge of that son of a bitch. You'd better haul ass. This ain't gonna be pretty."

Jules did not need encouraging. As Shah came hammering up the steps to warn them of the impending disaster, she flicked on the boat's PA system.

"Hey. Listen up, everyone. Get down low and grab something. I'm going to have to lay on some speed and do some rally driving."

Another long, shrieking blast on the container ship's horn pounded at them, and all around her, those ships that could put on speed suddenly did so, leaping up at their bows and churning up white wakes.

"You have seen?" asked Shah.

Julianne pushed the throttles to three-quarter power, and the boat leapt ahead.

"I'm on it," she cried out over the rising clamor of horns and the screaming of thousands of people in the water and on nearby boats.

Stray rounds from the firefight on the tanker splattered

against the boat inches from Fifi's head. She unlimbered the PKM and spat a stream of tracers back at them. "Fuckers!"

"Get down and stop arsing around!" Jules shouted.

Reefing the wheel to port, she narrowly avoided spearing an old wooden yacht that looked a lot like the *Diamantina*. It was certainly of the same vintage, and seemed to be crewed by three swimsuit models. Another sharp turn to starboard swept them around two more yachts, which had already collided with each other, and a bright yellow water taxi that was dangerously overloaded. The bow wave from her boat struck it amidships and it went over.

Jules was sorry, but there was nothing she could do about it.

Behind them the horns of both the tanker and the container ship roared in one long, deafening note.

Shah pointed her toward a stretch of slightly less crowded water, and Jules opened the boat's engines all the way. The massive bulk of the sixty-foot power craft lifted even higher in the water, and she gripped the silver wheel hard, concentrating on not running into anyone. A few blasts on her own horn began to scatter and clear some room up ahead, but then the warning was lost in a huge, world-ending uproar as the two giant ships collided. Risking a look back over the stern, she saw the container ship keel over violently. So great was the impact that dozens of the giant steel crates stacked high on its deck were thrown clear; those from the upper stacks described long slow arcs over the top of a few lucky ships before crashing down and utterly destroying a host of smaller boats. One rusted blue P&O container turned end over end and flew a good hundred meters before slamming amidships into the overcrowded garbage barge they had previously left in their wake. It struck like a giant fist, crushing hundreds of people instantly and cleaving the barge in two. Bow and stern folded up like a jackknife and sank in less than a minute. More and more of the massive steel boxes began to fall away as the ship tilted over. They rained down over the side, falling directly on top of those vessels and people who'd been initially spared as the first containers sailed well over their heads.

Jules flinched, expecting to hear the volcanic eruption of the oil tanker going up, but it never came. Then the thundering collision and avalanche of containers gave way to torturous tearing and grinding of steel plates as momentum crushed the two ships together.

"Awesome," said Fifi as Jules turned away from the spectacle to concentrate on threading their way through the pandemonium of fleeing craft.

Having hung back while she negotiated safe passage through the chaos of the collision, Shah appeared at her side as they finally swung out around the southern head of Acapulco Bay and got a little sea room in which to maneuver. To port stood the high, wooded slopes through which they'd driven back from Revolcadero Beach, and Jules made certain to maintain a safe distance from them. Twice they'd hit roadblocks rolling through there, and she didn't fancy getting sniped by some resentful bandito sitting up on the bluffs. Around them the smaller craft began to suffer in the open ocean. The cries of distress from hundreds of small boats suddenly swamped by the powerful and unruly ocean swell was distressing. She had seen a lot of children on some of those dinky little tubs, but she pushed them out of her mind. To stop and pick up anybody would mean getting swarmed by hundreds, possibly thousands of people. Julianne left the throttles open and brought them around to the southwest, heading for the rendezvous with Mr. Lee.

"I have spoken to Thapa," said Shah after a few moments. "As you asked, he has done some work back on shore. Investigating the attack on your vessel by this Shoeless Dan."

"Whoa," said Fifi. "He's cute *and* smart. Man, I'm gonna have to get me some of that later."

The way she was eyeballing the small, well-muscled Gurkha standing at the stern, Jules knew it was no idle threat.

"Did he find out anything useful?" she asked, as the towering Aztec pyramid of the Fairmont hove into view a few miles off the port bow. "It's okay if he didn't. I wasn't expecting much. Just wanted to cover our arses really."

Shah, who seemed able to maintain his balance in the rough conditions simply flexing at the knees, shook his head.

"It is his job. And mine. He discovered nothing specific about the attack on your boat, but there are at least three syndicates, criminal enterprises, that moved very quickly to capitalize on the Disappearance. Most of their activities were restricted to land, but one of them already had a history of maritime criminality. Perhaps this is how they came to know your shoeless friend."

"Makes sense." Jules shrugged. "Maritime criminality was Shoeless Dan's special power." She spun the wheel to take them on a long looping course around a paddle steamer that had somehow found itself blundering through the waves. It was nearly as badly overcrowded as the sunken garbage barge had been, and she wanted to give it a very wide berth. "But there's not much of a piracy culture around here," she added. "Not like parts of Asia. A lot of smuggling yes. But not piracy. The Americans would not have allowed it, even in Mexican waters. You think somebody's branching out? I mean, not that we'll be hanging around long enough for them to try their luck."

Shah bobbed and ducked quite comically to maintain his balance without ever once needing to grab on to anything to steady himself.

"You will if you insist on hugging the coastline to drop Pieraro's people anywhere," he said.

Jules frowned testily. "Look, I'm really pissed off about that. But I didn't see any way around it. Miguel had that Colombian nutter holding the crowds off us, and he could have very easily put us right in the poo if I'd cut up rough about the mariachi band."

"The what?"

"Sorry. In-joke."

Fifi produced another beer from an icebox on the flying deck and winked at Shah.

"They're cool with me," she said. "I think they're cute. Wanna brew?"

Both Jules and Shah answered at once. "No."

"They're not American citizens," Jules continued. "They're peasants. Nobody is going to take them in as genuine refugees. Even if we can get all the way across the Pacific with the rations we have on board—and, look, I suppose we can—Hawaii will not take them. They're shedding people at the moment. New Zealand might. Australia won't. And everybody else is just as likely to open fire on us as soon as we sail into view."

Shah held both hands up as if to show her that he had nothing left.

"I do not presume to tell you what you should do. But you have hired me to provide security, and I advise you now that heading back toward the coastline will be a very dangerous business."

"Fifi, you've been out on the *Rules* with Lee a lot more than me. How's our provisioning?"

She drained half the beer and burped.

" 'Scuse me. It's not bad, Julesy. That golfer had some good shit in the fridge, and plenty of it. And we topped up the larder nicely. There's like two frozen pigs and a couple of steer down there now. Plus, them Mexicans did bring plenty of food. Not like those other fucking snobs. All they brought was expensive luggage and heaps of attitude. I don't see a problem. Really. Come on. It'll be fun. Be like Carnivale every night."

Jules looked to Shah for support, but he remained entirely impassive.

"I just . . . it's just that . . . oh, I don't know . . . my father taught me that helping people was wrong. It never ended well. We're not philanthropists here. We're smugglers at best."

"Foxy fucking smugglers," said Fifi, saluting Julianne with her bottle. "And anyway, your old man ate his pistol one night just before the cops grabbed him. Should you really be looking to him for advice?"

Jules looked completely lost.

"That was my mother's fault," she said bitterly. "If she hadn't tipped off Scotland Yard about Daddy's diddling the tax man . . ."

Shah regarded her with some confusion.

"Your mother informed on your father?"

"After a less-than-satisfying divorce settlement failed to provide for her in the style to which she'd *so* been looking forward," Jules explained.

She was surprised to find it hard to speak, with her throat suddenly locking.

"I was his favorite," she said quietly.

34

Kuwait International Airport

The sutures in his butt made it all but impossible to run, and for a running-high junkie like Melton, that was becoming every bit as uncomfortable as his assorted injuries.

"You'll have to excuse my irritability, Sadie. I've been folded, spindled, *and* mutilated. Puts a man in a poor frame of mind."

The al-Jazeera correspondent clicked his coffee cup against Melton's and smiled.

"It is nothing. Really. Look at what is happening to the world. And you are worried about your manners."

"Well, perhaps if people were possessed of a few more manners, they wouldn't go around killing each other with such abandon."

Sayad al-Mirsaad's eyes flickered nervously around the departure lounge. Kuwait International Airport was swarming with armed personnel from a dozen different countries—mostly American, however—and the atmosphere was twitchy and dangerous. Dense knots of travelers, civilian and military, crowded around every available television screen to follow the war news. There had already been one unpleasant incident when al-Mirsaad had been recognized from a report he'd filed on the sinking of the USS *Hopper*. A couple of marines didn't think he was suitably respectful in tone, and Melton had been forced to intervene before the little Jordanian got stomped.

It had put the American in a bad mood, arguing with his own people, even if they were a couple of Podunk assholes who would have left the world a better place had they stayed home and been zapped by the Wave. He'd been snappy and irritable ever since, and his inability to break out of the blue funk simply made it all the worse.

He needed to piss, his wounded hand throbbed like a bastard, and he'd had no sleep in the thirty-six hours since the first Israeli warhead had gone off. He was grateful to Sayad for hauling his ass out of TRANSCOM limbo, though, especially so given the business-class ticket, paid for by BBC World, that his colleague had handed him.

"You're off to London, you lucky devil," said al-Mirsaad as he handed over the precious travel wallet. "You don't deserve it, of course, what with your whoring and drinking and your disgraceful attitude to the Prophet and his faithful. I should really be going in your place. After all, I am much more virtuous."

And behind his friend's twinkling eyes and ready smile Melton had seen real fear at being left behind to burn in a nuclear furnace. It made it all the more affecting that he had agreed to track Melton down for the British broadcasting company, which had lost contact with him when he was injured. Melton wondered whether he would have done the same thing in al-Mirsaad's place. The small coterie of full-time war correspondents tended to be close and unusually supportive of each other, but al-Mirsaad had spent days hunting him through the vast labyrinth of the U.S. Transport Command and, having found him in that transit hangar out in the desert, had insisted on personally driving the injured reporter three hundred miles to Kuwait City.

"Don't you have a job?" asked Melton as they waited in the lounge for his BA flight to England.

"I am a roving reporter." Al-Mirsaad grinned. "I rove, therefore I am. And I will file many stories on the reaction to the Israeli bombs and to the American pullout. Frankly, if it keeps me away from the bomb sites themselves, I am grateful. I have heard from colleagues sent into Egypt and Syria about the conditions there. Many of them are now very sick. The network has suspended operations in the irradiated areas until they are safe. Well, safer. For now, Kuwait and Qatar are my beats, as you say. I shall fly out to coalition headquarters when you have gone, for a briefing on the cease-fire."

Melton snorted.

"Not much of a cease-fire, Sadie. The Israelis wiped the field clean with a couple of airburst nukes. EMPs fried everything the Iranians had."

Al-Mirsaad's fragile smile fell away.

"You know, a lot of people are saying that if your government had not warned Tehran and the others, they would not have deployed all of their defenses to be wiped out. Many people think it was a conspiracy, a plot between Washington and Tel Aviv to steal all of the oil, not just Saddam's."

Melton regarded his friend warily.

"Sadie," he said in a gentle tone. "Washington's gone. Bush, Cheney, all of them. Gone. All of the oil company head offices. Gone. Car manufacturers. Gone. Arms companies. Gone. If there was a conspiracy it was a one-way street. Everything I've seen tells me the Israelis completely suckered Jim Ritchie. Iranian military doctrine is to throw everything at a threat. No reserves. They got an hour or so warning and put everything up. They tried to warn their own people with the end result that the entire country lit up in panic. Computers, phones, radio, TV, every goddamned piece of electronic equipment in the place, and none of it hardened against a pulse."

"So what you are really saying is that they didn't need to bomb the cities. They had already destroyed their enemies as functioning modern societies."

"Well, I wouldn't call them functioning or modern, but I see your point. Look, I don't condone it. Who would? By the time the final butcher's bill is totted they've probably killed, what, a hundred and fifty, two hundred million people. Christ only knows how many more if anybody else follows their lead. Possibly everyone, in the end. You know what that makes us? I mean the U.S. and the Disappearance? Old news."

"You are right," al-Mirsaad conceded. "I apologize. I sound like some ill-bred street Arab falling on conspiracy talk like a scabrous dog on a bone. Tell me truthfully, Bret, what do you think your military will do?"

He shook his head.

"I have no idea. Leave you all to it, I expect. We're out of the superpower business as of last week. Go ask the Chinese. Or whoever's running India. If Pakistan hasn't nuked them yet."

They fell into an uncomfortable silence as the PA called flights out to Paris, Rotterdam, and Bangkok. Melton attempted to find a position in which he could recline without putting pressure on his injured butt cheek or shoulder. It was difficult. At least for the first time in weeks he was clean, and dressed in luxuriously soft and well-fitting civilian clothes. The BBC had sent him payment in euros for the copy he'd filed before he was wounded, and had advanced him another, larger sum, on the basis of the interviews he had done at the transit facility out in the desert. As he'd expected they were most interested in any European angle.

For a wonder, their money was still worth something in Kuwait, at least in the hermetically sealed environment of the international airport. He was able to buy clothes and replace some of his lost and damaged equipment. Even better than that, he managed to fill a few prescriptions at a pharmacy on the main concourse and, now that he had escaped the Kafkaesque frustrations of the military transport system, he could eat when he felt like it.

"What will you do when you get to London?" asked al-Mirsaad.

"I got a bunch of studio interviews to do," he said. "You know, glamorously wounded foreign correspondent stuff. I've promised to write up a couple of thousand words for their website, and I really want to push ahead with this book I've been thinking about. I wouldn't be surprised, though, if they asked me to turn around and come right back. They lost a lot of people yesterday. Reporters in bureaus throughout the region. They're gonna be hiring, but it'll mean heading back here."

"Do you want to?"

"I don't know what I want. Something normal would be nice. Do you miss normal, Sadie? I do. I can't go home, so all of the conventional nostalgia bullshit is out. Truthfully? I'd just like to sit on my busted ass somewhere, write my book, and, I dunno, look around and not see guys armed to the fucking teeth. How about you?"

"I am an Arab," al-Mirsaad answered glumly. "I grew up surrounded by men who were armed to the teeth."

"Hey, I grew up in Kentucky. Me too."

The PA system announced that his flight to London was boarding, and Melton suddenly felt a soft pressure in his chest and throat.

"Well, Sadie. I gotta be going, bud. I might be back, but you know . . . I just want to say thanks for finding me. I think I might still be doing the zombie shuffle through TRANSCOM's twilight zone if you hadn't grabbed me up."

Al-Mirsaad stuck out his hand and they shook, awkwardly because of Melton's wounds.

"It was nothing, a trifling favor for a friend at the Beeb, and one I was happy to do, as it helped another friend . . . I hope we will stay friends, Bret. If we live."

"Yup. A big if, Sadie. Take care. I'll contact you through the network when I get settled."

The Jordanian patted him gently on the arm and picked up his bags for the short walk to the air bridge. Most of the passengers lining up there were civilians, their numbers split evenly between Arabs and Europeans, although, Melton reminded himself, they might well all be British citizens. Nobody looked happy to be traveling, either because of what they were heading toward—parts of England were under martial law and it was being strictly and harshly enforced—or perhaps because of a well-founded fear that they might never get there.

Thousands of people had died when their aircraft were knocked out of the sky by the same electromagnetic pulses the Israelis had set off to cripple their enemies.

Neither reporter spoke again until Melton had swiped his boarding pass. The BA hostess was as smooth and pleasant as ever, which only served to heighten the sense of brittle weirdness and impending doom.

"Good luck. And thanks again," said Melton.

"A safe journey to you, my friend, God willing," replied al-Mirsaad.

He was pathetically grateful for the business-class seat. It was like settling into an overstuffed hotel bed compared with the steel benches, hard plastic seats, and stinking kit bags on which he'd mostly sat while in transit. It was possible, while sipping at the complimentary orange juice and waiting to taxi, to imagine that things *were* entirely normal. The business-class section was full, but remained decadently spacious and agreeable. His fellow bizoids, with one exception, were all male. The one woman looked like a banker or lawyer, and had no sooner strapped in than she began opening files to work on. She plugged herself into an iPod and radiated a fierce repeller field lest anyone should attempt to approach or interrupt her. An old hand, then.

The man sitting next to him, in the window seat, nodded

brusquely before returning to his BlackBerry. He kept stabbing at the keyboard without any observable result. "It was working this morning," he kept muttering to himself. Melton ignored him all too easily. A hostess, noticing his injuries as he levered himself into place, offered extra pillows and a blanket to lie on. A long time ago in a galaxy far, far away he'd have derided such indulgences as snivel gear. It took him a long time, after getting out, to throw off some of the dumber attitudes of his time in service. He took the pillows and thanked her, settling into them after washing down a couple of painkillers with the last of the orange juice. As the engines spooled up, the captain came on to announce that they would be taking a very circuitous route to avoid any hazards from hostilities to the north. Melton didn't bother to pay attention to the announcements. He didn't care how they got out of this mess, only that they did so.

He was going to miss Sayad, and felt yet again that he was simply allowing events to sweep him along and away from another friend, one whose own future looked very bleak. Melton didn't see anything good happening in this part of the world any time soon. There was no way the U.S. could sustain a presence here, but it remained an area of vital importance to the surviving great powers. How long could it be before Chinese and Indian and Russian warships replaced the U.S. Navy on permanent station in the Gulf? As his eyelids drooped and he tried to suppress the snoring he knew was going to piss off his fellow passengers, he tried to get his head around the strategic and economic wreckage of the Israeli strike, but he was too tired and the seat was too comfortable and before long he was asleep.

He woke briefly, thousands of miles later in Gibraltar, but popped another couple of pills, drank some water, and went back to sleep. After that he didn't stir again until the plane began to descend. A stewardess appeared at his elbow to gently rouse him and the BlackBerry addict, and to ask that they put their seats into the upright position for landing.

"We're in London?" he croaked.

The young woman, a rare beauty of Caribbean heritage by the look of her, seemed distracted and anxious.

"No." She shook her head. "No. We're stopping in Paris. It's . . . unscheduled . . . but nothing to worry about. We'll refuel and be on our way."

That brought him awake.

"We won't be going to London," said his traveling companion, whom he'd avoided talking to so far.

"I've been out of it, sorry," said Melton. "I snore. Has something happened?"

The man, a young, nondescript-looking character with one of those weird Amish-style beards, shrugged and held up a pair of earphones.

"Sennheiser sound-canceling technology," he said. "Blocks out jet engines and loud snoring. Not a problem."

Okay, so he wasn't Amish, then.

"Britain's closed its borders," he explained. "They haven't told us yet." He waved a hand toward the front of the plane to indicate that he meant the flight crew. "But I snuck a look at a news feed in the toilet. Everything's locked down. Air and sea ports, ferries, the Chunnel. All of it."

Melton's head was clearing slowly because of the painkillers in his bloodstream.

"Why?" he asked.

BlackBerry guy folded his arms in obvious disgust.

"Blair's saying something about unrest spilling over the Channel. It's rubbish. I need to get home. Do you see any jihadi wack jobs on this plane? We're businesspeople. This is just bullshit."

"What unrest?" asked Melton. "I didn't think those riots in Paris were so bad, considering."

The man looked at him as if he were dealing with a retarded child. "You're kidding me, right? You've been out in the boonies, have you? Out of contact? Paris is on fire, man. All of France is. It's a civil war. And they're sending us into the middle of it."

ONE MONTH

April 14, 2003

35

"So, you missing Uncle Sugar yet? Nostalgia sucks the big one, don't it?"

Caitlin's voice cracked, and she smiled through split, swollen lips, with teeth stained cherry red by her own blood.

But the look on Reynard's face was totally worth it.

The Frenchman did his best to hold his feelings in check, but she'd struck a nerve and his anguish spilled out in a slight downturn at the corners of his mouth, the merest pout of his lips, and a hollowing of the cheeks as he tilted his head back in an effort to disengage emotionally from his prisoner. He would not beat Caitlin for her insolence. The Algerian would be back later on to do that. Reynard—not his name, but he *looked* like a Reynard, like a hungry fox licking shit from a wire brush, as her old man would have said—he was too important to get her blood on his hands.

"The doctors tell me you are a very sick little girl," he said in English. "We could help you. Your illness progresses, but it is not too late. Help us, so we can help you."

She laughed, a wet rattling sound that ended in a string of explosive, searingly painful coughs. They felt like phosphorous burns in her chest. Small gobbets of blood flew out and spotted his shirt and tie.

"Sorry," she said, and then added, "Red just isn't your color, is it, *Reynard*?" before hawking up a mouthful of phlegm and blood to spit at him. She had given him the name as soon as she realized that he was not going to identify himself, not even with a false name.

It was a cheap trick to increase her feelings of powerlessness and one easily countered by simply calling him something and sticking to it.

Hawking up blood clots to spit at him helped a little, too.

He held up a clipboard to protect himself but she let fly anyway, hitting his fingers with a satisfyingly lurid chunk.

He cursed her in French and stormed out of the cell, dragging the door closed behind him. A heavy iron cage, it slammed shut with a deafening clang.

Caitlin closed her eyes and smiled. A small victory. Not so long ago Reynard would simply have absorbed the abuse and bored in on her, attempting to undermine her defenses, all the time reminding her how utterly alone she was in the world. Enraging him was a small win. Possibly Pyrrhic, but a victory nonetheless. She breathed in slowly. The air was stale and dank. She remembered her last stay in the cells beneath Noisy-le-Sec as being uncomfortable because of the cold. Her interrogators had maintained the temperature just above freezing, but on this occasion there had been no attempts to manipulate her environment. She put that down to power shortages. The lights flickered off and on irregularly, often going out for minutes at a time. The fort would have its own generator, but even so, the directorate would need to ration supply if the wider grid had gone off-line.

Really, though, she had no idea. She had been held incommunicado for a month, and her captors had told her nothing of the outside world save for those details that suited their ends, and, of course, she could not necessarily believe them anyway. She could only trust what few minuscule scraps of reality came filtering through their control.

Time. They had tried to disconnect her from the flow of time. To impress upon her that she was adrift on the seas of eternity, and completely within their control. They were good, too. She had been trained to listen for any clues in their conversation, to try to catch a glimpse of any timepieces or watches that might stray into her field of view. But Reynard and his men were good. On each of their wrists she found only a tan line, and for a long time, lost in the haze of beatings and interrogation, she did lose track of the days and weeks. But of course there was one thing they could not take or hide from her.

She was a woman, and three weeks into her capture, her period arrived, weak but unmistakable.

It had since passed, marking a month since Monique had been killed, and she had collapsed in the hallway of the apartment block back on the rue d'Asnières, betrayed by her own failing body. She kept the small morsel of knowledge, that she knew how long she'd been held, to herself. It was a small prize to covet in her ongoing battle with Reynard. And not the only one either. She knew things about him that he would not want her to know.

The Frenchman, for instance, was losing weight. She had taken note of where he notched his belt the first time he had interrogated her. It was two notches in from there now. At first, too, he had always been clean-shaven, and his suits freshly dry-cleaned and pressed. Recently, however, he had once or twice sported a five o'clock shadow, and she noted that his collars and cuffs were growing dark with grime. He, like her, was suffering. Dark bags had appeared under his eyes, and he had chewed the skin around his left thumbnail quite ragged.

She could not know what was happening in the city outside the fortress walls, she did not even know what was happening in the cells near her own, but Caitlin was willing to bet on systemic collapse. And so she taunted him along those lines, finally eliciting the angered reaction of a few moments past. She would wait now for her punishment. She composed herself, a task made somewhat easier because today she was able to lie flat on her slab. She was naked, but she had long since grown used to that. And most important they did not have her trussed into a stress position, sitting with her knees pulled right up and bound, and her hands cuffed behind her back. It was excruciating after a while, and they had forced her to maintain the posture by having two men stand over her with lengths of heavy rubber tubing to hand out a beating whenever she attempted to alter position.

After a few days of that, however, pressure sores covered her buttocks and had become infected. That bought her a few days' respite while a medic treated her. After that they relented, in a fashion, resorting to a mix of stress positioning, waterboarding, and sensory bombardment, rotated in such a way as to maintain her torment without the inconvenience of needing to halt for treatment. It had almost broken her, but they had stopped after she sank her teeth into the wrist of a man who'd been attempting to place a hood over her head in preparation for another waterboarding session. Caitlin had bitten down as hard as she could, feeling the skin break, and hot, salty blood start flowing a split second before feeling the satisfying crack of a shattered bone.

The asshole had screamed a lot louder than she ever did, something she'd been quick to point out to Reynard. After that they had reverted to beatings for a couple of days.

Beatings she could handle, and she had even begun to goad them, holding out the hope that somebody might lose control and kill her with an uncontrolled blow.

Because Reynard was right about one thing.

She was doomed. There was no point hanging on for the sake of the mission. There was no mission, and there would be no deliverance.

Caitlin was refusing to break simply because that was all she had left in the world. The only choice that remained in her life was how she left it.

She released a lungful of infected breath, carefully, slowly, so as not to set off another round of racking coughs. Slowly breathing in, she kept her eyes closed and tried to imagine the harsh fluorescent light hanging from the bare stone ceiling of the cell to be the sun. Her myriad agonies she repackaged as the well-earned scars of a hard day's surfing over exposed reef in the Mentawais. She had been there not twelve months ago, on a two-week vacation with her brother and some of his college friends.

(All gone.)

They had surfed eight hours a day, and she had been pounded without mercy. Caitlin projected herself back there. She did not attempt to recall the entire trip, only one perfect ride, which she reconstructed from fragments of memory, recalling the kiss of warm tropical water flowing through her toes as she paddled out, the heat of the sun on her back, burning through a UV shirt, the salt spray in her mouth as she duck-dived through one broken wave after another, the tickle of bubbles she blew out through her nose while under the water, the . . .

"Dreaming of your mother's apple pie, Caitlin?"

She was too nerve-dead and exhausted to startle. But inside she fell through negative space, tumbling end over end. She knew who it was before opening her eyes. Her target.

Bilal Baumer.
Al-Banna.

"Are you an assassin, Willard?"

"What the fuck?"

"It's my Brando doing his Colonel Kurtz," said Baumer with a rich stagy laugh that bounced off the damp, moldy ceiling of her cell. He repeated the quote, amping up the grinding, nasal impersonation.

"Are *you* an assassin, Caitlin?"

(Okay. Just go with it.)

She indulged him. "I'm a soldier."

"You're neither." He smiled, dropping out of character, but staying with the quote. "You're an errand girl sent by grocery clerks to collect a bill."

She smiled back at him, all bloody teeth and cold eyes, a feral creature that has learned the trick of imitating a human being. "Yeah. And you'll pay in full."

"I don't think so."

It was Reynard. He had changed into a fresh shirt and now stood behind Baumer, regarding her with restrained enmity.

"These theatrics, they weary me, Miss Monroe. As they must weary you, too, *non*? It is time, don't you think, that we shook off our roles. Me the nameless interrogator . . ."

"Reynard'll do fine . . ."

"*You,* the lone wolf, the hunter, who will never give in. It is all bullshit. You have nothing to fight for."

"I didn't pick this fight," she said, suddenly angry. The sight of Baumer had brought back memories of Monique, and a more painful moral sensibility, a recognition of her abject failure to protect the girl.

"You sent your people in after me. I don't know why. Or I didn't, until he showed up."

"You still do not understand," Reynard assured her.

"What? So he belongs to you. He's a double? Big fucking deal."

"No," said Baumer. "*I* am not one of *his*."

Caitlin levered herself up a little farther, and fought down an urge to shield her naked body from Baumer. It would be an acknowledgment of weakness. She raised her cuffed hands to rub at her eyes. Her wrists were bound by plastic zip ties that had cut deeply into the skin. The wounds were raw in places, crusted over in others. Just another locus of pain to put in a box and hide far away at the back of her mind.

Her voice was faint and croaky, but she put as much strength into it as she could.

"What, you're telling me ol' Reynard here really *is* a cheese-eating surrender monkey? He's sold out to Osama?"

"No," said Baumer.

"So, what, he doesn't like cheese?"

The Frenchman squeezed his eyes shut and sucked in air through his nose.

"I have brought Bilal here to show you the futility of resistance," he explained. "The war you were fighting is over. Your country didn't lose. You lost your country. What is the point in clinging to ideas and loyalties that no longer exist? It is the definition of madness, Caitlin. Just tell us what you can of Echelon's operational structure in France and you can go. We understand you were no longer hunting Bilal. You are a stateless refugee. You need help. But we cannot do that until you help us."

Caitlin sucked her bruised and broken lower lip.

"Yeah, look, about that, weren't you the guy torturing me, the last few weeks? Why would I help you, exactly? And why would you let me go, when I did?"

Reynard sighed. "Caitlin. You are not an imbecile. Stop pretending otherwise. We are all serious people, and the work we do, the measures we must all take, they are serious, too. *Non?* You killed three innocent people during your cowboy shoot-out. You did not know that, did you? No, of course not. You could not know. But the postmortems put *your* bullets inside them, not ours."

She shrugged. He could be lying, probably was. Maybe she'd tagged that cyclist, but that was all, as best she recalled.

"Caitlin, we need to know what you know about Echelon. I understand that you work in cells. I am not expecting you to give me details you cannot provide. But even the most mundane of details might mean something to us while possibly meaning nothing to you. You have to understand, Caitlin. Your fellow agents are rogue operators now. They are more dangerous than ever. The situation outside is stable, but critical. There has been much unrest. Much distrust between peoples. Even bloodshed. Things have settled now, due to a great deal of effort and goodwill by all parties, but just one of your colleagues, carrying forward a single mission, hitting just one target, they could bring everything down. You *must* understand this. They must be stopped. For everyone's sake."

Bilal moved closer to the raised slab of concrete on which she lay.

He looked tired and stressed out, but he retained much of the easy, feline grace that she recalled from preop surveillance. He looked in much better shape than Reynard. An immature, irrational part of her wished that Monique could see him now, and could see that Caitlin had not been lying.

"Like you, Caitlin, I am merely a messenger," he said, sitting himself down carefully on the edge of her slab, keeping his eyes on her face and away from the bruises and wounds that covered her body. "I obey a Lord who is compassionate, who will make you a partner in peace or war."

Her mouth curved up in a vulpine sneer.

"Well, *Billy,* if you knew your Ibn Ishaq as well as your Coppola you would know the full context of that reference, that before whispering sweet nothings about peace and mung beans, the Prophet's companion Ubayy ibn Ka'b first spoke of settling matters with the sword at Khaybar, where the faithful would bring death to those who struggle against them. Or something like that. Maybe I'm getting confused with *Conan the Barbarian.* That was a great flick."

She had hoped to unsettle him, but Baumer nodded as though agreeing with her. He seemed almost pleased.

"So not just an errand girl, then," he said. "A scholar of the book, no less. In which case you would also know that Ishaq was not just a historian, but almost a prophet of sorts. A small-'p' prophet, if you like. What prescience he must have had, Caitlin, to write 'Evil was the state of our enemy so they lost the day. We slew them and left them in the dust. Those who escaped were choked with terror. A multitude of them were slain. This is Allah's war in which those who do not accept Islam will have no helper.' "

He reached out and brushed away a few matted strands of filthy hair that had fallen over her eyes. "I understand that you were a warrior, Caitlin Monroe. And you remain one. It is an honorable calling. But there is a time for war, and a time to put aside our swords and shields. The world has been wounded and it suffers gravely, Caitlin. We are all God's subjects, and we must bind up those wounds together. But we cannot do so without trust. That is why I am here, why 'Reynard' has invited me here, to make peace with my old enemies."

Her feet and hands were still bound, but if she could lock her arms around his head, she might still have a chance, with one wrenching pull, of separating his head from his spinal column.

"I can trust you, Caitlin, because I know you. Just like you know me. I know you must be calculating the odds of lashing out at me now. You must be measuring your strength against the damage and pain you have endured in here the last few weeks, perhaps weighing what residual skills you retain from all of your years of training, what strength of will you possess, even after Reynard has tried to break that will."

He grinned and flicked one eyebrow up in a gesture of camaraderie.

Then his hand shot out in a blur and he gripped one of hers, turning it back on her cuffed, bleeding wrists so quickly that a spike of pure white fire ran up her arms and she almost screamed, biting deeply into the inside of her cheek in a desperate attempt to draw her mind off the agony of the wrist lock.

The holy warrior known as al-Banna let her go.

"So, shall we stop fucking around?"

He drove a fist squarely into her face, a blow that detonated inside her head like shellfire. As the back of her skull hit the hard concrete slab, she felt his iron grip on her arms, wrenching her bodily over onto her stomach.

"Or shall we begin?" he snarled.

She tried to lash out with a feeble kick but only scraped more skin off her legs.

Another punch on the back of her neck stunned her, and she came to understand just how weakened she was by weeks of torture and illness. His hands clawed at her hips, dragging her toward him, confirming the worst.

The rape lasted only a few minutes, but she was still shaking hours later.

When Caitlin was a girl, maybe nine or ten years old, her family had traveled to California for a holiday, driving all the way from Charleston AFB, in South Carolina, where her daddy had been stationed with an airlift squadron. They had done all of the family things you do in California, visiting Disneyland, Hollywood, the beaches. But for her the standout memory had been climbing the bell tower on the Berkeley campus, just before the clock struck ten in the morning. The pealing of the bells was frighteningly loud, much louder than she had imagined it would be. She not only heard the thunderous clanging, she felt it, inside her chest and stomach, reverberating right down through her feet. The sensation, which was entirely unpleasant, remained with her ever after.

Lying on her slab, under a harsh flat white light in her cell at Noisy-le-Sec, she felt a powerful psychic echo of that same deep-body shock.

Her limbs quivered and shook, sometimes so violently that she resembled a victim of late-stage Parkinson's disease, but it was inside that she felt herself being torn apart by a quaking, shuddering violence that was entirely psychological.

Nobody had entered the room since her violation. In her rational, calculating mind, the cold, mechanical killer's mind that had been honed to such a dangerous edge, she knew that that was just part of the "tactical questioning phase." But she could not rid herself of the burning shame and humiliation she felt. As hard as she tried to control herself, the awful, nauseating tremors reminded her of that day in the bell tower, which naturally led to thoughts of her family, especially her father, and with them came more unutterable shame.

She tried to focus on something simple, some goal she might start working toward, like driving a stiffened sword hand strike into Baumer's throat at the first opportunity, but that only reminded her how weak and unable to resist him she had been in the first place. She was curled into a tight, shivering fetal ball when the lights went out.

It was so unexpected, so out of the ordinary that Caitlin suffered a moment of total disorientation. She had been kept for so long in a cell flooded with bright artificial light that the sudden fall of darkness was terrifying, as though her eyes had been put out by sorcery. And then she heard something so familiar, but, like the sudden inky darkness, so unexpected, that her mind seized up for an instant.

Gunfire.

It was muted at first, far off in the distance somewhere in the underground maze of Noisy-le-Sec's interrogation cells. But it soon grew louder, and with it came more familiar sounds. Boots running. Men cursing. More gunfire, the ripping snarl of automatic weapons and the crash of large-bore single-shot rifles and pistols. A grenade exploded with a deafening roar in the enclosed tunnels outside her cell. She could see the flashes in the dark now and pick out individual voices, none of them familiar, all of them French.

Men ran past the heavy iron cage door locking her in. One stopped, briefly, and fired in through the bars, a short wild burst that largely missed her, although a ricochet did rake a painful burning graze along one hip. She groaned and rolled off the slab, letting herself fall as a deadweight to the floor. In the pitch darkness of the cell nobody could see her, and whoever had stopped to finish her off rushed on. Muzzle flashes soon accompanied the crash and zip of bullets, which reached a crescendo as more men rushed past her cell carrying their fight deeper into the complex.

In the blackness, Caitlin crawled into a blind corner, where she might just avoid getting shot, if she was lucky. She huddled there, naked, bleeding, and all alone, for what felt a long time.

36

PACOM HQ, Hawaii

"My God, it looks like the seventh level of hell down there."

"Down there" meant the Valley of the Nile, for thousands of years a seat of human civilization, and now an eerie wasteland of oozing, radioactive mud dotted with the stubs of a few scattered ruins, both modern and ancient. To Ritchie it looked like nothing so much as an endless sea of black garden mulch littered with tens of millions of corpses being picked over by every vulture in northeast Africa. The few American recon teams that had ventured in described the buzzing of flies as being unbearably loud, something akin to a band saw. There were a handful of crazed survivors, one-in-ten-million lottery winners, of a sort. They were all, without exception, insane. The population of Egypt had been reduced to a few oasis dwellers deep in the Western Desert, and some wandering Bedouin, all moving south.

Ritchie stood grimfaced in front of the multipanel displays, many of them recently arrived from Qatar and the former headquarters of the coalition. The Pacific Command's war room was fully engaged monitoring the dozen or more chaotic conflicts now scattered across Ritchie's theater. This temporary facility had been constructed to maintain an overwatch of the former CENTCOM area, the nuclear wastelands of the Middle East. And as bad as the apocalyptic desolation of Egypt might have looked through the cameras of the two Global Hawks slowly circling above the Nile Valley and Delta, it was by no means the most horrifying vista arrayed in front of him.

On other screens smaller, more intimate, and, in a way, more dreadful images played out. In Iraq, Syria, Lebanon, and Iran the survivors were eating each other, literally. Thousands of burned and wounded but still living victims of the atomic strikes had swarmed out of the charred husks of their cities and fallen upon the rural hinterlands. With no reliable supplies of fuel, power, or even water in many areas, with almost no functioning transport system, the farming lands of those countries, already poisoned by fallout, had suffered an almost total collapse in their productivity. What little edible stores the smaller settlements had now needed to be defended against the hordes that fell upon them.

Ritchie had ordered that the worst of it not be allowed to run as a live feed. There was no tactical reason for having such grotesquerie on display. But as the senior officer he still had to view the unedited intelligence tape, which more often than not featured surveillance cover of village-level fratricide and cannibalism. It was heinous and terrible, disturbing at a cellular level, and it was repeated over and over again until he no longer possessed any moral capacity to react to the horror. It was all just pixels.

"Okay, I've seen enough," said General Franks.

The two men turned away as half of the video wall blinked out and switched over to standby feeds.

"I'm sorry," said Ritchie, as they left the room, dragging a tail of aides behind them. "Short of nuking the Israelis themselves I didn't see what I could . . ."

"Forget about it," growled Franks. "They blindsided you. Me too. The warning I passed on to Tehran just made it worse for them, meant they lost everything to the EMP. I guess we can count ourselves lucky they didn't fry us as collateral damage."

"There would have been consequences for that," said Ritchie.

"Yeah," Franks agreed. "Wouldn't have made any difference to me and my guys, though, would it? And that bullshit target list. Brilliant really. But now they have to live with what they've done. And the Israelis know they can't do it again. The Russians will nuke them, and we won't lift a finger in their defense."

Ritchie said nothing to that. Three days after Armageddon, as the one-sided atomic war had been christened by the Western press, an emergency session of the reconstituted UN Security Council in Geneva had passed a unanimous resolution authorizing member states to use "all necessary means" to respond to any further nuclear strikes. In contrast to the usual ambiguity surrounding such things, the Russian and Chinese ambassadors had made it clear that that meant a massive nuclear attack on Israel.

No other states had demurred.

"We still don't know where those other subs of theirs are hiding," said Ritchie.

"Not our problem," said Franks. "Not anymore. We're out of the world-policing business. Let the fucking French or the Brits find them. They have more to lose."

The small pod of military officers turned into a large briefing room that had been prepared for their arrival. Franks, the new acting chairman of the Joint Chiefs, waved everyone back to their seats as the assembled officers came to attention. He and Ritchie took their places at the head of the large conference table. There was no ceremony. Franks ordered the first briefer to the podium with a wave of his hand.

Colonel Maccomb nodded and smiled thinly at Ritchie as he moved around the table. The two men had seen a lot more of each other than their families in the last month. Ritchie had come to trust the intelligence man's judgment implicitly. He seemed able to read Jed Culver like an open book, for instance, and he'd warned of the possible Israeli strike days before it happened, which admittedly wasn't all that impressive, because the same predictions had been made many times in the press. But Maccomb had worked up a scenario predicting the attack almost exactly as it transpired. Unfortunately, the report had not made it to Ritchie's desk before Asher Warat arrived in his office. The admiral made certain that the much-chastened commander of the 500th Intelligence Brigade understood that he was never again to sit on any of Maccomb's reports if the colonel thought they should go up the line.

"Good morning, ladies and gentlemen," Maccomb began. "I have a number of points from each of the theater commands to cover quickly before we discuss any particular issue in depth. Firstly, CENTCOM. Our latest best estimate puts half the population of the area dead, and it is likely that seventy-five percent of the remainder are going to die within six months to a year."

There was no evident reaction to the statement. Everyone had become inured to the horror story of the Middle East what felt like a long time ago.

"Major combat operations have ceased entirely, both between our forces, which have now left the region, and our former combatants, and between Israel and her former combatants. Israel remains under martial law but we expect the state of emergency to be lifted within the next forty-eight hours, as decontamination procedures progress far enough to allow some of the population to return to work."

Maccomb thumbed a control stick and powered up a large flat-panel display on the wall behind him. A very familiar map of the Middle East appeared, with each of the atomic strikes clearly marked. Shaded areas of fallout stretched behind them.

"A combined British, French, Russian, and Chinese task force has arrived in Saudi Arabia to replace our own withdrawn forces. Smaller deployments have been made to various Gulf states to secure the surviving oil infrastructure. The Russian federation's missile forces targeting Israel remain on the highest state of alert. British and French submarines also remain on station in the eastern Mediterranean as a continued deterrent against further strikes by Tel Aviv. The future status of the French nuclear submarine *Le Triomphant* remains uncertain, however, dependent on the outcome of the struggle within France."

Ritchie had some trouble containing a snort of surprise at Colonel Maccomb's talent for understatement. The "struggle" he referred to had degenerated from incipient anarchy into civil war and from there into a confused and savage blood swarm. Tracking the movements of the country's nuclear submarines was consuming almost as much attention from the surviving great powers as speculating on the disposition of those assets should the French government finally succumb to the Intifada.

"The situation within EUCOM is fluid," said Maccomb, continuing with his penchant for understatement. "The British government continues to enforce a maritime exclusion zone and has secretly begun work to seal its end of the Channel Tunnel."

That *was* a surprise to Ritchie. Since Franks had returned from Qatar and replaced him as acting chairman, he was no longer briefed daily on developments in Europe. Last he'd seen, Tony Blair was still denying that the Brits intended doing any such thing.

"The state of emergency remains in place throughout Britain, but we are informed that it will be lifted in Northern Ireland as of 0600 tomorrow. Our best information to hand is that the Blair government will ignore the ultimatum from the EU to release all of the so-called emergency detainees and is in fact planning to deport significant numbers of them."

A murmur rippled around the table.

"With permission, General?" Ritchie asked Franks.

The chairman nodded. "Make it quick, Jim."

"Do you have any better information than just 'significant numbers,' Colonel?" asked Ritchie. "Are they talking about flying out a couple of crazy mullahs or are we looking at mass deportations?"

Ritchie's daughter was in England, having escaped the Disappearance by a matter of hours. She was in no immediate danger, but the news coming out of the UK was growing darker every day.

"My information is that the forced relocations will probably take place on a greater rather than lesser scale, Admiral. Much greater. They will probably involve a significant drain on the security forces. It will be a controversial policy."

Sitting next to Ritchie, General Franks grunted and leaned forward.

"Ha. You know how to sugarcoat a shit sandwich, don't you,

Colonel? It'll be a bloodbath. They're talking about deporting hundreds of thousands of second- and third-generation citizens. It's a pogrom, pure and simple. But," he sighed, "it's only our problem if it affects us operationally. What's your latest on the money Blair promised us?"

Colonel Maccomb coughed uncomfortably, and sipped from a glass of water by the podium before continuing.

"General, the best information I have is that the special appropriations bill will pass with the help of the Conservative Party. There are a hundred and thirty-four members of Blair's government who have publicly confirmed that they will vote against it, but the Tory Party leader has pledged his support so it will go through."

"And this little ethnic-cleansing program of theirs, what's your reading of that? Is it likely to bring down the government? And if so, can we expect the same level of support in the future?"

Ritchie thought Maccomb looked even more uncomfortable, being asked to read the storm clouds of British politics, but it was a fair question. For the moment at least most of the day-to-day cost of running the U.S. military was being met by alliance partners such as Britain and Japan. NATO was split on the issue, with some countries like Poland stumping up support in cash and kind, while others, like France, were so busy falling apart that they were worse than useless, as Ritchie knew all too well.

"The policy is supported by a clear majority of the British electorate," said Maccomb. "But the significant minority who oppose it can be expected to do so by all the means at their disposal. There will be bloodshed. From our point of view, however, both the government and opposition are committed to the supplementary appropriations process. So any change in government will not affect that. However, whether the UK can actually afford to maintain such outlays even in the short term is another matter entirely. And not one I am really qualified to discuss."

Franks smiled grimly.

"Nice buck pass, Colonel. Damn, I never thought I'd see out my days as a gun for hire. Okay. We'll put that on the back burner. Continue."

The intelligence officer returned to his notes and brought up a slide show of images culled from European news media.

380 • JOHN BIRMINGHAM

"Fighting in France has intensified over the last two weeks. Elements of the state are in open conflict with each other, while large-scale street-level clashes that began as food and race riots have developed into open, disorganized tribal warfare, largely based on ethnic lines, but exacerbated by the involvement of some criminal syndicates in Marseilles and Lyons, and by the arrival of outside agitators from throughout the EU. Most official border crossing points have been closed, but that means nothing. The borders aren't simply porous. They largely do not exist and haven't for years. Additionally, we have very strong indications of government-level assistance for some of this cross-border movement, especially of skinhead gangs from the eastern regions of Germany into the main metropolitan areas of France. The numbers involved are nontrivial. We tracked three trainloads of neo-Nazis from Berlin and Dresden all the way to Paris. In total, they numbered more than four thousand strong."

"Good Lord," muttered Ritchie. "You mentioned that these were government-sanctioned movements. Which government?"

Maccomb pressed his lips together as though chewing over something unpleasant.

"It is inaccurate to speak of a unitary state authority in France right now, but one bureau of the Direction Centrale des Renseignements Généraux, the general information service, has been in close and constant contact with the BND, the German government's foreign intelligence service, and the Russian FSB, which maintains extensive networks in the former East German provinces. It's significant because the GIS, as we call it, is the intelligence arm of the French police, which answers directly to the interior minister, Mr. Sarkozy. And of course, his Emergency Committee has assumed, or some would say usurped, responsibility for state security from the Élysée Palace since President Chirac was wounded in the suicide bombing of March 18."

Ritchie, who had privileged access to information about the situation in France that nobody in the room other than Franks enjoyed, still found Maccomb's line of explanation difficult to follow.

"I don't see how this all hangs together, Colonel. What is the point?"

Maccomb shrugged before bringing up video footage copied from a French news service, a hugely violent confrontation between thousands of rioters in Clichy-sous-Bois, a poor commune in the east of Paris. Hundreds of black-clad French riot police stood by as a wave of shaven-headed thugs appeared from a maze of side streets in a coordinated assault on a mass of dark-skinned rioters. Armed with clubs and even-edged weapons they cut a swath through their densely packed, and less-well-armed, opponents.

"The death toll from that one encounter was over two hundred," said Maccomb. "It didn't rate as a news story for more than a day because there were bigger and more violent riots elsewhere in the city, and the following day the first of the radioactive plumes from reactor meltdowns in CONUS crossed the French coast. The CRS, the French riot police, not only did not intervene, but actually facilitated the attack and later the safe withdrawal of the neo-Nazi street fighters."

Maccomb brought up footage of two police officers calmly chatting with a small number of fascist organizers, apparently giving them directions, while a murderous brawl took place a literal stone's throw away. The skinheads appeared to take a good deal of advice from the officers before running off to marshal their own forces.

"At no point in any of the clashes of the past weeks has the CRS decisively intervened to stop any major incidents of violence, *except* on those occasions where ultranationalist forces looked to be in trouble. I have a separate briefing note on this subject, and will cover it at length in due course, but for now I think it is reasonable to categorize the situation in France as a race war within the general population, and a civil war between some elements of the state security apparatus."

Franks and Ritchie exchanged a quick, wordless glance. They had their own angle on the French troubles, but it was not something they could discuss, even in this forum.

"Thank you, Colonel," said Franks. "It's fascinating, even a little satisfying, but we need to move on. You have a quick rundown on the Russian situation."

Maccomb nodded.

"Russian military forces either remain at the highest level of alert, or, in some cases such as Georgia and Chechnya, have been deployed on active duty. None of the deployments raise any threat to American forces or interests, however, and the Russian Defense Ministry has been assiduous in keeping us informed of any developments that might impact upon our interests. They are treading very carefully around us, and trying hard not to generate too much friction along the Chinese border . . ."

Maccomb glanced up at Ritchie before continuing.

"Which brings us to the Pacific Command."

There was a noticeable shifting of postures around the table. PACOM was home. At least half of the officers in the conference belonged to Ritchie's theater command.

"There are two serious flash points within PACOM," said Maccomb. "I would have said three until recently, but the Korean peninsula is one of the few areas where tensions seem to have *decreased* in the last month, most likely due to the volume of aid shipments heading north from Seoul. For now the bribes are working. For now, as well, there have been no calls from the north for the withdrawal of U.S. forces; however, there will be an emergency session of the National Assembly in two days, to discuss an urgent motion requiring the withdrawal of all foreign forces from the Republic."

Ritchie had known it was coming but most people in the room did not and, as much as a tightly controlled group of professional officers could descend instantly into uproar, they did, which is to say, an air force general swore under his breath and a Marine Corps colonel banged his water down a little bit too loudly.

"Get over it, people," barked Franks. "If they don't want us we can't stay. They're already picking up our drink tab and they can't afford it. Their economy has imploded. Vote or no vote, we'd be leaving. Go on, Colonel. Give us some bad news for a change."

Maccomb essayed a slight twitch of the mouth that might have been the ghost of a mirthless grin.

"India and Pakistan," he said. "The probability that one or the other will attempt a preemptive strike is approaching certainty. Their conventional forces have already clashed seriously on three occasions in the last month, all cooperation with Islamabad over the Afghan situation has effectively ceased, both sides have carried out proxy terror attacks approaching mass casualty levels, and satellite cover indicates that each has stepped up the readiness of its nuclear forces."

"Jesus wept, did they learn nothing?" exclaimed the same Marine Corps officer.

"You can skip the details of any likely exchange, Colonel," said Franks. "We know what one of these wars looks like now, and how it affects the rest of the globe. Admiral Ritchie, what's our Uplift status for the subcontinental region?"

Ritchie didn't need to consult his notes or an aide. He'd been living with Uplift for nearly a month.

"Ninety percent complete, General," he answered. "TRANSCOM has moved eighty-three thousand U.S. citizens from India, Pakistan, Sri Lanka, and Bangladesh to reception facilities in Australia and New Zealand. We're still shifting up to a thousand a week, but the flow has really tapered off."

"Anybody who's not out soon is going to get turned into an X-ray," said Franks. "We've done what we can. I don't want our people there in large numbers when one of those fools presses the button. I think we might put a deadline of this Friday local time for Uplift. After that, anyone dumb enough to hang around will be on their own. That timing sound right to you, Maccomb?"

"It's tight," said the briefer. "The Indians have begun to prepare their launch sites. A lot of embassies are already shutting up and getting out. The Brits and Aussies have upgraded their travel advisories to the highest level, warning of immediate interstate conflict."

"Okay. Wednesday. Midnight. That's the end of it for us. Go on."

"China," said Maccomb, pausing as if that was all that was needed. "While the People's Republic does not suffer from some of the ethnic division present in France, on our reading of the current situation its future is just as bleak. The economy hasn't imploded. It has just ceased to be. There were already imbalances and rigidities building up before the Disappearance. Thousands of state-run enterprises being propped just to keep the rural poor fed and housed. Now, hundreds of millions of people have no income and, in the cities, no means of supporting even a subsistence level of existence. China was a net food importer at the time of the Disappearance. It cannot feed itself now. The PLA, which had begun to move some force projection assets around the Taiwan Strait, is now fully engaged within the country's borders. The government has imposed a media blackout and expelled all but a handful of foreign journalists, and their movements are tightly controlled. Most of our in-country assets were managed from CONUS and are of little use now. But we do have access to British and some Russian intel, and they are convinced that a schism has opened both between the army and the Party and within those institutions. At 0230, the FSB's Beijing station was reporting that major combat had broken out within the city between elements of the People's Armed Police and at least two divisions of Army Group Six, including armored and artillery units. Admiral Ritchie will have more, in a few minutes."

Ritchie felt the weight of everyone's attention fall upon him.

"Very quickly, Jim. You think they're going to turn this inward, or out on the rest of us?"

"Inward," he said without hesitation. "At least in the short term. Command and control of the Chinese state is failing. Has failed. This is about reestablishing that control, but it won't be simple or easy or something that happens very quickly. Like the colonel said, they have hundreds of millions of people who might well starve to death in the next few weeks. Jumping across the strait will not change that. It will simply make dealing with it all the more difficult, and at any rate, the chain of command is broken. They can only fight among themselves, for now."

"Okay," said Franks. "That'll do for the wrap-up. Let's start grinding our way through the to-do list, shall we?"

They met privately during a break in the all-day conference.

Franks joined Ritchie in his office, where they shared a cup of powdered coffee. There wasn't a drop of the real stuff to be had on the islands.

"This French business, we're gonna have to do something about it," said Franks. "I wouldn't have believed it when you first told me, but this latest intelligence from the Brits nails it. We have to get that girl out."

Ritchie drained the last of his lukewarm java and pondered the view out of his window. Another beautiful Hawaiian day. It seemed perverse, given the state of the world, but he knew that even out there, things were going badly. Most of the island's nonresidential population had already been moved on to resettlement facilities elsewhere in the Pacific. Almost none had volunteered to return to the mainland.

"Well, it explains a lot," said Ritchie. "Especially about what

Blair has done, I suppose. How are we going to get her? She's dropped off the grid."

Franks shook his head.

"We've found her again. Sarkozy's people grabbed her up an hour ago."

37

Seattle, Washington

Jed had scored himself three adjoining rooms at the Hotel Monaco, and standing in the center suite, trying to listen to a CNN report out of the constitutional convention, he wondered if he should have grabbed a couple of spares for the overflow. There had to be more than a hundred people in here. The roar of such a crowd so closely confined was loud enough to bury the sound of the television unless you knelt down in front of the set and jacked up the volume. He'd done that a couple of times, but within a few minutes the background noise had simply grown in response.

Dozens of people pressed in close around him, trying to listen to the report, but their own cries of outrage drowned out the TV just as effectively as the background roar. On the screen a doughy-faced man with an unfortunate comb-over banged his fist on a podium and yelled, "It would only be temporary . . . a three-year sunset clause, with . . . extension *only* if the emergency requires it. But we need . . . measure now. We face annihilation without . . ."

A small band of type flashed up identifying him as Reggie Guertson, whom Jed now knew as a GOP mayor from some pissant burg out holding its breath right up against the edge of the Wave.

"The military got us through the worst of this," yelled an increasingly red-faced Guertson, "and they'll get us through the worst that is to come. But only if we give them what they need to get the job done."

"He's a poet and don't know it," cried out one of the hecklers behind Jed.

Onscreen, the camera panned around and the auditorium erupted with fierce catcalling and jeers, but Jed estimated that at least half of the howls of protest were directed against anyone who'd objected to Guertson's proposal to reserve a third of the new congressional seats for the armed forces. As an emergency measure.

The reaction behind him, in the hotel room, was uniformly negative. Deafeningly so. Nobody here was backing the idea. Jed frowned and tried to get some more volume out of the television, but it seemed to have been programmed by the hotel to prevent inconsiderate or hard-of-hearing guests from annoying their neighbors. He could just make out a rising cacophony as Guertson attempted to shout down a sizable chorus that was chanting over and over again, "*Sieg Heil! Sieg Heil!*" The image cut to a shot of the convention chairman, the newly elected Anchorage mayor Mark Begich, banging his gavel and calling for order, entirely without effect.

Culver shook his head and pushed himself up to his feet. His knees hurt, and he felt a little giddy, probably from all the smoke in the room.

All three suites were choked with cigarette smoke, despite all the nonsmoking signs, and the whole space reeked of wet clothes, body odor, rebreathed air, and stale farts. The carpets had disappeared under an inch-thick mat of crushed potato chips and pizza crust, and every flat surface was full of empty bottles and paper cups. Clear plastic bottles of spring water stood next to crushed cans of Canadian beer. He wondered sometimes how many people were here simply because he had a proven supply of snack foods and free beverages.

Well, not free.

There was nothing so gauche as a cover charge to get into Jed Culver's lair, but everyone in these rooms would pay a price for being here. Sometime, somewhere.

"Hey, Culver. Been looking for you."

He turned, looking for the owner of the harsh Brooklyn accent. Or Brooklyn by way of Warsaw, to Jed's well-traveled hearing.

"Mr. Cesky," he called back, over the din. "I've been looking for you, too. Wanted to thank you for your help yesterday."

Cesky, a short, thick-shouldered man with the hardened hands and beaten-down features of somebody who'd worked construction all his life, waved him off with one hairy, bandaged paw.

"Nah. Fuggedaboudit," he said. "What's money for if you can't fuckin' spend it to get what you want?"

Jed smiled but said nothing. For all of Cesky's two-fisted roughneck routine, he'd found him to be quite a shrewd operator. A hard nut, his old man would have called him. Not likely to crack under the hammer. The businessman was covered in suture marks and bandages from whatever misadventures he'd endured getting himself and his family out of southern Mexico. Cesky had said nothing to Jed, but the lawyer had done his background work before taking the man's favors, and he knew that after a couple of failed attempts, Henry Cesky had pulled off a remarkable escape from Acapulco, right in the middle of the city melting down. He had to have some kind of smarts, and he was obviously tough enough to have come through intact if not unharmed.

Like all men, however, he was cursed with his own particular weaknesses.

That crack about the money, for instance. That wasn't just for Jed's benefit, reminding him how much credit he'd poured into the lawyer's "discretionary account," his black-bag fund, for want of a gentler euphemism. It also let everyone within hearing distance know that Henry Cesky was no fucking chump. Henry Cesky had somehow managed to salvage a good deal of his personal fortune and what was left of his business, and Henry fucking Cesky was still a fucking player. Especially by the much-reduced standards of American politics, as it was now being played out in the surviving seat of power, the Pacific Northwest.

He slipped one of his heavy arms around Jed's shoulder. With Cesky's shirtsleeves rolled up, Jed could feel the thick mat of gorilla fur on the man's forearm tickling the back of his neck. He ignored it. Getting inside your personal space was a favored ploy of Cesky's, and as Jed had about four inches and a good number of pounds on him, he let it slide.

"What I wanted to talk to you about was them fucking army

engineers," said Cesky. "They're doing a lot of work for the city at the moment and I can't help thinking that it could be done a lot fucking quicker and cheaper by the private sector, you know. By people who don't need to cross every fucking 'i' and dot every fucking 't' if you know what I mean."

Jed didn't correct him. He knew what the construction magnate meant.

"I hear you, Henry," he bellowed back. "I'm a hundred percent behind you on that. But for now, at least, the army's a law unto themselves here. You've seen that. They're still running this place, really."

And Jed had to wonder at that, given what he'd been hearing about relations between the city and Fort Lewis over the last month.

Cesky took his arm away. He'd had to reach up a ways, and it couldn't have been comfortable for him.

"Well, they need to get back in their fucking box," he said. "Or someone needs to put them there. I heard about what they did with the council guys. Playing the fucking heavy like that. No fucking wonder they got the contracts locked up for this joint, eh?"

Jed wanted to shake his head in amazement. Another Henry Cesky weakness was a complete inability to see the world in terms other than his own. He honestly regarded the army as little more than a rival firm, undercutting him on his bids for city work. In their position, it's what he would have done, so obviously that's what they'd been doing when they "sequestered" the local councillors during the worst of the immediate crisis following the Disappearance. They were simply looking to do Cesky out of a buck.

Un-fucking-believable.

Jed held up both palms.

"No argument from me, Henry. I can see why they moved the way they did at first. It was probably the only way to keep things together here. But we're past that now, aren't we?"

Cesky nodded sagely, or in a manner that he obviously thought of as "sagely," if he even knew what the word meant.

"Fucking lotta work to be done here, Culver," he said as they threaded their way through the heaving crush and heat of the crowd. "Not just spadework neither. There's a lot of rebuilding up here, too," he added, tapping the side of his head with two thick fingers.

Culver nodded, a little surprised at his insight.

"That's why this week is important," said Jed. "It's why we need guys like you on our side, Henry. Things are at the tipping point, if you ask me. Could go either way. We could fuck this up, end up with Fort Lewis running everything, doing guys like you out of a job, or we could make a whole new start. And all this bullshit about giving the army seats in any government. That would be fucking things up, don't you think? That's Third World stuff."

Cesky nodded vigorously. He grabbed a bottle of Molson Old Style Pilsener off a tray as it wobbled past at eye level. Whether he bought Jed's argument as a point of high principle, or whether he saw his main chance being ruined by his major competitors getting their camouflaged butts into Congress was a moot point. From Jed Culver's point of view, Henry Cesky was an ally because like everyone else in this room, he was firmly in the "no" camp when it came to the question of rewriting the Constitution.

"I dunno what these assholes are so frightened of," declared Cesky. "I don't see anywhere dealing with the fucking Wave as good as us, and we got hammered flat by the fucker. Look at them French assholes, killing each other in the street. Fucking China, falling apart like a cheap fucking toy. And England, it's a fucking prison camp. None of that happened here, and never will, unless we let it."

Jed could have argued with him about some of the prison-camp aspects of post-Disappearance Seattle, but he let it go.

"Good man," he said, as he slapped Cesky hard on the back. "That's the spirit. Question is, though, what are we going to do about it? What are *you* going to do about it, Henry? The days when we could leave this stuff to the insiders and the Beltway crowd are over. Those assholes are gone. Well, mostly gone. There's a few of them hanging around like farts in a phone booth at the convention, let me tell you. But that just means we've got to step up. *You* have to."

"Hey, I'm doing my bit. I'm here, aren't I!"

"Yeah, but it's going to take more than standing around flapping our gums, Henry," said Culver, steering the smaller man into a makeshift alcove formed by a couple of a couches. He leaned forward conspiratorially. "Might come a time soon when we have to act," he said. "How would you feel about that?"

"What do you mean, act? You mean break some fucking heads? If that's what it takes, Culver. That's what it takes."

"Oh I'm sure it won't come to that," said Jed, moving again toward the door connecting two of the hotel suites. "There's no point butting heads with the army. You'll lose. But it's good to know, Henry, that if push comes to shove in some other way, we have you and your organization behind us."

Cesky stood a little taller and nodded emphatically.

"Six hundred guys I got on my payroll, Culver. Six hundred families I'm keeping fed and housed and warm at night. I'm fucking proud o' that, you know. It's not just about the money or my own family. It's what I can do for others. You need me to get out the vote, it's out. You need boots on the street, you got 'em. They're my people. They know who looks after them, and they know who's been trying to take food from their fucking tables, too."

Cesky frowned and waved his beer at a TV in the next suite.

Through a shifting mass of bodies, Jed could just make out somebody on the screen, wearing an army uniform.

"Mr. Culver. Mr. Culver."

He gratefully embraced the distraction. Looking for an excuse to break free of Cesky, Jed craned his head around searching for whoever was calling his name. Unfortunately the builder saw the guy first.

"Over there. Faggy-looking mope."

Jed saw him straightaway then. Aaron Metz from Microsoft.

He was attempting to cut a path through the tidal flow of the crowd and not doing so well. Jed could see that he was holding something aloft in one hand.

"Come on, make a fucking hole, would you," shouted Cesky, bruting his way into the crush and virtually hauling the fragile-looking Metz out of it by force.

"Not you, of course, buddy." Cesky grinned. "Wouldn't want you making free with any holes around me, eh?"

The very obviously gay Metz was both flustered and grateful, and chose to ignore the up-front homophobia of Cesky's comment.

"Thank you," he said. "So many people here, Mr. Culver. It's almost as mad as the convention floor. Not that I can get in, of course, but . . ."

"How can I help, Aaron?" Jed asked, cutting him off before he started to babble. He'd learned the hard way not to let Metz get up a head of steam.

"Oh, Mr. Ballmer wanted you to have this, sir, right away, Mr. Culver. It's one of our new smart phones. Well, not ours, it's an iMate, but it runs the Windows Mobile OS. It was still in development, you know, when . . ."

Jed nodded and waved off the rest of the explanation.

"Thanks, Aaron. You tell Steve it's greatly appreciated."

"It has some special security features, Mr. Culver . . ."

"I'm all over it, Aaron. Thanks again. Tell Steve and Bill, I *will* be in contact, later today."

Metz looked even more flustered than when Jed had first seen him, but he gushed and flapped around and even bowed at one point.

"What a bag of fruit," grunted Cesky as soon as he was out of earshot.

"To each their own," said Jed, pocketing the smart phone. "I'm grateful for their help, Henry. I'm grateful for anyone's help, given the mess we're in."

"So how come they're not here, then, those big software guys? You got a lot of corporate types here, Culver. Really heavy hitters, eh? You can't tell me there's anyone big enough in this town to put the fucking frighteners on Bill Gates. He's still richer than God."

"You wouldn't think so, would you?" Jed replied, but not with enough volume for Cesky to hear him. "You'll have to excuse me," he said, a little louder. "I have people I need to talk to. Now, as for you, Henry, I can count on you and your guys?"

"You bet, Culver. I'm not gonna get rolled over and ass-fucked without a fight."

"Great. And your family, they're good? There's nothing I can do to help out there?" he asked, studiously avoiding the actual reason Cesky had fronted him: his complaint about getting shut out of city work by the Army Corps of Engineers.

Cesky shook his head and flexed one bandaged hand.

"We had some trouble getting out of Acapulco," he said. "Some people I gotta settle up with about that one day. But my girls are all in Sydney now. They're safe. I don't have to worry about them if things get difficult around here."

He cracked the knuckles on his undamaged hand and jutted his chin out. Culver gave him a comradely squeeze on the shoulder, excused himself, and made for the nearest exit. As he muscled through, at least half a dozen or more people attempted to intercept him, but Jed shook them off with a smile and a wave of the smart phone that implied that he had A Very Important Call to make, which he did.

Out in the corridor, it wasn't nearly as hectic and crowded, but he was unsurprised to find a spillover crowd working the space just as intently as the folks back in his suite of rooms. It was a weird vibe, for an old hack like Culver. He saw figures he recognized from both the left and right of politics, some of them West Coast, some national figures who hadn't been caught by the Wave. Their heads bent together, their devious minds were plotting against a new enemy, this cross-party faction in favor of a total rewrite of the Constitution and the Bill of Rights, paring it back and ceding permanent powers of near-autarchy to a smaller, militarized executive, all of it sold in terms of the dire need to protect the Republic from annihilation or anarchy or some such bullshit.

Culver had seen it all before. Frightened people driven to mortal foolishness by the extreme situation in which they found themselves.

Well, not on my watch, buddy, he thought.

He'd been blindsided by how bad things were politically when he'd first arrived in Seattle. But Jed Culver was nothing if not adaptable.

The future of the country was being fought out in this city, and he was a large part of the battle. As Governor Lingle's personal envoy to the surviving representatives of the civil authority in what was left of mainland United States, he had driven the convention process harder and faster than anyone thought possible. And yes, he had to admit, to himself if nobody else, that the whole push to institutionalize a role for the military in the new system of government had caught him unawares.

It certainly wasn't coming from any of the uniformed guys he'd dealt with back in Hawaii. That wasn't their style, and they had their hands full anyway. And it wasn't coming from the military power structure here in the Northwest, as best he could tell. Not publicly anyway. That Blackstone asshole out at Fort Lewis—a real Captain Bligh character, thought Jed—even he was scrupulously careful not to be drawn into any political debate.

But then as someone who'd perpetrated all manner of villainy in his professional life, Jed was well aware of how easy it was to use cutouts and puppets to do your dirty work while you fronted the media, or the investigators or some nitpicking congressional committee, with your halo shining and hands washed free of blood.

Somebody, somewhere, was driving this madness, attempting to hijack *his* convention, and he'd be damned if they were going to get away with it.

He threaded through the hallway loiterers, smiling, waving, and glad-handing everyone as he went. A part of Jed seemed to float outside of himself, marveling that a fixer from the backwoods of Louisiana could find himself at the center of the storm that had destroyed so much already. He spotted a few Alaskan delegates he would need to corral later in the day, and a couple of Canadian diplomats who caught him by surprise. Jed made a mental note to investigate their presence but hurried on around the corner and into the fire escape. Two floors up he finally had some privacy.

The phone numbers were preloaded as arranged, and he found the one he was looking for without trouble. He was a bit of a gadget freak, if truth be known, and the chance to play with a new toy was reward enough in itself. But the call he had to make was important. The connection went through on the third ring.

"Hey, Bill, it's me, Jed Culver. I got your package. Thanks for that."

The strangely youthful voice at the other end came through with great clarity, in spite of all the filters and washers and heavy encryption he knew had been packed into the phone.

"Oh, hey, Jed. Good, that's great. I'm glad that got through to you."

"So, I don't want to come on as a nattering nabob of negativism, but you're sure this is secure?"

The man on the other end laughed.

"My guys are sure, Jed. As sure as they can be anyway. I'm

confident, if that helps. I am talking to you, after all. Some people in this town would consider that treason."

"Okay. Good enough," said Culver. "So, you can get more of these units out where they're needed?"

"Already on their way. Six hundred of them, give or take a few. They'll be distributed by nightfall. The network will light up when you want it."

"You sure? I understood the Net was terribly patchy now. Not at all reliable. Do we want it sitting there as a weak link?"

"It's fine. At least here, it's fine. There are massive holes everywhere else, but the local nodes in the Northwest are good. We made sure of that. You can rely on them. Especially for this. We've taken precautions."

"Okay," said Culver. "If you say so. We'll proceed. I can't tell you how important this is, what a difference it could make."

"I'm happy to help. It's important to do what you can. I've been here, remember. Could have flown out, but I stayed. All my people stayed. We're not ready to give up yet."

"That's the spirit," said Jed.

"Okay. Well, anything you need, you have my number."

"Thanks," said Jed. "I will be in touch."

"I hope so," said Bill Gates, before hanging up.

Jed studied the small piece of technology, wondering how long it would be before the appearance of such things, and the progress they spoke of, became commonplace again.

Possibly never, if he didn't win the confrontation he knew was coming.

He could feel it down in his guts.

He was confident of the alliance he was building up here in the city. In his quiet moments he was even proud of what he'd achieved since arriving. But he knew it wasn't enough.

Jed Culver understood humanity. He understood their baser, uglier nature, the way fear could rob them of reason and send them rushing over the cliff like lemmings. Look around the world and you had proof enough of that.

But he also knew that if led well, if led with some wisdom and just a modicum of courage, a frightened horde could rise above itself and act with outward calm and considered grace that completely belied any inward turmoil. But they had to be led, and he was not a leader.

He had come here knowing that he would need to find one and fast.

He opened the contacts file on the smart phone again and, yes, the name and number he had asked for were there.

He did not dial, however.

It was time to make contact, but he would have to do so personally.

Everything he had heard about this man, everything he'd learned since flying into Seattle, had only confirmed Jed's suspicion that he was the one. But because of that, he was not the sort of man to be played like Henry Cesky.

This one would have to be given the opportunity to make a choice. A real choice, for good or ill.

And if he was, Jed was certain he'd choose wisely.

He put the phone away and headed downstairs.

38

MV *Aussie Rules*, Robinson Crusoe Island

"I think we're probably right to go," said Jules.

Fifi agreed, and triggered a burst from the PKM.

"Yeah. I think you're probably right."

Tracer rounds zipped away over the heads of the islanders, forcing them all to duck below the gunwales of the small fleet of lobster boats heading toward the *Rules*. Jules hit the press-to-talk button on her headset.

"Mr. Lee, are those contacts still closing?"

The old pirate's voice came crackling back to her.

"They are still on a course to intercept us, Miss Julianne. In forty-two minutes if we do not leave now."

"Okay, Lee. Everyone's aboard. Let's get the hell out of here."

Jules felt the deck thrum under her feet as the engines growled into life, and she reached out for the handrail to steady herself against the inertia. The bow lifted appreciably as they thrust forward, adding their speed to the bluster of a freshening nor'wester. Jules and Fifi crouched instinctively as a few puffs of white smoke from the decks of the lobster boats told of a couple of ancient shotguns being fired in their direction. Fifi responded with another snarling burst from the heavy Russian machine gun. Again she aimed well over the mast of the lead boat, and again their pursuers all ducked. It would be a ridiculous pantomime were it not so serious. The islanders meant to delay them long enough for those radar contacts to close with them. Jules was now certain they were being chased by one of the Peruvian syndicates.

She pressed the talk button on her headset again.

"Sergeant Shah. Have your men stand ready. I don't think they'll be needed, but best we don't try our luck."

The Gurkha leader's voice came back to her.

"They are in position, Miss Julianne. The passengers have been secured below by Pieraro. He will join us on the boat deck."

Jules thanked him. She didn't bother looking for the small squad of mercenaries. The yacht was too large, and they were mostly arrayed on the lower decks toward the stern, giving them a clear field of fire over the heads of the lobster boats as the yacht came around. Fifi safed her weapon when she could no longer draw a bead on the little wooden tubs.

"You want me to head on down there, Julesy? Be a shame to waste the ammo, if we're not trying to hit them. Seven-point-six-two Eastern Bloc standard doesn't grow on trees, you know."

Julianne shook her head, trailing a regretful look back over the retreating vista of the Juan Fernández Archipelago.

"No, save your fire. We'll need it soon. And those guys are no real threat."

Behind the tiny, bobbing armada of trawlers the soaring peaks of the main landmass, Robinson Crusoe Island, knifed into a slate-gray sky above the village of San Juan Bautista. The lonely settlement, the only one anywhere in the archipelago, clung to the water's edge at the mouth of a steep valley that funneled bitter winds down into Cumberland Bay. The uppermost reaches of the jagged, volcanic mountains were lost inside a mass of scudding clouds. The gale roaring down on them had teeth and blew stinging salt spray into her face, but in spite of all that, it had been a great port in which to lay up and recover from the mad dash away from Acapulco and down the coast. Even more important, it had been about as far removed from the rest of the world as you could be, without pulling on your thermal knickers for a trip to the Antarctic. That had been the deal clincher after the Middle East went up. None of her passengers or crew had objected to the change in course. None of them wanted to be anywhere near a big city that might disappear inside a mushroom cloud.

Robinson Crusoe Island, a solitary fleck of volcanic rock in the vastness of the southern oceans, had seemed a perfect bolt-hole.

Too bad it hadn't worked out a little longer.

As the boat built up to its maximum speed, the muted pop of gunfire from astern was lost in the roar of the wind. Jules and Fifi remained on the flying bridge for the moment, wrapped in oilskin coats, taking in the view as they hastily exited Cumberland Bay.

"I can't believe they narked us out," said Fifi, sadly. "After they gave us those lobsters and everything!"

Jules shrugged.

"Lobsters they have an abundance of, Fifi. But diesel, food, medicine—those they're running out of fast. Shah said the boat from Valparaiso hasn't been here for two months. I don't think it's coming again."

"So what, dropping a dime on us to the fucking syndicates is their idea of self-help?"

Julianne lifted her hands in a gesture of resigned acceptance.

"What are they to do, Fi? We weren't part of the tribe. We're just a big shiny boat full of stuff they need and can't get anymore. These people are doomed, and our time with them was up. Get over it."

As Mr. Lee took them out into the exposed waters again, the yacht began to pitch and roll on the much rougher swell. The bow climbed larger and larger waves, smashing down into the dark trough on the other side with an enormous boom. Jules took one last look off to starboard at the wreath of funereal clouds gathering around the highest summits before motioning to Fifi to follow her inside. Lee was at the helm in the gleaming bridge, joyfully directing the other crew members present, Dietmar the German navigator they'd picked up in Acapulco along with the Rhino, who was chewing the stub of a much-abused cigar. Apart from a bag of clothes, his personal luggage consisted entirely of foul-smelling stogies, which he insisted on smoking at all times, right down to the nub. The smell of the Davidoffs reminded Jules of her father's library, so she indulged the old coast guard chief, over the protests of her passengers, who objected to his "secondhand carcinogens."

"How's it looking, Rhino?" asked Jules as she shook off the spray and slid the hatch closed behind her.

"Excellent. Just excellent, if you're in the market for an old-fashioned ass kicking today. Two boats. The lead vessel is making about eleven knots. Pulling away from the other, which is topping out at about eight."

"Any idea how big? How many of these hoodlums we might be dealing with?" she asked without any hope of an answer.

The Rhino puffed on his cigar, firing up the embers right under his nose. He shook his head. He was about fifty years old, and his face was a bright red relief map of broken blood vessels and sunspots.

"Sorry. They're not in visual range. I wouldn't have seen them until they were on us if we'd been anchored any farther inside the bay. The mountains were blocking the return."

She sucked the salt from her lip and thought it over. The *Rules* had a comfortable cruising speed of fifteen knots, which they could push out to seventeen and a bit for a while now that she had some engineers she could trust, but if they had any trouble in the hugely complicated engineering plant, or if they hit foul weather, their pursuers were likely going to catch up. Plus, of course, she'd burn through their fuel a lot quicker at top speed. Jules rubbed her temples, which were beginning to throb. This was not what she had planned when she'd agreed to soak a bunch of rich tourists for as much as she could get. She wondered what Pete would have done.

"Okay," she said at last. "I don't see this ending well. Fifi, let's get everyone together, shall we? Anyone who can hold a weapon, down in the main lounge. Lee, you just keep as much distance between us and them as you can. I'll be back soon."

She had one last look back toward the islands. A storm front was piling up to the southeast, smudging out the horizon. She was confident in the *Rules*'s ability to handle a big blow and could only hope that whoever was chasing them didn't enjoy such a pimped-out ride. Perhaps they could lose them in bad weather.

It really was an incongruous sight. She'd never really been taken with the fabulously overblown opulence of the main lounge area on the *Aussie Rules*. It was a bit too clubby and try-hard for her tastes. But she had to admit, she liked the sight of the half-dozen little village urchins who'd come on board with Miguel bouncing and leaping from one deep blue lounge chair to the next. Or rather she liked the look of utter dismay on the faces of some of her wealthier passengers.

Fifi followed her in, toting the PKM. It brought a level of decorum to the proceedings, with even the children stopping and pointing. They were experienced enough to know what it meant.

Pirates.

"All right. Listen up, everyone," Jules cried out. With all of the passengers and some crew gathered in there, she guesstimated that nearly thirty people were in the room. It held them comfortably. Miguel's villagers, who'd proven themselves less trouble and much more help than her paying guests, were mostly clustered together quietly under the oil paintings of Greg Norman's dogs, with just a few of the younger children still roaming around unleashed. Julianne subtracted them from her plans. They would need to be hidden away somewhere with a minder. Perhaps Granna Ana, who was the oldest of the Mexicans and spent most of her days shelling beans and peeling vegetables in the weak sun up on the pool deck. Jules had no doubt that she'd cut the throat of anyone who tried to harm the little ones, but she was virtually immobile. The rest of them, though, she'd come to appreciate. They worked hard. Ate little. Some of the men were good shots. They were reliable in a fight and would do whatever Miguel ordered them to, without demur. Plus, they'd proven themselves diabolically effective traders whenever the *Rules* had put into shore for resupply. Jules was still adamant that they would have to leave the boat at some point, but for the moment, she couldn't see her way clear to dropping them anywhere. The mainland, which they had now left behind anyway, was too dangerous, especially near any of the larger cities, and the villagers had proven themselves too useful.

Her small crew, recruited over half a dozen trading stops at smaller, self-sufficient towns and villages on the way down to Crusoe, were all handy with weapons in one form or another, while Shah's men, it went without saying, were utterly formidable. As she totted up the number of potential shooters in the lounge, Shah himself appeared at the main entrance and nodded silently to her. His men had the situation in hand for the moment.

The problem, as always, was the passengers, the rich, skiving dilettantes she had taken on board to fund the trip and provide her with a fig leaf of respectability when she arrived in Hawaii, or Sydney, or wherever they were headed. While some of them had proved themselves not completely odious, and one or two, such as Marc Unwin, the oil broker, had even brought some of their arcane skills to bear for the benefit of all, as a group they were a bunch of fucking oxygen thieves. The trust-fund brats, Phoebe and Jason, had alienated all of the crew by treating them like staff. Indeed, Jason still sported a black eye from one of the engineers. Moorhouse, the merchant banker, had become a virtual recluse as he had come to realize that the old world, and his fortune within it, was never coming back. The others simply made pains of themselves at every opportunity for want of anything better to do.

Well, she had work for them now.

"Okay," she said simply. "Pirates. Looks like we have two shiploads of them bearing down on us from the north."

A murmur surged through the adults, and some of the youngest began to chant, "Pirates pirates," but Granna Ana whacked one of them behind the ears and they all shut up quickly. Even the whackee held in his tears.

"We've had our problems with these guys before we got to Crusoe, and it looks like we've got them again."

"How?" asked the banker. "How'd they find us out here?"

Fifi shrugged. "Somebody on the island probably dropped a dime on us. Five'll get you ten one of the lobster boats chugged out of port and went looking for someone who'd be interested. They couldn't take us themselves . . ."

"But they sold us out to someone who could," Jules finished for her.

More audible concern, and a good deal of anxious muttering from the A-list passengers, greeted that. Jules held up her hands to forestall any panic.

"They *could* take us, if they caught us sleeping on the job. But they won't. You have all seen these sort of characters before. We chased them off then, we'll do it again now. I've only called everyone together because this time it looks like there's more of them and they have a bigger, faster ship. It makes sense," she explained. "Things have turned to custard on the mainland. People are killing each other for a handful of beans in the big cities. In a situation like that, you will always get bandits who group together to prey on the weak . . . But we are not the weak."

Fifi hoisted her large, ugly-looking Russian machine gun to emphasize Julianne's point. Shah folded his massive arms and allowed his solid granite head to dip once in a nod of agreement.

"We will try to outrun these guys," Jules continued. "One of them is already falling behind, and the weather is closing in. That will help. They'll have to fight a storm instead of us. But they have another vessel that could catch ours if we have any problems, and so we need to be ready. Everyone, and I mean *everyone*," she repeated, eyeing her American passengers, "will be armed and ready to repel any boarders."

She expected objections, but the statement simply dropped into a fearful silence.

"I do not expect you to get into machete fights. You'll lose. But we have enough small arms and ammunition to distribute amongst you, and you *will* defend the boat with them. That means you will have to shoot people. Dead. This is not something you can leave to Sergeant Shah and his men. There will be too many for them to handle on their own. No offense, Shah."

Shah smiled. None taken.

"I need you to divide yourselves into two groups. Those who are familiar with firearms and those who are not. Sergeant Shah and Birendra will give the latter a quick tutorial in how to pull a trigger. That's all we ask of you. The others will go with Fifi down to the gun lockers and arm yourselves appropriately. Do *not* panic. Whatever may happen will not happen for many hours yet, possibly even a day or two. Familiarize yourself with your weapons and whatever firing station you are assigned. Learn its blind spots and weaknesses. Identify a fallback route. And then get some rest. Watch a movie, hit the gym. Whatever does it for you. If you have to fight, it's best that you're not shagged out from running around like headless fucking chickens for half a day beforehand."

At least some of them laughed. Nervously.

Jules took a few steps toward them.

"It may not come to anything," she said. "We may outrun them. We have enough fuel for six thousand miles of cruising. Enough food stocks now for a month with some rationing. We may lose them in the storm that's brewing up out there. We may not."

She paused, very briefly, taking in the effect she was having. The faces of the older Mexican men were unreadable, their eyes black polished stones in a dark night. The women looked much more defiant, but also fearful for the children. Some of the younger men, boys really, looked excited.

Her A-listers, on the other hand, were quietly freaking out.

"You need to understand this, most of all," she concluded. "Anyone who steps onto this boat with hostile intentions will be cut down. They will be killed. And there will be no mercy shown them. Because we will receive none in return."

39

"We could let 'em loose," Stavros deadpanned. "About seventy-five miles north of here."

General Tusk Musso snorted softly. Yep, it would solve a few problems if he could just throw all of his prisoners into the Wave. But then what would the *New York Times* say?

Nothing. Not now.

Goddamn, but he needed a rest.

Musso pushed the tips of his fingers under his sunglasses and rubbed at his sore, bloodshot eyes. He could feel bristle growing on his cheeks. The camp had run out of razor blades. He'd have to do something about that. Have to maintain standards.

They had run out of Kiwi boot polish as well, hard as that was to believe. Most combat boots looked as if they had been polished with a Hershey bar, if at all. The general wore a pair of the new, now rare, suede tan Marine Corps boots. At least he didn't have to worry about spit and polish every night.

The afternoon sun was warm, but not uncomfortably so. Nonetheless it glinted off the steel and wire of Camp 4 with a fierceness that made the sunglasses necessary. It was quiet today. The next call to prayer was still an hour away, and the prisoners' initial excitement after the Disappearance had long since evaporated. The Israelis had made sure of that. Most of these humps were now as alone in the world as the Americans who still guarded them.

"I don't know what to do, George," he admitted. "Pearl wants this expedited. And that's the extent of their instructions. Except for Susan Pileggi's Uplift requirements we really don't rate as a priority anymore, and the refugee flow has slowed up anyway. God knows some of these losers really don't need to be here." He waved a dismissive hand back toward the detainees. "But, on the other hand, nobody's going to thank me for releasing a couple of hundred more lunatics onto the job market. So what do we do?"

"Don't know, General. That's why you make the *big* bucks."

That really was a joke. Neither of them had been paid in three weeks. Even if they had been, what use would they have for a dead, worthless currency?

"Okay, decision time. Let's set up a small review team. We'll do a quick and dirty study of each case. The really bad motherfuckers, like Khalid, we're going to try according to the laws of war. If convicted, they can be dealt with summarily."

Lieutenant Colonel Stavros looked wary.

"But, General, most of the personnel involved in the commission process were back home. Prosecutors. Defense. Most of their files. They're gone. What do we charge them with? How can we . . ."

Musso cut him off with a chopping hand gesture.

"I didn't say it'd be pretty, George. Just fast. Some of these guys need their necks stretched. Some of them don't belong here. Let's shake the box and see who falls out of which hole. I want it sorted in a month."

"A month . . . but, General, we've got hundreds of cases . . . And where are we going to send them?"

"A lot of them can be repatriated to their homelands, assuming the Israelis didn't turn them into a slag heap. We got a lot of Pakistanis here. Let Musharraf have them. We might even get lucky. India might nuke him as soon as they touch down. Most of the rest are Saudis, Jordanians, Afghanis. Let's send 'em home. What happens then is up to their governments. Frankly I don't think many of them will survive but that's not my problem. A month, Colonel. This is one issue I don't need to think about anymore. There's plenty that I do. Including this waste of space."

Stavros turned to look over his shoulder where Musso had glowered at two approaching civilians: Dr. Griffiths and his assistant, Tibor, universally known as Igor. They were stomping up the road in front of Camp 4, sweating profusely.

Griffiths began carping as soon as he was in pistol-shot range.

"Found you at last, *General*. I must protest again about the lack of cooperation from your staff with my research. Do I have to remind you that I was sent here by your superiors? I am supposed to be studying the phenomenon. Instead I spend most of my time getting jerked around by you or your minions."

"Good afternoon, Doctor. Always lovely to see you. And no, you don't have to remind me," said Musso. "I've heard that particular song so many times now that it has its own neural pathway that lights up every time I see you. If this is about your field trip, my staff aren't thwarting you, Doctor. They're simply following orders. They cannot go into the exclusion zone along the line of the Wave because they have been ordered not to. The Wave is dangerous, Doctor. It eats people. It ate one of yours the first week you were here. Left a little pile of goo in a white coat as I recall. It's not getting any more of mine."

Musso's voice was rising, and he could feel his anger slipping the leash. He pushed past the civilians and stomped over to where his driver and Humvee stood waiting on the small loop road in front of the camp. Brown, dried-out grass grew to knee height on the waste ground there, and Musso made a note to himself to have that seen to. It was getting to be a fire hazard. He was aware of Stavros crunching up behind him, but his thoughts were elsewhere, sailing out across the blue waters he could just glimpse between the prison camp buildings as he attempted to calm down. Increasingly he found that the fuse on his incendiary temper was burning way too quickly. He had once fancied himself the world's most patient man. Really. He was known for it. That's what made him a good lawyer. But he did have a temper, a foul one, and it had been running wild for weeks. Ever since the first shock had ebbed and he'd had time to really take in the enormity of the loss. Of his loss, personally.

He lay awake in his cot most nights, unable to sleep properly, tortured by the loss of his family. It was wrong, he knew, to feel their deaths so much more keenly than the hundreds of millions of lives snuffed out on that day and since. But that was just how people were. As each day went past, he found it more difficult to deal with their absence, not less. He often caught himself thinking irrationally of calling one of his boys, or his wife. And then he'd remember . . . and his mood would implode.

"Well, let the Cubans escort me, General," continued Griffiths, who was entirely oblivious of the needs of anyone but himself. "They don't have to follow your orders, do they? I'm sure some of them would love a chance to travel back into their own country."

Musso spun on him.

"Go ask them yourself, Doctor, but first, tell me what the fuck you have actually learned while you've been here. Tell me what anyone has learned, here or anywhere else, about that thing."

Griffiths staggered back one step and opened his mouth, but no words came out, because there was nothing to say. The Wave did not exist, at least not according to any instruments or sensor arrays currently available. The only evidence that it still sat squatting over the North American continent was available by looking north. There it soared, miles into the sky. Mute, terrible, and utterly impenetrable.

"Nobody is stopping you, Doctor. Off you go, if you wish. But do not bother my people about it. I have lost half a dozen of them to that thing. Not to mention the Cubans it's grabbed up. It's random. There is no safe distance within two thousand meters from it. People have been snatched from twenty feet away, and two klicks. You were told all of this, on arrival. Nothing has changed."

Griffiths, a small man afflicted with receding red hair, appeared likely to blow a gasket. But unlike Musso, he still had control of his temper.

"I am sorry for the loss of your men, General . . ."

"And women. Two of my marines were women, Corporal Crist and Lieutenant Kwan."

"Okay. I am sorry. But those casualties all predated my arrival. I do not need anyone to follow me into the exclusion zone. Entering is a risk I am willing to take. But I cannot get out there without an escort. There are simply too many bandits now. It is too dangerous."

Musso made a conscious effort not to explode. He tried to climb down from the heights of his rage. Perhaps Griffiths was right. Nobody had ever been taken beyond two thousand meters. The survey stations in the Pacific Northwest and Canada confirmed that, too. If the scientist had the nuts to take himself inside that safe, established perimeter, on his own, who was he to argue? After all, if the Wave gobbled him up it'd be one less headache for Musso to deal with.

"Okay. You can have an escort to within three thousand

meters. After that you're on your own. Even if you get nailed by bandits within clear sight of my people, if you're in the zone, you're on your own. See if you can remember that little rhyme. It'll help with your confusion when we don't come running to drag your ass out of trouble."

"General, your meeting with the French consul, sir, you're going to be late."

"Thanks, George," he grunted. It wasn't even a setup. He really did have a meeting, for which he was truly grateful. "Dr. Griffiths, if you don't mind, I have to sign off the last of the refugee convoys today. Perhaps when they are gone, there will be time for dealing with your issues."

That seemed to surprise and even mollify Griffiths somewhat, and Musso climbed into the Humvee without delay. He didn't offer the civilians a ride anywhere.

"These won't be the last refugees we get, you know, General."

"I know, but it will be the last big convoy the navy escorts anywhere. The word from Pearl is *finito*. It's been a month. From now on people will have to make their own arrangements. We're losing more of our power-projection capability with each passing day."

The midnight hour had long since passed, and Musso was back in his office, enjoying the chill of the air-conditioning and the absence of pests. He nursed a precious cup of coffee. At least in this part of the world it was still plentiful, if expensive. Colonel Pileggi sat across from him, just outside the cone of light thrown down by his desk lamp, half hidden in the gloom, an old-fashioned clipboard on her knee as she ticked off her checklist. Behind her the waters of the bay twinkled under a bright moon, and dozens of civilian craft of all sizes lay quietly at anchor, awaiting the departure of the next convoy for the Pacific. A few small light craft still plied a path between them, distributing stores, collecting passenger lists, and handing out information on convoy protocols. In contrast with the first few crazed days of his time at Gitmo, a skeleton crew was on deck at the headquarters building. The base slumbered out in the darkness.

"So we can expect the escorts here tomorrow?" she asked doubtfully. There had been problems recently transiting the

Canal. With the Panamanian government's collapse, Pearl had finally put in a brigade combat team to control the locks, but they were being pressed by an unknown number of criminal syndicates. Not a day went by without one or two casualties among the Americans. On the upside, though, the rules of engagement for the Canal zone were robust. Anybody approaching the American-controlled locks was immediately engaged and destroyed without warning.

Musso nodded.

"It should be cool. Principal escort's French, coming up from Guiana. An F-70-class ship on the way now, a frigate, although it's big enough that we'd call it a destroyer. I spoke with their guy out of Cayenne when he flew in late afternoon. It won't have to transit the Canal until the convoy gets there, and it has enough firepower to muscle through any parts where we can't provide cover. And a solid detachment of marine infantry for good measure. Our guys will pick them up on the other side. Then the French will split off with the smaller group for New Caledonia."

Pileggi raised one eyebrow but remained silent.

Musso shrugged. "I know. I know. Surprised me, too. I thought the French were too busy tearing each other apart to bother with helping anyone else, but Sarkozy's faction has been looking real hard at their Pacific territories. You want my opinion, there's going to be a lot of Frenchies opting out of food riots and ethnic cleansing for grass skirts and Gilligan's Island any day now."

"Damn," muttered Pileggi. "Is that the good dope you're smoking? Straight from Pearl?"

"Yeah," said Musso. "There have been talks, apparently. Very quiet talks. This consular guy confirmed as much. We may be in business as a transit point in the future. Assuming Sarkozy wins, of course."

"That's quite an assumption from what I've read," said Pileggi, as a new worry etched itself into the deep lines of her face, and shadows pooled under her eyes. "I've got a lot of my refugees bunking down in the French colonies. What's going to happen to them?"

"No idea. I guess there'll be more talks. Things are already pretty crowded in French Polynesia. For now, our problems are all here. We've got nigh on a hundred vessels to get out of the harbor and through the Canal. Are they going to be finished provisioning? You were having some trouble with supplies as I recall."

Pileggi tapped the clipboard with her pen.

"Those two big container ships that came in early this morning from Port-au-Spain declared a lot of stuff we could use. So I requisitioned their cargo. My guys are going to check them out in the morning and begin redistribution."

"Uh-huh. How were the captains about that?"

She waved the question off with a hand gesture.

"Relaxed. They even sent over a complete cargo manifest to help out. They're Panamanian-flagged with mostly Russian and Indian crews. The shipping line's gone out of business. They say they'll need some fuel and an escort to Australia. I'd guess they're going to sell what they can in Sydney. The Indians will want to go home from there, the Russians will probably jump ship and try to disappear into the crowd."

"Well, the crowds would be big enough, I imagine. Must be nearly two million displaced down there now."

Pileggi shook her head.

"Passed that last week. They're up to two point two, as of close of business yesterday. Two and a half if you count New Zealand. Mostly ours, but a fair number of Europeans, too. Clean-shaven and fair-skinned, of course," she added drily. "Don't bother knocking if your name is Mohammad."

Musso felt instinctive disapproval stirring in his gut, just as he disapproved of the British government's mass internment and deportation policies. It was ethnic cleansing by another name, or ethnic filtering, perhaps, Down Under. Racism cloaked as necessity when you got right down to it. But it was hardly the worst thing happening in the world today. And the Aussies had taken anyone with an American passport, regardless of background. While their motives were almost entirely selfish—just look at how much remnant U.S. military power had been redeployed down there to protect America's most precious asset, its remaining people—you couldn't argue with the result. Refugee allocations to Southern Hemisphere locations were among the most precious things in the world at the moment. The ecological catastrophe of the Disappearance was mostly confined to the northern latitudes. Nobody in their right mind wanted to go into the tribal slaughterhouse that was Africa. And with so many South American countries succumbing to the contagion of anarchy or military takeover, slots in the Australia and New Zealand programs were the most avidly sought. Fortunes in trade goods were being made smuggling people in there.

Musso was about to ask Pileggi for a rundown on the civilian flights out of Soto Cano, in Honduras, the other leg of her role in Operation Uplift, when he suddenly blinked in shock.

A freighter moored near the old fueling station down in the bay exploded. There was no warning. It simply lifted a few feet out of the water, a small dense blossom of white light cracking it amidships before flowering into a dark, oily orange ball of flame that lit up the entire harbor. The sundered bow and stern thumped back down, throwing up huge fantails of water before the vessel keeled over and started to sink.

"Motherfuck!"

Pileggi spun around in her chair, half raising herself as she did so.

Musso didn't bother with the formalities of ending the meeting. They were both already headed for the door when a navy lieutenant appeared, blocking their exit. She was holding a sheaf of paper and appeared goggle-eyed with surprise.

"General Musso. There's a message for you, sir. From President Chávez."

"Who?" He was tired, worn slick, and not firing on all cylinders.

"Hugo Chávez, sir, president of Venezuela."

She handed it across as more explosions ripped through the night, muted by distance. A crackle of small-arms fire resolved itself from the rolling thunder.

"What the fuck?"

He snatched the piece of paper and skimmed it.

"What is it, General?" asked Susan Pileggi.

"It's that commie wing nut down in Venezuela," said Musso as he finished rereading the transmission. "He's demanding that we leave Cuba. Says the External Committee of the Cuban Politburo in Caracas has requested the assistance of Venezuela in removing 'all imperialist chancres' from the body of Cuba."

"What?"

"He's a wack job, how do I know what he means?"

Pileggi's eyes suddenly flew wide open, just as Musso's had done a few seconds earlier.

"Those container ships," she said. "We haven't been able to inspect them yet. One of them's a ConRO vessel."

Musso shook his head, trying to clear the mud out and not having a lot of luck.

"A container ship with a roll-on/roll-off facility," she explained, quickly. "Just like an LHD. You could use it for putting troops ashore."

"Shit!"

Another officer appeared at the door. An Army Signal Corps captain.

"Excuse me, General, you need to see this, sir. It's a distress call from the French ship. The *Montcalm*. She says she's been torpedoed. Three hits and she's going down, requesting immediate SAR to this location."

The captain handed over another piece of paper with the grid coordinates.

"Venezuelan navy, Lieutenant. Do they even have submarines?" he asked the wide-eyed naval officer.

She seemed to stumble over the answer before composing herself.

"Two that I recall, General. A couple of Type 209 diesel electric attack boats. German design. Not a bad ship killer if you can't afford a top-shelf product."

Musso squeezed out a silent curse as the sound of gunfire escalated behind him. He hurried back to the window for a quick look-see. The previously calm moonlit setting had changed into a maelstrom of moving craft, all illuminated by the burning freighter. By pressing his face right up against the glass he could see far enough up the main branch of the bay to make out a big cargo vessel that appeared to have beached itself. An armored vehicle rolled down off the ramp, spewing tracer fire into the camp.

40

Noisy-le-Sec, Paris

The soup was a simple broth, a thin brown liquid in which floated a few chunks of carrot, some onion, and a little shredded meat, possibly beef, but to Caitlin it was heaven in a bowl. She sipped at the rim. Her hands shook too much to use the spoon they had given her, and she had already finished the small piece of bread that came with the meal.

"Thank you," she said again. "I'm afraid this place doesn't really deserve its Michelin star."

Captain Rolland smiled kindly and affected a very Gallic lift of the shoulders. "Standards are slipping everywhere, mademoiselle."

Caitlin returned the smile.

"I dunno. My last stay here wasn't much better either."

She finished the bowl and placed it on the small table in front of the old leather couch on which she sat, wrapped in a clean blanket and dressed for the first time in weeks. Rolland snapped his fingers, and a young soldier appeared from outside the office to clear away the dish and plate. They did not speak while he was in the room. Caitlin peered out the window, over a rain-slicked parking lot below. A bus burned in one corner, and a couple of bodies lay nearby in pools of blood, which became lighter and pinker as the rain diluted them. She appeared to be about three stories up, high enough to see over the red-tiled roofs of the surrounding buildings to the eastern suburbs of Paris. A few fires burned in a desultory fashion here and there, dwarfed by a huge tower of smoke about five miles away.

She couldn't see any movement in the streets, but she could hear gunfire. A lot of it.

"Sounds like Beirut. Or maybe the Mog," she said.

Rolland, a handsome thirty-something man with a full head of black hair swept back and oiled in a very old-fashioned style, lit a cigarette and then stopped himself.

"Excuse me, do you mind?"

The pain in her head was wretched, but it was no worse than any of her other manifold agonies.

"Knock yourself out, *mon capitaine*. I doubt those things will kill me. They're at the back of a very long line."

Rolland sat down across the coffee table from her and drew deeply on the unfiltered cigarette with evident pleasure. His uniform was filthy and his boots were caked with mud. He had not shaved in a few days.

"This is my first one all week," he said, waving the cigarette around. "And I had to take it from one of the jihadi pigs. It's Turkish. Not my blend. But what can one do?"

"Yeah, the jihadi pigs. About them. You want to tell me what my target was doing in your dungeons? You know, besides raping me."

Rolland shifted uncomfortably in his chair.

"I am sorry," he said. "It was a disgraceful thing. But, I am afraid, all too common these days. Monsieur Baumer, your target—and mine, as it transpires—he unfortunately escaped our net. We were hoping you might be able to help us find him. After all, you are the expert on al-Banna?"

She laughed, a short, joyless sound.

"I'm the world expert on getting my ass kicked by him. And I have to tell you, Rolland, the shape I'm in, I'd get it kicked all over again if we met. But you're not answering my questions. What was he doing here? What were any of them doing here? And what the hell's been going on out there? Reynard told me you guys had things under control." She nodded toward the city center. "But that's not under control. This place is dying."

Momentary confusion passed over the soldier's face as he shook his head. "Reynard? Oh, you mean Lacan. No, it is not under control, mademoiselle. It has not been for weeks. Half of the city's population has fled into the countryside, but things are worse out there. All the cities have emptied out. You can imagine what that means. Some of them took tents and provisions for a few days' camping. Most just fled when the Intifada and La Résistance began in earnest. Farms and villages have barricaded themselves off from the world, fought off everyone who seeks shelter or aid. It is a Dark Age again. There are bodies piling up in fields. Possibly a million of them by now. With thousands more dying every day. Many, many are the dead."

Caitlin was already dizzy with exhaustion and moral collapse, but Rolland was making her head spin. She imagined a host of totally unprepared urbanites swarming over the French countryside expecting to live off stolen eggs and wild berries. They'd have stripped the fields bare in days. She began shaking again, the same deep-body tremors that had seized her after being raped by al-Banna.

"S-sorry," she stuttered.

Rolland reached into his blood-smeared tunic and removed a silver flask.

"Here, drink some," he said. "It is brandy. Good brandy, not like the hospital disinfectant you are familiar with. And my battalion surgeon, he said these may help, too."

A small blister pack of tablets dropped to the tabletop. Half of them had already been popped.

"They will calm your nerves," he explained. "But should not dull your senses."

Caitlin briefly wondered whether she might react adversely to them, given her medical condition. Then she thought, what the hell, and downed two with a swig from Rolland's flask. The liquor burned softly and warmed her upper body. As she handed back the brandy, a jet suddenly screamed through the air nearby, the noise arcing up from a distant whine to a deafening shriek in mere seconds. A very short time later she heard the unmistakable crump of air-dropped munitions detonating within a few miles.

"So, things haven't gone as well as I was led to believe?"

Captain Rolland took a long draw on the harsh-smelling cigarette.

"I am afraid not. The situation remains . . . confused."

"Not as confused as me. Why don't you try explaining? You could start with Baumer. He was one of yours? That's why I was targeted?"

"A double agent? No. I am afraid not."

Caitlin's head felt as though it had been wrapped in old towels soaked in chloroform. She had trouble concentrating and holding her thoughts.

"But what was he doing here at the fort? What, are you saying that Reynard, sorry, what did you call him . . ."

"Lacan. Barnard Lacan. The second-in-charge of the action division."

"Okay. Lacan then. You're saying he'd sold out to the Intifada?"

Rolland waved his hands in a frustrated manner, as if trying to shoo a fly.

"It is not so simple, no. You have been out of contact for a long time, Caitlin. Do you mind if I call you Caitlin?"

"It's not the worst liberty's been taken with me recently. Go on."

"Lacan was working with Baumer's network, yes. But not just Lacan. And not just with one jihadi cell. It is difficult, Caitlin, this situation I must explain. Please bear with me. You will be aware of some of the history of the DGSE, your rival service, *non*?"

She leaned back against the arm of the lounge and pulled the blanket around to a more comfortable position. Outside the rain began to pick up, strongly enough to wash much of the blood from the courtyard. The pills hadn't kicked in yet, but the brandy was having a soothing effect. Rolland used the opportunity to light another cigarette.

"Unlike your CIA, and despite its name, the action division does not maintain a standing section of paramilitary covert operatives. When such skills are required it draws on what we call a 'tank' of operators from the army, mostly the special forces and commandos."

She nodded. The information wasn't new to her.

"Do you know of the original battalion on which the division relied?"

She searched her battered memory and came up with some fragment.

"Some paratroop regiment?"

"Very good." Rolland nodded. "Almost right. The Onzième Bataillon Parachutiste de Choc," he said. "The Shock Parachutist Battalion, as you would say, first raised in 1946. It was disbanded in 1963 because its officers were collaborators, supporters of French Algeria."

"Okay. That means they backed whitey, right? The *pieds noirs*. Ancient history, but go on."

"Ancient for you, young lady. Not for France. The Algerian

416 · JOHN BIRMINGHAM

war nearly destroyed us. It collapsed the Fourth Republic. Brought back the Gaullists, and forever changed our view of France as *une puissance musulmane.* Do you know the phrase?"

"A Muslim power," she replied. "Again, so what? A hundred years ago you wanted to lord it over the Arabs, because the Brits scarfed up all the good colonies for themselves."

He favored her with a lopsided smile.

"I had been told you were a difficult woman."

"I prefer to think of myself as challenging."

"Your American psychology betrays you, Caitlin. *Une puissance musulmane* does not just mean to wield power over the House of Peace. It means to hold that power in . . . how would you phrase it? . . . agreement, accordance, a sort of *entente cordiale* with the Islamic world itself. You and the British often described your filial bonds as a special relationship. Indeed, that relationship extended across all of the English-speaking world. Your employer, Echelon, it was a perfect expression of that dysfunctional Anglophone family, *non*? An alliance, a secret one, between the English-speaking powers, directed against *everyone* else. That is quite special when you think about it. Well, our special relationship, our particular delusion if you wish, was with the Dar al-Islam. Or so some thought."

"Captain," she said, as toxic rain began to patter against the windowpanes and the room became even gloomier, "you're going to have to help me out here. I have a brain tumor. I have trouble putting two and two together."

Rolland stood up and flicked on a light. He called out to one of his men stationed in the corridor, and they spoke in murmurs for a moment before he returned.

"Excuse me. I am expecting someone. Yes, I am sorry. It is the continental way of narrative. Much more elliptical than your own. Let me bottom-line it for you, to borrow from your own vernacular. Since the accommodation in Algeria, there has been a school of thought, a quiet but powerful clique within the state, that has believed that accommodation with Islam is the only way forward. At first this group was centered on the Quai d'Orsay, and they applied their doctrine within their own sphere, often in conflict with other actors in the state realm."

"Okay, so you had some surrender monkeys in the foreign ministry and they were rub-fucking the Arabs. I have to say, this isn't breaking news."

Rolland uncapped the brandy flask and took a swig for himself before offering one to Caitlin. She joined him. The pills, whatever they were, had begun to smooth her rough edges, and another drink seemed a good idea. Sitting on this magnificent old sofa, drinking fine spirits and chatting with the handsome French officer, she finally began to get some distance on the horror of the previous weeks.

"I believe similar tensions existed between your own State Department and military," Rolland countered. "It is the usual way between peacemakers and war fighters. But here in France there was a complicating factor, which grew more complicated with every year."

Caitlin nodded slowly. "Your own Muslim population."

"Quite so. Just as your country found that certain questionable policies and state activities initially carried out beyond your borders, say, in Southeast Asia, tended to return home in one form or another . . ."

"We called it blowback."

"How brutally elegant. Well, we, too, have discovered that a contagion, acquired in Algiers, transmitted itself to the body politic right here."

"Rolland, this would be a fascinating discussion if we were Jean-Paul and Simone sucking down Gitanes and black coffee in a Montmartre café, but how about you ditch all the context and sell me your pitch?"

Rolland leaned back and blew twin streams of blue smoke out through his nostrils.

"Betrayal, Caitlin. I am talking about betrayal. The man who held you here, Lacan, did not do so on his own recognizance. Nor did he operate as part of a small, traitorous cell. I am afraid that Monsieur Lacan was part of a much larger, and very well-organized, network of state officials, the Algerian School, as we know them, who had determined that the only possible, rational option for dealing in the long term with the rise of Muslim power in the Middle East, and within France herself, was accommodation."

"Appeasement, you mean."

"No, 'appeasement' is not a strong enough word, Caitlin. To appease is simply to make morally compromised concessions in order to maintain one's own tenuous status. That is not what the School's philosophy now entertains. 'Adaptation' is more apt. Although in your language it sounds rather bloodless. It is not. As practiced by the Algerian School it means to slowly adapt the French secular state to the brute realities of its future as an annex to the Dar al-Islam, as a true Muslim power."

"To convert."

"Yes. To convert. And to that end they have allied themselves with the Intifada, in which your target is a leading player."

"Holy shit," she said, impressed at last. "And the action division. How many of them were . . ."

Rolland shook his head.

"Enough. Say a third. The others were quickly dealt with in the first days of fighting."

"But you've got a civil war out there. Surely you can't have whole army divisions who've gone over."

Rolland shook his head.

"No. There is fighting between many arms of the military and other organs of the state. But most of those involved see nothing beyond their gunsights. An army regiment is ordered to put down a mutiny by the Foreign Legion and the individual soldiers do not understand that they are fighting an engagement to suit the ends of the conspiracy. To them it is just a civil war, and now it is so far advanced that all about chaos reigns. Accusations, counterclaims, propaganda. All is confusion."

He leaned forward and stubbed the butt of his cigarette.

"But this I do know, Caitlin. You can help stop it. Your target, Baumer, he is not the key, but he leads to the key, to the masters of the Algerian School. Take them down, and the Intifada is leaderless, nothing more than a rabble—a huge rabble, yes, but not one that can match an army that is not divided against itself."

"You want me to kill your own people?" she asked, still not believing it all.

A new voice spoke up from the door behind Rolland, startling her. An American voice.

"That was always going to be your next mission. That's why you were targeted."

"Wales? Goddamn, Wales!"

As sick in body and soul as she was, Caitlin pushed herself up off the couch and ran over to hug Wales Larrison, almost knocking him off his feet as she threw her arms around his neck.

"Goddamn, Wales, it's been . . . it's just . . ."

A small burning lump in her throat grew and grew, until it merged with the ache in her chest, and for the first time since she had been captured, Caitlin Monroe let herself go and poured out a torrent of tears.

Larrison, a rangy, silver-haired Nebraskan, enfolded her within a generous bear hug and made no attempt to calm her down as wretched, pitiable sobs and shudders racked her body.

"I'm s-s-sorry, Wales. I failed . . . and . . ."

He shushed her and stroked her head, patting down masses of thick dark hair still wet from the shower and smelling of cheap shampoo.

"It's all right, Cait. It's all right. You've been sick. I know. They told me. You shouldn't have been out in the field, let alone trussed up in this shithole . . . if you'll excuse my, er, French, Captain Rolland."

"But of course. It *is* a shithole."

Caitlin could feel Larrison's strong heartbeat through his suit jacket, and that strength flowed through his arms into her. She slowly regained her composure and pushed herself away.

"How did you get here?" she asked shakily, wiping her nose on a shirt cuff. "I thought they'd grabbed you, Wales. I thought they'd rolled up the whole network."

Larrison put one finger on her lip and bade her to be quiet. He led her back to the couch and eased her down, then sat himself at the other end.

"I was in London when everything happened," he said. "I had to sit on my ass and watch it from there. I'm sorry, Caitlin. I tried to get an overwatch team to you, twice, but DGSE had a legitimate counterintel responsibility for shadowing us. We did spy on them, after all. They never penetrated a cell, but their intelligence division was aware of us. That's how they grabbed you the first time you were here. And they blocked both teams I sent in. Wiped out one. Grabbed up the other one."

Caitlin pulled the blanket closer around her shoulders.

"What's left of us, Wales? Of Echelon, I mean."

He puffed out his cheeks.

"Every op we had running in France was taken down. Every one. With extreme prejudice. The Brits lost their people, too. Would have caused a quiet, dirty little war if we hadn't known about the School. So now, in France, I'm afraid you're it. Our last designated hitter."

He indicated the fort with a wave of the hand. Somewhere many miles away, more bombs exploded.

"Lacan had people all over," he said. "This Algerian School, it's like Rolland told you, they were everywhere. When we sent you after Baumer they stepped in. He was protected as part of the . . . accommodation. They were always going to try to keep you off him."

Captain Rolland put one muddy boot on the coffee table, leaned forward, and retrieved his packet of pills. "Normally you would have been detained, interrogated, the usual inconveniences," he explained. "But the Disappearance, it changed everything. A massive, world-changing shock."

"They had contingencies," said Larrison. "In the event of some foreseeable catastrophe that would cripple the U.S. Financial collapse. Nuclear strike, whatever. The Disappearance wasn't foreseeable, but it was also a hell of a lot more than a simple catastrophe. It wiped us out."

"And the contingency?" said Caitlin.

"To finish the work of Allah," answered Rolland. "As soon as it was confirmed what had happened in America, Lacan purged the action division and sent his trusted people out, to roll up your network. It was not just you, of course. The British also maintained Echelon cadre in France, as Monsieur Larrison explained. They, too, were targeted. Even your junior partners, the Canadians, Australians, and New Zealanders, all of them were smothered."

"So what, all the street fighting, the ethnic clashes, they were engineered by the School?" she asked. "That seems a bit far-fetched."

Larrison, who looked so much older than the last time they had spoken, just two months ago, shook his head sadly.

"Not all of them, Cait. A lot of violence arose naturally. Once the capstone was off, the geyser blew. But yes, some incidents were engineered to bring on a wider confrontation. An uprising. Even then it might not have worked. Conspiracies often don't, as you would know. But Israel nuking half of the Arab world, that was a deal breaker. Race war, holy war, civil war, whatever you want to call it. It was inevitable after that. Unavoidable. And people have been killing each other ever since."

She moved her head carefully to look out the windows again. The rain turned the suburbs outside into a bleary, gray netherworld, but some elements did resolve themselves. There was no traffic, vehicular or pedestrian. The only aircraft aloft were military, and of course she had already noted that they were attacking targets within the city. There seemed to be fewer fires burning than she remembered, but the rain was heavy, and on looking more closely she could see that whole districts had already been burned out.

She snuggled deeper into the sofa. It was strangely comforting. "You said something about my next mission?"

Wales Larrison clicked his tongue.

"Yup. I did. We didn't tell you, because you didn't need to know, not at that point. But the hit on Baumer was a joint operation with the DST, the intelligence arm of Sarkozy's interior ministry. Sarkozy had decided to move against the School and had asked us to help. It was unprecedented. Echelon does not play outside of the family. But in this case, we did, because the strategic consequences could affect the family generations down the line. The Brits were particularly gung-ho. Your mission was designed to shake out Baumer's contacts. To expose Lacan and his people. They were being monitored by the DST without their knowledge."

"Or so we thought," said Rolland.

"Or so we thought," sighed Larrison.

"There was a leak?" said Caitlin.

Larrison grunted. "There was. We still don't know where from. But Lacan found out, and that's why he bet so much on grabbing you up. He needed you to start unraveling the op against him and the other School masters."

"Son of a bitch," muttered Caitlin.

"I'm sorry, Cait, but you know the rules."

She waved away his apology.

"I'm not pissed at you, Wales. I know my job and I know it's not always what it seems. I'm a pawn. I can be sacrificed. It's just . . . I dunno. I'm sick, Wales, really sick. And it's messing with my head, the way I think and see things."

A weak breath escaped from her lips, and she deflated.

"I made a friend. An asset. I shouldn't have, but I did. I'm not well. And I got her killed because I wasn't good enough to save her."

The room broke up into a jeweled kaleidoscope as more tears came. Larrison leaned over and patted her on the knee. Her dad had done the same thing a thousand times, and it only served to deepen her sadness. Larrison's voice was soft, the way her father's had once been, but still hard with it.

"You're not a pawn, Caitlin," he said. "You're a knight. And you're still in play."

41

Sixteenth arrondissement, Paris

The BBC offices in Paris were an armed compound, with every window covered in steel plating. It did nothing to dull the arrhythmic tom-tom beat of heavy machine-gun fire or the dense, percussive thud of high-explosive ordnance pounding the rubble, just a few minutes' drive away. A sandbagged gun pit and razor wire guarded the main entrance, secured by a rotating team of gunned-up heavies from Sandline, a British-based "private military company." Dave, one of the operators, was American, and Melton had initially attempted to forge some kind of relationship with him, but entirely without luck. All he ever received in return for his stream of "howdys" and "hi theres" and "how ya doin's" were grunts and the blank, dead stare of the deeply disinterested.

"He's not really a people person, is he?" said Monty, the chief of staff. "Still, better than having every man and his mad dog wandering in, eh?"

Monty was a thirty-year veteran of war reporting, having cut his teeth on the Golan Heights all the way back in 1973, during the Yom Kippur War. Like most of the bureau staff he was newly arrived, a volunteer, in his case from Kabul. Paris was considered a war posting, which was how Melton had moved from freelancer to staffer almost as soon as he'd put his foot in the door with his collection of Iraq War interviews. Very few people had the desire, experience, and unique mix of skills that he brought to the table. Even among the grizzled veterans of the Beeb's first-rank war correspondents, he stood out because of his own combat experience.

"Tea?" asked Monty, as they gathered in the second-floor conference room, a windowless box in the center of the building. Next to the production studios down in the basement, it was one of the most secure areas in the building, but even so, every now and then a larger explosion nearby would shake flakes of plaster from the ceiling. Melton could feel the detonation through the soles of his shoes.

There was no coffee to be had, unfortunately, and Melton had noticed that the Brits really did seem to function a lot more effectively with just a cup or two of their weak, milky brew inside them. He had no idea where Barry, the office manager, sourced their supplies, but in a starving city riven by ethnic and civil warfare he somehow did keep the larder stocked and the teapots full. When Melton had complimented him on his scrounging chops Barry had grinned back and said, "If I can keep fucking Jim Muir's beer fridge full of fuckin' Boddington's in Beirut, a cup of fucking char in Paris isn't going to bovver me, is it, govnor!"

"But a decent cup of java's impossible?" Melton asked.

"All but," said Barry, in an apologetic tone. "Frogs is killing each other over moldy croissants and fucking Nescafé. So no, Mr. Melton. No fucking coffee. Learn to drink somefin' civilized, why don'tcha?"

The small team of correspondents and editors took their places around the table, most of them juggling papers and folders in one hand, and bone-china cups and saucers in the other. A packet of "biscuits," as they insisted on calling all forms of cookie life, sat in the center of the table, and Monty doled out one each to every tea drinker before carefully twisting the packet closed again and clamping it off with a wooden clothespin. The provenance of the clothespin was never explained. It was a peculiar ritual, which Melton had rather come to look forward to each day. He was offered one of the McVitie's wholemeal "bickies" to have with his glass of water, but again he turned it down.

"Couldn't get any Oreos, Barry?" he teased, only half in jest.

"Oh, I know where there's a whole warehouse of them, Mr. Melton. Just couldn't be fucked dickering for 'em. Why, do you want some?"

"Oh, no, don't put yourself out on my behalf." He smiled.

"Wasn't planning to, sir."

Other exchanges rolled back and forth across and around the table as everyone settled in. The morning news conference was about something more than simply assigning new stories and monitoring those already in progress. It was the only time each day when the entire team was in one place, and it served as an opportunity for everyone to touch base, for the tribe to hunker down and count its blessings that their numbers had not been thinned out once again. The Beeb had had seventeen journalists killed or simply disappeared in the last month, not counting those who'd been vaporized in the Middle East or the United States. The Paris bureau, however, was charmed, having lost nobody since Jon Sopel was killed in the first week of fighting. The bureau had grown like Topsy since then, and had taken the buildings on either side as they were abandoned, but only seasoned warcos and freelancers like Melton worked there now. He'd been hired on a twelve-month contract. It paid a fraction of his *Army Times* job, which hadn't been a great payer in the first place, but because of the hazardous posting status, he was guaranteed "room and board" at the Paris compound.

It seemed perverse, but he ate better and slept more securely than many people in England.

"Right then," Monty called out in his down-to-business voice. "What enchanting fripperies and puff pieces will we be filing from the city of light today then? Caroline, darlin', any chance of that interview with the blessed Sarko yet?"

Caroline Wyatt rolled her eyes up to the peeling paint of the high ceiling.

"His minders promised me I'd see him yesterday and I spent the whole bloody day in this wretched armored car roaring around from one bunker to the next, without ever actually managing to get anywhere near the little bugger. I'll stay on it, Monty, if you really wish, but I don't think he's going to roll over for us until he has some genuinely good news to crow about."

"Well, his armored boyos entered the old city last night. I'd have thought that was good enough."

"Yes, it is a feel-good story, isn't it, dozens of Leclerc main battle tanks crushing Arab street fighters under their treads in the Bois de Boulogne? I can't imagine why he wouldn't want to sit down and chat about that over a Pernod or two."

"Well, keep at it, sweetheart. I have faith in your charms. Bret, are you all squared away with the marines? London is super keen to see you embed with them after they cleaned out Lyons."

Melton tapped the point of his ballpoint on a Spirax writing pad.

"Soon as we're finished up here, I'm off to Suresnes. The marines—although you know, they're really more like army rangers—they laid up last night at Mont Valérien. It's an old fortress right next door. Parachuted in there when it was still full of jihadi. Pretty fucking hard-core. They'll have some good stories."

Normally, in a room full of BBC reporters, he'd have kept his mouth shut and just grunted, "Yeah, good to go." But these guys weren't normal. Even Caroline Wyatt, who still spent an hour in makeup every day, nodded appreciatively. He didn't need to sex it up for them. They all knew what a godless blood-swarm the drop into Mont Valérien would have been, and what the push into the city was going to be like. The clashes between rival elements of the French military were destructive in the extreme. Whole swaths of the suburbs had been gutted by collisions between main force units siding with either Sarkozy or the so-called Loyalist Committee. The blocks bordering the Bois de Boulogne parklands now looked like Stalingrad at the end of 1944. Those buildings still standing were mostly gutted and blackened, often with the upper floors sheared off by high explosives. They stuck up out of the ruined streetscape like broken teeth.

"It's bloody confusing, isn't it?" grumbled Monty. "Rebels, renegades, mutineers, loyalists. Hard to keep them all straight some days. And if someone could do me a favor and explain why we're still calling them fucking loyalists when it seems pretty obvious they've cut some sort of deal with the Intifada crew, I'd be very grateful."

Melton, who was idly sketching a rough map of the city center, with various lines of advance and defense marked out, just as he'd been taught so long ago, shrugged. "They self-identify as loyalists, Monty. It's only good manners. After all, Sarkozy did anoint himself boss hog when Chirac got whacked. Smart move or not, it was illegal. Shades of Napoleon grabbing the crown. Gotta figure most of the guys fighting for the committee think *they're* the ones protecting the Republic. The soldiers, at least. Sarko calling them all traitors and sellouts to the Intifada wouldn't have helped calm the matter down either. The jihadi, they're allies of convenience. It's all fucked up. Civil wars always are."

"Do you believe him, though?" asked Caroline.

"Sarko? Who knows?"

"It seems a little incredible, don't you think, accusing the Loyalists of treason? They seem rather less discriminating than that. Anyone in their way gets killed, no matter what their allegiance. Street gangs, neofascists, jihadis. They've cut them all down at one time or another."

"Like I said, Caroline, it's confused. It's a mistake to think of this thing in terms of massed armies maneuvering against each other. Alliances and loyalties are contingent. They can shift in minutes. An agreement negotiated at one level might have no effect at others, or farther down a city block. I think this is going to be one of those times where the winners definitely write the history."

"Well," Monty interrupted, "as another of your countrymen once pointed out, journalism is the first draft of history, and ours will be due in a few hours. So let's crack on, shall we?"

Leaving the office was no longer a matter of grabbing his equipment and stepping out to hail a cab. Melton didn't expect to see the compound again for a couple of days, and he packed accordingly. On the bottom of a small black rucksack he stuffed a layer of spare socks and underwear. On top of them some emergency rations, though he hoped he'd be eating with his embedded unit. On top of them went his equipment, a small digital camera and twenty-four hours' worth of videotape, three notebooks, and a couple of pens. He topped off with two handfuls of carefully hoarded chocolate bars and cigarettes, which he planned to share with "his" troops. He understood just how welcome an outsider with a small stash of luxuries could be.

It was raining again, quite heavily, enough to dull the sounds of close-quarters fighting. He couldn't see outside, but the steel plating that covered all the windows only served to magnify the sound of the downpour as the torrents hit the metal. He pulled on his rain slicker over a BBC-issue ballistic vest and snagged a pair of goggles to protect his eyes. The toxic rain wasn't nearly as bad as it had been a few weeks back, but letting the water run into your eyes still felt like swimming in a hideously overchlorinated pool. The last item, he took his time with. It was a controversial choice, a personal weapon. Some of the reporters, like Caroline and Adam Mynott, who'd arrived from Afghanistan with the last of NATO's returning contingent, refused to carry anything, and tried very hard to talk Melton out of doing so. They argued that their best protection was their noncombatant status.

In turn he insisted that nobody was playing by the Geneva conventions and cited at least three occasions in Paris where he'd been forced to defend himself. It was an unresolved dispute, with some of the older hands writing him off as a fossil from the Cowboy Age, while some of the younger ones quietly sought him out to ask his advice about how they might discreetly pack their own protection. It was telling, he thought, that Barry had scrounged him two spare magazines for the Fabrique Nationale Five-seveN pistol.

He stripped, cleaned, and rebuilt the handgun before slotting home a full mag. Safety on, it went into the holster on his right hip and disappeared under the slicker. He finished his packing with a fully charged cell phone, plugged into British Telecom's network and set to roam, but noted that—as usual—there was no signal available. Service was spotty at best. After a quick visit to Monty's cubicle for all the good-byes and good-luck wishes, he signed out at the security desk, lodging a rundown of his expected movements over the next forty-eight hours, the name of the French unit he would be with, and the number of the all-but-useless cell phone in his breast pocket.

From there he hurried out to the internal courtyard where his ride was waiting, a custom-built six-wheeled Land Rover with two armed guards and his driver, American Dave.

"Fantastic," Bret muttered to himself. More loudly, on approaching the vehicle he called out, "Morning! You guys got my route map this morning. We're gonna be skirting around some contested ground."

Dave, a chunky, dark-haired man with a short-cropped beard, continued chewing his gum and nodded. "Yup."

"Okay then. Drive on."

It took them all of four minutes to deviate from the route. Bret had mapped out a long, looping, circuitous path through the district's quieter streets to avoid the fighting between Avenue Foch and the huge traffic roundabout at the Place de la Porte Maillot. Within that area fourteen irregularly shaped city blocks had been reduced to a wasteland of shattered buildings, burning ruins, and rubble through which no armor could pass and over which thousands of men and women now fought. The rain had dampened hostilities somewhat, but the rolling thunder of combat never completely abated. At one point two jets screamed low overhead to unload their bombs on somebody. The air force was almost entirely behind Sarkozy, but even so, Melton flinched a little. Technically, they were still in Loyalist territory, and an armored Land Rover would make an excellent target of opportunity.

He didn't notice them veering off course because American Dave surprised him by initiating a conversation as he popped a CD into the stereo. Bret checked out the cover. *Dave Dudley's Truckin' Hits*.

"Gonna git bloody, soon," said American Dave.

Okay, it wasn't much of a conversation, but it was a start.

"Yeah," agreed Bret. "Always gets kinda biblical whenever you get a lot of irregulars tangling with main force. These guys'll be desperate, too. You got the marines and tankers coming in from the park, and those two grunt divisions hit Romaine and Noisy-le-Sec yesterday. The Loyalists are trapped."

Dave snorted in disgust.

"Fucking Loyalists. Bullshit. Nobody loyal to nothing but Allah ever partnered up with those raghead motherfuckers."

Melton let that one slide past. He had no idea what game plan the Loyalists were running and wouldn't be surprised to seem them turn on the Arab street fighters and massacre them wholesale if the need arose.

The Land Rover rumbled down a deserted street in which all of the trees had died. The rain was still heavy, reducing visibility to about thirty yards, and he could tell from the neglected appearance of the buildings, with gaping broken windows and doors left ajar, that most of them were empty. Every now and then a figure would dart furtively from cover, but only for a few seconds at most. In the back, Dave's companions kept their weapons at the ready.

"You don't think?" said Dave.

"Sorry. I don't think what?"

"You don't think the ragheads and Loyalists are teamed up?" Melton shrugged.

"They have a common enemy, but that doesn't make them friends or even allies. The Loyalists are fighting Sarkozy because they think he's a dictator. A fascist. The street Arabs from the outer suburbs are fighting him because he sent his troops into their neighborhoods and served 'em up a big bowl of smackdown. The skinheads are fighting them because they're skinheads. The other white gangs are fighting the Arabs because fighting's all there is now. You fight, you eat. You fight, you live. Maybe. Don't know that's there's much more to it."

Dave grunted and lapsed back into silence.

Mr. Dudley started singing that he was the king of the road.

And just out of the corner of his eye, Bret Melton saw the telltale, snaking smoke trail of an RPG round.

A warning cry was in his throat but never got out.

The world turned upside down with a head-cracking roar and a geyser of hot fire.

42

Seattle, Washington

It was raining, of course. Jed pulled his overcoat a little more tightly around his stout frame as he left the foyer of the Hotel Monaco. The caucus was still running in his suite. It ran 24/7 all week, forcing him to retain another, private room on a different floor. He scowled at the weather and tugged his hat down a bit more smugly, feeling like an extra from a B-grade film-noir feature. There was no avoiding it, though. The temperature had dropped away dramatically as spring succumbed to a "Disappearance fall," and a wide-brimmed hat was the only way to keep the acidic rain off one's face. For good measure he popped a large black umbrella as he stepped out onto the street. He had a four-block walk in front of him. Only the military and emergency services were getting any gas in Seattle, and they didn't rate Jed Culver's needs high enough to afford him a car and driver.

He rather missed Hawaii.

The Monaco might have been one of the hippest little boutique joints in the world a month ago. Now it was full of rowdy conventioneers and tobacco-chewing soldiers who clomped so much mud through the place that the management had given up attempting to keep the public areas clean, and had instead laid down massive canvas tarpaulins everywhere. When Culver left the hotel, he found a quartet of soldiers standing around one of the hotel's carpet-shampoo machines, trying to figure out how it worked. He overheard someone, probably a sergeant, he wasn't sure, saying he wanted to return the place better than they found it when they left.

If they leave, Culver thought as he stepped out into the quiet streets.

Huddled deep inside his coat, he shuffled quickly past an abandoned building site where oily water gathered in pools and dripped from torn plastic sheeting. Some locals had told him it would have been their new library but nobody expected it to be finished now. He walked on down Fourth Avenue, with his free hand jammed into a coat pocket. He pressed a leather document wallet up against his body with that arm. He wore thin leather gloves to protect his hands from the burning rain, but even so he preferred to keep them tucked away. The streets were quiet, save for a few city workers who all wore bright yellow ID laminates around their necks, and small groups of soldiers who tried to stay under cover at every street corner. Some managed a little respite under an awning or bus shelter. Those who didn't looked as miserable as Culver had ever seen grown men and women look. His own laminate, which guaranteed his passage through downtown, was an embarrassing hibiscus pink, identifying him as one of Governor Lingle's representatives to the convention.

A gust of wind, whipping through the canyons of the city,

threw a spray of toxic water into his face, forcing Jed to stop and wipe it down with a handkerchief, one of a collection he carried for just that purpose. He'd stopped outside Simon's Espresso Café, where he'd managed to score a quite decent prime-beef sandwich on his first day in the city. But between grousing about the "fascist pig dog maggots" who'd "taken over" the city, and muttering darkly about the secret military experiment that had caused the Disappearance in the first place, his waiter, a life-support system for 392 stainless-steel ringlets, studs, and spears, had warned him to enjoy the dead flesh, as it was one of the last sandwiches Simon's would serve. And sure enough the café was soon closed and dark, like most of the retail outlets in the city. As he wiped the stinging water from his face, Jed wondered idly what had happened to the freak with all the piercings.

Probably joined the "Resistance."

He had to laugh at the studied pretension of those losers styling themselves on the French Underground. As bad as things were in Seattle, it wasn't Paris under the Nazis. And when you got down to it, these Resistance idiots were simply making things worse. Every time they hacked a server at Fort Lewis, every time they broke into a food bank to "liberate" the supplies for the "common people," every fucking time they chopped down a tree or spread small iron spikes on a road to "deny" it to military traffic, they simply made things worse. They weren't achieving anything—a major sin in Jed's book— and they were handing Blackstone one rolled-gold opportunity after another to maintain martial law. What was worse, of course, they played right into the hands of the pinhead lobby that wanted to hijack the convention as the first step in reframing the Constitution, adapting it into something that Ferdinand Marcos or some Argentine general might have approved of in the 1970s.

Still, thought Jed as he shuffled down the road, dabbing away the stinging water on his face, they were an element of the game, another piece on the board, and they could be played, too.

That's why he had contact numbers and encrypted Net addresses for some of the larger cells in his smart phone.

"Hey, buddy. Got a mouthful, did you?"

The lawyer looked up with a start. He had no idea where the

432 • JOHN BIRMINGHAM

man standing beside him had come from. Correction: the soldier standing beside him.

"Sorry, hope I didn't scare you. Ty McCutcheon's the name. Major Ty McCutcheon. But you can call me Mac, if that suits."

"Uh-huh," said Culver, warily. He felt he'd been put off balance on purpose, but for what reason he wasn't sure.

"I've seen you at the convention," said McCutcheon. "I'm heading up there myself now if you'd like the company. It is kinda lonesome round here at the moment. I feel like the Omega Man some days."

"The what?" asked Culver in a flat voice.

"You know, Charlton Heston? End of the world. Last man alive. A great, great flick. Even with those dumbass hippie vampires. I'm telling you, Jed. They won't ever make 'em like that again."

"No," said Culver, wondering what game this character was into. He scrunched up the damp handkerchief with which he'd wiped off and jammed it deep into a pocket. He could feel the smart phone in there. Loaded with dozens of names and numbers, any one of which could see him hauled in by the military police for extended questioning.

That's how things ran in this city.

"Well, I am headed that way, Captain . . . uh . . ." Culver knew what the gold oak leaf on McCutcheon's Gore-Tex jacket represented.

"McCutcheon. Major McCutcheon." The man smiled. If he'd taken Jed's calculated affront to heart, he gave no sign of it.

"So you're an army man, then, McCutcheon," said Jed, even though he knew full well that that wasn't the case. Precisely modulated buffoonery seemed to be the appropriate response to this glad-handing mountebank.

"Nope. Air force," said McCutcheon as they continued toward the civic center, cutting across Marion into Fifth Avenue.

"Well, that's all right, too, I suppose," said Culver. "And what threat to national security are you dealing with down here, Major McCutcheon?"

"Oh, I'm just a humble liaison officer, Jed . . . You are Jed Culver, right? One of Governor Lingle's people. It's my job to know."

Culver's smile was knowing, but he allowed just a small twinkle of admiration to light up his eyes, too. This guy wasn't half bad. He certainly wasn't nearly as stupid as he pretended to be. It was telling that he'd referenced Culver's official designation as a Hawaiian delegate, and not his more infamous profile as the prime mover behind the "No" lobby, the makeshift alliance opposed to any radical change in the nation's constitutional arrangements.

They turned the corner into Fifth, where a line of trees leading up to the civic center had shed all their leaves and died. The exposed branches called up an image of a witch's hands, clawing at the poisoned sky.

"I suppose the big pink calling card gives me away," he conceded, fingering the laminate for emphasis. He had wondered who'd picked the colors for the laminate cards, which Culver had received when he had arrived two weeks ago. It certainly wouldn't have been his first choice, or Governor Lingle's for that matter.

Jed Culver stopped and turned to face McCutcheon directly. "But what gives *you* away, Major, is your nonregulation haircut, which is just a bit too close to the collar, your whole hail-fellow-well-met routine, which is a little too practiced at being a little too hip, the small, almost unnoticeable hole in your left earlobe, which tells me that at some point you had something stuck in there, possibly to fit in with some underground cell of Resistance nitwits or anarchist troublemakers. It was a nice save on the name, but I've been dealing with military people for weeks now, and none of them ever call me anything but 'Mr. Culver,' or 'sir.' So why don't you stop trying to jam ten pounds of horseshit into a five-pound bag and tell me what it is you want?"

McCutcheon appeared to regard him with detached amusement. Staying in character, then. *Okay,* thought Jed, *one point for him.*

"You're the guy set this gig up, aren't you, *Jed*?" He smiled, with just a hint of steel in his voice.

"The constitutional convention, you mean?"

"Yeah. The clusterfuck down at the Municipal Tower of Babel."

"No. I'm not the one who set it up, *Mac.* I think you'll find that the executive and legislative branches of the surviving states did that, in accordance with Article Five of the Constitution. I'm just an observer for Governor Lingle's office."

"Bullshit. Everyone knows what role you're playing. It's a dangerous game, Jed. Look at this place."

McCutcheon waved a gloved hand at the dead city lying in state around them. "More'n half a million people hunkered down like rats, living on subsistence handouts. An active underground resistance, which is this close to flipping over into major violence, and the only goddamned thing keeping the lid on is martial law. And that's just here. You know what it's like back in Hawaii. You must have heard about the refugee camps down in Chile and Brazil. America isn't a functioning nation anymore. It's a fucking shambles, which is *this* close to going under. Do you honestly believe we can afford to indulge ourselves in partisan bullshit and self-seeking politics anymore, the whole fucking spin cycle, red state blue state, inner-outer Beltway psychosis? We are this close to going under."

"No," sighed Jed. "You are *this close* to giving me a migraine. What are you, McCutcheon? Blackstone's lord chief assassin? His witch finder general? What is it exactly that you want from me?"

"It's not what I want from you, Jed. It's what you can do for your . . ."

"Oh, please, don't."

Culver turned and resumed his steady stride down toward the convention. He half expected McCutcheon to grab him by the elbow and muscle him into a black van or down an alleyway. But the air force man, if that's what he really was, didn't even bother to follow. He simply called out after McCutcheon, "Room 1209."

It took half a second for the significance to sink in, but when it did, Culver froze, almost comically, nearly pitching forward under his own momentum.

"That's where your family can be found, can't they? Room 1209 of the Embassy Suites."

It took all of Jed Culver's willpower not to spin around and fly back at McCutcheon. He was still a powerful man, in spite of years of fine living. His wrestler's physique had not run too badly to fat, and at that moment every nerve in his body was singing a high, sweet song of madness. He wanted to tear one of McCutcheon's arms out of its socket and beat him down with it.

Instead, he fixed a small vulpine smile on his face and walked back slowly.

"I don't know who you are, McCutcheon. Who you *really* are. I don't know what you really want. I'm going to do you the courtesy of presuming that your intentions are honorable and your means, like so much of what is happening in this city, are driven by the devils of necessity. But if you know about me, and what I am, what I've done, you'll know I neither make nor accept threats idly. Our business here today is done. But you and I, my friend, we are not."

And with that Jed Culver turned and walked away, wondering if he should continue with his planned meeting. Could he be under surveillance?

He wondered about McCutcheon's agenda.

It seemed a hell of risk, confronting Jed like that. What would happen if he walked up to a news crew at the convention and started bleating about being monstered by a military officer, who had threatened his family?

And then he smiled.

He knew what would happen. McCutcheon would produce half a dozen impeccable witnesses, probably backed up with electronic evidence—say, date-stamped video coverage—"proving" that he had been nowhere near the city at the time Culver alleged. Jed would be ridiculed as a fabulist and possibly as a fellow traveler with the subversives in the Resistance. His effectiveness as a backroom operator would be over.

He nodded in appreciation of the gambit, stopping and turning around.

McCutcheon, of course, was gone.

"You sly sumbitch," muttered Jed. "You're not half the fool you pretend to be, are you, boy?"

He snorted with wry amusement and resumed his progress toward the Municipal Tower.

His back muscles, clenched against a bullet, only relaxed a block later.

His stash of freeze-dried rations at home was beginning to look mighty good as James Kipper surveyed the buffet in the main convention hall. The military had stocked trestle tables with light tan, plastic-wrapped MREs while a couple of ancient urns, dug out of the city council dungeons, hissed and steamed, providing hot water for powdered coffee. First cup free, then you had to supply your own makings. Kipper ripped open a sachet of army coffee, wondering if the navy's would taste any better. He'd heard that once. Too bad if it did, because the army had a lock on the coffee market in Seattle now.

The air in the hall was hot and cloying. That was his doing. Power restrictions meant that the air-conditioning had to be dialed right back. The lighting had been dimmed, too. Kipper had taken a lot of grief for that decision, but every time some angry state congressman with three-day body odor harassed him about it he just shrugged and pointed out that the citizens of Seattle were restricted to eight hours of power a day for the foreseeable future. The city engineer made his one free powdered coffee and grabbed an army chocolate bar for his daughter to have later. The soldiers called them track pads, and after sampling one, he could understand why. They were hard as bricks, but they seemed to mollify his little girl. Kip looked at the MREs and tried to figure out which one had either Skittles or M&M's in it. He'd learned that you could never tell.

He was getting ready to make a clean getaway when a Mack truck in an expensive-looking three-piece suit suddenly blocked his way.

"Mr. Kipper, the city engineer?"

Kip kept his face neutral, wondering if he was going to get into trouble for stealing the chocolate bar. As one of the city's senior administrators he had unrestricted access to the conference floor—in case he had to speak urgently to any of the now-released city councillors—but he probably shouldn't have been grazing at the buffet. It had been laid out for the delegates. He palmed the chocolate bar, or attempted to anyway.

"Oh, don't sweat it, son. I have a sweet tooth myself." The suit grinned. "Culver is the name. Jed Culver, with the Hawaiian delegation. And you're James Kipper, aren't you?"

"City engineer, yeah," said Kipper, who felt the need to explain himself. "This, uh, this is for my daughter. She's six and . . ."

Culver held up his hand and shook his head.

"Say, no more. I have two of my own. Although they've moved on a bit in years now. Terrible teens, back in Honolulu, thank God. Listen, Mr. Kipper, I wonder if I might bother you for a few moments of your time."

Feeling as guilty as hell over the chocolate ration bar, Kip didn't feel that he could say no.

"Is there something I can help you with, Mr. Culver? I'm not a delegate. Not elected. I'm just the city engineer. I'm trying to keep things running."

Culver nodded. "I know. That's why I wanted to talk, briefly. But not here. Do you have an office? Or, even better, somewhere we could talk that isn't likely to be bugged."

Culver spoke in such a matter-of-fact way that the real meaning of his question took a second to register with Kip. He blinked and shook his head in surprise.

"I uh . . . well."

"I have good reason for caution, sir. Doesn't need to be anywhere special. Indeed, the less special the better. Somewhere you wouldn't normally transact business. Somewhere your elected officials would be unlikely to frequent."

"Somewhere not worth bugging?" said Kip.

"Yes," nodded Culver.

Kipper shrugged. "Okay, I suppose so, if you want to follow me."

"Tell you what. I understand that it may be an inconvenience for a busy man, but could you meet me in half an hour? Wherever you think best."

Kipper wasn't sure whether to be pissed off, intrigued, or worried. A little of each, perhaps. He gave Culver directions to an empty office on the twenty-ninth floor. An auditor had been working in there all last year, causing untold angst for all of the department heads. But he was gone now, and the office had not been reallocated. It was a bare space full of paper files awaiting the shredder.

Kipper had enough time to squeeze in a quick meeting with his own section heads, detailing their priorities for the day—sanitation and sewage were the new headaches—before excusing himself for ten minutes. To his surprise, he found Culver waiting for him in the empty office. He wasn't entirely happy with that.

"Do you mind if I ask how you made it up here, Mr. Culver? I mean, you're not really supposed to be on this floor."

"Nope. But in my experience just looking like you should be somewhere is ninety percent of the battle won. And you don't have any armed soldiers up on these floors, do you?"

Kipper released a deep breath from his nostrils.

"No. Not since they released the councillors. Military's handling security downstairs, but the city looks after its own up here now."

Culver seemed to chew this over.

"I hear tell you were the one who dragged this town through the worst of the aftermath. Heard you were the de facto mayor and governor."

Kipper shrugged it off.

"City employs a lot of people, Mr. Culver. They all worked long days after the Disappearance. I wasn't unique. There's thousands of city and state government workers, thousands more in private firms, tens of thousands of individual citizens who all pitched in to help. Most of my people haven't seen their families awake in a month."

"And the military," said Culver. "Do you mind if I ask how they . . . fitted in?"

Kipper snorted.

"Fitted in? More like stormed in. Was a time there I was seriously thinking about following one of my guys out the door. He quit after Blackstone arrested the councillors. Said it was fascism, no less. But his family came from Europe. I guess they had some history."

"But you didn't quit."

"How could I? The army is good at some things. Not others. You want something destroyed, they're your guys. You want something saved, preserved, built, whatever, not so much. Believe me, Mr. Culver, I had my doubts. But this place would have fallen apart if enough of us just threw up our hands on a point of politics. And it did get sorted out in the end."

※

Culver waited to see if Kipper claimed any credit for that. His sources told him the engineer was responsible for sorting out the "misunderstanding" between the city and Fort Lewis, and for ensuring that everybody moved on from it as quickly as possible. A remarkable piece of hog trading, in Jed's considered opinion.

But the engineer said nothing. He didn't even raise it.

Culver decided to nudge him.

"I have to say, Mr. Kipper, I am surprised it got sorted, as you put it. People must have been a tad upset with General Blackstone? I would have thought a lot of folks would have wanted him arrested and court-martialed. Or at least relieved of duty, or whatever they call it."

Kipper shrugged.

"Look, it's a tough call. Blackstone is an asshole. He shouldn't have done what he did. But he gets as much credit for pulling this place through the last month as anyone. More than most, really. I guess unusual times call for unusual methods."

Kipper checked his watch.

"Look, I don't want to be rude, Mr. Culver, but is there some reason we had to arrange such a cloak-and-dagger meeting for a conversation you could have a hundred times over down on the conference floor?"

Jed smiled.

"I'm sorry, Mr. Kipper, I know you're very busy. There was one thing. Have you ever dealt with a Major Ty McCutcheon?"

43

Guantánamo Bay naval base, Cuba

The screaming howl of turbines prompted Tusk Musso to dive for the floor, badly jarring his elbow and bruising a few ribs. Thunder struck the headquarters building. Windows shattered, and the floor seemed to jump beneath him as a computer screen crashed down off the desk. Smoke poured into the office from down the hallway, and dozens of phones rang as the base alert siren trumpeted the end of the world. The shouts of marines, sailors, and soldiers in and out of the building reached Musso dully through the ringing in his ears.

"Corpsman! Man down."

"What the fuck what the fuck what the . . ."

"The armory now, Gutteres . . ."

Colonel Pileggi picked herself up, checked for injuries while dusting off, and reached for one of the two ringing phones. Musso grabbed the other one as Pileggi shouted into her handset.

"Commanding officer," Musso yelled, finger to his ears. He heard an unfamiliar voice, gruff and powerful, as someone attempted to make himself heard over the crash of rockets and gunfire.

"Gunnery Sergeant Miles Price, base security, sir. Orders?"

"What's our status, Gunny?" coughed Musso as he caught a lungful of dust and smoke.

The room glowed bright orange from the flames in the bay, bright enough to blot out the stars and illuminate the panic of the civilians on the vessels crammed together down there. Their cries and screams registered faintly in the small spaces between the crash and roar of battle.

"Got a battalion-size landing force in the bay, sir. They've split into two groups. One headed for the airfield, the other for your position. My marines are scattered all over the base. It'll take at least fifteen minutes to get everyone up," the gunny shouted.

Musso carried the phone with him over to the window, taking care not to present an easy target. He could see a column of six-wheeled armored vehicles and amtracs rolling out of the bow of the beached container ship. Muzzle flashes twinkled from their gun mounts as long ropy arcs of tracer fire reached out for targets unseen in the night.

"Try to set up an antitank team and hit that column headed for headquarters. Colonel Pileggi's organizing a security force to handle the airfield. Get every swinging dick a weapon, I don't care what branch they are or what their MOS is, I want everyone armed. Grab any willing civilians, too. Anyone who can and will pull a trigger. We're in the shit deep, Gunny. You read me?" Musso asked.

"Yes, sir, we are indeed in the shit," the gunny replied. "I'll get on that antitank team."

"I'll keep someone on this line," Musso promised. He turned to the navy lieutenant by the door. "Lieutenant McCurry, man this phone."

"Aye, sir," barked McCurry, taking the handset from him.

Tusk watched as Pileggi yelled into her phone. "No, hold those fuckers off the airfield, Sergeant. And if you've got civilians volunteering to fight, then let them. I don't have time for any bullshit about whether or not it's kosher, just do it!"

"Can you hold it?" Musso asked her as she slammed the receiver down.

"I have no idea, sir. I'm not over there, I'm here," Pileggi said.

"Grab a couple of marines as close protection, a personal weapon, and go, Susan. You're my man out there."

She stood to attention and ripped out a salute. Then she was gone, barking out orders at men in the hallway he couldn't see.

Turning back to the shattered window on the second floor of his headquarters building, Musso watched tracer fire flickering across the airfield, some of it going astray into the bay, skipping across the water. A C-5 Galaxy was trying to climb off the runway and claw her way into the air. Ice water flooded Musso's veins as tracer fire reached out from the perimeter of the airfield to pepper the fuselage of the massive cargo transport plane.

Climb, Musso prayed to himself. *Climb.*

"Sir," McCurry shouted over the chaos. "I'm getting reports of two additional columns outside the base perimeter. Estimated time to contact is five minutes."

The tracer fire lost interest in the Galaxy and refocused on earthbound targets. Musso allowed himself a sigh of relief.

A missile zipped into the flank of the cargo plane at the wing root and exploded. The lost wing folded up and back over the top of the C-5, shearing off the tail section as the fuel exploded, engulfing the dying aircraft.

"Mother. Fucker," said Musso.

He watched the wreckage plummet toward a Carnival cruise ship, which was burning from a number of bomb strikes. Years later, when his body was stooped and his eyes dimmed by glaucoma, Musso would still wake at night and see children falling out of the belly of that burning Galaxy as it careened toward the ship.

"No," Musso whispered. "No, God."

The plane hit the bow of the cruise ship, shearing it off completely. Burning fuel and white-hot shrapnel shredded the upper decks. Adding to the carnage, an aircraft, a jet, swooped in low, strafing the growing funeral pyre in the bay, catching some burning passengers in midair as they flung themselves from the cruise ship and tried to find safety in the waters of Guantánamo Bay. Another container ship pushed past the wreckage for the beach only to be met by a couple of navy shore-patrol boats, gnats buzzing around a behemoth. Small-arms fire passed back and forth between the mayfly-quick adversaries and their lumbering prey, chopping up the water around the smaller boats where civilians were mixed in the fray.

"Got a firefight between base police and some infiltrators at the McDonald's, sir," McCurry said. "Another engagement is taking place up at base housing. Gunny Price says he's only got a third of his force under arms and maybe two dozen civilians. That's it."

"Where's that army commo puke?" Musso asked, as he stalked over to the doorway. "Captain Birch!" he roared.

A scuffle of boots through the smoke-filled corridors produced a large, somewhat overweight man in army BDUs. "Sir."

"We still have comms with Pearl, or the brigade in Panama?" Birch seemed pale, a bit stunned.

"Comms with Pearl, Birch. Or the Canal. Get with the fucking program," Musso said, resisting the urge to slap the man silly. "I need air cover over our AO."

"I'll check." Birch turned to leave. "Specialist Gibbs," he called out, "see if Pearl is . . ."

Birch's head exploded.

"Sniper!"

Pileggi, shepherded by two marines and a stray coast guard chief, made the airstrip on the bay's western headland by virtue of a white-knuckle high-speed run in a little Trabant, a Cuban vehicle parked outside the headquarters block that one of the marines, a Sergeant Gutteres, hot-wired with practiced ease. At times tracer fire zipped and crackled all around them, while at others, on short stretches of road, everything seemed eerily still. As they screeched around the last curve before the hangar buildings at the edge of the field, Gutteres pointed skyward and her heart sank as she saw dozens of parachute canopies popped open high in the air. A few lines of orange and green fire flicked up to crosshatch the descending paratroopers, but not enough. It was a feeble, poorly guided effort compared with the volume of fire on the ground.

Chief Lundquist, who had the wheel, swerved a few times to avoid burned-out vehicles and hastily erected firing positions before slamming on the brakes next to a long concrete pipe behind which a small group of marines seemed to be directing the defense of the airfield. Pileggi, still dressed in her office uniform, scrambled out and hurried over with her bodyguard right behind her. She was protected from the worst of the enemy's ground fire by the giant pipe, which stood at least six feet high, but she crouched almost double anyway, running to avoid getting picked off from above. A few of the Venezuelans were shooting from small handheld weapons as they came down. The fire was inaccurate, but getting heavier.

"You Sergeant Carlyon?" she asked the senior noncom, throwing herself up against the pipe.

"Yes, ma'am," he answered, reading her name tag and adding, "We spoke before, Colonel."

"Okay, what's your situation, Sergeant? I'm not going to run your fight for you. I'll just see what I can do to help."

Carlyon looked relieved.

"I have eight marines with me, Colonel. Only six have any ammo left. Around the base, I have less than fifty men. Some of them sailors. Some airmen. They're not trained for this. Some MPs, who are."

As he spoke, two of his men depleted their stocks even further by sniping at the Venezuelans dropping to earth beneath dozens of chutes.

"There's at least a platoon of hostiles on the ground already," explained the sergeant, raising his voice over the steady gunfire and more distant roar of the battle in the bay. "But they haven't consolidated. I think they came ashore in a couple of inflatable hulls, probably got split up, and haven't regrouped yet. We've got 'em pinned down behind a couple of shipping containers on the far side of the strip. But tactical's changing, ma'am."

He looked upward, stepped away from the cover of the pipe, calmly raised his rifle, and put two shots into a paratrooper a hundred yards up and slightly north of them.

"Well, you got my guys, here," said Pileggi. "Here, take my rifle, give it to one of your men. I'll make do."

She unholstered her pistol as Carlyon passed her M1 across to a grateful-looking marine.

"Thank you, Colonel. Much obliged."

Just behind her, Lundquist raised a Remington shotgun and fired twice. She turned briefly to see a human leg falling from beneath a writhing, screaming paratrooper, not fifty yards away.

"You're gonna need more men and guns," she said. "You got a radio?"

Carlyon shook his head and handed her a cell phone.

"It's still working. On and off."

"Okay. I'll see if I can round up some warm bodies. What happened to those civilians you had before?"

"They're dead."

PACOM HQ, Hawaii

Admiral Ritchie watched the four fifty-two-inch HDTV screens of the ad hoc war room of the re-formed Joint Chiefs of Staff at Fort Shafter. Center left displayed a real-time Keyhole satellite feed of the running battle at Guantánamo Bay. Center right displayed a live feed from some reporter on the scene, an embed from the government-run TVes network. He was covering Venezuelan marines as they tried to fight their way toward base headquarters and at that moment was speaking to the camera, framed by the burning light of an amtrac. The satellite feed was choppy and slow, breaking into bursts of static, but Ritchie could see that he looked terrified. He was also providing a constant stream of very useful information that a small team of marines were feeding right back to their colleagues at Gitmo.

On the last screen, on the far left screen, President Hugo Chávez pumped his fist in the air as he shouted cadenced beats of Spanish at the microphone. A running subtitle of translation tried to keep up, but Ritchie had long since given up on reading it. Most of his attention was focused on a real-time videoconference with the surviving senior officer of the Nimitz Battle Group, Captain Don Taylor. Lights flickered behind the master and commander of the wounded USS *Nimitz* as he gave his report to General Tommy Franks.

"I've got two cats up, and two-thirds of my air wing operational. However, we're still at half power and running on one screw. Additionally, the USS *Princeton* is trailing behind. We may have to scuttle her if we can't get flooding stabilized," Captain Taylor said.

"Captain"—Admiral Ritchie leaned forward—"you'll transition into the Atlantic later this afternoon your time, correct?"

"Yes, sir. Barring any trouble at Gibraltar. The Royal Navy tell me they still have things under control, but Morocco is a little too close for comfort. I estimate that we can be in Cuban waters, earliest, ten days," Taylor said.

General Franks shook his head. "This will be over long before then, Don."

Captain Taylor nodded. The thin man didn't appear to have an ounce of body fat on him. Most in the navy were, well, a little heavier than they ought to be, himself included.

"Don, do you think you can spare any elements of your battle group?" Ritchie asked. "Who can sprint away and arrive sooner?"

Captain Taylor rubbed the bridge of his nose, probably trying to clear his head or suppress a burning migraine, perhaps both. "Sir, if you think it will do some good, I'm sure the battle group is willing to make the sacrifice. However, I do not think we can suffer the loss of our remaining combat power without endangering either the *Nimitz* or the *Princeton*. Furthermore, I do have a convoy of my own refugee vessels trailing my battle group. Some of them have been vetted by our marine and navy boarding teams, some have not. There is no way to know whether or not one of them is a jack-in-the-box waiting to pop on us."

Franks looked at Ritchie. "Do you think it's worth it?"

Ritchie looked up at the paper map of the Atlantic area of operations. They were already falling back to paper, acetate, and colored markers to indicate their force dispositions. It wasn't for lack of computing power. It was lack of secure communications and data sources that forced the fallback to more primitive methods.

"No, sir," Ritchie concluded. "*Nimitz* should continue as planned. We'll have to try something else."

Franks turned to the commander of the U.S. Army in the Pacific, who had sat silently during the exchange. "Francis, what is your take on Guantánamo?"

General Murphy snorted. "They're well and truly fucked, sir. Civilians mixed into it and us with our cocks in our hands . . . Musso is a smart man. He'll see it pretty clear as well."

"You mean surrender," Franks said. "Right?"

Murphy couldn't bring himself to say it. He folded his arms and nodded.

"Sir." An army specialist approached the officers. "Gitmo on the line."

Guantánamo Bay naval base, Cuba

Susan Pileggi exhaled, and with the hot, stale breath went some of the tension cramping her arms and shoulders. Not that she *relaxed*. That would have been impossible. But as she saw the end coming, with no chance of escape or redemption, she accepted it for the first time, and some of the fear and the strain of the last few weeks ebbed away.

She waited in the gun pit. The muzzle of her M1, retrieved from the body of the marine she'd lent it to a few hours ago, tracked the small group of Venezuelan paratroopers as they cautiously rounded the huge mound of burning rubble a hundred yards away. It had been a chemical storehouse; for what she had no idea. But the stench was vile enough to blot out the smells of the base as it died around her. Burned meat, corpses crawling with carpets of black flies, the unwashed bodies of the men around her, napalm smoke and festering wounds—the evil stink of the warehouse blotted them all out.

"Sergeant Carlyon. A head count."

"Twenty-three friendly, ma'am. As of five minutes ago."

Pileggi nodded. They were spread out over a hundred-yard front, some fucking the earth in a drainage ditch, others taking cover behind broken machinery or piles of concrete barriers. They held on.

The enemy numbered in the hundreds now, but they still hadn't forced the issue, and in this failure had probably died in greater numbers than was necessary. *They could have plowed us under an hour back,* she thought. Carlyon popped up and squeezed off a three-round burst, and the reassuring boom of Lundquist's shotgun followed almost immediately. The volume of return fire was heavy, but poorly directed.

She followed the advance of the small party attempting to flank them to the north. Carlyon was aware of them, too.

Gitmo was dying. The little base had done so well to hold off against the sneak attack, but the colonel knew it would be over-run, probably in the next few hours, and her small band of brothers was sure to die with her. She was aware, without turn-ing to look at them, of the men in the firing pit next to her. Lundquist was hunkered down reloading his shotgun next to Jimbo Jamieson, a civilian who'd joined them in the middle of some of the worst fighting, pulling up in a Humvee full of sailors, carrying two boxes of ammo and, most precious of all, spare barrels for a squad automatic weapon. Jamieson was watching the enemy creeping through the dark, too, never tak-ing his eyes off them as they crept closer.

Even while concentrating so fiercely on the flankers, Pileggi remained unnaturally aware of other details.

A patch of red hair peeking out beneath the curve of a hel-met. The straight line of a bayonet. A muted cough in the next foxhole, barely audible under the freight-train scream of battle all around.

Their lives had only one meaning now: to delay a catastrophe that was otherwise inevitable. Attackers were pouring onto the headland from three sides, and they were going to take the strip. When they did, more would doubtless fly in, falling upon Guantánamo's defenders and the unarmed refugees with equal ferocity.

God only knew what sort of a bloodswarm that'd unleash, and Pileggi wasn't sorry to miss it. She'd already seen civilian boats targeted out on the bay, for no apparent reason other than that they made easier, more pleasing prey than armed marines and soldiers.

The atrocities, witnessed by everyone she'd managed to gather for the airfield defense, had doubtlessly hardened their resolve. Dozens of dead paratroopers lay on the tarmac as testi-mony to that.

She laid the cold iron sight of her weapon on the center of the group of men, who were now coming at them with much greater confidence and speed. They hadn't seen Carlyon's ambush yet. Good. Half a second telescoped out toward infinity. Susan Pileggi had plenty of time to examine the poor standard of their uniforms and the torn rubber shoes of the man in the lead. It spoke of a badly planned, hastily thrown-together attack. A three-legged dog suddenly bounded in front of the advancing

Venezuelans, spinning in circles, howling as though possessed by a demon. It was probably mad.

"Fire."

The dog exploded into a ball of hair and gore as the SAW opened up a short distance away. She heard cursing and saw Lundquist adjust his aim up a little. The attackers dispersed like startled rabbits, those who could anyway. An invisible wave swept over at least half of them, cutting some down, throwing others into the air, completely disassembling one from the groin up.

"Pour it on, boys!" Carlyon yelled over the uproar.

The dense crump of exploding hand grenades momentarily smothered the rattle and snarl of gunfire. The battle for Gitmo, a vast conflagration, fell away from the minds of the men around her. The whole world was now contained on the small stage of this burning, rubble-strewn airstrip. They started to take return fire from the enemy dug in all around them, and someone screamed as a round took him in the face. Pileggi squeezed off discrete shots from the rifle, picking her targets, waiting until she had a clear line, and sending two or three rounds downrange. The bullets hit hard, punching out chunks of meat and bone when they struck. Pileggi dropped three men in just a few seconds before having to duck behind the shattered masonry she'd built up in front of her firing position.

Lundquist cried out and flew backward. Gouts of dark red blood looped gracefully into the sky. The ground shook and heaved violently as mortar bombs began dropping on their position. None of them had any overhead protection.

"They're coming!" screamed Carlyon. "Get ready!" He emptied a whole magazine to give himself and his men some cover. The Venezuelans had gathered themselves at last and were charging at them en masse, running into their own mortar barrage with bayonets drawn. She was almost certain she heard a bugle faintly beneath the din of battle.

Pileggi changed magazines, rapidly, mechanically, firing again as quickly as possible. Four of the attackers fell in front of their pit. Two more leaped, sailed over the edge, and threw themselves onto Jimbo Jamieson, who swung wildly at the closest with a lump of wood. It connected with a hollow thunk that Pileggi heard quite clearly despite all the noise. She swung her own gun like a club, too, driving the heavy stock into the face of the other attacker. The man's nose collapsed with sickening ease as blood erupted from torn flesh.

Carlyon fell on her, driving her down.

She felt his dead weight, the terrible slackness of his limbs, and knew he was gone.

She tried to lift him clear so she could get back to her firing position, but he was too heavy. It was worse, much worse than having a drunken lover fall asleep on top of you. It was crushing, painful.

And then he was gone, the weight suddenly flying away, and she was looking up into the muzzle of a gun, wondering what it was, and realizing just before it flashed white.

"Pearl is up, sir," a marine private said, holding up a phone. "A lot of static."

Musso thanked the private and took the phone. "General Musso."

"Franks, this line secure?"

Musso shook his head. "I sorely doubt it. It's probably trailing across one of the sat news channels as we speak, sir."

He looked around the command bunker. Some of the screens were running live feeds from Venezuelan TV. The static on the phone connection grew in intensity. Musso shook the phone, even though he knew it didn't do any good. It made him feel better. "Say again, sir?"

"As a matter of fact, TVes is running us live, Musso. Bastards. What is your status?"

Musso rubbed his forehead and thought for a moment. If they were live on TVes, this conversation was going out to the world. He might be able to use this to his advantage. He couched his next words very carefully, trying to remember the lessons he was taught at Charm School when he received his first star.

"Enemy forces are aggressively targeting civilian refugees at my position, sir," Musso said. "I've got multiple civilian vessels burning in the bay or sinking. We lost a C-5 Galaxy as it tried it take off. My air liaison officer tells me more than two hundred U.S. civilians were on board. We're probably looking at upward of a thousand civilian casualties minimum, perhaps more. My own casualties are climbing as well."

"Any attempt to offer a cease-fire?" Franks asked. "To mitigate civilian casualties."

Musso blinked. Every fiber in his soul screamed at him to fight it out, resist to the last, make the enemy pay, but the civilians were his priority. They were his boss, his reason for being in the first place.

"By us or by them, sir?"

"Either."

"Negative, sir. I've not even had a chance to think about it," Musso said.

"The civilians need to be your top priority, General Musso," said Franks. "I'm ordering you to attempt to contact the enemy commander to seek terms of a cease-fire. We will try to do the same on our end. In the meantime, until you receive such a cease-fire, should it be forthcoming, resist with maximum effort. Do you understand?"

"Yes, sir," Musso said. What other choice did he have if the Venezuelans weren't willing to accept terms? Even though he'd moved underground, he could still hear a savage battle chewing up the base above him.

"Also know this." Franks paused for a moment. "If you go under, we will extract retribution from the Venezuelans at a time and place of our own choosing. We will make this night very expensive for them. Do you understand, General Musso?"

I'm not the only one playing to the media, then, Musso realized. "I do, sir."

"Carry on. Franks out."

Musso hung up the phone and found Lieutenant McCurry in front of him.

"We've lost the airfield, General," he said.

That meant Pileggi was probably dead. He nodded and hurried over to a display carrying security-cam vision of the area. He could see that the tracer fire at the field across the bay had flickered out. The burning hulks of civilian and military aircraft littered the runway.

On a separate display, the armored column was stalled out, harassed by ambushes set up by Gunny Sergeant Price's security teams. Musso felt like he was falling into a deep well, an abyss of despair that seemed to know no end. From the depths of this descent, he heard himself speak the words. They sounded faint and weak to his ears.

"We need to find a white sheet."

44

MV *Aussie Rules*, southern ocean

Mr. Lee heaved on the wheel and took the *Aussie Rules* up the face of the giant wave at about forty degrees. Jules held on, wedging herself into a corner of the bridge, unaware that she was clenching her teeth, willing the superyacht over the moving ridge of black, storm-tossed seawater. A force-eleven storm raged outside, reducing visibility to near zero as it hurled sheets of rain and ocean spume at the thick glass windows of the wheelhouse. Lightning strobed, followed almost immediately by the crash of thunder as Lee took them over the crest and down the other side, dropping so precipitously that Julianne had to hold on to the grab bars even more tightly to avoid having her head smashed into the ceiling.

"Nice work, Mr. Lee," she called out over the uproar.

The old Chinese helmsman did not reply, remaining steadfastly focused on trying to feel the heaving ocean beneath their keel.

"Radar, how we doing? Have we lost those cheeky fuckers yet?" she called out. The Rhino, who had strapped himself into his chair, gave her a ready thumbs-up and raised his voice over the shrieking of the storm, speaking around the newly lit cigar that was fugging up the air in the bridge.

"Hard to tell, Skipper, but I'd bet two inches of horn that they're losing contact. Slow but sure. Last time I had a good fix it looked like they're having real fucking problems with the storm. We had about eighteen nautical miles on them."

"But they weren't breaking off pursuit?"

"Afraid not, no, ma'am. Oh, and Boss Jules, is this a good time to ask about the location of the humidor? It's just that I couldn't find it in the library like you said and . . ."

Julianne silenced him with a warning look.

"Alrighty then," he hurried on. "We'll sort that out later."

The ship suddenly tilted precipitously, as a rogue wave took them abeam and tried to roll the vessel over. Lee cursed in Mandarin and spun the wheel again, calling for more power. Jules would not admit it, but her heart felt as though it might burst out of her rib cage. She took a deep, difficult breath and announced as calmly as she could, "I'm going to go check on everyone down below. Shout out if there's any change at all, for better or worse. Good work, everyone. We'll outrun these blaggers yet."

Lee didn't reply or even turn his head, so fiercely was he concentrating. He stood on the balls of his bare feet, knees flexing to meet the rise and fall of the deck, eyes seemingly unfocused, simply lost somewhere out in the dark and violence of the storm. The Rhino, by way of contrast, looked quietly pleased with himself. The bridge crew, Dietmar the navigator and Lars, the Norwegian backpacker turned first mate of the *Aussie Rules*, both grinned like stupid dogs given a pat on the head. They were among the younger members of her pickup crew, and even though they'd been shot at half a dozen times so far, they still seemed to think it was all just insane fun, a great story they couldn't wait to tell all the Helgas and Anyas at their next travelers' lodge. Nobody but Lee and herself seemed to be much bothered by any of it. Jules wondered how they'd be feeling if things turned bloody and personal in a few days, should the Peruvians get close enough to board. The *Rules* enjoyed a speed advantage of a few knots and had put some good distance between them, but they were hanging on doggedly.

She clawed her way out of the corner into which she'd been jammed and tried to roll out of the bridge and into the companionway, all in sync with the movements of the yacht. With seas running at ten meters, whipped up into a frenzy by sixty-knot winds, her progress was slow and extremely hazardous. She found the conventional stairwells and wide corridors of the

Aussie Rules more difficult in extreme weather than the cramped conditions she'd grown used to on Pete's little yacht. It was so much bigger that the chances of being thrown clear across a room or hallway by a particularly bad wave were significantly higher. As she proceeded toward the media center, she climbed up a steep, pitching rise, levitated into the air, and crashed back onto a plunging deck as Lee took them through another boiling ravine on the surface of the southern ocean.

Finally reaching her destination after a trek that took five minutes instead of the usual one, Jules launched herself through the door into the plush confines of the media room with a real sense of deliverance. She found Shah, Fifi, and Miguel there, all of them wedged deeply into the soft blue armchairs, talking among themselves, if somewhat volubly over the sound of the storm. The big screen was lit up with a feed from the Rhino's radar, showing a highly degraded image on which one sole vessel occasionally popped out, the giant trawler *Viarsa 1,* a toothfish poacher turned pirate raider.

"How's it goin'?" asked Fifi.

"Spiffing," said Jules. "They're holding on. I was really hoping we'd lose them in the storm, but Rhino says not. They're used to these conditions and worse. We're not."

"No," Fifi agreed. They really weren't. On the *Diamantina* they'd always run from big storms, or harbored up or anchored on the lee side of an island wherever they could, and ridden them out. Only once or twice had Pete been caught out in open seas when a big blow started up, and that had been nothing like this.

"Miguel. How're your guys hanging on?" she asked. "They wouldn't see a lot of ocean storms back in the village, I'd imagine."

The vaquero, whose face was a study in granite stoicism, shook his head almost imperceptibly.

"Very sick, Miss Julianne. The children are frightened. They are all frightened, but only the children admit so."

Jules saw the *Viarsa* appear as an indistinct, faraway blip on the big screen. It must have climbed a crest at the same time as the *Rules,* and been painted by the radar. She wondered if there was somebody on the other vessel, hunched over a screen, hanging on for a fleeting glimpse of them through the fury of the storm. There had to be. Otherwise they'd have lost them already.

"As soon as the weather calms down enough to get them out

of their bunks I want you and Shah to start training everyone again. And the Yanks, too. Just the basics, as we discussed. Aiming, firing, reloading, clearing jams. Over and over and over with every minute we have. These bastards may never get within a bee's willy of us, but if they do, I want to kick them so hard that their goolies pop out of their eye sockets."

"They will be fine, Miss Julianne," Shah assured her. "They did very well in their lessons before the storm. They understand what is required. And what will happen to them if the pirates get control. They will fight. All of them. Even the children if you let them."

She looked across at Miguel. Deep hollows under his eyes gave him a ghoulish appearance in the dim light of the room. The ship plunged and rolled again, forcing him to grab the arms of his deep, padded chair with white knuckles that stood out starkly against the blue fabric.

"I have discussed this with my wife and the old ones," he said. "We have agreed that only the very youngest will go with Ana and one of the crew in the big launch if the worst happens. The others will carry ammunition and if they can hold a weapon, they may fire it, too."

It was hard to be certain in the half-light, but she thought he might have been on the verge of tears.

"My daughters, they will fight," he said. "They must. Better for them to die quickly than to live out their years as a slave to some stinking Peruvian *cabron*."

"Miguel," said Jules, as softly as she could and still be heard. "I promised you safe passage for your family. The girls do not have to fight. If the *Viarsa* gets close enough we can put them in the sports fisher with Lars or Dietmar and Granna Ana. They would outrun any pursuit."

Miguel smiled sadly.

"And then what, Miss Julianne? How far are we from safe land? They would not survive a storm like this, and they would be heading into the weather. I told you I would hold you responsible for their safety, but I do not hold you responsible for this. You are not pursuing us. You did not bring the storm out of the skies."

Shah clapped his hands together, a thunderous sound.

"Enough of this talk! This will defeat us as surely as any man. How many of these monkeys have we seen off these last weeks?

They are desperate, foolish fishermen playing at pirates. Let me tell you what will happen if they should come alongside us. *We* will cut *them* down and take their stores for our own."

"Hooah!" cried Fifi, grinning hugely. "That's the spirit, mountain man!"

Julianne braced her back against one arm of her chair and her feet against the other as the *Rules* began another tumbling ride down a foaming summit. She glanced at the screen to see if they'd lost radar contact with the *Viarsa*, but it wasn't onscreen. It must have been hidden in some shifting valley of water at that moment. The seas were large enough to tower over both vessels at times, hiding them from each other.

"Okay," sighed Jules. "Shah's right. If you'll all excuse me, I'd best get on with my King Henry routine."

"I am sorry, Miss Julianne?" said Miguel.

"A little Shakespeare, darling. Benefits of what classical education I received before Daddy pissed away his ill-gotten gains and all of the family silver. 'For forth he goes and visits all his host . . . Upon his royal face there is no note, how dread an army hath enrounded him.' "

The Mexican was an intelligent man, but she could see that she'd lost him.

"Don't bother none about her, Miguel," said Fifi with good humor. "She gets all thinky and stuff sometimes. Your girls, they'll be fine. I will personally take apart any motherfucker who tries to interfere with them."

"You are kind, for one so fierce, Miss Fifi," said Miguel. "But in the last extremes I shall attend to my own family."

"Enough!" barked Shah, clapping his hands together again with a thunderous report.

"Yes," said Jules, "enough," and pushed herself up out of the chair with the momentum of the ship. "Try to get some sleep."

Her rounds of the ship took nearly an hour, a slow, difficult progression through all the decks, moving hand over hand along companionways that violently plunged and rolled and shifted as the storm tossed them about. Most of the passengers were in their bunks, many of them strapped in against the violence of the night. Down in the engine room her grease monkeys, a Sri Lankan and two Dutch merchant mariners she'd picked up in Costa Rica, were tending to the *Rules*'s gleaming white plant with the universally pissed-off look of all engineering crews.

The Sri Lankan, Pankesh, had one hand bandaged, the legacy of a fall against a steam conduit in the difficult conditions. She checked his burn, which seemed quite ghastly, but he insisted on remaining at his station.

In the main lounge, which looked very bare with most of the fittings stowed away, she found one half of the trust-fund brats, Phoebe, sitting with one of the village children. They'd wedged themselves into one of the heavily padded lounge chairs. Before Jules could ask them what the fuck they were doing, Phoebe spoke up.

"Maya was scared," she said. "She got lost looking for the little girls' room, didn't you sweetheart, and wandered into my cabin. I said I'd sit with her awhile."

Julianne wondered if Maya was the only one who'd been scared, but she let it go. The last thing she needed now was panic over a lost child.

"Thank you, Phoebe. Good show. But make sure you get her back to her bunk soon. I need everyone rested."

She had turned around and was about to claw her way back to her own sleeping quarters when Phoebe called after her, "Hey, Julianne."

"Yes?"

"Do you mind if I ask you something?"

There was a neediness in the girl's eyes that answered Jules's earlier, unspoken question.

"What's up?"

The little village girl, Maya, no more than five or six years old, snuggled in tight, burying her face in the young woman's chest.

"You used to be rich once, didn't you?"

Jules couldn't help but smirk.

"So did you."

"No," said Phoebe. "That's not what I mean. Before all of this. Before the Disappearance, before you *found* this yacht. Before whatever it was you were doing with Fifi and that Chinese man. You used to be rich. Like me. I can tell from your voice. From the way you run your crew. Like you were always meant to."

The ship dipped and plunged again, unbalancing Jules and propelling her forward. She let herself fall into another lounge, close to Phoebe, lest she get hurled out through the glass doors.

"Yes," she sighed. "My family had money. Old money. And my father stole a lot more. But never enough to fund his extravagant tastes, or to pay the upkeep on our estates."

"I knew it," said Phoebe with a note of triumph. "So you, like, grew up in a castle?"

"Something like that. It's not nearly as much fun as it sounds. We had to throw the place open to the public every other weekend just to pay for heating."

"And how did you end up doing, you know, whatever?"

Jules's smile was genuine now.

"Smuggling, Phoebe. I was a smuggler. I still am, I suppose. It's one of the few jobs still paying these days." Jules shrugged and settled deep into the safety and comfort of the chair. "I loved my father in spite of his faults. Because of them, in some ways. He was very different from the sort of people we mixed with. Or rather, he was just like them, but more honest about it."

"But you said he stole money."

Jules smiled, fondly. "He did. He was a terrible crook, but he only ever stole from the rich, and believe me, Phoebe, if your family has been rich for nine hundred years, somewhere some of that loot was stolen. Most of it, really."

Lightning and thunder flared and crashed so closely together that Jules was unaware of any lag between them. The flat white light illuminated a ghastly vision of the whole ocean in turmoil, of living waterborne mountain ranges boiling up around the ship.

"You didn't tell me how you became a smuggler," said Phoebe.

"No, I didn't," said Jules, who pushed herself up out of the chair and headed for the nearest grab bar. "Don't worry, Phoebe," she called back over her shoulder, "you'll be fine. The only reason you're on this boat is because you were quick enough and smart enough to react to the Disappearance. You got some of your old money out and turned it into new money, very quickly. Most people aren't like that. They'll sit and wait for the situation to bury them. You're a survivor. Plus, a family like yours, it would have had investments all over the world, wouldn't it? Not all of them would have tanked."

Phoebe said nothing to that, and Jules smiled again.

"Don't worry, sweetheart. You've paid for passage. I'm not going to ask for any more. But tomorrow, or the day after when this storm clears and those Peruvians have a clear run at us, if we can't outpace them, you'll have to *earn* your passage. So get some rest."

She pulled herself up the rising deck and out into the companionway. Her own cabin, the former owner's quarters, was a hand-over-hand trek that took another six minutes and came close to exhausting her.

"Maya? Maya?"

A woman's voice, Mexican, made her look up. Pieraro's wife, Mariella, was clawing her way along the corridor, a frantic look haunting her eyes.

"It's all right," Jules called out. "She's in the big lounge. With Phoebe."

The two women hauled themselves along, hand over hand, holding on to the safety rails that ran the length of the companionway. The look of animal panic disappeared from Mariella's face, but a deep, abiding fear remained. The storm, Jules supposed. Your first big storm at sea was always terrifying. How much more so must it be for a woman who had spent her life on the edge of a desert.

"Miss Julianne. I am . . . sorry . . . I . . . not to find her . . ."

The ship slipped sideways and Jules nearly lost her footing waving away the mother's concerns. Mariella didn't speak English with much confidence, although Jules did not know why. Her grasp of the language seemed fine, but after the scene at the Fairmont she and the other villagers had very much kept to themselves, doing everything asked of them, but trying to remain as unobtrusive as possible.

"Just down there a little way," Jules said. "Through the big doors. She went to the loo . . . to the toilet, sorry. And got lost. She is fine, Mariella."

Pieraro's wife nodded gratefully.

"I worry. I cannot see them and I worry."

"She's fine," Jules repeated.

The woman grabbed at her arm as they passed, a strong, almost viselike grip.

"You are a good person, yes? A good person to save my family. All of us. Thank you, thank you."

Embarrassed, as any Englishwoman would be by flagrant neediness and raw emotion, Jules blushed slightly and tried to shrug it off.

"No," insisted Mariella. "You did not have to take us all, but you did. You helped when no one else would. You are a good person, Miss Julianne. Good person."

"It's fine," said Jules, not knowing what else to say. "She's in the lounge. Best go get her."

"*Sí. Sí.*"

Mariella continued on her way, muttering "thank you" repeatedly as she receded. It was the longest conversation Julianne had had with her or any of Miguel's people, save for Pieraro himself, of course. Truth be known, she had avoided them, not wanting to grow attached to people she had promised herself she would cut loose at the first opportunity.

Putting the uncomfortable thought out of her head, she resumed the journey to her cabin, taking another few minutes to get there. She was sticky with salt and sweat, and filthy from the day's exertions, but the sea state was too rough to have a bath or shower. Instead Julianne stripped down to her underwear, crawled under the covers, and turned out the light.

There was nothing she could do about the storm or the men chasing them. The storm would pass. The men would not.

She fell asleep haunted by visions of the little girl called Maya being tortured by faceless ghouls.

45

Seattle, Washington

Jed Culver stood at the back of the auditorium, stirring a packet of Sweet 'n Low into his instant coffee, regarding the deteriorating fiasco of the convention with mute detachment.

Reggie Guertson had the call again. He'd firmed up as the point man for what Jed was calling the Beer Hall Putsch, the broad-based faction of neocon Democrats, national security fetishists, wing-nut Republicans, and a grab bag of survivalist nutters, chancers, urgers, and shameless self-aggrandizers who had all come together behind the banner of the so-called Reform Movement. They were his enemies. That was how he thought of them. His enemies, and the enemies of the old Republic.

And they were winning, at least on the floor of the convention.

Their crazy, fear-driven idea of a new Constitution, enshrining military representation at the heart of a civilian government, was actually gaining traction. If he didn't have such a low opinion of human nature he'd have a hard time believing it. Didn't these fools understand that the U.S. military couldn't even sustain itself now, let alone run what remained of the country?

The hard truth didn't seem to matter to them, though.

It was as though they had joined hands and stepped through the looking glass.

Up onstage, Guertson was haranguing a section of the audience attempting to shout him down. Spittle was flying from his lips, and the public-address system distorted every time he banged the podium with his fist. For their part, the hecklers were giving back as good as they got, screeching and even throwing things at him.

"This is what we're fighting against!" railed Guertson. "This sort of anarchy and subversion is what will destroy us all. It has to be stopped."

"*Sieg Heil, Sieg Heil,*" chanted his detractors.

"This is going well, then."

Culver wasn't surprised to find James Kipper at his elbow. He'd been expecting him here. He knew Kipper often cruised the buffet tables looking for treats to take home to his daughter. In fact, before Jed could speak, the engineer fessed up.

"Just came up looking for more army chocolate," he admitted sheepishly.

"Here. For your kid," said Culver, producing a carefully hoarded packet of Milk Duds. "I traded my cigarette ration for them."

Kipper blushed and began to shake his head but Culver waved off his objection.

"I don't smoke, Kip. And I'm diabetic. I just thought your little girl might like them."

"Well, she would," Kip admitted. "But it doesn't feel right. Things are so tight at the moment."

"What are you, a Catholic with all that guilt? Take the fucking Milk Duds. They'll kill me if I eat them. Do you have any idea how hard it is to get insulin at the moment?"

The engineer thanked him and pocketed the small treat.

"Suzie'll love them."

He had to raise his voice to be heard over the din.

"This is a first-class shambles, isn't it?" said Culver.

Kipper nodded. He surveyed the scene as if discovering a bedroom left in chaos by a naughty child. The convention chair was on his feet now, pointing his little wooden hammer at Guertson, demanding that he give up the podium. The "*Sieg Heil*" crew was being pushed around at the edges by a group of men who looked like they'd just come in from a logging mill, and at least two fistfights had broken out on the far side of the convention hall. Kipper muttered something, excused himself, and hurried away. A minute or so later, all power to the room was cut, plunging it into darkness.

The effect was nearly instant. A sudden change in tone from angry contention to confusion and surprise. After a short interval, the lights came up again, and when they did Kipper was standing at the podium, smiling at Mayor Guertson, asking nicely for the microphone. He got it and then spoke forcefully to the entire room.

"Sorry, folks. My bad. James Kipper, city engineer. We've had some trouble with relays from the power station, and this place is a major drain on the grid. The whole building is set to flip off when we get a spike. Perhaps a ten-minute break while my guys sort this out would be a good idea. It won't take long, I promise."

He flicked off the PA and waved a hand at a man in overalls, standing by a junction box at the rear of the hall. His technician dimmed the lights and cut power to the sound system with an audible pop. Kipper hopped down from the stage, holding both hands up, with his fingers splayed.

Ten minutes.

The crowd seemed to deflate as the malign energy that had been building up sluiced out of the room. Not entirely, but enough for everyone to climb down and retreat from their entrenched positions.

Culver stood to one side as a hundred or more people made straight for the coffee and sandwich tables where he was standing. He pushed through them, like a salmon swimming upstream, intent on catching Kipper before he disappeared again. He found the engineer loitering by a side exit, watching over the room with a censorious air.

"So. Mass psychology and creative bullshitting. I didn't realize the city engineer had to be so versatile."

Kipper raised an eyebrow and turned up his palms.

"Multitasking, Jed. It's all multitasking in today's go-go world of local government."

"Uh-huh, so you're going to switch off the lights and send them to the naughty corner every time they get out of hand?"

Kipper looked at a loss for words.

"I don't fucking know. I mean, what the hell is this about?" He waved a hand around to take in the entire auditorium. "I don't know that we're gonna get through this. You'd have thought that people would be pulling together, not trying to rip each other down."

Culver smiled gently.

"Do you know much history, Mr. Kipper? Do you know the battle of Salamis?"

Kipper looked slightly perplexed.

"Some civil-war thing?"

Culver shook his head.

"Most important battle in history. Gallant little ancient Greece versus the enormous, evil Persian Empire. If the Greeks had lost that battle, we would not be standing here today. There would be no such thing as Western civilization. Anyway, the point being, before the battle the Greeks looked a lot like the people in this room. Beating on each other, calling each other dumb fucks and ignorant assholes. The only thing they could agree on was the need to kick Persian ass. But nobody could agree how. In the end, though, they did. And it was partly all that aggravating back-and-forth that helped, as they sorted through their ideas. That and the fact that the Greeks all fought as free men, and the Persians as slaves to a God King."

Kipper sort of squinted and sucked air in through his teeth.

"I don't really get it. We're not about to fight a battle. We're just trying to rebuild a working country."

Culver leaned in closely.

"We *are* fighting a battle, Kip. And this . . ." He waved his hand at the room. "This is just a skirmish."

Suzie's squeal of delight was painfully, beautifully loud in the gloomy candlelit kitchen.

"Oh thank you, Daddy. Thank you!"

She hugged the bright yellow packet of Milk Duds to her chest.

"I'm going to have a tea party and share them with Barbie, and Big Teddy, and Daisy the horse and . . ."

Barbara Kipper stroked her daughter's bobbing head and tried to calm her down.

"That's lovely, sweetheart, but remember, Daddy may not be able to get any more, so don't *share* them all at once. Maybe just one tonight?"

"Oh, I know that, Mommy," she insisted. "I know that Milk Duds might not come back ever again. Or Oreos or Barney the Dinosaur. So I'll share mine for real with Sophie and Anna. Because they're sad."

"That's very generous of you," said Kip. "That's very good, darling. You go play, and let Mommy and Daddy talk."

The little girl flicked on her Scooby Doo flashlight, turned on a dime, and shot away up the darkened hall to set up a tea party with her A-list stuffed toys.

"Any chance she won't scarf them all down tonight?" asked Barb skeptically.

"Oh, she's pretty good. She did share that army chocolate with her friends."

"*And* she got in trouble for it, Kip. Remember? That asshole ration nazi at the school had her wait outside his office for an hour. A fucking hour . . ."

"Okay, honey. Calm down. It's a good thing, you know. She gets so little now. And she's so good about it. It's nice that we can still get her these little things."

"Nice for her, Kip, but you're not here every day dealing with the neighbors, and the school moms." Her voice hitched. "The th-things they say."

Tears welled up in Barb's eyes, and her face creased as she leaned forward into his chest, sobbing. She was like this so often now. Brittle and prone to emotional collapse. They stood like that, in the soft, guttering light of a half-melted candle, for nearly a minute. The house did have power, for the next two hours, but like most people they kept their energy usage to a minimum. Barb had the rice cooker plugged in on the bench, with some vegetables in the steamer basket, but that was it for appliances. They would turn on the battery-operated radio at nine for the Emergency Broadcast update, and then switch it right off again.

His wife was just calming down when three hard knocks rattled the door leading out to the porch and made them both jump.

Kip left Barbara to compose herself and peeked through the curtains to see who'd come by. Visitors were a rarity these days, because of the shortages. Everyone stayed close to home. There was no mistaking the mountain-size moonlit silhouette on the porch, however. It was his friend and former deputy, Barney Tench.

"Holy crap, Barn, what are you doing all the way over on this side of town? How'd you get the gas?"

"Can I come in?" asked Barney, with a hint of urgency.

"Sure, buddy. Come in. Hey Barb, look, it's Barn, reckon we could break out the emergency bourbon?"

Tench hustled in, keen to be off the street.

"'S okay. I don't need a drink, Kip. Although a glass of water would be nice."

Barbara wiped the last of her tears away and fetched him a glass from the cupboard. She drew the water from a five-gallon plastic bottle on the bench by the sink. It didn't matter how many times Kip assured her that the water supply was all right. She refused to drink straight from the tap anymore. She handed the glass to Barney, who was abashed to see that she'd been crying.

"Oh man, I hope I'm not interrupting anything."

Barbara kissed him on the cheek.

"Don't worry, Barn. I'm just being silly. Ignore me. I'll go look after Suzie. She gets lonesome in the dark after a while."

As his wife disappeared Kip pulled out a couple of chairs from the kitchen table.

"You sure I can't offer you a drink, buddy? Wouldn't mind one myself, the day I've had. The week, really."

Barney sat down and said no.

"I have to keep a clear head, Kip." He paused and looked his former boss in the eyes. "I'm sort of on the run."

"What?"

"It's Blackstone, Kip. There's a warrant for my arrest. Oh, man, I hope you don't mind me coming here. I don't want to get you in trouble."

"Don't be fucking ridiculous. You're always welcome in my house. What's going on? Is this another one of his stupid fucking games? I'd have thought he'd have learned after the last time."

Barney shook his head.

"The warrant is for sedition and sabotage. For aiding the Resistance. Specifically for cutting off the power to Fort Lewis last week."

Kip smacked his open palm down on the scarred oak table that Barbara had dragged all the way over from New York.

"Son of a bitch. Those assholes at Lewis . . ."

"Kipper," said Barney, talking over the top of him. "It's true. I was part of that. In fact, they couldn't have done it without my help."

"Oh."

An awkward moment followed, a hot uncomfortable silence broken in the end by Kipper.

"Well, they're still assholes. But why'd you do that, buddy? You'd know you couldn't really hurt them. Crews had that supply back on within hours. It's like poking a wild bear with a stick. You're gonna get your ass bit."

Barney rubbed his face and leaned forward, elbows on the table, a picture of desolation.

"I did it because it was the right thing to do, Kip. Even if it seemed pointless and made things even worse for me. And my family. They cut Lorraine and the kids off support, did you know that? After I left the department, they couldn't even get the food stamps that everyone else got. They had to live off the neighbors and her family. Church helped, too, for a while. Then their stamps got cut off, too."

"Damn, Barney. I'm sorry. I didn't know."

"You wouldn't, Kip. You've been too busy holding the city together. And I didn't want to put you in the shit by contacting you. They've been watching me pretty closely. I meant what I said when I left. I couldn't collaborate with a dictatorship. But I want you to know that I think what you've done for the city, for the people, that's been great."

"Oh come on, Barney. Don't piss in my pocket. That was my job. It was yours, too. I respect your reasons for going. But I couldn't agree with them, for myself, you know."

"I know. I . . . Look . . . I don't want to sound like a nut, but do you think we could go somewhere where I can't be seen from the door?"

Kipper was nonplussed, but Barney was so agitated, and his concern seemed so genuine, that he picked up the candle and led him through to the den. He could hear Barb and Suzie playing tea party upstairs, and thought about calling out that it was almost time for bed. But he kept his mouth shut. Barbara would probably put her down in the next half hour or so and crawl into bed with her. She'd been doing that most nights since the Disappearance.

The den was dark, and the curtains drawn. A small fire in the hearth threw a flickering glow over the room. Kip blew out the candle and placed it on an old plate that was already scummy with melted wax.

"Welcome to the new frontier," he said drily.

They took seats facing each other across a glass-topped coffee table, spread with Barb's old magazines. *New Yorker*s. *Vanity Fair*s. And a couple of *Vogue*s. None of them would ever be published again.

"Okay," said Kip. "What have you got yourself caught up in, Barney?"

Tench rubbed his palms on the knees of a pair of jeans that looked like they hadn't been washed in a long time.

"Like the arrest warrant says, Kip. The Resistance. That's what they call themselves. Frankly, I think it's a dumb name. It's all a bit *Get Smart* for me, but there's a hell of a lot of them out there. Normal people, you know. Some like me, worked for the city. Some used to work for the feds. Lots of businesspeople, too. But normal, Kip. Really normal people who just don't like the way this thing, this fucking Disappearance, has been used as an excuse to mess around with stuff, to start cutting off people's freedoms."

"But Barney, we're not free to live as we did. You can surely see that?"

Tench leaned forward.

"We're not free to run our plasma TVs twenty-four hours a day. No. We're not free to gorge ourselves to death on junk food and Vanilla Coke. No. We're not free to travel anywhere we want. We're not free to fill up our tanks and drive to Disneyland. We're not free from hunger or fear of being eaten alive by that fucking thing out there, whatever it is. You're right. None of those freedoms are ours to enjoy anymore. But the basic freedom, Kip, the freedom to say what you think, and to act on it, the freedom to control your own life, that is being taken from us."

Kipper was going to protest, but he had been at the convention when that blowhard mayor had moved an amendment to reserve thirty percent of the congressional seats for the military as an emergency measure. To ensure stability. He'd sniggered when he heard it, and then been flabbergasted as one speaker after another rose to support it. And the fact was, the city was still locked down. People were living on handouts and doing as they were told. Food stamps were the new currency. The movement of people and goods was closely vetted by the military. "Production committees" had been set up to allocate labor and resources where they were most needed. And the local media, although able to work again, were heavily constrained by "D notices," issued by the acting governor but countersigned by General Blackstone.

"Barney," he said, feeling very uncomfortable. "I work with these people every day. Some of them, sure they are sons a bitches. I wouldn't trust them with three dollars in change. But I can guarantee you, man, they are not doing these things because they're all little Hitlers in their hearts. They're doing it because they're scared. They're scared we're not gonna make it."

"We're not," said Barney. "Not like this. We might *survive.* But as what? What about you, Kip? Be honest. Do you think it's a good idea to just rope off a third of Congress for the military?"

"Well, of course not, Barney. It sucks the big one, but if you'd been there today and seen the chaos on the convention floor, man, I really don't know whether that is the way to go. I just . . ."

A thunderous hammering interrupted him. Barney blanched and muttered, "Oh, God."

"Open up," called out a harsh voice. "It's the police."

The two men locked eyes and a whole conversation passed between them without a word being spoken.

Kipper placed a finger to his lips and gestured for Barney to follow him, leading his friend into the hallway and pointing to the door under the stairs that led down to the cellar. Barney needed no telling. He hurried over to the door as the pounding began again.

"Open up, please. Police."

"I'm coming," Kipper yelled back. "But I'm not breaking a leg for you, so you can just fucking wait."

Barb appeared at the top of the stairs and Kip waved her back, shaking his head emphatically. There was no time to explain to her any of what Barney had just said. He could only hope she wouldn't give anything away. Kipper moved into the kitchen and deliberately banged his leg on the table, sending a cup crashing to the floor.

"Son of a bitch," he yelled, loud enough to be heard outside. Reefing open the back door he let his natural foul temper off the leash a little, surprising the two police officers who stood there, blocking his view of a small squad of soldiers.

"This better be fucking good and quick," he snarled. "I have to get up about three in the morning tomorrow and drive out to Fort Lewis."

One of the cops actually blinked and said, "Oh."

The other, older one didn't take a backward step.

"Mr. Kipper, eh? Sorry, sir. My name is Sergeant Banks. This is Officer Curlewis. But we're looking for agitators who've been reported in this area. We need to have a look around your place."

"What's going on, dear?"

Barb had appeared at his elbow.

"I dunno. Some crap. They think we've got someone here. Want to search the place."

"Well, that's ridiculous."

"Mrs. Kipper, ma'am," said Banks, the older cop. "I'm sorry. I have my orders. Do you mind?"

"Well, I do, but that's hardly going to make a damn bit of difference, is it?"

The policeman didn't bother replying to that, but he at least waited until Kip opened the door properly, rather than forcing his way in. His partner followed and the soldiers moved up the path, but Barb held up a hand.

"I'm sorry. I don't mind the police looking around, but you

boys have the filthiest shoes I've ever seen. Would you mind awfully just waiting for the police to do what they have to? You can stand on the porch if you want to get out of that drizzle. I could make you some cocoa if you'd like. It's powdered milk, though, I'm afraid."

A corporal raised one eyebrow at the cops, who shrugged it all off.

"Yeah, whatever. If you don't mind us poking around, Mrs. Kipper?"

Barb smiled sweetly, firing up her long-dormant Homecoming Queen charm.

"Well, if you could try not to wake my daughter. I've just put her down, and her sleep's been very disturbed since . . . you know."

When Kipper's wife felt like it she could be all eyes, tits, and teeth, and even the older cop was taken in by all the display.

"We'll try not to disturb her, ma'am," said Banks.

They padded through the kitchen, and Kip watched them head toward the cellar door with a lurching heart. Curlewis, the younger one, flicked on the lights as he went, and both Kip and Barbara flinched and squinted at the fierce glow. They hadn't had the place lit up in a month.

"So, would you boys like that cocoa?" she asked brightly.

Kip's heart was racing and he felt like his guilt must be writ large on his face, but the corporal only smiled and nodded enthusiastically at the offer of a hot drink.

"That'd be awesome, ma'am."

"Will you be out all night?" his wife asked as she set about fixing up their cocoa. "It's going to be terribly cold, I think. It's been so chilly and awful, hasn't it? Since the Wave came."

Kip tried not to look concerned as the police disappeared down into his cellar. He tried to imagine where Barney might have hidden himself away at such short notice. The place was a mess, with dozens of packing crates from their original move to Seattle still stored down there. But really, there weren't many places a grown man could hide himself.

"Who'd like a marshmallow?" trilled Barb.

His nuts felt like they were retracting inside his body as he heard the cops shifting boxes and talking to each other downstairs.

"Mr. Kipper? Sir? Could you come here?" called Banks.

Giddy and shaking ever so slightly Kip excused himself and walked down the hallway. He stopped at the head of the staircase. They hadn't been able to find the light switch, and the cellar was lit by two flashlight beams.

"Something I can help you with?" he asked, forcing the fear from his voice.

"Yeah. There is. Could you come down here, sir?"

He trod carefully, descending the steps.

"Something up?"

"Yeah," said Banks. "You know there's an emergency ordnance against hoarding, don't you, sir?"

Kipper almost stammered in reply.

"What?"

"You've got a lot of rations stowed down here, sir," said Banks. "I hope you didn't stock up recently."

"I . . . uh . . . I . . . no. I didn't, Sergeant. I'm a hiker. I got those supplies at least six months ago, in Spokane, when a camping warehouse closed down."

"Got receipts, Mr. Kipper?"

Completely flummoxed now, Kip could only shake his head.

"Uh. No . . . No, wait, I paid for them with my Visa. It'll be on the statement if you need to see them."

He felt like he was trapped in some absurdist East European play, one of those fuck-awful theater-of-pain things he'd seen with Barb when they first started dating.

Man, the things you do to get laid.

"Okay," said Banks. "That'll be fine then, if you could fax that through to me on this number."

He handed Kipper a card.

"I'm afraid I do have to report it, sir. But if you've got that statement you'll be okay."

"Great," said Kip.

The cops gave the room another once-over but seemed satisfied and picked their way through the clutter back toward the stairs. Kipper moved back and aside to let them up. He could smell the heady aroma of cocoa wafting in from the kitchen and hear the muffled voices of the troops as they thanked his wife. Banks and Curlewis checked every room downstairs before heading up to the second floor.

"My daughter's first room on the right," said Kip softly. "If you could just, you know, be quiet up there."

They stepped lightly up the stairs and pushed Suzie's door ajar carefully. She was wrapped up in her Barbie quilt, with just a tuft of hair poking out. He could see that her room, normally quite neat, was a shambles, with toys all over the floor and clothes strewn everywhere. Banks gestured to his younger, more agile partner to get down and check under the bed, which Curlewis did by shining a light under there.

He shook his head.

"No bogeymen. No terrorists."

The room had no cupboards, which had always been a source of frustration to Barb. Every drawer in Suzie's dresser was open, with items of clothing hanging out, and her jumbo toy box was open, but crammed full of furry friends, dress-up costumes, and an inflatable Barney the Dinosaur.

"Sorry about the mess," said Kip. "Kids, you know."

Banks rolled his eyes.

"I got three."

He searched the other bedrooms, and the bathroom, but without success. At last, with Kip's heart fit to burst out of his rib cage, the sergeant flicked off his flashlight.

"Think your wife has any cocoa left?" he asked.

"There's always some to spare," said Kipper.

They weren't long in staying. Just another five minutes, long enough to throw down a hot drink before heading out into the hard chill of the night. Barb smiled and waved them all the way down the drive and kept her mask in place. Then her act fell apart and she rushed to the sink and vomited up a stomach full of warm cocoa.

Kipper quickly flicked off the lights so they couldn't be seen from outside.

"Holy shit," he breathed. "Where the fuck is Barney?"

"Toy box, in Suzie's bedroom. I stashed him there. Covered in Barbies and fairy wings. God, he's so fucking big, I didn't think he was going to fit in. Oh man, I have never been so fucking glad we got the monster-size toy box," she grunted before hurling again.

Barb took a few seconds to gather herself.

"I told Suzie it was a game. That she had to pretend to be asleep. Oh, my God, Kip. What the hell was that about?"

"I'd better go get the Scarlet Pimpernel and let him tell you himself," he said.

"Better wait a while first, honey," she replied, wiping flecks of brown drool from her chin. "In case they come back."

But they didn't. Kipper peeked out once and saw them knocking on the door at Mrs. Heinemann's place. They seemed to be working the whole street, which gave him some confidence that he hadn't been specifically targeted. He gave it fifteen excruciating minutes before hurrying upstairs to rescue Barney. Suzie had fallen asleep for real while Barney hid in her toy stash. His legs had cramped painfully, and he'd had a lot of trouble breathing in there. He emerged with a flushed purple complexion and a plastic tiara on his head.

"You see, Kip. You see what we're reduced to," he said.

Kip put one finger to his lips to quiet him down.

"Come on. Don't wake Suzie. We have to get you out of here."

"I'm sorry, Kip. I'm real sorry. I shouldn't have come. I'm gonna get you in trouble."

"Just shut up, Barney, and come out of Suzie's room."

Barb was waiting outside in the hallway, looking terrified but angry with it.

"What the hell was that about?" she demanded to know.

"They were looking for me," Barney admitted, shamefacedly.

"No shit, Sherlock. What the fuck's going on, Kip? Barney?"

"Just what I said would happen," said Barney.

He grabbed Kip by the elbow.

"I'm . . . I can't thank you enough for helping me back there, Kip. But it's not just me. More people need help. They need *your* help, buddy. What d'you think now?"

Kip didn't answer.

He was looking at his wife's eyes.

Her frightened, haunted eyes.

46

His mother tucking him into bed. Patting down the blanket and making sure that Thumper, his stuffed corduroy kangaroo, was snuggled in tight. A fire crackling in the potbellied stove. Bret's head hanging over the edge of the bed as he stared into the flames. Heat. Smoke.

Rough hands. Cursing.

He came to in the wreck of the Land Rover, American Dave's caved-in head on his lap, as heavy as a medicine ball, spilling its glutinous contents over his legs. A dark man, without a face, leaning in over Dave rummaging in his jacket, looting his

(body)

No. He was alive. He stirred and the figure jumped and swore in Arabic. Hands closed around his throat and tightened. He gagged and tried to gulp down air, but could not. A struggle he couldn't hope to win ensued as Melton shot a hand out, reaching for the man's throat notch. He missed and struck a bristled cheekbone.

Flames licked at the back of his neck, and smoke poured out the rear of the wreckage. His hand, scrabbling like a giant fleshy spider, quickly felt its way up his would-be killer's face, finding an eye socket into which he dug his thumb, gritting his teeth against the inescapable revulsion as he felt it push in between the eyelid and socket.

The man screamed, rearing back and hitting his head on something. Melton could see his hands pawing at the injury. He lifted a leg and lashed out with one boot as best he could. Not a great kick, but enough to drive the man back another foot. The former ranger twisted, attempting to pull out his pistol, but pain, white fire, in his shoulder prevented him. Dark spots bloomed before his eyes, but he turned the other way and reached around with his good hand, reaching across his body and finding the weapon at his hip. Dave's ruined head turned up to stare at him. One side of his skull had been jellied by the impact of the rocket blast. Trying not to let the gnawing, twisting rat of panic get control of his mind, he drew the pistol as quickly as he could, thumbed off the safety, and fired two shots into the center mass of the looter. The man flew backward and down, hitting the pavement with a heavy thud.

Melton scrabbled at his seat belt, only to find that it was already disengaged. He had no idea how. Perhaps the guy he'd just killed. He couldn't get out the driver's-side door. American Dave was blocking the way. With his one good hand he attempted his own door, but it was buckled and jammed. Ammunition began to cook off in the rear of the vehicle. Or was that shooting from outside?

The heat was unbearable, and his eyes stung with acrid smoke. He levered himself around, drew up both legs, and piston-kicked the door. He was unbalanced by how easily it flew open, and suffered a painful blow on his shins as the door bounced back and struck him heavily just below the knee. Swearing loudly, he butt-shuffled across the seat and fell onto the cobblestone road.

Instantly the air cleared, at least compared with the smoke-choked interior of the Land Rover. Left arm dangling uselessly, Melton quickly checked for the other passengers. One was obviously dead, shredded by the RPG. The other was missing. He hurried away, making for the nearest doorway. With no idea where they were, disoriented by the blast and probably suffering a concussion, he took in his surroundings as a dizzy, discontinuous swirl of images. Burned vehicles. Gutted buildings. At least four bodies in the street. A wall of four- and five-story terrace buildings in front of him. Old but well maintained until recently. They were now pockmarked with bullet holes and disfigured by scorch marks. He was still in the old city. Somewhere near the BBC offices, he thought, but deep inside that jigsaw puzzle of irregularly shaped city blocks to which neither the Loyalists nor Sarkozy could lay claim.

Bullets spattered and caromed off the wreckage of the Land Rover, just as the fuel tank went up with a dense, hot *whump!*

Melton hobbled as fast as he could for cover. A doorway, hanging from its hinges, just in front of him.

"This is the last of them," said Caitlin. "If he's not here, or hasn't been here, I'm tapped out, *Capitaine.*"

The French officer patted her gently on the shoulder.

"You have done well. Better than we could have asked. Perhaps you should let us handle this now?"

Caitlin peered through the window of the ruined apartment across the street from the tenement where Baumer had met with English members of Hizb ut-Tahrir on three occasions.

"No. I don't think so. If that fucker turns up, there'll be a reckoning between him and me."

"You are still very weak, Miss Monroe. If we are to get him, it will mean a struggle."

"I'm strong enough to pull a trigger."

Rolland pulled her around to face him.

"We need him alive. Both him and Lacan. We need to know the extent of the School Masters' influence."

Caitlin folded her arms and leaned against the wet, peeling wallpaper. A bomb had damaged the upper floors of this building, letting in the elements. She was wrapped in a padded army jacket but still shivered at the unseasonable chill. Three French commandos kept watch on the street while staying well hidden from view. It had been a hellish business, just getting them into the neighborhood, let alone into this house across the street from the last of Baumer's known addresses. Three days they had been on his trail, using her knowledge of al-Banna's networks and contact nodes. Three days they had been scurrying like dump rats from one ruin to the next, avoiding all contact with the enemy, both uniformed and otherwise.

She felt much stronger in mind and body than she had for a long time, although her illness still weakened her, and she would be months fully recovering from Noisy-le-Sec. In truth, she should not have been out here, but there was no choice. She was the expert on al-Banna, and that meant being in on the hunt, no matter how damaged she might have been. A wet, dank-smelling armchair, covered in plaster and mouse droppings, sat in the nearest corner. After one more glance back out on the street she dropped into it. Outside she heard sporadic firing and the occasional shout, but the street was relatively quiet for now. A more distant thunder spoke of the pitched battle at the edge of the park, as Sarkozy's forces attempted to break into the heart of the old city.

"He may not come," she said, forcing the weariness she felt out of her voice.

"No," Rolland admitted. "Maybe not. He may have fled the city already. But we must do what we will. Would you like a coffee, Caitlin? I saw some in the kitchen before. I could have one of my men heat up some water. We may be waiting awhile."

They were.

It was not until night had fallen completely that any significant activity returned to the street. There had been a small explosion, earlier in the day and a cloud of dirty black smoke rose over the roofline of the buildings opposite, but nothing came of it. Just another skirmish in a city of a thousand myriad clashes. She dozed through the afternoon, fitfully, for a few hours, waking in the early evening as Rolland's men ate a cold meal of MREs. She'd been hoping the French might have better field rations than the U.S. version, but there was no discernible difference in quality.

It was all NATO standard slop, she supposed.

"Miss Monroe, come here, please."

She came fully awake with a start, and slid from the chair like a cat. Rolland stood by the window, narrowing his eyes, peering through the lace curtain.

"Those men, do you recognize any of them?"

She peered out. At least four young men, all civilians, all Arabic or African in appearance, were gathered outside the target address across and down the street a little ways. It was dark outside, but some of them smoked, and as they passed around a lighter she was pretty sure she recognized a couple of faces.

One in particular stood out.

Short. Round-shouldered, with a potbelly. Gray stringy beard with no mustache. His skin was dark brown, as though stained by tobacco juice. He smoked hand-rolled cigarettes, and in her imagination she could smell the fragrant blend. Some acne pits blemished the left side of his face, and melted skin from a homemade bomb gone wrong marred his other profile. The permanent squint to his right eye was a result of the same disfiguration. She couldn't see from here, but she knew he would have yellowed, crooked teeth, with two of the lower incisors missing, thanks to a beating from the Malaysian Special Branch five years ago. Powerful forearms and thighs from years of silat and karate training.

"The chunky-looking groover in the nasty gray acid-wash jeans and cheap vinyl jacket, his name's Noordim ul Haq. He's an Indonesian. Javanese. We call him Dr. Noo. He's a Jemaah Islamiyah commander. A bomb maker, too, but not a great one, as you can see from his pretty face."

"He is part of Baumer's network? I have not heard of him." Caitlin frowned.

"Nope. But they have met, twice that we knew of. Once in Singapore, August 1998, and later that year in Surabaya. We're not sure to what ends or if they ever met again under the radar. But the Doc there is a heavy hitter in Mantiki 3, the Jemaah Islamiyah franchise with responsibility for the Philippines and Central Indonesia."

Rolland looked lost.

"Sorry," said Caitlin. "I can be a bit of a fucking trainspotter, can't I? His CV doesn't matter. The fact that he's here does. He should be about ten thousand miles away, blowing up noodle shops in Jakarta for the glory of God."

"Well, we don't have many noodle shops in Paris anymore."

"You never did, Marcel. Not worth a pinch of shit anyway."

"So, this Noordim," said Rolland softly, peeking out into the dark again. "If he is here, there must be something important going on."

"Dude, if he's here, it's the end of the fucking world . . . Oh, wait. Sorry, we already did that, didn't we? Okay, look, it's not just delicious noodles and opportunities for mass murder that kept him in Mantiki 3. This guy, he doesn't like whitey. His father was a midlevel official in Golkar, the guys who put the party into Indonesia's one-party state under Suharto. His mother was a singer, but more important a second cousin to Tuk Tuk Suharto, the big guy's daughter. The family controlled the distribution of kretek cigarettes in East Timor and lost it all in the Australian takeover of '99. Dr. Noo was already into the whole jihad thing by then. His family may well have been funding him. But Timor pushed him right over. Ruined the family and put the zap on his head. So he really hates whitey."

She paused and Rolland took the hint.

"But?" he said.

"But," she continued. "He *really* fucking hates Arabs and resents their control of international jihad. To his way of thinking the Arabs never recovered from the crusader attacks after 9/11. All the best jihadi since then have been Asian or African, but in the mythology of the jihad, it is the Arabs who matter. And they make sure their little rice-eating cousins know about it, too. Our understanding was Noordim got assfucked three ways from Sunday while he was in the Northwest Territories and Afghanistan. The camel humpers really broke his balls. His raison d'être ever after was to be acknowledged as a player of equal importance to the likes of bin Laden and Zawahiri."

"So he blew up noodle shops?"

"Yeah. Lots and lots of noodle shops. Apparently Allah really fuckin' hates noodles."

Rolland smiled, an exhausted, washed-out smile. Caitlin watched the men in the street as they moved into the building.

"Tell your guys they need to be on the stick now," said Caitlin. "They need to . . ."

She trailed off as a car appeared.

Gasoline was so scarce that any moving vehicle was invested with significance. This one, a blue Passat with a cracked windshield, appeared to be full of passengers. She motioned Rolland over to the gap in the curtains.

As they watched, saying nothing, the car came to a halt and all four doors opened like insect wings. Heavily armed, unshaven young men stepped out and scanned the street. Neither Caitlin nor Rolland moved. Nobody pointed them out or paid anything but scant attention to the ruined building in which they stood. As a jet screamed overhead somewhere nearby the last of the passengers exited the rear of the Passat.

Baumer and Lacan.

Melton was lying in a child's bed, his head pillowed by a mildewed stuffed elephant. The room was dark and the multileveled house empty. Abandoned.

Or at least it had been.

As he came awake he heard voices on the lower floors. Men talking in a ghetto mixture of Arabic and French. He was jolted awake as all of his body's remaining adrenaline reserves sluiced into his nervous system. A cool ball of ice seemed to form in his stomach, making his balls contract and loosening his bowels.

He wondered if friends of the man he'd killed earlier had come looking for him, but the few snatches of conversation he heard clearly seemed to be about the civil war.

A quick scan of the room where he'd hidden out, far above the street, told him there were no obvious hiding places. He slowly, carefully eased himself up, fearful of a creaking bedspring that might give his presence away. For the same reason he dare not put his feet on the floor, as the boards would surely creak. Instead, he lay in darkness, straining to hear whatever he could pick up. He stroked his pistol for reassurance and checked that he still had the spare mags in his vest pocket. Not that a dinky little handgun would be much help if he'd woken up in a house full of jihadi street fighters. And really, who the hell else was left in this part of Paris?

As the minutes ticked by with infuriating slowness his heart rate began to slow down a little and he even managed to relax. Nobody had come up to check on his room. He hadn't been discovered. Indeed, there didn't appear to be anybody in this attic level of the house. But he found that hard to accept. It commanded a good view of the street below and some of the approaching roads. He would have put a lookout up here, even if he was just running a small gang of looters. Then again, his instructors at ranger school had probably drilled the basics into him with more alacrity than the towel-headed loser who'd trained these guys downstairs. If trained they had ever been. Judo rolls and paintball in the forest didn't really count.

Slowly, and as quietly as he possibly could, Melton eased himself off the bed and slid across to the door. He placed his ear against the cool wood for two minutes, straining to hear anything that might indicate he wasn't alone up here. After that, he gripped the old-fashioned brass knob and turned it gently but firmly until the door clunked open. It sounded as loud as a grenade to him, but there was no discernible change in the flow of conversation from downstairs. He was able to make out a lot more of what was being said, however, not that it did him much good. The men's French was heavily accented and their Arabic so guttural and fast-spoken that his very basic understanding of the language was all but useless.

Then someone spoke whom he could understand. A French-man, with a polished, well-educated voice. Again, Melton's French wasn't great, but he was certain this guy was giving them a pep talk. Something about how well the fight had gone in the suburbs and how they had to delay the fascist Sarkozy forces long enough to get their leaders out of this area. Or at least, that was what Melton *thought* he said. He simply couldn't be sure, and it made no sense. He had no context in which to frame the conversation.

It was infuriating, but there was nothing he could do about it.

"They will be here in fifteen minutes," said Rolland. "They are coming through the storm water drains. There is a . . . what do you call it . . . a man's hole in the rear courtyard of the tenement two down."

Caitlin snickered despite the seriousness of the situation.

"Okay. You got any floor plans?"

Rolland removed a set of drawings from a plastic tube.

"There has been some remodeling of the property in the last five years," he said. "These were lodged with the city archives. I had a devil's job getting them."

"Yeah, but God bless continental bureaucracy," said Caitlin. "Now, what've we got here?"

They scoped out the plans of the house across the street on a fold-up card table in a windowless room on the second floor of their own building. It looked like it might have been a store-room until recently. A few cardboard packing boxes, folded flat, remained.

The target property was not so different from the one in which they stood. Same number of floors, similar layout of rooms, save for the ground floor, which had been opened up into one vast living space. It was not bomb-damaged either, as far as they could tell.

"This will be very hard," said Rolland. "Getting them alive."

Caitlin nodded. "Like a hostage situation, where the hostage doesn't want to come with. And he's armed."

"We would normally train in a mock-up facility first. But there is no time."

"You could let me go in on my own," she offered. "I am renowned as a sneaky bitch, you know."

"You are renowned as an assassin, Miss Monroe. I have no doubt you could make it inside. But perhaps only you would come out, *non*?"

"Perhaps," she conceded. "But I could make it easier for you."

"How so?"

She explained what she would need, and although the plan was crazy, to his credit, Rolland heard her out.

When she was finished she folded her arms and shrugged.

"It is the only way I can think of to kick down the doors, kill everyone who needs killing, and maybe, *just* maybe keep Baumer and Lacan in one piece."

Rolland pinched his lip between thumb and forefinger, a gesture she recognized.

He was thinking of betting the pot.

47

MV *Aussie Rules*, southern ocean

"Oh, for fuck's sake."

"I am sorry, Captain, but the storm, it put much stress on the engines, yes, much stress on everything, and this can be repaired but it will take time."

Julianne examined the length of black steel mesh tubing that was going to kill them all. It was less than an inch thick and a foot long, and it carried coolant to one of the *Aussie Rules*'s twin 1,492-horsepower Caterpillar engines. Or rather, it would have were it not disconnected and dangling uselessly, having blown from running at maximum pressure for way too long. Her chief engineer, Pankesh the Sri Lankan, shook his head sadly, as though betrayed by his wife.

"How much time do you need to fix this?" asked Jules. "The truth. Don't underestimate the difficulty."

"It is a very specialized fitting, ma'am," said Pankesh as his two Dutch offsiders crowded in behind him, both of them looking equally despondent. "Three hours, minimum. Possibly up to five. You can run the other engine at half power but that is all."

She closed her eyes and breathed deeply. Her temples were throbbing. They had a lead of twenty nautical miles on the *Viarsa,* but she would eat that distance up in two hours. They were going to have to fight.

"Okay," she said, standing up and turning away from the mess of spilled coolant. The engine room gleamed as white as ever, but it was eerily still with the power plant shut down. "All three of you will work on this as fast as you have ever worked on anything in your fucking lives. Got me? Maybe you'll perform miracles. First, though, get to the armory and draw yourself a weapon. If they board we will need every hand we have, except for you, Pankesh. You keep working here. You don't stop until one of them comes through the door, understood?"

The Sri Lankan's white, frightened eyes were comically wide as he bobbed his head up and down.

"Rohan, Urvan, when I give the call to repel boarders you'll have to put down your tools here and come help out on deck. You understand that?"

The Dutchmen, both in their thirties, were veterans of the North Sea oil rig tenders, who'd been stranded in Ecuador by the collapse of the airline carrying them home from a sex tour of Bangkok. They nodded and tried to look resolute, but she could tell neither of them wanted to leave the relative security of the engine room.

"All right then. Get your weapons, then get back to work. If you can pull a miracle out of your arse we won't have to fight."

She moved from one handhold to the next, negotiating an exit with the engineers on her tail. They'd left the storm behind twelve hours ago, but the sea was still a vista of churning, mountainous waves. At least it would make any boarding difficult. When the Dutchmen headed aft to the gym-turned-armory, she hurried as best she could up to the main lounge, where she found Shah and Birendra engaged in the interminable process of teaching her passengers how to kill. She held on to the doorway to steady herself and beckoned Shah over when she caught his eye. He moved with fluid grace across the pitching deck, barely needing to check himself against the movement of the ship.

"Yes, miss. The engines, they are down?"

"Yeah, and I don't think we're getting them back any time soon. How're your pupils doing?"

"They do well, miss. Some of the Americans have guns at home. Moorhouse the banker hunts with a shotgun. I think we should arm him with one. The others should take the M16s. They are A2 models, quite reliable. We have seventeen of them and three thousand rounds of ammunition. I would suggest creating three fire teams. Pieraro can watch over one. Two of my men will take the others. Volume of fire, Miss Julianne. That will be crucial."

Jules had to agree. Even the Yanks who may have had pistol club or hunting experience would never have shot at another human being and, crucially, would never have been shot at. The decks were still heaving all over the place, and she knew from personal experience that firing from one unstable platform at another usually meant missing your target. Shah was right. Best just to throw up a wall of lead.

"Okay," she agreed. "Your guys and Miguel will need to run those teams, otherwise we'll fire off all our ammo and hit nothing but waves and sky. What about the crew and your chaps? What's happening with them?"

Shah looked behind him, where Birendra was instructing the village children how to reload an M16 magazine. He was making a game of it, laughing and clapping along as they pushed the rounds in. Jules shook her head sadly. *What a sight.*

"We have spent much time on this, Miss Julianne. I will lead the reaction force. We will have the heavy weapons, including the rocket launchers. Three RPG7s and eight warheads, deployed from the upper decks. Depending on how the enemy attempts to board we shall use them to interrupt the assault or interdict any heavy weapon crews on the *Viarsa*."

"Fifi's gonna be pissed." Jules smiled. "She loves rocket launchers."

"Miss Fifi will lead the fire team composed of crew members," said Shah. "She will also suppress any heavy weapon fire from the *Viarsa* with her machine gun. The crew I have divided up according to their levels of competence. She will take the best of them as a reserve, holding the pool deck and providing cover over the aft sections. If needed they have been trained to split into two sections, one to hold the pool level and the other to deploy as needed."

"Okay. Sounds like a plan. What about those kids, though? I'm really not comfortable having children in the thick of it."

Shah shook his head, frowning gravely.

"It is a bad business, miss. But unavoidable. They cannot run away, not in this sea state. And they are very useful. Birendra has trained them well to load and to clear blockages. They know to keep their heads down. And miss, remember, too, they are not spoiled little brats. They are village children, from the edge of the desert. They have all worked from their earliest days. Their lives have been hard, and sometimes violent. They will be scared but I think they will endure the battle more calmly than some of the others."

She rolled her eyes.

"I know what you're talking about, Sergeant. I'm really worried about some of my bigger dilettantes just going to pieces."

The deck dipped sharply as they slid over another crest. One of the kids Birendra was teaching rolled himself into a ball and tumbled across the thick woolen carpet in the empty lounge, squealing with laughter.

"Now roll back, roll back, little yeti," called out Birendra.

Jules had to admire his patience. She found the children a challenge, and was more than happy to have as little to do with them as possible.

"How long until we are intercepted?" asked Shah.

"Two to three hours, depending on how hard we can push the second engine. I don't want to blow it, too, though. If we get stuck without any propulsion at all, we're royally buggered."

"Then I shall take all of the civilians outside for a live fire exercise," said Shah. "It would be best if they hear the guns before the real shooting starts."

"Yes," agreed Jules. "It would be. Who knows? It might even put off our chasers."

It didn't, but the live fire did give Jules some hope and, she supposed, her charges, too. Shah gathered everyone on the boat deck at the stern and had them fire off three rounds, one individually, one in their fire teams, and one en masse. It was the latter that gave everyone some heart. Shah had assembled quite an armory for the yacht, and the roar of so many guns firing all at once was more than impressive. It was actually frightening. The youngest children, who had nothing to do with the fight, were all herded inside for the exercise, but it was still loud enough to upset them. Quite a few of the adults, too, Julianne thought.

But when the single crack of thunder had dissipated on the strong ocean breeze, what remained were forty-one people, most of whom were grinning like fools.

"Bring it on," yelled Fifi, leaping onto a diving locker and waving her arse at the small dot of the pursuing vessel. "You want some of this? Come and get it, baby."

The younger members of the crew laughed and grinned, and some of the Mexican village boys began smacking their own arses and crying out, "Bringing on, *sí*. Bringing on."

"Maybe we should be the pirates," said the Rhino, who stood beside Jules on the pool deck above the display. He was wearing a sidearm for the first time, and his eyes were hidden behind a pair of dark aviator glasses. His face was flushed but Jules couldn't smell any rum on his breath.

"How long, Rhino?"

"Less than an hour."

Julianne shaded her eyes against the sun and stared at the dark shape closing with them from astern. It was about twice the size it had been when last she checked.

First blood went to Fifi. As the *Viarsa 1,* a red-hulled two-thousand-ton former toothfish poacher, muscled through a seven-meter swell to put itself within a few hundred meters of the *Rules,* Fifi lay under a tarpaulin on the pool deck, tented to allow her spent cartridges to eject, with only the barrel of her Russian tripod-mounted machine gun poking out. Shah had deployed everyone to their fighting positions and then ordered them to remain under cover. The *Aussie Rules* appeared deserted as it wallowed about under reduced power. Fifi took her time, adjusting to the relative rise and fall of the two vessels. With the *Viarsa* coming up astern she had a clear view of the vessel's foredeck and bridge. She had intended to unload a magazine into the wheelhouse, hopefully cutting down some of the more important crew members, but as the distance between hunter and prey collapsed, an infinitely more tempting target presented itself. At least a dozen men, all armed, began to gather near the bow of the *Viarsa 1,* pointing at the *Rules* and occasionally firing the odd random shot.

Fifi waited in her little tent, patiently tracking the closely grouped cluster of men with her sights. Three times she imagined squeezing off a burst, but held her fire, waiting to see what the arrhythmic dance of the two ships did to her aim. Once, as the *Rules* fell hard aport into a boiling black trench, she would have missed completely. The second and third times, however, were fine.

On the fourth occasion that the two ships lined up, she fired.

The battered, rusting trawler had pulled to within two hundred yards. The boarding party had stopped firing, possibly at the behest of a large, bearded man who had just rushed down onto the deck. He was yelling and gesticulating, obviously warning them to move away. The eerie quiet of the *Rules* and the complete lack of any movement on deck had apparently unnerved him. The poacher heaved itself over a line of black swell shot through with steaks of dirty foam just as the *Rules* began to climb a wall of water large enough to steady the yacht's ceaseless tossing from side to side. For three precious seconds, as the trawler slid down the face of the wave behind, Fifi enjoyed a relative stable platform and an exposed slow-moving target.

She breathed out and squeezed the trigger.

The PKM began its harsh industrial jackhammering, and lines of tracer arced out across the southern ocean to kiss the bow of the *Viarsa 1.* She had a two-hundred-round box mag loaded with Russian standard 7.62 rifled cartridges and tracers. The long, whipping line of light ribboned across the gap between the ships almost instantly and tore the men apart. She fired in three separate bursts, as hot spent casings bounced off the tented tarpaulin and stung her whenever they touched exposed flesh. Only two survived: the bearded man who had rushed onto the deck to warn his comrades of the danger they faced, and another who dived for cover as soon as her first target disintegrated in a shower of blood and body pieces.

She noticed a twinkling light on the roof of the wheelhouse

and rolled off her perch a split second before the tarpaulin was chewed to pieces by the line of return fire.

Whump.

Whump.

Two lines of gray smoke reached out for the twinkling star on the *Viarsa 1,* which disappeared inside twinned explosions as the rocket-propelled grenades detonated, taking out the machine gun. Fifi heard another snarling burst of automatic fire and wondered whether Shah or one of his men had targeted the bridge, as she had intended to. Belly-crawling to her next firing station, where Dietmar waited with a fresh box of ammunition, she didn't dare put her head up to look.

The *Rules* was now taking fire from the length of the trawler.

Shah had disposed of his resources very well.

Five independent fire teams, providing coverage for the length of the yacht, with the least experienced and reliable given the best cover. Peering at the *Viarsa*, he had to wonder who was running things over there. As soon as Fifi had opened up on the fo'c'sle more men had emerged from the rear of the wheelhouse and begun to spread out on the aft decks, taking cover here and there, and firing in an uncoordinated, indiscriminate fashion. *Stupid fishermen,* he thought. His teams, all run by his own men or Pieraro, worked in concert and directed their fire onto specific targets.

"Blue barrels, aft," he called out, and his shooters sent a torrent of gunfire into the rear of the ship, where two men had just popped up and started firing at the bridge of the *Aussie Rules.* One of them flipped over backward as a dark fan of blood painted the white crane nearby. The other dropped straight down and didn't come back up.

Puffs of smoke appeared, and the occasional tracer zapped across, punching into the aluminum skin of the yacht with a terrible clang.

"Smokestack, aft," he called out again, sending a lethal stream of automatic-weapons fire across the gulf between the ships, a distance, he noted, that was narrowing rapidly.

*   *   *

Armed with her trusted shotgun, Julianne crouched in the entrance to the bridge, watching Mr. Lee as he hunkered down and attempted to steer them away from the *Viarsa* with only limited power. He was also handicapped by having to keep his head below the line of the windows lest he get shot. Dozens of rounds had already smashed through the glass and wounded the Rhino, who was bleeding heavily from one arm, cursing up a storm, and puffing rapidly on a new cigar.

"Apologies, Miss Julianne," cried out Lee as the whole ship rang like an iron bell.

The *Viarsa* had just struck them broadside.

Fifi's voice came through on her headset.

"Here they come, Julesy. Lots of them."

"On my way."

"Shoot them down," said Pieraro, without any urgency or, he hoped, trace of fear in his voice. It was difficult, however, to contain his marauding emotions. He was not leading some band of old seadogs or hardened mercenaries. His little fire team was composed entirely of men and boys from the village, and unlike him, most of them had never known violence beyond a trifling smack in the head from a parent or uncle. Now they were fighting for their lives.

"As they climb across, shoot them down," he said. "Do not linger. Stand up, shoot, and drop down again."

His small group of fighters, six in all, did as they were told and had been taught, popping up and firing short bursts at the Peruvians, before scuttling like bugs to another hiding place. Pieraro himself snapped up his M16 and squeezed off short bursts whenever a slow-moving Peruvian exposed himself.

Well, he assumed they were Peruvians.

It was possible, he supposed, that they may have been from anywhere.

All that mattered now, however, was that a small army of them appeared to be boiling up from the innards of the ship and attempting to board the ship where his family sheltered. Some threw grappling hooks and thick lines across. Others darted from cover as the two vessels banged together and attempted to leap from one to the other. He flinched as one man missed his jump and fell between the converging vessels. The crunch of steel plate on aluminum was slightly muffled as his body was pulped by the collision. Pieraro could not help but see the flattened remains peel away from the flanks of the trawler and fall into the sea.

"They are getting on board," cried Adolfo, one of the older men.

"Stay where you are. Keep firing. The others will take care of them," yelled Miguel.

"The boat deck!"

Jules hurried up behind the racing form of two Gurkhas as they headed aft to repel the first of the intruders. Doubled over to remain below the line of the gunwale, she moved as quickly as she could but had trouble keeping up with them. The uproar of the battle was enormous, much worse than anything she'd experienced before. Bullets whined and pinged around her, chewing huge pieces out of the yacht's superstructure. She did not dare lift her head. And all the time the vessel lurched up and down, dancing drunkenly on the huge waves.

A grappling hook clanged down in front her and bit deeply into the fiberglass walls of the gunnel. She didn't stop to look, instead whipping out her machete and slamming the edged weapon down on the line as she passed. An ululating scream fell away into the churning maelstrom and Jules moved on to where she could hear the bark of automatic weapons starting.

She found the Gurkhas, Sharma and Thapa, taking cover behind a couple of Jet Skis and engaging at least three boarders who'd leaped across and hidden themselves behind one of the smaller runabouts.

"Coming up behind," she cried out over the savage din.

"Please cover us from behind," Thapa yelled, and Jules dropped low, aiming her shotgun back up the exposed passageway along which she had just run. Less than two seconds later a man swung over the rail and dropped to the deck. She registered him as young, dark, and rake-thin. He was wearing cutoff, or possibly rotted, denim shorts, and his naked torso was covered in swirling, amateurish tattoos. She cut him down with one blast from the shotgun, tearing a football-size chunk of meat from his stomach and rib cage.

Behind her, she heard the Gurkhas scream something, but

could not turn as yet another man dropped to the deck beside his fallen mate. The *Rules* pitched over and before she could shoot him he tumbled back into the sea with a terrified scream.

A quick look over her shoulder and she saw a chromatic, disordered flicker of scenes. Thapa and Sharma leaping at the intruders with kukris drawn. A flash of silver blade. Gouts of blood. A shot and Thapa flying backward to slam into the side of a sportfisher.

Movement in front of her again. Two of them this time.

The yacht plunged and her shot went high and wild. Their guns cracked and spat at her.

She racked another round and squeezed the trigger again. The first man flew backward as she fired twice more without success. The dead man's body shielded his mate.

She was going to run out of ammunition before she finished him.

A thunderclap and a spray of wet, organic matter.

Both pirates dropped to the deck.

Jules blinked and saw Moorhouse the banker stick his head out of a hatch and look her way. His grin was feral, and he pumped his fist twice.

"Yessss!"

She flinched as bullets stitched up the hatchway and Moorhouse disappeared.

Fifi had lost two of her crew already. Dietmar was gone, shot in the throat. One of the engineers, Rohan or Urvan, she could never remember which was which, had died as soon as he'd stepped outside. She had two men left. A wounded Rhino, who had joined her from the bridge, and the surviving half of Rohan and Urvan.

She was also out of ammunition.

No more boarders were pouring out of the *Viarsa,* but from the sounds of the struggle on the lower decks there had to be more than enough of them on the *Rules* already.

"Rhino, your arm's fucked, gimme that 16, would you?" she yelled over the noise.

The old coast guard man readily handed over the weapon. His left arm dangled uselessly at his side, dripping blood through a makeshift tourniquet, and his normally ruddy com-

plexion was gray. Fifi led them aft again, hunkered over, shuffling forward until they could pour fire down on the boat deck.

Popping up quickly, she spied Jules and one of Shah's men
guarding a fallen Gurkha with about half a dozen boarders closing in on them. The conditions were so rough there was no point
attempting to pick them off with single shots. She pointed to a
couple of men and indicated to Rohan, or Urvan, that he should
draw a bead on them, before crying out, "Julesy! Heads down,
babe!"

She bobbed up and fired.

Dropped.

Moved, popped up, and fired again.

She'd cleaned four of them up when a single bullet from the
wheelhouse of the *Viarsa* blew out her brains.

Jules was out of ammo, curled up in a ball, under one of the
boats with Sharma, who was edging forward with his kukri. A
small lake of blood, thinned only slightly by salt water, sloshed
about the deck as she gripped her machete and followed the
Gurkha as he advanced on a pair of bare, filthy feet a couple of
meters away.

They were within arm's length, close enough to see all the
open sores on the man's deep brown, stringy calves when the
shooting seemed to reach a crescendo. The feet lifted off
the deck, and a body, riddled with bullets, crashed down on top
of a coil of rope.

A few isolated, individual shots followed and then, silence.

She had no idea who had carried the day until she heard
Pieraro's voice.

"Miss Julianne?"

48

Dawn rose over Guantánamo Bay, a bloodred shroud for the silent battlefield. Ships still burned in the water, and wrecked aircraft smoldered on the airfield over which the flag of Venezuela now flew. Few civilians remained in the bay. More than four thousand had been rounded up and herded out onto the salt flats beyond the base perimeter, where they sat in the sun, surrounded by soldiers and marines of the Venezuelan armed forces.

In the base commandant's office, never truly his to begin with, General Tusk Musso stared at his opposite number, who was seated behind a desk that wobbled precariously. It had been damaged in the fighting, and every time General Alano Salas leaned on it, the entire surface tilted precipitously. It made for a slightly ridiculous pantomime, but Salas seemed to think it important that he should be able to sit behind Musso's desk.

Lieutenant Colonel Stavros sat to Musso's left, sporting a bandage over one eye, while two aides to the Venezuelan commander stood behind the desk, flanking him at each shoulder. They were armed. The Americans were not. Next to the shattered window a Venezuelan soldier was recording the meeting with a large shoulder-mounted camera. There had been no sign of the TVes reporter for hours. His signal had cut out during an ambush of the small armored column by Sergeant Price.

Musso tried to remember who, exactly, had been the last American general to surrender on a battlefield. General Lee was the most notable example, but hardly the last. If memory served correctly, he was reasonably certain that Lieutenant General Jonathan Wainright was the last man to surrender. He had had an untenable situation as well, at Corregidor, after old Dugout Doug slipped away for Australia.

Musso's opposite number scribbled something onto a pad, signed it, and looked up. "My terms for the cessation of hostilities are explicit, General Musso. Unconditional surrender of all forces in Guantánamo Bay."

Salas presented the piece of paper with a flourish. Musso wondered why he'd bothered to write down such a simple thing. For the National Museum in Caracas, perhaps. Hugo Chávez had cracked down hard on his country, but it was one of the few in South America still functioning, which made him a major power in the hemisphere now. Perhaps *the* major power, for the foreseeable future. He would want his piece of paper for the archives. The marine officer ignored it.

"And what about safe passage for my civilian population?"

"Unconditional surrender, sir," Salas insisted. "I shall accept nothing less."

Musso shook his head. "That is unacceptable."

He leaned forward, and the two men on either side of Salas shifted their stance perceptibly.

"Allow me to explain what will happen if you do not agree to negotiate," Musso continued. "While my tactical situation is untenable and deteriorating, my ability to resist is not. I extended an offer of a cease-fire entirely out of concern for my refugee population, whom you have deliberately targeted in violation of the laws of war . . ."

Salas glanced over his shoulder and appeared to consider saying something to the cameraman, but turned back to Musso instead.

"That is a despicable lie."

Musso shrugged.

"You're not the only one with a camera, General Salas. Returning to the matter at hand, however, I have dispersed my remaining forces throughout the base and surrounding area. The better part of a marine brigade. Three thousand armed men, including a component of special-operations-capable personnel. You have not had much luck locating the majority of them as of yet."

"We will."

"I seriously doubt that. You will provide a guarantee of safe passage for the civilian population out of Guantánamo Bay. Furthermore, you will provide . . ."

Salas slammed his hand down on the desk, causing it to tilt

again and spill a couple of pens onto the floor in front of the Americans.

"Surrender is to be unconditional, General Musso!" he shouted.

Musso raised his voice and continued, ". . . You *will* provide safe passage for our military personnel. In return, we will surrender our remaining holdings in Cuba."

"We already hold your remaining holdings in Cuba."

Musso jerked his thumb at the shattered window behind him. "Three thousand of my marines say you don't. And if they do not hear from me within the next twelve hours, this marvelous silence we have enjoyed will come to an end. More to the point, the United States will not rest until the civilian population of this facility is evacuated to safe harbor. Those three thousand will be joined by other forces within days."

Salas laughed. Partly it was forced, but not entirely.

"The United States does not exist, you stupid man. Where have you been this last month? You do not make threats anymore. The Muslims were chasing you out of their lands before your Jewish friends murdered them all. As we shall chase you out of our territory now. Your threats are empty and worthless."

Musso shook his head. "Really? General Salas, I'll be the first to admit it: We're down. However, we still have the bulk of our navy. We have our submarines, and the majority of our armed forces were deployed overseas when the Disappearance took place. We are still strong. Stronger than you will ever be, and *we will not leave anyone behind, sir.*"

"It is an empty threat."

Musso decided to push his luck. "You have raised the issue of what the Israelis did recently. They had less than two hundred nuclear weapons. We, my friend, have far more than that, and more to the point, we really do not need your oil anymore."

Musso leaned forward and invested his voice with all the growling threat he could muster.

"How many ballistic-missile submarines does the Venezuelan navy have, General Salas?"

Stavros looked as if he was holding his breath. Musso rolled on.

"You tell that little cocksucker el Presidente of yours that if we do not get acceptable terms, we will atomize every major population center in Venezuela by the end of the day."

Salas turned pale.

"I . . . I'll need to consult my superiors," he stammered.

"You do that."

With Tommy Franks back in the top job, Admiral Ritchie found that many of the political calls he'd recently had to make could be passed up the line to his superior, a situation for which he was entirely grateful. He had even managed to get home for more than four hours and have a meal with his wife this week, after which they had spoken on the phone with Nancy, their daughter, for a few short but precious minutes. She was staying with a couple of college friends in Edinburgh, sharing an apartment rather than braving one of the American refugee camps in the south of England. It was a blessed relief to hear her voice again. It meant Ritchie could set aside personal worries and concentrate on his much greater professional ones.

He had his hands full coordinating refugee flows throughout the Pacific, while standing watch over the strategic situation in Asia, a fancy way of saying he was holding his breath and watching the collapse of China and the northeast Asian economies, hoping it wouldn't spill over into the wider world. His ability to do anything about it was disappearing fast. He simply couldn't sustain the Pacific fleet much longer, even with the help of allies such as Japan, who were themselves teetering on the edge of collapse.

But Musso's gambit had dragged him right back into the center of a purely political question. Would he be a party to authorizing a strategic interdiction?

Damn the euphemisms. Call it what it was: a nuclear attack.

He stood opposite Franks in the Joint Operations Center for the whole of the Pacific Command as they listened to the last of Musso's briefing on speakerphone. The room was a large space, but old-fashioned. It had been due to be replaced in a few months with a much larger, modern facility. Maybe it would happen. Probably not, though. For now, both men leaned forward to listen to their colleague as his disembodied voice crackled out of the old speakerphone.

"I really don't think we can let them put ten thousand hostages in the bag," said the marine. "They'll turn the civilians into human shields for certain. We either show them that they can't fuck with us right now, or I promise you they will. After Gitmo it'll be the Canal next. And they won't even have to land there. They can just start executing hostages on the hour until we leave. You know they'll do it."

Ritchie found himself agreeing, but he waited for Franks to speak.

The soldier's melancholy features seemed even more hangdog than usual, which was saying something. The new chairman of the Joint Chiefs had returned from the Middle East with enormous dark pouches under his eyes, and cheeks hollowed out by the stress. A flap of skin hung loose beneath his chin where he had lost a lot of weight.

"General, I do not know whether our submarines will even respond to an order to fire on Venezuela," said Franks. "Only the president can authorize a launch. What d'you think, Jim?" he asked, turning to Ritchie

Ritchie shook his head.

"Right back at the start of this I had the devil's own job getting my boomers to break protocol when I needed China boxed in. I didn't know whether they would have launched on my say-so even if I had ordered them to. I still don't. Only the president of the United States can authorize the use of nuclear weapons. The commanders in charge of those assets are trained not to respond to any other command authority."

"There's only one way to find out," said Musso.

He found Salas back in his office, arms folded, glaring out of the jagged hole where a window had been just yesterday. Lieutenant Colonel Stavros had remained seated and was watching the Venezuelans with mute hostility. He relaxed only slightly when Musso returned from the radio shack.

"I could just order my men to take this building, you know," said General Salas, keeping his back to them. "You could not hold it long, General Musso. I can see that from here. Perhaps that might be a better idea than allowing you to run off every few minutes to consult with your superiors. No?" he finished, turning to face him at last. It was very poor acting, thought

Musso. He'd seen much better dramatics at law school during moot season.

"No," he answered. "That would not be a very good idea, General. You're here under a flag of truce, to negotiate a surrender on acceptable terms. Perhaps if you faced up to your responsibilities as an officer and started behaving like a professional warrior rather than a gang lord, we might get somewhere."

The general's neck flushed noticeably, but his face froze in a cold fury. He sat himself very carefully down behind the damaged desk again.

"Have you spoken to Caracas?" asked Musso, all but ignoring the gross umbrage taken by Salas at his remark.

"*Sí,*" the Venezuelan general said, deciding in the end not to respond to the insult. "I am authorized to offer safe passage to all Americans in Cuba. We, in turn, will accept custodianship of the unaffected region of Cuba until the Cuban government reasserts itself."

Musso snorted. "We want more than just safe passage out of Cuban waters," he said. "It wouldn't do to have one of your submarines taking potshots at us as we try to sail out of the neighborhood. We want a guarantee of safe passage out of the Caribbean and Atlantic as well."

Salas narrowed his eyes. His lips turned white, and his nostrils flared.

"You are pushing your luck, General Musso," he said with a tightly clenched jaw.

"No," Musso corrected him. "You are pushing yours."

"Tell the president that it is not a bluff, Mr. Shapiro," said Franks. "Tell him we are deadly serious. The rules have changed. Hell, there are no rules anymore. Not when he feels free to fire on our civilians whenever it suits him . . . I don't give a damn that they deny it. That's one of the things that's changed. I don't have to give a damn anymore. Just tell him."

Ritchie stood quietly in the underground command center, listening to Franks as he talked on the phone to the American ambassador in Venezuela. *Now, there's a job I'm glad I didn't get stuck with,* he thought. Many of the screens in the room were blank, the workstations unmanned. Just behind Franks a navy commander silently updated the positions of three Ohio-class ballistic-missile submarines in the South Atlantic, moving their pins on an old-fashioned paper map. All three were well within striking distance of Caracas. One of them, the *Tennessee*, had only just responded to flash traffic, having gone silent on the day of the Disappearance. There were another two other boomers lurking somewhere in the Atlantic right then as well, but they had flatly refused Franks's request to put some bite into Musso's bluff, citing the launch protocol line and verse.

Only the president of the United States, using the correct and verified launch codes . . .

It didn't matter. They really only needed the ordnance of one Ohio-class submarine.

Franks appeared to listen to some long and winding passage of dialogue from Ambassador Shapiro before cutting him off.

"Look. I can see this is getting us nowhere, Mr. Ambassador. Can I suggest that you take cover, sir? Franks out." He hung up and turned to Ritchie. "Do it."

The admiral picked up a phone. He had expected his voice to shake but it was remarkably steady. "This is Ritchie," he said. "Patch me through to the *Tennessee*."

General Salas nodded and hung up his phone.

"It is not acceptable," he told Musso. "You impugn our honor with the very suggestion. To promise that we will not attack you as you flee, to imply that we would even consider such a thing, is to traduce our national reputation. Our very manhood."

Musso would have snorted in derision, but he was haunted by the awful sight of that C-130 spilling its precious human cargo into the night. So many children, hundreds of them. Their deaths had been confirmed by the light of dawn. It was a sight so gruesome he would never be free of it. What terror must have attended their last moments on earth?

If he had been wearing a sidearm, the general's brains would probably be dripping down the wall behind him right now.

"Do not talk to me of your honor," he said, slowly and carefully enunciating each word. "I have seen your honor, and it is a poor ragged fucking thing that barely hides the crude ugliness of your intentions and deeds. The lowest of my marines could not wipe his ass clean with your honor, General Salas. It would not be worth the effort of the rubbing. Now I suggest you stop

fucking around and agree to what is a very reasonable request."
Musso looked at his watch. "Time is running out."

Salas regarded him with lidded eyes, a snake sizing up a
scorpion for its dinner, weighing the risks.

"And how long do you imagine that the civilians we are holding, some four thousand of them I believe, how long do you
think they will survive in any . . . cross fire?"

Musso sneered openly.

"Those people are in your care, General, and I would warn
you to have a care for their safety. You, and every man under
your command, will be held personally responsible for their
fate. You keep telling me that things have changed, and you are
right. There will be no diplomatic solution to this question, no
Security Council meetings, no backroom deals. If you hurt
them you will be hunted down. Your men will be hunted down.
And your country will be laid to waste."

"I think you overestimate yourself, General Musso. You are
not the power you once were."

"No. We're not," said Musso. "We're something infinitely
worse now."

"Active track, package inbound," a staff officer replied. "One
minute to impact."

Ritchie watched the center left screen, which showed a view of
Caracas from the roof of the American embassy. The Venezuelan
capital sat high up in a valley of the Cordillera Central, separated
from the shores of the Caribbean by a ten-to-twelve-mile stretch
of national park. On a linked display the ocean could be seen in a
wide-angle shot sourced from the international airport, which lay
on the water's edge in the smaller city of Maiquetia a short distance away. The image looked benign, a pleasant scene of blue
water and a few plodding boats. Ritchie wondered if there were
people down by the water, taking in the fresh air. He didn't recall
Caracas being famous for any beaches. The embassy reported
that the streets of the capital were not overly crowded, although
there was a heavy and obvious military presence. But there was
none of the violence and chaos that was rampant throughout so
much of South America, or Europe for that matter.

Nobody in the command center spoke. Ritchie could hear the
blood rushing through his own head.

It seemed perverse that he had just unleashed a nuclear warhead. It could not be real.

At 0706 hours a second sunrise blossomed out over the horizon from Maiquetia, as three bright flashes flared up twenty miles offshore on the satellite feed.

"All weapons delivered."

The Venezuelan general looked ill as he put down the phone.

"S-safe passage out of the region is . . . assured, General Musso," he said. "But this isn't over. My government assures me this isn't over."

"It'd better be over," Musso said, rising from his seat. "The next time it won't be warning shots. Good day."

49

Sixteenth arrondissement, Paris

Caitlin wormed her way through the crawlspace, feeling nauseated and claustrophobic. The attic was a constricted geometric tangle of wooden beams, hundreds of years old, rendered into opalescent green by her borrowed night-vision goggles. She'd had three days to recover since her liberation from the cell, but at least two of those days she had spent on the move with Rolland and his small team, creeping through hostile territory, backtracking a year's surveillance of Bilal Baumer. Tight spaces had never bothered her before, but her heart felt as though it was being squeezed by a giant rubber hand. Yet another symptom of her physical decay.

And so it came to this, as always. Caitlin, on her own, inching carefully toward her prey in the dark.

She reached the little access panel after an hour of snaking through the roof space of the line of tenements in which Baumer was holed up. Her watch read 2:13 a.m., and although she could hear the rumble of a great battle in the distance, and even sense it vibrating up through the structure of the house, down below her all seemed quiet. She had no idea what Baumer and his men were doing down there. Chances were, it was just a layup point, a place to regroup before fleeing the city. She adjusted her headset and hit the push-to-talk button on the secure digital radio.

"In position," she reported quietly.

Rolland's voice came back in a brief crackle.

"No discernible movement inside. One guard at the front door. Sniper has him marked."

"I'm going in."

She cut the connection and carefully lifted the panel, just a crack, giving her access to a hallway on the top floor. Threading through a thin, black fiber-optic wire plugged into a handheld display, she was able to recon the hallway. It was clear.

Caitlin removed the hatchway and took a length of rope from the heavy utility belt she wore over black coveralls. Tying it to a beam, she rappelled down silently and took a moment to orient herself, imagining the floor plans Rolland had secured overlaid onto the glowing green setting in front of her. A narrow corridor leading to a stairwell. Two doors on the left, both closed.

A silenced handgun and a fighting knife appeared in her hands.

She glided over to the first door and inserted the fiber-optic wire through the old keyhole. The room appeared to be deserted. She turned the knob. Hinges creaked horribly and she side-stepped, bringing up the pistol. For two minutes she stood, ready to cut down anyone who appeared, but there was nobody inside.

She moved on and repeated the routine.

This time her pulse accelerated as the optic display unit showed her a low-light-amplified image of a man, crouched in the corner of the room, pointing a pistol at the door.

A large white male, with head and arm wounds field-dressed using torn bedsheets, if she was not mistaken. He seemed to be straining to hear any sound that might give away the position of someone in the corridor. Caitlin checked her exposure. Crouched low as she was, off to the side of the door, she was safely out of his line of fire. He was aiming for the center mass of anyone who walked through the door.

Fuck.

She had no idea who he was or what he was doing there. The man was a complication she did not need.

There was no going in and taking him down. This guy was primed for trouble.

She took a moment to examine him in the display screen again. He had a good firing position and held the gun as though it was an extension of his body. He didn't look nervous, self-conscious, or likely to hesitate if he needed to shoot.

He was clean-shaven, and wearing the sort of vest she'd often seen on press photographers. The image was not sharp, unfortunately, but she thought she could make out a notepad, some pens, and possibly a small Dictaphone in some of the pockets, the sort of thing that took little microcassettes. If only she could see the back of his vest—there might be an identifying logo or something. A lot of reporters used reflective tape to spell out PRESS or the acronym of their media affiliates on their backs.

Caitlin thought that just made them easier targets, but journalists were weird. They had some fucked-up ideas.

She had to come to a decision quickly.

The man was almost certainly not part of the group downstairs.

He was trapped in the room, probably by their unexpected arrival.

There was probably no way of getting in there without him firing off half a mag at the door.

She decided to leave him in place.

He disappeared from the screen as she withdrew the fiber-optic wire.

For thirty seconds she crouched, waiting, but no sound or movement came from within.

That was actually kind of impressive.

This guy was no amateur.

But he was not necessarily an ally either, and she began to edge away, eventually making the stairs, where she stood, adjusting herself to the sounds, to the feel of the house. It felt like an inhabited dwelling, but that wasn't down to any bullshit sixth sense. She knew the lower floors were occupied. What she didn't know was where her targets were holed up.

She listened, willing her nausea to recede to the edge of consciousness, breathing as she had been taught to settle her nervous system.

She could hear the angry rumble of battle.

A jet aircraft shrieking low to the west.

The creaking and settling of the building as the ground underneath moved fractionally in response to the pounding of high explosives and the grinding of heavy armor through streets no more than a mile distant.

A radio, playing Arabic music.

Snoring. Some muttering, but not conversational, probably someone talking in their sleep.

A clink of china cups or glasses.

Quiet laughter.

A ringing in her ears, which had been constant for two weeks.

Her pulse and heartbeat.

The silent advance of the tumor that was eating her from the inside out.

Caitlin floated down the stairs, using a technique she had studied under the ninjutsu master Harunaka Hoshino, who had trained her to cross a nightingale floor with a minimum of noise. There was no way to eliminate the singing of the boards, but Hoshino taught her to quiet its chirping. The stairs of the old French residence were no challenge after that.

She paused on the second-to-last step. The house was dark, the power grid having failed long ago, but with her NVGs she could make out a weak, fluttering light emanating from under two of the four doors on this floor. She stilled herself, becoming as stonelike as a human being could, and opening all of her senses wide to let the world rush in.

She smelled old food. Meat gone cold. And coffee.

A body shifted and rolled over on the floor nearby, lifting slightly and settling back down with a light thump.

A sheet or blanket rustled.

A windup clock ticked.

In one of the lighted rooms a page turned.

Every hair on Caitlin's body bristled, an ancient autonomic response to danger, a hangover from her animal ancestors.

She floated down the hallway to the door behind which she knew at least one man was awake and reading. Again she settled into stillness and allowed the life of the building, just a soft heartbeat and a murmured breath at this dead hour, to flow into her.

Another page turned and she heard mumbling in Arabic from the same room.

"O ye who believe! When ye meet the Unbelievers in hostile array, never turn your backs on them. If any do turn his back to them on such a day—unless it be in a stratagem of war, or to retreat to his own troop—he draws on himself the wrath of Allah and his abode is Hell, an evil refuge indeed."

Caitlin visualized the small room on the other side of the door. A single bedroom, probably given to a child in happier days. A window overlooking the street behind. No connecting doors to any room on either side.

She examined the handle. An old-fashioned brass knob without a keyhole.

There could be a latch on the other side, but of that she could not be certain.

There was only one thing for it.

Caitlin sheathed her fighting knife.

Powered down and raised her night-vision goggles.

And waited.

The mumbling and page turning continued.

She stood motionless for six minutes, until her opportunity arrived.

Another jet, roaring close overhead within a mile.

As the whining howl reached its maximum intensity she calmly reached out, opened the door, got a sight picture of one man, young and shirtless, sitting up in a small bed, leaning against a pillow, reading and looking up at her, all innocence and dawning bewilderment as the assassin raised a hand-tooled, frequency-shifting silenced pistol and squeezed the trigger twice.

Two muted clacks, almost like a stapler, and the subsonic .300 Whisper rounds left the muzzle of the weapon at about 980 feet per second, slowing only fractionally as they entered his brainpan and scattered the contents all over the room.

She swept the space automatically, but already knew it to be empty.

A quick puff to blow out his candle and she pulled the door closed and turned down toward the next lighted room.

This one was silent. No muttering. No page turning. Again she waited.

Closer to the stairwell this time, she could hear at least three voices down on the ground floor. Two spoke in rapid-fire Arabic; one was slower, polished, but heavily accented.

Lacan.

Okay, that was a bitch. She'd been hoping to find him in bed, but filtering out his voice, she did determine that Baumer's German accent was not part of that conversation, the only one in the house at the moment.

Caitlin returned to her vigil at the door.

The flutter of a light leaking out told her of a candle inside.

She concentrated, leaning her ear to the door, and waiting. After three minutes she was rewarded with a brief snore.

No jet fighters conveniently appeared to cover the sounds of murder this time, but when the voices downstairs rose and broke into laughter she repeated her actions of a few minutes earlier. Coolly opening the door, lining up a headshot, and double-tapping her victim, a slightly overweight balding man who had fallen asleep with a pair of headphones plugged into an iPod. His body shuddered violently as the bullets shredded his neocortex.

Dousing this second candle, she plunged the floor back into darkness and refitted the NVGs.

Two other rooms remained on this level. According to the building plans they were larger, possibly capable of taking more than one small bed.

Caitlin moved to the door through which she could hear the loudest snoring.

She sniffed the faintest trace of an earthy, familiar smell.

Kif.

A highly concentrated cannabis resin, popular among North African fighters.

That was enough for her to take a calculated risk, unshipping the fiber-optic set and sliding the wire under the door for a quick scan of the room.

Inside she found three men all asleep on the floor. There being no beds or other furniture, they had balled up clothes or bags and used them as pillows. Caitlin observed them until she was certain they were deeply asleep. She withdrew the surveillance device, and quietly swapped out her mag, which unfortunately only ran to six rounds. It was one of the drawbacks of using the bespoke no-name handgun.

This time, however, she kept the goggles powered up as she eased through the door and closed it behind her, covering the three prone forms all the time. A damp towel lay on the floor and she carefully toed it along the gap between the bottom of the door and the floorboards.

Then she quickly and methodically executed every man in the room.

Only the last one came awake, and then only enough to prop himself up on one elbow and squint into the dark. His sudden movement put her aim off and the first bullet struck him in the throat. Caitlin took two silent steps toward him and cut off his gargling death rattle with her last shot.

A hard, steel spike of pain was drilling into her head from a point about an inch behind her left eye, intensifying her nausea and giddiness.

She took a precious minute to center herself, to breathe deeply and detach from the barbed emotional tendrils of her bloody work.

The last of her six-shot magazines went into the pistol, and she replaced the suppressor with a new one taken from a slot on her belt. The silencers, unique to Echelon wet work cells, relied on a customized combination of austenitic nickel-based superalloy baffles, foam wipes, and carbon-nanotube mesh to reduce the sound of weapon fire by diverting and cooling the hot, rapidly expanding gases created by the detonation of the gunpowder. After she had burned out this one she would have to rely on her knife for silent killing.

She drifted to a halt in front of the next door, another darkened room outside which she waited for a minute before threading through the optical fiber again. When the display lit up this time ice water sluiced though her bowels. She could see Baumer, asleep on a mattress on the floor. Lying next to him was a woman she did not recognize. She had one leg draped over his thigh, and a thin arm lay across his chest.

Billy, Billy, Billy, she thought. *Monique was too good for you, buddy.*

She removed a one-use syringe from a leather pouch at her hip, uncapped the needle point, and pressed the plunger until a small stream of fluid squirted out.

Lacan was talking downstairs. In French now, cursing Sarkozy as a fascist and a half-Greek Jew, a comment that gave rise to an animated rant by one of his companions about the Jewish state and the revenge that was coming its way.

Seizing the opportunity, she entered the room, and came face-to-face with the woman, who had awoken and sat up. Her wide eyes searched the darkness, bulging when she saw Cailtin's outline: a silhouetted figure in black overalls, wearing night-vision gear and carrying a weapon. She was dead before she could scream, two bullets taking the top of her skull off and painting the wall behind them.

Baumer came awake instantly and rolled out from under the falling corpse, crying out as he did so. He launched himself at Cailtin's knees, knocking her back off her feet with a crash. She drove the syringe into his neck and squeezed, smashing the butt of her pistol up against his head for good measure. It didn't knock him out, but it stunned him enough for her to piston a boot into his chest and push him away from her.

"Crusaders," he cried out in Arabic. "Hurry, they're here."

He tried to launch himself at her again, but the fast-acting drug had already robbed him of any coordination, and he fell like a drunk into a heap at her feet.

"Not so tough now, are you, you rapist motherfucker," she said before hitting the PTT button on her headset and crying out.

"I'm blown, Rolland! I got Baumer. Third floor, first room on the left coming up. Possible civilian above us, armed. Hostiles below. Lacan is awake and unsecured."

"You . . ." said Baumer, mushily as he collapsed into a drugged stupor.

Caitlin heard the French commandos open fire on the ground floor.

The guard out there would be dropping to the ground, dead before he hit. Below her the sounds of riot and tumult erupted as men awoke and reached for their guns, unsure what was happening, but certain they were in mortal peril.

She holstered the silenced pistol and pulled her personal weapon around on its strap, an H&K MP-5. Feet thundered up the staircase below her and she darted from the room, all concern at stealth departed. The house had no power, but flashlights and electric lamps dazzled in her NVGs. She loosed two bursts from the submachine gun down the stairwell at the bobbing, moving sources of light. Two of them tumbled back down and the third stopped and dropped as the man carrying it let go.

Fire came back up at her, automatic and single shot, describing beautiful emerald traces in her enhanced night vision. She stripped a hand grenade from her belt while firing one-handed down the well, pulled the pin with her teeth, painfully cracking a filling as she did, and tossing the small bomb down into the maelstrom below. She closed her eyes, backing away and firing blindly. The grenade exploded with a roar that caused the spike of pain already drilling into her head to grow cruel thorns that raked at the back of her eyes and drove jagged spears deep into her brain stem.

Caitlin pitched over and vomited.

"Son of a bitch," she grunted, struggling to regain her feet.

The volume of fire downstairs was deafening, drowned out only by the deep bass percussion of exploding grenades on the ground floor. The boards beneath her shook and shuddered so much she feared they might collapse. And still she couldn't get up. Her head spun as though she'd stepped off a fairground ride, and she could not control her weapon anymore. Two figures appeared at the top of the stairs, one of them the squat, powerful outline of Dr. Noo.

He raised his weapon, a FAMAS assault rifle, at her and cried "Allahu Akbar!" just before his face exploded and he toppled backward onto the man behind him.

"Quick, come with me!"

The voice. Coming from above her. It was unfamiliar, but unmistakably American.

"Who the fuck . . . ?"

She gagged and choked again on a mouthful of bile and toppled sideways as she tried to stand.

"Can't go," she protested. "My target."

"Leave him!"

The stranger, the man upstairs, leaped down beside her, stripped the MP-5 from her grip, and wrested a fresh magazine from the utility belt. He swapped out the mag in the dark without trouble and moved over to the stairs to fire down on any approaching attackers. Three more grenades exploded in close succession and the uproar of automatic fire became unbearable.

Caitlin felt herself falling away into darkness.

50

No civilized man should ever be awake at this hour, thought Jed, as he waited in the darkened office for his last meeting of the night. Not unless he had a bottle of good champagne in one hand and couple of exotic dancers in the other.

He stayed away from the window, by habit now, but there wasn't that much to see.

The city center was in darkness save for a few buildings running on generators, one of them his own hotel, a few blocks away to the south. The never-ending caucus would still be in session there, as his delegates—he did think of them as his now—worked the phones and counted heads as they attempted to stave off defeat in the morning's vote.

But they would be defeated.

Jed Culver had stolen enough votes in his time to know when the situation was hopeless. The Putsch were going to get their amendments up. They were going to turn the United States government into something like a Third World junta. He shook his head at his own incompetence in not foreseeing this and aborting it at conception. But looking back, he could understand. He'd been so focused on his own, much humbler agenda that he simply had not been prepared for the depth of feeling, the visceral fear that had infected everything here in a way it hadn't back in Hawaii. That was understandable. You couldn't see the Wave in Hawaii. You didn't live every minute with the prospect of it moving and just eating you alive.

He should have factored that in.

"There is a tide in the affairs of men," he muttered to himself, "which, taken at the flood, leads on to fortune—but omitted, and all the voyage of your life is bound in shallows and in miseries."

"What's that, Jed?"

Culver turned around and was surprised to find a thin man, silhouetted in the doorway by the light of a small handheld phone. Two larger men, instantly recognizable as bodyguards, loomed a discreet distance behind him.

"Just mangling the bard, Bill," he said. "It always helps me when creeping murmur and the poring dark, fills the wide vessel of the universe."

Bill shrugged.

"Me, I like to read or play bridge. Golf 's pretty good, too. But not at this time of night."

"No," said Culver, who hadn't been expecting anyone like this. The others he'd met tonight had all been anonymous people. Quiet men and women.

"So . . . ah . . ."

The figure snickered in the gloom.

"I really threw you for a doozy, didn't I? Coming here, I mean."

Jed nodded.

"Yes, you did. I was expecting someone . . . lower down the food chain."

"Someone expendable?"

"If you like."

The man walked into the room. His bodyguards remained in the corridor.

"This is important, Jed. I have a lot invested in this venture. We all do. If it fails we're sunk. If it plays out, who knows, maybe people will remember us hundreds of years from now. Assuming there's anybody left, of course."

Culver shrugged. "People would remember you anyway."

"Not for something as cool as this, Jed. This is the sort of thing that ends up in oil paintings. Like Paul Revere's ride. It's that important."

Culver couldn't argue with that.

"You did bring your phone, right?" asked Bill.

Jed pulled it out of his suit pocket and handed it over. The man's face was underlit by the glow of the screen as he keyed in a series of codes.

"Okay," he said, as the smart phone beeped. "The network is active."

"And secure?"

"And secure."

Jed thanked him as he took the phone back.

He opened the message window and pressed a few buttons.

A single hard-encrypted message beamed out across the city to hundreds of identical devices.

"It's done," he said. "It's happening."

Most of the delegates at the convention had succumbed to the lack of air-conditioning and removed their jackets, loosened ties, and in some cases even removed them altogether. The atmosphere in the auditorium was sour, hot and rank, although partly that had to do with the split on the floor that was threatening to tear the whole process apart. Kipper pressed his lips together and tried to maintain his calm as some asshole from Spokane attempted to tell him how to do his job.

"This isn't how we would run things, let me tell you, Kipper. We'd have had this show wrapped up days ago, and there wouldn't have been any of this school camp bullshit with lights out and no air, either. How the hell do you expect people to make decisions under these conditions? It is impossible."

Kipper's jaw moved like he was chewing gum, which he wasn't. It was simply an old habit. He folded his arms and resisted the urge to tell this . . . Malcolm Vusevic, according to his name tag . . . that he was full of shit because Spokane, lying behind the Wave, wouldn't be organizing anything ever again.

He kept his mouth shut though, because in his experience, people who'd hailed from the dead zone tended to be a little sensitive about it, which was only reasonable. What wasn't reasonable was the delegates demanding that they get special treatment over and above what the rest of the city could expect.

"Not gonna happen, sir," said Kipper, resolutely shaking his head. "Redmond, Finn Hill, and North Creek are all on their allotted power-ups at the moment. If you want to turn up the air-con here, it means diverting grid power from those folks. I'm not going to do it. Not on your say-so."

"Well, on whose, then?" Vusevic demanded to know. "Would an order from General Blackstone do it for you?"

"Nope." Kipper shook his head equably. "I work for the city, not the military. Leastways not yet."

He instantly regretted the indiscretion. Vusevic's eyes lit up in triumph.

"Oh I see, one of those anarchists, eh? You're just doing this to delay the inevitable. What's a matter, buddy? Don't like losing a vote? Can't handle democracy?"

Kipper's shoulders and arms ached with the tension building up in them as he restrained a violent urge to beat this idiot into a pulp.

"None of my business, sir. City utilities are my business. And you're not getting any extra power."

With that he turned and walked away from the delegate from Spokane, wondering how the fuck anyone from Spokane got a ticket here in the first place. All Vusevic represented was a burned-out ruin of urban wasteland.

"*Whoa* there, Nelly. You're gonna throw a shoe, stomping off like that."

Kipper pulled up at the sight of Jed Culver, who'd just emerged from the crush around the refreshment table. He seemed to live there, and it was taking its toll. The guy looked like he hadn't slept. His face was puffy, and dark bags hung under his eyes.

"Sorry, Jed. Not today, man. I've got a world of fucking hurt on my shoulders."

"Who doesn't, Kip? Who doesn't? Just a word in your shell-like. Won't take a minute."

Kipper frowned at the odd phrasing, until he remembered that Culver had worked in London for a couple of years. Or he said he had. Sometimes with Jed you were never quite sure when he was feeding you a line. He sighed, exhausted. He really was buried by work, and being called down to the conference floor to get reamed out over the air-conditioning hadn't improved his mood. He hadn't slept last night, after the Gestapo, as Barb called them, had left. Partly because Barney had stayed for another three hours, attempting to win him over to the cause. His friend had left just before dawn, in a police cruiser of all things.

"Not everyone in uniform wants to be the Führer," Barney explained, winking, before he disappeared.

Kipper shook off Jed's guiding hand and continued on his way to the exit.

The lawyer fell in beside him, not saying anything. Grinning and waving at the other delegates as he passed them, even those Kip knew for a fact he hated. How the hell he did that was a mystery for the ages. When James Kipper didn't like someone they didn't die wondering.

"You going back to your office?" asked Jed, as they left the auditorium behind.

"Yes, I am, but . . ."

"Great. I'll come with you. Come on."

"Don't you want to be here for the vote? It's on soon, isn't it?"

"Already lost that one, Kip. So no, I have other plans, my friend, come on."

He reluctantly allowed Culver to tag along with him, mostly because he knew the man was congenitally incapable of taking no for an answer. He could blow him off, but by the time he reached his office many floors above, this expensively suited fixer would be waiting in his chair with a big, dumb grin on his face.

"That doesn't sound like you, Jed, giving up because you can't win."

"Who says I'm giving up?"

Kipper spared him a glance and was disturbed by the wolfish smile he found there.

"What's happening, Jed? This really isn't the morning for it."

"No. That's where you're wrong, Kip. This is very much the morning for it. This is the morning the American people, what's left of 'em, God help us, take back their government."

They entered the elevator, which Kipper had tried to shut down without success—the city councillors had balked at that power-saving measure—and Jed punched in the number for his floor, smiling graciously and using his arm to bar the way of a young woman who'd rushed up behind them to share the ride.

"Sorry, darlin'. Do you mind?"

She did, but there was nothing to be done about it as the doors slid shut.

Kipper bristled at the impoliteness.

"That wasn't very nice, Jed. And it was wasteful. And what are you crapping on about anyway? You already said you were going down in that vote this morning. Blackstone is gonna get his congressmen, whether the rest of the army wants them or not."

Jed put a finger to his lips before gesturing around the elevator. Kip sighed with exasperation, but after last night he wasn't
so quick to dismiss paranoid speculation about surveillance.

The lawyer nodded.

"Well, you're right about one thing. Not all of the military
wants this situation. Ritchie and Franks are dead against it."

Culver looked around as if addressing an unseen audience.

"And nobody in uniform is arguing in favor of it, of course.
But in the end they'll accede to the wishes of the people."

"But people don't want this," Kipper said without thinking.

"Some people maybe. But not everyone. This is just fear and
craziness."

"Well, fear whispers loudly downstairs, my friend. Come on."

A bell dinged as the elevator came to a stop at his floor. Kip
made to step out and head for his office, but Culver grabbed his
arm and directed him toward another.

"I had this one swept fifteen minutes ago," he said quietly,
pulling the door closed behind him.

"You what!"

"Found this," he said, pulling a small electronic device from
his breast pocket. "Don't worry, it's been disabled."

Kip stared at the tiny piece of technology as hackles rose on
his back.

"Sons of bitches."

Culver shook his head.

"Nah. Amateurs, Kip. Rank fucking amateurs playing at big
boys' games. Now, come to the window. I want you to see the
sort of view you miss when you work indoors all the time."

The chief engineer followed Culver to the window and
looked down on his city. It was a relatively clear morning, the
first in a while. A few gray clouds scudded out near the mountains to the east, but otherwise the sky was clear, save for two
army helicopters holding position over the bridges across Lake
Washington. And then he saw them, a sea of color, a teeming,
seething mass of humanity streaming onto the bridges and
heading for the city center.

"What the hell?"

The crowd had already swept past a small army roadblock at
the eastern end of the crossing and was beginning to string out
in a long procession that took up every available lane.

"The wishes of the people, Kip. I didn't think they were

being heard downstairs either. So I invited them all here to have their say."

"I don't . . . you what?"

"You're a local? How long do you think it will take to walk that distance, Kip? To get them here, I mean, beating on the doors of the convention?"

Kipper shook his head.

"Not long, I guess. If they're allowed."

Jed Culver snorted.

"If they're allowed! What, did I wake up in Soviet Russia this morning? They're American citizens down there, Kip. Your neighbors and friends. Nobody tells them what they can and can't do, and for sure as shit nobody tells them how they're gonna govern themselves."

Kipper pressed his head to the glass, which felt cool against his sweating brow.

"How did you do this, Jed? Without anyone knowing?"

"Without Blackstone knowing, you mean? Or his stalking horses? I had some friends. Some of them friends of yours actually."

"Hey, buddy, sorry to keep dropping in like this."

"Hello, sweetie."

He spun around to find Barney standing by the office door. And next to him was Barb, holding Suzie on one hip.

"Holy crap, Barn, they'll fucking lock you up, man! And Barbara . . ."

"Daddy said the rude word!" squealed his daughter.

He pulled up, realizing he had just dropped an F-bomb in front of his six-year-old child.

Damn.

"I'm sorry," he said. "Daddy shouldn't have done that, darlin'. It's just that he was a little . . . surprised. And kind of upset. What's going on here?"

Barney peered out back along the corridor, where his former coworkers were beginning to gather and point at the slow-moving crowd snaking across the bridges. One or two saw him and waved. He smiled back.

"I told you last night there were a lot of people involved in the Resistance, Kip. Some wack jobs for sure. You know, commies and anarchists, just like you hear all the time, but a shitload more decent folk. Guys who used to work for the media. The telecoms companies. The government. Moms and dads."

Barbara nodded as she carefully lowered Suzie to the ground.

"You run along, princess," she said. "Find some paper to draw on. One of Daddy's work friends will help you. See if you can find Ronnie."

"I like Ronnie!" she cried before dashing out of the office.

Kip stared at his wife. It was as though he didn't recognize her.

"You too, Barb. You were part of this?"

"I'm sorry, Kip, yes. Well, I'm not sorry for being part of it, but I am sorry I had to keep it from you."

"But why?" he asked plaintively. "Couldn't you trust me?"

She smiled sadly.

"It wasn't safe, Kip. If you knew I was helping Barney and the others, how could you have come in here every day and faced Blackstone? You're a lot of things, Kip. But you're not a liar. You couldn't have done it."

Kipper turned on the lawyer. His head was an angry swirling mess of emotions.

"You knew about this? About my family being involved?"

Culver nodded. For once he wasn't smiling.

"I've had contact with a number of opposition cells. Your wife's was one."

"You had a *cell*?" he asked Barbara. His voice rose with incredulity.

Barbara sniffed. "You make it sound like a spy movie, Kip. It was just me and some of the moms from school. Some of our friends. People I could trust."

"Jesus Christ . . ."

"They're down there, Kip," she said, pointing out the window. "They're coming. Because they have to."

Barney walked over to the window and looked down on the massing crowd.

"We've been waiting for this, Kip," he said. "Waiting for the right moment when those assholes downstairs would go just a bit too far. I thought they'd done it when they locked up the councillors, but people were still frightened out of their minds back then, willing to give up anything just to feel safe. That just isn't so, now. They've had enough, and they want their country back. The little bit they have left anyway."

Kipper was stunned.

Never would he have imagined the day turning out like this. He kept his opinions private, but he was expecting a bleak and wretched day.

"We need your help, Kip," said Barney.

"Mine? What do you need me for?" He waved a hand at the window. "You look like you have it all locked down."

Culver answered his question. "We need you to shut off power to the city, and to Fort Lewis. And we need it done now. We have to knock the legs out from under these idiots before they have a chance to get to their feet."

"But they'll have their own backup plans," he protested.

"Everyone has backup plans." Culver smiled silkily.

"What about it, Kip?" Barney Tench implored. "You saved this city once. You can save your country if you act right now."

"Come on, honey," added Barbara. "You know what's right."

Kipper turned back and gazed out of the window.

The crowd looked to be hundreds of thousands strong. He could see them bunched up at the bottleneck of Faben Point, a great mass of people emerging from the suburbs. He could see a similar crowd heading over the Evergreen Point Bridge to the north.

Phones began to ring all over the floor, as voices rose in confusion, surprise, and even awe. His secretary, Rhonda, came bustling down the hallway and into the room with Suzie trailing behind her. She looked surprised and delighted.

"Barney!" she cried out. "And Barb!"

"Hey, Ronnie."

"Hiya, Ron."

His secretary turned her attention back to Kipper and said, "I'm sorry, Jimmy, but it's General Blackstone's office on the phone. They desperately need to talk to you and the other department heads. What should I tell them?"

Kipper smiled.

EPILOGUE

One Day

The killer awoke, to find a stranger by her bed.

No, not a stranger, the guy who had saved her. The civilian in the room on the top floor. She could see him clearly now, as she blinked the sleep out of her eyes.

"Where am I?" asked Caitlin, her voice cracking in her dry throat.

"London," said the man. "A special hospital. They had to operate on you."

"My friend the tumor," she said. "Don't tell me he's gone."

The man shrugged.

"I'm not a doctor, so I don't know. Or a relative, so they won't tell me."

"Who are you?"

"Name's Melton," he said. "Bret Melton."

Caitlin tried to lever herself up but found that she had no strength in her arms at all.

"Well, Bret Melton, thank you for saving my sorry ass. And to think I might have popped a cap in yours."

He seemed to take that without offense.

"You probably saved mine, Miss Mercure. I holed up in that joint after my vehicle got hit by an RPG. I was pretty much out of it, just trying to get as far away from the street as possible. If those guys had been even half competent they'd have checked and found me unconscious up top. Probably would have cut my head off."

"Probably," she agreed. "And my name's not Cathy Mercure, by the way. That's a cover. I'm sorry they felt the need to tell you that. My name is Caitlin."

Melton took that without obvious concern, too.

"In my experience," he said with a half smile, "ladies who sneak into snake pits and twist the heads off vipers can pretty well call themselves whatever they feel like. You should know, by the way, that I'm a reporter. I'm not going to write about you. Not even going to ask what went down in that house. They made me sign a piece of paper says I lose my nuts if I do. But I just wanted to get that out there for you."

Caitlin felt a wave of lassitude steal through her body. She was aware of great damage that had been done.

"Thank you, Bret," she said weakly. "But it's all right. I'm retired now, a lady of leisure, as of two minutes ago."

"Okay then." He nodded and they lapsed into silence. Her eyelids fluttered heavily, and she felt herself drifting back toward sleep.

"Bret," she said. "Did they get him? Did they get my guy?"

His voice seemed to come from far away.

"I don't know, Caitlin. They got a lot of guys."

She forced her eyes open.

For the first time she noticed the window off to the side of her bed. It opened onto a garden scene, although the trees were leafless and the grass had all died off.

"What are you going to do, Bret?" she asked. "Will you go home?"

He shrugged.

"I don't know."

She started to fade out again.

"Me neither."

One Week

They buried their dead according to whatever beliefs the departed had lived by. Gathered on the heavily damaged boat deck at the stern of the *Aussie Rules,* the surviving passengers and crew said their prayers or quiet good-byes for friends and loved ones who hadn't made it. Jules had never known Fifi or Pete to be in the slightest way religious, but in tidying Fifi's quarters in the days after the last battle, she found an old Gideon's Bible, stolen from a motel somewhere, annotated by her lost friend's large, childlike script. The story of Noah and his ark had come in for a lot of attention.

That's just like us, except for all the animals, she had written.

And, *Please Lord, smite that asshole Larry Zood* was followed in a different ink by *Damn! This prayer shit really works!*

It was evidence of a secret, inner life Jules would never have imagined of Fifi, and she asked Miguel to add a few Hail Marys to the endless rosaries his extended family were sending skyward for old Adolfo, the only casualty their party had suffered. Dead of a heart attack a full day after the gunfight.

"Hail Mary, mother of God, blessed art thou and blessed be the fruit of thy womb Jesus . . ."

Granna Ana smiled and nodded sadly at Jules and then the two bundles that had been her friends, and she realized that Miguel's family, who had been praying in Spanish, had changed to English without her noticing. Granna Ana waved a thin brown hand at Pete and Fifi's bodies, indicating that the change was for their sake. An earlier, more cynical Jules would have reflexively smirked and rolled her eyes at the idea of an omniscient God needing a translation, but now, all alone, on a morning that was bright and cold, she let tears come freely as the age-old prayer to the mother of Jesus was whipped away on a freshening southerly breeze.

The sea state had dropped to long, rolling swell, and only a few wisps of cirrus cloud spoiled an otherwise perfect sky. Eight bodies lay wrapped in sheets and blankets on the large, bullet-pocked diving platform at the stern. Fifi and Pete she had placed there herself, the last two bundles on the starboard side, with a lot of help from Shah and Pieraro. The gravity and sorrow of the moment was undercut somewhat by the frozen stiffness of Pete's remains. He'd been lying in the largest of the galley freezers for more than a month, and Jules wasn't sure she'd have been able to contemplate moving him had Shah and Mr. Lee not helped.

"Mr. Pete, he would have loved this," said Lee, as they struggled with his body. "Would have laughed his *gweilo* anus right off, yes."

And he would have, thought Jules, with a private smile and an involuntary hitching sob.

Fifi, though, she would have been pissed. Of all of them, Jules thought her friend had most easily dealt with everything that had happened. Perhaps because she had been alone and fighting for herself most of her life. Mute and numb, staring at the inert swaddle of sheets in which the redneck princess lay, Jules could not help but indulge herself in a small, bitter moment of self-loathing. If she had been smarter, if she had in any way been worthy of the trust that everyone had placed in her, Fifi would still be with them. Still grinning and shining and lighting up the face of everyone who encountered her.

". . . Holy Mary, Mother of God, pray for us sinners, now and at the hour of our death. Amen . . . Hail Mary, mother of God . . ."

She was shaking. A slight tremor at first that she didn't really notice until it had spread through most of her body. She shivered inside her thick, dark oilskins, and her throat felt so tight she could not swallow. Beside her, the Gurkhas quietly sang a funeral song for their fallen comrades, Thapa and Birendra, that seemed to magnify the power of the Mexicans' rosary chant. Her American passengers mumbled along, all of them except for the banker Moorhouse, who lay on the diving platform next to Birendra, shot down after saving her life during the battle. His mistress, the boob job, as Fifi once called her, had found a black cocktail dress somewhere for her mourning outfit, creating an incongruous effect under a yellow rain slicker. She dabbed at dramatically running mascara, but, regarding her from within the depths of her own misery, Jules thought she was going through the motions of grief, rather than its reality. The presence of Jason's hand massaging her arse to help her over the trauma did detract somewhat from the air of decorous remembrance she was trying so hard to create. She had already moved cabins to take up with the trust-fund delinquent, much to the chagrin of his sister Phoebe, who was now refusing to talk with him.

Jules sighed at the petty, meaningless nature of it all.

You would think that people could put aside all of the silly wretchedness and just pull together, but no. They couldn't. Her father would have said it simply wasn't in their nature. He was an old villain, there was no denying that. But in his own strange way he had a good heart, and he never stole from anyone who couldn't afford it. There was even a spark of noblesse oblige in him, and he made sure that all of his children were raised to think of themselves as no better than anyone else, because as he so often told her "in the end, Julianne, we were all just as bad as each other."

"Miss Jules."

Lee's voice in her ear dragged her out of these reveries.

"It is a warship, Miss Jules. On the radio. From New Zealand."

She excused herself with a brief hand on Shah's arm, turning and leaving the funeral scene, secretly glad not to have to witness the dumping of the bodies into the deep.

"He wishes to speak with our captain," said Lee, who had contented himself with just a few private words over the bodies of his comrades before everyone came together for the ceremony.

Our captain, thought Jules. *How risible.*

"What does he want?" she asked.

"Oh, it is nothing bad. I have told him we have Uplifted Americans on board. He asks if we need assistance, and whether we will be berthing in Auckland or proceeding to Sydney."

"Okay, thanks, Lee."

She stopped before climbing the stairs up to the next deck.

"What do you want to do, Lee? When we get there. They probably won't let us keep this boat, you know. It's not ours."

Her one surviving friend shook his head sadly.

"No. They will not, Miss Jules."

"You can't go home. Indonesia is a godawful mess now."

"Yes, miss."

"So what will you do?"

He looked completely lost for the first time ever.

"What will you do, Miss Jules? Maybe I could come, too."

"I don't know, Lee. These last few weeks, they've really taken it out of me. I don't want to go home, I know that much. England looks nightmarish right now. A giant bloody jail if you ask me. Not at all the sort of place for the likes of us."

"No, miss. Foreign Johnnies not welcome anymore."

She started the long climb up toward the bridge, stopping just once to look back toward the stern and say her last goodbye. From here, against the vastness of the southern ocean, her little group of seafarers and survivors looked so vulnerable and sad. Like the last people on earth.

But at least they still lived.

Daddy would have been proud, she thought.

He'd have been so proud of her, for bringing the ship and

all of these people home safe, wherever that might turn out to be.

"Don't worry, Lee," she said. "We'll muddle through."

One Year

The president of the United States was hunkered down over a small mountain of paperwork in the Oval Office of the Western White House. Of course, it wasn't oval-shaped at all, but he felt it important to retain a link with the past, something to give people hope that they might be able to reclaim some of the advantages and even a fraction of the glory that the past had once gifted them as a nation.

He read the summation of the reports from the high-energy physics lab into the latest investigations of the Wave, but they all boiled down to the same thing.

Nobody knew shit.

He leaned back and rubbed at his eyes. His chief scientist and national security advisor waited quietly on him, as they sat in the bright yellow armchairs arranged in front of his desk. He had no idea from where the governor of Washington had retrieved them, just before he "gave up" his accommodations for the needs of the federal government, but they were suitably hideous. A parting fuck-you of exquisite eloquence.

"So, no change," said the president.

"No."

"Not in the slightest, sir," they agreed.

"Okay, thanks guys. Send in the secretary of state on your way out, would you? Thanks for your efforts anyway."

The two men excused themselves and departed.

The president gazed out over the gardens of the former governor's mansion. They had recovered well as the environment had returned to normal. Better than normal, actually. The total collapse of the world economy had given the planet a breather, but at a terrible cost. He'd actually heard that some of the deep green nutjobs in the all-powerful state legislature next door had been saying that on balance, the Disappearance was a good thing.

Of course, they never said so on the record. They'd be

lynched. But he didn't doubt for a minute that some of them thought as much.

He tidied the scientific reports and pulled over a tottering sheaf of folders dealing with the expatriate population. Most Americans still lived overseas, and tending to their needs and the demands of their host governments was about half of what he did nowadays. The Brits were looking for territorial concessions, pressuring him to give up the U.S. claims over the Antarctic oil fields. The Australian prime minister wanted him to visit to "discuss" the future cofunding arrangements of the Pacific fleet.

A dull pain was growing behind his left eye when his personal secretary burst into the office.

"Mr. President! Mr. President! You have to come, sir. Right away!"

"What's up, Ronnie?" he asked, suddenly worried.

Two Secret Service agents bustled past her into the room and demanded he come with them immediately.

"No, goddammit, I won't. What the hell is going on?"

"We need to get you away from here, right now, Mr. President, we'll explain on the way."

"Oh, no, you don't." President James Kipper jumped up from his desk. "I'm not going anywhere with anyone until you tell me exactly what is happening right now."

"It's the Wave, sir," cried Ronnie. "It's gone."

Acknowledgments

You know who you are. All the unusual suspects. My editors and publishers, who put up with so much. Cate. Bri. Jono. Betsy. And all of the serried ranks behind them, too. Marketing mavens, publicists (Hi, Annie!), cover designers. I loves y'all. A big tip o' the propellor beanie to Russ Galen, too, for making me think this idea through properly before he went and sold it.

Then there's my family, who put up with so much. Jane, Anna, and Thomas. Every book I promise to be a bit less monstrous come deadline. Every book I lie. And there's all those friends and neighbors who stepped in at crucial moments to help get me off Planet Parenthood long enough to get a few more pages written. My parents, Jane's mum Pat, and a swag of uncles and aunts helped out there, too. They all put up with so much.

For this book, there was also the hard-chargin' crew at Clayton Utz, the rockingest little great big law firm anywhere, anytime, who put up with so much from me as their writer-in-residence. I'm still not sure why. I guess they're just cool. While on that topic, the happy funsters at Avid Reader in West End also, possibly unwisely, gave me some valuable writing space while I was itinerant by virtue of renovations. My thanks. I was pretty well behaved there though, so I guess, for once, they really didn't have to put up with too much.

There's Murph—or Mr. Murphy to you. Mister S. F. Murphy of the great state of Missouri—who put up with so much as my principal researcher and at one point even graduated to coauthor for a couple of pages in one particular battle. I owe him for pulling my fat out of the fire so many times it just ain't funny. Which reminds me to thank my good friend Mr. Andrew McKinney of the Texas bar, who provided Lord knows how many thousands of dollars' worth of free legal advice re the line of succession, among other things. Add Mr. Steve Sterling, for some timely advice on what the end of the world really looks like.

And finally there's my blog buddies. The Burgers. Too numerous to name the guilty parties. And man, do they put up with too much, especially as deadline closes in and all they get, day after day, is entry after entry bitchin' about how tough I got it. Luckily, they're a ferociously disrespectful bunch of scurvy dogs and they don't let me get away with much. I bounce a lot of ideas off them. Get them to do a lot of unpaid research. And generally take them way too much for granted. But I'd be lost without them.

As always when I write my acknowledgments, I can't help but feel that I've left someone out. I really shouldn't do these late at night with a drink in hand. Whoever it is that I've forgotten this time, my apologies. Drop into the blog and tear me a new one. I'll give you a cameo in the next book.

Here is an excerpt from
John Birmingham's next novel,

AFTER AMERICA

the sequel to *Without Warning*

Coming from Del Rey Books

"These are no banditos," Miguel said quietly. "They are road agents."

He passed the night-vision goggles to the Mormon, Aaronson. They were an excellent tool, he thought. It would be well worth stopping in the next large town they might pass to salvage a pair from a hunting supply store or an army surplus outlet. He could easily make out a wealth of detail around the Hy Top Club, a slumping structure of old wooden slats with a broken-back roofline and a half-collapsed awning dropping down over a front veranda.

"Road agents?" said Aaronson, also quietly, although without whispering. "Is there a difference between these bandits and any other?"

Miguel took back the NVGs and resumed his surveillance of the old nightclub, or dive bar, or whatever it had been. It was the only place in Crockett displaying signs of life, but the agents who had attacked the Mormons' party, stolen the better part of their Longhorn herd, and ridden off with half a dozen of their women were doing their best to push back the darkness. The small town may have been a mausoleum, haunted by the seven thousand souls of those who had Disappeared here, but you would not have known it if all you could see of Crockett, Texas, was the Hy Top Club of South Cottonwood Street. It roared with life: rude, vicious, drunken, and barbarous, but life nonetheless. Miguel estimated the road agents' fighting company at twenty strong, give or take, and in addition to the six Mormon women they had taken, there appeared to be another seven or eight camp whores with them. All of them were female, but some were not really old enough to be called women. About the age of his own daughter, Sofia, he thought with a glare that was hidden by the absolute darkness of the night.

"The banditos are all from the south," he explained to Aaronson. "They raid into Texas, but they do not base here. Some say they are sent by my old friend Roberto Morales. I once knew him, you know. Before he became so famous."

He smiled at the frank disbelief on Aaronson's face. It was discernible even by starlight.

"I joke, of course," Miguel continued. "He was not my friend at all. But I did know him for a short while, long before he knifed Hugo in the back. Whatever the case, the banditos, they come and they go, taking what they can and doing their best to avoid Blackstone's troopers. If caught, they are hung . . . what is the word . . . summary?"

"Summarily," Aaronson corrected him. The man's face writhed with warring emotions: anxiety, fear, impacted fury, all of them barely contained by the need to remain hidden from the men who had taken everything from him. Screams intermittently reached them in their hiding spot, a thicket of loblolly pine and pecan trees a block west of the club. Miguel could sense the Mormon tense up every time. He wondered if Aaronson was able to recognize any of the ragged, terrorized cries and prayed that he could not. It would be too much for any man to bear. Certainly if his own daughter or wife were being held and abused by such human filth he doubted he would be able to remain calm and detached.

Such thoughts, however, could only lead to questions about exactly how his family was doing on the road to Corpus Christi, so he suppressed them with an act of great will.

"For banditos, Blackstone's Texas is a hard country," he explained patiently. "Deadly, if they are caught. For these men, however, not so much."

He jerked his chin in the direction of the Hy Top, which was illuminated by fire burning in oil drums. Rock music thumped and howled from inside. Gringo music. Crunching guitars and pounding drums to drown out all but the loudest wailing of the female prisoners. He stilled his sense of outrage, which was considerable, and regarded the scene with a heart crusted in salt and black ice. The camp followers were easy to tell from the Mormon women. Although just as likely to be struck or kicked or even dragged into the darkness by the road agents, they did enjoy a noticeable freedom of movement not granted to the newest captives. They also enjoyed the privilege of kicking down on the Mormon women. As he watched through the NVGs, two of the camp whores delighted a small number of agents by tripping one of the captives after she had delivered a tray of beers outside. They fell on her, pinning her struggling form to the ground, as one sat on her face and shook her ass, laughing and yelling something that Miguel couldn't make out, but which he was certain could only be a cruel and unusual taunt. It reduced the audience of road agents to helpless laughter.

Lying on the thick carpet of pine needles, he felt Aaronson go tense and start to move. Miguel reached over and grabbed the man's upper arm, digging into the flesh with fingers as hard as rail spikes.

"No," he said firmly but quietly. "Now is not the time."

"But . . . they're . . . that's Jenny Booker over there. Willem's betrothed."

Miguel drilled the tip of his thumb into a nerve bundle beneath Aaronson's bicep. The Mormon was not a soft man, but the pain would be excruciating, and it overwhelmed any other considerations. When Miguel was certain he was subdued again, he let go.

"I am sorry, Aaronson, but if you move against them now, she will die. Possibly all of your women will be killed. And not quickly. The agents will make sport of it. We must wait. The others will not move until we report back, and we need all of them."

Aaronson was silent for a moment allowing more screams and reports of debauchery to reach them from South Cottonwood Street.

"This is intolerable," he said at last in a weak, broken voice.

Miguel nodded in the dark.

"For you, yes. We should withdraw for now, back to the meeting place. I can return and watch the agents' camp by myself. It might be better anyway. I need to move around them, and I want to scout out the field where they have left the cattle. We must find out how many of them are on guard there, and I can do that without being caught. Probably. You, probably not. Let us go then."

He took one last look through the night-vision glasses. Two Mormon women, battered and bloodied, were being dragged by a pair of overweight road agents toward a steel door attached to the back of the Hy Top Club. Miguel watched the agents throw the women through the opening. One of them stood in the door, unzipped his fly, and relieved himself in the dark room. The stream caught the firelight and twinkled in the green haze of Miguel's night-vision goggles.

"What do you see?" Aaronson asked, his hand out for the goggles.

"Wait," Miguel replied. He watched the agent give himself a wiggle and zip himself up. Laughing, both agents slammed the door and kicked against it a few times. Only then did they put a padlock onto the latch.

Without allowing the poor man another second to think about it, Miguel was up, drawing the Mormon to his feet and exiting the overgrown lot from which they had been conducting their surveillance. The agents had set themselves up in a poor area of town, southwest of the main business center. He thought perhaps that even before the Wave it would have been home to the poorer folk of Crockett. Many of the houses that still stood looked small and mean, especially on the western side of Cottonwood Street, where remnant forests covered the hills and fields. A good deal of refuse and rusted machinery lay where it had been abandoned in gardens and driveways long before the inhabitants Disappeared, but fire and looters had not ravaged this area as completely as it had the town center and some of the more affluent neighborhoods. Nor—to judge from the scenes he had witnessed—had the Hy Top Club been relieved of its liquor supply in the years since the Wave swept away its clientele.

He pondered that.

Perhaps one of the road agents was a fortunate local, someone who had been out of the country in 2003. Perhaps with the army in Iraq? If so, he could have led his comrades here after they had attacked Aaronson's people. In the post-Wave world, a little local knowledge could often be a very precious resource.

The two men retreated carefully through the darkness. This far from the club, with so much scrubland in the way, not much light made it through from the burning oil drums, but the stars twinkled with cold brilliance high above and a half moon laid an opalescent glow over the ruins of the town, allowing them to pick their way through. They took it slowly, retracing their steps of an hour before, finally emerging into a small open area where the surrounding forest of hickory, elm, and sweet gum gave way to knee-high grass and a few thin saplings. In twenty years, thought Miguel, it would all be forest again.

Aaronson whistled, a trilling call like a night bird, and five silhouettes rose from the grass in front of them. Miguel was impressed. Had he not known the Mormons were secreted in the little glade, he would not have spotted them unless he was especially alert. He recognized the outline of Willem D'Age as the man spoke in a low, anxious voice.

"What have you seen, Brother Aaronson? Are our women alive? Are they well?"

"They are alive, for now," said Miguel, before the other man could start a panic among his fellows or tell D'Age anything that might send him into a righteous fury. "And they will stay that way if we keep our heads about us. Come. Gather round."

The group, all men—although two of them were barely old enough for the designation—clustered around the returned scouts. Miguel demurred to Aaronson, who delivered a competent report of what they had observed. He managed to contain his obvious distress at the state of their women and shaded the details to spare his comrades. Nonetheless they could not help themselves.

"So these animals, they have taken the women as chattel?" asked D'Age.

"They treat them very roughly, brother," said Aaronson.

"Then we should go now and release them from this veil," piped up another voice, high and reedy. "We shall lay the Lord's vengeance on them for their trespasses."

The speaker was young, and Miguel recognized him as one of the boys, Orrin. He was waving around a military assault weapon, and Miguel could tell, even in the starlight, that every line in his body was tensed up and quivering like a bow drawn too far and held too long. Miguel reached over and placed his hand over the lad's where it gripped the front end of the rifle: some sort of carbine, as he remembered.

"Boy," he said quietly but with great firmness, "this is no game. We shall kill these men tonight. Or they shall kill us. It is not play. Put your weapon away until it is needed. Until blood is the only end."

Miguel hoisted his own rifle, his much-loved Winchester, and held it in front of the youngster.

"This gun has been leveled at five men, Orrin. They are all dead now. Do you understand? That is how serious tonight is. I have never pointed this gun at a man and failed to take his life."

Not only the overexcited Orrin fell still, but all of the men around him.

"Good," said Miguel. "Then we can prepare."